N E W

Genesee River

Chemung R.

que Isle

uf

Allegheny River

enango
Salter's

P E N N S Y L V A N I A

West Branch Susquehanna River

Kittanning

Chartiers Old Town

Guyasuta's town

rt Pitt

FORBES'S RD.

Ft. Ligonier

RIDGE

LAUREL RIDGE

ALLEGHENY MTS.

Ft. Shirley

Juniata River

Carlisle

Ft. Littleton

Ft. Augusta

Easton

River

Harris Ferry

Trenton

Philadelphia

N E W   J E R S E Y

Ft. Bedford

Ft. Loudon

Susquehanna

River

Delaware

Ft. Necessity

Cumberland

Hagerstown

Wilmington

D E L A W A R E

Potomac River

Baltimore

M A R Y L A N D

Annapolis

MTS.

BLUE RIDGE MTS.

C H E S A P E A K E   B A Y

V I R G I N I A

Rappahannock River

A T L A N T I C   O C E A N

Lynchburg

James River

Appomattox

Richmond
(WORLD'S END)

River

York R.

Holden Hall

Yorktown

Williamsburg

Petersburg

Norfolk

0   25   50   75   100

Scale of Miles

ONKEN

Unconquered

A NOVEL OF THE
PONTIAC CONSPIRACY

Neil H. Swanson

DOUBLEDAY & COMPANY, INC.

GARDEN CITY, NEW YORK

To Hildegarde, my wife, with love

> . . . and to her adventurous forebears who settled in
> the ancient Kingdom of Accomac on Chesapeake Bay
> fifty years before the first Xtopher Holden landed in
> Virginia and built Holden Hall on the James River.

The Continental Congress has declared the independency of these united states. But it would be folly to suppose that all the troubles which afflict us will be removed or abated by the act of setting up a new form of government as replacement for another.

It has been easy and self-gratifying to blame British ministers and royal governors for every evil that has come upon us. The plain truth is that many of these troubles have been brought about by the selfish acts of our own people—by the rapacity of merchants engaged in trading with the Indians, the greed of unscrupulous land speculators, the deliberate cheating by which representatives of our colonial assemblies have induced the Indian nations to sign treaties they did not understand.

It is easy to put blame on these men also. They are convenient to be blamed; they are prominent by reason of their wealth or their position. And a portion of the blame is just. They have a share of the responsibility for the turmoils, civil war, and Indian attacks that have beset us in the thirteen years since the siege of Pittsburgh by the Mingoes, Shawnees, Delawares, and Caughnawagas.

But the plain truth also is that common men must take upon themselves a large part of the blame. Self-interest is not confined to men of wealth and power. For every merchant who was guilty of smuggling arms and ammunition to the savages, there were a hundred ordinary men who were quite willing to profit by that lawless trade—to be wagoners and clerks and pack-train drivers for those same greedy merchants. For every British officer whose stupidity or arrogance made him incompetent to deal with savages, there were a hundred ordinary men to carry liquor to the Indian towns in spite of laws and warnings, to abuse and cheat the savages who traded with them, and to debauch their women. For every self-serving politician and land speculator, there were thousands of common men who were eager to profit by their swindles and to seize lands which they well knew had not been purchased from the Indians.

The greed and selfishness of ordinary men are not so easy to be seen as those of men who are more prominent. But the accumulated consequences of their selfish acts are often more important than the misdeeds of the great and powerful. The time has come when each of us must take stock of himself. We must now resolve to so conduct ourselves as to be worthy of the independence which we pledge ourselves to uphold with our lives.

Self-government begins with government of self.

—Xtopher Holden to the Associators of Westmoreland County, Pennsylvania, on the occasion of the receipt of news of the Declaration of Independence.

My great-grandmother was a slave.

She was white. She was an English girl. Yet she was exhibited and sold at auction, not by barbarous Algerines but by the brutal laws of her own people. For it was even possible, in those days, for a man who had grown weary of his wife to put a rope around her neck, lead her to a public market, and there sell her.

This girl was a virgin. She was accused of murder, tried, found guilty, sentenced to the gallows—and then given the harsh choice of death by hanging or of slavery. To live was to hope. She chose life, and so became the property of a man who lusted for her, though he had a wife.

She was young when these things happened—only seventeen—and it is said that she was very lovely. I tell you of her so that you may see how far a journey we have come from the day when, in America, a white girl could be sold and bought as you would sell or buy a cow, a horse, a dog—could be lawfully and publicly stripped naked, whipped, shamed, and degraded.

—being part of a remarkable letter concerning the Holdens of Virginia, written by one of their descendants in the frontier village of St. Anthony in Minnesota, at the great falls of the Mississippi, in the summer of 1862 —one hundred years after the beginning of this story.

Preface

Men create their own disasters. There are times when the "accumulated consequences of their selfish acts" explode with all the violence of a phenomenon of nature.

The conspiracy of Pontiac was one of these man-made disasters. It was also a phenomenon of nature. Like the eruption of a volcano, it was an explosion of deep, pent-up forces.

Unconquered is a companion novel to *The Judas Tree*. Some of the people of that book appear again in this one, as they have appeared already in *The Silent Drum* and as they will appear in other novels—*The Rock in the Sun*, *The Vandals* and *The Stubborn Flesh*, *The Calico Tree* and *The Precious Hour*, *The Broadhorn* and *The Temporary Gentleman*.

Certain episodes will be familiar. An example is the dice game on the blanket spread out in the King's Road. In *The Judas Tree*, it was quite incidental; in *Unconquered*, it becomes important. Such scenes have been introduced on purpose, and the purpose is to tie these books together.

For *Unconquered* is an integral part of the lifetime enterprise to which I set myself some fifteen years ago—to re-create the life of Maryland and Virginia, Delaware, Pennsylvania, and the Ohio country during the critical years of the making of America, in a group of thirty novels. Each of these novels is—or will be—a complete story in itself and independent of the others, but all of them deal with one central, gradually expanding group of characters, their friends and neighbors, their forebears and their descendants. If I live to finish what I have attempted, the completed series will emerge at last as one continuous narrative of the advance of the American frontier from the Atlantic to the Mississippi.

In writing *Unconquered*, I have returned deliberately to the dreadful summer of 1763 when, in a blow as sudden and disastrous as Pearl Harbor, the frontier was driven eastward from the Allegheny River almost to the Susquehanna. The final scenes are played out on the same stage where Diantha Gaillard married Arnett Leslie—the burning fort where hungry men and women fought despairingly behind the barricades of rum kegs and molasses barrels, fur bales, cabin doors and tables. But the stage is crowded with a thousand people, the besieged and the besiegers. *The Judas Tree* saw only a few of them, and it was concerned primarily with certain incidents and with their consequences in the lives of one man and one woman.

Unconquered is concerned with causes also—with the tangled web of human motives that made possible the conquest of a continent—with the surging violence of a new kind of people who did not yet call themselves Americans. It is a story of "those clamoring, demanding, unwashed and unshaven, evil-smelling and foul-talking men who swarmed across five mountain ranges in profane and matter-of-fact disregard" of death and danger. It is also a story of people caught up by forces beyond their control and thrown together in the midst of a disaster for which each of them, in varying degree, had some share of the blame.

Some of the people in this book are real. Some are imaginary, but even these are of the essence of reality. They are composites of the men and women who appear—brief tantalizing glimpses—in old letters and dispatches, in the daily journal kept by one shrewd and observant trader in besieged Fort Pitt, and in the file of its commander's orders carefully preserved in London.

The Mason-Dixon survey was stopped by force in 1767, not in 1762. James Thompson was killed and scalped within the sight of defenders of Fort Pitt on June 22nd, not July 28th. But the basic premise of *Unconquered* is factually sound. History to the contrary notwithstanding, the Pontiac War did not burst upon the frontier without warning. The fact is that Sir William Johnson was warned repeatedly during the fourteen months preceding the massacre at Clapham's.

Even in the smallest details of life as it was in Newgate prison and at Norfolk, Williamsburg, Venango, and the Forks of the Ohio, I have tried to re-create the past exactly.

Justice Grenfell's threat that Abby might be burned alive for treason was no idle bluster. Under English law, the crime of "treason" was astonishingly broad; and burning at the stake was a refinement graciously reserved for women for almost three decades after Abby Hale was sentenced.

Will Ramsey actually built the swivel-jointed paddle-wheel boat in which the terrified schoolmaster, Ten Eyck, ferried Holden over the Monongahela. The first teacher at the Forks of the Ohio kept school, just as Ten Eyck said, in Colonel James Burd's cabin. A Delaware chief blacked the eye of the king's deputy commissioner, George Croghan. The "hipt or Lunatick" surgeon of the Fort Pitt garrison, James Miller, cut his own throat "with two Rayzors." Lieutenant Baillie suffered from the itch. And James Kenny, the young Quaker who kept store in Pitt's Town, amused himself by fetching home a sack of human bones from the old battlefield on Grant's Hill and tried fitting them together. Indian girls stoned his cabin when he would not let them use it for a brothel.

If you doubt me when I say that Fort Venango was left open and defenseless by the lack of hinges for its main gates, you will find the proof in a dispatch from Major Robert Stewart, First Virginia Militia, written in that miserable stockade on December 20, 1760.

If you are surprised to find Fort Pitt commanded by a British officer who speaks French much more easily than English, at a time when France was still at war with England, go to Captain Simeon Ecuyer's correspondence. He wrote his official letters in the enemy's own language.

And if you believe that biological warfare is a new and devilish invention, turn again to the contemporary records. It is devilish enough; but it is not new. The defenders of Fort Pitt fought Indians by spreading small-pox.

If Captain Steele's behavior seems implausible, my witness is Bouquet himself. Colonel Bouquet did not use so gentle a word as "implausible" in dealing with the conduct of another officer that summer—Ensign John Christie, who surrendered Presque Isle. In dispatches to Captain Ecuyer at Fort Pitt and Captain Lewis Ourry at Fort Bedford, he used words that scalded—"infamous" and "shameful conduct" and "a lasting Blot." He even wrote, to Ourry, that "Humanity makes me hope that Christie is dead, as his scandalous Capitulation for a Post of that Consequence, and so impregnable to Savages, deserves the most severe Punishment." Captain Steele is an imaginary character; but the incident of the theft from Ecuyer is true, and the stolen money was found hidden in the barrel of a cannon.

Again, if Martin Garth seems ruthless beyond credence, bear in mind that other white men of his time not only roused the savages to massacre but personally led Indian war parties in attacks on their own neighbors. If his towering ambition seems fantastic, look at the old maps where other men marked out the boundaries of their dreams and gave them names—Vandalia, New Wales, and Pittsylvania.

You will find in our colonial records that one man, by private treaty, got his hands on seven million seven hundred thousand acres—a region as large as the state of Maryland and larger than the states of Delaware, Rhode Island, and New Jersey put together. Great wars have been fought for areas much smaller. Alsace and Lorraine combined are less than half as large as the lands ceded to George Croghan by the Iroquois.

After many years of writing history and fiction, I have come to the conclusion that truth cannot be outdone by the imagination. Life has a fascinating and sometimes frightening way of repeating itself. When *The Judas Tree* was published, I was amazed to find myself accused of rattling skeletons in certain closets. In that novel, Arnett Leslie's discovery that his bride-to-be had married his father was a product of my own invention. I had even been a little worried lest the situation seem too far-fetched. I am less naïve now. In several instances that have been called to my attention, that same situation has been repeated in real life.

Therefore, in publishing *Unconquered,* I make no apology either for its coincidences and parallels or for its most improbable events. I do not even claim to have invented them. The least plausible of all its situations—the means by which Christopher Holden and the girl he loved attempted to escape from the pursuing Senecas—was already an old legend in the land of the Dacotah in my boyhood.

Chapter 1

Cerne Abbas is a town in Dorset. It has been there for a long time.

It was old on Doomsday. It was very old when Columbus sailed over the flat world's rim and proved that ships would not fall off into a void inhabited by demons.

The town had been there for eight centuries when Canute was king in England and his vikings came roaring over the Wessex downs to sack its abbey and hunt girls to earth in the wild thyme thickets.

Cerne Abbas, on the autumn evening in the year 1762, when Abigail Martha set fire to the Angel, had been there more than a thousand years.

Abigail Martha was the descendant of some village girl who was raped in that viking raid. The proof is not written; the records do not go back nearly so far. Even if they did, parish registers seldom make mention of rape. And the rape of Cerne Abbas was only an ancient legend when Abigail Martha was born.

The proof of her ancestry was her hair and her eyes. For her eyes were the blue of the deep Norse fjords and her hair was a Norseman's torch. Not red, though men called it so. Not the red of a torch in the night, but the clean bright gold of a flame in the midday sun—gold with that touch of copper so burnished it looks alive.

Alive. If one word can encompass a woman, that word was Abigail Martha's word. It was meant for her, made for her, and it took on a new special meaning because it was hers. Other folk in Cerne Abbas lived, but she was *alive.*

She was "the shiningest, springingest, eagerest thing on earth." A woman said that about her. It is the more remarkable because the woman who said it saw her own husband, Jude Ingle, cry like a heartbroken boy when they heard the news that Abigail Martha must hang by the neck until dead.

But there was more to it—much more—than the bright gleam of her hair and the deep dark blue of her eyes. When the sea is still, the blue of the fjords is cold; it draws the sun deep but it is not warmed by the sun; and under the blue-black cliffs and under the storms the fjord water is sullen and black. This girl's eyes were alive and warm. Oh, they could go dark! They could darken with anger as swiftly as squalls wipe the sun from the sea and leave it dull. But there was no dullness in Abigail Martha's anger. There was nothing sullen about her eyes.

"She blazed," a Lord Justice of England wrote. "Had her eyes been branding irons, you could have heard my flesh sizz. The trollop is well

1

done for." But Sir Bernard Grenfell, having passed sentence upon her, could not get her out of his mind. "She was a spirited baggage and luscious though slimly made, not meaty as you would expect out of Dorset." And then he added, as if in envy: "I wonder who has her now?"

There was no proof whatever that she was a trollop. Only one man, greatly blessed, ever knew the fire that was in her.

Sir Bernard Grenfell, king's justice, had only the evidence that she had been taken up for nightwalking in Turnmill Street and thrown into jail among strumpets. That—and the sight of her as she came into his court in Old Bailey.

It is strange how many self-righteous men condemn the thing they covet, having missed it perhaps in their wives and feeling that they have been cheated of life by life. Justice Grenfell's weary, unsatisfied eyes, looking down at the girl in the dock, read meanings that were not in her. Before she had spoken a word, Abigail Martha was witness against herself.

There was her way of walking. Her walk was the flowing of wind across treetops—and the man who described her thus was no poet but only a soldier in trouble. There was the eager lift of her head as she looked for Jude Ingle's face in the justice hall, and the valiant smile that resisted and hid her disappointment and terror.

There was her glowing flesh. Months in the horrible fetor of Newgate had not turned her sallow. She was, as Jude's wife said, "the shiningest thing." For hers was that luminous golden flesh—rare even in golden-haired women but possessed by no other women at all—like peaches ripe in the sun and rich with the sun's own life, smooth, sweetly rounded, and firm, not soft but suggesting a yielding softness, suggesting a ripeness not quite revealed.

Few women forgive such a girl for existing. Susannah Ingle was an extraordinary woman.

There was, also, the quick yearning gesture of Abigail Martha's whole body toward Jeffrey whenever she saw him, as if she would take him into her arms and somehow surround him with herself and protect him from the world that was forever bruising him.

It was a gesture that Grenfell, of course, never saw. It was also the key to the truth. But the record of her trial—so meticulous in its pretenses of fairness—makes it callously clear that the truth would have made no difference.

The court had no need for keys to unlock closed doors. One door, splintered and wrenched from its hinges, lay on the bloody floor. The room beyond it contained all the evidence Sir Bernard Grenfell needed.

Even if the whole story had come out in court, the verdict would not have been changed.

The story began in Cerne Abbas near the end of a gray-wool day. It was five and a half of the clock when Abigail Martha opened the kitchen door of the Angel and stepped out into the windy coach yard.

The wind smelled of chalk from the High Stoy hills and the downs above Mintern Magna. It was stripping gobbets of hay from the two-wheeled cart backed up to the cowkeep shed; the cart's canvas cover, blown loose, was flapping between the shafts. Wisps of spilled fodder were swirling around the stone well. A leaf from the beeches beyond the gate came toppling into the horse trough and scudded away over the ruffled water like a hoy with a brown lug sail. A harder gust rustled the wheat-straw thatch just above the girl's head and twitched at the long-handled virgin she carried. The warming-pan handle was slender and round and worn to a metal smoothness; she needed both hands to hold it against the tug of the wind. The door blew open again behind her.

"Bundle, now!" The girl smiled at Susannah Ingle's sharp voice from the kitchen. The sharpness was seldom meant; the word itself was a randy sort of a word—a little joke, all by itself. As far back as she could think, Mrs. Ingle had shouted it at her, not because she needed urging to hurry but because, most times, she didn't. "Don't be standen till ye're a-stooded! The poor lady's a-froze. She's a-bibber with cold—an' you dawdlen!"

Abigail Martha reached back for the latch and pulled shut the low, nail-studded door. Without needing to look, she felt with one bare foot for her own wooden shoes in the row at the edge of the stoop. She took her time wriggling them on while she watched the hurly and burly around the London coach. The shoes felt dampish against her toes, they had the blue-moldy feel that came with the wet-chalk wind; but she stretched her toes to hold the shoes snug to her feet and ran up the clattering outdoor stairs that led to the chamber gallery.

The gallery hung like a small flat bustle across the backside of the Angel. It was old, like the rest of the inn; and it sagged a little, like a bustle coming untied. The girl stopped at the head of the stairs and rested the brassen pan on the weather-veined, sagging rail. This was the time of day she loved. The evenings were always best, with new folk coming in; they were better than mornings, when everyone went away. And this was the best place to be; for the gallery, high as the roofs of the kitchen wing on one side and the spinning house on the other, overhung the square coach yard. It was like being in a stall at the theater, with the yard for the stage and the pit. Abigail Martha never had seen a theater but she thought that it must be like this—a little like this, at least.

She lingered now, curling her toes in the shoes to get them away from the dampy chill of the wood. She wasn't dawdling. Not *just* dawdling, anyway: she had a great good reason. The fine lady in the gallery chamber might be shivering with cold, although it was more likely the road sickness from riding so long in the staging coach over the joppety-joppety hills. She surely was not a-froze; people didn't freeze in October, in Dorsetshire. And a minute or two or three might make all the difference in the world. If Abigail Martha lagged just a little in fetching the warming pan, the lady might be undressing.

Ladies in London gowns could be seen every week or two, billowing out of a coach or a chaise or a rich gentleman's chariot to walk about under the beeches while the post horses were being changed, or even to sit awhile at the Angel's chimney place, sipping the best of Jude Ingle's wine and filling the low-beamed room with their highty-tighty voices. Their gowns were wondrous to see, though of course not their best. But Abigail Martha longed to know what such ladies wore underneath: to see

3

with her own eyes the ribbons and laces and furbelows, and the curious London fashion of tying a garter.

Strange stories came down from London. The bagmen brought most of them, for these traveling salesmen and hagglers were always as full of brags as their saddle packs were full of the cheaper sorts of tabbies and paduasoys, bob wigs and grizzles, stockings and high-lows and whatnot. But the traveling law clerks, the young sprigs of the gentry, and the officers on their way to join the king's frigates at Plymouth brought some of the tallest tales to impress the Cerne Abbas girls—to show what accomplished fellows they were and what a figure they cut with the ladies at Vauxhall and Drury Lane. Their stories, in the sly fashion of men on the prowl, served to turn their talk in directions that suited their purpose.

Abigail Martha heard few of these tales at first hand. The Angel's kitchen wenches and serving maids might do as they pleased, with a decent discretion; but let some peart bagman or navy lieutenant come ogling and ruffling it too close to David Hale's orphan daughter . . . there would be Jude Ingle, randily smiling but earnest, to rowse him off, or Susannah to send the girl bundling away on an errand. But the tales were repeated, with giggles, over the hum of the wheels in the Angel's spinning room and over the clatter of kettles around the hearth.

There was the rumor that London court ladies were wearing a garment called drawers. Even a scullery wench knew that that was the overright of the truth; it was a lie as plain as the nose on your face or the hand on the Cerne Abbas giant, whose fingers were seven feet long. Only sailors wore drawers. Drawers were made of coarse canvas and they possessed two virtues: they were cheaper than breeches and somewhat less drafty than the blue petticoats issued to navy seamen.

There was even a rumor that some of the finest fine ladies in London were taking up with a strange and intriguing French notion—shifts made of embroidered linen to wear when you slept. Abigail Martha had seen, once, a breath-catching negligee fashioned of crimson tabby so crusted with delicate silver threads that it looked as if silver spiders had spun their webs over the cloth. But clothes made for nothing but wearing in bed! It passed all believing.

A wondering, hungering look touched the girl's face now as she leaned on the gallery rail. Not unhappy. An eager, expecting look.

There was no special reason for it. There was, really, nothing at all to expect. There was nothing exciting, to anyone else, about the commotion in the coach yard below. It was all familiar. It was like a play seen again and again. But Abigail Martha loved it. The three horses had been unhitched from the claret-and-black-painted coach; the stableboys were leading them toward the trough; the postboy was strutting behind them and yopping shrill orders in cockney. The passengers had disappeared into the Angel—all but the weazened scrimp of a man with the peckish nose and no chin at all till you came to his Adam's apple. He was still sniffing about the courtyard as if it offended him somehow; his hands kept dab-dabbing at his black smallclothes as if he thought every bit of blown straw in the wind was intending to settle there. The coach guard, with his blunderbuss under one arm and his bugle horn under the other, was hurrying to warm

4

himself in the common room of the Angel. And that great man, the driver, was standing as stiff as a noble milord between the coach and the gate where the stage wagon up from Weymouth was turning in. He strutted just standing still, daring the wagon driver to spatter his Lincoln-green gilt-laced coat or come within whiplash reach of the elegant coach.

The eight stage-wagon horses swung wide. The wagon stopped humbly alongside the stable mixen and settled itself with a groan. The great man turned his back upon it and came lumbering toward the well and the tap-room door in the opposite wing of the tavern. Abigail Martha laughed: he looked like a coach himself, with his belly in front for the boot and his buttocks lumping behind as big as the basket for carrying trunks. London coachmen fascinated her—not for themselves but for what they implied. If a post driver took such high-mighty airs, what must a real London coffeehouse gentleman be! Would she ever know? Would she ever see that wonderful, magical city? She must. *Oh, she must!* She would never be sure till she did.

She was not quite sure what it was that she longed to be sure of. Life itself, perhaps. But life was a day, and a day, and another day, and the days were always the same. They piled up like bricks in a wall, and you couldn't see over tomorrow.

Her father, before he died, had given her just enough distant glimpses to let her see that Cerne Abbas was not the whole world and life in a Dorset market town not all the life that there was. Being a schoolmaster, he had known many wonderful things—but most of them secondhand, out of books. He had not known a great deal about his young, motherless daughter. He had not understood how hungry those glimpses made her, nor understood the thing in her that would not let her be satisfied with any second-best world or with life secondhand.

While she was only a child he had taught her Latin and Greek—a scandalous business, unheard of for even a gentleman's daughter. But he had gone even deeper in folly, reading aloud to her out of theater plays and queer poetry books and the tupenny London papers he got, now and then, from a haggler. He had shown her a world in which men were different, somehow, from those who lived in Cerne Abbas or stopped at the Angel an hour or a night and went on.

Not that she thought overmuch about men. She thought about them no more—and no less, perhaps—than any other sixteen-year-old girl in a little town.

But her conscious thoughts had been shaped by her special hunger—shaped not by instinct alone nor by adolescent curious wonder, but by those distant glimpses of a world far beyond her reach. Other Cerne Abbas girls might walk out on Old Midsummer's Eve with garden rakes over their shoulders and hemp seed in apron pockets. Abigail Martha didn't. She had never thrown the seed over her shoulder and said the old Dorset spell:

Hemp seed I set, hemp seed I sow,
The man who is my true love come to me now.

The reason was that she was afraid. She believed in the spell just as she believed in fairies and fairy rings and the wishing well by the ruined abbey. She was afraid that the spell of the hemp might work and a man appear in the moonlight. The risk was too great. The man might be one of the men she knew, and she might be bound forever. She wouldn't be bound. She *wouldn't*. Not to a man like any man she had seen. Not even a man like her father, gentle and kind, making dreams out of things other men had set down in books but not dreaming of making one dream come true.

She had dreams of her own—strange dreams for a small-town girl in the shut-away hills of Dorsetshire—a mixture of old English folk tales and Virgil and Horace and Suckling and Lovelace and Shakespeare and gay John Gay. She had learned just enough to know that the bagmen, for all their bold talk, were small pease and few in the pod, and that swanking young officers off the king's ships were not perfect knights riding down from Tintagel. And the gentlemen in the fine paneled chariots had a way of being old and fat, or pimply if young, or toothy or spindly-legged or empty-eyed. There was no room in her dreams for such men. Not even Jude Ingle—who pridefully called her "the choosy un"—suspected how high she was setting her cap, in those dreams. Not even Susannah Ingle suspected the goings-on in the girl's tiny garret room, nor knew what was hidden away in the cuddyhole under the eaves. That was Abigail Martha's secret.

It was a beautiful secret, exciting and precious and treasured. It wasn't quite perfect yet. But it could be, soon. It would be if only the lady . . . She wanted to hurry, she wanted to run to that chamber door at the gallery's end. But she made herself wait. She would wait just another half smidge of a minute. It took time for a lady to get undone, with her stays and all.

The stage-wagon driver had set up his steps at the tail of the wagon now, but he hadn't fetched any great hauling of folk—Wynn Lulorth, the cattle buyer from Wareham, with his coiled whip around his neck; a leather-cheeked country woman half again as wide as the hamper of squawking chickens she carried; two young apprentices coming home from a duty visit to their gran'ther in Nether Abbas; and an itinerant cobbler clutching his bench to his belly and trying in vain to see what his feet were doing as they felt for the wagon steps.

An eddy of wind, curling along the gallery, lifted her hair from her shoulders and swept it across her face. She flung it back with a toss of her head, but one lock clung to her parted lips. She nipped at it with her teeth, caught it, and bit it to teach it manners. Then, as she turned her head to blow the perverse lock back where it ought to be, she saw Jeffrey coming in at the gate with the tannery men.

She stopped. Her body yearned toward him—a quick small protecting gesture, almost too quick and small to be seen.

Abigail Martha herself did not know that her body moved. Shielding this older brother—trying to shield him—was part of her life. Almost from cradlehood she had been fighting the battles that Jeff wouldn't fight. The gesture was part of her too. It was instinctive; it was a habit now. She was as unconscious of it as Jude Ingle was of the habit that went with his years of keeping the Angel—his hand always reaching out to wipe at the bar or a table, no matter how clean it might be or how newly washed.

Some of the brightness went out of the girl's face now. The eager aliveness stayed, but there was a shadow on it as if a cloud had brushed quickly between the sun and the earth, not changing the earth but leaving it somehow changed like cloth that is brushed the wrong way. Poor Jeff. . . .

The tannery hands were stopping by at the Angel as they always did, for a bite and a drop. Jeffrey, as always, was with them. And yet he was not, somehow, *with* them. He didn't belong. He was different somehow, although he was as dirty as they from the vats and the hides, and as tired as they—even more tired, by the weary droop of his shoulders. Hides were heavy; they stank; and Jeff was not strong, and he hated the tannery stench that the others seemed never to mind. That was one reason, likely, why he was never really a part of the crowd but always, as now, on the edge of the taddle of men scuffing into the Angel's coach yard.

The tannery men didn't like him. Neither did Jude Ingle's hostlers and stableboys, nor the coachmen and wagon drivers, nor anyone in the town. Nor even Jude Ingle, really. But it was worse than that—it was worse than not being liked. Jeffrey Hale was not even disliked. To the men in Cerne Abbas he didn't seem worth the bother. They tolerated him with a kind of amused contempt.

The sudden tightening in the girl's throat now was as uncontrollable as the instinctive protecting gesture of her body. The difference was that she was conscious of the lump of unhappiness and anger and helplessness and pity in her throat. It was familiar. It was too familiar; and it hurt again now as it always hurt. Why did Jeff have to be the kind of man that he was? Why must he let people bully him and deride him and shut him out? It smalled him so; and it wasn't decent nor right. Why didn't he shut *them* out? Why didn't he keep clear away from them? Why did he have to take their sly, undercreepen tricks? It was a shameful thing for any man to be treated so and to take it and always be there for more. Why? *Why?*

They weren't questions, really. She knew what the answers were. Without needing to think about it, she knew that Jeff was hungry to be liked, to belong, to be let into things—so hungry that he would take crumbs anywhen they were dropped, because they were better than nothing. She understood hunger that couldn't be fed with food; but Abigail Martha would rather have starved than take the contemptuous crumbs that Jeff seemed contented to take.

No, he wasn't content; she knew that. He was terribly hurt and unhappy. And yet all these years, ever since he was twelve, he had been like this. If he would only *fight*. . . . But he wouldn't. He couldn't. Something was gone out of Jeff, and it wasn't his fault. It was *their* fault, not his. They had killed something in him, and Abigail Martha remembered exactly how they had done it.

She had been five then, going on six, but she had never forgotten. It was the first thing she remembered happening in her life—the first and the worst thing of all. After eleven years she could still see, almost as plainly as if it was happening over again, Jeff's face like a small white chip in the dark swirling boil of the river; she could still hear his choked, terrified cries and the laughter and hoots of the crowd that stood on the bank and watched; she could still feel her own choking terror.

It had happened on Processioning Day—the day when the Cerne Abbas elders assembled to walk the boundaries of the town and mark out exactly the land that belonged to the parish. They didn't make records on paper, for paper might burn or be stolen. They didn't use boundary stones, for the stones might be moved. They used children instead.

There had been a great faddle of children that day—a hundred or more, all whooping and running and bundling about in the outpour of grown folk who trooped along behind the solemn, important elders. For Processioning Day was a rare grand day and a great time for eating and drinking and gossip. It was better than a fair or a marriage or even a burying, almost. Half of the town turned out in its Sunday best to take part in the ancient rite. As Abigail Martha remembered it—trudging across the fields with her hand in her father's hand—it had been very gay and exciting. And then, suddenly, it had been frightening; it had been ugly and cruel. There had been, suddenly, agonized cries. There had been a boy writhing and sobbing under the blows of a stick that was more like a club or an ox goad. There had been the sound that the stick made . . . *swish* . . . as it rose, and the sound that it made . . . *whuck* . . . as it fell again and again on the small boy's back. Swish . . . *whuck*. Swish . . . *whuck*. And the wailing that wouldn't stop, but went on and on. That was the way the parish recorded its landmarks.

When the procession came to the great oak behind the abbey, another boy was chosen; he was fetched to the foot of the oak tree and held with his face against it and whipped till he howled with pain. And then he was beaten again, and again, and again, so that there would be no chance whatever that he would forget, as long as he lived, that the oak was a boundary mark. At the gray chalk ledge in Sharpe's meadow, a third boy was whipped; and at Up Cerne crossroads, another. Abigail Martha, clinging to her father's hand with numb fingers, had wondered why all the boys stayed, why they didn't run. When she asked, David Hale had smiled and shaken his head and said that it wouldn't do. She knew, now, that it was a kind of game; nobody could tell which boy would be chosen next; there was a good chance for most of the boys to see all the fun without ever getting a beating. And even if a boy was afraid, it was no good to run away: he would only disgrace himself and his father and earn a worse hiding at home.

When they came to the deep Cerne pool at the river bend, the elders chose Jeffrey Hale; and Abigail Martha remembered that she had cried and her father had picked her up and held her in his arms. She remembered the hoots that went up from the other boys, and the murmurs amongst the grown folk . . . *ay, schoolmaster's young'un . . . too good f'r a beatin'.* . . . Her father, too, had objected; he wanted no favors, he said, for his son. But the elders had had their way. The boy picked out to remember the river bend as a boundary mark was not whipped: he was picked up by the arms and legs and swung by two men and thrown head-long into the pool. The boys who had had their beatings and those who

8

might still be beaten thought Jeff was being let off too easy. But Jeff had been panic-stricken. He began to cry when the men picked him up and swung him; and when they threw him, he screamed—not a young boy's scream, not a human sound at all, but a series of quavering yelps like a small hurt dog's. It was funny; the grownups laughed, and the town boys mocked his terror by yelping like dogs.

But the river was high, and the current was running faster than anyone knew. It tumbled Jeff over and over, all arms and legs and now and again a glimpse of his white small face. Then it sucked him down and he didn't come up, and Abigail Martha was standing alone in the hooting crowd and her father was kicking his shoes off and fighting his way through the crowd and trying to undo his coat as he ran. She had seen her father, too, disappear in the ugly water. The laughter and yelping stopped. In the sudden quiet, her voice was the only sound—a sound so sharp that it hurt like knives in her throat and head. Other men had plunged into the river then; they joined hands and they made a chain all the way across the pool, they found David Hale and his son. Jeff looked dead when they carried him out and hung him head down over a low stone wall like a dripping, half-empty sack. She had never forgotten her father's face, pinched and sick, as he knelt by the brambly wall and pushed his fingers into Jeff's mouth, trying to find Jeff's tongue with his fingers and pull it out and hold it.

Jeff hadn't been dead. But he hadn't been Jeff, after that. He was never the same again.

It had been a long time—years and years—before Abigail Martha began to understand what had happened to him. But she knew, now, that something inside him had died. They had killed his spirit, they had drowned it as surely as if it had stayed in the deep Cerne pool and only his body was walking down there in the coach yard now. There were times when she hated Cerne Abbas and what it had done to her brother—times like now, when she saw him sidling toward the well, being so careful not to get in the way of the tannery men or even the stableboys, reaching out for the pewter cup where it hung by its rusty chain to the windlass post, and then letting his hand drop humbly because Wynn Lulorth shoved past him and seized the cup. *Oh, Jeff. . . .* Her hands winced on the warming-pan handle. *Don't just stand there. Don't take it . . . don't ever take any more insults.*

Jeff stood there. His meekness wasn't respect for an older man. It wasn't politeness. It was weakness and fear, and there was a fawning about it. She saw Jeffrey's mouth twist into a shamed, weak smile that pretended nothing had happened, and his eyes shift this way and that in ashamed furtive glances that tried to find out whether anyone else had noticed. It wasn't even a sensible fear of Wynn Lulorth's bull-like body or of his hands that made fists like dark speckled cheeses. It would have been the same if the burly drover had been the scrawniest stableboy. *Blessed are the meek for they shall inherit the earth.* There were times when Abigail Martha, too, was afraid—times like now, when she frightened herself: it was an awful thing to believe that the Bible told lies. She didn't believe that, really; she didn't want to believe it, but sometimes the thought sprang up; it was there, and she couldn't help it. Jeff had inherited nothing but trouble and cuffs and derision.

Wynn Lulorth had thrust the cup into the wooden bucket that stood on the stone coping of the well and he brought it out brimming now and stooped like a bull to drink. He had lips like those of the cattle he dealt in. His thick mouth devoured the cup and his meaty nose was pressed down on the opposite rim. Black hairs grew singly and stiff on the sides of his nose and like brambles inside his nostrils. The girl could not see the hairs now but she knew how they were pushing out of his nose and fringing the edge of the cup; she had seen him drink before. And he wasn't a tidy man. He was drinking in gulps and the water was running out the sides of his mouth and down his cheeks and dripping from his jaws to make black bright streaks down his hairy throat. He swashed the last gulp of water around in his mouth and spat it out, and when he was finished he let the cup fall dangling and bumping and spattering on its chain.

Jeff picked it up. Holding the cup, he looked to see whether Lulorth was watching before he wiped the outside of it carefully on his sleeve. He dipped it into the bucket and wiped his thumb on his breeches and used the thumb to wipe the inside of the rim. He swirled the water to rinse the cup. And then it happened—the thing that would end his life and four other lives in strange violent ways in unforeseen distant places—the thing that would change Abigail Martha's life and the lives of two men she had never seen.

Chapter 2

Abigail Martha saw it beginning to happen. Wynn Lulorth was walking away and he hadn't bothered to wipe the drip from his chin. Behind him, the post-coach driver had stopped by the end of the trough; he was standing there, watching the horses. Two of the horses had finished their drinking; the third one—the gelded roan leader—also had finished but he was still muzzling the water, hacking his head up and down and blowing. Jeff gave up rinsing the cup; he emptied it on the ground with a peevish impatient jerk that was partly anger at Lulorth but mostly his own futile shame at himself. And just then the gelding lifted his head and shook it. The water flung from his muzzle spattered the coachman's face and made a dark pattern across the front of the Lincoln-green coat. The great man's face seemed to swell. He bellowed:

"Ye damned country lout!"

His green sleeve came up and dabbed at his spattered face. Then he struck without lowering his arm, with the back of his hand.

Jeff's face was half turned away. He was dipping the cup in the bucket again and he didn't know what had happened; he didn't see the blow coming. It fell on his cheek. Abigail Martha saw his head jerk up and his face go blank with surprise and his cheek turn white around the red splotch where the knuckles had struck. The coachman drew back his arm to strike again.

"Ye whore's son!" he bellowed. "Ye maggotty cow-pimp! Douse *me,* will ye?" His knuckles slashed at Jeff's mouth. "Ye will, will ye?"

There was blood on Jeff's lips and a smear of it on his cheek and a slow moving streak of blood creeping down from the corner of his mouth. He looked blind. He stood there and stared at the coachman as if he saw nothing at all, and his face seemed to lose its shape and become a blur. It was blurred by a sudden blind fury, instinctive, too sudden for reason. Jeff's tongue came out and licked at the oozing blood. He raised his hand, holding the cup.

"Yes," he said. It was not Jeff's voice; it was not like Jeff's voice at all; it was thin and squeezed. "Yes." It was like a squeak. "Yes, I will." He hurled the full cup at the coachman's face.

"Good!" Abigail Martha hardly knew that she said it. Surprise was too great. Jeff had done it at last . . . at last, after all these years, he had dared to strike back. "Good! Oh, *good!*"

But it wasn't good. Nothing ever seemed to turn out, for Jeff, as he meant it to; he had bungled this as he always bungled whatever he tried to do, for himself. He had forgotten the chain. The chain snubbed the cup and turned it, and part of the water splashed his own face and smeared the blood over his chin and neck; the rest of it spattered the stableboy holding the gelding. The stableboy looked pleased.

"Here, take un," he said, and twisted the gelding's head down. "I been waitin' f'r this." The postboy, grinning, reached up and took the headstall. The stableboy spat on his hands and rubbed the palms slowly together and took a slow step toward the end of the trough, past the coachman. He wasn't really a boy; he was a full-grown lout of a man though only a hostler's apprentice—a good head taller than Jeff and two keg staves wider across the shoulders. A slow, pleased smile peeled his mouth away from his teeth as he spoke to the coachman. "He'll pay f'r it, Mr. Houck. Us'll teach un his manners, sure." Then he looked at Jeff and took another step.

"Ye been axing f'r it, ye weazen-faced, footy scrimp." He took another slow step, and Jeff backed away. "Ye ramshacklum, dead-alive croop." Another slow step. "It's time we came upsides with ye. Sloppin' y'r betters. . . . It's time ye're a-teached, ye sly, creepit mealymouth."

The tightness in Abigail Martha's throat was a hard, aching knot and her knuckles were white on the warming-pan handle. She had seen it so many times, this baiting of Jeff like a cornered and friendless dog or a terrified fox in a trap. Jeff . . . *Jeff!* Oh, stand up to him! *Fight!*

But Jeff was backing away. The stable hand was stalking him with short, mincing, menacing steps and Jeff was shuffling backward and cowering and his arms were huddled against his ribs. Jeff's face was no longer blurred; it was sharp and pinched with the old abject cringing fear. His brief moment of courage was gone. It hadn't been courage at all, but fear and surprise and blind instinct that overcame his habitual shameful meekness and the strange unexplainable terror that dwelt within him and had dwelt there ever since he was twelve years old. Wynn Lulorth had turned and was walking back to enjoy the sport, and the driver was watching with an ugly expectant look on his lumpy face. Behind Jeff, the tannery men were grinning and jostling and closing in to trap him between the trough and the well. They were egging the stableboy on:

"Chimp him, Jem! Break him to flinders!"

"Make un eat horse drop!"

"Taken his breeks down an' see what he is, Jem . . . for why . . . naah, there's no need o' lookin' . . . put petticoats on him; they're fitter . . . by God, no . . . he beant enough of a man t' make even a woman . . . ahhh, duck him . . . give un the cuckin' stool; that be the thing f'r the bletherin' likes o' him."

"Ay." The stable lout wet his lips with his tongue and drew the palm of his hand down over the pushed-out lip; he wet the other palm and washed them slowly together. "Ay; he's right fond o' water. Ye are, ain't ye? Free with it, ain't ye? Dousin' us. . . . There's a plenty o' water a-down the well. Would ye like t' climb in, or will we be throwin' ye down?"

"No!" Jeff's cry was shrill with panic. His eyes darted this way and that way, seeking escape, but the grinning crowd hemmed him in. "No! No!"

Abigail Martha said the same word. Not aloud. Her lips did not move. Her teeth had dug into her lower lip; they held it; it could not move. *No. No; they mustn't do that.* But she saw that they meant to do it. They had threatened to do it for years. It had been the town joke. It was the thing that had helped to make Jeff what he was—the old terror constantly kept alive. *No!* Always before they had been content to threaten and pretend; it had been sport enough to terrify him, to make him beg.

But they rushed him now, and he yelped like a small hurt dog. He struggled, crazy with fear; he was helpless against so many. They lifted him, writhing and twisting and pleading, by arms and legs; swung him once, twice, and a third time toward the well; and then dropped him into the horse trough and thrust him under and held him.

Abigail Martha kicked off her shoes. She sat down on the gallery railing, swung her legs over, caught her heels on the edge of the gallery floor, and jumped with the warming pan still in her hands. She jumped like a boy, half crouched, leaning forward, and she was as lithe and as sure as a boy. Her skirts, whipping up, showed her bare legs bent to break the shock of the jump. She seemed to be running the instant her feet touched the ground.

Nobody saw her jump, and nobody saw her coming nor heard her. For Abigail Martha had her own way of fighting. She had found out long ago —almost as long ago as she had found out that feet had been made for kicking and fists for hitting—that threats were a waste of breath, they only made people laugh. Fists, feet, knees, and teeth were all useful, but silence improved them: surprise was almost as good as a knotty stick or a stone or a wagon whip.

The horses were in her way now. They were snorting and pulling back from the laughter and yells and the frantic thing in the water. But the stable hands and the postboy weren't willing to miss the fun; they were holding hard to the bridles. Wynn Lulorth's bulk and the coachman's blocked off the rest of the trough. Abigail Martha swerved past the roan's

12

dancing legs. Her knee took the postboy hard in the saddle-soiled seat of his breeches. The knee and the roan's head, jerking, lifted him off his feet; the horse snatched him out of the way.

The far side of the trough was a jostle of men leaning over, holding Jeff's arms and legs and yelping at him, mocking his cries that they couldn't hear. Jeff's cries were bubbles now; his face was a blur in the water. The girl turned the warming pan upside down and thrust it across the trough. The brass bottom glowed with the heat of the coals inside. She raised the pan into the nearest face. The man yelped like a small hurt dog. Then he cursed her wildly . . . *ye devil . . . ye hagrod bitch!* Startled heads came up. Abigail Martha picked out, in the gawking row, the face that she wanted most.

The stable lout's wits were too slow to take in what was going on. He stayed there, bent, holding Jeff under. The girl brought the pan up into his grinning face and held it and pressed it, hard. He howled and flung himself backward and clutched his seared mouth. But he couldn't escape: the crowd held him. Abigail Martha laid the hot glow of the pan on the back of his hand. When he snatched the hand down, she burned him again on the cheek. Then she lifted the pan and hit him. Sparks flew from the pattern of holes in the lid. She lifted the pan again and hit the next head in the row and its hat came off and tumbled into the trough. Jeff, floundering, clutched at the floating hat and pulled it under the water. He sat up, retching, while Abigail Martha hit the next head and the next as they shrank away. The warming pan smoked and clanged.

A hostler came edging toward her around the end of the trough. She ran to meet him, and the full sweep of the pan caught him flat on the side of the head so hard that the latch on the brassen lid chattered like teeth knocked loose. He stopped and looked foolish.

The tannery men, too, looked foolish. They stood like a caddle of sheep, gawping at her, and one and then one and another one gave her a wheedling grin. The girl's anger flared. There wasn't one sorry, shamed face in the lot. They thought what they'd done was funny; they'd do it again. They had never been hurt in their lives the way Jeff had been hurt. *I'll hurt them.* . . . Tears stung her eyes. *I'll hurt them.* . . . The brass stung her fingertips as she twisted the latch of the pan and turned it away from the lid. She ran blindly, crying, to throw the coals into their faces.

A hand from behind caught her hair. An arm slid around her and lifted her off the ground. The reek of Wynn Lulorth's body came up like an uncleaned stable.

She kicked, and hurt only herself. She struggled, and only slid downward a little, inside her clothes, and the crushing arm lifted her breasts. Lynn Lulorth's hand moved on her body, opened, and closed again over her breast. His other hand, twisted into her hair, dragged her head up and back when she tried to bite, and the animal sound in his throat was not a sound only; she felt it; his hairy throat was against her cheek and his mouth was reaching down for her mouth and his lips were wet. His lips had the rubbery shine of an animal's mouth. He was chuckling and talking:

"Naah, then. Naah, then. Ye've had y'r fun. Naah pay y'r score like a good un."

Her body was helpless, but both of her arms were free. She swung the warming pan upwards and backwards, back of her head, upside down. She heard the coals fall on the lid and the lid drop open; it clanged once against the handle. She closed her eyes. Hot ashes came shifting down on her upturned face and over the front of her bodice. They burned on her face and her breasts. There were sparks in her hair, she felt them begin to sting through the pain of Wynn Lulorth's fingers twisting her hair. There was one fierce burrowing pain in the hollow between her neck and her lifted arm, and Lulorth's breath on her neck made the burning worse, his startled bawl fanned the coal that clung to her skin.

But he let her go. His rough sleeve smeared the ashes across her face. Her hands lost the warming pan; it was wrenched away. She brushed at the coal on her shoulder; it stuck to her flesh; she picked it off with her fingers and felt the coarse cloth of her blouse stiff and brittle with char. It broke, and her finger went through.

The tears came again. Behind her, Lulorth was cursing. It didn't sound right. *He'd ought to be yelling louder, he'd ought to be making more noise.* Then she knew that the cattle buyer was bawling as loudly as one of his bulls and that he didn't sound loud because the whole jostle of folk in the coach yard was yelling and whooping with laughter.

She turned and saw that Wynn Lulorth was doubled over. His thick body wove back and forth and his heavy legs moved in a kind of shuffling dance. His shirt was pulled out of his breeches behind. He was holding it half of the way up his hairy back with one hand while his other hand dug at his waistband. Some of the coals must have gone down the back of his shirt, inside, all the way to his breeches. But the crowd wasn't laughing at Lulorth—not at him, just. It was laughing at Houck.

The girl gasped at the terrible thing she had done. Most of the embers and ashes had taken the post driver fair. The fine Lincoln-green coat was covered with dirty gray, black-speckled dust. There were neat little piles of ashes caught behind each of the big brass buttons and two bigger piles on his shoulders and gray-dirty drifts in every crease and fold. When he brushed them, they smeared, and more ashes fell out of his cuffs to bedraggle his waistcoat. His lumpy face had turned purple; it seemed to be coming apart. All the lumps of his cheeks and his nose and his chins stood out swollen and dark. His face looked like a basket of plums that was ready to spill. He stood there in a thin cloud of settling dust and moved his face slowly from side to side to glower at the hooting circle that penned him in.

He didn't know, yet, the real why of the taunting laughter. He was so concerned about his smeared coat that he hadn't yet taken thought to his elegant hat. The hat was on fire. There was one redly glowing coal on the top of the crown, and smoke was beginning to rise from the deep cocked folds. It was funny. Abigail Martha felt laughter rise in her throat. But it was frightening too. She had never done anything nearly so awful as this, and she would be punished somehow. Mr. Houck would demand to be paid for his ruined coat and his hat and she couldn't pay and she might be

14

put in jail and stay there the rest of her life. Was burning somebody's clothes as bad as stealing? She didn't know. But if it was, they would put her in jail and whip her and maybe brand her. They might even hang her the same as they did the serving girl down at Weymouth who stole a cap and two kerchiefs out of a neighbor's wash.

She was frightened sick. But, terrified as she was, she knew there was something else besides fear that made her feel queer and troubled and not like herself. What was happening wasn't just funny and frightening at the same time. It was pitiful too. She felt sorry—not for what she had done, but for Houck. And she shouldn't feel sorry for him; there wasn't the smallest reason. The trouble was all his fault; he had struck Jeff, twice, for something that Jeff hadn't done; he had started it all. But now she was sorry for him, standing there disheveled and laughed at and taunted. Without really thinking about him, she knew that he was pathetic—not frightened as Jeff had been, but almost as bewildered and helpless. All his dignity was gone; and without knowing anything about him, she knew that his dignity had been his whole importance. She knew that the man was changing before her eyes.

One moment he had been a great man; the next, he was ridiculous and all his admirers had turned on him, hooting and laughing, and he was a clown for sour-smelling tannery men and the stable hands of a country inn. He might get a new coat and a new cocked hat, but he would never be a great man in Cerne Abbas again. And the postboy, capering now with his hand clapped over his mouth to keep in his laughter, would spread the story in every coach yard from Plymouth up to London. And Houck was shrinking and shriveling somehow; he would never be the same man again—not even to himself. He didn't know, yet, what was happening to him, any more than he knew that his hat was on fire. But the girl had a strange, troubled feeling of knowing.

For there are some people who have the gift or the curse of insight—sudden flashes of unsought and unwanted knowledge of others. Abigail Martha was one of these people. Perhaps all her childhood years of trying to shelter her brother and understand him had made her more sensitive to the feelings of others and more understanding of the secret and terrible ways in which they could be hurt. But such cursed or gifted people are not often given the same insight into themselves. Abigail Martha did not understand what was happening, now, to her.

What was happening was that in the space of a few hurrying minutes she was changing from girl into woman. For the first time she was getting a glimpse of life as it was—not a little personal thing touching only herself and Jeffrey and Jude and Susannah Ingle and not a bright-colored, exciting and comforting dream made of stories in books. She was seeing it now for the first time, blurred but whole—an impersonal and frightening immensity into which little lives were snatched up and twisted and changed—an implacable something as wide and as high as the sky that you couldn't touch. But the sky touched *you*. It sent rain, harmless drops that made little soft splashes upon your face, not as big as tears. And then the drops were Cerne River, boiling in flood and rolling Jeff over and over and making him something he hadn't been. For the first time she was seeing human cruelty for what it was—not merely small and personal, singling her brother out for abuse and derision, but impersonal and immense and a part of nature and no more to be controlled than the rain and the flood. She had seen the cruelty of the tannery men and the hostlers turn from Jeff to the post-coach driver as quickly as the Cerne River turned from tormenting one bank to the other as soon as it found that the other was weaker.

She saw now that Jeff had climbed out of the trough. He was sitting on the edge of it now with both hands pressed to his throat as if his throat ached from his screaming and choking and retching. Water ran down from his hair, over his face and his fingers, and dripped from his clothes and spread in a pool at his feet. His face was turned half away, she could see only the cheek with the marks of Houck's knuckles still on it. He wasn't watching the coachman: the crowd was between him and Houck. He was looking toward the low wing of the cowkeep shed and his face was startled. He jumped up and pointed. His lips moved, but the sound that came out was a croak, and he retched again. He wiped his mouth with one hand while he used the other to point. A thin stream of water ran brightly down both his thin arms and dribbled from his sharp elbows. He croaked again:

"Fire!"

And then Jeff was plucking and pulling at the backs of the tannery men, and they were turning their heads impatiently and turning away again, because Houck at last had found out that his hat was burning. He snatched it off. He was shaking it, upside down, and beating it on his legs and making noises that sounded like Jeffrey's croaks.

The crowd was in a spasm of noisy delight The men whose backs Jeff was plucking ignored him. One of them thrust him off with a crousty elbow:

"Garn! Get away, ye scrimp!"

Jeff seized the elbow and dragged him back. Abby saw who it was— Nolly Hintock, the tetchiest, peevishest one of the lot. Jeff took Nolly Hintock's face in his hands and pushed it and twisted his head on his neck. Jeff . . . *Jeff*, of all people, to *dare!* He was becalling and rating the man in a thin, cracked voice:

"Ye goocoo! Ye great noggerhead! Ye blind coof! *Will ye see?* The hay's burnin'! The cowkeep's afire!"

Hintock's mouth fell open. He bawled without closing it:

"Fire!"

The crowd stood a moment, gawking, and then it broke and was running. Abigail Martha's heart seemed to stop, and then it turned over slowly and dropped into bottomless nothing. The hay on the tilt cart was blazing. One long yellow tongue of flame was licking the cowkeep shed and scorching the old oak beams than ran crooked across the plaster. The plaster was black already in sooty streaks.

The yard was a blather of shouting. *A line . . . make a line from the trough . . . buckets . . . take 'en from under the wagon!* Noll Hintock's shouts were the loudest. *Get the horses away . . . wag y'rsel's . . get to the well, there, Lulorth . . . the trough beant enough. . . .* The long yellow tongue of fire touched the old yellow thatch of the eaves. It curled back, and then licked again, and the straw and the flame were no longer yellow but red. The girl felt her heart squeezed small as if Lulorth's hand had gone through her blouse and her flesh and his dark speckled fingers were squeezing it into nothing. *The roof . . . the roof's took . . . run for a ladder, you!*

There was a row of men already between the trough and the cart. The first brimming bucket was jerking along the row. But the heat was fierce; the last man in the line was edging away and shielding his face with his arm; the dark red glow was eating up through the thatch and the gray-weathered straw on top was turning brown in a widening patch. It would burst into flame in a minute, in half a minute. The ladder would be too late.

Abigail Martha ran toward the blazing cart. There on the ground, twenty feet past the well, the warming pan lay where Wynn Lulorth had flung it when he wrenched it out of her hands. A pattern of black ash beyond it showed where an ember had fallen and kindled a wisp of spilled hay. There were droppings of ash to show how the wind had rolled it and picked it up and whisked it into the cart. The girl sobbed as she ran.

Drops from the first flung bucketful spattered her neck as she passed the last man in the line. The canvas tilt cover still lay between the shafts of the cart. It was covered with gobbets of ash, and the thong that had fastened it to its hoop was burned through and one edge was brittle and charred like the hole in her blouse. But it wasn't on fire. She snatched it, and felt the heat like a blow in her eyes and saw her hair, swinging down past her face, suddenly crinkle and blacken around the ends. She slapped at it as she ran on to the door of the spinning room and up the steep stairs to the loft.

She unlatched the dormer window and pushed it open, and saw that the thatch of the shed had burst into flame. The roof was steep. She had to back out of the window. Her petticoats caught on the ledge, but there was no time to be modest. She squirmed backward onto the roof, on her hands and knees, dragged the stiff canvas after her, stood up and ran toward the blazing thatch. The edged straw cut her feet when she tried to stop, and she couldn't stop, the roof was too steep, she was running straight into the fire. She threw herself backward and slid, and rolled over and had to let go of the canvas to check herself by digging her hands into the thatch, tearing it loose, and digging her hands in again. Both hands were slippery with blood when she raised herself on her knees and crawled back up the roof for the cover and crawled back again. She got to her feet and began to beat at the flames with the canvas. Bits of the burning straw flew up and were whirled away. Nolly Hintock was roaring at her:

"Stop! Stop, girl! Ye'll spread it! Smother it—that's the thing!"

And then she heard Jude Ingle's voice, not roaring but only big as it always was:

"Abby . . . Abby, go back. *Go back.*"

She looked down and saw him below her. He was the last in the row now, close to the fire. Too close. He had come from the taproom; he still had his white apron on. But he looked different somehow; his face looked empty and gone. She knew why: all that he had was going. And it was her fault, and yet he was thinking of her. She wouldn't go back. She couldn't.

She lifted the heavy canvas and shook it out like a sheet to be spread on a bed. It flapped and jerked in the wind of the fire, but it settled down slowly over the burning thatch. She threw herself down upon it and rolled on it, squeezing the air out from under it, holding the edges and spreading them, pushing them down to smother the fire. The canvas was hot in an instant. She felt the heat coming up through her clothes and rising around her and clutching her belly. It seemed to be pulling her down. She tried to raise herself on her knees and elbows and lift her belly and breasts away from the clutching heat but she couldn't, she couldn't do that and still keep the cover stretched out and the edges flat. She let her body sag down on the canvas again, and it seemed to take a long time for her stomach to touch it again and the canvas felt hard, like hot metal, and hollow and curved like a shallow iron saucepan.

The fire was eating the thatch underneath and the canvas was sinking down into the hollow it made. She thought of the brittle-black hole in her blouse where the coal had burned through. When the canvas charred, it would crumble; the fire would come through.

She could feel the hollow grow deeper. The tilt-cover edges slid down. Little flames wriggled out and licked at her fingers. She snatched her fingers away and the canvas slid farther down and the fire curled up. She gripped the edge of the cover again and pushed it back over the fire and held it and felt the pain going through her in long sick shudders. She couldn't lie still but she had to. She couldn't. *She must.* Wherever her arms and her thighs touched the canvas, it scorched her bare flesh. The sleeves of her blouse were too short to protect her arms; she couldn't let go of the canvas to push down her wanton skirts. The wind was cold on her buttocks. If she could only turn over and let the wind touch her thighs for a moment . . . just one little moment . . . But she couldn't. If ever the wind got under the tilt cover now, the fire would run wild and nobody could stop it until the whole inn was gone. Nobody could stop it but her.

And then something struck her clenched hand and the pain was worse and she couldn't keep her hand clenched on the canvas. She snatched it away and held it against her mouth to soothe it and keep back the noise she was making.

The hand wasn't hot. It was cold. It was cold and wet. And water was running and glistening all down the sooty hollow in which she lay and running under her body, and where the fire had been curling out from under the edge of the cover, smoke curled instead, and the blackened ends of the straw were wet. Jude Ingle's voice was behind her:

"Abby. . . . Abby, d'ye hear me? *Abby!* Ye've got t' roll. Ye must roll whilst the reeds are sogged. The ladder's just here t' y'r rightwards. *Roll* . . . rightwards, mind, on t' y'r back, an' slide down here agean thc ladder."

She never had doubted Jude Ingle. She rolled, and as she began to slide she saw Jude at the eaves, on the ladder, bent over the topmost rung with his arms reaching out to catch her. His big hand closed on her ankle and guided her foot to the rung where his own feet were.

"Can ye lie so a minute?" He didn't wait to be answered. He turned away, reaching down for another bucket passed up from man to man on the ladder behind him. Abigail Martha lay on the wet straw, trembling, smelling the sour burned smell and feeling the dampness seep up through the back of her dress. Only it wasn't like that: it was more like her body seeping down into the straw, all the strength running out and leaving her weak, and then even the weakness was running out and there was nothing at all but the stinging bright pain in her hands.

She wanted to look at her hands, but her arms were like limp wet strings; it was hard to pull her hands up by the strings. When she saw them, they weren't bright at all, they were black, except in the places where blood came out in a slow dark ooze. She put them down again, carefully, on the straw, and lay watching Jude as he stooped for the buckets and raised them and slashed the water upon the roof. She saw now why his face had looked different, down in the yard.

His eyebrows and lashes were gone and the curling black hair was burned far back from his forehead; the hair that was left looked like a wig that had slipped and uncovered a shaven skull that was sprouting stiff reddish-brown fuzz; and his merry eyes were like slits under swollen lids. Jude . . . so patient . . . so kind . . . always the litsomest, handsomest man in his tavern, no matter who else might be there. *I did it. I did that to him. His face looks so gone.* Then she thought: *It is gone. From me, it is. He must hate and despise me. He hasn't looked at me once.* The weak tears trickled down her cheeks.

Jude lifted another bucket. It caught on the top of the ladder and part of the water splashed out. She felt the cold, burning spatter of drops on her flesh. She looked to see why they burned—and then the blood was burning up into her neck and face like the heat that had surged through the charring tilt cover, and even her breasts were hot. She was half unrayed from her rolling and sliding. Her short-gown was wadded under her back, and the blue wincey petticoat was a tight-pulled tangle around her hips. Her legs and her thighs were bare. The pain sparkled up through her fingers and into her arms as she tugged at the shameless skirt. Jude was leaning down toward her again over the top of the ladder and talking to her:

"The fire's douted, Abby. Ye'd nigh put it out before the first bucket came up. Ye're a clever brave girl. Gie me y'r hand, now. We'll get ye down." He looked at the blackened hand and took her instead by the wrist and pulled her up. She winced when her feet touched the thatch. "Ay, it hurts. Can ye bear y'r feet on the ladder?"

"Yes." But she couldn't bear his praise and his being so kind.

"I'll go before so t' steady ye, Abby. Ye'll not need t' use y'r hands." He stepped down two rungs to make room for her. "Gie me y'r wrist again."

"No." All the folk in the yard were clustered around the ladder and staring up. "No. Make them go away."

She shouldn't have said it. She knew, not more than a minute later, that it was the worst of all the wrong things she had done—that it was one more of those small trifling terrible things that could change people's lives. But she didn't know that when she said, *Make them go away.* And she couldn't go down the ladder with Lulorth and Nolly Hintock and all the tannery men and the hostlers and stableboys staring up at her legs. The blue wincey was heavy and wet and it covered her legs, but they didn't feel covered. She felt stripped and naked and shamed, and the words were said, and Jude Ingle had understood them. He turned his head over his shoulder and called:

"Stand away. Get away from the ladder."

The men didn't move. Jude was climbing down. He swung around on the ladder and jumped to the ground.

"Stand away!" His voice was not big and calm. It shook, for he was shaking all over now with exhaustion and strain and the sudden release from his fear that the Angel and all he owned was to be destroyed. "Get back, all of ye, now. F'r shame! The girl's sick with her burns. Will ye use a hurt girl f'r a peep show? Stand away, I said!"

There were titters and mutters and one gangling laugh and an angry word from Jude—the name of the man who had laughed. But the circle was shrinking back and the faces were not so close. The girl started down the ladder.

"Oh, " she heard Lulorth say, "stand away f'r Jude's nammet. Her be a main way too fine f'r the likes o' we. Her be Jude's peep show."

The murmurs and titters were louder, but nobody spoke till she stood on the ground, trembling and sickened with shame and wanting to run and hide and wanting the muddied earth under her feet to open and take her in.

"Come, now." Susannah Ingle was putting both arms around her. "There's a crock o' new butter waiten, not salted yet. It'll ease y'r poor hands. Come, child."

"Susannah," Jude said. "Susannah . . . wait. I've a word f'r Lulorth that ye must hear." His feet made slow, sucking sounds in the puddled dirt. "Wynn Lulorth, I've had enough trouble this day, but ye said a thing that I'll not let pass. Do ye tak' 'en back?"

Lulorth's lips made a wet bubbly sound like a horse blowing into a trough. Abigail Martha lifted her head from Susannah's shoulder and saw Jude's left hand go out and grip the coiled whip where it hung on Lulorth's chest. The drover stepped toward him, body to body.

"Ye don't flummocks me, Jude Ingle. I said what the whole town knows, barrin' maybe y'r wife. The girl is your girl. She be no cow-lease, Ingle. Ye've colled her. She be nought but y'r leasin' now."

Jude's fist made a sound on Wynn Lulorth's face like the stamp of a horse's hoof on hard dirt. Lulorth's head jerked backward against the loops of the whip. Jude jerked it toward him again and his fist made a different sound—soft and wet, like a hoof in mud. Lulorth's head hung backward over the whip. The coils held him, his face upturned. His nose was not where it had been, and his face was a bloody puddle around the crushed lump of his nose.

The whiplash began to slide through Jude Ingle's hand. Lulorth sagged as the loop grew longer. His face came up like a puddle standing on edge. It began to run. Then the loosening coils slid up over his head and he fell.

Chapter 3

This wasn't the first time Jude Ingle had carried her up the steep stairs to her little room under the eaves. The first time was long ago—the night after her father died. The room had been hers ever since.

She had been eight years old then, and alone and lost, and Jude's arms had shut out the empty and frightening world. Now she was lost and alone and frightened again, and his arms couldn't shut the world out. They were not the same. They never would be again.

She knew what Wynn Lulorth had meant. She could not help but know. For knowledge came early to girls who were born in Cerne Abbas. It came long before innocence went. It came before the first promptings of nature and the awareness of instinct—before the first stirrings of wonder concerning life and the first vague imaginings. And the Cerne giant left little to be imagined. No girl, seeing the monstrous male figure carved into the hill that threw its long shadow across the river at dawnen, could possibly misunderstand.

The figure was inescapable. It was a hundred and eighty feet tall, and the club in its hand was a hundred and twenty feet long. It was old. It was very old, it went back beyond time. The Cerne giant had been carved into the chalk of the hill by men of some vanished tribe, by heathens whose only religion was life and the making of life. It was a natural primitive symbol of life, made by men in a state of nature—decently ancient and yet obscene, enormous, exaggerated.

It was also a natural part of Cerne Abbas life, like the sky and the barren downs, the ruined abbey and the Eleven Apostles, the being born and the marrying and the giving birth and the dying. Because it was always there and had always been there, it was an outstep thing—it was something a great way off. Its very nearness, there at the edge of the town, seemed to make it remote. Its familiarity made it of no great importance. You were no more aware of it, most of the time, than you were aware of the rest of the landscape or of yourself.

But now, all the way up the stairs behind the stiff little flame of the candle Susannah carried, Abigail Martha held her neck stiff so to keep her head from touching Jude Ingle's shoulder. All the way up the stairs, she tried to make herself small—to lie in Jude's arms as lightly as when she was eight years old.

They were maggoty notions, the both. They were foolish and fanciful thoughts and she knew that they were. But she couldn't help that the notions were there, in her head.

No—that was wrong. The thoughts were not just in her head. They were all around her, outside, like the ugly dark shapeless shapes of the shadows the candle threw on the ceiling and walls of the stairs—obscene and enormous, exaggerated—like the ugly dark wings of the bats that hung under the eaves of the stable by day and emerged at blue dusk to swoop and swirl over the coach yard. The thoughts were not even her own. They were other people's. They were the thoughts of the stable hands and the tannery men and the girls in the Angel's kitchen, and she knew now that the ugly thoughts must have been in their minds a long time. If they hadn't been, Lulorth would never have dared to coll her and try to kiss her, to handle and fondle her body.

What the whole town knows, barrin' maybe y'r wife. She couldn't bear to look at Jude Ingle's face, or his wife's, or the satisfied, smugly excited, I-told-you-so faces of the two scullery maids who were following Jude up the stairs with pitchers of water and huckaback towels and pieces of frayed soft linen laid over the tops of the pitchers. *She be no cow-lease, Ingle*—no unmown field. She couldn't bear, ever, to look at any Cerne Abbas face. She would know that the faces knew. *She be nought but y'r leasin' now*—nothing but gleanings, left after Jude had reaped her.

It wasn't true. Jude wasn't like that. But she couldn't escape from the rise and fall of his broad, deep chest and the quiver and quob of his arms. She couldn't escape from her thoughts.

One after one, the dark thoughts swooped into her mind and fastened themselves by the words Wynn Lulorth had said. She tried to drive them away. *It's not true. Oh, it's not! How could anyone think——* But the words were as dirty and sharp and as hooked as the claws on the wings of bats. The thoughts hung, ugly and dreadful, under the eaves of her mind. Jude must be thinking now of what Lulorth had said. And Susannah, too, must be thinking. And how could Susannah know that it wasn't true?

She can't know. She wonders. She hates me. And Jude hates me too. He can't help it. He couldn't possibly help it, because he couldn't help knowing what Susannah was thinking—because he couldn't help knowing that his wife would never be sure that the words weren't a terrible lie. *Please, God, make my hands hurt worse. Oh, please! Please punish me, God!*

Her hands were two bright blossoms of pain as they lay in her lap. Her legs, tilted up to the crook of Jude's arm, held her hands with their palms toward her face, and the fingers were half-opened petals of pain above the muddy-streaked stems of her wrists.

They were black when she looked at them. When she didn't look, they seemed yellow. They must be yellow—the fingers were little separate flames. And she thought that her hands were like muddy flowers that she had plucked in a wet, miry place where the dead stems of last year's sedge were brittly and sharp. She could feel them growing, the pain unfolding and stiffening, and she must have pulled them up roots and all, just as she pulled up the bright yellow cowslips in the quaggy places along Cerne Pool when she was a little girl and came home with her hands full of grubby blossoms and her feet and her hands and her frock all pucksy and smeared with mud.

She could feel the thin ache of their roots growing down through her arms and into her breast and twisting into the hard, knotted ache of her heart. It was almost as if God was granting her mean little selfish prayer. When she thought of her hands like that, it helped her feel small—as small as the child who hadn't hurt Jude or Susannah or anyone else excepting the boys she had kicked or scratched when they taunted Jeff. She began to cry, slow tears for the little girl she had been a long time ago, and for the handfuls of cowslips that died because she loved them so much.

And now she was in the little room with the low, slant ceiling and the one window set so close under the eaves that the thatch made an eyebrow for it. Jude was setting her down on the stool by her bed, and the scullery maids were gone and the pitchers of water were here on the floor at her feet along with the crock of new butter Susannah had fetched. Jude started to go, and then he stopped in the doorway and turned around. He wiped with one hand at his sooted face and then looked at his hand and wiped the back of it on his apron. It made a long smear of blood.

"Abby . . ."

Susannah rebuked him.

"Be off with ye! Bundle y'rself. There's the kitchen t' see to, and folk to be fed. And I'll not have ye frettin' Abby."

"There's Houck t' be seen to," Jude said. "I've got t' settle with him. I count it would be a help if I knew how the gwains-on started."

Abby began to tell him.

"Oh, ees," Jude broke in when she came to her brother. "Jeff. *Him* again."

"It wasn't his fault!" Quick flash of anger, bright in her voice. The anger dark in her eyes. Dark, too, in her heart.

"No. It's never Jeff's fault."

Abby sat on the stool and listened to Jude Ingle's footsteps going away down the stairs. They sounded, somehow, as if they would never come back.

Susannah, so quick the most times with her tongue, was silent now. Only her fingers were brisk on the lacings of Abby's bodice and at the waist string of the blue wincey skirt. Even when they were loosed, the sogged cloth still clung to her body.

"Can ye stand on y'r feet f'r a bit?"

She stood up. The petticoat dropped. Susannah drew the bodice and blouse gently down her arms and peeled the wet shift up her body and over her head. There were streaks and smooches and puddles of fine straw ash on her body, and gritty dark charcoal ash in the hollow between her breasts. The charcoal had come from the warming pan, but how had the other ash come through her bodice and blouse and shift to soil her so quickly? It had seemed like hours when she lay with the hot canvas searing her thighs, and her body arching and sinking deeper and deeper into the hollow of burning thatch, but she knew it had been only minutes—maybe not even a minute. *So soiled.* . . . Susannah was dipping soft linen into a pitcher and washing her now. Susannah was trying to make her clean. But she couldn't. Nobody could. The tears came again.

"What? Weepen! That's not like ye, Abby. There's no harm done—a bit place on the roof that'll be the better when it's thatched new."

"I might have burned everything!"

"But ye didn't. Ye put it out." Susannah went down on her knees. She reached for one muddy foot. Abby tucked it swiftly under the stool.

"Oh *no! No!* That man . . . You heard what he said."

"It's not true. Here, now. Gi' me y'r foot." She began to wash it gently. "With some, it could be the truth. I know Jude. I know you. Would ye have me let the overright of the truth change my feelen f'r ye? I've loved ye these many years, and Jude's loved ye. He loved ye afore he ever laid eyes on me. Ye're like his own flesh and blood. *Tschhh . . .* y're poor foot's all cut. Jude's a girt fool, as all men are in their times. He was a girt fool this day, anigh t' killen Wynn Lulorth. He would have done better t' laugh. There'll be no end t' the talken now. But what's done is done, and I'll stand by Jude. Ye'll stand by him too, Abby. Ye'll stand up t' the gab and ye'll laugh and I'll laugh, and maybe in his own time Jude will laugh, though he's been hurt deep. Abby . . ."

"Yes."

"Ye mind what Jude said about Jeff? He has the right of it, child."

"But it *wasn't* Jeff's fault!"

"Fault or no, a man's his own man. Ye can't be the man f'r Jeff."

"They're all set against him . . . becalling him . . ."

"There's no one can change that but Jeff."

"How can he? He can't fight them all."

"I know, Abby. But it's him must stand up t' his trouble. Ye weaken him when ye do what he will not do. Ye shame him. Ye make it worse."

She couldn't argue and ballyrag at Susannah—not now—not ever, after Susannah had been so kind. But Abby's thoughts ran swiftly to Jeff's defense. He wasn't like other men. Expecting Jeff to fight was the same as expecting a clubfooted man to climb a hay staddle as quickly as other men. It wasn't fair. It was cruel. Nobody—nobody decent—taunted and tortured a cripple. Nobody blamed a man for being maimed or misshaped. People could understand the stump of an arm or a crooked back. But they couldn't see that Jeff was somehow crippled inside. Not even Jude and Susannah could understand that he had been warped and changed, when he was thrown into Cerne Pool, just as surely as if his legs had been broken or one of his arms had been cut on a scythe blade so badly it had to be taken off. They blamed Jeff for not being something he couldn't be. *If we only could go away . . . somewhere . . . where nobody knows. Why can't we? Oh, why couldn't we have gone a long time ago? It could have been so easy if . . .*

There was always that *if* in the way. She thought of her father's brother. It seemed so strange that her only kin in the world that she knew of, excepting Jeff, lived in London. But that had brought London no nearer. Jonathan Hale had not even troubled to answer the letters that Jude Ingle sent to London when David Hale died. It made London seem farther away.

"There, Abby, ye're clean." Susannah picked up the crock and one of the pitchers. "Ye're buttered like any bun f'r the oven. Get ye t' bed and sleep. Get that blather o' Lulorth's out o' y'r head. Ye'll feel better the morn." She bustled out.

Abby lay down on the bed that was made like a shallow box, only deep enough to hold the thin pallet of straw. She was used to the straw. She didn't mind it, most times. But it kept her wakeful now. Her legs felt tender and cooked. She put her heels carefully on the edges of the low boards at each side of the narrow bed so to ease the prickle of straw on the backs of her legs. But she couldn't sleep. She thought of what Susannah had said about Jude: *He loved ye afore he ever laid eyes on me.* It had been a long time—five years even before he married Susannah. She was six and Jude Ingle was twenty-three when she first saw him, brown and wide-shouldered and happy, filling the door of the Angel the day her father had walked her down to the inn to buy her a ha'penny sweet. She had stopped. She had squirmed her hand out of her father's hand. She had stood in the midst of the street looking up at Jude—at his clean white apron, his big thumbs hooked into the apron string, his long-sleeved waistcoat unbuttoned upon his chest like a gentleman's coat and his shirt pushing out between like a gentleman's ruffles. She took him in from his high-low shoes to his randy, smiling face. Even when Jude stopped smiling, to tease her by matching her solemn stare, the merry looked stayed in his eyes. And she had bundled across the street and hurled herself at him; and Jude Ingle caught her, mid-air, between his two hands, and swung her high and held her. They had laughed at each other. "She be the litsome un," Jude had said, past her shining head, to her father.

And after David Hale died, Jude Ingle had taken his place. Her own father hadn't been kinder. *Ye're like his own flesh and blood.* That was what Susannah had said. But now she thought of what Wynn Lulorth had called her. *Jude's nammet.* Jude's daytime meat. The ugly words, and the laughter. Suddenly, lying here, she was aware of herself as she never had been before. Of her breasts and her thighs. Of her whole naked body, flung out on the bed. She put her hands on her body, wondering at it. She drew them up over her thighs and her stomach and up to her breasts, feeling the tingle all through her—the tingle that wasn't at all like the prickle straw on her skin, but deeper—deep inside her and stronger now and vibrant. She felt it in her throat and in her arms and her fingertips and her legs. With a sudden spasmodic motion she drew her feet from the sides of the low box bed and crossed them over each other. She covered her breasts with her arms and suddenly she was sobbing, shaking with sobs.

She had never cried like that in her life before. She shook with this awful truth. She loved Jude. And what Lulorth had said was true. In her thoughts it was true. She hadn't known that she'd thought of Jude Ingle till now—till Wynn Lulorth's words pulled the thought out from amongst the unbidden, unformed secret thoughts stored under the eaves of her conscious mind and she knew it was there and had been there. She felt the shamed flush burn up through her cheeks and into her temples and forehead and down through her neck and her shoulders and into her breasts and turn into a kind of shuddering, deep inside. It burned her flesh like the touch of the scorching tilt cover.

And then it turned into a different fire. Not shame. Anger. A fierce indignation. She hated Jude Ingle. She hated all men. They had soiled her with words. With their greedy looks. They had soiled her, just thinking about her. They'd dirtied her, just being men. They had invaded her, handling her with their thoughts. She was smooched with their thoughts and their talk.

She flung herself off the bed and snatched up the towel Susannah had left on the pitcher. She plunged the towel into the water, slopping the water, burning herself with the slosh of cold water splashing upon her body. She scrubbed herself fiercely, hurting herself, hating herself for her thoughts. Oh, wicked . . . *wicked!* And then her anger lay like the towel on the floor at her feet and she moved to the bed and sat on it, staring at nothing, her hands lying loose on her thighs. Everything was changed—everything suddenly broken and gone—and nothing would ever again be the same. It was as if the Angel itself had collapsed and the spinning house and the wagon sheds and the stables, the wall and the gate —the whole safe, close courtyard—had fallen to pieces and even the pieces were gone. Jude and Susannah Ingle had been like a wall around her. She knew that the wall was gone. Oh, it would look the same. It would seem to be there. Susannah and Jude wouldn't change. But they had been changed. Ugly words, letting Jude's anger loose. *It's never Jeff's fault.* And Susannah blaming Jeff. Blaming her for defending him. Letting the truth come out.

Abby's fingers curled into fists. They hurt, and she made them hurt. They lay tight on her thighs. They beat, little blows, on her flesh. She knew the truth now. Jeffrey had been a trouble to Jude, and she was a trouble too. They must go away. Oh, they *must!* But how ever could they? How? *How?*

Her thoughts went to the only refuge she knew—to the wishing well by the abbey. And that was a wicked thought too. The ruined abbey was more like a church to her than the proper church where she went a-Sunday with Jude and Susannah. But feeling like that about it couldn't be wrong. It *couldn't.* The wishes she made were like prayers. They were a kind of comfort. She needed the comfort now.

The room had grown dark. The damp stain of spilled water was lost in the shadows spilling across the floor. The low window was blue.

She stood up. She moved through the room, a sweet ghost of a girl in the dusk. An unhappy ghost, lost now as she had never been lost before. She took her spare shift from its peg on the wall and slipped it over her head. Her hand reached for the drab stuff gown on the other peg, and touched it, and came away. She went quickly to the small chest of drawers and dragged it out from the wall and squeezed herself into the angle it made. She knelt and turned the wooden latch of the cuddy door in the wall and took out her precious secret—the dress she had made like a London gown—the dress she had tried so hard to make look like a fine lady's gown.

Her fingers caressed it. They knew every stitch, every pleat. It wasn't what she had wanted—she'd wanted rich, rustling blue paduasoy instead of the coarse brown tabby. But the blue watered silk was too costly. The only other thing she owned in the world was the yellow cow that had been a calf when her father died—and her pet, so they'd let her keep it. And she didn't get a wage like the scullery maids—but that was right, because Jude had given both her and Jeffrey a home and provided her clothes and her food. The only money she had was what she got by selling Lady Agatha's milk. It had taken a very long time to save enough farthings and pennies to buy even the cheapest brown tabby.

She knew that the dress wasn't right, but it was as nearly right as it could be made without lace and real side hoops. She'd had to make the side hoops herself. She had made them out of the hoops of a keg that she found in the cellar. They were sewed into a kind of cloth harness that went over her shoulders before she put on the dress.

She didn't have anything dainty to go underneath. No stays—and she didn't think of her lovely young body not needing stays at all. No clocked silken stockings—but she could leave her legs bare, and the scratches would do for the clocks. No kerchief as fine as gauze for her breast. No slippers. Not even her own wooden shoes—they likely were still on the gallery where she had kicked them off, and she didn't dare hunt for them now. If Jude or Susannah heard her, she would be bundled back to her room. Susannah might even think she was stealing out to meet Jude. Susannah didn't believe . . . Susannah had been so kind, but hurting both with the words that she said and the hands that had been so gentle. Susannah had said . . . But the thoughts in your mind weren't always the words you said.

She put the dress on over her one spare shift. She stole barefooted down the stairs and out into the mizzly dark. When she turned into the lane that led to the ruined abbey she felt the mist like a fine gauzy kerchief against her breast. The paduasoy rustled against her legs, and you couldn't see in the dark that the dress was brown and the silk was the cheapest silk. But she knew. And this wasn't at all like her secret dream.

She had dreamed of walking in silver slippers, with painted pattens to keep them clean. She had dreamed of a gown as blue as the sea. And wide. Not as wide as the sea but much—oh, *much*—too wide for a door. It would have wondrously light steel side hoops that moved up and down on secret miraculous hinges. And the gown would be laced in front, all the way from the billowing ruffles about her feet to the swell of her breast, with blue satin ribbons that shimmered like ripples under a sunny wind. And then, at the top, there would be a whole froth of white ribbons like foam from a wind-blown wave. Her shoulders would be all bare in the satiny foam, and she would be as lovely as Venus rising out of the sea. This dress wasn't like that at all, and she wasn't like that.

She had dreamed of a painted coach and a palace ball, and linkboys with flaring torches, and liveried footmen more haughty than any ship captain or Dorsetshire baronet who ever had stopped at the Angel. She would step out of the coach and her pattens would go *tap . . . t-tap-tap* on the wide stone blocks of the London footway and up the stone stairs to the door, and the haughty footmen would all be flummocksed because the king's door was not as wide as her dress. She would stand at the drashel a minute and let them worry—but only a minute, because she would always be kind, no matter how fess and fine. She would touch the side hoops of the gown and the hoops would rise on their secret hinges and she would be as slim as a young beech tree. She would walk in between the dirns as lightly as any beech leaf sailing the wind, and even the king would be daddered to see her so slender and litty.[1] Then the dress would be wide again. And the music would start.

[1] Litty, in Dorset, means graceful of body. Flummocksed means frightened. Drashel is threshold, and the dirns are the doorposts. Fess is proud. Daddered means bewildered.

But there was no music now. She came to the broken wall of the abbey and to the eleven trees. There had been twelve trees, once. They had been called the Twelve Apostles. But one had been wicked and so it had been cut down and was gone and you couldn't tell where it had been. She wanted now to be gone. She, too, had been terribly wicked. That first awful intimate consciousness of her body must be a sin, and what Lulorth had said was true. It was true in her secret mind. *As a man thinketh . . .* It must mean a woman too. And what Jude said about Jeff was true, in Jude's mind, and that made it true. And Susannah had said that she made things worse for Jeff by defending him, and she must be a wicked girl and she had to go, she had to go quickly and Jeff must go too—she couldn't leave Jeff behind. He was all that she really had, and she was all that he had.

She plucked a leaf from the laurel tree by the well and rolled it into a tiny cup. You had to do that when you wished. She didn't know why. It was one of a many things that people weren't meant to know.

She wasn't sure who it was that considered and granted the wishes or didn't grant them—the fairies, or God, or a kind of town meeting of angels. But she had always been sure that someday her wish would come true. It was hard to be sure tonight. Her mind was as dark as the unseen water below the rim of the mist-wet stones, and her mind was shaken now by her crowding thoughts as the water was shaken by ripples she couldn't see as she dipped the laurel leaf into the well and made her wish.

It was the same one she'd wished now a thousand times. To go somehow to London. To be a fine lady and ride in a painted coach and marry a gentleman who was tall and dark. She thought: *Jude isn't dark. He's not tall.* He was only strong and merry and kind. She hadn't dreamed that the man she loved would look like Jude Ingle at all. *I didn't know. I only just knew tonight. I've got to go away. I've got to go somehow. Somehow.* The wish had been wistful and longing and hopeful, before. It was different now. It was desperate now. And it seemed wicked even to wish. Everything that you did was wicked, if you were bad. And it didn't make you less wicked because you hadn't known how wicked you really were.

Her mind was all of a caddle, and her fingers ached now, she felt the ache high in her arms. The little stones in the lane hurt the cuts in her feet as she walked back to the Angel. The dark and the hurt in her heart made this seem like the other dream that wasn't a daydream but came, sometimes, in her sleep. It seemed, those times, that she was in that same wondrous fine ballroom. And then, as she started to dance, she heard the *t-tap . . . tap* again. *She'd forgotten to take off the pattens. She'd tried to dance in the wooden clogs.* And there was a dreadful moment when everyone knew that she wasn't a lady at all—when everyone knew that the hoops of her gown were made from the hoops of a keg. *And they laughed.* . . . It was a terrible dream. It seemed real tonight, even though she was wide awake.

There was still the sour smell of smoke in the mist as she came past the back of the cowkeep shed. And there was a darker shadow among the shadows by the side door of the Angel. It moved.

"Abby," it said.

"Oh, Jeff! You daddered me."

"Where've ye been?"

"To the well."

"You've no call to go dapping about. It looks—— After what Lulorth said——"

"I only went to wish we could get away. You and I. To London or somewhere."

"Coof! You an' y'r wishes." But he didn't sound crousty the way he did the most times. His voice wasn't so shacklen and dead-alive. "I count we can go, if you want."

"Jeff! You don't mean—— You don't mean you'd go to London!"

"Ees."

Even in her amazement Abby felt the quick pang that always came when Jeff used that countrified Dorset word—Jeff, who knew Latin and Greek, trying to wheedle favor with tannery men by saying *ees* instead of yes, and calling a turnip a *turmit,* a wasp a *wopsy,* and a farthing a *varden.* It was different, somehow, for her. She was only a girl, but Jeff was a man and he had a gentleman's learning. If they went away, they'd surely find some place where he could be what he ought to be. But she didn't see how. . . .

"We been a-waiten for ye. Jude said ye'd ought to be let to sleep, but Susannah said likely ye'd sleep the better for knowen." The familiar petulance itched again in his voice. "Ye weren't in y'r chammer. Come along—he's in the kitchen, and he's a-wearied of waiten. He's the tilty one anyhow."

"Who?" A sudden small clamor began to beat in her throat. Silent sound of excitement, and she was beginning to know that this wasn't just Jeffrey, willing to go away. It was something more. "Jeff—*who?*"

"The scrimpy fellow that came in the London coach. He's a lawyer's clerk. Father's brother is dead."

"Yes? Yes?" Clamor all through her now. Tingling, making her lips feel stiff. "He didn't care about us. He didn't answer. . . ."

"He left me a house."

"*Jeff!* Not in London, Jeff? Never a house in *London?*"

"Ees. In Turnmill Street, by Cow Cross."

"It's not true! Oh, Jeff—it's *not!*"

Chapter 4

But it was true. The clumsy iron key to the door of Jeff's house hung on a leather string at her neck. It was heavy between her breasts. She loved it.

The purse lay heavy upon the key. Its cord had made a crease at the back of her neck. Jude Ingle had given her a wondrous great sum. She could hardly believe it when he had said: "Ten pound. Ye've earned it, Abby. Did ye think I'd been letten ye work f'r no wage at all? I've been layin' it by agean the time when ye'd marry."

It was like a weight on her heart—the kindness, and being gone from Jude and Susannah. They hadn't wanted that she should go.

"We'd not have ye goin'—Susannah and me—on account o' what happened this day," Jude had said as she sat in the Angel's kitchen, hugging the key and reading the London lawyer's letter again after the clerk had insisted on reading it to her aloud. "We'd not have ye runnin' away on account o' what Lulorth said."

"I'm not!" She remembered now the quick flash of anger. *That.* She'd forgotten *that.* She had forgotten that there was a reason for going. And then she had known that there wasn't a reason. If she had loved Jude Ingle like that, she wouldn't have wanted to go. She would have gone. But she wouldn't have wanted to. She wasn't wicked. And knowing suddenly that she wasn't had made her happiness almost perfect.

It would be really perfect today. The last milestone said: "Lond. 4 M."

She tugged gently at Lady Agatha's halter. The cart creaked on. The road was climbing another hill. The hills weren't a much any more, but the cow was tired and Jeff was tired. Cows weren't meant to pull carts. And Jeff had been sick on the road. He had been too sick to sleep on the ground; they'd had to stay the last three nights at inns. She thought now that it might have been best to take the stage wagon instead of walking to London to save their money. But Lady Agatha couldn't ride in a wagon. She rubbed Lady Agatha's ear.

The girl and the brindle cow and the cart with the scorched tilt cover came to the top of the hill. The girl stopped. The cart pushed the cow. The cow's tarred hoofs slid in the muddy road. The rope harness went slack.

"Jeff," Abby said softly. And then again, breathless, insistent: "Jeff. It's London."

He didn't answer. She turned. He was leaning against the tail of the cart. His head lay on his arms. His hair lay on his sleeve like wind-frayed thatch, and the cheek she could see had the sickly bleached look of old thatch. Poor Jeff. . . . She knew, now, that he hadn't really wanted to come.

"Jeff, would you like to rest?"

He moved his head. Barely moved it. The hair hardly stirred on his sleeve.

"It's not noon yet. We're almost there. We have time. We've all the time we want now. All our lives. Oh, Jeff, don't you want to look? You can see the dome of St. Paul's."

He straightened up, but he didn't look.

"Oh, *go* on." He was peevish and tilty again. But she didn't mind. She didn't blame him. Two weeks of traipsing the roads in November hadn't been easy, with the cold rain, and the hills so slippery and steep that they'd both had to push the cart. But tonight they'd be sleeping in their own house, and Jeff would feel better, and nothing could keep her from being happy. Nothing now, ever. She spoke to the cow:

"If your ladyship pleases." She laughed, tasting the happiness in the sound. It tingled on her tongue. "Will you step into London, m' lady?"

The cow went patiently down the hill, her hoofs making hisses and sucklings. The road turned into a kind of causeway across Lambeth marsh. It wasn't at all like what Abby had thought it would be. It wasn't at all like coming to a great city. Just empty marshland, and ponds steely-blue, and other roads distantly crawling between the ponds. No people. She had supposed that there would be crowds of people—thousands of people, hundreds of carriages, hurrying on to London. There was only one other cart, lonely, a great way off on another road.

But the rain was done, and the sun was shining. The broom and gorse glistened with bright beads of mist; the ponds gleamed like jewels; the very mud of the road was soft brown velvet; and Lambeth marsh was like the rich folds of a paduasoy gown spread out, it was watered silk embroidered with costly gems. And under the pale gold light of the winter sun, the curving city made a girdle woven of golden thread, and the girdle was broidered with the gleaming jewels of windows. *Oh no!* The girl laughed again. There was even a better way to think of that lovely city. It was stretching out arms in brocaded sleeves. And the smoke and the mist were a fine Indies shawl about the shoulders of London—like gossamer, you could see through it, you could see the crease of a street like the crease between a fine lady's breasts when her stays were laced tight and her breasts were veiled by a smoke-thin kerchief, immodest and modest all at the one time. And the dome of St. Paul's was a high coiffure in the latest fashion, and the hills shining beyond were a coronet. London was a fine, gracious, lovely lady waiting with outstretched, embracing arms to welcome Abigail Martha Hale.

Abby loved it with her eyes. But she couldn't be welcomed in a stuff gown all pucksy from muddy roads and wrinkled from sleeping behind the hedgerows. She knew what she must do. It was foolish . . . but this was a day to be foolish. And there, just ahead, was a little hillock and a copse of trees, and the broom growing thick to hide her. She led the cow to the side of the road. She took a clean shift and the brown tabby dress from the cart and hurried into the thicket. It took only a minute to slip off the old stuff gown. She felt the wind's hands on her naked body. They were cold. They were like the sudden cold touches of fear she had felt, times and times again, in these last two weeks. But she wasn't afraid when the brown tabby covered her body. It warmed her. You couldn't tell, from outside, that it didn't have proper hoops.

She sighed a little as she started back to the road. It would be nice if the cart and the cow were a coach and three, and Jeff was a tall, handsome gentleman to hand her down at the door of a fine London inn. Furnival's, maybe, or . . . She scolded herself. She was a greedy girl, always wanting more than she had. And she had so much! She and Jeff could go to Furnival's someday. And not such a far day, either. They would have a plenty of money. They could keep school in Jeff's house. Or they could let rooms. Or they could even set up a tavern and call it the Angel. Her head was full of plans, and she was glad that she'd never lost faith in the wishing well even once in all the long time when it seemed that her wishing was foolish.

31

The roads were beginning to come together. Long fingers of houses reached out. And now she was walking between rows of houses, and the road was a village street. But such a dirty village! And here was a fork, and she didn't know which turning they ought to take to find London Bridge. There was a tavern, but it was a slatternly place, and she didn't want to go in and ask. She took the turning that seemed to lead toward the dome of St. Paul's.

The cart had been five minutes gone when a man in a purple coat came out of the tavern and followed. He was in no hurry. He sauntered. He didn't catch up until the street came to the river.

Abby knew, by then, that the street she'd taken was wrong. The Thames was wrong too. A broad band of black slime sloped down to black, scummy water. Houses stood on stilts, and the stilts were slick and drippy with slime. This wasn't London. It couldn't be! She heard the man speak to Jeff. When she turned and saw him, she thought that he looked like a rutabaga. He was all purple and yellow and shaped like a rutabaga—one that had just been pulled but not washed—purple coat, yellow waistcoat brocaded with yellow-brown smears of spilled wine and droppings of food, and his stock stained yellowish-brown with a many sweatings. Purple veins crawled over his face and made knots in his nose. Even his eyelids were purple, they gave the same tinge to his bloodshot eyes.

"Name of Siddell, young gentleman. Oakley Siddell. It goes with fiddle, ma'am. Servant, ma'am. Ye're only just come t' Lunnon? A far journey, belike." He was eying her dress. "Nah, happen somebody asked me I'd sye ye had come from Winchester."

Jeff didn't bother to answer. It didn't seem right to be rude to the very first person that spoke them kindly in London. Mr. Siddell was pleasant and mannerly, for all that he wasn't clean. And the dress was a great success. It must be. Mr. Siddell thought they had come from Winchester, and that was a fine big town. She owed him a decent politeness.

"We've come farther than that," she said. "From Cerne Abbas. It's in Dorset. We—we were looking for London Bridge."

"Hoh! Missed the turning, ma'am. Might be ye c'd take a wherry. Depends where ye're bound in Lunnon, up river or down."

"Turnmill Street." Mr. Siddell looked blank. "It's by Cow Cross. It's in Saffron Hill."

"Ay. Saffron 'ill." The purple lids almost closed. "Ye wouldn't climb a cove's leg, nah, would ye? Ye're not on the snaffling lay?"

All her reading in books hadn't told her what the snaffling lay was. It hadn't told her that Saffron Hill was a warren of thief-runs and rogue-hides, where secret tunnels led from one house to another, and naked bodies were sometimes found in the filth of Fleet Ditch.

"We've got a house there," she said. "Our uncle died and left my brother a house. It's three doors past the Cross Keys. Is there—is there anything wrong about it?"

"Wrong abaht it? Nah wot'd be wrong? There ayn't no better tavern in Lunnon."

"But the street. You said——"

32

"Wot'd I sye? I said nought abaht streets I was thinkin', that's wot. Y'r 'ouse is aw'y on t' other side o' the city. I was thinkin' abaht the time ye'd 'ave findin' it—bein' stryngers an' all."

"I know how to find it from London Bridge."

"Oh, ay. Do ye, nah? There's two bridges across Lunnon river. If ye can't find one o' the two, 'ow will ye find a street when there's hundreds o' streets?"

"I know how to go." The lawyer's clerk had written it down, but she'd taken no chances on losing the paper. She knew the whole way by heart. "Leftwards from London Bridge to Water Lane, and right-handed to Ludgate Hill and Great Old Bailey and Giltspur Street——"

"Nymes! D'ye think them streets'll speak out an' tell ye their nymes when y'r lydyship passes by? Hoh! They might, when they see ye, ma'am. But happen they do, they'll be lyin' as likely as not. Ye can't go by nymes. Not in Lunnon, ye can't. Ye tyke Pudding Lane, nah. Think ye'd get somethin' fine t' eat. But ye'd not—ye'd be walkin' in hog guts up t' y'r pretty ankles. Butchers in Pudding Lane. Kill hogs . . . dump hogs' puddings in street. Or ye tyke Love Lane. Sounds a bit of all right. But Lord love ye, miss, I'd sooner see ye dead than alive in that street. Pinch me blue, I would."

She thought absurdly that, being already purple, he couldn't turn blue no matter how hard he was pinched.

"I tell ye wot, miss. I'm abaht goin' over the river. Goin' by wherry, I was, but no matter. They'd charge a fortune t' lay the two o' ye on the other side, with the cart an' the cow. Come along. I'll tyke ye 'cross Lunnon Bridge."

"Oh no. We can't put you out. If you'd be so kind to show us the turning——"

"Put me aht? Rabbit me, ma'am. Ye're savin' me rhino, ma'am. Ye're savin' me sixpence a tilt boat would cost. An' comp'ny beside. I like comp'ny, I do. Like t' talk t' folk. It's my business, it is. I write things f'r the newspypers."

"Oh." That explained Mr. Siddell. She knew about people like that. They were called hacks, and they lived in attics in Grub Street, and mostly they starved. Mr. Siddell didn't look starved, but he was shabby enough.

They turned the cow and the cart around and went back up the street, and made a many turnings through other streets that were narrow and ugly and stank.

"There ye are, miss. There's Lunnon Bridge."

"That's not London Bridge!"

"Oh, ayn't it, nah? An' wot makes ye think it ayn't?"

"There aren't any houses." She knew exactly how it should be, from pictures. Not like a bridge at all, but like a thin thread of an alley hung over the river, with queer crooked houses crowding close on both sides. "There aren't any shops." This was just a bridge.

"Shops an' 'ouses, eh? They've been gone this long while. Torn down five years ago. Too 'eavy, they was. The bridge is fair rotten, ma'am."

She was disappointed. A part of *her* London was gone. But she supposed it was better. If there had been houses and shops, she couldn't have seen the river. She could see it now for a great way in both directions, and it looked as it ought to look. Like a broad highway cut through a forest. The thick forests of masts grew tall on both banks—masts and yardarms mostly bare, like the trunks and branches of trees at this time of the year. But some had sails that hung slack, and there were flags everywhere, every color. And she thought the white sails made the tangle of masts and spars look like a woods with the hoarfrost on it, and the flags made them look like a woods when the most of the leaves had fallen but those that still clung were painted brightly with frost.

But there was never a road so busy. The Thames was a swarming street. Wherries, sharp-nosed and sharp-tailed for sliding themselves up onto the low tide flats. Painted barges with flashing oars—barges with bright blue cabins on them, like little houses—coal barges, smutty and black—other barges so high-piled with hay that you couldn't tell they were boats, they looked like hay staddles floating. Small boats darting about, with white hoods like cart covers on them: those must be the London tilt boats she'd read of. And still smaller boats that skittered like bugs on the water. They ran with their tails: men stood in the back end and wriggled a single oar. Fishing smacks, galliots, schooners, sloops of war, frigates, fat Indiamen a-far down by the bend of the river—she knew a many names for the ships that came to London, and if she didn't know which was which now, she would find out in time. And there was the Tower of London!

They came to the end of the bridge. Leftwards now, with the bowsprits of ships leaning over the street and all pointing to the wonderful city piled up on the other side. And the people! People by thousands—dozens of Cerne Abbases swarming and jostling, shouting, hustling boxes and bales and barrels, loading wagons and carts. Stacks of cork. Yellow bins of sulphur. Sugar spilled in the street. Strange smells—and one day she would know what each of them was.

"Nah, 'ere ye are. Yon's Trig Stairs comin' up from the river, an' 'ere's Friday Street. Tyke us t' Cheapside, it will. No need o' goin' all th' w'y up t' Water Lane. Save ye time, it will. Lost? Nah, miss, don't ye fret y'rself. I'll see ye safe t' Cow Cross."

She hesitated.

"Ay, ye're right t' be stiff with a strynger. I meant no 'arm, miss."

She hadn't meant to be stiff.

"Nights especial, miss. There's footpads an' scourers an' Mohocks an' them that'd slit y'r throat. Not a throat like yours, miss. They'd steal ye whole. Mind, nah, don't ye go abroad nights. But supposin' I wished ye ill, wot 'arm c'd I do ye 'ere in the midst o' Lunnon in full daylight?"

He couldn't do any harm. She wasn't afraid. Her heart sang. It bubbled and swelled in her throat. This was the London she'd wanted so long. She feasted her eyes on the city—her eyes and her ears. Her nose too. She'd never seen it nor heard it nor smelled it, but it was familiar.

It was all here. It was just as John Gay had set down in his verses—the streets paved with hugeous humped blocks of stone—the stone footwalks with rows of posts to keep folk from under the wheels. And so many wheels! Great wagons and horse carts and pushcarts, lumbering coaches, hackneys—and muddy water spirting up from the wheels as Gay said it did. And the noise! Rattling, clattering, groaning, rumbling, thunderous wheels—sledges screeching over the cobbles—carters roaring at footmen in powdered wigs a-top the elegant painted coaches, and footmen roaring back even louder without unbending their pikestaff backs or unfolding their arms—shrill cries and bawlings and singsongs. And here was a blue-smocked butcher with legs of lamb over his shoulder and he was shouting: "Trotters! Fine trotters! Who'll buy?" And a girl with a board on her head and tarts on the board, miraculously staying there somehow. And a man with stockings fluttering from a pole, and a man crying "Bellows to mend," and a sweep-boy scuttling amongst the legs and the legs shrinking away from his sooted broom.

"Oh, Jeff! Isn't it wonderful?"

"Oh, ees." His whine was sarcastic. "Your London's a wondrous fine place. Blather an' bleat! Jostle an' shog! I'd give the ten pounds t' be back where we should ha' stayed. Streets peasen with muck! It's worse than a stable mixen. It's a dunghill, your London is."

"Jeff, it's not!" London *did* look dirty. Jude Ingle would beat the breeches of any stableboy who let such filth lie. But she loved it, turmoil and dirt and all.

"It won't be like this when we're home, Jeff. Turnmill Street's not in the city. It's more like country—like Tottenham Court. Isn't it, Mr Siddell?"

"Same direction, miss."

"Aren't we almost there?"

"Ay. Ten minutes, brisk. Likely 'arf a nower, with the cow so slow."

"D'you hear, Jeff? Half an hour. It'll be better in Turnmill Street."

But it wasn't better. They came by Cock Lane to a place that Mr. Siddell said was Pie Corner, and suddenly London had changed.

"Right 'ere's where the fire stopped, miss. We're out o' the new city. From 'ere on it's the old."

It was very old. It was dirtier. The houses were meaner-looking.

"Nah, miss, 'ere ye are. This 'ere's Turnmill Street." Her heart sank. The grimy houses leaned together over the narrow, darkening street. "Yon's the Cross Keys." The frowsty tavern leered at her out of windows encrusted with dirt. "Three doors beyond, did ye sye? I ayn't been t' Saffron 'ill in a good long time, but I mind now which 'ouse it is. It sets across the end o' the little lane. An alley, like. It goes under the 'ouses yonder. Didn't I tell ye Oak Siddell'd set ye right? Ye can't lose y'r wye now, miss. I'll just stop in an' tyke me supper in the Cross Keys afore I start back. Would ye do me the honor—a dram f'r y'r brother an' a sup o' the small f'r y'rself? An' a bit o' cheese, m'ybe?"

"Oh no." She was sick with dread of the street and the alley that made a dark cavern through the walls of the grimy houses. She fought back the dread. It could still be a fine great house, being set back off the street. "We have food in the cart. We're anxious to see——"

"In course ye are. No 'arm askin', miss."

"I can't thank you. You've been so kind."

"Nothin' kind abaht it. I'd count it a pleasure t' do ye a kindness one day. Might be I could. I get abaht. I 'ear things. Y'r brother'll be wantin' t' turn a shillin' nah an' again. If ye'll give me y'r nymes—I've a bit o' pyper abaht me. Quill an' ink, too, seein' as how I myke my livin' by writin'."

He unbuttoned the yellow waistcoat and drew out a small inkhorn hung to a chain. He laid a piece of paper against the side of the cart.

"Jeffrey Hale," she tóld him.

"Wot's the good o' writin' out nymes if the writin's mine? If I 'ear of a plyce f'r y'r brother, I show 'is own fist t' prove he c'n write. Mykes a diff'rence, it does." He gave the frayed quill to Jeff. "Right 'ere, sir."

She didn't know what made her afraid. Jude's warnings, perhaps. Or Will Hogarth's pictures of terrible things that happened to people in London.

"Jeff, don't!" She took the paper. It was folded; she turned it over. There was writing above the fold.

" 'ere, nah!" Siddell moved toward her. "Wot's this all abaht?"

She backed away. She was reading: *for the sum of five pounds in hand paid . . . doth hereby covenant . . . East India Company . . . seven years. . . .* An indenture for seven years!

"You! *You!*" She tore the paper across. She crumpled the pieces and threw them into the purple face. "I know what you are! You're a crimp!" There was a cobble loose at her feet. She picked it up. She threw it. The inkhorn spattered the yellow waistcoat. The stone bounced. And Siddell was bowing. He doubled over, holding his belly. Abby stooped for the stone again. Siddell shrank back against the wall of the inn. Then he turned and ran, still holding his belly with both his hands. She heard Jeffrey being sick.

He clung to the cart as they went into the alley under the low, dirty beams of the houses built over it. No cobbles here. Mud, and heaps of garbage, fish heads, broken bottles, slops dumped from the windows above. The house at the end of the alley sagged toward them. Its windows sagged, and the most of the windows were broken. And she would be sick in a minute . . . another minute.

She took the key from her neck. It fitted the rusty lock. But it wouldn't turn. *This isn't the house. He lied.* But when she twisted the key the opposite way, it turned. The tongue of the lock went *chnkk.* The door hadn't been locked. And Siddell hadn't lied. This was the house. She wanted then to be sick. She wanted to, but she couldn't.

This wasn't a house. It was the corpse of a house. When she opened the door, the smell of decay was waiting—musty, moldy, like earth that was always damp under the floor of a stable. She stepped over the threshold and knew why it smelled of earth. The floor was gone, there was only dirt underfoot. Even the joists were gone; you could see where they had been chopped away with an ax. And the stairs were gone—all the treads gone, the banister gone, only the framework left like a skeleton in the dark hall. She didn't know that it was only what frequently happened to houses left empty in London. She only knew that it was a wrecked, ruined house—the insides of it stolen and carried away—all the furniture gone—all her hopes ruined and wrecked. They couldn't keep school. They couldn't let rooms.

They couldn't live in the house. And she couldn't bear to look at Jeff's face. She had to be to herself before she broke down.

She walked blindly past the gaping stairs, along the hall where even the walls had been broken in and the laths had been taken away. There was a blur at the end of the hall—an open door that she hardly could see for her tears. She pushed the tears back with her fists. There was a small, brick-walled close littered with trash that must have been there a hundred years. Warped shingles. Ashes. Bones. A pile of old boards. Why had they wrecked the house and left boards in the close?

She went back into the house. Jeff was still standing in the front doorway.

"There's a courtyard," she told him. "There's a place for the cow." She touched his arm. "We'll be all right, Jeff. We'll find work. They're bound to need teachers in London. They're bound to." He didn't answer. He drew away from her hand.

She unhitched the cow and led her into the house, through the hall to the close. When she came back, Jeff was still standing there, leaning against the doorpost. She said again:

"We'll be all right. It's a place to stay. We've money. If I can't do anything else, I can work in a tavern."

"And be a fine lady," Jeff sneered. But at least he had spoken to her.

"We can sell Lady Agatha's milk."

"Little milk ye'll get out of a cow, anywhen ye've dragged her a hundred and fifty miles. Jude said she'd go dry."

"But she hasn't."

"She will. And no matter. Jude said nobody in London drinks aught but gin."

"Jude said! Jude's never been to London. Of course they drink milk." She called Gay's verses to witness: " 'On doors the sallow milkmaid chalks her gains; ah! how unlike the milkmaid of the plains.' *I'm* not sallow. I'll say my complexion comes from drinking the milk. They'll buy! I'll set myself up for a doctor. 'These grave physicians with their milky cheer the lovesick maid and dwindling beau repair' . . . remember?"

Jeffrey remembered too well. He knew Gay as well as she did.

"That wasn't cows. It was asses. And you've got the ears for one—taking up with that crimp."

"I didn't take up with him! He took up with us."

"You were willing enough." Oh, *Jeff.* "It was you that toled him along with your gab. You might have sent him packing."

"I did!"

"You might have done it straight off." He mimicked her. " 'We'll sell Lady Agatha's milk.' " His whine made a peevish ghost of the words that had tried to be hopeful and brave. He sneered: "*Lady Agatha.* Fetching a cow to London . . Where d'ye think the fodder's to come from? What d'ye think she's to eat? I'll tell ye! She'll eat our ten pounds, and we'll starve. By God, we'll eat her before she eats us."

"Jeff . . . you'd not!" But she mustn't quarrel with him. He didn't mean it, really. "She won't go dry. You'll see."

But she was afraid of what she would see as she took the wooden noggin and went out to the darkening close to milk the cow. The stream was thin, the teats were flabby and thin. She laid her face against Lady Agatha's flank and tried to fight back the tears. There wasn't ten pounds for a cow to eat, or for anyone else to eat. Jeff's being sick on the road had cost a great sum. There was only seven pounds six. It was terrifying to think that two pounds and fourteen shillings had gone in only two weeks. And the house that would be so fine . . . the awful, wrecked, empty house . . . and all her hopes empty and wrecked. *We can always go back to Cerne Abbas.* Already she wanted to go. *Oh, never!* Creeping back . . . hungry beggars. *Never!*

She stood up with the noggin only half filled in her hand. Her dress! She'd forgotten the precious dress. It had lain in the mud while she milked, and the hem was pucksy and stained. It flopped, cold and wet, on her ankles as she went back to the house. Jeff hadn't even begun to unload the cart. He had found a piece of broken board and laid it across where the lowest stair tread had been; he was sitting there with his head in his hands. He drank the milk, but he didn't get up. He put his face into his hands again and didn't watch her while she fetched in the tilt cover and spread it out on the dirt and laid his pallet on it and made a bed.

"You can lie down now, Jeff." He shambled across to the make-do bed and dropped down in a dead-alive, whindlen heap. She pulled up the covers around him. "I'll fetch you your dinner in bed."

He said bitterly: "*Dinner.* Still above y'rself, aren't ye? Evemet, ye mean." The Dorsetshire word for supper. The peasant word. And she'd thought he had changed. He'd been willing to come to London. He'd been as eager as she. But she knew now that it hadn't been coming to London, it had been running away from Cerne Abbas. He hadn't changed. He wouldn't fight, ever. He wouldn't be his own man. *Crippled inside.*

She finished unloading the cart. She went out to the close and gathered up pieces of moldy wet boards in the dark and fetched them into the house. She lighted the candle—their one stump of candle, too precious now to be used for more than the fewest minutes. She laid the pieces of board on the skeleton of the stairs. They teetered and slipped, and twice she was near to falling. But she got upstairs.

It was better upstairs. Musty and old and empty, but the most of the floor was there. Not quite empty, either—there was a great gloomy wardrobe in the back room, and it must have been too clumsy and heavy to steal. There was a third story—a garret, at least—up steep narrow stairs that hadn't been stolen either. Thick cobwebs matted against her face. Thick smells webbed themselves in her nose. She didn't dare to go up, alone, in the dark. But her hopes were climbing again. She went back down the teetering slippery boards she had laid for steps.

"Jeff . . ." He didn't answer. She knew he wasn't asleep. "Jeff, it's all right abovestairs. There's wood—a plenty of wood. We can fix the house. We can make benches and stools. Don't you want to come up? It's damp, sleeping here." He made a petulant flop in the blankets. "Jeff, d'you mind if I sleep upstairs?"

"Oh, for God's sake. Blather and chat. . . ."

She carried her pallet and comfort up to the room where the wardrobe was. Not so dreadfully empty there. There were pegs in the wardrobe. She hung her dress on a peg and the wooden-hoop harness over another peg. She lay down in her shift. And then she remembered her prayers. She began to say her prayers as she lay shivering on the damp pallet. But she had a feeling that it wasn't right to pray lying down. God would know that she was a drawlatcheten lazy girl. She knelt on the pallet. No—even that was too easy. She crept out till her knees were bare on the bare, veined, splintery planks. But when she crawled back to the pallet the terror came crawling with her and over her, and she bit her arm so to forget the fear and stifle the sound of her sobs.

She didn't know that she'd slept. But she suddenly knew that she was awake and that there had been a sound, wrenching and hard. Red fingers of light were feeling into the room. They were sticky with dark. She heard a shrill, frantic cry. *Jeff* . . . She thought the house was on fire and Jeff was trying to rouse her.

She ran to the head of the stairs, into red smoky light. A torch flared in the hall below, and shadows wrestled around it, and the shadows were men. The door she had locked was still locked—one narrow piece of the door. The rest had been smashed from its hinges and broken and battered down. It lay on the floor. And Jeff was struggling and crying out—shapeless cries, no words at all. She saw a fist come out of the dark. Pale flash in the dark, suddenly red in the flame of the link. She heard it on Jeffrey's face. He screamed. And then she was screaming. Thin thread of sound, pulled out of her throat. It pulled faces up to her. She could see them, surprised. And then grinning. Blue shadow said: "Hah! The place is a pigeon roost." Purple shadow answered: "Ay. Wot'd I sye? There's a plenty o' whore lofts in Turnmill Street. The 'ouses that ain't blood cellars is lay stalls, an' the most o' them both." And why was that purple coat here? Why was that face like a rutabaga here, grinning and pleased?

She knew. She screamed again:

"You can't take him! He didn't sign! He lied—Siddell lied. He's a crimp, but he didn't sign." He . . . he . . . all mixed up . . . they wouldn't know which one lied and which one didn't sign. "He's got no paper. I tore the indenture up."

"Fetch her down," the blue shadow said.

A head with a black stiff pigtail began to come up the stairs. She drew back. *Undressed,* she thought wildly. *I'm in my shift.* Men, looking up at her. Like standing on the roof of the cowkeep shed. Laughter now. *Make them go away.* But Jude wasn't here. And Jeff was still struggling and crying out.

She moved close to the wall. She took a step down. The pig-tailed man reached for her. She dodged. Another step. Two. Hand clutching her shift. She struck at the hand. The loose board began to tilt under her feet. It slid. Hoarse, startled shout in her ear. No stair rail to hold by, and she was falling into the flaring torch.

She fell into stunning blackness. Her body knocked a man down, and the link went out. She crawled among legs in the dirt. She beat at the legs until hands caught her arms and dragged her up to her feet. Hands mauling her, pawing her body. Hot breath on her face—reek of old sweat and

39

new gin. Hot, stinking mouth on her mouth. Hand under her shift, at her breast. But not closing over her breast. Jerking . . . She felt the string of the purse cut into her neck. The string broke. It was gone. She opened her mouth and set her teeth into flesh—wet, smooth flesh of an underlip, soft as her teeth went in, bristly against her tongue. It tore as it jerked away. Wild yell: *"Ye God-damned——"* Word she had never heard. But the hands were gone. She stood free.

"Jeff! *Jeff! Run!* You can get away!" He could, if she could. He didn't answer.

Red light flared again. Another man coming in with another torch, walking the length of the splintered door on the floor. And she wasn't free. They were all around her. And Jeff couldn't get away. He stood with his arms straight down at his sides, tightly held, and his head was tilted up and an arm was locked around his throat from behind. She thought he was choking to death. She could hear the gurgle of breath. But it wasn't Jeff's breath.

The light slid greasily over bright metal buttons on a blue lifted sleeve. The buttons winked toward the stairs. One word: *"God!"* And then silence. Nobody touching her. Nobody looking at her or at Jeff. All the faces sliding greasily toward the stairs and the face that hung there and gurgled. Face hanging crookedly. Legs running on nothing, running crazily there under the frame of the stairs. Again:

"God! Bennett . . . he fell."

"The girl pushed him. I saw——"

". . . ain't stairs. Just loose boards laid on. Push or fall, his jaw caught on a nail. He's got a spike through his throat. Blood like it was out of a pump."

She saw the blue sleeve come up. She saw its hand in the light of the link. Hair on the fisted hand, all fuzzy with the red flame—reddish brown and fuzzy the way the scorched hair had been on Jude Ingle's head. Something heavy and dark in the fist. Like a club. . . . It struck at Jeff's upturned face. The arm that was locked around Jeff's neck let go. She saw his face sliding down. White. And so *still*. She felt the stillness soak through her and fill her slowly. She floated on it. *Like water.* . . . Like water in the trough in the Angel's coach yard. *They held Jeff under,* she thought. *He drowned.* Voices drowned in the terrible stillness.

"Must have had a head like an egg."

"Resisted, didn't he? Justifiable force."

"Ay. Fetch the bitch along. Where——"

She was out the door. She was running down the black cavern between the houses and crying for help as she ran. Feet trampled the broken door, they splashed in the mud of the alley, they beat on the stones of the street. She couldn't think, but the instinct of hunted things made her shrewd. Her feet were bare. They couldn't hear her running. They wouldn't know where she was if she didn't cry out. It was no good to cry to these darkened houses.

She ran on, silent. Only the stillness, roaring inside her head. They would surely hear that.

She took the first turning she found. And the next. She twisted and turned through one short, crooked alley after another. All empty. A cobbled street, then. A stone footway. The sound of a man's heels—not hurrying, walking slowly, not hunting for her. She ran toward the sound. She caught the man by the cape of his coat.

"The night watch! Help me find the watch!"

He caught her arm and held it.

"Now there's a new dodge. Clever, ain't ye?"

"Oh, please," she panted. "My brother——"

"How much have ye got?" He twisted her arm. "It'd best be a pound, or ye'll get more watch than ye want." His other arm came to her shift. "What's this? Where's y'r clo'es?"

"I told you!" She hadn't. She'd tried. "Scourers . . . broke in . . . he fought them——"

"Oh, ay. An' where was all this?" His hand was searching her body. "Ye ain't got no money."

"In Turnmill Street. He's hurt. Oh, he's badly hurt. I don't know. Might be he's——"

"This is Turnmill Street. Ye're too clever by half, my girl. New at it, ain't ye? Nobody in Saffron Hill ever called the watch yet." He whistled shrilly. "Oh no, ye don't!"

"Let me go!"

"Ay, to Giltspur Compter." His hands were strong. They held her, and held her off. "Don't try bitin', ye slut." A lantern came swinging. Its speckled light sprinkled men's legs and the shafts of long staves. "Here's another one for ye, cullies. Not a shillin' on her. Nor much else neither. All of a mind for business. She'll learn the rest of her trade. Warm her back at the Bridewell, she'll pay up the next time she's asked."

Chapter 5

Abigail Martha Hale, spinster, aged seventeen, was brought to trial in Justice Hall Court in the Old Bailey on the fifth day of January, 1763. She had been seventeen for two days.

She did not know, until she stood in the dock, that she was accused of murder. She had thought that she was in jail for being those things they had called her—a doxie, a trull, a tear-sheet, a whore, a nightwalker. It had seemed like a judgment upon her for being so wicked—for thinking she loved Jude Ingle, who had a wife. God punished you for your evil thoughts, even though you found out that the thoughts were not true. It was right that she should be punished.

But then she had heard the clerk read from the paper that said she had murdered "one Abide-All Bennett, an able seaman, the Abide-All Bennett aforesaid being there and then upon and about his duty under the lawful orders of the aforesaid impressment officer of His Majesty's ship *Arethusa* . . . and so the aforesaid Abigail Martha Hale did as aforesaid there and then shog and jostle upon the body of him the aforesaid Bennett and there and then, in the manner and form aforesaid, willing, feloniously, and of malice forethought did kill against the peace of His Majesty. . . ."

She had thought, until then, that the men who broke into the house were robbers and scourers and Mohocks.

The trial lasted nineteen minutes. The judges were much annoyed. The most of the trials at that session had lasted no more than four minutes.

When it was over, the warders had taken her back to the prison to wait for sentence. They had put a different kind of chains on her arms and legs —heavier chains that ran from the manacles on her wrists to the iron belt around her waist, and iron bars an inch and a half thick that were riveted to the belt and to the iron hoops on her ankles. The belt was too big for her waist. It was made with six hasps that fitted in six small slots, but even when they put the padlock through the last of the hasps, the belt lay on the bones of her hips. It had chafed through the skin and made deep sores in the flesh. But the iron bars were too short for her legs. When she stood up, they bent her knees, and she couldn't walk. The warders had to lift her out of the dock and half carry her out of the court.

And now she was in the same dock again. It was like being in a cage. She had been in a many cages.

The first was the place that was called a compter and smelled of slops. The night watch had taken her there. She'd been put into a room with twenty more girls and women. The room was no bigger than hers had been at the Angel, and one of the girls was only thirteen and one was entirely naked. The women shrieked and blasphemed all night. In the morning they had been cuffed and herded and driven into a kind of railed pen, like a sty, and she had seen a wrinkled heap of brown tabby flung down on a table outside the pen.

"That's mine," she had cried, because she was so ashamed in her shift. "That's my dress!"

And a man who wore a blue coat with bright buttons spoke to the man who sat at the raised-up desk:

"That saves us a deal of trouble. It proves she's the one. We found the dress in the house."

"Let me have those names again."

"Abide-All Bennett." The man at the desk wrote it down. "Jeffrey Hale."

"Both dead, you say."

"Yes, sir."

"Remanded to Newgate."

They had let her out of the pen and a bailiff threw the brown bundle into her arms. And it came undone and the hoops were on top, and everybody saw that the side hoops were made from the hoops of a keg. The women had screamed with laughter. She hadn't heard it, then. Jeff was dead, and all she could see was his white, still face sliding down, and all she could hear was the stillness inside her. But afterward she had known that the screaming laughter had been there.

The bailiffs wouldn't let her put on the dress. They had walked her through the town in her shift, with the dress and the hoops huddled against her breast. They had taken her through a door with iron spikes on the top, and she had been hustled into a dark stone cage where the smell was as solid as stone. The cage was for women, but it was called waterman's hall because the floor always was wet. Sometimes the water was two inches deep and the straw on the floor floated until it was sogged and sank. The women lay in two rows on the floor, of nights; there was no other where to lie.

There were fifty-nine women. She hadn't known that there were women like that—like beasts in an uncleaned stable. They said she had to pay something called chummage. She couldn't pay, so they took her dress. They made a fire of the hoops. It was the only fire they had in more than a sennight, until the girl who was called Fanny Swivens was taken out of the cell one night by two of the warders. After that they had coals for a fire, and Fanny Swivens was taken out every night.

And then, after the trial, there had been a different cage. The condemned cell, it was called. It wasn't so wet, but it was colder. There was never a fire, and the windows had only iron bars, they had no glass and no shutters. When she could sleep at all, she had slept huddled close to Margaret Dyckett, who had been convicted for wearing a pair of thread stockings. The court said Margaret's husband had stolen ten pairs, although Margaret said he hadn't; she had sworn that they were a bridal gift; she said Ben Dyckett had paid for them three times over, working nights for the stocking man after he'd worked all day as a carter. It hadn't done any good, the court hadn't believed her. But Abby believed. She was wearing Maggie Dyckett's dress now, so she would be decent in court, and Maggie was naked in the stone cage.

This was a better cage. It was made of wood, waist high, and it had a row of thick, sharp-pointed iron spikes set into the wood on both sides and in front. You could let the chains clank down on the wooden ledge and ease the pain of the shackles in the raw flesh of your wrists. You could hold to the spikes with your hands so to keep the weight of the leg irons from pulling you down. You could look at the withered bunches of rue that lay between the iron spikes. You could think of gathering bunches of cowslips when you were a little girl and there was only mud on your hands and not blood from the scabs that the shackles had gouged a-fresh.

"Prisoner at the bar. . . ."

She looked up from the sprigs of rue. She looked over the heads of the bailiffs and clerks to the row of judges in the tall chairs. There were six chairs and only five judges. There was a sword on the wall over the empty chair. She knew that the sword was for justice. She didn't know that the chair was for the Lord Mayor of London or that it was empty because the house in Turnmill Street was in Middlesex, not in London. She didn't know that if the house had been only a few hundred feet farther south, it would have been in the city and the press gang would not have dared to break in.

"Abigail Martha Hale. . . ." The judge who was saying her name was old. He looked as old as the house. His eyes were dim windows that sagged. He had a nosegay of flowers in his hand. When he said her name, he put the flowers to his nose as if even her name smelled bad. She didn't mind the smell much any more. It was part of her now—all the smells of a hundred years of slop buckets, and cells where there weren't any

43

buckets and the floors never were cleaned, and the bodies of women who hadn't been washed in years. They said there were people who'd been in Newgate for forty years and never been washed.

"You have been found guilty of the heinous crime of murder." The judge's voice was hollow and musty-sounding, the way the empty house had made your voice sound when you talked. "It is my duty to pass upon you the sentence which our just law enjoins."

The judge wore a scarlet robe. He wore a wig that hung down in long flaps on both sides of his face and down over the robe. The woolly flaps made her think of the legs of a sheep just before shearing time. He had a long face like a sheep. Sheep were stupid things. He was stupid too. *Our just law.* . . . A man in a long black robe was putting a flat black cap on the judge's head. The point hung down over his forehead.

"The sentence of the Court is——"

"My lord!" She heard the chains clatter against the spikes. "That's a lie." A judge shouldn't tell lies. There had been so many lies. All lies.

Something rapped her elbow. It hurt. The bailiff standing behind her in the dock had struck her with the iron-headed mace he carried.

"Woman, be still!"

"I'll not! The law isn't just! I tried to tell you. You wouldn't let me. My brother . . . he was asleep when the press gang broke in. He didn't know . . . We didn't either of us know——"

"You had your trial, girl."

"I wasn't allowed to speak. I had no counsel to speak for me." No money to pay a warder for taking a message to the lawyer's clerk who had come to Cerne Abbas. No money to send a letter to Jude. No money even for paper to write a letter.

The judge waved the wilted flowers under his nose. He talked wearily to the flowers:

"That has nothing to do with your case. Counsel is not permitted to speak at the trial of a felon. The prisoner is here to receive sentence for the murder of one of His Majesty's seamen, not to presume on the patience and dignity of the court."

"I didn't kill him! *I didn't!*"

"He is dead."

"My brother is dead too." She heard the clank of the chains in the swimming stillness. She gripped the spikes to keep the stillness from sucking her down. "I deserve to be punished, my lord. But not for kill-ing——" She didn't know how she should call the seaman. "Not for killing Mr. Bennett. It was my brother I killed."

"What's that?"

"I made him come to London. He'd be alive but for me." She shud-dered. "I killed him."

"Girl, do you know what you say? You are seventeen. Your brother was your only relation. You were under his authority and control. If it pleased this court to take notice of what you have said, you would not be held guilty of murder. You would be guilty of petit treason. You would be burned."

She must be shaking. The chains made little hard shuddering sounds.

"The sentence of the court is that you be taken from this place to a lawful prison, and thence——"

The bailiff jostled against her. He was putting a looped string around her thumb.

". . . to a place of execution, and that you there be hanged by the neck until you are dead . . . dead . . . dead."

The bailiff pulled the string tight.

"And may the Lord have mercy upon your soul."

She was swaying. The bailiff put his hands under her arms and began to drag her backward toward the steps of the dock.

"One word more. The law is not only just. It is merciful. It gives this court the power to offer you the gracious mercy of our Sovereign Lord the King. Instead of hanging, you may be transported to His Majesty's colonies in North America. . . ."

Voice swimming up out of the drowning stillness. Her own voice. Thin, like water. Trickling slowly, like water.

"Not—to die—my lord?"

"There to be sold at public auction to the highest bidder, and to serve not less than fourteen years under the pains and penalties for prisoners so transported. Well, speak up, girl. The choice is yours."

The same words. She could think of no other words:

"Not—to die—my lord."

Chapter 6

She was on a ship. She had been on it now for five weeks. But it was still new and strange. For almost four of those weeks the ship had plunged and rolled like a crazy thing, and the convicts hadn't been let to come up on deck. She hadn't been sick, though the other women were sick. She hadn't minded the wildest plungings—they made her think of a colt turned loose in the spring, rolling and kicking and squealing because he was free.

It was so strange and wonderful to be free of the chains—to feel the clean wind on her face and her body—to feel it whipping her hair and her clothes, beating them clean of the awful smell.

There were marks of the shackles yet on her ankles and wrists. She wondered whether they ever would go away or whether, as long as she lived, a stranger need only to look at her wrists to know what she had been. There were marks inside of her too. They would never go. But she tried not to think about them. Margaret Dyckett and Jeremy Love said you mustn't ever think back. You must think always ahead. But she was sure they were wrong. You couldn't be sure of happiness still ahead. It was best to think of the times when you'd really been happy. You *knew* about those.

The ship and the ocean helped. Now that the storms were done, the sea was all green and it was piled up in row upon row of great swelling waves like the Dorsetshire hills in spring, and the foam on their tops was like mist blowing away over the downs of a morning and it was white like the chalk where the downs were bare. And being on a ship, going up and up over the waves and swooping into the valleys between them, must be very much like riding in a post coach over the joppety hills.

And the ship made her think of the Angel. There was a place along the bulwark where boards had been laid for a kind of footway. A gangboard, Jeremy Love said it was. But she called it a gallery, in her mind. It was like the small gallery at the back of the Angel, and the bulwark was like the railing—curved so that it seemed to sag. The bulwark was painted red, but the red was dull now with weather, and the wood felt old and ridgy and veined. It felt familiar under her hands.

Of course the ship wasn't quite the same. She couldn't look over the rail into a neat closed space like the Angel's coach yard. The space was behind her. It was called the waist of the ship. But Abby called it the coach yard, and that seemed a sensible name—as sensible as the other. That part of the ship was low, and the other parts rose up like buildings at either end—forecastle, they called them, and poop—and the space between was walled in by the bulwarks, and there was always a hurly and burly of people. The poop was a kind of house where the gentry and officers lived. There was a low arched door leading in, and the name of the ship was carved above it—*Star of London.* Curving stairs led up to the roof. Jeremy laughed when she called it the roof. It was the quarter-deck, really. Gentlemen walked about there, leaning this way and that to the roll of the ship and staggering sometimes the way gentlemen did when they'd taken too much of Jude Ingle's negus.

Jude! He had come to her after all, in spite of getting no letter to tell him about . . . *Don't think about that. Think about Jude.* She had seen him for just an hour, the night she was taken away from the prison, down to the boat on the river. Mr. Houck had told him—not glad that Jeffrey was dead and that she was in terrible trouble. He had fetched Jude a London newspaper and he had been sorry, Jude said. Mr. Houck, whose coat she had ruined, whose hat she had set on fire. He had taken Jude on the box of the coach, and he had driven the miles to London faster than any post driver had ever done them before.

Susannah had sent her the clothes she wore now—Susannah's own best dress—and a little trunk with shifts and stockings and shoes. Jude had paid a great sum to the warder to let him see her. And then, when she had tried to run to him and had fallen instead because the leg irons had just been struck off and her legs felt so light and so far away, the warder tapped Jude on the shoulder and winked and said:

"There's a room w'ere y'r honor c'n 'ave 'er private. A nower, ye c'n 'ave. A fine soft bed, y'r honor, an' none t' disturb ye till 'er time comes t' go. Only a pound, y'r honor."

She had thought that Jude was going to crush the smirking face the way he had crushed Wynn Lulorth's. He had the same look. But he paid the pound. He carried her to the room that was only another stone cage, small and cold and evil-smelling and dark. He had sat on the edge of the bed and cradled her in his arms as he did when she was a little girl.

"Ye'll not be gone, Abby," he'd told her again and again. "Ye'll not

46

really be gone. There'll be letters. We'll never lose ye—Susannah an' me."

She had been a little less frightened and lost and alone when the time came to go. And Jude had walked beside her all the way to the river, in the clabbery yellow fog, his arm around her in the roped column of convicts. They wouldn't let him go down the Thames in the barge. But she knew that he had been standing there on the water stairs, looking after her, when she could no longer see him. It was a kind of happiness, knowing that. And there would be letters. She was so much luckier than the most of the convicts, who couldn't read or write and would never have any letters from home.

Sitting here on the bulwark now as she used to sit on the gallery railing evenings, she held tight to one of the strands in the mazy weaving of ropes and looked down at others who weren't so lucky. The men were tramping the deck in a circle, around and around, to the *rap-rap-rap* of Mr. Leach's cane. Mr. Leach was a kind of keeper. The soul-driver, Jeremy called him. But he wasn't like the bailiffs or the warders in Newgate. He was a timid kind of a man, with a meager face that was always twitching as if it was trying to pull his chin and his forehead together. He had even been kind to her, though he made out that it wasn't kindness: he'd said that she caused the trouble. But she hadn't been made to walk in the circle since the day Jack Rundle pinched her as he shuffled behind her and Jeremy Love had flown into him like a scolding hen, shrill and futile and funny, and the nice Purvis boy wrapped his arms around Rundle's head and wouldn't let go until Leach beat all three of them with his cane.

Jeremy Love was the funniest, cheeriest little old man she had ever seen. And almost the raggedest, too. They were elegant rags—the finest of white silk stockings held together with pieces of string, satin breeches split in a dozen places, waistcoat embroidered with tarnished gilt thread, and a silk drugget coat so old that its once-modish cuffs came all the way up to his elbows.

The cuffs were his place of business, he said; they were full of old ribbons and thimbles and greasy cards; there was even a china saucer in one of them, but you never knew which. He was sixty years old and he had seven years to serve, but he was trotting along in the circle and smiling happily to himself as he kept his small clever fingers in practice by juggling the pewter button that he had plucked from Leach's coat by pretending to stumble against him. He persisted in playing with it even when Leach was looking. It was a kind of game, and Abby thought that Jeremy Love was a deal like the little boys who risked beatings by following the Cerne Abbas elders when they processioned the parish. But Leach didn't notice the button—perhaps because it was polished from Jeremy's fingers now and so much brighter than the rest of the buttons on Leach's coat.

"Step out! Step out brisk now!" The cane began to rap faster. "Stir y'r stumps an' work y'r pumps. Get y'r blood movin'. Ye'll fetch better prices at Norfolk t'morrow. Better price, better master."

Tomorrow! She saw Margaret Dyckett's hand fumbling to find her husband's. Most of the convicts seemed to be unconcerned. Some of them even seemed eager. Wherever the Purvis boy was in the circle, his eyes watched the horizon where the new world would appear. Fanny Swivens was flirting her eyes and her head and her hips at every sailor who passed. The girl from Lancashire was staring at space with the placid content of a cow at the gate at nightfall. But the Dycketts were frightened. Their hands clung, and Abby knew that they lived in terror of being sold to different people and never seeing each other again.

Leach whacked the deck with his cane.

"A'right. Break y'r ranks an' save y'r shanks."

Jeremy Love came trotting toward her. The Purvis boy was beside him, talking, his face all a-light.

"Seven years, Jerry, an' I'll be free. I'll only be twenty-two. If I could get me a bit o' land . . . Is it true a man can get land without paying money? Are ye sure it's true?"

"Beyond the least shadow of doubt. Why, thousands of folk that have land and fine houses started the same as we're starting." Jeremy—sixty, and talking of *starting!* "There's a many with coats of arms that by rights ought to have a broken chain on 'em, or open shackles—argent, say—or a gallows and a rope with the noose untied."

She shivered. Jeremy leaned on the bulwark beside her.

"What about me, Jeremy? What will I be in fourteen years?"

"Fourteen years older, my dear."

"Don't, Jeremy. Please . . . don't joke. I'm afraid."

"Mathematics is not a joke. It's a science—a most precise and exacting science. You'll be thirty-three. You'll be married. You'll have seven children. A wonderful thing, mathematics."

"How could I be married? A convict! A—a *slave!*"

"There's a plenty of wives are slaves. Half as many as husbands, likely. Whole shiploads of convict women been sent out to the colonies, Abby. More men than women. The women get married. Mathematics again."

"Oh, Jerry . . . castles in Spain."

"Why in Spain, when those Dorsetshire fairies of yours have sent you a castle right here?" He flourished one flapping arm toward the quarter gallery that overhung the ship's side near the stern like a turret high on a castle wall. "It's all in your mind, child. Like this button." He showed it to her in the palm of his childlike hand. "Take it."

She reached. The button was gone. His hand had not moved at all. She had not seen it move.

"Here it is." He plucked the button out of her ear. Absurd as it was, she thought she had felt the button lying there in her ear a smitch of a second before his hand ever touched her. "D'you see? Of course you don't. The human eye cannot follow even the human hand. How much less can it follow the human mind! My mind assures me that I am dressed in satin and drugget. My eyes see the rents, but my mind has already mended them. That, my child, is the essence of philosophy. It is the essence and the quintessence of living. Now suppose there's a gentleman in that fine gilded cabin. Suppose——"

"There is. I've seen him."

"Bad manners. Peeping and spying. Most deplorable manners." Jeremy leaned on the bulwark to look. "You can't see."

"Not when the sun's on the windows. I think he is old. Or sick. He lies

48

the most of the time a-bed. There's another gentleman sits with him. The one that wears the monstrous fine lavender coat."

"Ay, he's the dimber cove. Owns the ship."

"I've wondered. . . . That night they took us down the Thames to the ship. There was another boat."

The scene came back. The dark and the fog, and the rain beginning to fall. The rain making quick little snipping noises in the invisible river, snipping and snipping until the fog was cut into pieces and strips as ragged as Jeremy's coat. The ship's lantern high overhead as the convict barge slid under the stern, and the glimpse of another boat lying there and a man being hoisted out of it by a rope tied under his arms. His body swinging. And the awful stillness beginning again, and the judge's voice beginning again in her mind: *hanged by the neck until you are dead . . dead . . . dead.* And then the rope catching somehow on the carved stern rail of the ship, and being let down a little. Light from the great cabin windows, smoky with fog. Greasy light on the face of the man who hung by the rope. The face sliding a little—the way Jeff's had slid. And Jeffrey was dead . . . dead . . . dead.

"Oh, Jeremy! I killed him! I did!"

"Now, child. Now. Now. We settled all that."

"We didn't. We can't. Nobody ever can."

"I told you—never think back. Think ahead."

"Ahead! Tomorrow's ahead."

"Ah! That's better! Chin up. Be angry with Jeremy John Love. Come down from the rail, Abby. I am about to cheat you at cards—for practice, of course. Not very good practice, at that. Not at all a reliable test of my skill. Much too easy. No effort at all. I really need someone who isn't stupid. Good! Better and better! You flare up like tinder, Abby. Tinder to light us a fire. You're a pretty girl when you're sad. But when you're angry, you're a beautiful woman. Never fear—Jeremy Love will find ways of making you very angry tomorrow."

Chapter 7

Behind the sun-dazzled windows of the ship's starboard quarter-gallery cabin, Christopher Holden also was reliving a part of his life.

For seven years now the dream had been always the same. It was so familiar that even when he was deeply asleep he knew it for what it was. But the knowledge that he was dreaming did not make the nightmare seem any less real. There was always a moment when his subconscious mind refused to believe what it knew. There was always a moment when fear took complete possession.

He felt weighted down. He was choking. Something smelled foul. His head roared to a tumult of sound that washed over him solidly and was gone and came back and was pierced with thin jagged screams, and the pierced sound emptied itself with the liquid gurgle of breath in a mouth that was filling with blood. It wasn't his mouth. It was somebody else's mouth. But it would be his in a moment. Something was gouging the flesh at the edge of his ribs, and his fingers were losing their grip on the oily wrist, and he had no strength left to drag the knife out of his flesh.

Again and again he struggled to heave himself up. Again and again the weight on his chest bore him helplessly down, and the sharp gouging pain was repeated.

He struck out wildly—and came half awake to find that it was not the slippery painted Seneca holding him down, choking him with intolerable stench and hunting for the life at the top of his belly with the knife that was already stained and wet. It was only the quilt, slippery with satin, wadded around his arms and his neck and across his face. The smell was only the remembered and intolerable stink of London. The tumult was not made of shots and scalp yells and the cries of frantic white men and the groans of dying white men: it was only the soft-solid pounding of the sea against the ship's side, and the cries and groanings of its timbers, and the breathy gurgle of the water streaming down the quarter pieces and the munions of the cabin. The pain at his ribs was only his own clumsiness in sleeping with his fists clenched and his bony knuckles digging into the thin, crinkly-brittle tissue of the old knife scar. The sense of despairing and futile struggle was only the slow, rolling heave of the ship to the endless waves and its inexorably repeated plunges into the troughs between them.

But he was sweating now as if this were July ninth again, in 1755, and not the last week of March in 1763. He was drenched with his sweat, and clammy and cold with fear, and savage and sick with disgust.

Christopher Holden, captain of rangers in His Britannic Majesty's colony known as the Old Dominion, was no great admirer of himself. He had missed inheriting Holden Hundred on the James River, but he had inherited fully the Holden habit of self-derision. It was a trait that gave him, at times, a curious feeling of being detached from himself—as if somehow there were two Christopher Holdens—as if somehow he was outside himself and looking on at everything that he did. He was seldom impressed.

Now, as always when he woke up from that nightmare of Braddock's ford, he was ashamed and contemptuous of himself because he had been so afraid in his sleep.

What the devil would happen if the scene ever changed just a little—if sometime he dreamed that his hand lost its hold on the Mingo's wrist and the knife slid into the flesh at the tip of the scar? Would it kill him? *Yes,* he thought, mocking himself. *It likely would. It likely would scare you to death.* But the dream never changed. It was never finished. The terrible fear always shocked him partly awake just before John Fraser's black-hairy hands closed over the Mingo's face, from behind, and the face began coming apart. *What the devil's wrong with you, Holden?*

The answer taunted him. *You're afraid. You don't want to go back. You're afraid of trouble. That's why you're hiding from Garth.*

God damn it! He wasn't hiding. Or, if he was, the hiding was not his idea. It had been Pollexfen's idea.

But he told himself savagely now that the rest of the self-accusation was true. He did not want to go back to that lovely and ugly and smiling and merciless, treacherous wilderness where he had spent almost the whole of his manhood.

He'd had enough. He had never intended to be a soldier—but what you intended or didn't intend had only a little to do with the final shape of your life. One day, by the favor of young Major Washington, he had been an apprentice surveyor. The next, he had been a militiaman: he had been part of an "army" of forty-three men and boys hurrying over the mountains to take and keep a patch of red-yellow mud that had caught Major Washington's fancy. The Forks of Ohio. . . . That first puny fort with the high-sounding name. . . . And they hadn't kept it. They'd had to surrender Fort Prince George even before it was finished. *Nine years,* he thought. *I was seventeen.* It didn't seem possible that he had lived to be twenty-six without feeling that he had lived.

He had gone back again and again. Excitedly. Eagerly, even, at first. And then never eagerly after the massacre on the Monongahela. But he had gone. He had been willing to go. He had been reluctant and willing at the same time, because it seemed to him that he had some kind of an obligation to other men who had died. No—that was too glib. It wasn't a feeling that he could put into words, or would if he could. Any words at all would be mawkish and glib. He'd simply felt that it wasn't decent to quit. He'd simply felt that a man who had any guts would stay till he saw the end of the thing he had helped to start. And now . . . Now, at the end, something had happened to him. Something was wrong with a man who sweated and froze with that reasonless fear in his sleep.

There was no reasonable reason why the dream should be always the same. There were other memories just as ugly . . . the raid on McCord's, and the children trapped in the burning cabin . . . the stockade at Fort Granville after the French and the Delawares finished with it . . . Herman Unger's young wife a charred, screaming, shapeless thing in the Delaware fire. There were other memories much more recent . . . the Billingsgate scourers beating him to his knees, beating him senseless, stamping his face into the stinking gutter on his last night in London. There was the summerhouse at Hap Hazard . . . a girl's arms drawing him urgently down into concealing darkness . . . and the paragraph in the Williamsburg *Gazette* . . . the smug, smirking, viciously innocent words that would sting for the rest of his life. . . .

Suddenly and angrily Christopher Holden was wide awake. For seven months now he had been trying to shut Diana Travers out of his mind. But neither London nor six thousand miles of the storm-blurred Atlantic had blurred his last moment with her. Neither Ellerby Pollexfen's blandly insistent kindness nor Martin Garth's devious scheming had been enough to make him forget the girl who had chosen the cruellest possible moment to tell him that she had decided to marry his brother.

It likely was just as well that he couldn't forget. If he stopped remembering—if he buried his thoughts of Diana as deeply as he had finally managed to bury his conscious thoughts of the massacre on the Mon—he would likely start dreaming about her. And that would be worse. It would be an uglier nightmare. And it, too, would be unfinished. There was nothing to finish. He ought to have known that she was amusing herself. Yes . . . and others too. My God, what a joke it had been! How the tidewater must have laughed at the thought of Diana Travers taking a husband whose only estate was an old house in Norfolk and two thousand acres of un-cleared land at World's End, by the falls of the James!

But if he dreamed of her, he would believe again that he was coming home from the Forks of Ohio to marry her. And his longing for her would not let him stop at Holden Hall—he would not stop even to change his clothes after the ten-day journey across the mountains. He would ride straight on through Williamsburg and out by the Yorktown road, and even before he could smell York River he would be seeing the halo of light in the sky high above Hap Hazard. It would seem like a promise. And he would think: *It looks like a rainbow.* And then, with a smile, he would think: *You're a fool, Chris Holden. You can't see a rainbow at night.* But he could. A rainbow with music.

His amazed delight at her demanding hunger would come back again too. And it would be as false now, if he dreamed it, as it had been then. *No! No, damn it. Not false.* Despising her now, and despising himself for still wanting her, he knew that the eagerness and the desire had been real. They had been both the truth and a lie. When the fire and the hunger in her had set him on fire and he was starving for her and there was noth-ing in all the world but this unexpected and dazzling glory, Diana had said it coolly. *Judas!* How damnation coolly she said it:

"Chris, I've got something to tell you. I'm going to marry Jimmy."

She had been the one to be amazed then. He had left her lying on the cushions of the summerhouse bench. He didn't know what she expected, but it was not that. He had simply walked off and left her, and her voice had been incredulous: "Chris . . ." It had followed him: *"Chris!"*

He had been surprised at her surprise. Even now it was the only feeling that he could remember until much later—hours and days later—when the numbness began to wear off. Oh damn. Damn! *Damn!*

Christopher Holden flopped over angrily on his back. The satin quilt hissed and slid off the bunk. When it was gone he saw that he had at least a half-decent reason for being cold. His long legs had burst loose the covers again and his feet were out. He swore at them peevishly. And then, know-ing what would happen, he pulled them up into the hollow of the feather beds and watched his sharp knees lifting the blankets like tent poles.

Cold air came flooding in over his clammy body and all the damp hairs lifted his skin with an icy prickling. He shivered. He wanted to shiver. It gave him a reason for swearing in deadly earnest—a reason that had no connection with either Diana or Jimmy. *God's teeth and God's toenails!* Why in the name of the low-legged Judas couldn't his carcass have been put together neatly and sensibly? For as long as he could remember, his ungainly shanks had been a damned nuisance to him.

They were practical legs, he supposed. They fitted a horse—if the horse was big in the barrel and stood at least eighteen hands. And they were useful also for measuring distance. They had measured, in nine years of wilderness war, some thousands of the roughest miles a man was likely to find between the Blue Ridge and the Maumee. On three occasions they had saved his life by their superior ability at running. But he threw off the covers now and, sitting up naked in Mr. Pollexfen's luxurious berth that was gilded and painted and carved like a London coach, he looked down with a surly dislike at his gaunt, knobby shanks. Ugly dog. . . . Damned mongrelly, clumsy hound. . . .

Small wonder Diana Travers, along with some dozens of other women, had found James Holden so much more desirable than his uncouth younger brother whose mouth was too wide for his bony face, whose hands were forever losing their hold on teacups, and whose legs were not meant for tables or beds or ballrooms. He'd always been clumsy. He still had that recollection—absurdly painful—of his first Assembly ball in the Apollo Room of the Raleigh at Williamsburg. A gentleman must wear a sword when he danced, and Chris Holden had worn his sword like a tail between his legs. It had tripped him flat. He could still hear the laughter at young Mr. Holden funny-side-up on the floor.

He jeered at himself: *They're laughing at you again.* And that taunt also was true. He had made it true. He had left Virginia by the first ship he could find after that unbelievable moment when Diana said, "I'm going to marry Jimmy." He had been sick with revulsion. He'd wanted to hide. Not because he was still the sensitive gawk of a boy who had tripped on his sword and been shamed and humiliated. He could bear the humiliation. But he knew his older brother too well to bear the thought of Diana . . .

Even his closest friends must have laughed at his sudden desire to travel. And every tidewater dinner and fox-hunt breakfast and ball had been spiced with delighted laughter at the cool, perfect joke with which Diana had taken all pride and all dignity out of his flight. He could still see that smarting small paragraph in the *Gazette:*

Being no longer otherwise engaged, Captain Christopher Holden has engaged himself to purchase a trousseau for Miss Diana Travers of Hap Hazard Manor against her forthcoming marriage to his brother, James Holden, Esq., of Holden Hundred. He will make shift to do so in London, having taken passage for the 2nd October in Captain Lilly, the *Sally.*

The editor of the *Gazette* had not missed the chance to work the word *shift* into the paragraph somehow. He had done it before. And Shiftless Jimmy always regarded it as a wondrous fine jest. He was proud of his nauseous nickname! How could Diana—— Damn her. Damn Jimmy. And damn Pollexfen for fetching that Paris trunk into the cabin! *And damn that girl!*

Christopher Holden snatched at the huddled blankets and dragged them up to cover his naked body. He didn't know that the sun made the gallery windows opaque, from outside. He could see the girl plainly enough. He could see her too God-damned plainly. She was perched there again on the dull red bulwark above the main chainwales amidships. He didn't know how long she'd been there this morning, nor how many other days she had stared at the cabin windows, nor what she had seen. She likely had seen a plenty.

To Christopher Holden the most part of this voyage homeward was something that hadn't happened. Four weeks of the five were a blank. But the blank was not clean. It was a dirty-yellow-gray dizzying void into which he had been pitched and in which he had been beaten and kicked and blinded, and smothered and sickened with stench that was solid and foul. He knew, now, that his skull had been cracked: Pollexfen had told him that. And he remembered the yellow-gray fog by East Indian docks, and the riding chair that had been so handily waiting when he came down the stairs from Laurens, Taylor & Ensley's counting room with one more item of curious information about Martin Garth tucked into his waistcoat pocket. He knew, now, that the bearers had carried him into a Wapping alley. He remembered quite clearly the riding chair toppling over, and the crashing glass, and the blows. The stench that still seemed to be deep inside him was the unspeakable filth of the alley, ground into his nose and mouth. He knew—he was convinced, at least—that the Billingsgate scourers had left him for dead in the muck.

He remembered, vaguely, the hours he had fumbled and floundered along the streets from one footwalk post to another, trying to find his lodgings in Temple Bar Without. He knew that when he had found them, Pollexfen was there. He remembered Pollexfen's hands taking him by the shoulders. They hurt. They had shaken him, and Pollexfen's voice had come from a long way off:

"Garth . . . gone . . . gave us the slip. All my fault. Had other ships watched . . . never thought about watching our own. He's in *Star of London* . . . lying at Deptford . . . catch her. . . ."

The rest was only the plump yellow blob of Pollexfen's face in the candlelight, turning gray and dirty and vaguer and vaguer and drifting away like fog, and Pollexfen's voice drifting away. He hadn't known, until a few days ago, that he was aboard a ship. Even now, when he tried to remember, he had no recollection at all of being lifted into Pollexfen's coach, or the wild night ride to Deptford, or of being hoisted aboard like a bale of strouds. The weeks were a piece that was gone from his life. And why the devil couldn't some other pieces of his life be just as conveniently gone? Every day, since his wits came back to him after that beating in London, the trunk and the girl had been here to remind him of things he preferred to forget.

The trunk, not much more than arm's length away in the narrow cabin, was a suggestively beautiful thing such as only a Frenchman would make. Its sides were varnished in glowing red, but the color paled when it came to the high, arched lid. It was like rosy flesh, there, and the lid did not rise to a single dome: it swelled roundly and gracefully into two, like a woman's breasts, and the tiny round silver handles set into the top of each dome had been deftly, suggestively touched with the warm red lacquer. It was, so Pollexfen assured him, quite the most elegant bridal trunk to be had in London—and not to be had at all except by the lucky chance that the treaty of peace with France had been signed in February. That was another joke. By God, but it was! Nine years of a war that had changed his life[1]—and now it had ended just in time to let him fetch home a trunkful

[1]Historians may find fault with Christopher Holden's perverse notion that the Seven Years' War had lasted nine years. Captain Holden was no historian: he was merely a

54

of Paris clothes for the woman he loved to wear when she married another man.

He shifted his glare from the trunk to the girl who sat on the bulwark. He knew—without wanting to know—that she too was suggestively lovely. She held by one hand to a shroud, and her arm was lifted and bare, and her body was held in the hard embrace of the wind. Her hair whipped back from her lifted face, and her hair was like Diana's. *The hell it is!* Diana's hair did not blow loose in the wind: it was always perfect: it had the cool color of gold in an old worn ring—in a ring handed down through generations of weddings. He had wondered, a many times, how it would be when their own wedding was over, when Diana's hair was no longer piled high on her head, when her lifted hands loosed her hair and it fell and it was her only garment. Perfect, then. . . . Not cool. . . . And this other girl's hair was not cool. It was like a blown flame in the sun. It was hot, molten gold in the sun. *Pah!* He sneered at himself and the girl. *Brass!* That was more like it. She was as brazen as any trollop prowling the streets around Covent Garden. *Well, if she is, she might be a remedy, Holden. Hair of the dog that bit you.* Other men had been cast aside by one woman and instantly gone to another. *Remedy . . . hell!* That was one cure that he wouldn't try. He was sickened of women. Not of Diana only, but of the lot. There would be no wenching at Crisscross. There would be no woman, ever, in the manor house he would build on the new plantation out at World's End.

He wadded the blankets and hurled them at the detestable trunk. They spread as they fell. They covered the trunk completely. The cabin was much improved. And when he scowled at the window again, the girl was gone. He had only himself to scowl at.

He slid off the bunk and stood up, and saw his own face glowering back at him out of the mirror bolted between the stanchions. In spite of himself, he grinned. He had resigned himself long ago to what he considered his odd assortment of features. It was, he admitted, a useful face. It frequently kept him from taking Chris Holden too seriously. But that last night in London hadn't improved his looks. The bruises and swellings were gone, but the small ragged scar on his temple would always be there. It lifted one eyebrow a little. *Mmm.* . . . It might be an improvement, at that. It might make his face even more useful. He rather approved of that mocking, sardonic eyebrow.

He was experimenting with it and soaping his face for the razor when he heard Pollexfen being excessively quiet at the latch of the door, and then being excessively cheerful and hearty:

"*Good* morning!"

"Morning."

Pollexfen, who never missed anything, noticed the missing word.

"Better morning for you than it is for me, Chris."

"Umff," Holden said over the blade of the razor, and watched his scarred eyebrow lift itself skeptically.

---

participant. In his mind the war began in the spring of 1754, when Fort Prince George at the Forks of the Ohio was taken and destroyed by a French army under Pierre Claude de Contrecoeur.

"Be rid of me, this time tomorrow."

"Tomorrow!" The razor stopped scraping. "D'you mean——"

"Mean we're beating up for the capes. Wind's foul, but Brookes thinks we'll make Norfolk tonight. Damme"—Pollexfen was plaintive—"you might be politer about it. There's no need for looking so pleased."

"I'm not."

"Certainly are," Pollexfen corrected him blandly. "Don't blame you. I've stuck to you like a plaster."

"Yes, damn you." But for the first time that morning Chris Holden's swearing was neither angry nor sullen. It was affectionate, rather. Ellerby Pollexfen was junior partner in the eminently ancient, substantial house that had served the Holdens for three generations as London agent. He was young, but he too was substantial. He was a big, heavy man—not fat, but plump in the London fashion, so that he bulged in all of the proper places. Even his eyes bulged a little. His face was so plump it looked buttered. There had been a time when Christopher Holden considered him more than a little plumpish about the head. But that time was past. It was Pollexfen who had uncovered Martin Garth's trail in London. It was Pollexfen who had dropped everything, on barely a half hour's notice, to fetch Chris Holden across the Atlantic because he wasn't fit to travel alone.

"Can't say that I did you much good with my sticking. Never got you into St. Paul's. Never got you to look at Wren's buildings. 'S shame, Chris. Culture. All that. Ought to know about Wren."

"You still think we're savages, don't you?"

"Provincials? Don't know about all of 'em. Know about you. Carry knife in your sleeve."

"I never did, east of the Blues, till I got to London. Talk about Wren . . . can't you get it through your thick head that I went to school in one of Wren's buildings?" He grinned. "D'you know what I'm going to do? I'm going to take you to Williamsburg and rub your nose on every brick in that building. I owe you that." Then he sobered. "I owe you a good deal more than I'll ever be able to pay."

"Intend to collect. Made bargain, Chris. Said I'd help you find out about Garth if you'd teach me how to throw knife. Haven't taught me yet. Thought maybe you'd do it today. Got target rigged up on deck."

"Don't tell me you're letting me out. Isn't Garth on deck?"

"Was, few minutes ago. Might be good idea to let him see you. Surprise him, what? Last day at sea—up you pop. Might throw him off balance. Might make him try to cover his tracks when he gets ashore. Watch him—find tracks. Or d'you think your Ohio Company people have already done it? They should have done. Wrote to them, didn't you? Fraser. That Washington fellow."

"Yes. But I didn't tell them enough. I don't know enough yet. I've got to have proof. I'm going to trace a few of Garth's damned queer cargoes before I go out to Crisscross."

"Odd name, Crisscross. It's for the old boy, eh? Your grandfather, I mean."

"Yes."

"Looked him up." Pollexfen paused at the startled look on Christopher

Holden's face. "Surprised? Shouldn't be. All in a way of business. Like to know much as I can about people I do business with. Got out the old letter books when I heard you were coming to England. Tried to see what you'd be like. Stout fellow, that old boy was. Always signed his name with an X. Know what took me? You sign your name the same way."

"Yes," Holden said again, and bent to buckle the knees of his London breeches. Stooping, he hid from Pollexfen whatever emotion might show in his face. That signature—*Xtopher Holden*—was one of the things in his life that was still unspoiled. There was something assuring about it—assuring and reassuring—a staunchness, a rugged strength that was gone from the Holdens now. His grandfather had not learned to read or write until he was nearly thirty; and, having learned, he would not break the habit of making his mark. Even when he became a member of the governor's council in Virginia, he had still used the X at the start of his name.

"Never knew him, did you? No—silly. Couldn't."

"No." Chris Holden came back to himself with a start. "He died twenty years before I was born."

"Shame. Had the old blood in him. Drake—Raleigh—fellows like that. Kept going."

"Yes." It seemed strange that Pollexfen should say what he had been thinking himself. At eighty Xtopher Holden had been full of plans for that new plantation at the falls of the James. "He left his Norfolk house and a parcel of land at World's End to me. Not to *me*, of course. To the second-born son of the third generation—or of the fourth or fifth if no second-born son came sooner. Sometimes . . ." It wasn't easy to say. It would sound sentimental and foolish. "Sometimes I think it's more than just house and land. Norfolk's old, but World's End was still the frontier when he bought the land. It's a kind of pattern. It's like his own life—solid, but going on. I think, sometimes, he felt that a second-born son who had only a little to start with might make a life that would be like his. I think he hoped that whoever got the old house and the wild land would—well, keep going."

"Wouldn't be surprised. Makes sense. So does name—Crisscross. Brother's name doesn't. Often wondered about it. Why the devil's your brother called Shiftless Jimmy?"

It was a natural question. He had expected it, sooner or later. But it was a question he had no intention of answering truthfully.

"Names go by contraries, sometimes. Holden Hundred's a good plantation. It's just the reverse of shiftless."

"That's right. Thought it might be that."

But Christopher Holden's moment of pride was gone. He thought of his brother, darkly handsome and headstrong and strongly built, cynical, shameless, and proud—proud of his shamelessness. Theirs had been a strange boyhood together, fatherless, motherless, under the slender restraint of a guardian much too concerned with his share of Holden Hundred's tobacco crop to be greatly concerned about them. James Holden, too, had inherited the family habit of self-derision. But it had not been, in his case, a kind of censorious conscience. It had been an excuse for doing whatever he wanted to do.

57

Having only a low opinion concerning himself, James Holden had undertaken to justify the opinion. He had lived down to it boldly. At seventeen, in college in Williamsburg, he was already known as a six-bottle man and three different kinds of a devil. He was a reckless devil on horseback, a lucky devil at hazard and loo, and an even bolder and luckier devil with other men's wives. The town girls did not count, although he kept count for a while, carving new notches in the mahogany posts of his bed each time he came home and telling his younger brother the gaudier, bawdier details. He did not bother to keep a tally of the redemptioner women or slave girls: they were a mere convenience; he took them for granted.

A man only a little less strong might have destroyed himself before he became a man. A man only a little less rich might have become an outcast. But James Holden was not a weakling. The Holden name was a stout tradition. The heir to the colony's third largest fortune was not only tolerated; he had such friends as he found congenial. His excesses—and his successes with women and horses and cards—brought him the scandalized admiration and even the envy of at least some of the hard-drinking, hard-riding, hard-gaming tidewater gentry.

To Christopher Holden, at twelve, the notched bedposts meant nothing. The details were not disgusting; they were not even interesting. He had been much too busy cutting notches for deer in the stock of his first long rifle. But the summer when he was sixteen and his brother came into complete possession of Holden Hundred, he had ridden away as an apprentice surveyor for the Ohio Company. He had come back to Holden Hall only five times in nine years. In his thoughts it had still been home. But each time he returned it had somehow receded a little farther into the past. It had seemed somehow less real, when he saw it again, than it had been in his mind.

But he could not tell Pollexfen that Holden Hall had another name on Virginia tongues—a scandalous name that was either amusing or ugly, according to taste, but always contemptuous. It was called Holden Ordinary, after the fashion of taverns that kept a fixed scale of prices. Such prices and what they bought was known as "the ordinary." He could not tell Pollexfen that his brother was called Shiftless Jimmy because his fixed scale of prices for women was a joke all the way from the meanest cabins in the Great Dismal to the tall manor houses on the Potomac—five shillings if the girl kept her shift on, ten if she took it off.

Chapter 8

Chris Holden was stonily silent as he followed Pollexfen out to the deck. Bright sun on his face. White sails soaring up. Vast circle of sparkling sea. Bright wind, warm with Virginia spring. And the dark cold mood, taking possession again.

That damnable question. . . . Today, of all days, when he was almost home. Why couldn't Pollexfen have asked it a month ago? Five months ago? And why must he be reminded at all that his brother had dirtied the

Holden name? His evil mood was not eased by the knowledge that he had no need of reminders.

But Pollexfen was blandly unconscious that he had given offense. Or was he? He hadn't become a partner in Abernethy & Griswold by being unconscious. He was a shrewd man of business, and even his rudenesses had their purpose. Chris Holden felt a temptation to use his foot rudely now on the noble expanse of lavender velvet breeches that swelled the skirts of Pollexfen's darker lavender lutestring coat.

"There. . . ." Pollexfen waved a plump hand, and his voice was as plump as his hand and as full of cheer as his breeches were full of himself. "Think you owe me something, eh, Chris? It's not sixpence to what you owe *them*."

Over the gallooned cuff of Pollexfen's sleeve, Holden looked at a row of scarecrows huddled along the gangboard, out of the way of the sailors swarming around the open hatch in the waist. Scarecrows left out in the fields all winter and now gathered up for some improbable reason. *Or two winters, or three.* One year's weather couldn't have made them as dirty and tatterdemalion as that. You wouldn't take a horse or a cow to market in any such shape as that: you'd curry the horse; you'd wipe the muck off the cow and pull the burrs out of its tail. But human beings for sale . . . Fluttering rags. Other rags so stiff that they couldn't flutter but only flopped in the wind. Seamed faces, with dirt in the seams. Woman's face, sleazily innocent above a dress that had been blue taffeta once but had never been innocent. Fat old man's face like a raffish cherub's under a frizzled wig. Other faces—bold, sly, furtive, frank, or only vacant. Some of them decent enough. But lank, greasy hair, uncut and uncombed. Hard to tell the men's hair from the women's. Except that girl's. . . . *So that's what she is.* A trull and a convict. *You're doing better, Holden.* For once his judgment about a girl had been right. He felt Pollexfen nudge him.

"There's the reason why *Star of London* was waiting at Deptford. Waiting for convicts. We'd have missed the ship, else. Missed Garth, if it wasn't for them. There he is. Hasn't seen you yet. Will in a minute. Know more about him, then. Know whether he hired those Mohocks to break your head."

"No," Holden said. "You won't."

"If he did it, he'll think he's seeing a ghost."

"I doubt that he's frightened of ghosts. He's planning to make too many. Whatever he thinks, you won't know."

"Lay you a crown piece, even."

"Thanks. You'll lose. There isn't an Indian in the Ohio country can hide his feelings as well as Garth—when he's got something to hide. He must have been hiding this scheme of his for at least three years—ever since the French burned their forts and pulled out."

Tackle squealed in the sheave of a snatch block. A cargo net rose with slow jerks from the hatch. By the mainmast a thick-bodied man in dark wine-colored broadcloth and gray waistcoat and smallclothes followed it with his eyes. His face came up with the same slow jerks. Chris Holden, watching him, felt a doubt creep into his mind again. Martin Garth's was not the face of a man who could plan a cold-blooded crime and perfect it slowly and patiently, year after year. It was an oldly young face—as if Garth, well into his thirties, had kept the moon look of a greedy small boy. Only the solidness of his face, now, kept it from looking pudgy—that, and the two deeply scored lines which began at the base of his nose and curved downward to match the curve of his rounded jaw. They contained his small thick lips and his chin as firmly as the taut ropes of the cargo net contained the small solid boxes of pig lead.

The boom swung the net across the coaming. Above it Garth's eyes came to Holden's and stayed for a casual moment. The cargo net touched the deck, and the ropes relaxed. Garth's face neither relaxed nor tightened. He flicked his hand to his hat in a careless gesture of recognition. Holden nodded. Then, neither too slowly nor quickly, Garth was looking again at his freight.

"I'll take that crown piece, Polly."

Pollexfen handed it over. Holden, slipping it into his pocket, saw the fat little man in the frizzled wig watching with button-bright eyes behind withered lids that were like shabby buttonholes that hadn't been fastened.

"Come along." Pollexfen was taking his arm. "Oughtn't act too in- t'rested, Chris. Make Garth think something is up."

"He already knows."

"Mightn't. Look here . . . what d'you think of my target? All right? Brookes found me a spare dolphin striker."

The slushed spar hung in a sling of ropes from the mizzen yard and was lashed, near its butt, to the mast. The butt was no more than ten inches across.

"It'll do."

"Here's Captain Brookes." He already knew Brookes: the captain of the *Star of London* had paid him a call in the gallery cabin as a matter of duty to a friend of the owners. But he was obliged now to make his manners to the smug little purser whose name was Ellis, to a rabbity fellow who had no forehead at all—Leach, he was called—and to certain gentlemen pas- sengers whose names he promptly forgot. And Pollexfen was bound and determined to turn him into a raree show for their amusement. "Carries a knife in his weskit. Straighter shot with knife than most men with pistol and best French powder. Has clothes cut to measure for knife. Ought t've seen tailor chaps gawp when he told 'em to cut armhole low so to leave room for the handle." Pollexfen had a gift for enthusiasm, and no com- punctions at all about pushing the gift upon others. "Show 'em, Chris."

Reluctantly, Holden took off his coat. He drew the hunting knife out of its sheath at his armpit.

"Look at that weazand sticker! Long as your arm!" The blade was only eight inches long. "Captain Holden can cut a knave's throat at a dozen paces. Did it at White's. Knave of hearts. Won forty quid on him." The gentlemen murmured, politely incredulous. Pollexfen produced a card.

"Never mind that." Holden tried to conceal his irritation and failed. "This isn't White's. I was sober enough so the floor didn't heave like a ship."

He laid the knife on his palm and lifted his arm and threw. The point went *hht* in the butt of the spar and the gentlemen murmured again.

Holden walked over and pulled the knife out. He handed it to Pollexfen.

"Go ahead. This isn't a show. It's a lesson. No—not like that! You're not playing mumbledy-peg. Let the weight keep it snug in your palm."

Pollexfen threw. The knife missed the spar by three feet and slid clattering down the deck. A grinning sailor fetched it back.

"Must've done something wrong." But Pollexfen was nothing shamed. "What?"

"Mostly everything. Not your fault. I can't show you properly here. The way this knife's balanced, it makes one turn in a fifty-foot cast. No room for that here." He fitted the knife into Pollexfen's soft hand. "It's all in the forearm and wrist. Chop your forearm down and then give it a flick with your wrist."

Pollexfen tried again. The flat of the knife smacked the mast. Holden, stooping to pick it up, heard another but duller and heavier metal sound. A stave-bound bale had slipped from the hoisting tackle and crashed to the deck between the hatch and the gangboard.

"Garth's," Pollexfen said.

"Yes, I see it is." A gleam of steel showed through a bursted seam in the end of the oiled-canvas wrapping.

"That budge rascal sees it too."

The cherubic old ragamuffin was bending over the bale. He plucked out a long-handled hatchet with a long, narrow, curved blade. He was waddling back to the huddle of convicts and showing it to the girl with the bright, blown hair.

Something burst in Chris Holden's brain. No; not in his brain. It was something that lay beneath conscious thought and burst suddenly into his thought—an explosion of pent-up, unsatisfied angers. The old angers came hurrying now. Washington's forced night march to surround the French camp . . . the quick sharp fight in the dark and the moment of heady triumph . . . the moment that didn't last . . . the false and ugly talk of assassination. Fort Necessity. The cold rain pouring down, the trenches dug in the swamp, the mud to his crotch, the comic-pathetic surrender, the Mingoes yelping like dogs gone crazy over a cornered fox. He'd never cared much for fox hunting after that, after he got a notion of how the fox felt. Braddock. And then the desperate march on Kittanning, the charge through the corn . . . not a charge at all, but only a few tired farmers running slowly and clumsily up a hill, and firing, and falling down. The fight in the snow on Sidelong. The fight on the Loyal Hanna. The fight on Grant's Hill. The steel hatchets chopping the necks of Grant's Highlanders, chopping their heads from their living bodies. French hatchets, then. And now English hatchets. Nine years . . .

Nine years of backbreaking toil and heartbreaking defeat, of rations and powder that never came, of endless nights in blankets soggy with mud or stiff with frost and the hair of your wrists and your neck frozen fast to the wool. Nine years of danger and wounding and death. And now Martin Garth was gathering up the bones and turning them into cash. Bones of men he knew. And if he was right about Garth, there would be more bones.

"Soul-driver!" Martin Garth's voice. It was more than a year since he'd heard it, in Garth's frowzy tavern and trading post at the Forks of Ohio. But it was not a voice that you'd ever forget. It made a sound like chips being stirred in woven-splint basket. "You . . . Leach. Come here!"

So. The rabbity fellow was the indenture agent in charge of the convicts. He scuttled across the deck now. He twittered at Garth:

"Eh? Eh? What? Service, sir. Nothing wrong, I hope."

"No! No indeed!" Harsh, breathy, dry voice. "Only a thief that's not learned his lesson yet." Garth had the fat, flabby rogue by his dirty neckband. "He'll do with another lesson. He stole this hatchet." Garth brandished it under the soul-driver's twitching nose. "I know the law. Ten lashes at least."

"No!" Young voice, clear, with a curious brightness in it. The girl had jumped down from the gangboard. "He didn't steal it! He was but showing it to me."

"Mind your tongue." Garth's voice, rasping at her. Softening suddenly as he looked down at her: "Who are you?"

The raffish old man broke in before she could answer.

"My daughter, sir." He was bowing as well as he could with Garth's hand twisted into his neckcloth. "The devoted daughter of Jeremy John Love."

"I'm not!" the girl cried.

"Not in fact, but in spirit, sir." The cherubic face beamed at Garth. "Ah! What a spirit she has! And you, sir, are one to appreciate it. You are a gentleman, sir—a gentleman of discernment. In spite of these . . . ah . . . unfortunate circumstances, your eye was not deceived. It was unerring, if I may say so, sir." Jeremy Love felt gingerly of his throat. Apparently out of Garth's own hand, three grimy cards appeared in his grimier fingers. "Can you always spot a queen?"

"Always." Garth let him go. "And if I do?"

"The stake is yours to name, sir."

"A pound?"

"A pound." The cheerful rogue was not in the least abashed. "If I had foreseen . . . I do not carry large sums on my person when traveling, sir. But between gentlemen, sir . . . Shall we say a matter of honor?"

"No." Garth's eyes were still on the girl. "You have better assets than that." He tossed a coin on the bale. "We'll say a gold sovereign against a kiss from your daughter in—kindred spirit."

"Jeremy . . . no!"

"Hush, child. Would you shame me?" Jeremy Love fanned the cards. His hand, brushing over them, brushed the girl's protest away.

"There you are, sir. There is the queen. Now you see her . . ." The cards flitted along his fingers. "And now you don't." The cards fell face down on the bale. "Can you spot her now?"

"Yes." The solid face was still and its eyes were still and there was a sudden stillness in Abby's heart. The wine-colored sleeve reached out. The thick fingers . . . She thought of Wynn Lulorth's fingers. But these weren't hairy, like Lulorth's. Only meaty and strong. They went to the biggest hole in Jeremy's tattered coat. They pulled out the queen. "I can spot a knave too." The breathy laugh was like the harsh rustle of the

62

thatch in the cold chalk-wind, one day long ago. "And that will be thirty lashes instead of ten."

She saw the frightened crumpling of Jeremy's face.

"You wouldn't dare!"

"*Dare?*" He drew the word out. It lay on his hard lower lip. "That's an odd word from you, my girl."

"But he's an old man. You wouldn't——"

"Wouldn't I? Leach!"

"Wait." She couldn't help Jeremy with her fists that were clenched so tight that they ached. But she wasn't a girl any more. She was a woman now. There were other ways. Other men had kissed her. Lulorth. That man who had held her in the dark house and bruised her mouth while his hand bruised her breast and broke the string of Jude Ingle's purse. That leering warder in Newgate. It didn't matter. Nothing could ever matter again. "I'll give you the kiss."

"You can't give it. I won it." He stooped to pick up the coin. She kissed him quickly. Solid flesh under her lips. Cold. . . . And a cold solid anger looking at her. "Another cheat."

"I paid you."

"I like full value. You can do better than that." His arms were as hard as Lulorth's. Harder. It wasn't his arm that was hard. It was the shaft of the hatchet he held. It pressed into her back. His mouth pressed into her mouth. When he let her go she struck out as blindly as Jeffrey had struck. Her fingers stung. She saw the print of them, white on his mouth. The mark didn't stay the way the print of Houck's knuckles had stayed on Jeff's cheek. The mouth smiled, and the mark went away.

"Leach, is this woman for sale?"

"Yes. Yes, Mr. Garth." Twitter and squeak. "Certainly. Certainly, sir."

"Name your price. I'll take her." His mouth lingered over the *take*.

"Uh . . . uh, sorry, sir. Law, you know. Public auction required."

"Quite right. We'll have an auction right here. Gentlemen . . ." Rasp like a file in his voice. "Do you care to bid for this girl? As a matter of form? Stand her up on this bale here, Leach. Let them look her over." Rustling laugh again. "Matter of form. I'm starting at twenty pounds."

Pollexfen's arm was up, but he didn't throw. He looked at Holden.

"Damme, Chris. I was right. Got savages in the colonies. White ones."

"Garth isn't white. He's part Mingo. Oh, not by birth. By choice. I told you he'd exchanged blood with a Mingo chief."

"Won't have business like that on this ship. By God, I won't. Stop it, Brookes."

"No," Holden said. "Don't."

"Blister me! D'you want——"

"The girl? Hardly. But I'd pay a small sum to put a blister on Garth."

"Outbid him? You can't afford it."

"Plague take you! That's the trouble with London agents. They know too much. Don't worry. I'll not ask to borrow on crops I've not planted yet. I've got enough left to make Garth pay high for his fun."

Pollexfen shrugged. The soul-driver's cane rapped the deck. Then it tapped the girl's chin.

"Hold y'r head up. Give 'em a smile. Twenty pounds bid for Abigail Martha Hale, serving fourteen years. Going once . . ." The cane rapped again. "Going twice . . . For the third and last time, twenty pounds——"

"And sixpence," Chris Holden said. "You can't say I'm extravagant, Polly." He grinned at Pollexfen, but there was small humor about the grin. There was none in Garth's tight smile.

"Amusing yourself, Holden?"

"No. Just making it legal. You wanted an auction, Garth."

"Thirty."

"You can do better than that. Your own words, I believe."

"Make the sale, Leach! I said thirty pounds."

"And sixpence."

Garth lifted the hatchet and rested his chin on the long curved spike at the back of the blade. He spoke over it casually:

"Would your sense of humor be satisfied, Captain Holden, with fifty pounds?"

"It's unpredictable, Garth. It might——"

"Fifty!"

"And then it might not. No, I don't think it is. Go on, Polly. Throw. Mmm . . . a little high."

"A little high for a girl that's done murder," Pollexfen said.

"Murder?"

"She's the one, isn't she, Ellis?"

"Yes, sir. Confessed. Spoke out in court and admitted she killed her brother."

"Mmm. . . ." Holden walked toward the target. He didn't care what she had done. She was a tool to his hand, and Garth was a more satisfactory target than the butt of a spar. He reached for the knife. "And sixpence."

Wind that came from the wrong direction stirred the hair at his neck. It lifted the hair on the back of his hand. Where his hand had been, the hatchet stood quivering in the wood. He heard Pollexfen's breath draw in, hard and quick like the rush of the tomahawk past his ear. Garth said: "Seventy-five!" And Leach was twitching and squeaking and squirming about like a rabbit caught in a snare.

"Seventy-five! Seventy-five pounds bid for this girl!" More like an excited rat than a rabbit, Holden thought—and thought then, contemptuously, that Leach was likely half out of his wits between fear of Garth and the prospect of pocketing most of the price himself. "Look at her, gentlemen. Look at her!" The soul-driver laid his cane on her hip and drew it downward along the curve of her thigh. "Look at her ankles." The tip of the cane raised her skirt. "Her face is her fortune, gentlemen. And the rest of her's the good fortune of any man that buys her. She——"

Pollexfen took a step toward him.

"That will be all of that, Leach!"

Garth sneered.

"Are you in this too?"

"I happen to own this ship, and I'll have no more nastiness on it. D'you care to argue the matter?"

"I never argue."

"If there is any doubt in your mind," Pollexfen said deliberately, "I prefer to remove it. I said 'nastiness,' Mr. Garth. The word includes you."

"Polly!" Holden stepped quickly between them. "Let be! This is my affair. I've got first rights." He glanced at the hatchet stuck in the spar. "You might say I've got a tomahawk claim. And I've still got that sixpence, Garth."

"How much more have you got?"

"Bid, if you care to find out."

"Cash on the barrel, Holden."

"One of your powder barrels?" He had touched Garth there. By Judas, he had! He had fetched a wariness into those cold gray eyes. And the wariness wouldn't be there unless his suspicions were right.

"Let's settle this, Holden." Garth was pulling out notes and coins. "Leach! Here's my bid. One hundred and three pounds."

"And sixpence, Garth."

"I'll double that bid in Norfolk tomorrow morning."

"Cash on the barrel. Your own words again. And here are some others you used: *Make the sale, Leach.* Make it, I said! My money is in the ship's strongbox." There would be two pounds left. He couldn't resist the temptation to say it. He could, but he wouldn't. "You lost by two pounds, Garth. Oh yes—and a crown. I almost forgot." He patted his pocket. "I made a wager on you this morning. It won me a five-shilling piece."

"A dangerous practice, Holden." Garth's face was pleasant, polite, completely controlled. "You may not always be lucky. I trust the crown piece doesn't burn you." He swung away and came face to face with the girl. "If it doesn't, this other piece will."

The girl smiled. *Brazen. . . . Pretending she didn't hear.* She had heard, right enough. *Making out that she didn't know what Garth meant.* She was pretending now to hang back, and the raffish old rogue was urging her on. *Innocence fresh out of Newgate.*

"Captain Holden, if you will permit me——"

He wouldn't. He had no intention whatever of standing here, making a spectacle of himself, talking to a trull and being jostled and pawed by a greasy thief. He was grateful when Pollexfen took him by the arm and walked him firmly away. But he knew, as he went, that the girl's smile had died and there had been a kind of shadow across her face. Like anger, he thought. Eyes suddenly dark. And what the hell did she have to be angry about? He thought: *She's young.* He thought: *The wind's falling. I hadn't noticed.* The wind now was hardly a breeze. *We won't make Norfolk tonight. My God, but she's young.*

"Well, Chris."

"Well, what?"

"Now that you've got her, what will you do with the wench?"

"I don't know. You might give me time to think."

"Stab me, you'd better think. You've bought a problem, my friend."

Holden scowled at the bright blade lying along his palm. Already the satisfaction of angering Garth was losing its edge. The joke was losing its point.

"What the devil *can* I do with her?"

"There's not much doubt in Garth's mind what you mean to do. Nor in most other minds—including hers, I dare say. You've bought you a concubine. That's what your friends will say when you fetch her ashore tomorrow."

"Let them say! They'll be wrong. And you're wrong. She's not a problem. She's the answer to one."

All the mocking, unhumorous humor was gone from Chris Holden's face. His mouth was flattened and grim.

"We got off from London in such a rush I forgot something rather important." The mockery stayed in his voice. Pollexfen, who did not know what was coming, knew Holden well enough now to know he was taunting himself. "There was something I meant to buy. I just bought it."

The knife flashed. The point sank deep in the wood. The blade shuddered there with the sudden passion that drove it.

"She'll be my wedding gift to Diana and Jimmy. One of them ought to like it."

"You can't do that, Chris."

"The devil I can't."

"Not to Diana. You'd set the whole province laughing. And not to yourself. You'd regret it. You love her. You must, to hate her so much."

Chapter 9

The faint breeze failed completely at dusk. The *Star of London,* at anchor against the ebb, was a gleaming white obelisk rising out of the flat moonlit desert of Chesapeake Bay. The Virginia shore was a low black smudge across the track of the moon.

Vague and blurred as it was, Chris Holden could see it clearly. He leaned alone on the quarter-deck rail and watched it, remembering it. He didn't need eyes to see the high gullied banks or the yellow orange earth or the narrow strips of the black sand beaches below the banks. He had seen the tide flats of the Thames and had smelled them too. He could smell Virginia now, with the tide running out to the sea, and it wasn't unpleasant like London's river.

It smelled fresh, damp, and clean, and new. It smelled, somehow, as if it had just been washed, or had just been born.

He breathed deeply, pulling Virginia far down into his body, trying to hold it, not wanting to let it go. But there was nothing, he knew, to hold. This was no home-coming. This was a loneliness worse than any he ever had known.

He was almost glad when he heard Pollexfen's brisk heels on the deck and felt the plump shoulder settle itself beside him.

"Feel like talking, Chris?"

"Yes. Of course."

"Good. I've taken a notion about you. About you and us. We're your London agents."

"Not mine. It'll be a long time before Crisscross has need for an agent."

"Wasn't thinking of that. Thinking the other way—upside down. Always think upside down. You don't need a London agent. We need an American one."

"You've got an agent in Norfolk."

"Got one in Philadelphia too. Got one in New York. All English. Good men—wrong places. How'd you like to be our American agent?"

"Me? Polly, you're crazy."

"No. Don't think so. Never have been yet, in the way of business. D'you know how I got to be partner? By thinking up new ideas. Any new idea is crazy. It's got to be. Wouldn't be new if it wasn't. Simple."

"This one's simple, all right."

"Surely is," Pollexfen agreed. "D'you know how I got my notions? Simplest thing ever heard of. I take an old one and turn it over—see how it looks bottom up. That's how I came onto this one. Good for you Americans to have English company looking out for you in England. Well, then. Good for English company to have a colonial looking out for it in the colonies. Plain as the nose on your face."

"Confound it, Polly, I don't know a customs receipt from a bill of lading."

"Hire a clerk to tell you the diff'rence. We've got a plenty of clerks. Haven't got one that knows what you know about North American colonies."

"There's more to know than any one man can ever find out. It's a big place, Polly. I've never been farther north than Philadelphia. I've never seen York province or Massachusetts or Maine. I've never——"

"Know tobacco, don't you?"

"I know something about how to grow it."

"Know more than that. Know more than you think you do, Chris. You know who's got the best ground. You know enough not mix the prime leaf with stem."

"Anybody knows that."

"The devil they do! You'd be surprised what trash we get from some of your biggest plantations. That's one place you'd be a help."

"Grading tobacco? You can hire——"

"No. Grading people. That's the real trick in business. Pick best ones, you'll have the best business. Know fur too, don't you? Know where it comes from. Know all about Indians."

"Nobody knows all about Indians."

" 'Nother thing, you've been out with our army people. Know how to get on with them. Important, isn't it?"

"Yes. But I'm still the wrong man. They're not overfond of provincial militia."

"Respect you, though. Bound to, with those scars you've got."

Holden laughed.

"I can see myself now, walking into General Amherst's headquarters and taking my clothes off so he can look over my scars. What d'you want me to do? Run around stark naked?" He sobered. "I'm grateful, Polly. But I'm no agent for you. I can bell a buzzard, but——"

67

"Bell a buzzard? Do you do that? Why?"

"For the fun of it, mostly. It's useful, too, in its way. Say a colt or a calf gets mired in a swamp and you're hunting for it. If you see buzzards circling, likely as not they've found it. But they don't always circle. They might be huddled on tree limbs, watching the poor brute, waiting for it to die. You can't see them, in the thick woods. But happen one of them has been belled, you'll know where they are."

"Sounds silly. Bad business. Put bell on the colt—be better."

"No, it wouldn't. First thing that happens, when a belled cow or horse gets to floundering in a swamp, the bell fills up with mud."

"You see? I'm right. Wrong about buzzard—right about you. That's the reason I want you. Keep us straight on things we don't know. Pinch me, Chris." Pollexfen was plaintive about it. "You're the one that gave me the blue bloody blazes because you said Englishmen don't understand provincials—don't know a thing about 'em. Now you won't take me up."

"I don't want to take you in. I'm no man of business. Confound it, I proved that this morning. A hundred and three pounds——"

"And sixpence."

"I could afford the sixpence. No. You're generous, Polly. I'm grateful but I can't accept. I'd only do harm."

"You're more like to do harm if you go ashore with that girl at Norfolk tomorrow. I know what small towns are like. I know how tongues waggle and clack."

"What's the odds, if I give her away?"

"To Diana and Jimmy?"

"Yes."

"The odds," Pollexfen said, "are five thousand to one that you don't."

"Be careful, I might take you up on *that*. It would be a way to recoup."

"The odds stand."

"Oh, you win," Chris said wearily. "I'm not quite a savage yet. But if the tongues waggle, let them. Who's to care, if I don't?"

"Diana, maybe."

"Pah!"

"Pah" all you like. You've got her as deep inside you now as you had half a year ago."

"The hell I have."

"It's a kind of hell that I'd like to see you out of. Women can change. My wife changed her mind twenty times before she decided to have me. What's more, she's been changing it nine times a day ever since. You'll be in worse hell if you find out Diana has changed her mind and is ready to turn back to you—and then see her turn away again because you've bought a neat bedpiece for Crisscross."

"I haven't. Dammit!"

"She'll think you have."

"I doubt that she'd mind."

"Because she didn't mind about Shiftless Jimmy and how he came by his name?" Pollexfen's hand lay on Holden's arm a moment. The arm was rigid and ridged with the lean hard muscles drawn taut by an angry fist. He couldn't see Holden's face. The young moon had set while they talked;

68

there was only the faint sheen of starlight laid over the sheen of black water. But he was quite sure that the face beside him was as hard and angry and taut as the arm he touched. "Thought I didn't know about that, eh, Chris? I did. Had a reason for asking you why he was called Shiftless Jimmy. I already knew. Wondered whether you'd tell me. You didn't. D'you see?"

"No." It was grim and flat.

Pollexfen sighed. He had laid careful plans for distracting Chris Holden's mind from unhappiness, and the plans were not working out as well as they should.

"Wasn't interested in Jimmy. We knew a plenty about him. Didn't know about you. Had a notion, though. Found out. You're loyal."

"Loyal?" The question sounded astonished. "To Jimmy? No! He didn't have one damned thing to do with what I told you or didn't."

"Right. Thought so. Been thinking so all along. Remember the first time we talked about roots—yours—mine? About your grandfather, I mean— how he was starting out new, in Virginia, at the same time my grandfather was a clerk for Abernethy & Griswold. You've got the old boy in your blood. Abernethy says you're like him."

"How does he know?" But Pollexfen detected the pleasure and pride that came into the voice beside him. "He couldn't. It's been fifty years."

"Letters. Letter books full of him. Told you that. He felt pretty much the same about this new world of yours as you do. Wrote about Virginia same way you talk about the frontier. One thing about him—he knew where he was going. Went. You can go too. Same places. Higher, maybe. Another thing—he knew what to leave behind. He wasn't afraid to throw things away. Left England behind. Threw his business away. Chris . . ." Pollexfen's hand touched Holden's arm lightly again. "D'you know what finally made me sure about you? It was what you did this morning— throwing away the last hundred pounds you had."

"My God!"

"You're not the only one that's thrown money away today. I've thrown more than you. There's good profit in handling indentured convicts. But so help me, Chris, no ship of ours will ever carry another man, woman, or child to be auctioned off like a beast. It's too much like being a slaver. And that's your doing, my friend."

"I never once mentioned carrying convicts. I never once thought about it."

"Thought about something else. Freedom. New world and new hope. New chance. New kind of people. Horizons—all that."

"Oh." And then, slowly: "I can't take the credit for that—or the blame, whichever it is. I didn't know I believed those things, till I said them."

"Not surprised. Dare say you believe that you bought the wench to plague Garth."

"I did."

"No," Pollexfen said, "you didn't. Oh, partly. Not mostly, though. Little reason sometimes has bigger reason behind it. Can't see the woods for the trees. You hate Garth, but mostly you hate what he stands for. You don't like what he's trying to do to your precious Ohio country. Ready to fight about it. Spent the most of your London holiday getting ready to fight. Damn near got yourself killed."

"D'you call that good business?"

"Doesn't look much like it, but could be. Too early to tell. Peace treaty signed . . . French pulling out . . . whole continent opening up . . . no end to what it can mean. Garth sees one kind of a future. You see another kind. One of you'll win. What about the little wench, Chris?"

"What about her?"

"Ought to get shut of her. Where's the hope for her, once it's known that Christopher Holden has fetched home a concubine fresh out of Newgate?"

"God damn it!"

"I know. She's not, in your mind. But she will be in most other minds."

"What d'you want me to do? Set her free?"

"She's a felon. You can't. Not now. Much too risky. Might do it, someday, if you make up your mind she deserves it. And if you handle things right—if people don't find out about her. There are ways, lawful or not. That another surprise? Respectable merchant conspiring to break the law? I'm not."

"Not respectable?" Holden asked.

Pollexfen chuckled.

"Not very. You'd be surprised how many Pollexfens there'd be on the Old Bailey docket if they had been caught. Smugglers a long way back. That's where the money came from to make us respectable. And as far as that goes, thousands and ten thousands of decent Englishmen make their living at smuggling. The Pollexfens have been law-abiding for three or four generations—though God knows there's a plenty of laws that I can't abide. Dare say the smuggling is still in my blood. That's what I've been thinking about—smuggling the girl ashore so that neither you nor she will be dirtied with talk. How far out are we?"

"Five or six miles."

"Not too bad. Brookes is sending the gig ashore. Sending Ellis in with ship's papers and such. Save time if he's there in the morning. Know the river, don't you? Awkward place to come into at night, Brookes says. Thought you might handle the tiller."

"That's a damned thin excuse. Polly, what the devil am I to do with the girl after I take her ashore?"

"Got a house in Norfolk, you said. Empty. Closed up. No reason she couldn't stay there awhile, is there, and no one the wiser? Must know some decent family that'd be willing to take her in for the work she'd do. Might hire her out at wages—get interest on your money."

"It's nonsense, Polly."

"Interest's never nonsense. Miss paying it—you'll find out."

"Besides, it won't work."

"Why won't it?"

"She'd be missed as soon as the rest of the convicts got off. The souldriver's got to account for the lot."

"Simple. Say she was sold on board. That's the truth. Say owner took her ashore. That's truth too. Perfectly legal. Records complete. All she is then is a name on a list. Nobody knows how pretty she is. Diff'rent from having whole town look her over, there on the wharf. No talk."

"It still sounds like damned nonsense to me."

"Sorry." Abruptly Pollexfen became abrupt. "Thought you meant what you said."

"I didn't say what you've been saying."

"Got the notion from you. New chance in new world. Good notion. No good if it's not made to work. Thought I'd like to see if it would."

"Oh, damn you," Chris said. "You stick like a plaster. All right."

"Good. I'll tell Ellis to send her up. Look here, Chris. Think about being agent."

"Don't forget there's a buzzard I've got to bell."

"Give you plenty of time."

"Thanks, Polly. I'll think about it."

"Fine. Gig ought to be getting away. See you tomorrow. Be on the wharf, eh? Good night, Chris."

"Good night."

Pollexfen hurried away. Holden leaned on the rail alone and wondered why he had let himself be bullied, and what old Xtopher Holden would think if he could know that his grandson was fetching a girl out of Newgate to hide in his house. He heard the trample of feet on the deck and the clatter and bump of the boat being hoisted out. The falls screeked. Ellis stood at his elbow.

"The gig's ready. The girl's in it, along with her trunk. Never fear, sir. There'll be no talk. Mr. Pollexfen's dealt handsomely with the gig's crew— very handsomely, sir. I suppose you'll want her in the stern sheets?"

Damn him! Had he borne down a little too heavily on that last word? Holden said sharply:

"No! Put her up in the bow."

"She may cut and run for it, sir, the minute we touch shore."

"She'll not run." He wouldn't care if she did. But he wished that he hadn't said it.

Chapter 10

The river was a darker darkness. It was almost solid. It was too confounded solid, he decided glumly, to be blundering about it in the small hours of the morning on this damned fool's errand.

There would be half a hundred vessels in the town reach, likely, and another half a hundred small craft—and all of them anchored every which way. No London street could get itself worse tangled with sedan chairs, carts and wagons, chariots and chaises than the eastern branch of the Elizabeth with pinks and shallops, snows and pungeys, square-riggers out of England and sloops from the islands, Carolina schooners and New England brigs, double-ended Chesapeake batteaux and Hampton flatties and periaguas. And not one in ten of them would ever trouble to hang out a lantern.

Somewhere he heard rudder pintles working in their gudgeons, sensed the bulk of a moored vessel without seeing it, and jammed the tiller over in bare time to sheer off from a low Patapsco schooner. He knew she was from Baltimore by the way her raked stern hung above him, as steep-pitched as an attic ceiling. One of the starboard oars rapped sharply on her counter and the oarsman muttered. To the left, ahead, a distant glimmer pricked the darkness. It was fainter than it ought to be, and lower. He had held on too long toward Craney, and the gig was much too far out in the stream.

He swung the tiller over till the prickly glimmer turned into a pin-cushion of light from the patterned holes of a tin lantern. The pattern repeated itself, dark streaks and yellow speckles on the round stern of a plump snow. He knew, now, where he was. For half a mile there would be wharves with ships tied in them like so many animals in barn stalls, the floor spattered with the droppings of light from their lanterns.

All the stalls were filled. That vague shape slipping by was a Bermuda sloop. He could not see her raised quarter-deck or her high bulwarks, but the tangy odor of red-cedar strakes and timbers could not be mistaken. In the next slip, also dark, lay a Barbadoes schooner with the reek of rum about her: it was different from either the Jamaica or Antigua. Then another schooner, down from the Potomac, smelling of dried herring. And one up from Carolina, with the mingled smells of barreled pitch and hides and brine casks filled with salt pork, and—faintly, quickly gone—the clean sweet scent of myrtle-berry wax in boxes on her deck.

In the borough dock a horn lantern spilled out greasy light that glistened sleekly on the stern of a ship larger than the *Star of London* and dripped down into the water rippling past the rudder. Its reflection ran and spread and vanished, as if a crock of grease was being tipped at intervals to let a blob splash out upon a warm black griddle and lie there a moment and then melt and run. The broad basin of the dock was crowded. There was no room even for a gig to squeeze in, here, to a wharf ladder.

A man might scramble up without a ladder, with another man to heave him; but the girl . . . He certainly did not intend to pick her up, his arms around her legs, and lift her up and hold her while she squirmed and wriggled. It would be, he thought, an excellent preliminary. Any man in his right mind would think so. Ellis would jump at a chance to help her up the wharf. The purser—and the sailors too—would doubtlessly enjoy it. For all he knew, *she* might. *The little trollop.* . . .

He almost missed Boush's Landing. The long timber that projected from the wharf there, with the ducking stool fixed to it, was above his head before he saw it.

"Easy," he said. "Easy, now."

The gig bumped a piling, slid off, bumped again. He put out his hand and touched rough wood and knew it—a barge gunwale slivered by the hoofs of horses. He had hoped that it would be there, but it was a long time since he last rowed up the river as far as Boush's ferry; he had not been certain that the barges still tied up, nights, at the same place. Finding them here gave him an unreasonable pleasure. It was like a welcome. Some things had not changed. Some things were still dependable and solid.

"This will do." He stood up. "You can walk ashore here on the scows. Or there's a ladder, about two scows in." He stepped across the gunwale. "You'll find a tavern open somewhere. I'll say good night. If you'll hand up the trunk . . . Obliged."

The trunk astonished him. By the feel of it as he tucked it underneath his arm, it must be nearly empty. The girl probably had no clothes but the dress she sat in. *Good Lord!* He couldn't turn her loose, in a strange place, with nothing. He felt excitement tingling in him, creeping upward through him as he walked toward the gig's bow.

"All right," he said into the darkness. "Come along."

He put out his hand, and the girl's hand came up obediently to find it. Her fingers touched his wrist. The tingling rushed together there like bubbles. Then her hand slipped into his and it surprised him. It was such a small hand. *Dammit.* She was nothing but a child. And . . . *dammit* . . . she was trusting him. Or was she? Was she merely willing?

He found, presently, the ladder. The first rung he touched was dripping wet and slimy, and the one above still slippery from the ebbing tide. He guided her hand:

"Can you climb it?"

"Yes. The trunk, though . . ."

"It's nothing. I can manage."

He thought, climbing, that he should not have said the trunk was nothing. It sounded as if he had been taunting her with its pathetic emptiness . . . as if, almost, he had been warning her that she was helpless, utterly at his disposal. The trunk must be important to her, and he wondered why. It could not possibly contain more than a petticoat, a pair of stockings, a spare shift . . .

His mind pounced upon them. She had not been wearing stockings. The soul-driver's cane, lifting her skirts, had showed her ankles bare. And his brother had a notion about women's shifts. . . . *God's life, Holden, so you're down to that now. So you're down to Jimmy's level.* Shiftless Jimmy! Five shillings if she keeps her shift on, ten shillings if she takes it off. *Well, Holden, how you'd like it? Shiftless Chris . . . how d'you like the sound of that? You don't? You've got some decency about you, eh? Or have you? She's a child. She's not a trollop.* That's it! If she were, you wouldn't want her. *I don't want her.* Oh no? Besides, how d'you know she's not a trollop? Some of those streetwalkers in the Bridewell were as young as she is. Younger, some of them. Sweet and innocent as angels, till you heard their voices and their gutter language. *Child! Child of the devil, likely.*

But her voice was different. Even with the note of worry in it, this girl's voice was low and gentle. It had no sharp edges. It was like her, softly rounded. *Dammit!* He did not want to see her that way. He did not want to undress her that way, in his mind.

His mind continued to undress her. She was coming up the ladder now. Her face and shoulders were a pale blur in the darkness, rising toward him. He could hear her garments brushing on the ladder, her legs stirring in them, and the bubbling tingle of excitement rose up through his body till it tightened in his chest and throat. He turned away without a word, his heels dully hollow on the ancient planks, and heard the girl's heels like obedient small echoes following him.

The wharf ended. The soft, intermingled ruts of Water Street were underfoot. He could feel the black sand, fine as sifted corn meal, like a yielding carpet; it made hushing noises—his steps and the girl's together. She was not following him now: she was beside him. He could not see her face unless he turned his head, but he could see her breast; he could see, at least, the white blouse covering her breasts.

The street, he thought, was lighter than the river. There were no lights, but the darkness seemed less solid. It was a phenomenon he had forgotten. In the wilderness the nights were always less dark on the rivers than they were on land: the hills and forests multiplied the darkness. Here in the low tidewater country, in the flat towns where the streets and houses left no room for trees, the rivers seemed to draw the night down into them and hold it.

The forgotten fact, remembered, lost its strangeness quickly. It became familiar, and the town became familiar. He could not actually see the town, but he could feel it all around him. His grandfather had walked this same street, with the low wharf sheds on the river side and, on the other, the low hip-roofed houses that looked right and wrong at the same time— right because they had been there for a hundred years and were familiar and belonged there, but wrong because they also looked more Dutch than English. He had smelled the same smells—the hemp in the ropewalks, citron, coffee, juniper shingles from the great swamp, tar and turpentine and cheeses, bags of feathers, and the mingled odors of rum and tobacco that soaked through them all as if the whole town had been steeped in rum and smoke-cured with tobacco.

To the right now, sharply. The market house loomed up ahead, a sprawling blackness; its broad roof, projecting to the colonnade of timber pillars, seemed to fill the street. There was the pine pump, standing sentry, leaning on its long iron handle like a soldier half asleep and leaning on his musket. And here was the blunt turn into Church Street. The name was new. In his grandfather's day it had been simply "the street going out of town."

His eagerness was still a-tingle in him. But it was now, somehow, much more pleasant. It was rising through him like continuous fine streams of bubbles in his blood, but they no longer tightened in his chest and throat; they flowed easily and pleasantly and freely. The anticipation mounting in him was compounded partly of the girl beside him, of his knowledge of power over her, of his possession of her, and her tacit and obedient admission of possession. But it was compounded also of innumerable small unimportant sensuous impressions—of his having piloted the gig up the dark river intricate with ships, and of the touch of the old splintered gunwale of the ferry—of the feeling of returning, not to Norfolk merely or Virginia or to America, but to the place of his beginnings and to stout old Xtopher. Now here, unexpectedly, he was not alone.

He had no idea whether the sense of companionship came from the rustle of the girl's skirts, from her nearness, from anticipation of her, or from being home and feeling that it *was* home. When he came to his grandfather's house and put his hand on the low rounded coping of the garden wall, he was not thinking of the girl at all. He was barely conscious of a thin, vague thought that came into him without effort, without conscious thinking: she was here beside him, she would be here when the proper time came, but the time was not yet. There was something, for a moment yet, that was much more important. The moment of returning was here now, and it would not return. There would never be in all his life a time precisely like this.

When he drew the gate toward him, he could feel its old familiar slow reluctance—as if he had disturbed it in its sleep—as if it did not, at the first touch, know him. He could feel the weight of the twenty-four-pound round shot on the chain inside it rising. It rose sluggishly at first and then, by some law of physics he did not pretend to understand, the chain on which it hung began to lift it quickly and more quickly, as if it weighed less as it rose higher. It seemed, at the last, to welcome him—to be almost eager. He stepped through the wall and kept his hand behind him on the gate to let the girl come in and then kept it there another moment to prevent the gate from slamming. And then he remembered that it would not slam. The round shot on its chain, descending, drew it swiftly shut until the last two inches and then seemed to have been overpowered by drowsiness again. The gate closed as softly as a feather.

A sprawling rose bush brushed his knee. Thorns ripped across his breeches. The old rose walk was in need of trimming. Well, if he listened to Pollexfen, if he settled down to be a merchant, the old house would come back to its proper function. He would use the old man's office and his chamber; and the rose walk would be trimmed. He liked the notion. And found himself wondering whether, if he ever got the money, Jimmy would sell Jason to him.

Black Jason was the last living link with the man who built this house; he had helped to build it. Jason had been in the prime of manhood when his master died. He was an old man now: he must be seventy at least, or eighty. He was fit only to trim rose walks now, or potter in a kitchen, or sit at the tiller of the Holden Hundred longboat. But he remembered much about old Xtopher. It occurred to Chris now that old Jason probably could teach him a good deal about how to be a man of business.

He'd buy Jason from his brother and then set him free. He'd make a partner of him, and to hell with everybody. Jason's memories of his master would make him a valuable partner. It would be almost like having old Xtopher himself for partner—a sleeping partner. The thought made him suddenly acutely conscious of the girl beside him.

"Wait," he told her. "Wait here."

The house was his, but Jimmy sometimes used it. The possibility that the house might not be empty struck him for the first time. It wasn't likely, but . . . Great zooks, how Jimmy would enjoy *this!* He found the low brick step and took the key out of his pocket and set the girl's trunk on the step. His hand felt the old oak planking of the door, the planks not set straight up or straight across, but slanting. It was a thing worth knowing: planks set slantwise kept a door from warping.

The heavy door swung open easily, with a small sound like sighing.

Warm air from within the house brushed out across his face. It was almost as if the house breathed. And it smelled clean. Opening this house was like opening a tidy box. The warm breathing of the house swung the door softly shut behind him, and he let it stay.

His heels made solid, satisfying noises on the bare ax-hewn planks. The candlestand was in its place against the wall, but . . . Christopher Holden was suddenly and unreasonably annoyed. There should be three brass candleholders on the stand, one for each chamber above stairs, with the brass tinderbox precisely in the center of the stand. Coming into a dark house at night, a man always knew exactly where to find the box. He always knew, too, that the end with the wheel inside it was toward his right hand. He could lift the lid and spin the wheel and know that there was shredded tow to catch the sparks.

The tinderbox was gone now. There was only one brass candleholder, and no candle in it. Not that he needed any candle to find his way up these familiar stairs. There was no doubt about it . . . he could feel the foot-worn hollows in them. And they creaked at the right places—the third stair, the sixth, the seventh. He was smiling to himself as he climbed toward the last one: it had always been the loudest. It still was. It was almost peevish in its loud complaining about being roused at this time of the night.

"Jez'bel——"

He stopped, frozen, with one foot still on the plaintive step. His weight came onto it again, and it objected.

"Jez'bel! Mammy Jez'bel?"

Even with the weight of drowsiness upon it, he could not mistake that voice—light, quick, gay, confident. It was not gay now. It was not quite confident. It was impatient and a little frightened.

He heard bedcords creaking. *His* bed. Bare feet whispered on the floor. He saw a misty grayness in the place that would be the doorway to his chamber—his grandfather's chamber. All the bubbling eagerness swept up into his brain and burst there.

"Diana," he said, not believing. Not believing, *knowing*. She was there, within reach. He could take three steps and touch her. The sheer unexpectedness of hearing her voice made him feel lightheaded and lightbodied. All the sensuous awareness and anticipation of the last hour lifted him and thrust him toward her. He said again: "Diana . . ."

"Chris! Chris . . . it can't be. Oh, *Chris* . . . how wonderful!"

Her arms came up to him. His hands reached for her and found her. The thin filmy negligee she wore was nothing. It kept nothing from him. She was warm and smooth, and the curves of her body in his hands flowed smoothly downward, outward. She was taller than he had remembered. His hands had not found her waist, they were on the first slim curving of her hips. His hands felt as if they held her naked body.

But there was a hesitance about her body as he drew her to him—a slow heaviness, as if she were still half asleep, as if a weight were holding her. It was not resistance, it was not reluctance; it was drowsy willingness without will. And then, suddenly, he felt her body shaken, and the weight was gone and all suggestion of reluctance. She was whispering:

"Your hands . . . They're like ice."

Her body shrank from them. It could not shrink away, it could move only toward him. She could not escape his hands. They drove her close and held her shuddering against him, her whole body trembling and collapsing into his as he bent over her. His mouth found hers and held it till her trembling was no longer violent and helpless but a vibrance weaving her whole body closer to him. She was in his arms, warm, soft, pliant, acquiescent. She was, suddenly, not acquiescent. She was seeking him as he sought her.

"Chris . . ." Her mouth moved against his with the same vibrant weaving urgency. "Chris, I'm cold. Take me to bed. There's no one in the house but Jez'bel. *Take me. . . .*"

He picked her up and carried her across the room to the high bed. Her lips still clung to him when he had put her down, but her hands hurried him away. The old walnut ladder-back was by the window where it should be. He found it in the dark quite easily and laid his coat upon it, and saw beyond the chair the two geese cut into the shutters. It was almost morning, but not light enough to see the carved geese clearly; he was seeing them more clearly in his memory than in the pattern of gray twilight that they made.

There was a small mysterious struggling in the bed. The cords creaked and were still again. He saw a pale mist drifting, settling slowly to the floor, and he put out his hand and touched it as it floated down: the thin lawn of her negligee was light as mist but it was not cold like mist, it was warm from her body. Where it had been, there was a white blur in the darkness. It leaned toward him. When he went to meet it, eager, reaching, it retreated from him. He forgot the three steps that stood by the bed. He barked his shin on the sharp edge of them, and swore, and heard Diana's laughter from the pillow.

"Clumsy. . . ."

Her hand came to find him, touched him. Both of her hands lay upon his chest, flat. Almost, for a moment, they resisted. Then they slipped across the sensitive thin tissue of the scar and up, around his body. Her arms opened to him, and her hands were anxious.

Chapter 11

His body had come back to him. He did not know how long it had been gone. But it had changed—he knew that. It had lost the sense of being lifted up and carried weightlessly and irresistibly, of being powerless to resist. It lay relaxed and comfortably warm and comfortably heavy. He could even feel it growing heavier—slowly, pleasantly, more slowly—sinking deep and deeper into some dark deep contentment just as the weighted chain upon the gate had settled slowly and more slowly down into the dark until it drew the gate solidly and softly and completely shut.

He felt as if a gate had closed behind him. He felt enclosed, shut in, and at the same time delightfully released. Shut in . . . released. They were contrary words. They couldn't go together, but they did. They couldn't. But they did. It seemed quite reasonable, in the same way that the most impossible experiences in a dream seemed real and reasonable in the first unreal moment of awaking.

Even with Diana in his arms, he felt as if he was still more than half asleep and just beginning to awaken—as if in a moment now he would wake up completely and know that it had been a dream—as if she would be gone and he would be lying here alone.

He did not want to be alone. His arm beneath her lifted her and swept her hard against his breast; his hand rushed down her body and drew all of it against him. His hands held her fiercely.

"You're not here! You can't be!"

"Sshhh!" Her breathing laughter was a gusty warmth and sweetness on his face. "I'm here." She proved it with herself.

"You're so damned beautiful." Those words, together. He had not meant to say them. They were said.

"You can't see me." The low, delicious whisper of her laughter touched his mouth. Her mouth was murmuring against his, and the words were kisses.

"It's daylight. I can open the shutters. I can kick off the covers." He pretended to, and was imprisoned instantly. "I don't like mysteries."

"Oh, don't you?" She drew herself away a little. His hands brought her back. "Truly, *don't* you?"

"Yes! *Yes!* But to come home and find you here . . . as if it had been planned . . ."

"A rendezvous. It could have been. I was thinking of you while I was undressing. I was looking at your bed and thinking."

"But——"

"How did it happen I was here, waiting for you? There's no mystery about that. Only a ball at Fair Lea. You know how it is—a hundred guests in a house meant for twenty. The girls are sleeping seven to the bed at Fair Lea—sleeping crosswise. I don't like that; it's all right for little girls, but I'm tall. Did you know?" She pressed herself against him. "So I came here. I'd barely gone to sleep—I hadn't, quite—when I heard the stairs creak. I thought it was Jez'bel. She's so old. She wanders about, nights. Sometimes I wonder if she sleeps at all."

"Where's Jimmy?"

"I don't know. Up-river somewhere. Shirley Hundred, or at Riverview. Does it matter where he is? It doesn't. Don't you know it doesn't? Don't you know . . . now?"

"Yes."

"Don't speak of him. Don't think of him. I don't. Don't ever think of him again."

Relief flooded over him and through him. His arms held her closely. His mouth found the hollow of her neck.

"Chris, *don't*. You prickle. Chris?"

"Yes?"

78

"Did you fetch my new gowns? All the list I made you? Are they lovely?"

"Gowns!" He laughed at the absurdity. His hands, too, dismissed them. His hands stripped her of the possibility of garments. "Don't speak of them. Don't think of them. Don't ever think of them!"

"But there's the governor's ball three days from now. You'd not want me at the governor's ball like this?"

"*Want you!* I'd not have you go to any ball. I'd keep you here. I'd——"

"But there *is* a ball gown? There's one special ball gown?"

"Yes. From Paris. It's by Forgel." He chuckled. "That's the way they put it, like a painting—*by* Forgel."

"Paris! Darling! But who's Forgel? Is he man, or woman?"

"I don't know." He felt her stir. There was something disapproving in the quick withdrawing of her body. "So help me, I don't know. I never thought to ask."

His arms still held her, but she was withheld. She had not broken from the circle of his arms; she lay back against them, looking at him. But something had been broken, something was no longer perfect. She had found a flaw in him. *Not just in me,* he thought: *between us.* It took him by surprise.

"All I know," he said, "is that Forgel is dressmaker to La Pompadour. To the king's mistress."

"Oh, wonderful! Oh, perfect!" She returned to him completely. "You brought the dresses with you? They're here, in the house?"

"No. They're still on the *Star of London.* She's in the roads, becalmed. I came ashore——"

"But there's a breeze now. Listen." She drew herself firmly from his arms. Not away from them: up through them. She sat up, looking toward the shuttered window. "Listen. . . ."

He saw bright sunlight shining through the carved geese in the shutters. But it was not shining straight in. It was sharply angled, steeply slanted, and he knew what that meant. Eleven. . . . It was past eleven.

"Great damnation!" He flung off the covers. Sitting on the edge of the high bed, he could not reach his stockings in the frothy pool of negligee upon the floor. He felt Diana's hands upon his back, caressing him. Her arms slipped around his body and her hands clasped to hold him. She was murmuring against him:

"It's not so important. Of course I want to see my new gowns: I'm a girl." He felt the vibrance of her laughter. "You know that, don't you? But the gowns can wait a little."

"There's other things that can't." He took her wrists and parted her hands firmly and slid off the bed and heard the quick resentment in her voice:

"Chris! You'd not!"

"I'm sorry. I can't help it. I've got to get down to the ship. I should have been there when she came in."

"My lud! What's so tremendous about a ship you've been aboard for weeks? They'll take care of your baggage."

"It's not that." He couldn't tell her he had bought a seventeen-year-old girl and brought her to this house and left her waiting in the garden and forgotten her. "There's someone on board I oughn't to be rude to. I——"

"Oh?"

"A man. Ellerby Pollexfen." He was sitting on the bottom bed step, cramped and awkward, struggling with his stockings. His face felt hot. He felt as if the flush was covering his body. "Pollexfen," he said carefully, "is a partner in our firm of London agents. He came over with me. I'm going to work for him."

"You're going to *work* for him?"

"I'm going to be their factor in America."

"But why?"

"Why?" He was dragging on his breeches. The untrimmed rose branch in the garden, he saw, had pulled the threads in two long streaks across the knee. "Because I need the money."

"But you don't . . ." She hesitated. "You don't need it badly enough to do that. Lud! A grubby merchant like Niel Jamieson or Captain Tatum or the Tuckers. You've no need to——" She stopped altogether.

"I've the need, right enough. I've spent every penny that I owned, except one crown piece. I can't even make a start at clearing Crisscross till I whistle up some more."

"So you haven't given *that* up."

"Good Lord! Give it up? I can't. I've too much in it. That's where the money went—to get what I need to start a new plantation. At least," he amended, "that's where most of it went." He hadn't, so far, had to lie outrightly.

"Oh. And you're still bound to live there? At the world's end?"

"But it's not. The world's gone a good way past it. There's plantations all the way from Richmond to the mountains. And a plenty of fine houses on them. Tuckahoe——"

"Tuckahoe! There's a far difference between Tuckahoe and Holden Hall. Why, Chris, it's nought but plain boards!"

"I know." It seemed unbelievable. Not five minutes past she had been lying in his arms. Now they were disputing about houses . . . other people's houses. "But I'll not be living out at Crisscross for a long time, likely. I've been planning to live here. Would you mind that?"

"I haven't minded it too much"—her smile seemed to be remembering —"so far." Her half-lifted arms invited him again. "I'd ought to be sure, I suppose."

He dropped the ends of his stock, still untied, and went to her and snatched her up out of the bed and held her pliant body crushed against him.

"*Di . . . Di . . .* Stop it, sweetheart. *Stop it.*"

"I'll not. I'll not stop it, ever. No one can make me stop it. Not . . . even . . . you."

"I must. I must, now, Di." He laid her down among the pillows. "If you're not sure"—he stood smiling down at her—"I'll make you sure as soon as I come back."

"But you can't come back here!" She sat up again, abruptly. "You can't possibly come back here."

"It's my house," he said. He realized that he could not come back to it while she was in it, but it pleased him to insist. "It's my office too. I'm a man of business. Haven't I the right to choose my partner?"

"Sir, your most obedient!" She made him, sitting in the bed, the pretense of a curtsy. "I vow, sir, I'm flattered. You mean, of course, a sleeping partner. That is what they call a secret partner, isn't it?" Then: "Chris, how *am* I going to see those gowns?"

"I'll have the trunks sent here."

"No. No, I don't think so." Beyond his shoulder in the glass, he saw her frowning.

"There's no reason why I shouldn't send them. There's no reason why I shouldn't come here with them. If I'm still on the ship——"

"You're not, though."

"I'm supposed to be. I'd have no way of knowing that you're here. It would be only natural to come to my own house. When I find you here, I can go to Gay's Inn."

"And have people wondering how much of your time you spend at the inn and how much here?"

"We'll get someone for a chaperone, then. You said there's a mob at Fair Lea."

"And have them see my new gowns? Never!"

"I thought you'd want them seen."

"Chris! Are men really as stupid as they make out sometimes? I wouldn't for the life of me let any woman see my Forgel gown until I sail into the governor's ball. Late," she added. "Quite late. La, they'll swoon in windrows when they see me. They will, won't they?"

"They should. It cost a hundred eighty-seven pounds—the dress and what goes under it."

"D'you think that's expensive?"

"Well . . ."

"For me, darling? Have you forgot so soon? *I'm* what goes under it."

"There's a deal of you that doesn't. It comes right low."

"How d'you know how low it comes? D'you mean you tried it on some other woman?"

"No. *I* didn't. But a man can't go buying women's doodads without help. If it hadn't been for Polly——"

"Polly? And who's Polly, may I ask?"

"Jealous!" He laughed at her in the mirror. "Polly is Pollexfen. His wife helped choose the gowns. She was right proud about the Forgel. She put it on to show me. There's no doubt it's low. She wore a kerchief with it, but her husband didn't like it, even so."

"Show me."

He made vaguish gestures.

"Not on you, silly! On me." She squirmed about until her back was to him. "No, show me where it comes."

He picked out a place in the smooth hollow of her back and put his finger on it.

"But that's not *low!* You're wrong. You must be wrong. A *Paris* gown? The front, then. Show me how it is in front." She leaned back against him, her head tilted and her mouth provocative. "Well, aren't you going to show me?"

His hands cupped her breasts.

"You devil." He bent over her. She let her head slip down into the curving of his arm. Her mouth was waiting for him. "You've a devil in you, darling . . . darling. . . ."

His arms must have hurt her, he thought. And his mouth too. But she was talking eagerly the instant she was free.

"I've thought it out. We'll go to Holden Hall. Don't scowl, now. Listen. . . . I know what you think of Jimmy, but he's not there. I'm quite sure he's not there. If he is, you needn't stay. But I've got the longboat. Jimmy took my barge; it's bigger, and he wanted to make up a party for a hunt at Shirley, so we traded." She laughed lightly. "You know what *he's* hunting. I've got Jason and a crew from Holden Hundred. They've got to go back sometime. Just think of it . . . all night on the river. We'll be home by morning, Chris . . . another morning . . . just like this one. Shall we?"

"Yes!" He hadn't thought that he would feel so soon again the keening tingle of excitement racing through him. "Yes, Di!"

"You'll not be long with this Pollexfen person?"

"No. I should be, but I'll not. He'll understand. He's not staying in Virginia anyway; he's going on to Baltimore as soon as the ship sails."

"Then hurry. Hurry, Chris. You'll be surprised how quickly I can dress me when I want to. I'll come down in the boat, and you'll be so amazed to see me! You must be properly amazed, you know."

"I will be. I still am."

"Be off with you, then. Hurry . . . I can't wait to see my Forgel gown."

But when he had put on his coat, her arms reached out to him again. Her body lifted itself to him.

"You *will* hurry," she whispered. "You will, won't you? I can't wait to see . . . tomorrow morning."

He forgot, until he was halfway downstairs, that he might find another woman waiting for him on the doorstep. The door, he saw, was tightly closed. Had she done that? Or had it been the wind? Or Jez'bel? He saw, also, that the brass tinderbox had been misplaced. Someone had left it on the table by the door, where visitors were meant to lay their hats.

He moved the box into its proper place upon the candlestand—and thought, as he set it down precisely in its place, that his grandfather's house would never be so orderly again. Diana would not keep a tidy house. He did not know exactly how he knew it, but he knew.

It occurred to him that he had taken time to move the tinderbox because he dreaded opening the door. When he opened it, the girl was not there on the step. She was not in the garden either. She had gone, and she had taken her trunk with her. He felt enormously relieved. He felt, also, just a little foolish.

Chapter 12

The *Star of London* was already in. He guessed it by the empty street and the deserted market and the sour face of the tavern keeper glooming at him through the window of the Three Tuns. At this hour the taproom should be filled with merchants, lawyers, and shopkeepers nooning over beef and oysters, mugs of beer, and the *Intelligencer* or last week's *Virginia Gazette* come down from Williamsburg. But a three-master out of England, tying up at midday, sucked the Main Street inns dry. A good half of Norfolk would be swarming on the river front, and gentlemen not handicapped with ladies would be rattling dice and clinking half joes on the tables of the meaner taverns along Water Street.

Mr. Holden had small liking for the prospect of shouldering his way through a mob of townfolk. His eyes were stiff with sleeplessness: they felt exactly as if they had hoops around them, like the hoops of wooden noggins. They smarted. When he rubbed them, the stiff bristles on his cheekbones were like slivers prickling on his fingers. And the ladder at the ferry landing had put smears on both his stockings and a sourish-looking stain above the left knee of his breeches. He felt and looked as if he'd spent the night at Mrs. Valentine's. *Great Judas . . . what a thing to think of.*

Before he reached the market house he saw the gold harp of the *Star of London's* house flag fluttering above the Norfolk chimney tops. She was lying in the borough dock, he saw when he had made the turning. Her bowsprit hung across the breadth of Water Street like the trunk of a great blasted pine tree that had been stripped of its bark by lightning and come crashing down upon the hip roof of the Tucker house. It seemed to lean upon the house. The squatty roof looked crushed.

The down-thrusting dolphin striker made an eddy in the crowded street beneath the ponderous timber. A cluster of town urchins dangled from the bowsprit martingales like monkeys, working themselves hand over hand along the ropes, their bare feet walking air amongst the cocked hats and the ladies' bonnets and the apprehensive ears of horses waiting in the shafts of two-wheeled carts and warehouse sledges. A gentleman's long ebony cane rose from the crowd and thwacked a squirming backside and fetched dust out of its breeches. A carter twirled his whip. The cane whacked again. With sharp, shrill cries, the boys dropped off the ropes.

When they were gone, the shrill complaints continued: the wheels squealing in the hoisting blocks amidships. A cargo net swung out across the rail. A mate bellowed: "Lower away!" The bulging net dropped down into a circle of upraised, sweat-glistening black arms of stevedores. Above the piles of freight already on the wharf he saw Ellis standing on the *Star of London's* gangboard, checking manifests. The purser grinned at him familiarly as he came up the landing stage.

"Good morning, Mr. Holden—or good afternoon, I should say. A man loses track of time." His grin grew broader and so did his meaning. "I trust you got some sleep."

Holden's embarrassment flared hotly into anger.

"Damn!" He meant to say, *Damn your infernal impudence,* but an unpleasant notion checked him: he could not afford the luxury of damning Ellis. If the fellow hadn't talked too much already, it would be a very luxury of folly to offend him into talking. The purser's voice descended to an intimate and sympathetic murmur:

"Led you quite a chase, eh? I was sure she meant to slip you. You'll recall I said so."

"You said so. But she didn't."

"Uh? You say she didn't."

"She had no cause to. She's free."

"You mean you've given her her freedom?"

"I intend to."

"Well! The minx should have told me. She said nought about it— not one word about it. She seemed to feel—um—uh—still bound." The plague take the fellow! He was grinning like a pleased cat. He was purring like an obscene tomcat on a back fence. "A sense of obligation, I've no doubt. Uh—yes indeed. That would explain it. I'd have said she seemed to feel more bound to you than ever."

Holden wanted savagely to hit him.

"What the devil are you talking about? Where'd you see her?"

"On the street. I came out of the Old Borough tavern about seven of the clock and there she was—walking along bold as you please on the main street in daylight, with her trunk and all. I can't say it surprised me. She's a bad un. Bold as brass. My God, didn't she confess to murder? Well—when I saw her marching down the street I figured it was just the thing she *would* do. Brazening it out, I said. I made a mistake. If I had known——"

"What kind of a mistake?"

"Why, seizing her. She told the truth, mind. I can see that now. Said she was going to the wharf to wait there. I took it for granted she was lying."

"Where is she?"

"In the hold, sir. I fetched her to the wharf and turned her back to Leach, soon as the ship came in. He locked her up."

"Confound it! Couldn't you have asked Pollexfen?"

"But Mr. Pollexfen wasn't on the ship. He'd gone."

"Gone!"

"Yes, sir. He was in a fever to get north, sir, as you know. A Patapsco schooner that was lying in the river dropped down to the roads at daylight. Mr. Pollexfen was on deck with Captain Brookes; and when Brookes told him what she was, nothing would do but he must hail and ask if she had room to take a passenger to Baltimore. She had, and Mr. Pollexfen was off and aboard her in no time at all. He left a message for you. It's locked in the strongbox. If you like, I'll fetch it."

"I'd be obliged." Walking across the deck, Chris Holden was no more than half aware that Ellis was still talking.

". . . a rule of the house. Soon as an Abernethy, Griswold, and Pollexfen ship puts into any port, she sends off a man to pick up news. Papers, gossip, anything. We always ask for letters; it makes a great impression on a passenger to fetch him letters that he isn't looking for. Considering how suddenly you sailed, I'd not have thought that there'd be anything for you. But there it was, in the master of post's office. Seen hard travel, by the look of it."

Holden saw the dirty crumpled paper poking out at him and knew, without even looking at the writing, that it was a letter from John Fraser. It was sealed with a great blob of candle wax pressed down by the hairy knuckles of John Fraser's two enormous middle fingers. The hairs had left their pattern in the wax—the Fraser coat of hand, John called it, and maintained that it was more distinctive than a coat of arms. Chris chuckled, looking at it, and felt better instantly. But it was odd that Fraser should have tried to reach him through the master of the post at Norfolk. He had told John definitely that he'd look for letters at the Raleigh when he got to Williamsburg.

He was sliding his thumb underneath the fold to break the seal when he saw Garth by the mainmast, watching him above the stiff rim of a beaver pelt. There was something odd about that also. Where the devil had Garth got a beaver? And why was he interested in it? Norfolk's fur trade was a trifling business, certainly not worth the notice of a man who claimed the whole Ohio country. Then he saw the opened bale of fur at Garth's feet, muddy boots beyond it, a shag jacket, and a face that was unpleasantly familiar.

"Wel-l-ll . . . Dave Bone!" He pretended a surprise that he did not feel. There was nothing odd about *this*—about seeing Martin Garth's right-hand man here, two weeks' hard journeying a-horseback from the Forks of the Ohio. It fitted perfectly with certain pieces of unfinished business that he had forgotten in these last few hours. "You're getting to be quite a traveler, aren't you, Niggerhead?"

Using Bone's nickname, he could not help thinking how suitable it was. The man's head looked as if it had been sorted from a pile of boulders of the kind back-countrymen called niggerheads; and his face was like a chunk of yellowish gray limestone roughed out with a sledge. His little eyes, under yellow lashes, were the cold hard gray of agates, and they had dirt in their corners. Holden prodded him again:

"What's happened, Niggerhead? You're not traveling for your health? Or are you? Did the army run you out of Pittsburgh? Don't tell me that you're freighting fur four hundred miles to Norfolk."

"I doubt very much," Garth said, "that Dave will tell you anything."

"I doubt very much that I'd believe him if he did."

Bone's hands clenched. His little eyes sought Garth.

"No," Garth said. "Not this time. Don't mind him, Dave. He's had a bad night. Lost a piece of property. A pretty piece—and pretty costly too. It's curious how people who can't tend to their own business want to tend to other people's. Captain Holden is a very curious fellow."

"That's right." Holden nodded amiably. "I'll see you again, *gentlemen*. And first, I hope." He was smiling, though not with amusement, as he walked into the captain's cabin. That half minute on the deck had been extremely interesting. He had not expected Bone to tell him anything worth hearing; he had asked his questions to annoy Garth. And he had succeeded. That was the surprising thing about it. Without intending to, he had pricked Garth into making an admission. He knew, now, that Garth had been informed about his inquiries in London. It was a thing worth knowing.

Leach, he saw, was writing at the little table under the racked charts. The indenture agent's scrawny figure left the chair half empty. Leach, preparing for his moment of importance when he marched his column of chained convicts down the landing stage, had laid off his dingy scratch wig and unpacked a bagwig that was some years cleaner. He had hung both wigs on the corners of the chair back, so that they seemed to be peering down across his shoulders. His shaved skull was egg shaped, with his pointed features squeezed together at the small end. The collar of his coat bulged up behind his ears and pushed them forward. He looked, crouching there, like an aged rodent with a hairless head, emerging from a hole. Chris Holden, walking toward the table, half expected him to scurry back into his hole.

"Good morning, Leach."

The quill jerked and squealed. It scratched like small scrambling feet upon the paper.

"Ah . . . good morning, Captain Holden. A fine morning. A fine, fortunate morning for that girl too. Yes. Yes. There's not many that get such a master. I've just finished with her bill of sale, sir."

"I'm afraid you haven't. Sorry. I've got more work for you."

"Ah-hhh? You've sold her, then? But not at a profit, surely. You paid dear for her. *Tchh, tchh.* And found her unsatisfactory. A pity. Who——"

"I haven't sold her. I want her indenture canceled. She's to go free."

"What? What say? *Free!* My God, sir, you can't do that!"

"What's to stop me?"

"Why—why—she's a convict. She's done murder. Why—why—she barely missed the gallows. Fourteen years was light, sir, very light."

"And at going rates, I've paid for forty years. There's nothing light about that. She's my property, isn't she?"

"Yes, yes. Certainly. But——"

"I can sell her, can't I? And at any price that I can get?"

"Yes, yes. Certainly."

"I can lose her at a game of hazard, can't I? Lend her to a neighbor for a housemaid . . . hire her out to any tavern keeper . . . give her away as a free gift to anyone I choose. I can, can't I?"

"Yes, yes. Cer——"

Stop squeaking at me! If you say *certainly* again I'll—— Sorry. It so happens that I'm in a hurry. I bought the girl, and I'll dispose of her as I see fit."

"But you can't free a convict felon, Captain."

"There must be some way."

"You might marry her."

"Confound you!"

"That's the only legal way it could be done, sir. A nice point of law —the bonds of matrimony substituted for bonds of indenture. I can think of instances——"

"Let be, Leach! I'm marrying someone else. Now let's get on with it."

"Ah-h-hhh!" Leach hunched forward in the chair as if he found new interest in the matter. "Congratulations. I see your difficulty. Yes, yes. I see it all now. If—— No. No. It's quite impossible. Quite. Quite. I couldn't turn in a report that she'd been freed. I wouldn't dare. My God, sir, it could cost me dear. It would be the finish of me. Cost me my place, it would."

It occurred to Holden that Leach kept those two words—*cost me*—on his tongue a little longer than the others. And he had a single crown piece in his pocket! His knuckles rapped the table angrily. At the least, they sounded angry. He misliked what he was doing, but there was no choice about it. Lacking means to bribe Leach, he must bully him.

"That's a plenty!" Half the indignation in his voice was for himself for being caught in such a situation. "That's more than a plenty! I'll not have you putting your damned squeeze on me!"

"Squeeze!" There was no doubt, this time, about the squeak. Holden felt a twinge of shame. But he pressed on.

"Don't think you can come it over me because I'm a provincial. I know when I've been solicited for a bribe! You're not in England now, you're in Virginia. A word to the governor . . ." The bullying, he thought, was having its effect. "You've got your money for the girl, Leach. Your records show her sold. I wonder if they show you got a hundred and three pounds." They didn't. The wild guess, he saw, had come close to the truth. The soul-driver seemed to have grown smaller in the big chair. "A low trick, Leach. But it might come high for you—as high, say, as the Tyburn gallows."

"Beg pardon, sir." Ellis stood beside him. "I'd ought to be on deck. If you'll step with me to the door a moment . . . *Thank* you. Here you are, sir . . . Mr. Pollexfen's letter. Quite a long one, by the thickness." Ellis winked. His voice became a murmur. "If I may say so, sir, you've taken the right road with Leach. He's a mangy rat. But don't follow him too close, sir. Give him room to dodge. I'd not be saying this to everyone, but seeing that you're going to be with us . . . Here's a dodge he might not think of." Ellis's murmur dwindled to a whisper. Then, heartily: "You'll want your baggage on the wharf, of course."

"No. At the port rail, if you please, and ready to hoist over—the trunks and boxes, that is. There'll be a boat alongside presently to take me off. The gear in the hold will have to go by shallop. Archer's Hope Creek—the town landing, if you'll see to it."

"No trouble about that, sir. And the girl . . . you'll want a word with her? I'll see that she's on deck."

Holden turned back to the table.

"Well, Leach?"

"I can't send the wench ashore free. They'd not let her land. They'd hold up the whole lot."

"Don't quibble, man. I know that." He hadn't known it until Ellis told him; nor known, either, how to get around it. "She'll go ashore under the indenture you've made out to me. But you'll make out another one exactly like it—name, age, sold to me, and fourteen years to serve. Exactly the same, Leach, except that you'll leave out the line that says she is a convict. An ordinary bond for service, do you understand? And you'll write an endorsement on it that I've set her free. Bring it to me in my cabin and I'll sign it, and you'll give it to her when she's gone ashore and the port officers have cleared her. I'll not ask what price you set down in your records, *unless* . . ." He let the word hang. Leach reached for a sheet of paper, and the quill began to twitter.

Chapter 13

Christopher Holden felt even dirtier, after he left Leach, than he had felt already in his smeared stockings and stained breeches. He stripped them off, in the cabin he had shared with Ellerby Pollexfen, before he read Pollexfen's letter. It was not long:

CHRIS—I am seized by another of my crazy notions and am gone to Baltimore. The Vessel I go by is one of Smith & Speare's. A good Opport^y to make Acquaintance. Brookes tells me they are near to being Rated Sharpest of y^r men of capital & Speare is aboard of Her. I w^d be a nuisance to you y^r first days at Home & greater than I was in London. Don't deny it I was. I take liberty to Leave you some Advance upon y^r first Year as factor for A G & P wh^{ch} gives me further cause to Fly—being gone, you Can Not refuse me. I intend for Phil^a & N. York and will return to Philadel^a. Meet me if you will at the Indian Queen tavern there three months from this I pray you. I w^d wish to Go with you to the Ohio & so roundabout into Virgin^a. We shall go Great things believe me.

I am Etc Etc y^r most h^{ble} sv^t

ELLERBY POLLEXFEN

Pollexfen had dashed his pen across the signature and then scrawled below it: *Polly, damn you.* The rest of the packet was a sheaf of ten-pound bank notes. There were twenty of them. Mr. Holden, looking from them to the scratched-out name and the profane amendment, found that he was seeing them with difficulty. He found, also, some obstruction in his throat. In the circumstances, it took him an unreasonable length of time to read John Fraser's letter, although it was no more than five lines:

Connygojug 16 M^{ch}

You guessed Right I think. A meeting will be Williams^{bg} on the 3^d April. I send this to Norfolk in a Hoap to Ketch you thare if you are come in time. Look me at the Fair. All Beaver gone to Mackinac.

There was no signature, but none was necessary. A man might counterfeit John Fraser's seal but not his penmanship. Holden, puzzling out the sidehill writing, found himself still puzzled about what it meant.

Some parts of it were clear enough. John Fraser had received Chris Holden's letter, sent from London in November; and he had discovered something, somewhere, that bore out the worst of the suspicions in it. But what had John been doing at the Conococheague settlement on the Potomac, a hundred and eighty miles from Pitt's Town, when he wrote this message? Whatever it might be that Fraser had discovered, he must think it was important—as important as the errand that had fetched

Garth's right-hand man to Norfolk. The "meeting will be Williams[bg]" was reasonably clear: it meant, likely, that the gentlemen of the Ohio Company were gathering to talk about the state of their affairs. But what had been in Fraser's mind when he set down that final sentence? "All Beaver gone to Mackinac" meant something. The five words hid, probably, the meat of the whole message.

Holden was still puzzling over Fraser's closing sentence while he shaved and dressed and finished with his packing, closed the trunk, and picked up his caped coat. He remembered Leach and the indenture papers, walked aft to the captain's cabin, listened with half his mind to Leach's whining explanation that the task had been a long one, and picked up the quill. He read the papers hastily and signed them. At the door he swung about:

"And no chains, mind you. I'll not have her ironed. If anybody questions it, you've got the reason: she's mine and I gave the orders."

There. That was done with. He put the shabby business from his mind. When he came out on the deck he forgot John Fraser and his letter also, Martin Garth and Dave Bone and all else that was unpleasant. The port gangboard was piled with his baggage. Two of the ship's hands were looping slings around it. The trunk with the high-domed, silver-handled lid was already swinging out across the bulwark. *The longboat was there . . . it was alongside . . . he couldn't see it but it must be there . . . Diana had come quickly . . . she was waiting for him.* He went toward the gangway eagerly.

"Captain Holden."

Judas! He had clean forgot about *her*. He had brushed right past her and not seen her.

"Good morning, sir." She smiled. She had some kind of blue hood on her head. There was a little cape thing, the same color, on her shoulders. Cape and hood together were tied with a blue bow under her small chin. The blue was like her eyes. *For God's sake! What a thing to think now.* He said brusquely:

"Morning."

"You're not angry with me?" The smile trembled. "Mr. Ellis thought that I was running off. I wasn't. I—I did what I thought you'd want."

"Yes. Yes. Certainly." Plague take it! He was talking like that twittering mouse, Leach. The girl was looking at him anxiously, but she *knew*. He felt the flush sweep up into his face. "Where did you go?" He didn't give a damn where she had gone. He only wanted to be gone himself.

"I walked. I didn't mind. It was——" Oh, good Lord! She was going to weep. The smile was quivering. "It was wonderful! It was the first time I'd walked free in so long! Five months. You can't know what it meant. You can't! If only . . . Could you?"

"Could I what?"

"Buy Mr. Love too. He's been so kind to me." There was a pathetic earnestness about her. "He's not really bad. He's very clever. He——"

"I'm sorry. I can't. I can't take you, either."

"But you bought me! All that money! You did buy me, didn't you?"

"Yes. But I've just set you free."

"Free!" Her voice was unbelieving. "Oh no! Not *free*. Not really free."

"Yes. You will be, in a few hours. There's a little trick about it; you'll have to be careful what you do and say. It's not lawful to release a—um—an indentured person sent out by a court. You'll go ashore among the others. But as soon as you *are* ashore, you'll be free. Leach will give you a new set of papers. I've just signed them. There's nothing in them about being sentenced. Watch your tongue and you'll be safe enough; remember, you're a girl that bound herself for service and was bought and then freed. You'll have the canceled indenture for your proof, and no one will know otherwise."

"I can't believe—— Of—of course I do. But it's hard to believe that anyone could be so kind. So—terribly—kind."

"Zooks, child, there's nought to cry about."

"I'm not. I'm not crying. But I can't let you do it. I'm grateful. I couldn't ever tell you . . . But I won't accept my freedom."

"Great Judas! I'm afraid you'll have to."

"No. No, please. I owe you a hundred and three pounds and sixpence. I can work it off. *Please.*"

"Fourteen years?"

"I don't care!"

"But I do. You're much too pretty for a man to fetch along to pass the porridge on his honeymoon. Too pretty for the man's wife, anyway."

"Oh. Oh, I see."

"Well . . ." Thank God *that* was over. "Good-by—good-by, Miss—uh——"

"You don't even know my name."

"It's——" There was no damned reason why he should be standing here, talking to her, with Diana waiting. "It's Abby." He felt like a fool. "Abigail Martha Hale." Then he remembered something else. "I can't set you free with nothing. Here." He fumbled in the pocket of his coat and slid one of the notes out of the sheaf Pollexfen had left for him.

"I can't take it."

"Nonsense. This is my great day, child. Let me celebrate. Mmm . . . you may have trouble getting change for that." He put his hand into first one outside pocket and then another. "I had a King Charles crown. What did I do with it?" The girl's head turned. He saw her looking at the cherub-faced man she had wanted him to buy, and Love was looking at the deck. Her eyes came back. She held out her hand, and there was a crown piece in it.

"Oh." His mouth went grim.

"I didn't steal it! You don't think—— I didn't!"

"It doesn't matter. But you'd best find honest work, my girl. They're no easier on thieves here than they are in England." He walked away.

He was out of sight before the girl moved. But she ran then. Captain Holden was already halfway down the gangway. She raised her hand to throw the crown piece after him—and thought, for an instant, that she saw her own reflection in the shining water. There was a girl's face, looking up at her. There was a girl's arm lifted, just as hers was lifted. She could see the anger in the girl's face. The froth of lace about the smooth bare elbow *could* be only bright spray floating on the water. The girl *could* be her reflection. But the lifted hand was open. There was no coin in it. And that girl was wearing a wide hat of woven straw with lace and roses on it and a dainty cap of white lace underneath. That girl was dressed in lemon-yellow taffeta . . . her arms weren't bare, she wore long yellow silken gloves that had no fingers to them . . . and she had hair that was like new honey.

Abby saw the boat then. It was white and dazzling. There were black men in it, with blue jerseys all alike; the jerseys matched the pale blue pillows in the boat's stern where the girl was standing. The girl had a soft, smooth, slender face. The face smiled suddenly and was no longer looking upward. It was watching Captain Holden as he swung about from the last step. The girl put out both hands to greet him. *She is still angry,* Abby thought, not thinking. *She's still very angry, but she's hiding it. Not very well.* The smile was bright as sun on shallow water; it was thin; it covered her expression the way water seemed to cover a reflection in it, thinly.

Captain Holden took the outstretched hands. But he didn't hold them. He used them only to draw the girl swiftly toward him, as if he could not wait to take the last small step himself. His arms took possession of her, and his head bent over her and hid her face. Her hands crept around his back. They pressed. Their fingertips made shadows on the pale blue coat, they pressed so hard—one dented shadow for each straining fingertip. *She saw me,* Abby thought. *That's why she was angry.* There had been so little need for anger.

"Abby." It was Jeremy's voice, troubled. "What happened, Abby?"

"Nothing."

"Aren't you going with him?"

"No."

"But the blunt—the money!" Jeremy was outraged. "Ye're not telling me he tossed away the rhino that you cost him! Ye're not telling me he just walked off and left it?"

"*You* wouldn't, would you?"

"It don't stand to reason."

"You wouldn't leave a crown piece in a pocket, would you? Not in anybody's pocket. No matter who he was. No matter how kind he had been to you—or to your friends."

"Chive me! Spit and baste me! So *that* did it. He's not sending for you? He's not coming back?"

"Look. See for yourself."

Jeremy looked.

"Oons! So that's what he's gone on. Who's she?"

"His wife."

"Did he tell you?"

"No. But I was——" She stopped. "He said he couldn't take me on his honeymoon. He didn't want her to know anything about me. Money didn't matter. He set me free, and gave me ten pounds more."

"Free? *Free!* God love me, and you stand here mooning!" Then he sobered. "Abby!"

"Yes."

"Last night. You went ashore with him. What happened last night?"

"Nothing."

"D'ye mean he sets you free—he gives you ten pounds—and asked nothing from you? Look here, Abby. I'm an old man. You can tell an old man."

"There's nothing to tell."

"D'ye mean he didn't try? D'ye mean he didn't even kiss you?"

"No, Jeremy. He . . . didn't . . . even . . . kiss me. He didn't even want to."

"Hah! And you wish he had."

"I don't!"

"Women." Jeremy lifted helpless hands. *"Women.* Where's your papers, if he set you free?"

"He said Leach would give them to me, when we go ashore."

"Ashore? *Ashore?* Now what kind of snaffling lay is that? Why wait till you're ashore?"

"He said——"

"No matter what he said. You go see Leach. You go right now and see him."

"You don't think—— Oh *no!*"

"I don't think anything. A man's a man, though. And a pound's a pound. No harm in asking, is there?"

"No. No, of course not. But it isn't true! The whole world's not like that. Not the whole world!" She ran toward the quarter-deck door.

"Mind yourself," Love called. "Garth's in there. I saw him going in."

"I'm not afraid of him!"

In the after cabin Martin Garth had requisitioned Leach's chair and pen. The beaver pelt that he had dropped upon the table covered most of the indenture agent's papers. Garth had been signing manifests and sealing them with wax dripped from the candle. Leach was holding for him; and he had just got an interesting answer to a question.

"So he turned her loose, eh? Took his value of her quickly. Captain Holden's quite a man, Leach."

"I don't know about the value. She was on the wharf this morning, and she didn't look——"

"Look? A wench out of Newgate? You expect too much, Leach."

"If you ask me, she looked as if she thought she had been done, not undone. I know 'em. She looked disappointed."

"You amaze me." Garth laid the quill down and set his elbows on the table. His thumbs ruffled the fur of the beaver pelt. He leaned over it and blew into the fur as if he had not quite made up his mind about it. "Leach," he asked, still rubbing at the beaver with his thumbs, "how would you like to finish up your business in a hurry?" His eyes flicked to Dave Bone, slouched against the closed door. "My friend here deals in anything that offers profit. Mr. Bone might take your whole lot. Twenty-three—fourteen men and nine women—four hundred pounds, say, for the lot."

"Done. But it's twenty-two, sir. Four hundred for the lot, except the girl that Holden——"

"Except no one, Leach."

"My God, Mr. Garth, that's double-selling! I've made out her papers."

"Yes. I see you have. I've just been looking at them. Very interesting. Very interesting to the judges at Old Bailey, don't you think, Leach? Let's be reasonable."

"But she's free!"

"Free by a trick, Leach. An illegal trick. And your name's on the papers."

"If she isn't free, she still belongs to Holden. She's sold. There were witnesses."

"Exactly. Mr. Bone just bought her. I'm the witness."

"But it's hanging!"

"And what's this?" Garth waved the fresh indenture at him. "I thought you were up to something of the sort. Why d'you think I hustled you out of this chair? To do a little signing? Pah! Why d'you think I dropped this beaver on the table? To cover up your papers so you couldn't snatch them, Leach. Now let's—— Damn you, put that candle down! You're spattering me!"

The candleholder chattered on the table. The soul-driver's lips twitched up and down his slanting teeth. His hands twitched, clinging to each other.

"Scared, are you?" Garth laughed contemptuously. "What's the matter, Leach? A sore throat? You're clawing at it as if you could feel the rope already. Here." He thrust the beaver pelt into the agent's hands. "Maybe that will keep the hemp from scratching. Now, Leach . . ." Garth's fingers fiddled with the paper. They began to twist it. "I can send to fetch the sheriff. I can send you back to England in irons." He laughed again. "In your own irons, Leach. I can send this indenture along with you, and my own sworn evidence and Mr. Bone's. Or"—he showed Leach the paper, twisted now into a tight quill—"I can touch it to the candle. It will burn much quicker than you will in hell. I can put four hundred pounds into your hand and let you keep the price you got from Holden."

"Somebody's comin'," Bone said at the door. "A woman, sounds like. She's a-runnin'."

"Interesting," Garth said. "If it's the Hale wench, Holden's gone. Keep her out, Dave. Well, Leach, make up your mind."

The sound of running ceased. Dave Bone leaned his weight against the door. The knob turned. Then it turned again. Bone grinned. Knuckles touched the door uncertainly.

"Well, Leach," Garth said softly. "A hundred and three pounds for your own pocket, Leach." His voice coiled and struck: *"Now earn it."*

Chapter 14

The longboat, dropping down the river, left the town behind it quickly. It seemed almost to have left the world behind. The cockpit was a small world by itself, alone in space, suspended and remote. It had its own white canopy of sky. It even had its own clouds; they were made of light: the shimmering reflections of the sun upon the river, striking upward, streamed across the undersurface of the canopy in endless infinitely various processions.

He could not see the oars completely. He could see the wet blades only, at the end of each stroke, at the moment of withdrawal. If he did not turn his head to see the river, there was nothing in the world but this delicious vibrant motion and emotion and the knowledge of the girl beside him, and the sleek smooth softness of her garments.

He moved his hand until it lay against Diana's leg—and felt her move away. He saw her frowning at him, her eyes warning him. *Plague.* He'd forgotten Jez'bel, crouching almost at his feet between the woven willow hamper and the charcoal brazier. He looked down at her now—a lean, long-boned nigra woman with a face that was not like a nigra's: lean and long-boned also; fierce, almost hawklike, with the muddy-yellow-lidded, wrinkle-lidded eyes of an old fish hawk. On the slave list at Hap Hazard she was written down as an Ashantee from Buntakoo, but there was some other blood besides Ashantee in her—Arab, probably, or Berber. Her eyes were closed now, and she seemed asleep. She was, he thought, no more asleep than a hawk on a limb above an eddy of the river. Diana had said, *Sometimes I wonder if she sleeps at all.* He, too, was wondering. She had been hearing, he thought, every word Diana said—and thought, also, that Diana had been saying most of them for Jez'bel.

From the moment he had stepped into the boat and kissed her, Diana had been talking, talking. Lightly. Quickly. Gaily. Talking about dancing until almost dawn at Fair Lea, and how she had helped herself to the key of his house at Norfolk, from the hook it hung on underneath the cover of the well.

". . . though why nobody's lost it down the well is more than I can tell you. What a place to hide it!"

"It's been a right good place," he'd told her. "It's about the last place anybody'd think of looking. For that matter, it's about the last place I'd have thought of finding you—in my house, I mean."

"La, Chris, I'm certainly not ready for the well. Life is much too wonderful. It's wonderful to have you home again too. I scarce believe it."

"Neither do I. But here I am. At least I think I am."

"Don't you know? Lud, sir, I assure you *I* do. I may scarce believe it, but I *know.* I feel quite undressed. And all on your account. In all my days I've never combed and laced and tied me in half such a frantic hurry on account of any man."

Her voice was as bright and shallow as the river on the sand bars over against Craney Island, slipping by now. Her words slipped by as unimportantly. The double meanings in them could be nothing, to the ears of the Ashantee woman, but the daring raillery that was the fashion of the gay tidewater manors.

Her face showed nothing but its perfect profile, pure and delicate against the jade-green water. It was as delicate and perfect, he thought, as a cameo—a cameo cut out of palest coral and set into a jade mounting. It had the same fragile purity of coral and it had also, now, the same cool remoteness. Her eyes, too, were cool. They were green, like jade. They glanced down at Jez'bel quickly. And then, briefly, they were not cool

94

nor hard nor shallow: they admitted him to depths he knew. But her talk rippled on, light as the breeze across the river:

"If you don't know you're home, the half of Norfolk does. I was but half awake this morning when here comes Tom Allerdice a-galloping to tell me there's a ship just come in from England, and you on her. The gentlemen at Fair Lea hadn't gone to bed at all. At least, that's their story. They'd gone out for air, when the dancing finished. Airs, more likely—the kind of airs they find at Mrs. Valentine's. D'you know, I wonder if that is her real name? It's almost *too* appropriate, for the house she keeps. No matter. . . . They saw the ship at dock, and Tom came hurrying to tell me. Think! We might have missed—each other."

Lambert's Point dropped away to starboard and the breeze came strongly and the broad reach of Hampton Roads lay spread before him, ruffled with the breeze and laced with foam and shimmering with sunlight. As if, he thought, a woman in a gown of shimmering green padua-soy had just stepped through a doorway with her hoops drawn up against her body and had let go the hoops and let the rippling silks spread out in rustling, shining folds. On the distant shore, toward Newport News, the wind and tide were drawing a white frill of foam like a modestly immodest kerchief over the full bosom of the harbor. The twin swellings of the headlands were almost suggestive.

Then the longboat's foresail, creeping upward, hid them. He was suddenly intensely conscious of the swelling of Diana's breasts above the white lace. The Paris gown, he thought, would come a little lower than the yellow taffeta that she was wearing, and there was no kerchief with it and no lacy froth to hide her. There were only satin flowers in garlands—tiny rosebuds—they would look like. . . . They would look like part of her.

"Chris . . ."

"M-mm?"

"You didn't bring all of your baggage, did you?"

"Hardly. We'd have been considerably crowded."

"Oh? Yes, probably we would."

"It's scarcely suitable for Jimmy's longboat."

"I'd have thought it would be perfect."

"Good Lord! Plowshares, falling axes, sledges . . . Why, I've even got an anvil."

"But I thought that you were bringing someone with you."

"He'd gone. He wants me to meet him in three months in Philadelphia. What d'you think about that? It would be a right nice journey." It would be, he thought, a perfect wedding journey.

"But your other baggage . . . Oh, Chris, don't be so innocent! I know all about your other business. How could I help but know? That girl—she followed you quite to the rail. I thought, for a minute, she was coming after you. And don't look so baffled, either. It's the same as looking guilty. What did you do to her?"

"Nothing. I——"

"Nothing." It was not a question; it was merely repetition, slightly speculative, casually thoughtful. "Yes, that could be the reason. That could make her very angry, if she'd been expecting something else. She's pretty.

Very pretty, in a back-country kind of way. Was that why you bought her? Was she great fun, Chris?" Her laughter was as bright and rippling as the sparkling river. "Oh, lud! Now you *do* look guilty."

"I've nothing to look guilty for."

"Then why did you buy her?"

"To keep a man named Garth from getting her."

"Garth. . . . Who's Garth?"

"Someone I don't like. He tried to buy the girl to punish her."

"To punish her for what?"

"For not appreciating him. He kissed her, and she slapped him."

"How quaint! Do you buy every girl that doesn't appreciate the men you don't like? You'll have quite a harem when *that* gets about. You'll be like Jimmy." She frowned, speculating. "I wonder if you aren't. Perhaps that's the reason you dislike him so—because, underneath, you're like him. He's a better man of business, though. I doubt he'd pay a hundred and three pounds for any wench."

"How the devil——"

"—did I know that? You're not in London, Chris. You're home. Have you forgot that everybody in Virginia knows everybody else's business? Tom Allerdice was fairly panting with it—how the solemn one of the two Holdens had at last fallen from grace. A hundred and three pounds. . . . Was she *that* good? Or bad?"

"Damn Allerdice!"

"Why? *I* don't mind. I think she was likely worth it. You have improved, you know. Is that her doing?"

"It is not."

"Or Polly's? Oh, Polly's a man, isn't he? He had a wife, though."

"Good Lord, Di!"

"Meaning that she's a good woman? For the lud, Chris! Don't you know that there's no difference? Except, when she wants to be, a good woman's more a wanton than a bad one; she enjoys the guilt more—she's not so used to it. All it wants is the right man at the right moment. But whichever 'twas, I'm grateful. You'd not have kissed me, a few months ago, the way you kissed me when you sprang down off the ladder. You'd not have known how. What are you going to do with her?"

"I set her free."

"Oh." She sounded disapproving. "Then you *are* fond of her."

"No. Of course not."

"When'd you do it?"

"This morning."

"But was it necessary? What a waste, Chris! And you setting up to be a man of business! I think, Mr. Holden, I had best find out what kind of merchant you will make. I'll see my gowns, sir, if you please."

It took her hours to see her fill of them. While she turned the cockpit of the longboat into a London shop with silks and paduasoys and tabbies everywhere, and fans and gloves and slippers strewn amongst them, the water overside was changing subtly. There were stains like spilled tea on the jade-green satin of the harbor. The stains spread and darkened and the water was no longer jade, but amber; and the amber, too, in its turn, darkened. On either hand the low shore line closed in. The harbor narrowed and became another river. It was copper-colored; and its orange-yellow banks were daubed with streaks of red earth and with the black stripes of narrow beaches, with green splotches of the swamp reeds and the deeper green of pine trees.

Chris Holden stood up eagerly, knee deep in gowns, to see it. *This* was home. More than the house in Norfolk, even, this was *his*. The house belonged to him, but he belonged to this—the first beginnings of the forest. The air here was filled with smells compounded of the piney woods, the sassafras, the locust and the dogwood, fern and leaf mold. And the James . . . it was a very painted Shawnee of a river. He stretched and laughed, and yawned into the middle of his happy laughter.

"Jason," he called. "Jason." The old slave huddled in the bow, a seamed and weathered dark stump of a man with long arms like gnarled roots stretched out to the tiller ropes, looked back at him. "I'm sleepy. You used to carry me when I got sleepy, Jason. And you sang to me—*de raccoon's tail*. Remember?"

"Yassuh. Ain' much singin' lef' in me, Mist' Chris."

"One or the other, Jason. If you can't carry the old tune, you'll have to carry me. I've got a little heavy."

"Does yo' need carryin', Mist' Chris, ol' Jason he make out to do hit some way."

"I know you would. I've been thinking a good deal about you. I——"

"Oh, sit *down*, Chris. Please. You're standing on my dress."

"Which one?"

"Does it matter which one? Jez'bel can't get them put away, with you standing in the midst of everything. You're not the only one that's sleepy, either. And I'm hungry."

He sat down. There would be time, later, to tell Jason he was going to be free. The high, curved lid closed on the Forgel gown. Jez'bel, crouching at their feet, undid the willow hamper. They ate ham and biscuits, and drank wine from silver goblets.

The long straight reach of river was no longer copper. It was burnished brass now. Far upstream the setting sun lay on it. The river was a great brass candlestick with ruddy gleams upon it, but the candle was burned low. The sun made a reddish-golden flame the way the fire did on a stub of candle just before it burned out. Where the river touched the setting sun it was still brassy but it was not metal; it was liquid, and it glowed and stirred like melted wax around a guttering wick. Close by, a cleft among the darkening trees disclosed a winding tide creek and a leaning wharf and the white gleam of pillars marching in close ranks. The nigras at the oars began to sing:

> *De raccoon got er long, ringed tail;*
> *De possum tail, he bare;*
> *De rabbit got no tail at all*
> *But a little bush ob hair.*

He lay back on the cushions with his arms flung wide upon them. It was good . . . *good* . . . just to lie here, just to feel the old song humming in his throat, just to watch the darkening and changing river. It turned, finally, completely black. And yet the night was not completely dark. The young moon began to spread a faint pale phosphorescence down the sky. Only the curved space beneath the longboat's canopy was solid darkness. It was like a cave now.

A dry, scaly sound came out of it to startle him absurdly. There were times when his acquired frontiersman's instincts could mislead him: he felt, momentarily, almost ashamed. The scaly sound was not the warning a man listened for before he entered a cave in the mountains; it was not the noise of a snake's body crawling over shale and gravel; it was only the dry whirring of a fire wheel.

It repeated itself now, and he saw the little jet of streaming sparks and then a tiny red glow where they caught the tinder. Jez'bel was making ready to kindle a fire in the brazier. The round glow broadened . . . it was as big as a shilling now . . . a crown piece . . . and now it was gone as quickly as if Jez'bel's hand had picked the pocket of the darkness. She had thrust the burning tow into the charcoal and was blowing on it.

Quick gleams came and went. At each slow expulsion of her breath, her face appeared; then it was gone again. The charcoal in the brazier caught. The round pan of the brazier was an eye, enormous, red, and angry, looking at him without blinking. Jez'bel sank back on her haunches. Her hands moved above the glowing charcoal, dropping sweet herbs on it. The Ashantee woman, crouching there, seemed a fantastic sorceress from Buntakoo performing savage rites before a fetish in a cave, her long hands weaving spells.

Chapter 15

The pungent herb smoke drew up into Holden's nostrils. It brought him back, a little way, out of his drowsiness. He put his arm around Diana's shoulders.

At his touch, her body stiffened and resisted. Then it yielded to him, and he drew her close against him. But her mouth eluded him. She turned her face into the hollow of his arm and laid her hand, instead, upon his lips.

He kissed a finger, silently, and she moved her hand so that he could kiss all her fingers, one by one. The nigras at the oars began to chant again. Their voices seemed to come from far away:

> *Moon is in her glory,*
> *Stars to light de way;*
> *Open wide de gates ob home,*
> *Marsa's come to stay. . . .*

His arm tightened on Diana's body. She had opened gates to him that would be home now. He turned his face against her hair and saw, through it, that the stars were out. They were blooming low upon the wooded riverbank—as low and white as if the dogwood blossoms had turned into stars. He wondered at them: they were all square. They were candle-

98

lighted windows in a cluster of slave cabins, but he was too drowsy now to know it. On a hill above them and beyond them the great manor hall of a plantation opened a broad fan of light. The fan seemed to stir as if a lady held it in her hand and moved it gently. But he did not see it. He was sleeping.

He did not know how long he had been sleeping. But when he awoke the world had changed again. The river had been touched by the philosopher's stone. It was not copper now, nor brass; it was miraculously silver. The James was an enormous silver platter, and the low moon was a silvered oval mirror on a wall of dark blue damask. Almost in the moment of awakening he knew exactly where he was. The moon was over his left shoulder; if he shrugged his shoulder, he could touch it. The longboat was pulling almost north now: it was in the great broadening of the James, with Burwell Bay astern. They would easily be home two hours before the dawn.

He lay with his eyes half closed but all his senses open. He was not drowsy. He was more awake than he had ever been in all his life, and more alive. He was ravished with the admirable sweetness of the springtime. Who had said that? Someone, long ago. Some settler come from England to this new clean world. And it was still true. It was even truer now. Diana's head lay on his arm, Diana's body lay against him. He had loved her a long time . . . hated her . . . despised her . . . wanted her. He wanted her again now.

They would be married, he supposed, at Bruton. The day after tomorrow, when he went to Williamsburg, he would stop at the parish house and see about the banns.

"Darling . . ."

"Mmm?" She stirred sleepily. "Did you say something?"

"I said *darling*. But I want to ask you something. Is old Dr. Caswell still at Bruton?"

"You never woke me up to ask *that!* Paint and patches, Chris, you *have* improved. You're positively devious. Yes, Dr. Caswell's still there, but he's on his holiday. There's a young man come to fill in for him—a tall, hungry-looking, fierce man. He's full of the devil. La, that's all he talks about—the devil and damnation and hell-fire, as if he'd fright us into heaven. Why do they make heaven such a cold place? It's so funny—all the warmth in hell and none in heaven. I'd like *some* fire."

"I wonder if you know what hell is."

"Do you?"

"Yes. I've been there. It's a big place. There's an ocean in it, and a city larger than any you have seen. They call it London."

"Are you telling me you missed me that much? You don't need to. You've already told me. I was quite convinced."

"That was a long time ago. It seems so."

Her head pressed hard against his arm. He thought at first that it was a caress, and then knew it for a warning. She lay still, and he felt a tenseness in her. She was listening, he thought, for the sound of Jez'bel's breathing. Then she whispered:

"It could have been a long time ago—it could have happened seven months ago, before you went to London. You could have had me, that night in the garden. Don't you know you could have, Chris? Have you any doubt now? Had you any doubt then?"

"Not now. I did then. At the proper time—at just the wrong time—you said you were going to marry Jimmy. I've wondered whether you did that on purpose."

He felt laughter quiver through her.

"Chris," she breathed, "you're funny."

"Am I?"

"But of course you are. Thinking that I led you on. . . . I did lead you on. You know that, don't you? But thinking that I'd lead you on so far and then try to stop you! Oh, my stays and garters, darling . . . could I dream that then, just *then,* you'd stop for his sake? For *Jimmy?* It wasn't flattering, Chris. A woman thinks she's more desirable than that."

"He was my brother."

"Was? He still is, isn't he? You didn't stop to think of that this morning."

"No."

"Your brother, fiddlesticks! A most excellent and upright brother. Shiftless Jimmy! Oh, don't look so shocked. You are, you know. I don't have to see your face to know you are. Poh! Do you think I don't know all about him and his scale of prices? Well, I do."

"Oh." That accounted for it—for her gladness, for her yielding, for her eager welcome. "When did you find that out?"

"Lud, I've known it all the time."

"Before I went away?"

"Of course."

"And still meant to marry him?"

"Oh, Chris, stop asking questions! Please don't spoil things. You're so damned serious! You're like a Quaker—the round hat and all. And never smiling with your eyes. Forever looking, when you smile, as if you think you shouldn't. And making love as if it is some desperate encounter with your Indians. Love's not like that! It's gay. What was it made for, Chris, if not to pleasure us?" He felt again the quiver of her laughter. "You were so desperate that night seven months ago . . . in such desperate earnest."

"I'd have said that you were."

"Not in the same way. I wanted you. I wanted to be loved. I wanted you to love me. It was the waiting I was desperate about. The waiting and the wanting . . . wanting the moment to come quickly and wanting it to never end. But you . . . You weren't thinking about *that.* You were thinking *past* it, you were thinking about what came afterward, about marrying me. You weren't like that this morning. You——"

He felt the sudden tightening and stillness of her body. He listened with her and did not hear the Ashantee woman's breathing. Diana drew herself out of his arms.

"Jez'bel," she said. "Jez'bel. . . ." There was no response. "Are you asleep?" Her voice was low, soft. No; not soft. It was like a silk thread. A silk thread could cut. "You are not sleeping, are you?"

"No." The Ashantee woman's voice was not like a nigra's. The word came quick and sharp, like a knife snipping a silk thread.

"Spying. Pretending to be sleeping. Lying to me. I will not be lied to, Jez'bel. I will not be spied on. I've had you whipped for it before. Have you forgot?"

"No."

"I will have you whipped again. If you say so much as one word, I will have you whipped until there's not an inch of whole flesh on your body— front or back—from your head to your feet. And then I'll have you rubbed with salt. You know that I will do that, don't you?"

"Yes. I know."

"Then get up! *Move!* Get forward with the other blacks, where you belong. D'you hear me?"

"Yes." The woman stood up. "Yes, I hear you, Mrs. Holden."

He did not know which of the two shocks had numbed him. He had been, he thought, a little numb already when he heard the woman say it. He had been a little stupefied by the obscene silken cruelty of Diana's voice when she talked of whipping. His only surprise now was that, for a moment, he had been surprised either by her threats to Jez'bel or by her pleasure in them. He had not been surprised at all when Jez'bel called her Mrs. Holden. He felt almost as if he had already known that she was married to his brother. It explained so many things—her use of the Holden longboat and the Holden slaves, and her unwillingness to speak of Jimmy, and her uneasiness and her tense listening for the Ashantee woman's breathing. She was Mrs. James Holden. In a few minutes now he would feel the pain of it beginning. Good God! She was his sister now by marriage. *His sister.* He asked numbly:

"When?" As if it made some difference.

"A month after you sailed." The answer had a tremor in it. Laughter . . . she was *laughing.* "As if you didn't know."

"I didn't."

"Oh, Chris!"

"How could I know?"

"He wrote to you."

"I didn't get it."

"Oh." Then, slowly: "Are you very sure you didn't get it? I see. That accounts for it. So long as you pretend you didn't know, you are still innocent and good and proper. Oh, what a hypocrite you are! You're worse than Jimmy. You're much worse. He doesn't go about pretending to be what he isn't. That's why he's talked about . . . because talking about him that way makes him seem different from other men . . . as if the men who talk about him are much better . . . as if they had never touched a girl or wanted to. What hypocrites you all are! As if women don't know why a pretty quadroon always fetches the high price. As if we don't know about Mrs. Valentine's or about Anne Lucas in the little house on Francis Street." She came to him with a rush that flung her body close against him on the cushions. "No! No, Chris, I didn't mean it! I know you're not pretending. I believe you didn't get the letter. And I'm glad you didn't. If you had, you'd not have taken me. But you have . . . *you have!* What's done is done. You can't undo it, can you?"

"I wish to God I could."

"You don't! And it *is* done. Don't you see, Chris? All the doubts behind you. You're not sorry. You're glad, really. Oh, I love you so . . . *I love you*."

He said dully:

"You bitch."

"Oh, *Chris*." There was no anger in it; there was only an impatience, as if he were being unimaginably stupid.

"You married him." He marveled at her. "You knew what he is. You love me——" He stopped abruptly. Amazingly, he knew that it was true. So far as she was capable of knowing love, she loved him. He felt the pain at last. "And so you sold yourself for Holden Hundred and ten thousand pounds a year."

"Do you think that's high?"

"I think that for a price like that you might have kept your bargain."

"I intend to keep it. Listen to me! Do you think that Jimmy will be faithful to me? You know better. Do you think that he expects me to be faithful? *He* knows better. There's more to the bargain than you'd ever guess. He's settled twenty thousand pounds on you. I——"

"Do you think I'll touch it?"

"If you care for me, you will. Chris, *can't* you see? It was the only way. If I sold myself, it was for both of us."

"God's teeth, you *are* a bitch!"

"Go on. Call me names. But if you'd stop to think, you'd know I don't deserve them. Or if I do, *you* do. Chris, we're very much alike."

"Thanks."

"Don't be sarcastic. It's true. What you find so shocking in me you find quite admirable in yourself. We both take what we want. Oh yes, you do! You wanted to explore, to run the woods, to be a soldier. You wanted to build your own manor house and clear your own plantation. You wanted those things much more than you wanted me. You wouldn't give them up. I wanted something too. I wanted you. But I can't live the kind of life that you'd have given me. I wasn't meant for the frontier——"

"Frontier! Crisscross isn't——"

"But it is, to me. A raw plantation hacked out of the woods and miles from anywhere! A shack to live in! Oh, call it what you like, but anything we could have had in years would be a shack compared to Holden Hall. I'd hate it, and in time I'd hate the man who brought me to it. I don't want to hate you, Chris. I couldn't bear it. Both of us have what we want now, darling. Life can't chain us. We're *free*."

"And I make free with my brother's wife. Is that it?"

"You did this morning. Did it matter? Did you know the difference? You didn't, and you know you didn't. And you never will."

She turned toward him, her whole body turning. Her arms went around his neck and her hands crept up into his hair, caressing him, entwining themselves in it. She lay half upon him, softly, warmly. Her mouth came to his and stayed there till he took her by the shoulders and thrust her away and held her. Her face, in the moonlight, was pure, gentle, innocent. Her lips parted, smiling at him.

"Darling, it's a wonderful arrangement, truly. And I'll not be selfish and not ever jealous, so long as I know you love me. Why, Chris, you can even marry some girl, if you want to, and have company at Crisscross. I'll not mind, if you don't stay there with her *too* much. And don't fall in love with her! You might get that little convict girl back. *She'd* go with you. Just imagine . . . sleeping with a girl that had done murder. You could even bring her with you when you came to Holden Hall—in case Jimmy happened to be there and have no special company. Even Jimmy may get notions, sometimes, about wifely duties." Her bright laughter danced across the water. "Well, why don't you say it? Why don't you ask me if I have no shame?"

"Is there any need to ask?"

"No."

It was unbelievable. He was not really hearing this soft, innocent, lascivious voice. His hands released her, and her whole weight came upon him. He put his arm around her, lifted her, and laid her down upon the cushions. The moon shining on her showed the yellow silk gown molded to her body, like her own flesh. He put his hand on her thigh and stroked the silk. It hissed and rustled.

"Diana . . ."

"Yes?"

"I knew that you would be like this. I should have known. Have you ever seen a den of rattlesnakes in spring?" Deliberately he ran his hand along the roundness of her leg and made the silk repeat its hissing and its rustle. "They sound like that. Smooth . . . and scaly. Soft . . . hard. Cold. They're poisonous. You make me think of them." He raised his voice. "Jason . . ."

"Yassuh, Mist' Chris."

"Where are we?"

"Nearabout Blount's Landin'. Way de tide feel, we jes' by de creek now. Archer's Hope, he pushin' right strong on de sta'board."

"Put me ashore, Jason. Blount's, if you can find it. Anywhere."

"Chris, you wouldn't!" She began to struggle, and he held her with his body. "Chris, are you *insane?*"

"No. Not now. Not any more." Deliberately, coldly, he put both his arms around her and her mouth upon hers. When he let her go, she put her hand up to her mouth and turned her face into the cushion. "I regret I haven't the five shillings."

The oars splashed the shoaling water. The bow nudged a low log landing.

"Jason, I've got two trunks and a ship chest. See you get the right ones."

"Yassuh."

He stepped from the gunwale to the landing and found Jason there beside him. The old man was crying.

"Take me wid you, Mist' Chris."

"I can't, Jason. You're not mine to take. But I'll come back for you. I'm going to buy you and give you your freedom."

"Don' need freedom, Mist' Chris, kin I be wid you."

"You're going to be. I need you to teach me how to be a man of business. You taught me most of what I know . . . to swim, and shoot, and how to break a colt. I wish to God you'd taught me something about women."

"Ain' no teachin' for dat. On'y learnin'. Dey ain' but one woman for some men. You's one ob dem, Mist' Chris. Ain' no woman no good for you till you finds de one."

"Maybe." He hugged the old man. "Thank you, Jason. I'll be back to get you."

The boat pulled away. He watched it disappear. Then he sat down upon the nearest trunk—and burst, abruptly, into an enormous laughter. The trunk was enormously uncomfortable. It was enormously and unbelievably and completely funny. It had a high, curved lid. It had twin handles let into the lid. The handles bit him as he sat upon them. He continued to sit on them and enjoy them while he roared with laughter. The gown made by Forgel for the king's own mistress was here underneath him on the landing of a muddy tide creek. He patted the amusing trunk, approving of it. For a long time—for as much as fifteen minutes—it kept him from feeling the complete cold emptiness inside him.

Chapter 16

Mr. Holden was hung over. He admitted it without shame. It was merely a phenomenon of nature—one he had looked forward to and hastened. It was also reassuring. There were some things that a man could still depend on. Good Jamaica rum was one of them, and Selden Blount the other.

Fetched down to his door at dawn, in cap and bedgown, by Chris Holden's knocking, Selden Blount had needed but one glance to grasp the situation and a bottle.

"Hair 'f the dog," he had prescribed instinctively. "Where've you been? Don't tell me—not till you're in shape to know you want to."

"I'm all right," Chris had assured him. "I'm not high."

"You're low, then. Never saw a man on his two legs much lower. If you ain't drunk, you should be."

"I'm just back from London," Chris had told him, as if that was ample explanation.

"Rough place, London." Selden's glance took in the red muck of the tide flats at Blount's Landing, plastered thick on Mr. Holden's slippers. "Must've walked." He picked up the bottle and ran both the glasses over.

It had been a very hairy dog. Even after fourteen hours' sleep and a breakfast that moved Selden Blount to envy, Chris Holden was still high. He felt higher than the plank seat of the wagon he had borrowed; and the borrowed horses, too, seemed far below him, they seemed to be floating on a cloud of yellow dust. He could hear the wagon jolting, but the jolts did not disturb him. They did not even touch him. Even his mind was comfortable, and that was the only part of the phenomenon that puzzled him. His head ought to ache. It didn't. His conscience ought to hurt. It didn't. His mind ought to be filled with regret and bitterness and an enormous sense of loss and loneliness. It wasn't.

Christopher Holden came to the conclusion that rum was a wonderful invention. It was undoubtedly superior to laudanum, and pleasanter to take. He was wide awake, but he was numb all over. He couldn't feel the losing of Diana any more than he could feel the jolting of the wagon. *By zooks!* It was quite a drink that could numb a man's mind and his backside at the same time.

He began to like the dusty yellow road much better. It wound through a pine wood where the sun came thinly and the wagon wheels were all but soundless in soft, tawny sand. He could feel the mingled smells of resin and warm earth and old pine needles seeping through his mind. He felt the stiffness going out of it.

The tall pines dwindled into scrubby second growth and the scrub into sassafras and chicken oak and fernlike thickets of young locust. Across familiar fields he saw Williamsburg's white paling fences, and the peak-roofed well sheds, and the neat white peaked-roof necessaries[1] of the town deployed like sentries in the back yards of the houses along Gloucester Street. He could see, beyond them, the bright glints of small-paned windows under the magnolias and elms and tulips, and the slim white cupola of Bruton.

To the left, as the road from Archer's Hope Creek landing drifted into Henry Street, he saw through ancient trees the warm red glow of brick walls with the flush of orange in them—Chris Wren's nobly gracious building where he'd gone to college—the same building that he'd bragged about to Ellerby Pollexfen. *Dammit.* He missed Polly. If he had the big lunk here now, he would take him over to the college and rub some of the cocksureness off him. He'd rub Polly's nose on Chris Wren's building. And then they would take up the matter of Jamaica rum. They would sit down in the taproom of the Raleigh and devote their whole attention to it.

But he didn't have Pollexfen with him, and the admirable effects of Selden Blount's rum were beginning to wear off. The thing to do was to find Fraser quickly. Next to Ellerby Pollexfen and a bottle, he decided, he preferred John Fraser and a bottle. He swung the horses into Francis Street and headed for the fair.

The street was lined with coaches, two-wheeled farm carts, wagons, gigs, berlins, and chaises. People swarmed among them; children, white, black, scuttled underneath them. In pens by the roadside, cattle bawled and pigs squealed. Tethered horses cropped grass in the Custis wood lot. The poor debtors' prison and the keeper's house showed only their sharp gables above booths walled and thatched with leafy oak boughs. Beyond them, across England Street, the eight-sided red brick Powder Horn was all but overwhelmed; its steep pointed roof protruded, but the eight-sided wall that matched and guarded the provincial arsenal was hidden in the maze of rustic bowers with drooping wilted leaves, of tents and peep shows, puppet theaters, raised platforms with signs stretched across them, and the white, sway-backed, bulging tops of Conestogas.

[1] Colonial Virginia's politer name for privies.

The crowd kept shifting, changing, as if currents moved it; at each booth and tent it tightened into eddies; but the eddies, too, kept changing and dissolving. Blue and buff and scarlet uniforms of the Virginia militia matched the bright gowns and the ribboned bonnets of the women. Gentlemen in silk coats and brocaded waistcoats elbowed ribs in somber broadcloth, checkered shirts and roundabouts, and plain frieze jackets, and were getting their own ribs jogged by irreverent bare elbows of apprentices in smocks and countrymen in rolled-up sleeves. From Chris Holden's high perch on the wagon seat, the crowd looked like a crazy quilt spread out for its spring cleaning, being shaken gently. Puffs of dust came out of it.

At the turning into England Street the jam was worse. The crowd overflowed the roadway, pushing through crosscurrents of more gigs and wagons, lumbering plantation coaches, gentlemen on high-stepping nervous horses, and whole families on farm nags. Vendors hawked paste buckles, stockings, sweetmeats, needles, buttons, fried fish, and queue ribbons. In a canvas booth a Judy in a red-yarn wig belabored a disheveled Punch whose nose had lost a splinter. The screech of an ax blade on a tinder's grindstone mingled with the Judy's shrill cries. A harness maker cracked a whip in each hand to draw customers On a rope hung slack between two trees a swarthy, oily-haired young man in red slippers, white hose, and red satin breeches danced a minuet with an imaginary partner.

A lanky hunter from across the Blues, in moccasins and clout and a new ruffled shirt, stood spraddle-legged, peering through the peephole of a raree show. He pawed the dirt with one foot, and his dangling clout tail waggled with excitement. A buxom young girl on a pillion behind her smiling husband nursed a baby, unabashed by the applause of three pigtailed sailors. Rough planks, laid across two barrels, made a platform with another barrel on it. A sign, crudely lettered, showed a grisly humor:

> Fool the Injins
> Wear a Wigg & Save y' Hair
> 6 d. a Head

The war with the French and Indians was over; Williamsburg had been a long way from it; the townfolk thought the joke was funny, and the owner of the barrel kept his small crowd laughing:

"Read it! Read it! You there—quit pretendin'. I c'n see y'r lips move, an' they're makin' the wrong letters. Finest wigs in all Virginny in this bar'l here. Bob wigs. Grizzles. Grizzle majors. Bagwigs. Little wigs an' big wigs. Hair that's been wore by some of the biggest wigs in England. Step right up here! They's a keg t' step on. Sixpence, an' shove in y'r hand. No tellin' whose scalp ye may get—the gov'nor's, likely, or a duke's or a prime minister's. They're all prime."

A farmerish youth parted with a coin and climbed up to the platform. The wig raffler tied a fold of cloth across his eyes:

"No peekin'. This here ain't no peep show. Pay y'r money, take y'r chance."

The blindfolded youth groped in the barrel and fetched out an enormous bagwig. The crowd jeered and hooted:

"Take keer, boy, ye'll get lost . . . build a kitchen onto it, ye got y'rself
a house . . . ye mean a stable, it's got livestock in it. . . ."

But the young countryman seemed satisfied. The wig fitted—though his
hat, now, didn't. A girl in a flower-sprigged apron came sauntering by with
gingerbread squares on a tray slung from her shoulders. She was singing:

> *Gingercake, hot. Square a penny.*
> *When it's gone I'll not have any.*

She smiled at the farm boy as he stepped down from the platform:
"A cake for the gentleman?"

The boy grinned and produced a penny. The girl wandered on. Chris
Holden, edging his team into England Street, saw another white-topped
broadwheel rocking toward him, coming from Woodpecker Lane or from
the York River landing on Queen's Creek. It turned off into the Powder
Horn field, toward the other Conestogas, and Chris wondered why the
driver's face had looked familiar.

On an upturned tobacco cask a schoolmasterish thin man flourished a
long ferrule in his right hand while his other arm made stiff, pump-
handle gestures. His face was small and narrow, his mouth round and
large; his lower jaw protruded like a trough beneath a pump spout. His
skinny arm worked up and down. Words came in gushes:

". . . worships and ladyships . . . today fo' the fust time . . . in this
great metropolis of No'th America . . . in this heah Athens of the New
World . . . the oppo'tunity that comes once in a lifetime . . . the
wondeh of the age . . . the Boukabekabus, the far-famed monsteh captured in the wilds of Madagascah . . ." He paused. He drew a flask from
the skirt pocket of his coat and primed himself. The ferrule tapped the
gaudy painted strip of canvas hung above the entrance of the tent behind
him. "The head of a unicorn, the body of the fabled Minotaur . . . his
belly is red hot, his eyes glow with hell-fire . . . smoke comes from his
nostrils.[2] Like the unicorn, he craves hay fo' his diet . . . but unfo'tch
nately it is impossible fo' him to digest it . . . his breath tu'ns it into
ashes befo' he can swallow. Thehfo', like the Minotaur, he has a pref'rence
fo' young ladies. Positively no young lady undeh the age of thuhty-five can
be admitted unless accompanied by a gentleman to fuhnish her protection.
One shilling the couple to behold this wondeh . . . two bits . . . just one
bit apiece . . . the eighth paht of a Spanish dollah."

Women giggled. Men looked sheepish. Two bits was a great price for a
tent show. The cadaverous barker looked down on his audience with
sorrow:

"Is this Vuhginia?" he demanded. "Don't tell me Ah have lost mah way
and find mahself in Pennsylvania province or in No'th Ca'lina! Can it be
that in Vuhginia . . . in *Vuhginia* . . . a gentleman holds womanhood so
cheap that he will not invest the eighth paht of a measly Spanish dollah in
its ed'fication? Don't tell me that ev'ry lady in this heah assembly has
passed the advanced age of thuhty-five yeahs!"

Chris Holden chuckled, but not at the barker's oratory. He had caught

[2]The Boukabekabus is no imaginary monster. There is an authentic contemporary
record of his appearance in Captain Jonathan Hager's town in Maryland.

a glimpse of massive homespun shoulders weaving through the crowd ahead. John Fraser, at least, had been spending money freely on a woman. He was hugging a new spinning wheel against his chest with one arm, and the other clutched three bright new bolts of calimanco. Townfolk, dodging his projecting elbows, put out mischievous hands to twirl the wheel; his head bobbed and swayed to see between the whirling spokes. John Fraser looked, from behind, a good deal like a trained bear walking on its hind legs. Holden slapped the reins. The wagon locked hubs with a red-lacquered coach. A face with red-lacquered lips peered at him from the window.

"Clumsy!" And then: "Slitterkins! Chris Holden! What in tophet are you doing? Playing farmer? There's a ball tonight at the Apollo. I'll save you the Landers."

Mr. Holden raised his hat. As well as he could, sitting on the wagon seat, he bowed to Mistress Colonel Chiswell who had been Betsy Randolph and his mother's friend. But his smile was stiffer than his bow. Two days ago another woman lovelier and younger than John Chiswell's wife had called him clumsy; and the woman was a wife too.

His mouth was flat and grim as he watched the paneled coach roll by him. When it had passed he saw John Fraser climbing the steps of a high square platform just beyond the tent in which the Boukabekabus was stabled. John was stripping off his coat. The crowd was yelling. Behind him, at the bottom of the steps, a lean lank-haired man in a white ruffled shirt and beaded breechclout held John Fraser's bolts of calimanco; another, with the thongs of pouch and powder horn crisscrossing on the back of his long linsey hunting shirt, cradled the spinning wheel in both of his thrummed arms.

Almost against his will, a grin unloosed the tightness of Chris Holden's mouth. The last time he'd seen Dan McCoy's back, he had been riding on it, head down, and Joe Lovatt had been shirtless; Joe's shirt had been a blood-soaked bandage on Chris Holden's belly.

His grin widened. He felt suddenly quite happy. He was *home*. Home wasn't a place; it was being where you belong. There was a sharper sense of home-coming in the sight of Fraser's homespun shoulders and McCoy's fringed hunting shirt than there had been even in the touch of the familiar gate in Norfolk. It was pleasant to be irritated once more with John Fraser for his incurable delight in fighting. And this fight would be a good one. Above Fraser's head, between two peeled saplings that were lashed to the front corners of the platform, a wrinkled dirty sailcloth sign proclaimed:

THE TERRIBLE TURK
*The Giant of Asia Minor
& the Master of the Cudgell
6 d. a Go
1 £ to Break his Head
2 Dols. if You Stay 2 Minutes*

The half-naked giant waited on the platform. His arms, as thick as any ordinary man's legs and as smooth as any woman's, were folded on his hairless chest. His head, too, was hairless: it was plucked bare like a

Shawnee's except for an absurd small tuft on the back slope of it, between his bulging ears. The meager tuft was tightly wrapped in eelskin. His mouth, grinning at John Fraser, showed black gaps among his teeth—like nailheads, Holden thought: like the heads of square nails driven into a pine block. The giant's swollen, gnarled ears looked like pine knots where dead branches had been broken off.

On the edge of the platform, legs a-dangle and head sagging, sat another man, half naked; a flap of skin hung loose across his forehead; blood poured down his face. He dabbed at it with uncertain fingers, looked at them, and wiped them on the planks. Then he looked up at Fraser and waved him away with his gory hand. But Fraser was emerging backward from his shirt. The shirt fluttered down the steps; the lank hunter caught it. The Turk stooped and picked up two six-foot cudgels.

Fraser took one, brandished it in both fists, stood on one leg, and brought the staff down hard across his lifted thigh. The cudgel snapped, and the crowd yelled again. Fraser sent the splintered pieces flying toward the white-topped Conestogas ranged behind the platform. He walked over to one of the peeled oak posts that held the sign and ripped the post loose from its lashings and tore off the sign. The Turk grinned and wrenched up the other nine-foot post that matched it.

The yelling stopped. The hundreds of upturned white faces framed the platform as John Fraser closed in. A boy hunkered on the tail gate of one of the wagons turned a minute glass.

Stripped to the waist, John Fraser looked more like a bear than ever. His great arms and shoulders and his broad back were a mat of black hair, and his hands clenched on the peeled white pole were black and hairy paws. He shuffled, circling. His head swayed and nodded. His legs, wide apart, were too short for his body. His feet in their soft woods moccasins were planted flatly. He looked slow and awkward, like a tame bear dancing. And the Turk was quick and agile as the slack-rope dancer; his oak sapling whirled in front of Fraser's face with the blurring swiftness of the spinning-wheel spokes. The long end of it flashed up and struck at Fraser's head.

Fraser seemed to be falling forward. His whole body drooped. But he had only moved in underneath the blow. His own sapling trunk cracked on the giant's ribs. As the Turk grunted and the yells burst out again, John Fraser shuffled back, crouched, and drove the butt end of the pole into his adversary's midriff. The Turk doubled over. Fraser circled, swung the pole again, and spanked him on his buttocks. The crowd roared with laughter. But the giant spun around and came in savagely. His pole chopped at Fraser's head. John met it. The two oak trunks crashed together, and the Turk's broke just above his left hand; the upper half of it bent forward on a hinge of splinters.

Fraser stepped back. Blood dripped from his knuckles: slivers bursting from the giant's pole had flayed his hand and laid the tendons bare. He raised the hand and licked the running blood and, over the heads of the crowd, he caught sight of Chris Holden.

"Chris!" he bellowed. "Coo-wigh-h-hh! Chris, ye old buffalo!"

He tossed his weapon clattering across the platform and made for the steps. His blood-dabbled mouth grinned broadly and his Caughnawaga war cry was a joyful whoop:

"Coo-weegh-hh-hhh!"

The Turk, behind him, swung the broken sapling like an ax. It made, on John Fraser's head, the sound of an ax being driven into hard wood.

Fraser took three steps, each step a little slower than the one before it. He did not fall. He seemed to be preparing to sit down—to be sitting down and walking at the same time. When the platform ended, he was on his feet, but there was nothing for his feet to walk on. The woods runner in the white shirt dropped the bolts of cloth and caught him as he toppled.

Chris Holden sprang down from the wagon, pushed the reins into the surprised hands of a man whose face he did not see, and went plowing through the crowd.

Chapter 17

Fraser was sitting on the ground below the platform with his legs spread and the spinning wheel between them. His chin was on his chest, and his big hands lay limply on his thighs. He was staring cross-eyed at the slowly turning wheel spokes, and his face was thoughtful and a little puzzled.

McCoy and Lovatt squatted on their heels and took turns at examining John's head. They looked up gravely.

"Mornin', Cap'n. Hi, Chris . . . Cap'n Holden."

They were not men to show surprise. Their greeting was as matter-of-fact as if they had expected him.

"Hello, Dan. Hello, Joe. Did it crack his skull?"

"I allow not," Lovatt said. "Only man that's got a harder head than his'n is Dave Bone. He'll come out'n it in two-three minutes an' he'll climb that bugger's smokehouse. I allow he'll spread his chitlin's over seven acres. You got any whisky on you, Cap'n?"

"No. He'll have a bad enough head without any whisky. Fetch him over to my wagon."

"Aw, Chris," Dan McCoy protested, "John ain't go'n' t' like that. He'll be all right in a couple minutes. He c'n use that dang Turk f'r a stake an' drive him neck-deep into solid rock. He c'n——"

"Not today, he can't. I need him. That's a noble shirt, Joe. I saw you a while back, taking in the raree show, but I didn't recognize the ruffles."

"Joe's been callin' on the ladies," Dan said. "There's a lady in that peep show that's half fish. Tail like a sturgeon, an' the purtiest . . . Well, anyhow, the rest of her's right neat. Joe's been t' see her three times. He can't figger out——"

"An' now lookit me," Joe Lovatt mourned. "Look how John's bloodied up them ruffles. I ain't decent." He slapped Fraser gently. "Damn ye, John, ye near t' ruined me. What you think you were—a polecat, fightin' backwards thataway?"

"Your shirt don't make no diff'rence," McCoy comforted him. "That mermaid ain't got no shirt a-tall. All she's got on is two clamshells, an' one little clamshell in her belly button. Take a-holt, Joe."

They heaved Fraser to his feet and walked him toward the wagon. His feet dragged, but his head came up:

"Is all them wagons yourn, Chris?"

"Only one," Chris told him. "The one in the middle."

"Don't climb my leg. My legs ain't in shape t' stand it. You know damn well that there ain't no middle t' four wagons." He blinked.

"How many heads d' you think you've got, John?"

"I dunno. I lost track."

Chris unhooked the bucket that hung underneath the wagon, turned it over, and they sat Fraser on it with his back against the front wheel.

"I'll look after him," Chris said. "Go on and have your fun. Meet me at the Raleigh about sundown and I'll stand you supper."

"I don't know's the Raleigh's our fit, Cap'n."

"Then we'll make it bigger. It won't be the first tight place that we've been in together. Nor the last one, maybe."

"Yeah? You got a notion? So've I. Things don't feel right, 'crost th' mountains. I've been savin' room f'r somethin'. Look a' here—you ain't seen this lately." McCoy pulled his powder horn up on his chest and tapped it with a horny finger. It was covered with fine carving that began at the wide bottom and wound down toward the stopper in a graceful spiral. "I sort of fetched it up t' date. This here's the Loyal Hanna, an' that there's Bouquet's camp with the abattis round it, an' right here's the Frenchies. In between 'em's Shelby an' the Seneca he fought the dool with. An' here—see that? That's you, time they creased you on the belly."

Holden saw himself, crouching in carved underbrush, with two puffs of carved smoke spurting at him from behind trees. He said seriously:

"That's good, Dan. That's damned good. I've seen things in London, in museums, couldn't hold a candle to it. That's a linn tree, there. And that one's a sycamore."

"Why, certain. That's the kind o' trees they were. I wouldn't put no slipp'ry elm nor pawpaw on no hardwood ridge like that was. An' here's me an' Joe, carryin' you like a meal sack. Say . . . this notion ye've got—is it somethin' big?"

"Yes. I'm afraid it is."

"Hmm." McCoy looked troubled. "I only got about five inches left f'r carvin'. Ye think I'd ought t' get me a new horn?"

"No. You'd best hang onto that one, Dan. It's lucky."

"It is, at that. Well, so long. Joe's got t' get him a new shirt an' try his bait again on that she-sturgeon."

They ambled away. John Fraser put both hands up to his head and rocked it as a man might rock a jug to find out how much was left in it.

"You look," Chris said, grinning at him, "like a Mingo buck that's waiting to hear from his dinner."

"Anyways, my brains don't seem t' slosh none. That Turk bastard—he ain't no more a Turk than I'm a Mingo. He's a Swede from up in Jersey. The last time I seen him, he was out to Bone's place—to the Gilded Beaver. Ye get my letter, Chris?"

"Yes. I've seen Bone too. He met Garth at Norfolk."

"So *he's* back."

"Yes, on the same ship with me."

"Which was trailin' which?"

"I did the trailing, but I'm not proud of it. I almost missed him."

"Damn good thing ye didn't." Fraser took his hands down cautiously. His eyes rolled up into his head as if to make sure it was staying where his hands had left it. "Garth's here. Bone's here. Hesselgart's here——"

"Jake Hesselgart?" Holden remembered wondering why the face of the broadwheel wagon driver looked familiar.

"Yah. Garth's got his ugliest buzzards roostin' handy. The Turk's one of 'em. Williamson's another—yah, the bugger that was keepin' three squaws at Pitt's Town till the army's morals got offended an' they cut him down t' two. Anyways, you're here. God A'mighty, am I glad that *you're* here! You c'n talk their language."

"Whose language?"

"Carroll's. Washington's."

"Good Lord, John, you can talk to Washington."

"I c'n talk, sure. But I ain't sure he'll listen. An' it ain't only Washington, though. It's Bouquet, too, an' Sir William Johnson."

"Here? For the meeting?"

"Yah."

"You didn't tell me that. I thought you meant it was a meeting of the Ohio Company."

"I did. It started off t' be. It was the company that sent f'r me. But somethin' happened; I ain't sure what. I ain't sure they know what I know. Chris, let's get away from here." Fraser stood up. "I don't aim t' show you what I got t' show you with a half o' the whole province gawpin' at us." He hung the bucket on its hook, laid one hand on the rim of the wagon wheel, and vaulted to the seat. "D'ye see? That Swede Turk didn't tap me scarcely. Anyways, he didn't hurt my legs none. Pull 'round into that little street the other side of the church. Only place that you c'n get away from people in a town, it seems like, is a church."

The wagon jolted down into the stony gutter, jolted up again into Gloucester Street, and rolled slowly past the Bruton parish churchyard and turned into Nassau Street. The hubbub of the fair receded. Holden reined in under one of the great elms. Fraser took from the skirt pocket of his coat a blue faded handkerchief with its corners tied together. He undid the knots and laid the corners back.

"Damn," Holden said. His mouth was hard. "Oh, damn . . . *damn*. So I was right. I was as right as that."

"Yah. Pretty, ain't it? Like a red an' black snake, all curled up an' waitin'. An' red ribbons f'r its tail—they must've learnt that from the Frenchies."

Fraser poked the roll of painted seawan with one hairy finger. The coils loosened as if stirred to life. They seemed to ripple. With a faint slithering sound, the broad yard-long band of wampum crawled across his thighs. It lay there, uncurled and glistening.

"Chris, that's the elegantest war belt ever I laid eyes on—an' I've seen some good ones. I seen the one that Guyasuta sent up to the Wyandots at Detroit two years ago. Ye know Cap'n Campbell got it off the Wyandot chiefs an' sent it on t' Amherst. It couldn't touch this here one."

"No Seneca made this."

"Ye're right. F'r one thing, it's sewed with sinew. Mingoes wouldn't go t' all that trouble, long as they could get thread off a trader. An' besides, they're scairt. They're sore as a mink that's lost toes in a steel trap, but they're scairt too. After the way Johnson rubbed their noses in the dirt an' set the rest o' the Six Nations onto 'em f'r tryin' t' start up a war two years ago, it ain't the Mingoes that'll start it this time. This here's an Ottawa belt. Ye see that little critter worked in beads there? That's Pontiac's sign."

"So that's what you meant. All beaver gone to Mackinac. It stumped me."

"My God, Chris! It never! An' that ain't no beaver; it's an otter. God A'mighty, you——"

"I remember all right now, John. Where'd you get this?"

"On the Venango path, about six miles past the forkin' t' Kuskuski. The buck that had it aimed a little high. An Ottawa, he was. He was so damn close I never got my rifle up. I shot him from the hip."

"When?"

"Goin' on four weeks. I didn't get y'r letter till the first week in March. We had a ring-tailed hellion of a winter—snow ten feet deep on the Forbes road, no expresses through in two months. Letter laid in Bedford six weeks. An' the same express that brought it fetched another one, from George. Said he'd had some news from London. Didn't name you, but I figured where the news had come from. Said the company wanted me t' Williamsburg t' tell 'em what I knew. It graveled me; I didn't know a thing. So I took a swing down t' Logstown, an' I wasn't a mite wiser— nobody left there but a few mangy Delawares. I was headin' north t' talk t' Custaloga when I got jumped. After that it didn't seem worth while; I a'ready knew a damn sight more than Custaloga'd ever tell me."

"Did you show this to Ecuyer?"

"No. He was off somewheres, inspectin'. Cap'n Steele was in command at Fort Pitt. He's a new one. When I get around to it, I'll tell ye about *him*. If I'd showed this belt t' him, I wouldn't be here. I ain't showed it to Washington, neither. George is at the Scotchman's[1] where he always stays, but I figured it could wait until the meetin'. Figured it might jar 'em if you sprang it on 'em. I kept hopin' ye'd turn up. Ye find out any more about Garth?"

"Some. Not as much as I'd like, but it may be enough—with this. It ought to be."

"By God, it ought! War belts passin' in the winter—ye know what *that* means. It means that the redsticks ain't go'n' t' wait until July, the way they did the last time. That's what wrecked 'em—waitin'. It gave Campbell time t' find out they were gettin' ready."

"It gave him time to warn the other forts."

"Yah. An' then what? Finish it, why don't ye? It gave the army a whole

[1] A tavern purchased four years later by one Richard Charlton and known thereafter as Charlton's Inn.

month t' sit on its behind without tellin' Johnson what was goin' on."

"I still think you should have told Steele."

"An' got put in irons an' throwed down into one o' them damn dungeons? Don't forget I killed that Ottawa. An' don't forget there's some of us the army doesn't like a damn bit better than it likes Sir William Johnson. Steele might not have hanged me, but it would have pleasured him t' let me drown."

"Drown?"

"I've been near to it a dozen times, Chris, comin' through the mountains. Ye've never seen the rivers higher. There was a worse flood at the Forks three weeks ago than the one that hit us last year. Water four feet deep on the parade, an' batteaux poled in through the gate t' take the troops off if it kept on risin'. The rivers didn't just come inside, this time; they took half the fort right with 'em. The walls held, on the two landward faces where the brick is; but on the other three sides the walls are in the ditch. I tell ye, Chris, I get the shakes just thinkin' o' those dungeons. I wouldn't put it past Steele t' forget he had a pris'ner in 'em. There were three men in the guardhouse—Royals—an' he left 'em there until the water was up past the buckles of their crossbelts."

"He sounds like Val Arnold."

"Arnold! Valentine Arnold ain't a circumstance t' Steele. An' what's happened t' Fort Pitt ain't a circumstance t' what's been happenin' t' the army. It's been changin'. Seems like soldiers always change when a war's over. There's too many new officers like Cap'n Arnold an' young Steele that think an Indian is lower than a cur dog. An' the men are gettin' slack. Why wouldn't they get slack? How c'n ye keep the rank an' file from roughin' up drunk Indians an' kickin' 'em, when they hear their own officers damnin' 'em an' sneerin' at 'em? How c'n ye keep buggers like Williamson an' Bone from sneakin' liquor t' the Indians, an' soldiers from tumblin' every Indian girl that comes along, when everybody in the place is sayin' Boyd's a rum-pot an' Steele's a thief an' Arnold's a whoremaster?"

"That's pretty strong."

"Sure it is. I ain't sure Steele's a thief, but I know a thousand dollars Pennsylvania currency was stole out of Ecuyer's quarters an' the talk is that Steele done it. An' I know Steele likes t' gamble."

"Is it only soldiers that are roughing up the Indians?"

"Far as I know. Even Bone ain't that much of a fool."

"But men like Bone and Williamson might egg them on. They're all Garth's men. It fits. The talk about Steele fits too. If Garth's doing what I think he's doing, it would suit his plans to tear the army down at the same time the Indians are being set against it."

"It don't take much tearin' down, with men like Boyd an' Steele an' Arnold in it. Ye know Surgeon Boyd's drunk two thirds of the time, an' I say Arnold's a whoremaster. Fetched out a wench from Philadelphia—Peg Sargent, her name is. The men call her Sergeant Peggy, from the airs she takes.[2] I know a bad one when I see her."

---

[2] A different—and more nearly correct—version of Peggy Sargent's relationship with Captain Arnold was recounted in *The Judas Tree*. She will appear again in *The Temporary Gentleman*.

"Do you? I wish I did."

Fraser rushed on without listening:

"An' Steele's worse, in a diff'rent way. He's one of those high-mighty, sulky-faced young rakehells whose families bought 'em commissions in the army t' get 'em out of England. How c'n ye have a decent army if young good-f'r-nothings c'n be shoved in over men like Carre an' Phillips? Sure, there's some good officers. There's Gladwyn an' Campbell at Detroit, an' Price up at Le Boeuf. An' there's Ecuyer an' Bouquet. There's a man— Bouquet! He's the best damn soldier in the army, an' he knows as much about the Indians as Johnson. I ain't sure he don't know more than Johnson. Funny, ain't it? Englishmen think they're ten times smarter'n anybody else, but they had t' get an Irishman t' keep peace with the redsticks an' a Swiss t' fight 'em.'"

"Maybe," Chris said, "that's the proof that they *are* smarter."

"Huh? I dunno. Hadn't thought about it that way. But they ain't smart about some of their other officers. There's Gordon at Venango. He ought not t' be there. By the Lord, he oughtn't! He's a babe in the woods, an' the way he keeps his men runnin' errands an' fetchin' letters down t' Fort Pitt, ye'd think the Forks of the Ohio was acrost the street, not eighty miles away. He's like a man that's got the trots, an' a man that's got the trots is weak; he's bound t' be. An' there's Walters at Niagara—he's the man that couldn't bother t' send on the word t' Johnson that the Mingoes had been passin' war belts. Campbell told Walters, but Walters was too all-fired proud an' jealous t' tell Johnson, the man that needed most t' know. That's the trouble; there's too many officers that don't know the first thing about handlin' neither Indians nor soldiers—nor anybody else. They're so stiff-necked they can't look down their noses. They can't even see Sir William Johnson. They're jealous—the whole army's jealous, all the way from Gen'ral Amherst down t' pukes like Steele an' Arnold—because the army doesn't want Sir William an' the Indian Department t' have anything t' say about the Indians. They want t' hog it all—an' the most of 'em ain't got no more notion about how t' handle redsticks than Braddock an' that pig-headed fool Grant[3] had about how t' fight 'em! It ain't just traders soakin' Indians with rum an' robbin' 'em. It ain't just soldiers kickin' drunken Indians around an' rollin' with their women. It's officers that ought t' know a hell of a sight better that are stirrin' up the western nations—callin' 'em subjects of the king when ye know damn well an Indian don't figure t' be anybody's subject—swaggerin' around an' actin' like they'd licked the world when all they licked was a few measly Frenchmen. I tell ye, Chris, the Shawnees an' the Hurons an' the Ottawas an' 'Jibways haven't got the foggiest notion that we licked 'em—an' we didn't.

"Thank God all the officers on the frontier ain't Englishmen. If the frontier's saved, it won't be Englishmen that save it. It'll be foreigners— men like Ecuyer an' Bouquet. It'll be people like you an' me an' Arm-

[3]Major James Grant, who led a blundering attack against Fort Duquesne in 1758, fell into a trap, saw his troops massacred, was captured, and thereby gave his name to Grant's Hill in early Pitt's Town and to Grant Street in the modern city. *The Perilous Fight* records a curious coincidence in which he figured in the life of Sam Smith, merchant-banker-politician-soldier who commanded the defense of Baltimore in 1814 and made it possible for Francis Scott Key to write "The Star-Spangled Banner."

strong, Doc Mercer an' Parson Brown with his militia company, an' Arn Leslie an' Yeardley an' Evan Shelby, the same as it's always been. I'm getting tired of mindin' other people's business. I'm gettin' *damned* tired."

"You'll be getting damned dry if you keep on making speeches."

"I ain't makin' no speech. I'm just talkin'. My God, I been holdin' in so long I'm bloated! I don't know what Martin Garth's been doin', but I know if trouble comes on the frontier it won't be *all* his doin'. Ye can't make a fire without sparks; ye can't make a war just by peddlin' guns an' powder. Ye got t' have a reason, an' Sir William Johnson gave the Ottawas a good one. D'ye know what he did? He told the Wyandot nation that it was the top dog of the Ottawa Confederacy. That was an insult t' the Ottawas. It made 'em fightin' mad. That's why Pontiac is sendin' out his war belts."

"Are you sure?"

"Sure I'm sure. I know an Ottawa belt when I see one. An' old Custaloga himself told me, more'n a year ago, that Johnson had made trouble with the Ottawas."

"You'll have a chance to tell him that today."

"No, *sir!* I don't make no speeches in no meetings. You're the one that's got t' do that. You know how t' gab, Chris."

"That's what it would be, to Sir William. Gab. So far as he and Bouquet are concerned, I'm just another provincial militiaman. And what's worse, I'm a Virginia militiaman, and they know that I've been mixed up with the Ohio Company. They still think the Ohio Company started the last war. You're right when you say the army doesn't like us. It's suspicious of anything and anybody that's involved in the Ohio Company. Even Bouquet is suspicious of us. No, John. I'm a poor one to make speeches to Bouquet and Johnson. They'll think it's the Ohio Company that's talking, trying to get some advantage."

"Ye've made speeches t' the Mingoes an' the Shawnees an' the Cherokees. They listened, didn't they? Johnson an' Bouquet will listen."

"I wonder. What I know—what I *think* I know about Garth is so unbelievable that I'm not sure *I'd* listen."

"By the Lord, they'll listen! They will, if I've got t' hold 'em. Ye know, Chris, I'm glad all this is happenin'. In a way, I am."

"Glad!"

"It'll settle things a little. Drivin' out the Frenchies didn't settle nothin'. They're still stirrin' things up. An' Garth's usin' some of 'em t' poke his own fire. He's hired half of the woods runners in the Illinois, Chris."

"Yes. He bragged of it, in London."

"It'll settle somethin' else too—fellow by the name of Holden."

"Thanks."

"I mean it. This'll get ye back acrost the mountains where ye'd ought t' be. Tidewater ain't no place f'r ye. By God, it ain't. Ye need a honin', bad. Ye're duller than the backside of a butter paddle, an' ye ain't go'n' t' skin Garth with no wooden ladle. Damn it, Chris, ye'd ought t' have learned *somethin'*. An' remembered it. Ye were out with Washington the first time, an' with Braddock an' Old Iron Head an' with Evan Shelby an' that damn fool Grant an'——"

"Don't forget John Fraser."

"I ain't. Ye're the one that's doin' the forgettin'. God A'mighty, I can't get over you thinkin' that an otter is a beaver. An' I can't get over you forgettin' about beaver too—about how the redsticks say the beaver go t' Mackinac in summer an' turn into rattlesnakes. I told ye that myself, Chris. What's got into ye? Don't tell me; I know. Ye've got women on the brain."

"Like hell I have."

"They c'n be hell, all right."

"I'll remember that, John. I'll remember to tell that to Half Pint."

"Go ahead an' tell her. I ain't talkin' about women like her. There *ain't* no woman like her. My wife ain't no fancy-nancy out of y'r tidewater cities or y'r dandiprat plantations. She's a woman fitten f'r a real man."

"Yes. She is. She surely is, John."

"Then ye ought t' know what a real woman is. But do ye? No! Ye go gettin' y'rself caught in a damn box trap like a year-old rabbit with hot britches. My God, what's that swell-top trunk ye fetched back if it ain't a box trap? Ye got she-bait in it! Any time a man goes baitin' traps like that t' catch a woman, it means he's been caught a'ready. Ye ain't got no anvils in that trunk, Chris."

"No. You're right, I haven't. And that's not all you're right about. I should have known exactly what you meant about the beaver and the snakes. I was so close to it I couldn't see it." Holden began coiling the belt neatly. The beads rustled. "It sounds scaly, doesn't it? Smooth. Cold too. Have you ever noticed how much warmer a snake's skin is *after* the snake sheds it?"

"Yah. I've noticed somethin' else too. They don't like to have you catch 'em when they're changin' skins. They're dangerousest then."

"Not always, John. There's some that never change."

"I heard about her marryin' your brother. You poisoned, Chris?"

"A little. Didn't you once tell me that if a man's bitten and it doesn't kill him, he's immune from then on?"

"Bein' bit once ain't no surety he won't be bit again. A new bite won't kill him, but he'll feel it. He'll be nearabout as fevered as he was the first time."

"I doubt that."

"You'll see."

"No, John. I'm done. I'll not be bit again. But if I am, I've got the certain cure. The Shawnees say the way to cure a snake bite is to make a poultice of the snake that bit you."

"Sure. It draws the poison. But you got to catch the snake."

"You're wrong. The skin is just as good. I've got it in that trunk there—a nice new one, John, from Paris. I was half a mind to send it back to her, or sell it. But I think I'll keep it to remind me."

"That's a damn poor way to cure a fever."

"Do you know a better?"

"Whisky."

"It's an idea."

"Trouble with you, Chris, you been drinkin' hogwash. It's enough to make a man sick. It made *me* sick at the Raleigh last night. An' I wasn't drinkin', neither. I was only watchin' what y'r fine tidewater gentry slosh their insides with—negus, cherry bounce, Maderia sack, flip, rum with sugar in it, an' peach brandy all fouled up with honey! Burn me if I didn't see a bottle that said 'Cordial' on it! There ain't nothin' cordial to a man's guts about stuff like that."

"In London," Chris said gravely, "they've a drink called fustian. You take a quart of strong beer and a pint of gin, a dozen eggs——"

"The hell I do!"

"—a bottle of good sherry, lemon, sugar, and a nutmeg, and you mix 'em up together."

"An' you wash hogs with it. Ain't that what I told you? Hogwash. Even a drunk Mingo wouldn't touch it. Chris, I'd sooner boil a Mingo's blanket with the crawlies in it."

"Well, they use snails sometimes. There's a drink called asses' milk. It isn't; that's just what they call it. They put hartshorn shavings, barley, China root, eringo, and a handful of cured ginger in a pot and boil it. When it's bubbling, they drop in a dozen and a half of bruised snails——"

"Judas! Do they have t' bruise 'em? They'd die nat'ral, wouldn't they?"

"—shells and all. And then a pint of cow's milk and an ounce or so of balsam."

"Asses' milk," John Fraser marveled. "I c'n see where the name comes from. Englishmen are mostly asses, ain't they? Ye take Gen'ral Amherst. Ye take things he's done, like shuttin down on presents f'r the Indians, rilin' 'em f'r no good reason. Ye take——" A look of deep concern spread over Fraser's face. "Snails! Shavin's! Asses' milk! Great God A'mighty, Chris, no wonder ye got poisoned! Start them horses, quick. We got a couple hours until the meetin'. We ain't goin' t' the Raleigh, neither—not until we got to. There's a place up at the end of town where they got whisky. Pennsylvania whisky."

Chapter 18

Whisky poured into John Fraser had the same effect it had when it was poured into a barrel.

A little of it only splashed around, it only made him feel the way a barrel with a little whisky in it sounded—emptier than empty. But in proper quantity, it made him solider and more substantial. It made him feel as if he couldn't be tipped over. To his way of thinking, no man in his right mind would fill up a barrel part way; he would fill it right up to the top until it couldn't gurgle.

Fraser knew exactly where his own top was, and he had quit exactly where he ought to. But he wasn't sure about Chris Holden. Walking down the street now from the noisy, satisfying tavern in Woodpecker Lane, past the round-topped brick wall with the red brick capitol behind it, Fraser kept looking sidewise at him, wondering how much he'd had to drink before they started on the whisky.

Holden didn't look drunk and he didn't act drunk. But he'd surely had his mind on something other than drinking: he had poured the whisky into him like water, without noticing it scarcely. And you couldn't notice any more effect than if it had been water—except, maybe, he had got a little taller. He was walking light and tall and easy, and his eyes were pinched up thin the way they'd be if he was in the woods and stalking something, coming up-wind on a deer or watching out for Mingoes in an ambush. *By damn,* Fraser thought, *he looks like a cocked rifle walkin' down the street.*

A blue-paneled chariot behind four glossy bays in silver-mounted harness edged in toward the swinging sign from which Sir Walter Raleigh stared disdainfully in ruff and doublet. A boy shrilled: "The gov'nor!" The crowd surged in around the coach and raised a straggling cheer. Blue-liveried footmen scrambled down. The chariot swayed heavily as a big beefy man in a plum-colored coat with gold-laced cuffs and buttonholes stepped out with heavy dignity. The cheer trailed off. Fraser jogged Chris Holden's elbow:

"There, that's Johnson. Ye ain't never seen him, have ye? Neither've tnese folk. Thought he was the gov'nor, an' now they don't know whether he's worth hollerin' about. He's changed some. Looks like he's got a keg inside his weskit—anyways a half keg. Not Bouquet, though." An officer, impeccable in powdered wig and scarlet tunic turned up with the dark, white-slashed blue of the Royal American regiment, had stepped down from the chariot. His mouth was girlish in his lean, still face. "Bouquet's meals ain't settled on him like Sir William's. He looks about the same as he did on the Loyal Hanna, except he's cleaner an' he ain't two-thirds starved like the lot of us was then."

"He's in worse company," Chris said. "Will you look who's with him?"

Fraser looked, and swore.

"Good God A'mighty . . . *no!* Garth, ridin' with Bouquet an' Johnson in the gov'nor's carriage! An' contented as a snake that's swallowed seven bullfrogs. How'd he horn in on 'em?"

"By doing what I should have done, instead of listening to you make speeches."

"There's George, comin' down the steps t' meet 'em. An' there's Lee an' Carroll. Sa-ay, they've got a Quaker with 'em. Looks like Andrews, that was at the meetin' with the Delawares at Croghan's Castle last year. What's *he* doin' here? D'ye know any of them others, Chris?"

"The one in the dark red coat is Jenifer, from Maryland. Daniel of St. Thomas Jenifer. He's a member of the boundary commission. And that's Barclay with him; he's another."

"Pennsylvania. Maryland. Virginia. An' Johnson's from York province. Sounds like another congress, like they had at Albany. God A'mighty, Chris, ye must've thrown a fine fright into 'em with what ye wrote to Washington from London."

They were on the steps. Wide shoulders in a caped horizon-blue coat leaned out from the press above them and young Colonel Washington's big hand reached down to Fraser's.

"So you made it, John. I wasn't sure that you'd get through. The freight-ers tell me it's bad going in the mountains."

"Bad enough. It's worse'n when ye went t' Fort Le Boeuf t' tell that old one-eyed French commandant t' pull foot."

"Legardeur de St. Pierre." Washington smiled, remembering. "He looked like an owl that had been badly stuffed. But he had good brandy."

"An' used some of it t' get ye killed."

"I've never quite believed that. If he did, he used too much. The Indian that drank it missed me."

A white-topped broadwheel wagon was lumbering by, plowing a wide furrow through the thronged street. Holden was still on the first step, staring at it. He looked up at Fraser briefly.

"Williamson," he said, low, and went back to staring at the wagon. There was a girl on the swaying seat beside the driver. Her hands were clasped in her lap and she was looking down at them, her face half hidden in her blue hood.

"What's bitin' ye, Chris?" Fraser plucked him by the sleeve. "Ye ain't figurin' t' buy a female bond slave, are ye? That's what they been haulin'—convicts."

"No." Chris started up the steps. "That girl looked like one I—one that picked my pocket."

"Picked you pretty clean, eh, Holden?" Garth stood, smiling faintly, at Sir William Johnson's elbow. His voice sounded more than ever like chips rustling in a basket. "It would be surprising if there wasn't a resemblance. She's the same girl. She came straight to me the minute you were gone."

"I see," Chris said, and did not like what he was seeing. This made three times. Three times in two days he had been made a fool of. "I thought she was only a thief."

He turned away, hot with anger and uncomfortably conscious of amused and curious glances, and heard Fraser, loudly cheerful:

"Here he is, George. I've had him an' Dan McCoy an' Lovatt on my hands at once. Joe Lovatt's got his heart set on a mermaid he seen in a raree show, an'——"

"Hello, Chris. I'm glad to see you." Washington's handclasp was strong and friendly. "Sir William . . . Captain Holden, who served with me. Colonel Bouquet, you remember Holden; he had our Virginia rangers. Chris, the last time I saw you, you were in a blanket slung between two rifles and you had a bullet in you. You looked like a ghost. Now you look as if you'd seen one."

"Be easy with him, Colonel Washington," Garth said. "It was an expensive ghost he saw—a hundred and three pounds' worth."

"Hazard, Chris? Or whisk? You always held bad cards."

"You do him an injustice," Garth protested, and Chris Holden thought, as he had thought before, of a great tree cat purring. "To a Pennsylvanian, you Virginians are an amazing people. Openhanded and high-minded—and high-spirited too. I tried to outbid Mr. Holden for a bond slave and lost, as I might have known. A hundred and three pounds and sixpence."

"My God," Jenifer said blankly. "That's ten hogsheads, prime."

"Not tobacco, sir. Hard money. And he freed her."

"My God," Jenifer repeated.

Holden knew that Garth had made him absurd. He could see the carefully controlled amusement on the faces of the men around him. Repressing their smiles, they repressed also the contempt that might have been there. Washington was trying to pass off the awkward moment.

"I've known some bond servants that were worth a stiff price," he was saying. "My teacher was an indentured convict. A fine man." He chuckled. "But he never did succeed in teaching me to spell."

Johnson, too, was helping:

"My wife was a bond slave, gentlemen." His voice was good-humored, but his wide mouth shut down, thin and hard, behind the words. His blunt face seemed to wait, as if it challenged anyone to recollect the gossip that the servant girl he bought bore him three children before he got around to marrying her, on her deathbed.

There was a polite, wordless murmur. Holden thought: *He didn't need to say that. There aren't many men who would have said a thing like that, to ease a stranger.* Then it occurred to him that possibly Sir William had not thought of him at all and had not spoken out of kindness but out of an old anger and resentment, because the tolerant contemptuous amusement of these men reminded him of similar experiences of his own. "Well, gentlemen," Lee said across the murmur, "we have business to attend to. Shall we go in?"

Standing at the door of the Apollo, looking at the dull blue paneling with the strange effect of warmth and sunlight in it, at the maroon marble hearth frame and the dark red damask curtains looped back from the white blinds, Holden found no welcome in the pleasant room. It had not changed; it was all familiar. Cards were strewn on the loo table; the ivory fish lay in the shallow ponds carved into the mahogany before each chair; the last chalk scribblings in the black oblong scorekeeps at the corners had not been wiped off. The chessmen waited on their board, the long clays in the pipe rack on the wall. The four brass candlesticks still marched across the narrow mantel.

The gentlemen were in no hurry to be at their business. Carroll picked up a tobacco journal from a pile of London and colonial gazettes and *Gentleman's Magazines* and moved to a window. Jenifer sat down at the long table and toyed with a tapered dicebox. The Quaker, a round dumpy little man, trundled across the room to stand teetering before the great parchment map laced in its frame upon the wall; his thin legs, in their dark gray hose and breeches, did not seem to be supporting his plump body; rather, they protruded from it like a pair of silver toothpicks stuck into a Spanish olive.

A stocky man in a moss-green coat had settled himself at the loo table with his paunch snug against it, his feet hooked around the chair legs, and his short forearms planted firmly. His small hands scooped up the cards. He lowered his jowled, sharp-nosed face to peer at them. Above him leaned a lank, loose-jointed figure all in bright blue smallclothes, coat and waistcoat above brown thread stockings. Chris Holden thought of a fat bullfrog catching flies, unconscious of a blue heron watching him with anticipation.

Washington pulled out the tall spindle-back chair at the head of the long table and stood by it, tapping his knuckles on the green baize throw and frowning at the group around the fireplace—Garth in one chair and John Fraser in the other, and Sir William Johnson between Richard Lee and Bouquet. Fraser had produced a small pine block and an enormous knife and gone to whittling. But it was Johnson who was holding things up. He was backing himself to the hearth and spreading out his coat skirts to the blaze. Garth made as if to rise, but Johnson rumbled at him:

"No, no. Keep your seat. Sitting down is no proof that a man has lead in his behind. I'm the one that has it." Lee laughed, and Garth smiled politely. "The French bullet I acquired at Lake George is still in my carcass. Eight years. You have some interest in natural philosophy and science, Mr. Lee? I'll tell you an odd thing. That bullet gets cold with the first frost and stays cold until midsummer. Hazards of war. We have to take the dice the way they fall. Did you know that after the battle of Lake George we found French bullets that had been carved into dice? I wonder, sometimes, if that Frenchman threw a deuce into me."

"He didn't make his point," Lee said. "It wasn't your number that came up, thanks be."

"Speaking of science," Johnson rumbled on, "we may be on the verge of a discovery of great importance." His bluff, handsome face was turned to the loo table. The loose-jointed man was sitting down now, helping to arrange the cards in neat rows. "Andrews and Jenifer should see what their astronomers are up to. Look at them—Mason and Dixon figuring how to take the hazard out of loo. Brother Andrews," he called, "look here. We can't tolerate this." The Quaker trotted toward him. "Dangerous thing, science. Got to keep these fellows in hand. What would life be with the risks gone?"

"Thee still has the Indians."

Sir William chuckled.

"Even that will be a simpler game now. The treaty's signed, you know. With the French out for good, it's only a two-handed game. Not half so interesting."

Smocked Negro servants came in carrying decanters, trays with glasses and halved lemons, sugar loaves and sticks of cinnamon, steaming luster pitchers, a platter piled with cold meats, bowls of nuts, tobacco in a brass box with an oiled wick and a fire wheel mounted on it. Garth spoke to one of them, and a tray was set down on the round-topped table by his chair. Johnson took a stubby black pipe from his pocket, dipped it into the brass box, and tamped it with his thumb. Fraser slipped out of his chair, squatted on his heels to spear a live coal on his knife point, and stood up to offer it to Johnson. Andrews stooped to look at the pine block in Fraser's hand.

"May I ask what thee is making?"

"Somethin' that ye won't approve of. Bullet holder. Hangs around y'r neck. Ye see, there's slots in it f'r bullets. Saves time when ye're in a hurry. Ye c'n hold six bullets in between the fingers of y'r left hand, and six-eight more in y'r mouth; but when ye've used 'em all, a bullet holder's handier than fishin' in y'r pouch."

"Science again," Johnson said around his pipestem. "Bouquet, why the devil don't you fit the Royals out with those things? Regulations? Fiddlesticks! You've broken half the regulations in the book. You've had to."

"We break them sometimes, yes." Bouquet smiled dryly. "But we do not hang them on our necks for everyone to see."

Johnson roared with laughter. He seemed to be enjoying himself hugely. Chris Holden, remembering the endless ceremonial preliminaries to an Indian council, understood why Johnson saw no need for an unseemly haste in opening a meeting. But Washington's impatience got the better of him:

"Mr. Lee, we'd best get on with it. I promised Wetherburn that we'd be out by four o'clock. There's a ball tonight, and he's all a-quiver to be at his polishing."

"Yes. Yes, of course. Gentlemen, if you will find chairs . . . No formality. Come, Mr. Mason. Mr. Dixon . . . Take the head, Sir William. Colonel Bouquet, if you'll sit beside him . . ."

"No, no," Johnson protested. "Not the head. I'm not here officially, you understand."

"We're none of us here officially, Sir William. If you please, sir. Even if Maryland and Pennsylvania lock horns, you will be safe there, with two colonels flanking you."

"Or outflanking me," Johnson said. "I'm never sure, you know. The Indian Department and the army are forever getting in each other's breeches." But he took the chair that Washington had drawn out for him.

Carroll, still absorbed in his tobacco journal, sat down in the first place that he came to. Holden found himself with Jenifer on one side and John Fraser on the other. He saw that Garth, with a nice show of deference, had waited until all the others had been seated; but he noticed, too, that Garth had stood so close behind the chair at the end of the table opposite Sir William that nobody else could have sat down there. Holden felt John Fraser nudge him as Garth set his tray down on the table and pulled out the chair.

"How d'ye like that?" Fraser muttered. "He's got brass guts, riveted with copper. Who's head an' who's tail now—him or Johnson?"

"Sir William," Lee was saying, "this is altogether an informal meeting. It has been customary for those of us who hold shares in the Ohio Company to meet in Williamsburg at public time each spring. This year certain unusual circumstances brought about a correspondence with others who are interested, in one way or another, in the western lands. The fortunate result has been that we are here together. I say 'fortunate' because the colonies—especially the middle colonies—have many interests in common; they cannot be dealt with separately. We discovered that fact in the late war, and we are discovering that it is still a fact. Indeed, it was the effort to establish the precise line of separation between Pennsylvania and Maryland that has brought us together.

"As you know, gentlemen, Mr. Charles Mason and Mr. Jeremiah Dixon were engaged to run the boundary between the Penns' proprietary and Lord Baltimore's. Some people thought that it was going to extremes to bring astronomers from London just to show us how to draw a straight line. And some others"—he gave Washington a sly smile—"thought that it reflected on our native talent."

Washington chuckled at the gibe.

"Mr. Mason and his colleague," Lee continued, "are impartial. And—what's more important—everyone admits that they're impartial. Even Mr. Andrews, I believe, will trust them when they tell him that Pittsburgh is in Virginia."

The little Quaker's faded eyes blinked placidly.

"And will thee also trust them?"

"Certainly—when they say it's in Virginia," Lee answered. There was a small stir of laughter. But the jest, Chris Holden thought, was more than half in earnest. "They'll find it's in Virginia—unless you move it, Mr. Andrews. Pennsylvania may move the town, but you can't move the Forks of the Ohio far enough to hide them from two mathematicians who have measured space between the planets." Lee's voice lost its lightness. "In some ways that was a much simpler task than running boundaries across our mountains. There are no Indians between the earth and Mars. It is not generally known yet, but the fact is that the survey has been stopped."

Here and there a man leaned forward. Two or three asked questions sharply:

"Stopped? Where?"

"Who the devil stopped it?"

But the news, Chris Holden saw, was no surprise to most of the men about the table. His quick glance at Fraser brought an angry grumble:

"Ye heard what he said. It ain't known gen'rally. If they ain't told the gen'rals, how the hell would I know?"

"Mr. Mason," Lee was saying, "suppose you——"

"Yes. Stopped completely. Dunkard's Creek. The tenth day of October." Mason ticked the questions off with mathematical precision. "Painted aborigines. They informed us we must not proceed beyond the warpath that runs east of Dunkard's. They were our own escort, provided by Sir William Johnson, but they were quite firm about it. Quite." He shuddered gently. "One of them wore horns."

"Hear that?" Fraser whispered. "Ottawa."

Carroll folded his tobacco journal slowly, with his finger thrust between the pages.

"Mr. Lee, you say this isn't widely known." His tone was disapproving. "Why hasn't it been known? Why haven't the back settlements been warned?"

"I'll answer that, sir," Johnson said. "We've seen too many panics on the frontier. I don't care to start another."

"A panic's better than a massacre."

"Yes, Mr. Carroll. But there's been no massacre. I have no reason to believe there will be. But a sign of weakness might produce one."

"Then there *is* a danger?"

"There is always danger." Sir William stared at his pipe for a moment, silent, and then rose. "This may be as good a time as any to say what I have to say. For fifteen years now it has been my business to deal with the danger—to watch it, measure it, and try to keep it within bounds. My responsibility as Indian commissioner would rest easier on me if our two astronomers here could draw me a boundary line between proper caution and an undue risk. They can't. Nobody can. It takes more than a star-gazer to tell what Indians will do. I think, sometimes, that nobody but an Irishman can understand the red man."

He paused as if he knew that there would be another stir of laughter. It came. Johnson's voice was graver when he went on:

"You gentlemen remember what happened after Braddock's fight on the Monongahela. If you have forgotten, Colonel Washington can tell you—the frontier collapsing, towns and farms and crops abandoned, the back-country people running by the thousands, and the scalping parties within thirty miles of Baltimore and Winchester. A panic's like a chimney draft; it can suck fire out of a few embers bedded in cold ashes."

Fraser's knife jabbed furiously at his pine block.

"Chimney draft!" he muttered. "It was Dunbar started *that* draft, runnin' f'r two hundred miles with a half of Braddock's army that hadn't even heard a gun go off. An' it wasn't no 'few embers,' neither. I'd like to of seen Sir William Johnson set *his* backside in them embers. They sure would've warmed that bullet in his britches. He'd know what a panic is, by God! He wouldn't be so quick t' blame the settlers when they pull foot."

"I'll not deny," Sir William said, "that this business of the survey is disturbing. Disturbing, mind you—not alarming. If the stopping of the survey became known, it would increase the nervousness on the frontier. We have some men out there who think it's wise to shoot an Indian first and ask his business later. Any provocation might cause trouble."

"Are there any other signs of trouble?" Lee asked.

Johnson shrugged.

"The usual. Indians stealing horses. White man in armed parties going out to get them back. It's hard to convince Indians, holding property in common, that they shouldn't help themselves to horses. And it's harder to convince a white man that it may be cheaper to lose a horse than to risk the losing of a hundred lives—especially when the horse is his and the lives aren't. Then we've put a stop to selling guns and powder to the tribes; they don't like that. Between us, French and English, we've taught the Indians to depend on muskets and gunpowder for their hunting. Now they can't buy 'em, and they're irritated. We've almost put a stop to selling rum. Every time a trader is caught doing it, Bouquet's troops pull his cabin down and stave in his barrels. The Indians don't like that, either. Every now and then we hear about some chief or other digging up the hatchet. Colonel Bouquet tells me that for weeks at a time Ecuyer at Fort Pitt has had his gunners on the walls all night, with their matches lighted. And all false alarms. I think Bouquet agrees with me that it's bad business. It suggests to the Indians that we are not sure of our strength. Settlers have been moving west again, these last two years; if suddenly they started moving east, it would be taken as a sign of weakness. That's why we've said nothing about the survey being stopped. The question is, what shall we *do* about it?"

Daniel of St. Thomas Jenifer, sprawled across the table with his chin almost upon the green baize, turned the dicebox round and round with thumb and finger. Lee, with his chair tilted back, drummed thoughtfully on one knee. Garth was pouring hot water from a luster pitcher on the sugar in his porter, stirring the while with a stick of cinnamon. Barclay was sucking soberly at his clay pipe. Nehemiah Andrews clasped and unclasped his thin hands on his round stomach. Washington had unfastened the mahogany lid of his pocket compass and was watching the gyrations of the needle as he passed an iron nutcracker back and forth above it.

"Well, gentlemen," Sir William prodded them, "I've come a long way. I had hoped for some suggestions. What are we to do about the survey?"

"Why do anything about it?"

Heads turned, startled. Carroll's finger lost its place in the tobacco journal. Jenifer sat up abruptly, and the dicebox rattled as if he was shaking it to make a cast. The front legs of Richard Lee's chair came down with a crash. The two Maryland commissioners looked at Andrews, and the quick suspicion of their glances said that Garth, too, was a Pennsylvanian.

"I'm sorry, gentlemen." Garth smiled above his lifted glass. "Is my question out of order?"

"It's out of my comprehension," Barclay snapped.

"Is it?" Garth sipped at his negus. "A little weak," he said, and reached for the decanter.

"So is the policy that you suggest."

"Policy?" Garth wondered at the word. "You misunderstand me, Mr. Barclay. I suggested nothing."

"Exactly," Barclay said. "That is what I understood. The Indians defy the government, and you'd do nothing."

"Why," Garth answered mildly, "that depends."

"On what, sir?"

"If I may borrow from the language of our two surveyor friends, here, it depends entirely on the accuracy of your observation."

"I don't take you."

"You made the observation that the Indians have defied the government. But have they?"

"Certainly they have!"

"Oh well, then . . ." Garth shrugged. He sat tapping his glass with the stick of cinnamon.

"Is there any doubt about it?" Jenifer demanded.

"Doubt? No, sir. There's no doubt whatever. If you'll look at the map . . ." He shrugged again. "After all, gentlemen, I'm an intruder here. Sir William was so kind as to invite me because I know something of the western Indians. I have no right to force my notions on you." Then, as if he felt an obligation to speak out in spite of his reluctance, he pushed back his chair. His manner was apologetic. "By your leave, Sir William . . . Mr. Lee . . ."

He walked briskly to the parchment map and stood beside it.

"Mr. Barclay, you say the government has been defied. Whose government? Maryland's?" He swung to Andrews. "Pennsylvania's?" The corner of his mouth twitched as he looked at Lee. "Or Virginia's? Let's see." He laid the tip of the long cinnamon stick on the map. "Take Maryland first. Here's Dunkard's Creek. And here"—he moved the stick a little to the right and downward—"is the Laurel Ridge. I know nothing of surveying, gentlemen, but I do know something of this country out here. I ought to; I've been back and forth across it now for fifteen years. There's one thing we can all agree on: water doesn't run uphill. West of Laurel Ridge the streams run west. Here, east of it, is Savage River. Turn south from the Savage and you come to Hope Good Creek and then to Spruce Run and then Laurel River." The cinnamon stick was tapping down the map. "Flat Run. Moss Run. The Cherrybrook. They all flow into the Potomac and they're all in Maryland. But right here"—the stick stopped—"is the source of the Potomac—and the end of Maryland."

"What?" Jenifer was on his feet. "What's that you say?"

"Are you so surprised? 'The first fountain of the river of Pattowmack'— by the royal charter, that's the western limit of your province. Here it is, sir. Dunkard's Creek is twenty miles beyond it."

Jenifer strode anxiously across the room, and Barclay came to stand beside him, staring at the crooked spiderweb of streams and ridges.

"Is this map right?" Jenifer demanded.

"Lewis Evans signed it," Garth said, "and it's right. You see now why I asked whose government had been defied. Not Maryland's. I dare say Lord Baltimore will be surprised to hear his money has been spent to run a boundary line that's no concern of his. But if you are called to answer for it, there is a good answer."

"My God," Barclay prayed, "I hope so."

"I saw something of Lord Baltimore in London," Garth said dryly. "He has other uses for his money than to draw lines through an empty wilderness. He's much more concerned with women, and he draws no line there. Twenty miles of wasted survey may displease him, but you can point out that you have saved him money."

"Saved him money? Dammit——"

"A good deal of money, Mr. Barclay. After all, it was your energy and foresight—and Mr. Jenifer's—that led you to attend this meeting and so find the error. You have saved Lord Baltimore the cost of carrying the survey on to the Ohio for no purpose but to settle a dispute between Virginia and Pennsylvania. Brother Andrews, your assembly has made every effort to keep peace with the tribes. Surely you'll not say that Pennsylvania's government has been defied." The tight-laced deer hide strummed as Garth's hand slapped the map. "Pennsylvania has no interest whatever in that country out there. My God, you've disowned it! And not once, but twice! Ten years ago, to get out of paying Croghan's bills for dealing with the Indians, the Pennsylvania assembly decided that the Forks of the Ohio are outside the western limits of the province. And eight years ago it did the same thing. It not only decided that the Forks do not belong to Pennsylvania; it said plainly that it doesn't want them!"

Garth paused to take a long sip of the negus. Over the rim of his glass his eyes traveled slowly from Lee to Carroll and then on to Washington.

"And that leaves Virginia," he said at last. "What right has Virginia to say the survey should go on? Virginia hasn't paid one farthing of the cost."

Washington looked up from his compass:

"Mr. Garth, until the survey reached the source of the Potomac, there was no occasion for Virginia to share the cost. I can't speak for the assembly, but I think you may be sure that it will take an interest in the matter. You overlook one thing, sir—Virginia has *not* disowned the Forks of the Ohio."

"I'm sorry if I have upset you, Colonel Washington. I know that you selected that site, but"—Garth shrugged—"a fort at the end of nowhere, guarding nothing . . ."

"That triangle of land may be the most vital spot in this whole country, Mr. Garth."

"My dear colonel"—Garth's mouth twitched—"a mudbank between two useless rivers, flooded every spring, poisonous with fogs and marsh gas. And in summer it's an oven—a confounded brick kiln."

"And a gateway. Don't forget that. It's a gateway to the whole west, and the rivers are not useless. They will mean as much, one day, as the York and James have meant to the Peninsula of Virginia. They may mean more. When I visited Fraser's forge I saw——"

"Coal!" Fraser blurted. "Coal an' iron! Pitt's Town's like a hen settin' on more coal than she c'n hatch out in a thousand years. Cook iron with the coal an' what've ye got? Steel! That town'll sprout into a city bigger'n Williamsburg. Go on—laugh! I'm tellin' ye."

"I'm no blacksmith," Garth said. "And I'm no more a lawyer than I'm a surveyor. But I do know something about Indians and their treaties and their land deeds. The plain fact is, gentlemen, that Virginia has no interest in the Forks."

"No interest!" Carroll cried. "Virginia fought for them! Virginians have died for them, and——"

"Why?" Garth asked blandly.

"Why? *Why?*" Carroll was as blank as Garth was bland. "My God, sir."

"Pennsylvanians and Marylanders died for them too, Mr. Carroll—not to mention Englishmen and Irishmen and Dutchmen. I was not speaking of a sentimental interest. I meant a legal interest. Virginia's whole claim to that region is based on the king's grant to the Ohio Company—an invalid grant based on a false assumption."

Carroll tried to speak and only stammered in his anger. Richard Lee rose:

"Mr. Garth, we are not accustomed to hearing His Majesty's acts described as worthless. Will you please explain that statement?"

"I intended to. The king's grant of certain western lands to the Ohio Company was based on the assumption that Virginia had already bought them from the Indians and paid for them. The royal grant was nothing more than recognition of that purchase. But the purchase, sir, had not been made."

"The purchase, sir, was made at Lancaster in '44."

"Yes. Yes, I know. The gentlemen of the Ohio Company *thought* it had been made. Far be it from me, Mr. Lee, to suggest that His Majesty was purposely misled. But what you got and what you thought you got are quite different matters. You *thought* you got everything from the Tuscarora Mountain all the way to the Pacific Ocean."

"To the Ohio River, sir."

"My apologies, Mr. Lee. I was merely stating the impression that has been given—gained, perhaps I ought to say—in London. But the language of the treaty—'all the lands that are or shall be by His Majesty's appointment in the colony of Virginia as far as it is settled, and back from thence to the sun setting'—that sounds like a lot of territory. To the Iroquois who signed the deed, its language has a very different meaning. 'Back from thence to the sun setting' doesn't mean Pacific Ocean and it doesn't mean Ohio River. It means only the next hilltop. What you *got,* gentlemen, was title to a strip of land between the Blue Mountains and the Allegheny Ridge—and that's all you got. That's why the Indians have stopped the survey. They weren't defying government. They were expelling trespassers!"

Across Jenifer's empty chair Chris Holden saw Washington glance toward him. The quick gleam of the blue eyes acknowledged that he had been right in what he wrote from London.

"Trespassers," Lee was repeating. "You apply that term to a surveying party working under the direction of two provincial governments and sponsored by the Indian commissioner. Sir William Johnson acts for the king's ministers. I would suppose that the king's law extended to the Forks of the Ohio. Or is it no man's land? Is that what you're trying to tell us?"

"The king's law moves with the king's muskets, and there aren't enough troops west of the mountains to keep back the squatters, let alone take on an Indian war. As for the land—it's mine."

"Yours, Mr. Garth?"

"Yes, sir. Mine. I own it. Barring two small parcels, I own everything from Laurel Ridge to the Ohio, from Venango down to Logstown. And south of the Ohio River I own everything from the Greenbrier River to the mouth of the Scioto."

"Impossible!"

"Not at all, sir. I have bought it, paid for it, and I hold deeds to it. And the deeds are valid. They weren't got by trickery, and there's no fancy language in them like 'from thence to the sun setting.' They were granted by the Indians in council, and their proper chiefs have signed them."

Washington closed his compass with a sudden small crash that was loud in the dead silence.

"Indian's can't deed land to individuals, Mr. Garth."

"I mislike to contradict you, Colonel," Garth said, "but you're wrong. They *have* sold land to individuals. I assure you, sir, there is sound legal precedent behind my deeds—the very soundest precedent."

"You mean Croghan?"

"Yes—for one. George Croghan holds deeds to several thousand acres, one tract on the Youghiogheny where he has gone into partnership with Colonel Chapham, and the other on the Allegheny four miles above Pitt's Town. He got both tracts from the Indians by private purchase."

John Fraser snorted.

"But when?" he demanded. *"When?* I'll tell ye. Fourteen years ago! Fourteen years ago there wasn't any gov'ment west of Tuscarora Mountain, an' there wasn't half a dozen traders west of Laurel Ridge."

"I was one of them," Garth said.

"An' I was another. I know all about them land deals. Anybody could buy anything f'r a tin whistle—and his title wasn't worth it. Things have changed since then, Garth."

"They have indeed. I am obliged to you for reminding your employers of it. Now that the war's over and the government acknowledges his titles, Croghan's land is worth a good deal more than a tin whistle. So is——" He broke off abruptly. "Have I said something to surprise you, Mr. Carroll?"

The dismay in Carroll's face was answer. Croghan's "purchase" lay within the royal grant to the Ohio Company. Lee asked sharply:

"Is that true, Sir William? Has the government accepted Croghan's titles?"

"It has had no reason to dispute them," Johnson answered smoothly. "And the army acquiesces. Croghan has been one of His Majesty's most faithful servants. In the Indian Department he has been invaluable."

And, Chris Holden told himself, Sir William Johnson would not be the one to find a reason for disputing Croghan's titles. Johnson himself had laid his hands on too much Indian land to raise awkward questions touching his own deputy commissioner.

"The Indian Department has no right to pass on land claims," Lee protested. "And the army has no right to acquiesce. The law——"

"The law!" Garth rasped. "The army and the Indian Department *are* the law, across the mountains. I'm sorry, gentlemen. I understand what this means to the Ohio Company. It's not the first time that a thing like this has happened. Maps change. Land grants are withdrawn. Why, the whole proprietary of Maryland has been carved out of what was once Virginia—and the Penns believe that it was carved out of land that had been granted to them by the king. I wonder . . . I had understood this meeting was concerned with danger on the frontier. If it is, you should be reassured. What I have done will go a long way to eliminate the danger."

"How?" Carroll snapped.

"By keeping out the settlers. They're the root of all the trouble. They're the reason why the survey was turned back. To the Indians, a surveyor today means a new settlement tomorrow. That's why they sold the land to me—because I'm a trader, and they know *I* know that settlers ruin trade. If there's danger on the frontier, blame the settlers. Settlers! Squatters is the better word. And thieves is a still better. That's what they are —thieves. Licensed robbers! There are thieves in England, but they are not licensed. They're hanged! It took our colonial assemblies to improve on English justice. When a squatter steals land from the Indians, our assemblies pass a law to prove that it was his from the beginning. There were a thousand squatters in the Cumberland five years before the land was purchased from the Indians. And what did Pennsylvania do about it? Licensed them! Connived at thievery, and tried to profit by it! Sold land warrants—deeds for land it didn't own. But in the end, it lost. When the Indians came back, the squatters ran squealing to the government, and Pennsylvania had to send troops to protect its land thieves."

Holden, staring at his clasped hands, saw the knuckles whiten. What Garth said was true, but it was truth so misshaped and distorted to his purpose that it was more false than a complete lie. The Cumberland had been bought and paid for eight years before the Indians came down upon it in the wake of Dunbar's panic-stricken, fleeing army. If the settlers of the Cumberland had begged for help, they got none. They had raised their own militia and stood like a palisade between the savage horror and the eastern towns, while the British Army ran and the Penns clutched their purse strings and the Quakers solemnly debated whether it was not unlawful for a farmer to possess a gun that might be used to shoot the Indian who scalped his children. They had even dared to strike back. Three hundred settlers—less than a tenth of the strength of Braddock's army—had accomplished more than Braddock. They had marched across the mountains and wiped out the Delaware town of Kittanning on the Allegheny. And Garth called them thieves and mocked them! His rasping voice was still denouncing the back-country settlers:

"They're the ones who drive the Indians to desperation. They're doing it again. Colonel Bouquet, how many squatters are there now between the Allegheny Ridge and the Ohio?"

"I do not know. Hundreds. Thousands, perhaps. It is a large country. We do what we can to keep them out, but——"

Johnson's pipe jerked as he nodded:

"Yes, they push in and they push in. They'll not heed the army nor the danger. Those that have been through one Indian trouble are the hardest-headed. They seem to think a massacre is like the smallpox—if they've lived through it once, they are immune."

"They'll find out how immune they are. They've got to be kept out."

"Colonel Bouquet hasn't enough troops to do it."

"General Amherst should give him enough troops," Garth said harshly. "A few companies to drive the squatters out would be cheaper than an army to protect them—when it's too late. That's my opinion. If it is rejected, I wash my hands clean of the matter."

"I hope they stay clean," Chris said, and knew instantly that he had blundered.

Chapter 19

The angry words had set the room on edge. Chris Holden saw the faces turning toward him, surprised, puzzled, disapproving, some of them indignant. Only Garth's expression did not change; his face, now, seemed to wait. But Johnson's changed. The color surged up in his weathered cheeks like blood bubbling underneath the brown-crisp surface of a rare beef roast.

"Captain Holden! Mr. Garth is here by my request. I asked him to give his opinion because he knows the Indians——"

"He ought to," Holden said. "He's blood brother to the Mingoes."

"Watch your words, sir!"

"They're true! I'll repeat them. Garth exchanged blood with the Mingo war chief that sent out the red belts last time—Guyasuta. And his wife is Guyasuta's daughter."

Johnson's voice came coldly through the startled murmur:

"Captain Holden, I assume you know that I am a blood brother to the Mohawks. I assume you know that my wife is a Mohawk."

"Yes, sir. I do. I had no intention to insult you, sir. And"—deliberately, slowly—"I don't believe it's possible to insult Garth. He knows what he's doing. Garth, you've threatened us with an Indian war——"

"Threatened!" Richard Lee made an impatient gesture. "My God, Holden, he but spoke the thought that's been in all our minds."

"It sounded like a threat to me, sir. He's too sure. He knows too much about it. If war comes, Garth, which side will you be on?"

The composure of Garth's face was undisturbed. It was as if the harsh lines in his face were the deep marks of strings that tied his features tightly so that nothing possibly could move them. Deliberately, slowly, Garth said:

"I've killed men for less than that."

"Yes. Much less. Only I believe you prefer hiring it done for you."

"Chris! *Chris!*" He felt Washington's hand grip his shoulder. "Have you lost your senses?"

"No. I haven't. I've just realized how dangerous this man is. I thought, for a while in London, he was just a swindler, but——"

Johnson's fist crashed on the table.

"That will be all, Holden! I'm amazed—amazed, sir. If you can't see that you are doing me and all of us a serious disservice, you should see at least that you're embarrassing your superior officer. You've been drinking, I suppose. There's no other explanation."

Holden's face was fiery as he thrust himself up.

"Sir William——"

"Sit down or withdraw, sir. You've said all we care to hear."

"I don't doubt it!" He leaned toward Sir William, his clenched knuckles on the table. "You'll care less for what I'm going to say. I don't want to embarrass Colonel Washington, and he knows it. He'd be more embarrassed if he thought an officer of his was guilty of concealing information."

"Information?" He heard the relief in Washington's surprised voice.

"Yes. I didn't tell you. I should have, as soon as I got here, but I didn't realize the nature of this meeting. And I wasn't ready. I'm not ready now, but it can't wait. I've been to London——"

"To visit the queen!" Garth's face was quivering with silent laughter.

"I had expected to stay there a year. I came back after five months because I found——"

"A redheaded convict, gentlemen! That's what he found."

"Well, Garth, are you quite through?" Holden saw the distaste and the faint contemptuous amusement on the faces clustering across the table. Garth had discredited him and discredited, as well, whatever he might say. He struck back with a sense of hopelessness: "A red-haired woman makes a good red herring. I admit my error, but I doubt that Garth can understand the reason why I bought her. She was put up for sale on shipboard. That was *his* idea, not mine. He kissed her, and she slapped him. He called for an auction. I outbid him."

"And why did thee do that?" Andrews inquired gently.

"Because I don't like him—I admit that too—and because I can't get used to women being auctioned like mares for a stud lot. You may believe that or not, as you like."

"My God," Fraser blurted, "I believe it! He's that kind of a damn fool!"

The cloud of smoke in front of Johnson's face exploded with his laughter. Jenifer was chuckling. Even Bouquet smiled his tight smile. But the little Quaker was not smiling; his sharp nose seemed to have discovered something that it did not like; his withered cheeks had turned pink. Chris Holden, going on, thought his crude answer had offended the one man who was concerned enough to ask a question.

"I found certain information while I was in London. It was an accident, at first. I wasn't looking for it—I didn't know Garth was in England till the man who handles the affairs of Holden Hundred mentioned him. He said Garth was cutting a wide swath in London . . . making high connections . . . on the way to being one of the most powerful men in all the colonies——"

"So that's my crime," Garth said. "London's a great place for wild talk. Englishmen aren't the cold-blooded, calculating people they're made out to be. They're gullible. Not"—he smiled disarmingly—"that I tried to gull them. Though I think I could have. They're quite certain the Ohio country's paved with gold."

"They must be," Chris said. "I know sixteen London merchants who gave Garth credit on Ohio land——"

"What's wrong with that?"

"Land he doesn't own. Land he claims is not for sale, for settlement."

"We'll see who owns it," Garth retorted, almost amiably. "The rest of your remark just shows how little the real value of those lands is understood. I understand it. The longer the army keeps the settlers out, the better I'll be pleased."

"Go on, Chris." Washington, at least, was interested. "What are you driving at? There are dozens of speculators in these colonies selling land that they've no title to except hope. Including"—wryly—"some of us in this room—if Mr. Garth is right in what he says."

"*Caveat emptor,*" someone murmured.

Chris picked up the words:

"Yes, let the buyer beware. I'm not concerned about what happens to the London speculators. I'm concerned about the use Garth has been making of his credit."

"Captain Holden's curiosity about my business is . . . ah . . . flattering. You'd think he had an interest in it."

"I have, Garth. I find it very interesting—very. You——"

"I'm a trader, gentlemen. At least, I was. I hope to be again. I've used my credit in exactly the same way as a Virginia planter orders bills of goods in London against credit on his next year's crop."

"But in Virginia we grow tobacco. You're planting a strange crop, Garth. Colonel Washington, you asked me what I'm driving at." He plunged. "It's this—someone is stirring up the tribes. Not the Mingoes only, nor the Delawares, but the western Indians——"

"Some of the French traders in the Illinois, yes," Johnson said. "They'll not succeed. The news of the French treaty'll put an end to that. Besides, there's no one who could pull those western tribes together."

"I believe there is someone, sir—Pontiac."

"Pontiac! That's nonsense," Garth said. "Pontiac is one of the best friends the white man has."

"Which white man?" Holden did not wait for Garth to answer. "Mr. Mason said that one of the savages who stopped the survey wore horns. That's the headdress of the Ottawas. What brought the Ottawas east of the Allegheny River, two hundred miles from their own hunting grounds? What interest did they have in the survey? Dunkard's Creek is Delaware and Mingo country. Something's happened when the Ottawas make common cause with a tribe of the Iroquois—with one of the Six Nations. Someone *has* pulled the tribes together. And someone is arming them. *I believe it's Garth.*"

The charge was shocking. Hearing it in words, in his own voice, Holden himself was shocked by the enormity of the accusation. For a moment there was a stunned silence. And then, after the first impact of the words, Chris Holden saw the disbelief come slowly into all the faces. Jenifer cried out incredulously. The tobacco journal crumpled under Carroll's fingers. One after another, all the faces turned expectantly to Garth, still sitting calmly in his place. Garth said, almost mildly:

"It is not true." Then, as if anger lifted him, he lunged up from his chair. He half raised his clenched hands, let them open, dropped them. Hanging, they said eloquently that he had been subjected to a gross indignity. As if he had just realized how gross it was, he burst out hoarsely:

"It's a damned lie!"

"Is it?"

"I said so, and I'll answer for it!"

"Very well." He had not dared to hope that Garth would fight him. "I'm at your service."

"We'll have none of that," Sir William broke in. "You'll not settle private grudges here. Mr. Garth, I consider that your offer is withdrawn. Captain Holden, if you see fit to follow it up later, and I hear of it, I shall be forced to say that you gave provocation—extreme provocation. Thank God I'm not a gentleman to find my honor damaged every time a Huron says I've got a forked tongue or an Onondaga talks about my big feet." Deftly, shrewdly, out of his experience with hotly wrangling savages at council fires, Johnson was easing the unbearable tension. "When I told the Onondagas I was coming with an army to take possession of Detroit, they reminded me that I'd be passing through their country. Warned me to be careful what I stepped on with my broad feet. That's what they called 'em —broad. Now, Captain Holden, I assume you'll have some explanation for this extraordinary conduct?"

"Yes, sir. I said Garth is planting a strange crop." He took the slip of paper from his pocket. "In the last ten months Garth has bought in London twenty gross of hatchets, eighteen gross of sheath knives—scalping knives, they're called in the back country—and two hundred thirty bullet molds——"

"Great God!" Garth cried. "What nonsense!"

"—twenty-seven hundredweight of bar lead, three thousand flints, forty-two hundredweight of powder, and eight hundred sixty-seven muskets."

"Have you finished, Captain Holden?" Johnson asked. "Is that all?"

"No, sir," Chris said. "I don't think so. But that's all I know of."

"Well, Mr. Garth . . ." Sir William waited.

"Am I on trial?" Garth demanded.

"You are not. But I asked Captain Holden for an explanation and he gave it. I'd assume——"

"The explanation is this hothead's jealousy. I never dreamed he'd carry it so far."

"That's no explanation for eight hundred muskets," Washington was saying sternly, "or two tons of powder. How do you explain those figures?"

"I do not explain them," Garth said blandly. "I deny them. My accounts are in my baggage. I can have them here in fifteen minutes; you can look at them and welcome. What more can I do than open my account books to you?"

"Well, Chris?"

"Colonel Washington, no ledger that Garth shows you will contain those figures. He bought the goods—but not in his own name."

"O-ohh! That's it," Garth sneered.

"He was buying in a dozen different names. He shipped freight to a dozen landings along Chesapeake Bay—two dozen, for all I know."

"For all you know?" Washington was grave. "You're not prepared with proof, then?"

"I can prove it if I have time. I came home to prove it. I know where some of these shipments went. I can find out what became of them. I——"

"Then the fact is," Johnson interrupted heavily, "that you have made this accusation without evidence."

"I have the evidence that was available in London."

"Written evidence? Affidavits? Oh, the list!" Johnson waved it away angrily, and Garth took advantage of his intervention:

"I, for one, would like to know how that list was made up."

"Our agent has many connections in London. My father and my grandfather had others. I made inquiry through all of them. They gave me information, a piece here, a piece there——"

"And all of a piece!" Garth said. If, behind the dark mask of his face, he had been shaken for a moment, he was confident again now. "All flimsy nonsense! A monstrosity, made out of whole cloth." Of a sudden he was laughing. "A Boukabekabus, gentlemen! That's what it is. Has any of you seen my monster? You must. Since the trade's been stopped, I have been put to it to keep my men together. They're good men—too good to lose. When the trade's reopened, as it will be someday, I'll have need of them. So I've turned my hand to anything—freight hauling, odds and ends of fur wherever I can find them, speculations in tobacco, lumber, even bond slaves. And I've got a traveling tent show to help pay expenses. I've got a Boukabekabus—a monster straight from Madagascar —made of buffalo hides, barrel hoops, and sailcloth. He's so big he takes two wagons, but he's worth it; the back-country people flock to see him. He reads, writes, and roars. I've been looking for a man to put inside him that knows Latin. D'you know Latin, Holden? Lord . . . if I could hire Chris Holden, he could tell some more of these tall stories. We could add a sixpence to the price and make a cleaning. Oh, this is rich . . . *rich!* Let's hear some of those names I used in London. Let's find out about me! I insist, Sir William. I insist that I be given the means of disproving this fantastic nonsense."

"Holden——"

"On September sixth, last year, Garth ordered forty muskets and two hundredweight of powder from Thorp, Fleming Company."

"False."

"It's Redding Thorp's word against yours."

"And Thorp isn't here!"

"You ordered the shipment sent to one John Armiger at Fredericksburg."

"Never heard of him."

"Ellerby Pollexfen saw the order."

"And Pollexfen's not here either. You took good care, Holden, not to have these witnesses of yours where they could be questioned."

"Mr. Pollexfen can be questioned. He's but gone to Baltimore. He'll be glad to come back; he'll be glad to furnish affidavits. But there isn't time!"

"Oh, naturally not," Garth said.

"This thing has gone too far." But Holden knew that he could not convince these men. He tried again, hopelessly: "Here's one item that Pollexfen could make oath to—on October third, by the ship *Elephant,* Garth consigned another hundredweight of powder and two hundredweight of bar lead to George Sample at Annapolis. He gave the order in his own hand to Ford Talbot in Red Maid Lane."

With complete astonishment, he heard Garth say:

"That's right. I did. I'll help you out with your list, Holden. The totals are fantastic, but I see now where you got your false start. I also ordered from Laurens, Taylor, and Ensley, by East India docks, twenty condemned muskets and a hundredweight of powder to be shipped to Henry Pollins in Conococheague. You know Pollins, Mr. Andrews. He's one of the little traders who lost everything in the last Indian trouble. His credit's gone; he's bankrupt, and his only chance of getting on his feet again is to have goods ready when the trade's reopened. I arranged the purchase for him, and I guaranteed the payment. I helped several small traders who have been less fortunate than I've been."

"Is thee so fond of competition, Mr. Garth?"

136

"I don't mind their kind, Mr. Andrews. They're too small to hurt me. Oh, I'm not so tender! I know what I'm doing. I believe in trade. I've staked everything I've got on trade as the best means of keeping peace on the frontier; and the small trader has his place. Great God, gentlemen! My crime is that I helped a few poor men—to my possible disadvantage. Men who were ruined by the war—men who have been petitioning the Pennsylvania assembly for relief. You know that is true, Andrews. They begged for an indemnity to make good their losses, and they didn't get it. Now——"

"In London," Chris said, "you were hot against indemnities."

"For the big traders, yes. For Trent and Croghan and men like them, yes. But these little fellows—why, they've been reduced to begging for an act to keep them out of debtors' jail—to give them time to pay back the money that they owe for goods destroyed or stolen in the last war. And they haven't got *that*, either. That's what Indian war means to traders —ruin, poverty, and jail! And now *I'm* stirring up the tribes! Now *I* want another war! It's insane! Trouble on the frontier now would wipe me out. I've more to lose than any twenty men that you can name. My God, think of it! My trading store in Pitt's Town is the least of it. What would happen to my station up the Allegheny—to my posts on Beaver Creek and the Muskingum, at Kuskuski and the Scioto towns and Pickawillani?"

There was a murmur of agreement. Holden felt the great relief around the table. Jenifer had gone back to playing with the dicebox. Bouquet picked up a knife and drew the platter of meat toward him.

"Captain Holden," Johnson began coldly, "I consider that your reckless statements——"

But Garth interrupted:

"By your leave, Sir William, a rebuke now would be useless. I appreciate your confidence, but what I want is proof that I deserve it. I want this nonsense stopped! I don't want it coming up five years from now as an excuse for challenging my trading license. I suggest that Holden should be given time to produce evidence. I suggest that he be *ordered* to produce it! When he fails, we'll see what comes next."

"There isn't time," Chris said again. "You know that, Garth." He put his hand into his pocket.

"No. You'll not live long enough to furnish proof——"

"Thanks for the warning."

"—even if you live to be a hundred. You see, now I'm threatening to kill him! Thank God the Indians don't let young hotheads run their councils. If they did, the war belt would have passed before this."

"It *has* passed," Holden said, and flung the blood-red band of wampum on the table.

Chapter 20

The white-hooded wagon with the blue-hooded girl on the seat beside the driver had turned left, off Duke of Gloucester Street, past the red brick Powder Horn. Now, unhitched, it stood between the cudgel platform and the raree-show tent where the Madagascar monster bellowed.

Like the finding of the last piece missing from a puzzle, its arrival in precisely that position gave a pattern and a purpose to the casual arrangement of the other white-topped wagons. It formed, now, the fourth side of a hollow square of Conestogas—like a little village with its own small green.

The men and women huddled there stood quietly, waiting numbly or despairingly or curiously for the thing that was about to happen to them. The poles that Fraser and the Turk had ripped loose from the platform had been replaced. A new sign, lettered hastily with axle grease, was already turning yellow with the dust encrusted on it. The indentured convicts could see only the back of the cloth sign, but the letters showed through faintly. Those among them who knew how to read could puzzle out the letters backward:

PUBLICK SALE
Fine Servants new from England

If they wearied of the fateful sign, or dreaded it, they could watch the man whose face was pocked and shaped and colored like a hatchet pitted with rust. Williamson had taken off his shirt. He was sweating, and the sweat was running down his thickly freckled back in rusty streams. He was crouching over a small anvil, cutting manacles and leg irons off the convicts with a sledge and chisel. And he was not being gentle.

The burly fellow in the remnants of a velvet coat was kneeling by the anvil. The sledge fell. The wrist iron sprang open, and Jack Rundle stood back cursing.

"Ye bloody bowman![1] Ye slit-weasand cully! Ye don't have t' break a man's arm."

He sucked his wrist, licking the raw, ridged place where the sledge had pinched the flesh between it and the handcuff. Williamson swore back at him.

"Save y'r squawllin', ye cheap scourer. I'll give ye cause t' howl. If y'r new master wants ye manacled, I'll see them irons is hot. We got a nice forge here t' warm 'em f'r ye. Happen ye hain't sold, by God, I'll heat 'em so damned hot they'll roast the marrow in y'r armbones."

"He'll sell," Bone said from the wheel where he was leaning. He had a long coiled trail whip in his hand. "There's a plenty overseers c'n use that carcass in their fields." He grinned at Rundle's helpless fury. "When they've wore him out, there'll still be meat enough t' feed a pack o' hounds." He slapped the coiled whip on his leg. "They cut the meat up for 'em with this, Rundle. An' when the dogs are fed, they've got the bones left t' plow under. The gentry likes that kind o' slave. They get their crops worked an' their dogs fed an' their fields fertilized, all f'r the one price. Last about four years, ye will. Six, maybe."

[1] In the jargon of London's underworld, a bowman was a Bow Street runner—a combination of policeman and detective much more feared than the ineffectual town watchmen and thief-takers, and therefore more violently hated. A cully was a bailiff. And a scourer was the lowest kind of a thief, and the word therefore an insult to Jack Rundle who had been a highwayman, a "hightoby."

Bone walked across the grassy square, climbed to the platform, and began haranguing the crowd.

Rundle was still babbling oaths around his welted wrist. Williamson casually dropped the iron sledge on his bare foot. Rundle yelled.

"Get away, ye bastard," Williamson said. "Get back t' y'r corner, if ye want y'r toes. Come on. Next!"

Margaret Dyckett was the next in line. Her husband stood behind her, close, his chained hands holding to her wrist to comfort her. She moved forward fearfully.

"Squat, blast ye!"

"Be easy," Ben begged. "For the love of God, go easy with that sledge."

"I might f'r the love o' Maggie. How about it, Mag?"

She shrank back. Williamson swung the sledge. It brushed Dyckett's breeches. Margaret went down on her knees and laid one arm across the anvil.

There were two clanging blows. The handcuffs clattered on the ground. The wrist chains clashed upon them.

"A'right," Williamson said. "Up on y'r pins. Let's have y'r gam, wench."

Her husband's arm steadied her as she lifted one leg. Williamson grasped her ankle, jerked it, laid it on the anvil. He pulled Margaret's skirt up over the leg shackle. It slid down again.

"Hist y'r dress."

She fumbled blindly at her petticoat.

"Hist it, I said!" With an oath, Williamson seized the skirt and flung it back above her knee, exposing half her thigh. She made a small, soundless gasp. The freckled hand slid down the flesh. She cringed.

"Skittish, hain't ye?" He leered up at her. "The more fun f'r him that gets ye." Then he saw the desperation in Ben Dyckett's face. "Ye would, would ye?" He juggled the sledge, flipped it, caught it by the head. The hickory handle rapped against Ben's shinbone. "Give me another look like that, ye'll get the other end."

He held the handle of the sledge above the girl's bare knee.

"Ye want I should give her a dose of the same? Keep y'r mouth shut then, God damn ye. An' ye keep y'r blasted skirts out o' my way, girl. I might buy ye f'r myself, an' then ye'd have y'r fret f'r nothin'."

The chisel clinked against the leg iron. The sledge fell. Williamson wrenched off the iron band.

"A'right. Let's have the other one."

She wavered and leaned back against her husband as she raised her other leg and laid the ankle on the anvil. She pulled the petticoat clear, almost to her knee.

Williamson swung the sledge in a swift menace toward Ben's shin. Margaret Dyckett drew the skirt up over her thigh swiftly. Williamson laughed.

"Ye'd learn," he said. "Ye'd learn in no time—in a half a night."

Then she stood free of the chains.

"Now," Williamson said softly. "Now, my fine fellow . . ."

The girl watched with terror on her face while the sledge crashed against her husband's manacles. But Ben was a valuable piece of goods. When the irons were off, he was no worse bruised than Rundle.

Bone's face reappeared. He was holding to a corner post and leaning forward to peer down into the square.

"Ain't ye got some ready, Williamson? I can't hold this crowd all day. You, there—you that's got y'r irons off—come up here. Brisk, now! Bustle 'em up, Oeste."

The huddle of convicts stirred uneasily. It began moving toward the gap between the wheels—the tall Purvis boy first, Mrs. Swivens, Jeremy Love, the broad-hipped Lancashire girl, Rundle, and the Dycketts. They moved slowly, stiffly, awkward in the sudden freedom from their shackles. The Lancashire girl slipped and fell and lay face downward on the platform, her legs dangling over the projecting ends of the rough planking, and Bone stooped and hit her with the coiled whip. The blow shaped her torn skirt briefly to her buttocks.

"Get on up here, ye fat bitch!" Bone hit her again as she tried to crawl on knees and elbows. "Williamson! Where in hell's that Hale girl? If the little slut's run off, I'll lace her bloody!"

She had not run off, nor tried to. Bone's eyes found her where she stood, small, desolate, and frightened, holding to one dusty wheel spoke of the farthest wagon, behind the convicts who still waited their turn at the anvil.

"Hidin', are ye? By the Lord, I'll hide ye! Come—an' come a-runnin'."

She could not run. She was numb with terror at what Williamson had done to Maggie Dyckett.

"Ye heard me!" There was sudden fury in Bone's face. "Just b'cause I've favored ye by leavin' the irons off ye, don't try gullin' me. Ye're mine. *Run!*"

She walked toward him slowly. Bone leaned down and snatched her by the arm and swung her by it, up onto the platform. While she stood there, holding her bruised wrist against her breast, he hit her as he had hit Jenny Brenn, across the buttocks. She heard men guffawing.

"Get up front where they c'n see ye." Bone's hand shoved her. "Ye're the bait. Smile at 'em."

She was walking blindly past a barrel with a wooden cover on it. She was standing on the last plank of the platform, and men's eyes were reaching for her. Like hands . . . fingers at the lacings of her bodice . . . Williamson's hands pawing Maggie Dyckett. She tried not to see them. She tried not to think about them. *There's another barrel on the ground there. Think about that.* It was only a part of a barrel. It had been sawed half across, and a board lay on the sawed place. A man sat on an upturned keg and used the barrel for a desk. He had papers spread out on it, and a quill pen and an inkhorn.

"Smile, I told ye," Bone growled, close behind her.

Abby picked out, in the swimming mass of faces, the one face that she could smile at. It was not a kind face. It was broad and red and sweaty and it had hair on it. But it was a woman's. Abby's stiff smile pleaded with it, and the woman began pushing toward the platform. Behind her came a gawky youth who was all sunburned ears, sharp elbows, and hair like a carelessly made haycock.

"Mister . . ." She rapped on the plank at Abby's feet with man-hard knuckles. "Hey, mister . . ." Bone walked over to her. "I'm a-lookin' f'r a girl that's mule strong. Ye got one that's good f'r somethin'? I want one c'n spin an' weave an' tend cows."

"I can." Abby's voice was desperately eager. "I know how to milk cows. I can——"

"Tlhh!" The thick ruddy face turned toward her. It closed like a door against her.

"Ma . . ." The gangling young man poked the woman. "You hear what she said, Ma? She knows how t' do things."

"Ay. I'll warrant. I ain't a-lookin' f'r no fancy woman. When it comes t' that, one girl's same as another. All ye need's a stout back." There was a new gust of laughter. "That wench wouldn't be no good f'r nothin' after a day's hoein'. See here, mister . . . I'm a widow woman, an' I can't afford a lot o' nigras. Only way poor folk c'n crop their ground is t' raise a crop o' brats first. I want t' buy a stout wife f'r my son here."

Abby's smile died.

"Here y'are, ma'am." Bone prodded Jenny forward. "Heres' a wench c'n outwork any mule ye ever seen. Kind an' lovin' as a dove, too. Make y'r son a good affectionable wife, ma'am."

"Aw, Ma!" The son drooled at Abby. "Buy that there one."

"She's been spoke a'ready," Bone said.

"Tlhh! I wouldn't take her as a free gift. She's been free, I'll warrant!" The woman waggled her broad face at Jenny. "I might take this here one, if ye make the price right. Lea' me talk t' this one, private."

"Help y'rself, ma'am. Hunker down there, Jen, so she c'n talk t' ye. Look her over good, ma'am. Can't take chances when ye're buyin' brood mares."

Jenny Brenn crouched down obediently. Bone slapped the coiled whip on the barrel cover.

"Now, then. Now, then, gentlemen, we'll get t' business. We got some fine goods here. The lady wanted a girl that's strong as a mule; she's gettin' one. Now here's a feller strong as two mules." He flourished the whip at Jack Rundle. "Look a' them there shoulders! Look a' that chest! Pull a plow all by himself, he can. Hoe from sunup till sunsettin', an' then tend y'r livestock. Smart, too. Took the Bow Street runners seven years t' catch him. Indentured f'r life, gentlemen! What's y'r pleasure?"

Bids came quickly. Ten pounds . . . twelve . . . fourteen . . . fourteen six.

"By God," Bone swore, "this ain't no five-year indenture. It's life! Ye c'n make it long or short's ye want to."

Rundle went for twenty-two pounds, and the overseer who made the bid said curtly:

"Iron him."

"That'll cost ye extra, mister."

"It will not. I got my own irons. Put 'em on him or no sale."

"A'right. Toss y'r irons up. Pay y'r money to the notary an' get y'r papers." He caught the jangling chains. "Here, Oeste. Take 'em. Take this hightoby down 't Williamson an' see he's well nipped. Now, gentlemen . . ." Bone turned toward Ben Dyckett and his wife. "Here's a young coppersmith'll mend y'r kettles. Times there's no work in y'r fields, ye c'n rent him out an' make a profit on him. Get y'r money back in no time." He touched Margaret Dyckett with the whip. "Offered with this maid of all work. Ye'll find uses f'r her. Who'll start off with twenty?"

"Twelve."

"Thirteen."

"Thirteen pound f'r as handy a pair as ye'll ever see this side Cape Henry," Bone cried. "The girl alone's worth that."

The overseer who had bought Rundle said, "Fourteen."

"Ye may want her," Bone leered, "but ye don't want her the worst way." There was a smothered laugh.

"I'm bidding fourteen for the man. I don't want the woman."

"She's yours, mister, f'r six pounds more."

Margaret Dyckett had moved close to Ben. Her shoulders pressed his arm. Ben's hand slipped out and found her hand and held it.

"For God's sake," he begged. "For God's sake, Mr. Bone, don't sell us apart."

"Ye'd be apart if ye'd been hanged. Fourteen . . . fourteen . . . an' sold t' this gentleman here. Now who says six f'r the woman?"

Maggie Dyckett moaned. She put her hands up to her face and covered it. Bone pulled them down. Abby felt her throat close. Words came crowding out of it. They were useless words. She knew it, but they came:

"It's not right! It's not decent to sell her by herself."

"Shut y'r mouth!"

She saw the overseer's hard eyes. They did not soften, but they watched her.

"Don't buy him alone," she begged. "Please, sir! She's his wife. They're married."

The overseer looked up at Dave Bone coldly.

"You never said they're man and wife."

"They're slaves, ain't they?"

"I'm not breakin' up a family. I'm not takin' the man, neither. I don't like swindlers, mister. Sellin' a man without sayin' his wife's in the lot is swindlin'. You know damn well a man that's sold that way won't be no good. He'll pine worse'n any nigra, an' he'll run off the first chance he gets. I'm done."

He turned away. The crowd shuffled, loosened, murmured. Abby felt Bone's hand close on her arm. It jerked her.

"Get down off o' here." His voice was not loud. He was smothering his fury, choking on the need to smother it before the curious, half-hostile crowd.

His hand spun her. It set all the faces spinning. Margaret Dyckett's face, wet, streaked with tears. Maggie Dyckett whispering: "Oh, thank you! *Thank you!*" Wet voice saying: "Mr. Bone! Don't! Please don't whip her!" Voice full of tears. Streaky and smeared, like the face. Voice hard and crushing: "Ye keep out o' this!" Hand, hard, crushing the face out of sight. The hand had a coiled whip in it.

Here was the edge of the platform. Here was the thick post that held it. Here was the half-naked giant with the shaved head, and the naked head was the same color and the same shape and the same size as the top of the pine post.

"Get on up here, Oeste," Bone said. "Talk to the crowd. Hold 'em. Sell that Purvis boy next. Sell the widow."

Oeste sprang. The shaved head soared past her, and it was as if the post itself had suddenly leaped up. It sickened her. Where the giant had stood there was the ground between the wagon wheels, a long way down. She reached out to the post and clung to it.

"Get down!" Bone put his hand against her back and pushed. She fell, and as the distant earth came toward her she felt her dress catch and tighten and she thought: *It's trying to hold me.* Then she heard it tear.

She fell face down between the wheels, into the dusty grass. *Not so far,* she thought. *It wasn't as far as it seemed to be.* But perhaps it was. Her dress was falling a long way. It took the torn petticoat a long time to catch up with her body. She felt it settling down upon her slowly. It felt like a gentle warm wind. When the dress had finished falling, she could still feel the intimacy of the sun and wind upon her—on the back of her leg and in the hollow of her knee and on her thigh. The moving warmth stroked her flesh and she thought of Maggie Dyckett and the rusty-hatchet-faced man. She huddled herself tight against the earth.

Hard hand on her arm again, squeezing the flesh, pinching it between the sharp chisels of fingernails and the slim bones inside the arm. The hand jerked her up and thrust her, dragged her through the narrow space between the wheels into the small square walled in by the wagons and the tent. The square was empty now except for the anvil and the pile of chains, and Williamson was sitting on the anvil. Hard voice:

"Truss this bitch up. Tie her to the wagon tail there."

For once Williamson's obedience was eager. This was something that he was prepared for. He was pulling thin cords from his pocket. The first cord bit deep into her wrist. It dragged her arm up, over her head.

Hard hand in the hollow of her back. It pushed her toward the wagon, and the slanting tail gate came against her face and pushed her head back.

The cord flipping over the iron hook in the blue-painted, faded, dirty tail gate. Freckled hands tying it there, jerking. Thin cords biting deep into her other wrist. Both arms dragged up now, straight up and strained and tingling-numb. Her toes only touching the ground and her body hanging from her bound wrists, and again the intimacy of the warm wind on her flesh—the stir of air as Williamson stood back from the last knot, the wind of his quick motion fanning through the long rip in her dress and running up her body.

Fingers on her shoulder now. On her left shoulder. Knuckles, hairy, scratching her skin. And the fingers knotting, bulging into her. The fist jerking with a sudden savage eagerness.

The blouse and the bodice tore together. The sleeve tore away. She felt the air, cool on the moist skin, and then sun, warm, warmer.

The warmth crawled down into the deep curved hollow of her back. She was naked to the waist.

She pressed herself against the wagon. Tried to hide herself against it, but the wagon was too high. Only her face and her shoulders touched the slanted tail gate. Emptiness slanted away underneath it. She arched her body into the concealing emptiness.

"Ay, cringe," Bone said. "Much good that'll do ye. Ye'll curl when ye feel this!"

There was a thump somewhere behind her. There was a voice, anxious. Jeremy's voice. *Mr. Bone . . . Mr. Bone . . . not her!* Jeremy had jumped down from the platform. *As one gentleman to another, Mr. Bone, sir, not the whip for that sweet back.* Another thump—a longer, sprawling noise. Bone had struck the old man. He had knocked him headlong.

"Tom! Keep that he-polly-parrot till I get around to clippin' his wings —an' his tongue. I'm sick of his damn mealy mouth. He's got too much mouth an' too much guts. By God, we'll make guts of him! Put him into that damn Boukabekabus thing, Tom. He c'n use his gab there. Hey, Love . . . d'ye talk any foreign lingo?"

Jeremy retched. He spat, and the sound was sputtery, as if some of his teeth were gone or hanging loose. He said faintly, rapidly:

"Pax vobiscum anno domini . . ."

"A'right. Talk it, then. Williamson, ye have him listen to that other bugger's jabber, an' then shove him in. See't he gives 'em a good gab. See't he bellers good an' loud. If he don't . . . He will."

"God damn it," Williamson said.

"Get goin'. I c'n tend to this piece without none o' y'r help. No-o-ow . . ." Bone dragged the word out, tasting it. "No-o-oww . . ."

The whip coils flopped into the grass. He began to drag the long lash through his fingers.

With her face pressed against the worn boards of the tail gate, Abby could see Bone's arm moving backwards, drawing the whip through the rustling grass. She could see it with her eyes closed.

"Now, ye little slut!"

The swift slashing whisper of the whip through the air and the swift slashing pain across her back arrived together.

The sound and the pain crowded into her ears at the same time and her ears rang, and they crowded into her throat at the same time and choked her, and her body curved itself into the hollow dimness underneath the wagon.

The whip followed her there.

Chapter 21

In the Apollo room Chris Holden had the most of the long table to himself. He sat on the edge of it, alone, his legs crossed and one long leg swinging, while he cracked nuts with the hinged lid of a pewter tankard and wondered how much longer these men could endure the sound of their own voices.

He held the tankard on his thigh and let the broken shells fall mostly anywhere. Now and then, when he thought about it, he brushed some of the brown dust and the bits of hickory and walnut fibers off his waist-coat. And every now and then he turned the pewter tankard upside down, quite carefully, and added more shells to the litter on the floor.

The mess that he had made there pleased him. Somebody else would have to clean it up. It wasn't his floor. It was Wetherburn's floor. All a man got, when he tried to clean up messes, was a lot of trouble. He had learned his lesson. From now on he intended to stay clear of trouble—most particularly other people's trouble.

The talk had been going on for upwards of an hour now, Lee and Washington and Carroll, Jenifer and Andrews, Barclay and Bouquet and Fraser in a circle around Johnson. And Garth! Garth was one of them. He had the devil's own gall and knew how to use it. When he spoke, they listened; and Bouquet and Johnson were still treating him as if they owed him an apology.

The talk, too, went in circles. *Fraser should have given the alarm at once.* . . . No. Johnson didn't think so. It was a matter for the Indian Department, he had said, and Chris Holden noticed Bouquet's grimace at Sir William's instant, jealous grasping for authority. *The forts must be warned.* . . . Bouquet answered stiffly that the garrisons were constantly alert. *The settlers, then.* . . . No. Johnson spoke again of panic. Any sign of weakness, he repeated, would increase the danger.

And now, for the third or fourth time, Washington was saying something about reinforcements. *At least reinforce the small forts.* Bouquet shrugged. Reinforce them with what? A detachment had been ordered to Detroit—Lieutenant Cuyler and a hundred Royals and Queen's Independent Rangers with a convoy of provisions. The only other troops he had, Bouquet said, were the remnants of the Highlanders sent up from Cuba —two skeleton battalions of men who were but skeletons themselves, worn out in the long siege of Havana, decimated in the final storming, wasted now by fever. They could reinforce a hospital, he said, but not a fort three hundred miles away across the mountains. In four months, perhaps . . .

The walnut caught between the tankard's rim and lid crushed under Holden's hands. The flying pieces pattered on the floor. *Good God . . . they're letting Garth hear that! They're telling him the frontier can't get help till August!* What Martin Garth had heard in the last hour, he thought, had given him a weapon deadlier than his eight hundred muskets. *When the tribes hear that . . .*

Holden set the tankard down. The lid, he saw, would never fit again. And Chris Holden, he thought savagely, would never fit this company again.

Even with the war belt in their hands, these men had not believed him. He had, suddenly, a feeling that they had not listened to him—that they had been listening *against* him.

They had not wanted to believe him. He could understand that. He understood now a great many things he had not even thought of a few hours ago. It was less unpleasant—and much less unreasonable—for these men to believe that Christopher Holden, on the loose in London, had become enamored of a worthless woman and let jealousy destroy his judgment than to believe that Martin Garth was guilty of a cold-blooded and inhuman crime.

The Garth they saw was a man of their own kind—mature, strong, self-controlled, respectable, successful. He was not a gentleman, but Washington and Lee and Jenifer and Carroll would not be the ones to blame a man for his beginnings. They would lean over backward to be just to him. And they could understand Garth's lust for land: it was a lust they shared. They could comprehend his towering ambition: it was an ambition that the Calverts and the Penns had realized. A proprietary carved out of the wilderness was no fantastic notion; it was not, in fact, much more fantastic than the dreams of the Ohio Company. They could admire and even envy the shrewd skill, the patience and the boldness with which Garth had wangled land deeds from the Indians. He had actually strengthened his position with the gentlemen of the Ohio Company by his challenge to their titles. The Virginians would lean still farther backward to be scrupulously just to the man who threatened to defeat their own ambition.

Johnson, too, could comprehend Garth. In many ways their lives ran parallel. Both had come from small beginnings. Both had dared the wilderness and wrested success from it. Johnson, too, was a landholder—one of the greatest in the colonies. He had been a trader; there were rumors that he still was, secretly, behind the names of others. And he had his own strong appetite for power. For years now he had fretted under the superior authority of Amherst and the army; he had pulled strings endlessly to set himself up as head of a new Indian department that would supersede the army. He had married a bond servant. He had mingled his blood with the Mohawks. He had taken Indian women: it was whispered that he was the father of a hundred half-breed children. And a Mohawk girl was Lady Johnson now. This man would see, in what Garth had admitted doing, only a man's natural desires and a shrewd trader's judgment—a quite admirable mingling of good business with much pleasure.

And the Pennsylvanian, Andrews, was a part and product of the Quakers' principles and policies. His thoughts were colored by dislike of force—and it was an aversion that extended even to the symbols of force, to militia uniforms and log forts. It was also an aversion that saved money. He was one of those who had left Pennsylvania's frontier defenseless, refused help to Forbes and Braddock, even given up the Allegheny Valley and the Forks of the Ohio rather than spend money on stockades and men to hold them.

And all of these men—Quaker, planter, soldier, merchant, politician, and land speculator—had one thing in common. All of them feared trouble on the frontier.

Holden knew now that everything he said had outraged them. They had not wanted to be made uncomfortable. If what he said was true, it meant that Johnson's work as Indian commissioner had failed; it meant that he had suffered an enormous personal defeat. It meant almost as much to Henry Bouquet, responsible for holding the frontier but not prepared to hold it. And to Andrews it meant that the Quaker policy of compromise, delay, and penny-pinching had failed yet again. Nehemiah Andrews would receive a cold reception if he went back to his colleagues with news that another Indian uprising was about to burst upon them. They would act as if he had somehow betrayed them, as if he were an apostate.

It seemed to Holden that now, for the first time, he was seeing the breadth and the depth of the gulf that separated the tidewater cities and plantations from the frontier. For the first time he was seeing the vast web of ignorance and selfishness and carelessness in which the problem of the frontier was entangled. For the first time he was seeing the inextricably complicated pattern of men's motives—seeing how birth and wealth and comfort and tradition and experience, ambition and self-interest and politics and even honest principles had pulled and plucked at these men's minds and warped them.

There was something outrageous and indecent in the spectacle of these tidewater gentlemen and politicians solemnly debating life and death for others. They found it so easy to put all the blame upon the little settlers, to agree with Garth and Johnson that the squatters building their one-room log cabins in an empty wilderness were responsible for bringing on the danger of a new war. It was true; but it was only partly true, and therefore false as hell.

Johnson with his Indian grants, Garth with his twelve million acres, and the gentlemen of the Ohio Company with their half million—all these men with their great gaudy dreams—condemned the little man who dreamed of owning fifty acres and would risk his life to get them. It was easier to blame the settlers than it was to blame the men who let them come—the royal ministers who granted lands that were not theirs to grant, the colonial politicians who winked at settlement on lands they had not bought, the British politicians who were too far away to know or care and who clung to their jobs by shaving shillings off the taxes of the English merchants and landholders and would not give Bouquet enough troops to keep the settlers out or Johnson enough money to deal with the Indians in the one language that was useful—presents. They were as guilty, in their way, as Garth.

And if the settlers shared the guilt, they were the ones who paid the penalty. If squatters helped to bring on Indian war, they brought it on themselves. They paid for their guilt in blood and fire and torment. The others who were guilty did not pay; they only blamed and criticized.

Not one of these gentlemen, excepting Washington, had ever seen a massacre. They hadn't seen McCord's Fort when the Delawares had finished with it, nor McConnellsburg, nor Granville. They didn't have the faintest notion what it was to be a settler west of the Blue Ridge—to wake and eat and plow and sow and reap, and make love even, with death not a dim remote thing that must happen sometime in the far-off future but a thing that waited behind any stump or brush pile or crouched in the laurel by the spring behind the cabin or dug under the sill log at night and came in. . . .

He slid off the table, his heels crunching in the littered shells, and walked over to the map and stood there, staring at it, seeing things that were not on it.

The tidewater country was like a great broad shelf hung on a wall. The high wall was the Allegheny Mountains. And the shelf now was weighted down with towns and people. It was cluttered with brick houses and great manors, with furnaces and mills and warehouses and fat lumbering coaches; with women who fattened out their hips with hoops and their behinds with bustles; with mellon-bellied little merchant-politicians like the Quaker, Andrews, and thick-bellied and ambition-swollen politicians like Sir William Johnson, and with ignorant crowds that thought an Indian was some kind of freak and laughed and hooted at him.

For a hundred years now civilization had been piling its accumulated litter onto the broad shelf of the tidewater. The load had become too heavy. The shelf was being wrenched loose from the wall by its own weight. The tidewater country—the safe, settled, comfortable east—was being separated from the frontier. It was being separated from the rest of the whole continent. *And I don't gave a damn. I don't give a damn if the whole tidewater slides into the ocean. There's nothing here I want. John Fraser's right. I don't belong. I'm finished with it, and I'm getting out.*

Instantly his mind protested. It had made no such decision. This was the life he had been born to. These men—the Virginians and the Marylanders, Lee and Washington and Carroll, Jenifer and Barclay—were his kind of people. He was like them, he had been born to be like them. They had stood for everything he had looked forward to possessing and to being—for broad lawns and pillared houses, sangaree in silver goblets, loo and hazard, race days and hunt breakfasts, comfort, dignity, and broadcloth and brocaded waistcoats and silk-damask walls and lovely gracious gaily laughing women. He had planned Crisscross plantation in the image of their ample manors. He had even planned himself in their own image.

His mind did not want to leave this world in which he had been born. His mind did not want to exchange this pleasant, leisurely tidewater for the restless west, for the unstable, dangerous frontier. It was not reasonable that a man should find more peace and comfort there. It was not reasonable that he should feel a stranger here, that he should feel homesick for the wilderness where he had never actually had a home but only rain-sopped tents, or half-faced brush shelters, or his blankets wrapped around him underneath the sky, or at the most a cabin. He had never seen, on the frontier, a woman he had wanted. He had seen one here. . . .

Now, suddenly, he had a feeling that the land he knew had cast him out.

He did not wish to stay. But he had no desire to go back to the wilderness. The decision to go, he realized, was not actually a decision. It was, rather, the discovery of a conviction that had been there for a long time. He knew now that his sense of being different from these tidewater gentlemen was not a sudden thing. It had been growing imperceptibly for years. One by one, the ties that bound him to this way of life had been cut or broken or had simply frayed and disappeared. His mother's death, and then his father's. The knowledge that Holden Hall was his home only at the pleasure of his older brother. And his brother's furious pursuit of gaiety and women—and, finally, of one certain woman. He thought now that Diana had been the last of all the ties. What Fraser had said to him was true. He did not belong here. He belonged across the mountains, on the frontier. *Did he? Would John Fraser still believe that?*

Fraser had counted on him to convince these men that the frontier was in great danger. He had not convinced them. He had bungled. He had not behaved with the forthright directness of a man like Fraser; he had behaved exactly like a strutting actor in the theater on the governor's palace green. John Fraser had expected him to be a weapon—and he had turned out to be about as useful as a plantation dandy's dress sword. *Flat on your face again. . . .* John Fraser, who made rifles, had no use for ineffective weapons, for a rifle that you couldn't trust, for men who bungled things. It would not be surprising if John Fraser felt the same scorn for Chris Holden now that he felt for Major Walters and Lieutenant Gordon, Captain Steele and Arnold.

Holden was aware of a lost feeling—a sense of belonging nowhere. As if, trying to be a backwoodsman and a gentleman at the same time, he had ended up by being neither. Behind him—a long way behind him, it seemed —he heard Garth saying:

"There may be no danger, but I've got thirty men in the Ohio country —traders, pack-train drivers. I would like to warn them. The forts should be warned too."

"They have been warned." Bouquet's voice sounded prickly. "They have had many warnings."

Good God, he thought, *they're back to that again.* Talk . . . talk. Higgle . . . haggle . . . hmm . . . well . . . yes . . . no. Words. *Words!* A rank thicket of words, overgrowing and concealing the plain trail of facts, and men thrashing through it blindly, wandering in circles, getting nowhere. And now Garth's voice again, dry and breathy, like the sound of moccasins moving cautiously and slowly over dry leaves:

"I am not a soldier, but I do not see what harm can come of warning them again."

Chris Holden thought: *Garth said that once before . . . at least once before.* He was not sure how often Garth had said it. He had not been listening. But he thought that Martin Garth had been deliberately complicating and confusing these men's thinking—leading the talk around and around and bringing it back again and again to the same futile place. It was a trick that Indians used to delay pursuit by doubling on their trail, traveling in circles and crossing their own tracks again and again until whoever was pursuing them could not tell which track was the fresh one. And Bouquet was off now on the old track:

"You are not a soldier, no. But I am. It is not all guns and fighting. It is morale also. The men in the western posts are Royals. They are not—how do you say?—greenhorns. Would you require to be warned to be alert if you were at Le Boeuf, a hundred miles from nowhere, in the midst of Indians? No. You would be irritated. You would think that your commanding officer did not trust you. You would think he was a fool, and nervous."

"A sound logic," Washington said dryly.

"I am glad that you agree."

"I don't."

Bouquet looked bewildered.

"Men will be careless even with their lives, sir," Washington said. "I have found too many sentinels scalped, mornings, to believe that there can be too many warnings."

Bouquet answered stiffly:

"The posts will not be taken by surprise. And if not by surprise, they cannot be taken."

"I can take them," Chris said, without turning. He was still staring at the map, at the little dots like flyspecks in the maze of streams and ridges. The dots were forts. There were not many of them. One sluggish fly could have made them all in a few minutes, crawling. And some of the dots had no more meaning than so many flyspecks. They marked nothing but the places where forts had been when the map was made. Granville —burned and taken. McCord's—burned and taken. Loudon—empty, long abandoned. Shirley—not a fort at all, a trading station. Prince George— lost before it could be finished. Even Fort Necessity was still there on the map. It made him want to laugh and cry and swear at the same time. The high hopes and the high adventure and the heartbreak. Folly and futility and failure. "Washington's rabbit trap," people used to call it. And some of the new forts were not much better. He turned to the clustered faces:

"I could take Venango or Le Boeuf with twenty men." The faces disapproved of him. "That goes for Redstone and Sandusky too. I could take Presque Isle with fifty—and I don't mean rangers. I mean Indians. Any Indians. Catawbas, even. But that's not the point. Colonel Bouquet, you say the forts have had repeated warnings. Why? What kind of warnings?"

A slow flush was creeping up into Bouquet's face.

"To be alert," he said with a hard-held politeness.

"Is that all? I thought you said that kind of warning only made men nervous. It's eighty miles from Fort Pitt to Venango. It's forty-six miles farther to Le Boeuf, and a hundred fifty more to Fort Sandusky. That's a long way to send messengers with warnings to be alert"—he picked up Bouquet's language—"many warnings."

"You question my word?"

"No, sir. I don't mean to be disrespectful, Colonel, but there's something I don't understand. I was in command at Fort Venango for eight months. I was sent up there in December, 1760, with a platoon of the Virginia regiment—a sergeant and ten men. I got a lot of messages in those eight months. Orders about buying deer meat from the Indians. Orders about how to make out sick reports. I even got an order about how to feed hogs! But I didn't get one message warning me to be alert."

"It was not necessary," Bouquet said.

"But it is now?"

Bouquet did not answer. The flush had ebbed out of his cheeks. It stayed, a rim of bright pink, just above the outline of his jaw, as if he had settled his chin into the high collar of his tunic.

Holden saw Washington's eyes, blue and sharp as steel now, watching Bouquet's face; and he knew that Washington, too, was trying to pick up a trail. The blue eyes traveled from Bouquet to Johnson.

"I'd like to hear the answer to that question," Washington said. "We'd all like to hear it."

Sir William Johnson's face looked thick, thickened somehow, as if the blood underneath the surface of his roast-beef cheeks was welling up and pushing on them. The Indian commissioner had his pipe clenched in his teeth and his mouth clenched around the stem. When he spoke his tone was heavy with sarcasm:

"I suppose it is exciting for a young man to have war belts in his pocket. I suppose it makes him feel important. I have felt that way—when I was younger. Captain Holden is just back from London. Doubtless he has been to theaters and seen plays. It is good play-acting to throw war belts on a table. I am afraid we were a disappointment to him—Colonel Bouquet and I. We were not surprised enough to suit him. If we had been surprised, there would be good reason for excitement. It would have meant that both the army and the Indian Department are blind. We are not blind. I apologize for pricking Mr. Holden's bubble, but . . ."

Sir William hesitated. The smoke from his pipe thinned to a straight wisp that climbed toward the ceiling like a blue thread being unwound from a bobbin, being pulled off. When he spoke again, his voice sounded as if what he said was being pulled out of him against his will:

"This isn't the first war belt that has passed. They have been passing since November."

Lee cried out incredulously. Barclay's teeth bit through the stem of his long clay. He took the broken piece out of his mouth and looked at it. John Fraser said *Christ!* very softly. Jenifer was fumbling at his pocket. He pulled out a blue watch.

"Since November," Lee said. "Five months." He held the words and looked at them the way Barclay looked at his snapped pipe. Daniel of St. Thomas Jenifer was looking at his watch and then at Johnson with the same incredulous expression.

"We've been here for two hours and you didn't tell us. You didn't mention it till now. Why?" Jenifer's face reddened. "In God's name, why?"

"It is official information. This is not an official meeting. I considered it improper——"

"Christ!" Fraser said again, not softly. "Jesus Christ . . . *official!*" He pushed past Sir William Johnson and snatched up the war belt. "This here belt ain't official neither. It's got ribbons on it. Red ones. But it ain't official if it ain't got red *tape* on it!" He stuffed the band of wampum under his coat quickly. "I'm gettin' out of here! I'm goin' back to the Kuskuski path an' find the Ottawa that was deliverin' it. I sort of feel obliged to tell him he ain't dead. Officially, he ain't."

Washington said quietly:

"Sit down, John."

"Set, hell! There's been too God damned much settin'." Fraser's face worked as he looked from man to man around the circle. "Settin' like a flock o' brood hens. Like a flock o' squawllin' peahens. Come along, Chris. You an' me are hittin' for the mountains. We're go'n' to tell a lot o' people that they'll be dead pretty soon but that they ain't to mind it. It won't hurt 'em. *It won't be official!* By the time these peahens hatch out somethin', there won't be no forts left, nor no settlers neither. We're go'n' to warn 'em, an' if any peewit of a peahen tries to stop us . . . Are you comin', Chris?"

"Yes. I'll meet you at the wagon."

"If you ain't there in half an hour, you won't. I got a wife in Pitt's Town. I ain't waitin' for nobody." He lunged to the door. It slammed behind him.

"You see?" Johnson asked. "You see why we cannot talk about these matters. But that does not mean we have done nothing."

"Just what has been done?" Lee asked him.

"We are calling all the nations to a council. The western tribes as well as the Six Nations."

"When?"

"In July. We must wait until General Amherst——"

Chris Holden felt sick. Anger swept him. It was such an anger as he had not known before—a violent upheaval of disgust and outrage and contempt that was like a surge of nausea inside him. His insides felt as if John Fraser's whisky and Blount's rum had curdled in him and were coming up and he could not control himself. If he could, he wouldn't. The mere prospect of relief was a relief. He was walking toward the table, hurrying, half running, as a sick man hurried when he had to find a basin to be sick in. Words came, hot and bitter. He could taste them:

"Stop this nonsense! *Stop it!* Do you think you've got all summer? I raised hell with Fraser for not showing that belt to Ecuyer. I raised hell with him for wasting two weeks bringing it across the mountains. Two weeks! *And you've wasted five months!*" He lifted clenched fists to Sir William's face. "Wait . . . wait . . . you've got to wait! Have you ever seen a woman staked out naked with fire burning on her belly? I have. *She* knew what waiting meant. It wasn't a big fire. It burned a long time. Time . . . *time!* Do you know what time is? It's lives—other people's lives, not your life! Have you ever seen a man that had been buried to his neck and roasted, with a slow fire two feet from his face, until his eyes boiled in his head and bursted? I have."

He saw Johnson's face beyond his clenched hands. Johnson's face was sweating. It looked like roast beef with a thin gravy on it.

"They had cut his lips off. They had cut his tongue out. They had stuck his tongue up on a green stick just in front of him so he could watch it cooking. He could see it till his eyes boiled and ran over. Like that. . . ." Holden put one finger on the sweating face and drew it downward through the sweat and made a streak there. "Like that."

Then he wiped the finger on his waistcoat. It would not get dry. His whole hand felt wet. When he looked down at it, curiously, he saw his own sweat strung like beads of wampum on the black hairs of his wrist and knuckles. The edge of his cuff was damp. The lace hung there limply.

He felt like the wrist lace, limp, damp, all the starch gone out of him. All the anger had gone out of him now too. It had left him drained and empty and he felt ashamed, the way a man felt when he had been sick in public. It was a God's wonder that Sir William Johnson had done nothing and said nothing when he laid his finger on the sweating face and made a streak between the pouched eye and the big mouth. *I oughtn't to have done that,* he thought. It was a thing a gentleman did not do. Or if he did, he made amends as soon as he was sober.

Chris Holden was completely sober now. But he had no desire to make amends. It was a curious thing. Then he remembered that he had decided he was not a gentleman.

But there was something else that was more curious than Johnson's silence or his own reluctance to apologize. The talk had stopped. These men were looking at him with a kind of sober stillness in their faces. But there was no disapproval in them. He began to realize that this time they had listened to him. His crazy outburst of unbridled anger had been more convincing than all he had said when he was trying hard to keep his self-control.

"Was that why you left the frontier, Captain Holden?"

He could not believe that he had heard the question. He could not believe that Washington had asked it. He said stiffly:

"No, sir. It was seven years ago, at Granville."

"You've remembered it a long time."

"You don't forget a thing like that."

"How old were you?"

"Eighteen."

"You were not a captain then?"

"I was a private."

"And you stayed on the frontier? You continued to serve with the rangers?"

"Yes, sir."

"You were wounded, I believe."

"Yes." *God's teeth!* What the devil was he driving at?

"More than once?"

"Three times, sir."

"If my memory is correct, you were promoted sergeant after the attack on Cumberland, and ensign at the Loyal Hanna. You commanded the Virginia rangers in the massacre on Grant's Hill. And you managed to get most of them out. Colonel Bouquet thought that you should be a captain. He entrusted you with the command of Fort Venango."

"Yes, sir."

"While there, did you send me a report?"

"Yes."

"Do you recall what was in it?"

"I said Venango couldn't be defended if the Indians attacked in earnest."

"Did you say that you intended to surrender?"

"No, sir. I said if I thought that an attack was coming, I did not intend to wait for it. I said I would try to stop it."

"Hmm. You would try to stop it. May I ask how?"

"The same way Captain Campbell stopped the Hurons and the Senecas the next year." He saw now what was back of all these questions. He did not like what he saw. "Campbell didn't wait five months. He didn't wait five hours. He called a council. He sent out belts on his own responsibility."

"You planned to do that?"

"No, sir. Not to send them. I had no interpreter to go along. It was a thing I had to do myself. I could talk a little of their language. I was going to go myself. I'll go now." He had not meant to say it. He had said it. "If you'll send belts now, I'll take them."

"Good man, Chris! I thought you'd say that. Well, Sir William . . . there's your answer. Is there any possible objection?"

There was.

"We have no belts here, sir."

"They've been made in Williamsburg before this. They can be made here and Captain Holden can be off in three days. He can be at the Forks of the Ohio by the time you could reach either Croghan or Sir Jeffrey Amherst. The Nemacolin path . . ." Washington let the sentence go unfinished.

"One man is not enough."

"There's Fraser. He was living with the Delawares before the French came in."

"No," Holden said. "Not Fraser. Fraser's married. But there's . . ." Over Johnson's shoulder, Martin Garth was looking at him blandly. "I can find the men."

"I'll be glad to help," Garth offered. "I have several men here and a dozen more in Pitt's Town. They're at your disposal. So am I, Sir William. After all, I have some standing with the Senecas and Hurons—with all the Ohio nations. I can be in Guyasuta's town in ten days and on the Muskingum in a fortnight." He shrugged. "If you care to trust me."

"Thank you," Washington said bleakly. "In the circumstances, I believe it will be better to use men who are under military orders. You agree, Sir William? Captain Holden will be called back into active service."

Johnson hesitated and then nodded.

"That man Fraser, too," Bouquet said. "We can't have him talking. He is still in the Virginia militia? Good. Good. You will see to it, Colonel Washington? Now, Captain Holden——"

"Your pardon, Colonel Bouquet." Garth was deferent, apologetic. "In the circumstances . . ." He put no emphasis upon the words that Washington had used; but, using them, he changed their meaning. "I ask your permission to withdraw, Sir William. I shall be in town for some days." He was bowing. "Gentlemen, your servant."

They were silent, watching him until the door closed. Daniel of St. Thomas Jenifer swore softly.

"Holden," he said, "if you're right about that fellow . . . It's incredible. You can't be! But right or wrong, sir, I don't envy you!"

Chapter 22

Bone had started auctioning the bond slaves about half after three. It was four less a quarter when Garth came out of the Raleigh, murmuring apologies to the gentlemen he jostled on the broad steps, and cut across the Powder Horn square toward the clamor of the barkers.

The sale looked to be going well. If Bone had lined up all the convicts on the platform as he had been told to do, the most of them had been sold off already. There was still a good crowd. But he could not hear it bidding. He could not see Bone.

The raffish slut in gin-stained finery was standing on the barrel, flirting the soiled ribbons of her cap and swiveling her hips. Only a few of the men were watching her. Even they were not much interested. They had the look of men who were waiting for something. There was a kind of listening look about the crowd.

Bone knew better than to let that London tattersheet parade herself. Not a man in Williamsburg would have the gall to buy the woman now. The only way to sell that sort of trull at a tidewater fair was to fright the drab soul out of her until she looked abused and humble and half decent. Bone could have managed it; he knew how. But he had lost a sale now; he was giving up. A hand seized the Swivens woman's arm and dragged her off the barrel, and Garth saw beyond her the eeled pigtail dangling from the naked slab of Oeste's head.

Garth's mouth folded inward. His lips, for a moment, were a white welt. He damned Bone in a luxury of anger that he had denied himself for two hours.

But it was a luxury that he could not afford yet. Someday . . . He elbowed his way through the crowd and swung himself up by the corner post.

"Where's Dave?"

Oeste's broken teeth showed through his grin.

"Down there."

"Why?"

"Dave don't like public time. He's havin' his fun private."

Garth ran across the platform. He came to the edge of it in time to see the third weal sink into the bare back of the girl tied to the wagon. The mark of the whip was a white crease across her flesh. And then, as the lash flopped down into the grass, the crease reddened and began to swell.

That lash mark wasn't where Dave Bone had meant for it to be. It was lower down than he'd intended. The whip had taken her across the slimming hollow of her back, above the waist string of her petticoat. If he'd realized how small she was, he would have tied her higher, he'd have swung her right up off the ground by her two arms and let her kick. Bone watched her while he laid the lash out on the grass behind him, getting it just so, enjoying it. She was a little thing, but she was made nice. If he wanted to, he could whip that skirt right off her. He could break the string of it with one good slash. She had nice legs. That would be the way to whip her proper. He could see what he was doing.

He lifted his arm slowly. The lash crawled a little way and hung. He licked his lips.

"Ye little bitch. Ye'll find out who's master."

Garth sprang down. His hand caught the whip.

"It's time you found out, Dave."

The jerk of the whip pulled Bone around. Garth stepped up close to him.

"You fool! Loose her."

"She spiked a sale."

155

"Loose her, I said."

Bone went sullenly to the wagon. Even after she was free the girl stood huddled to the tail gate. One hand clutched the bodice to her breast. The other tried to pull the torn blouse up to cover her wealed back.

"Abby," Garth said.

She turned her shamed face toward him and then turned away. Her whole body shook.

"Go into the tent. You can fix your dress there."

She went into the tent blindly.

"Are you out of your head, Dave?"

"You said to gentle her."

"I didn't say to use a trail whip! Don't forget she's mine. Keep your whip off her—and your hands too. There's a hundred people out there. You'd have had her screaming in a minute, and the crowd swarming in."

"Not past Jake an' them."

"You could have started trouble," Garth said. "Holden's here."

"The hell! Has he seen her? Does he know ye've got her?"

"Yes."

"Ye might've thought of that. He lives here, don't he? Why the hell did ye want to land at Norfolk anyhow?"

"Because I've used most of the other Chesapeake Bay landings. I couldn't be sure all the shipments had got through."

"Ye let me take the chance on findin' that out. Lyin'. Usin' other men's names. Signin' 'em to bills of ladin'. Runnin' guns acrost the mountains, past the forts."

"Don't get above yourself, Dave. It wasn't important whether you were caught or not. It isn't now."

"It ain't, huh? I could talk."

"But you wouldn't."

"Ye're damn' sure o' y'rself, ain't ye?"

"I am. And I'm sure of you too. You're in a hole so deep nobody'd pay attention if you yelled."

"Ye're in deeper'n I am."

"But in a different hole, Dave. There's the little matter of Ecuyer's money."

"Ye're in *that* hole, by God!"

"You think so?"

"Ye got y'r share. Steele paid ye. All I got was a hundred."

"I said you were a fool, Dave. Do you think I kept it? If you weren't a fool, you would have done what I did."

"Wha'd ye do?"

"You'd like to know that, wouldn't you? I'll tell you this much—it's in a place where it can be found, if I want it found. And if it's found, there'll be no doubt that Dave Bone put it there."

"God damn ye!"

"There's another thing you might remember. You signed the girl's indenture papers, not I. You sold her to me. That's two hangings you've got coming, Dave—stealing money from Ecuyer's quarters, and selling a bond wench that wasn't yours to sell. I'll keep the rope loose on your dirty neck, Dave, but remember that it's there."

"Ye're more Mingo than ye are white, Garth."

"That's what the Mingoes think. So does Holden. He was at the meeting."

"Yeah?"

"He found out some things in London, and he's guessed more." And then, slowly: "Damn them. They're like children. They're like babies with a sugar tit."

"Who is?"

"Indians. All of them."

"Mean babies," Bone said.

"They've got the brains of children. They've got to have their ceremony. Last time it was the Senecas. This time it's the Ottawas. They had to send out belts! They had to send a belt to Guyasuta—Pontiac to Guyasuta, with both of their signs worked in it. The damned fools!"

"Who knew about it? Holden?"

"Hell's fire, he had it with him! Fraser fetched it to him."

"That damn nosy tinker. I wish Oeste'd killed him."

"I wish to God he had. It was the belt that did the damage. Until they saw that, they thought Holden was a crazy young fool. They were ready to laugh him out of the Apollo. They still think he's a fool—most of them. But they're not laughing. He and the Ohio Company crowd talked Johnson into sending him in to the tribes with peace belts and a call to a council."

"Which tribes?"

"All of them. All that matter."

"That'll take him a while. When's the council?"

"July."

"There ain't no harm in that. Not in July, there ain't."

"There's harm in it if it works. Handling Indians is like handling quicksilver. They like talk. They like presents. They might decide to wait until the council's over."

"If ye're worried——"

"I'm not worried. Holden can be stopped."

"That's right. A lot o' things c'n happen to a man between here an' the Kiskeminetas. A lot o' things c'n happen to him between here an' that graveyard down the street there. I'll see t' Holden. He won't even start."

"You *are* a fool, Dave. That's all it would take—Holden killed a few hours after he attacked me in that meeting. You're like him."

"The hell I am!"

"You both go too fast. Holden overplayed his hand. But if something happens to him in the wrong place, they'll begin believing him."

"Where d'ye want that it should happen?"

"He's going by the Nemacolin path."

"Did he say that?"

"They talked about it."

"Then he ain't."

"Yes. He'll think I'm stupid enough to believe he'll go some other way

157

because the Nemacolin path was mentioned. He's smart. He's halfway smart. That's how he'll go. He'll have someone with him. Fraser, probably. He took the trouble to deny it would be Fraser."

"It could be McCoy an' Lovatt. They're in town. How soon's he goin'?"

"I don't know. I want all of them watched—Fraser and McCoy and Lovatt."

"I'm takin' Holden."

"No. Put Williamson on him. Hesselgart will be enough for those two rangers; where one is the other is, or will be. Let the Swede take Fraser. It would be a waste of your peculiar talents, Dave. I don't want Holden shot. I don't want him stopped—yet. All I want to know is when he goes, and where. If he's ever found dead, I don't want rifle bullets in him. . . . Where's Killbuck?"

"Sleepin' in the wagon—the one other side y'r tent."

"Drunk?"

"Not enough to matter."

"How about Mamaultee? Has he stayed out of town?"

"I ain't seen him. Far as I know he's still in the gum woods where I left him, up beyond Burnt Ordinary."

"He's got to start tonight. I'll talk to Killbuck now."

Garth climbed the front wheel of the wagon. The hood was laced tight in the front. There was only a small opening behind the seat. Crawling through it was like crawling through the low door of an Ojibway wigwam.

An Indian lay on a pile of blankets with the shaggy hide of a woods buffalo thrown over them. He was naked except for his clout and moccasins and the five wide silver bracelets on his right arm.

Garth squatted down beside him. It was not a comfortable position for a man in boots and a tight-fitting coat. The boots cramped his legs behind the knees. The coat bound his arms. His sleeves pulled up and showed a silver bracelet on his wrist. The bracelet was like those the Indian was wearing, split across to fit a girl's wrist or a man's arm or an ankle.

He felt the discomfort in his mind as much as in his legs and arms. It was not a dignified position. Coming from the Apollo room made a difference. Gentlemen did not squat on their hunkers waiting for a naked savage to wake up.

He had a feeling that the Indian was not asleep. It was another of their childish games.

"Killbuck."

He knew then that the Indian had been awake. Killbuck rolled over and sat up and pulled his feet under him in a single motion. The short Delaware crest fuzzed out from his plucked skull like a worn-out clothesbrush. The trade bracelets clashed as he put his hand up to his neck and found the string that went around it. He pulled on the string, and a piece of red cloth flopped down across his shoulder. He smoothed it on his chest. It was cut in the shape of an officer's gorget—like a quarter moon with round horns. It had its own insignia. Instead of the engraving on a gorget, it had a pattern of bear's claws sewed onto it.

The red cloth lay there on his oiled skin like a piece of flannel on a chest that had been greased to cure the croup. But the damned Indian, naked to his clout, with hairs from the buffalo robe sticking to his damp hide and his belly button showing, had acquired a dignity by rolling over and sitting up.

"My brother is hungry?" It was the conventional question, the necessary opening move.

Killbuck passed his hand over his belly.

"Much beef. Go now." He was all for business.

Garth was aware of an old irritation. An Indian, even a chief, got as full of importance out of being full of other people's food as a white man got out of being full of whisky. Holden, for instance.

"Tonight," he said. "Killbuck goes tonight."

"You go?"

"No."

"Killbuck travel many suns. Wait many suns. Mamaultee wait. Guyasuta wait. Wingenum wait. Windahola wait. Pontiac wait. No good."

In the dusty light Garth's face and the Indian's were alike in their lack of expression.

"Can my brother take a message when the thing he is to tell has not yet happened?"

"Long time," Killbuck insisted. "Garth give promise."

"Everything I promised has been done. Can Guyasuta melt the snow and empty the streams? Did Guyasuta make the path smooth? Wagons must have smooth paths. Because the streams were high and the road washed away, it was necessary to use horses without wagons. Many horses. Killbuck knows this."

"Guyasuta want more muskets."

"They are on the way now. And Killbuck must take a message. Listen." It was coming back now—the old habit of speech he had almost lost in London. "Listen, brother. This is the message Killbuck will take to Mamaultee and to Guyasuta. White men come who are not friends to Garth and Guyasuta. Killbuck knows one of these white men. He is the captain who was at Venango—Holden."

"No good."

"Other white men will come with him. It is not decided which ones. Probably the long knife who is called Fire Walking—the ranger with much red hair on his face."

Killbuck grunted.

"Also the one who is always with him."

"Good. Joe. No good."

"Yes. Joe. Also the gunmaker. They are sent to tell lies to the Shawnee and the Caughnawaga and the Ottawa and the Miami. To do this it is necessary for them to pass through the country of the Delaware and Seneca."

"Not go?"

"Mamaultee has his young men with him. It is time for the spring hunting. Nemacolin's path is a good place for hunting."

"Killbuck young man. Watch path."

"No. Killbuck is young man, but he is also a wise man. There are other paths—the Iron Head's road, the Kiskeminetas path, the path to Kittanning. It is best that Killbuck shall go quickly to Guyasuta and then to his own town and bring many young men to watch all these paths."

The Indian stared somberly at nothing for a minute. Then:

"Good. Go now."

"Not yet. When the sun sets. Before many fires are lighted. It is not good if the white men here see Killbuck going."

"Give red coat. Give hat. Look like Catawba." He spat gravely on the buffalo robe. "Garth give."

"All right." The damned mink had been working up to that coat all along.

Garth climbed out over the tail of the wagon and went into the tent. Four trade blankets, hung across a rope, divided the tent into halves. He had a field bed in the back half. Here in the front half there was a pine table with gate legs and a hinged top, made to take up little space in wagons. It was scratched and battered from much loading and unloading, and one edge of it was splintered where some fool—Oeste, probably—had banged it on a rock or on the iron rim of a wheel. There was a wooden bucket with a rope handle and hoops split from saplings. There were two stools. On the table lay part of a loaf of bread and the butt end of a baked ham with a knife beside it.

The girl was sitting on one of the stools, bending forward with one arm on the table and her face on her arm. There was a place on the edge of the table where a splinter had been broken off. She had fastened her torn dress together with it. She had used the knife to fine the splinter. The knife was not where he left it; he had left it sticking in the ham. There was a faint sprinkle of thin shavings in the trodden grass.

"Abby."

She sprang up and backed away from him. One hand went to her dress to hold it. She held to the table with the other.

"I'm sorry I was so long coming," he said. "If I'd been here . . . Bone's a brute."

"You stopped him. Why did you do that?"

"I don't want you hurt, Abby." He moved toward her. "Your back . . ."

"No!"

"Those whips make nasty cuts. They ought to be washed."

"No. I'm all right. It—doesn't hurt. Now."

"They've got to be clean. We can't have them mortifying." He picked up the bucket and set it on the table. He took out a handkerchief and dipped it in the water. "It's clean," he said. "After all, I saw your back."

"No! Please. . . ." She put up her hand to keep him off. There was a broad red weal around the wrist where the rope had dug in.

"At least I can do something about that." He caught her hand and held it firmly. "Must you be afraid of me? I've given you no cause. Oh . . . on the ship. I'm sorry about that. A man doesn't like to be slapped. But if I had bought you, this would not have happened."

He sat on the edge of the table and pulled her to him.

"I wish I'd found out sooner that it was a joke." He dabbed at her wrist with the dripping handkerchief.

"Joke," she whispered. Her mouth quivered. But Bone hadn't taken all the spirit out of her yet. Her eyes darkened to a gust of anger. "You call it a joke!"

"No. Not I. It was Holden said that." He wet the handkerchief again and squeezed it till the dripping stopped. He wrapped the cloth around her wrist and held it. "By the time I found out, Bone had already bought you with the rest."

"Would you——"

"Would I what, Abby?"

"Help me."

"I'll do anything I can."

"Help me get away."

"Getting away wouldn't help you. There's not a town in these colonies big enough to hide that hair of yours. You're a beautiful girl, Abby. You know that. Much too beautiful for——"

"You won't help me?"

"Not to run away. I'd only make things worse for you. Much worse."

"No! They couldn't be!" She shuddered. "Fourteen years. *With him.*"

"He'd find you. The law's not gentle with a runaway. Bone had no right to use the whip on you today. But if you run off and are caught— and you'd be caught—he'd have the right. It's not pleasant, Abby, what they do to runaways. There's such a thing as branding. Let me see your other wrist."

She kept her hand behind her, holding to the dress.

"You can change hands," he told her.

She put the damp hand behind her and held out the other. It was worse burned. In her struggle to escape the whip, the rope had chafed away the skin and left the flesh raw to the quick. Blood lay in dark speckles under it.

"Damn Bone!" Garth wet the handkerchief again and wrung it and wrapped it carefully around her wrist. He took the silver bracelet off his arm and slipped it over her hand and squeezed it small to hold the bandage. His hand held her arm above it. "Abby, there's one way I might help."

"How?"

"I can buy you from Bone. I can try." He pulled her close to him. "I'm not a rich man, but if you want me to——"

"Would you set me free?"

"No, Abby. I couldn't. No one can do that. Holden lied to you. A transported convict can't just be turned loose. A redemptioner, yes. But you're not that. Fourteen years, Abby—they'd be easier with me than with Dave Bone. There'd be no whippings. As for freeing you . . ." He let her wait. "There's only one way a transported girl can be set free. That's if the man who buys her marries her."

Her eyes watched him. They were frightened but he thought they had changed color. They were not so dark now.

"You mean . . ."

Then she was not looking at him. She was looking past him. Garth turned his head and saw the woman standing in the parting of the blanket curtain.

"Hannah!"

She was young. She was not as dark-skinned as most women of the

Seneca, and she was not made like them. She was taller, and she was as slender as this white girl he was holding, and her body under the quilled doeskin was as softly rounded. The two shining braids of her black hair curved over her full breasts. In silk and side hoops, with her hair piled high and powdered, she might pass for a white woman. She would not have a white girl's prettiness; her forehead was too high, her dark brows were too straight, the bones beneath her eyes too strong for prettiness. But even with her hair in braids, and the blue strouding wrapped around her like a tartan, and the absurdity of the short calimanco skirt above the fringed and quill-embroidered leggings, she was a handsome woman.

"I didn't know you were here, Hannah. You should not have come."

She let the parted blankets fall. The gesture that released them was a graceful motion that flowed into the lifting of her hand to the loop of glass beads at her neck. Her eyes, watching him, were not like an Indian's at all —not the small, flint-brown, flint-hard, unchanging eyes. They were as large as Abby's, and they had their own kind of darkness. There was a patience in them and a fire too. He knew how quickly they changed from one to the other. He had tried both her patience and her fire.

"Mamaultee waits," she said. "You tell him not come here. I come."

"I'm sending Killbuck to him."

"Killbuck waits."

God damn it . . . as if that was the only word they knew. *Wait . . . wait.*

"I've talked to him. He's going."

"Not go yet. You promised coat."

He forced the stillness back into his face. He waited now himself till he was sure that it was there.

"That is true. I'll get it." He walked past her to the curtain. With the blanket in his hand, he turned. "That girl has been hurt, Hannah. See to her."

The blanket dropped. They heard Garth leave the tent. Hannah came slowly toward the table.

"White one pretty. Who?"

"A bond slave."

"Slave. I know slave. Garth not look at white one like slave." She touched the bracelet. "His."

"My wrist . . ." Abby held out her other hand. "They tied me." There was something terrifying in those eyes. They were as soft and placid as a dog's. They were as hard as Bone's eyes. "Bone was whipping me. He made Bone stop."

"Why? You not his."

"No."

Hannah repeated the word:

"No!"

With a swift, fierce motion, her hands came to Abby's arm. They were soft. Hard. They were gone again. Hannah was clasping the bracelet on her own arm.

"Who are you?"

"His wife."

Chapter 23

It was over. It was all decided, every detail settled for him. The gentlemen were leaving the Apollo room now, and their going lacked the dignity of Garth's departure. They were being hurried. They were almost being swept out. Three of Henry Wetherburn's house nigras waited with brooms in the doorway.

Holden's feet crunched in the broken nutshells he had scattered on the floor. They no longer pleased him. All the satisfaction had gone out of knowing that somebody else would have to clean them up. He thought: *I was going to stay clear of trouble.* He thought: *All a man gets when he tries to clean up messes is a lot of trouble.*

The odd part of it was that now, when he had got himself into a thorough mess, so many other people were picking up the pieces of responsibility. Jenifer was carrying a note to Fraser in his pocket. Washington was undertaking to find moccasins and buckskins. Lee thought he remembered that a quantity of ceremonial belts and wampum strings—as essential in diplomacy at Wakatomica and Pickawillani as red sealing wax at Paris—had been left over from the last Catawba council. Carroll was attending to the matter of the horses.

A hand touched Holden's arm. He saw that Washington had waited for him in the hall.

"You'd best get some sleep, Chris. If you spent the night with Selden Blount, you spent the most of it awake. Use my room. It's at the right, back, and the bed's not bad—what there is of it."

The bed wasn't bad. But it wasn't good. There wasn't enough of it. His feet pushed against the footboard, and the board pushed back. He tried to sleep. He tried to push the thoughts out of his mind; they, too, kept pushing back. He had made himself ridiculous today. That foolishness on shipboard had made him vulnerable to Garth's ridicule; and in spite of that he had been overconfident; he had been dramatic, like a boy showing off. Small wonder they had not believed him. He had only himself to blame for his failure. And now, likely, he would pay for it in some Mingo or Shawnee or Twightwee town.

He was not afraid. *The hell I'm not.* He knew too much about it not to be afraid. Washington had put him in a box. He'd had no choice. He had to take those belts or knuckle down. He saw now that George had been testing him, and he resented it. After nine years it wasn't reasonable. Nine years was time enough to find out whether a man was worth trusting and believing in and backing up. He had a feeling that George was aware of his resentment—that he had been trying, toward the last, to make amends for not believing him. Inviting him to supper. It would take more than a cold cut of mutton and a mug of porter for amends. George was fond of cold roast mutton. Holden wasn't. *Oh, to hell with it! To hell with everything.*

He heard the creaking of the stairs. The door opened soundlessly. Light from the stair well splashed upon the ceiling. Fraser's whisper hunted for him in the lower darkness:

"Chris? Chris, you sleepin'?"

"No."

"You'd ought to locked this door."

"For God's sake."

"After what you done to Garth?" Fraser slid the bolt.

"What did I do to him?"

"You sort of crowded him a little."

"I'm the one got crowded."

He heard Fraser pawing at the table, and the click and sputter of his flint. Sparks spilled. The smell of burning tow was in the room. One candle caught and then the other.

Fraser laid his wool hat on the bed. He sat down on the bed and jounced it, trying out the mattress and the cords. The cords squealed.

"George crowded you, a' right. He backed you up, though. He backed you up so hard he pushed you into somethin'. That's the way he is." The bed squealed again. "You'd think they'd grease them cords. They sound like pigs. Y' know, Chris, that meetin' t'day put me in mind of a greased-pig chase."

"The pig got away."

"That ain't your fault. Every time you got a holt on Garth, somebody jostled you. But you sure as all hell scairt him. He'll run like a greased shoat now. He'll get word to Pontiac an' Guyasuta. Maybe it'll make them redsticks start things sooner than they aimed to."

"It might. I don't know . . . it might even be a good thing. A small rising's better than a big one."

"By God, it had better be a small one! You heard what Bouquet said. Four months! He's got about the smallest army anybody could say *is* an army, an' the little that he's got ain't ready. What you figurin' to do, Chris?"

"Right now I'm figuring to have some supper, if George ever gets here."

"The plague take ye! You know what I mean."

"After that I aim to walk across the street and ask Wetherburn to have my horse brought around. Then I'm riding out for Holden Hundred."

"Don't try me, Chris." Fraser said it earnestly. "F'r God's sake, don't. I been tried a plenty f'r one day."

"I'm not going to stay at the Hall, if that's what you think I mean. But I'm riding out the Jamestown road as if it's what I intend to do. That's natural, isn't it, for a man that's been away from home for seven months?"

"Nat'ral or unnat'ral, you ain't go'n' to do it."

"Why? What's wrong about it?"

"What's wrong about it? Ever'thing's wrong! Ridin' out that road alone. Wearin' that God-damn white shirt frill so to show up like a deer's hind end. You might's well hang a lanthorn to y'r neck an' make certain they can't miss you. Garth's got a dozen men in town here. He'll have 'em watchin' when you leave. They'll follow you."

"That's what I'm counting on."

"F'r God's sake!"

"They'll not catch me. Carroll's horse is fast. I'll be ahead of them at Holden Hall—just far enough ahead. They won't know whether I've stopped there or not."

"They can ask, can't they?"

"When they've asked, they won't believe the answer. They'll have seen the horse."

"Huh?"

"I'll leave it by the front lane hitching rail. A horse that does six furlongs in one twelve is too good to be ruined in the mountains. My own's in the stables. If it isn't, there'll be others." He had already made free with his brother's wife. A stolen horse could hardly matter. "They'll not trail me from there to Burnt Ordinary. Not through those woods, at night. Did you find Dan and Joe?"

"I found 'em. I give 'em my rifle f'r you. They'll be waitin' in the first stand o' gum trees past Burnt Ord'nary, two hours b'fore daylight."

The door latch chattered.

"Who's there?" Fraser growled. He sounded sore and savage.

"Washington. With rations, if you're interested."

Fraser slapped the bolt back with a jerk.

Washington had two nigras with him. The one in the smock was carrying a wooden platter with plates and knives and glasses on it, and a loaf of bread. The other, in the governor's livery, had a woven hamper covered with a huge white napkin. The slaves set their burdens on the table and backed out.

"Mutton," Chris said. "Cold."

"Don't you like cold mutton?"

"Yes." He lied like a gentleman. It was one thing white gentlemen and Indians had in common. If they were guests, they liked the food no matter how much they disliked it. But he took a dig at Washington. "It's possible to know some things without seeing them."

"That's true." Washington flipped the napkin off the basket and spread it on the table.

"God A'mighty," Fraser said. "That's big enough to diaper a grown man."

"The governor loaned it to me," Washington said.

"He must be a sloppy eater."

"He provided the cold joint, too, and the wine. I found the buckskins, Chris, and two pairs of moccasins. They ought to fit you. They fit me. They're in the stable, in the saddlebags." The big hands lifted out a silver tray with the roast of mutton on it. They set three dark bottles on the table. The hamper was still nearly half full. "Lee sent a case of pistols. They're French, but they're good. The rest is wampum. Lee and the governor between them dug up forty white strings and a dozen and a half belts. Will that be enough?"

"It'll be enough as far's he's goin'," Fraser said. "George, you got to help me get the hobbles on this fellow. He's as hardmouthed as a pack mule. He's figurin' to ride out the Jimtown road in front of God an' ever'body."

"Barrett's Ford?"

"No." Chris told him what he planned to do.

Washington sliced mutton while he listened.

"That sounds sensible to me," he said.

"Sensible! *Sensible!* He won't get two miles! Garth's buzzards will layway him."

"I don't think so," Chris said. "Garth will see that nothing happens to me for a while yet. If something happened now—too soon and too near—it might seem a little odd. It might even make George think I told the truth about Garth."

"I think you think you did."

"He did!" Fraser cried. "God damn it, George——"

"Let be," Chris said. "It doesn't matter now. I'd say Garth will be glad to see me gone. I'd say he was relieved this afternoon. He'd rather have me peddling belts for Johnson than trying to find out what happened to the trade goods he bought for his bankrupt friends."

"Friends!" Fraser snorted. "Friends! I don't know them others, but I know Henry Pollins ain't no friend of Garth's, nor Garth of his. Pollins ain't no trader, neither, an' he never has been. He's a tavern keeper. What he mostly keeps is bed lice. Even pack-train drivers won't sleep in his blankets. Garth wouldn't spit on him. Yes, he would! That's about what he *would* do. Not his own spit, though. That ain't Garth's way. He'd get Bone or Williamson or that Swede-Turk or Hesselgart to do it. But any one of 'em would sooner spit in an Ohio Company man's eye—an' then gouge the eye out an' play cat-in-the-hole with it. You ain't been acrost the mountains in three years, George. You ain't got no notion how them Pennsylvania traders hate us."

"Not Croghan, surely. Not Will Trent. Both of them have worked with us. Not the Butlers nor such trading companies as Simon, Levy, and Franks. Trent's a partner of theirs."

"You'll see, one of these days. They ain't go'n' to let Virginia get them western lands. They hate our guts."[1]

"Then they should hate Martin Garth worse, if he's got those deeds he boasts of."

"If! If! There ain't no *if* about it! The only reason the Pennsylvania tradin' companies don't hate him bad as they do us is that they ain't got onto him yet. But they hate us bad enough not to give a damn when Garth sets his Mingoes to laywayin' the Ohio Company's men. Happen Chris gets into trouble an' needs help bad, he ain't go'n' to get it from them Pennsylvanians. If you had to push this business onto Chris, I wish to God you'd done it so Garth didn't know it."

"I don't think Garth will expect Chris to be leaving so soon. There was some mention of delay about the belts. I said three days."

"They'll be watchin' him," Fraser repeated stubbornly. "My God, I bet you even told him what trail Chris would take."

---

[1]If Fraser's prophecy was based on prejudice and was not quite accurate, it was nevertheless more nearly correct than most prophecies. The struggle between Virginia and Pennsylvania for the Forks of the Ohio broke out into civil war in 1774. Virginia troops invaded what is now western Pennsylvania and seized Fort Pitt. The little known story of that struggle will be told in *The Temporary Gentleman,* the next book in Mr. Swanson's series of historical novels dealing with the making of America.

"No. I mentioned the Nemacolin path. It seemed obvious. It seemed too obvious for him to use. Which way are you going, Chris?"

"By Nemacolin's path."

"Great jumpin' pink-toed Judas!"

"Garth will remember that the path was mentioned. I hope he'll think I've gone some other way."

"He won't! He ain't just slipp'rier than a greased pig. He's a damned sight cuter. He——"

"Let be," Chris said again. "If there's trouble, I'll have Dan McCoy and Lovatt. I'm not worrying about Garth and his buzzards."

"I am! An' I'm worryin' about them Delawares an' Mingoes. You can handle the Shawnees an' Caughnawagas good as anybody, an' Dan knows the lake tribes. But I know the Delawares an' Mingoes better'n all of you together. By the Lord, I'm goin' with you! I'm go'n' to show that belt o' Pontiac's in every town from Winchester right on to Bedford an' Fort Ligonier an' Clapham's."

"No, John," Washington said quietly. "You're not."

"Who's go'n' to stop me?"

"You've been stopped already. You're in orders, John." Washington laid down his knife and put his hand into his coat. "Here."

Fraser snatched the paper. There were two sheets. He spread them in the circle of light from the nearest candle.

"They're both of 'em the same. They are, ain't they?"

"Yes. There's a copy for you and one for Chris. Johnson and Bouquet each have one and I've got another."

"Sayin' the same thing five times don't make it so. Whyn't you get a clerk to write this so's a man could read it?"

"Then the clerk would know what's in it."

"By God, they ain't nobody go'n' to know what's in it from these turkey tracks of yours, George. You write bad as Croghan. You can spell some better, but y'r fist looks like turkeys had been scratchin' in dead leaves, huntin' nuts." The coarse fibers of the paper stood up where the pen had scratched them. They threw shadows down the paper. "There's some droppin's, too." Fraser's thumb commented on the blots. He began to read:

" 'Wmsbg.' That's a good trick, happen you can't spell it. '3 April 1763. Captain Christopher Holden, First Regiment, Virginia Militia, is this day recalled to active duty and assigned to special duty . . .' Which in hell is it? All he's got is the one duty—to get out there. I bet this here order don't say nothin' about gettin' back. That's his own damn lookout . . . 'special duty under the direction of the officer commanding the Western Department.' Whyn't you say Bouquet an' get done with it? 'Captain Holden's ass—assmt——' What the hell kind of talk is that? Assignment, you mean, huh? Assignment 'is of a most confidential nature. All intelligence in his possession will be communicated only to the Indian commissioner or to the officer commanding the Department. The above sentence to include Lieutenant Fraser.' " He crumpled the sheet in his fist. "I'm resignin'!"

"Resignation not accepted," Washington said.

167

"It's a damn dirty trick. You done it just to gag me. It's the first time an off'cer was ever bucked an' gagged. I'm shut out an' I'm shut up! God A'mighty, d'you think I can go out to Pitt's Town an' keep my mouth shut? D'you think I can run f'r cover without tellin' them folks out there that hell's go'n' to break loose? Well, I can't."

"You'll have to, John. Bouquet and Johnson insisted on including you. They're concerned about——"

"Don't say it! I've heard what they're concerned about. I've heard it till I'm sick. Panic. They're the ones that's got the panic. It's their own tails they're concerned about. They don't want anybody findin' out the mess they've got themselves in. Of all the fool orders!" Fraser's big fists slammed upon the table. The wine shivered in the glasses. The fists pushed Fraser up out of his chair.

"Where d'you think you're going, John?"

"I'm goin' over to the Raleigh an' get Wetherburn to mix up some asses' milk. I'm goin' to get me two kegs of it—one f'r Johnson an' one f'r Bouquet. They'll need it. Not to drink—to cool off the place they're goin' to get burned on." He ground his fists against his thighs. "George, f'r God's sake, I got to do somethin'. *Somethin'!*"

"There's something you can do for me," Chris said. "You can take that wagon that I borrowed back to Selden Blount."

"That's a help," Fraser said.

"It will be a help to me. There's another thing that you can do too, if you will. You or George. My brother owns a slave named Jason. I'd like to buy him." He took out Pollexfen's sheaf of ten-pound notes and laid it on the table. He took off two of the notes and put them back into his pocket. "I'd like it to be done soon. Tomorrow."

"How high do you want to go?"

"As high as need be. There's a hundred seventy pounds there."

"Great heavens, Chris!"

He knew that Washington was thinking of the price he had paid for the convict girl—thinking once more that he was a fool. But he could not explain.

"John," he said, "if there's money enough left, I wish you'd buy a team and wagon with it and pick up my gear at Archer's Hope wharf. I'd like you to freight it out to Pitt's Town."

"You mean you're go'n' stay there?" Fraser's voice was eager. It dulled. "If you get out of this alive."

"Yes. I'm going to stay."

"What about Crisscross?" Washington asked. "You're not giving that up?"

"It's for sale, if you care to buy it."

"Why? Because we doubted you today?"

"No." Why the devil should he be polite about it? Why the devil should he lie? "Yes. That's part of it."

"I'm sorry, Chris. I've felt the same way sometimes."

Holden thought that he meant Sally Fairfax who'd been Sally Cary. Washington imagined he had kept his feelings hidden, but there had been a deal of smiling gossip. It was not at all the same. Fancying himself in love with a friend's wife, and behaving honorably, was very different from loving your own brother's wife and taking her, not knowing she was married. But Washington had not suffered greatly over Sally Fairfax. He had married Martha Custis.

"Have you forgotten what they said about me after the Great Meadows? After Jumonville was killed? Murderer. Assassin. Even my friends, Chris. Not you. Not John. But a plenty of them. It's hard for even your best friends to know what to believe sometimes."

"You still think I'm wrong about Garth."

"Let's say I hope you are. I can't see," he said doggedly, "what Garth could gain."

"He might gain a good deal. In the first place, he could ruin every other trader. He's already proved that's possible. When Croghan and Trent and the rest were losing everything they had, Garth lost nothing. God knows how he managed it, but the fact is that the French Indians protected his men; they didn't even steal his goods. That's why he could afford to make a show in London of opposing the relief grant to the traders who'd been ruined. He lost nothing then and he'll lose nothing this time. And he'll bankrupt all the others."

"An Indian war might bankrupt some of them. All of them, even. But for every trader ruined this year, there will be a new one next year. I can well believe he is a liar when he says he will not sell the land he claims to have the deeds for. It's worthless to him unless he can sell it. And it can't be sold unless it can be settled. Settlements are barred now. If there's a new war, they will be barred years longer. No, Chris, I can't see it."

"His Indian grants carry more than land, George. They give him the exclusive right to trade—a monopoly along two hundred miles of the Ohio. I'm not saying he expects the Indians to drive us out. He's not a fool. He knows the Indians will be beaten—sometime. But a war will do more than keep out squatters; it will keep the Ohio Company out too. And when the war ends, somebody will make peace. I think he expects to gain credit for himself there too. He'll be the go-between. He knows that in the end the army'll have a firmer grip on the Ohio country. He can wait. He knows that in the end the land will be reopened. There's his profit. It's a double profit. He'll skim the cream off the Ohio trade for years; and when that's done and settlements are allowed again, his land will be worth a hundred times what it's worth now—a thousand times—ten thousand times whatever he has paid for it."

"But no white man could pull all the tribes together, Chris. The French tried it. We tried."

"I don't think Garth's trying. I don't think he needs to. It has been done for him."

"It's impossible, Chris. Except for the Iroquois, they can't hang together. Even the Iroquois Confederacy couldn't hold the Senecas two years ago. That's their weakness. They're too independent."

"There are the clans," Holden said. They were one source of strength that white men overlooked. Even men like Bouquet found it difficult to believe that Indians could act together, because they thought of them as separated into dozens of tribes speaking different tongues. But in the

American wilderness there were whole nations of families superimposed upon the tribal nations, and they were inextricably mingled, the one system with the other. "The clans . . ." But he saw that Washington was busy with the mutton. There was no use talking. *To hell with it*. He pushed back his chair.

"I might as well start."

He took his waistcoat and his coat down from the bedpost and put them on. He put on his hat. When he turned back to the table he saw the case of pistols, lying open, and two plain militia pouches. The pouches bulged. They would bulge his coat as if he had on side hoops.

He took off his coat again and laid it on the chair. He put the pistols in the armholes of his waistcoat with the curved butts turned forward. He slung the pouches, one across each shoulder. When he put on his coat again, they made him as broad in the beam as Johnson.

"Well," he said. He felt fat and clumsy and absurd.

"G'by, Chris. I'll see to y'r gear."

Fraser's hand slipped away. Washington's was waiting. It had the old mahogany compass in it.

"Take this along, Chris. You may need it, crossing Gloucester Street."

"Thanks, George." That was the nearest he had ever heard Washington come to making a joke of his own.

He didn't want the compass. He had never felt the need of one. It would be one more thing to bulge. But he meant the thanks. He knew that George had had that compass a long time.

Chapter 24

They had traveled fast. It was getting on into midmorning of the fifth day since they passed World's End and saw the last of the tide-water country. They had put Fort Cumberland sixty miles behind them.

Joe Lovatt didn't like the Nemacolin path. He didn't like anything about it, even to its name. In the first place, it wasn't a path: it was a wagon road. In the second place, it was a tomfool notion in the first place.

"Folks that can't travel without wagons ain't got no damn business in the woods," he had argued. "Look what happened to Ed Braddock. Look what happened to old Iron Head. He'd of stuck there in the mountains till he froze his privates an' his off'cers too, if Armstrong an' Shelby an' Doc Mercer hadn't pried him loose from his damn wagons an' his damn road-cuttin'.

"In the third place, it's a God-damn insult to me. It's an insult to all white men to name any white man's road or path or fice dog f'r a greasy Injin. In especial, it's an insult to Tom Cresap an' Chris Gist. They laid the path out, didn't they? Nemacolin wasn't no surveyor, was he? All the mangy, flea-bit, misbegot son of a polecat done was set on his behind an' eat their grub an' watch them work."

"How do you know?" Dan had asked him.

"B'cause I was settin' there on *my* behind an' doin' the same thing. They didn't name no paths f'r *me*. I've set on my butt end all over this damn country, an' they ain't named so much as a swamp crick f'r Joe Lovatt. In the fourth place, Nemacolin never went no further than the Youghiogheny. From there on, it ain't his path at all. An' in the fifth, sixth, an' eighty-seventh places, it's the damnedest poorest excuse f'r a road I ever seen yet."

"You left out some quite few places."

"Them's the places where it ain't a road nor a path neither. An' that's what it ain't the most part of the ways. It's a sinkhole or a slashin' the tomfoolest squatter would take shame at, or else it's a deer run. I've fetched me too many meals, just settin' by a deer run with my rifle laid along my leg, to go rammin' up this Nemacolin path a-horseback in the daytime."

They were climbing the east slope of Laurel Ridge now. Holden rode ahead. Ten yards behind him he could hear Joe Lovatt swearing about deer runs. McCoy was another ten yards back, behind the pack horse on Joe's lead rope.

The path made, here, a mile-long straight slash down the broad flank of the ridge. It was like a knife wound on the body of the forest—a wound that had not healed in a raised welt but had left, instead, a narrow sunken scar as if the lips of a deep gash had not quite grown together.

It had never been a clean wound. It had never been a good road. All the stumps were still here, and they weren't stumps that a decent axman could take pride in. They were beavered off close to the ground so that the running gear of wagons would not hang up on them. The cut trees lay every which way. Smaller trees had been bent, doubled over, twisted, slivered, snapped off when the big trees crashed down. With the underbrush that sprung up among them, the dead branches and the splintery trunks of the mangled saplings made an abattis on both sides of the path.

A man on foot could wriggle his way through. If he had to leave the path fast, he could crash through in some places. But a man on horseback couldn't. Holden began looking for breaks in the tangle and remembering them. There weren't many to remember. He didn't blame Joe Lovatt for his plaintive swearing.

But Chris Holden was feeling better than he had felt in a long time. He was thinking now about the last few nights in blankets on bough beds in the piney woods, and about the feel and smell of the raw earth beneath him and around him, and about the earthy talk of these two middle-aged backwoodsmen who called him Cap'n with a casual respect but felt quite free to poke fun at his highfalutin manners and would disobey him, just as casually and naturally, if they knew that he was wrong. But they wouldn't let him down.

They had saved his life twice. Both the times were carefully recorded on Dan's powder horn. Now they were risking their lives again on his account. It was good to be back with them. It was good to be back where the streams knew what they wanted and where they were going—where they brawled and wrestled with the hills instead of shifting back and forth with every tide. It was good to be shut of women—to be back in a man's world.

A deer flashed across the path ahead. It cleared the open space in one bound and was gone.

"I don't like that, neither," Lovatt whispered. "I been smellin' Injins the whole mornin'."

"Ye been smellin' y'rself," McCoy told him.

"I c'n tell the diff'rence. I been smellin' Injins ever since we passed Burnt Ordinary."

"Ye been seein' deer, too. That's about the eighty-seventh deer that's run acrost the road these last four days. Anyway, ye're in the middle."

"The middle's a damn bad place to be caught in."

"Cap'n Holden's up ahead. If they're layin' for us, they'll get him first. Cap'n, ye got any feelin' in y'r wishbone?"

"No," Chris said. "If they were going to jump us on this straight stretch, they would likely wait till we were past."

"That's right," Dan said. "They'd get us from behind. They'd get all three of us that way."

There was a sudden airy threshing in the woods, a rush of wings, a bumbling in the brush.

"Turkeys," Lovatt whispered.

"By God," McCoy said, low, "I c'd use me a fat turkey. Chris . . ."

"No. No fire tonight. No fires after we cross Laurel. I don't fancy a raw turkey."

He heard Dan grunt.

Maybe he was being foolish. It wouldn't take Dan long to fetch one of those birds. They could pull off the road before they topped the crest; they could stop and make a fire in daylight. Any fire that Dan or Joe made would not lift its smoke above the treetops. And there was one wild turkey that was not content yet. He could hear it stirring in the bushes. *Close,* he thought. *It's close.*

The hard windy whirring seemed to brush his cheek. He knew, before he heard the *ughh* sound, that it was not wings. It was thin and feathery, but there was a whimper in it.

When he turned his head, Joe Lovatt was already sagging in his saddle. The arrow stuck out from Joe's chest, above the wolverine-fur pouch. The feathered end of it bowed slowly toward the saddle horn. Joe died sitting in the saddle. He did not cry out or even whisper. The only sound was the rush of the arrow. Holden could still hear it. There were other arrows. He could hear them whickering in the dead branches. The familiar yelping started.

"Horses!" McCoy shouted. "They've got horses!"

McCoy was crowding alongside the pack horse. As he passed it he leaned down and cut the lashings of the packs with two quick slashes of his knife. A third slash slit one pack. It nicked the pack horse. The horse squealed and squirmed. The packs tumbled off.

"That'll maybe hold 'em." One Indian couldn't stand to see another Indian get first pickings. "We got to git out o' here."

McCoy had his arm around Joe Lovatt. He was easing Joe down.

"The pouch," Chris said. "Get his pouch." Half of the seawan belts were in it.

He saw Dan jerk the pouch. The rawhide loop broke. Dan shoved the pouch into his shirt. The string dangled, swinging. His horse was trying to rear and Dan was fighting him down and trying to slide Joe's body to the ground. He wouldn't let Joe fall if he could help it, dead or not.

The path ahead was a boiling flood of naked Indians and streaming manes. It was a narrow flood between the banks of woods, but it was coming like a spring fresh down a mountain gully. It made the same kind of sound—the swift drumming rush, the bent bushes hissing underneath the horses, the hoofs pounding like dead tree trunks and rocks tumbled by a wall of water. The high yelping rode it like a blown froth, thin and breaking loose and flung ahead.

Holden fired at the first horse and rolled it. The Indian shot over its head like a log tossed on a flood crest. He fell like a log and slid. The flood swept over him.

"Come on!" Dan's horse was carrying on. He couldn't shoot. "Let's git." He swung the horse down hill.

"The woods," Chris shouted after him. "Left! Left! There's a place——"

McCoy found it. He had disappeared. A jagged branch raked Holden's leg as he crashed through the hole in the tangle of down timber. The yells spattered and were thinner.

The underbrush was thinner too. The woods opened up. The hill pitched downward to a long slope under oaks and chestnuts. A dark streak in the earth flashed by. A deer trail—one of Lovatt's deer runs. The Indians had stopped yelling now. They were getting down to business. The soft woods mold dulled the drumming hoofs, but he could hear them. He could hear the whip and crackle of the brush.

He saw McCoy's horse check. McCoy flung up his right hand with the rifle in it. *Dan's hurt,* he thought. *There were a lot of arrows, but I didn't see . . .* McCoy reined abruptly to the right. *He's badly hurt.* The horse was walking. It walked off into the woods. McCoy looked back and jerked his head, and Holden saw that whether he was hurt or not he knew what he was doing.

There was an abrupt round shoulder to the hill here. McCoy was circling it, walking his horse, picking the way carefully among the bushes. *It's no good,* he thought. *They're too close. The woods are too open.* He thought: *Let the horses go.* But the woods were too open for that, either, to be any good.

They were around the shoulder of the hill when the first of the rush went by. In a minute—in a half a minute—the Indians would know it was a trick. McCoy knew they'd know. He put his horse to a run up the hill, still circling.

The narrow dark smudge of the deer trail flashed by again. *We ought to try that.* But McCoy plunged ahead. The horses were on a dead run when they crossed their own tracks. He could hear the Indians yelping again. The yelps came from both sides of them, up the hill and down. Some of the Indians had stopped to loot the packs. But down the slope he made out two or three of them. They were coming back up.

Circling on your tracks was a useful trick, if you had a long enough lead.

But it couldn't work now. The circle was too small. The red devils were too close.

McCoy knew that too. Here was the deer run again. Dan was turning into it. That was what he had been aiming to do, all along, from the minute he first saw it. Circling around the shoulder of the hill was only a small trick to gain time. If they had turned into it the first time they came to it, they would have had the Indians right on them. Dan had taken a long chance that the Indians would override their tracks.

Holden couldn't hear the hoofs behind now for the soft-hard pounding of the hoofs beneath him. They had gained two hundred yards. Three hundred, maybe. But if those Indians were smart, they'd figure out the shaping of the hill and how the deer trail ran. They'd cut them off.

Holden thought they were beginning to do it. They had quit yelling again now. They were working the thing out.

The deer run made a turn. There was a short straight stretch on level ground. Great oaks spread rugged branches. Grapevines hung down, thick and woven-looking like ship cables, dark as anchor cables being hauled up. Scurfs of bark hung dripping on them. Ahead, the woods closed in. The hill pitched down. There would be a stream, a ravine clogged with underbrush, steep shaly banks, rocks. A stumble and a snapped leg . . . *Let the horses go. Stop here. Fight it out. I can hold them a few minutes. Let Dan get away. One of us . . . Dan's the one. He's lived with tribes I've never seen. He talks more languages. I'm glad Dan's ahead.* He began to rein in.

McCoy's arm went up. His left arm. It was flailing ahead, pointing. An oak limb, thicker than a man's leg, overhung the trail. He saw Dan kick free from the stirrups. He saw Dan's horse swerve and both of Dan's arms fling upward. They locked around the oak limb. His legs swung underneath it, out of sight. Then the horse was gone. Dan's legs swung back again.

Holden slid his feet out of the stirrups. He held the rifle high. He twisted his wrist and thrust the barrel forward. He bent his arms to hook the branch against the insides of his elbows. He threw himself upward in a clumsy jump. The oak limb, swinging to McCoy's weight, slammed into his chest. It knocked his breath out, but his arms clamped over it. He hung there dangling.

McCoy swung one leg over the thick branch. He got one hand against the trunk of the tree and dug his fingers into the rough bark and drew himself up, on his knees. His fingers found another limb above. He was on his feet and the branch he stood on jiggled. Holden clung to it. The jiggling squeezed out all the breath he had dragged back into his lungs.

Dan's legs swung past his face, and then Dan's moccasins. They were drawn up slowly. Dan was whispering above him:

"Chris . . . Chris, can ye make it?"

He got a leg over the thick branch, straddling it. McCoy's hand reached down and grasped his wrist. He got his feet under him. Dan took his rifle. He began to climb.

They stood on another branch high up the tree and saw the Indians below them—plucked heads, Mingo scalplocks like thin manes, the long back hair streaming as they rode. There were a lot of them, but they were riding hard; they passed in a long streak of dull coppery bodies and black flying hair and pale glints of twirling feathers. The splashes of sun on the empty trail showed the deep prints of hoofs. Holden felt Dan's fingers on his arm. Then Dan was pointing.

"Jesus!" he breathed.

On the next to the lowest limb, where McCoy had crouched to draw Holden up, Joe Lovatt's wolverine-fur pouch hung by its broken string. The string was wound once around the limb.

The pouch swung a little. There was no wind high up in the tree, but there was a small breeze drawing down the deer run. The string slipped. Holden thought it slipped. He thought he saw it moving. He could not be sure.

The thudding hoofs were quiet now. There was a thrashing in the brush beyond the turn, down the hill somewhere. He could hear the Indians talking back and forth. They knew that they had been tricked somehow. They were casting about now for signs.

"Here." McCoy passed his rifle over. "I got to get that pouch." Then he froze.

An Indian was walking down the trail. His horse had gone lame. He was leading it. A Mingo didn't care how badly a horse was hurt so long as it could travel, but this horse was hobbling on three legs. Its front knees were scraped raw.

The Indian walked underneath the dangling pouch. He walked on down the trail. Holden felt Dan's body letting go of itself. His own body began letting go. And then the Indian turned around. He left the horse and came walking slowly back. He stopped just before he came to the thick oak limb and stood looking up into the tree.

McCoy pulled the flap of his shirt across his rifle lock and hooked his thumb around the lock, with the leather under it to muffle the click when it cocked. Holden touched Dan's arm and shook his head. He slid his knife out of its sheath. He put his mouth to Dan's ear:

"Steady me."

McCoy's eyes said he couldn't make a throw like that. But McCoy's big hand slipped underneath his belt and took a grip.

He let go of the thin limb overhead, slowly, carefully, so that it wouldn't move. He lifted his right foot and turned it. Doing right-about-face on a tree limb with a Mingo underneath it was a thing that wasn't in drill regulations. Throwing a knife almost straight downward, through a haze of leaves, was a thing he'd never tried or heard of.

When he got turned around he saw that the Mingo was holding his musket pointed up into the tree. The butt was not quite to his shoulder. He wasn't sure yet. He was almost sure. In a moment he would shoot. Or else he'd yell and bring the others back. He'd likely yell first, watching the tree all the time to see whether the yell fetched a quiver.

Holden laid the knife along his hand. He raised his arm. Thank God there were no branches close enough to bother. Thank God he wasn't next to the trunk of the tree. If he was standing where Dan was, the throw would be impossible. It was probably impossible anyway. The only place he could do that Mingo any real harm was in the throat. The left side of the throat. If the Indian stopped looking up when he let fly, he'd only nick an ear.

He chopped his arm down hard and let the knife go. The blade flashed. It whicked through the layered leaves and he lost it. But he heard it hit. It made a rapping sound. He'd missed. The weighted handle of the knife had hit a root.

The Indian still stood there, looking up.

"Jesus," McCoy said. "I never seen nothin' like that. I ain't seen it yet. It rapped him on the head an' then went in."

The Mingo dropped his musket. He began to sway—once backward and once forward. Swaying, he put one hand up to his neck. He took hold of the handle of the knife and pulled it out. The blood poured down his chest. He was red from neck to belly when he fell.

"We got to git out o' here. F'r God's sake, Chris, don't twist an ankle when ye light."

They scrambled down. As Dan's feet touched the limb where the pouch hung, the string slipped again. It unwound itself and crawled off the limb and the pouch dropped.

Dan snatched it up.

"Come on, Chris."

"I want this knife."

He had to pry it from the Mingo's hand. He thrust it, slippery and wet, into the sheath. He took the Mingo's horse by the rawhide bridle and turned its head into the brush on the downhill side of the deer trail and hit it hard across the rump with the barrel of his rifle. It went crashing away. The Indians yelled. Dan grinned.

"That ought to help."

They began to run uphill, up the long flank of Laurel.

Chapter 25

He had been running for eleven days. This was the first time he had really rested.

He lay back against the slanting outcrop of gray-tawny rock and felt the muscles of his legs let go like raveled strings. They trembled. The weak quivering crawled up the insides of his thighs. It gave him a frayed feeling in the bottom of his belly where the tendons of his legs were hitched on.

His heart was like an angry fist. It was like a tired man's hard fist, striking at him slowly. The blows jolted him. There was something queer about them. His heart was inside him, but he felt the pounding outside At each weary blow he felt the rock behind him, through his shirt.

There must be one place on his shirt that wasn't stiff with blood. He didn't know. He hadn't had his shirt off in five weeks. He hadn't dared to take the chance. If the Indians had jumped him when he had his shirt off, and he'd lost it, he would likely have been finished. The saw-edged swamp grass would have flayed him, and the bramble tangles would have fetched more blood to dribble on the grass and show his trail.

He hadn't run the whole time. He had slept, of course. A man couldn't travel from Maumee to the Forks of the Ohio without stopping. But he wasn't sure how often he had rested, or how long, or where. There were some parts of the last eleven days and nights that weren't clear in his mind. He didn't know yet how he'd got away. The hatchet blow had dazed him. He had no notion about what had happened from the time he woke up a little before daylight in the Ottawa lodge, and saw the hatchet coming, till he floundered into the old beaver pond and crept into the ruins of the dam and lay there under water with his face pressed up against the rotting sticks and his mouth sucking air between them. All he knew was that the long-gone beaver colony had saved his life.

He had been chased by Indians before, but that was the first time there had been enough of them to make a ring hunt of it. They spread themselves out in a circle two miles wide around the place where they had lost him, and he needed every trick he knew to get through. It had taken him three days to shake them, and by that time he had been on the wrong side of the Miami River. He had been two hundred fifty or three hundred miles from Pitt's Town. *If I'd been a crow.* It was nearer to four hundred, likely, the way he had traveled. Four hundred miles in eight days. . . .

This was the first time he had not felt driven. Even after he shook off the Ottawas he had been driven—days, nights—by the fear that he would be too late. He hadn't been sure, till he climbed the bluff of the Mononga-hela and looked down across the river, that the town was still there

He lay back now full length against the slanted jut of limestone, with his eyes closed and his arms spread loose, and let the smooth rock pound him through his shirt. The sun was warm and heavy on his eyes. The warmth soothed his empty belly. It pushed through the clammy leather of his leggings. They began to steam.

He dozed. His knees buckled, and he slid, and waked himself up. He made his knees straighten themselves out. They pushed his shoulders up the slanting rock, and he dozed, and slid, and waked himself again.

It wasn't the most comfortable way to sleep. But it was the only way he could afford until he had climbed down the bluff and got across the river to the fort and told Ecuyer what he had found out. If ever he lay down on the ground, under the warm blanket of the sun, he would sleep all day—unless he got the hunger cramps again. He'd likely sleep until the Indians came along and found him lying there and helped themselves to his front hair.

They were coming. That was certain. They were coming by the thousands. There wasn't any guesswork to it now. He knew. He had been howled down in councils. He had listened to the drums, nights. He had seen the splintered war posts. All the western tribes were up. The only nations that he didn't know about for sure now were the Wyandots and the Erics and the Mingoes. Dan McCoy would know about them. *If he isn't dead. . . .*

The sun was burning his eyes. The insides of the lids were two red blurs.

like fire. He hoped the Mingoes hadn't put the fire to Dan McCoy. Sometimes, when they got a man as tough as Dan, they dragged it out for days. Especially if the man was someone that they knew.

He laid his arm across his eyes to shield them from the sun. The red blurs swirled and darkened. They turned black, like the thick clotted smoke that tipped the flame of a pine splinter burning. When the swirling stopped, he opened his eyes and looked out under the scuffed leather of his sleeve.

He couldn't see the town now. The sharp brink of the bluff concealed it. Lying here, he could see nothing but a strip of laurel thicket and a strip of gray rock at the cliff's rim and a strip of sky beyond it.

The sky was pale with morning. It looked soft and peaceful; but the peacefulness was an illusion. He knew what it hid. In his mind he saw the little log forts lonely in the forest. Fort Venango, eighty miles north—he had starved and frozen there one winter, while the icy wind howled through the loopholes, and the hewn-timber gate leaned uselessly against the wall because the army hadn't bothered to send hinges for it. Le Boeuf, forty-six miles farther northward—not a fort at all, but two log houses lost in a morass. And then Presque Isle . . . Sandusky . . . Detroit . . . Mackinac . . . Wiatenon . . . Green Bay . . .

He swore fiercely, silently. *God damn you, Holden.* He had been within a hundred miles of Fort Sandusky when the Ottawas had tried to kill him. *You could have got through them, damn you. If you'd gone east . . .*

It had been impossible. He knew it. But he blamed himself now, savagely, for failing.

The bland sky condemned him. He swore at it, and the wild sound of his own voice startled him. He had been lightheaded, off and on, for two days; but he hadn't realized, until he heard the crazy cursing, that he was so close to breaking.

He pulled his eyes away from the accusing sky. He pulled them back until they came to his own body, and he saw himself half naked. His breechclout had gone first. When his moccasins gave out, he had used the breechclout to make wrappings for his feet. He wasn't sure when that was—sometime after he swam the Ohio River but before he crossed the Licking. He had cut the long thrums off the shirt and knotted them together into strings to tie the wrappings. But no matter how he tied them, the knots gouged his feet and started to raise blisters; he had had to cut two long strips off the bottom of his shirt instead.

He made the doeskin wrappings last as long as possible, but by the time he came to the Kanawha they were ground to shreds like deer-meat that a Shawnee squaw had pounded to make pemmican. Running with those pulpy bundles on his feet had been like running with his feet in bags of pemmican. He'd had to stop and hack off two more long, wider pieces of the shirt to make new wrappings. They were clumsier than the the soft doeskin of the clout had been, but the worst thing about them was that when he had to ford a stream they sopped up water, and the water stayed inside them and his feet cooked in it. He hadn't seen his feet in four days, but he knew what they would look like when he saw them. They would look like parboiled fat back.

He settled the two useless pistols in his belt and tugged the remnant of his shirt down over his hipbones as far as it would stretch. With his breechclout gone, there was hardly enough left of the shirt to keep him decent. There were women in Pitt's Town. When he crossed the river and came to the town he would have to remember to keep pulling his shirt down. *Have to remember,* he thought. *Women . . .*

The idea annoyed him. There was some reason why he disliked women. But he was too tired now to remember what it was.

He was walking toward the cliff's edge, and his legs were ripping through the laurel tangle. The laurel was in full bloom. Wading through it was like wading through a gloss-green river stained bright pink with sunrise. His knees kicked up a pink-white froth of blossoms.

As he walked, the sky began to slide up from behind the cliff. It was drawn upward smoothly, like a painted picture on a roller in a peep show. The green wooded hills beneath the sky slid up where he could see them, and then came the Allegheny River and the abrupt broken ledges of Grant's Hill and the beginnings of Pitt's Town below the hill, and then the brown, sleek, sluggish flow of the Monongahela with the long thin island in it, pale green with young marsh grass. Five hundred feet below him lay the Forks of the Ohio and the town and fort named for a politician who had never seen them.

Neither Pitt's Town nor its fortress was impressive. The triangle of low land between the meeting rivers looked, from this height, like a wedge of pie dropped into the deep dish of hills, with its juice oozing out around it. The Allegheny River, shining in the sun, was a bright streak of thin juice. The Monongahela was dark, reddish-brown like cinnamon, and thick and sticky-looking.

The pie had been cut carelessly. Both edges were uneven. They had broken off, in places, and slid down into the brown juice. At the broad end of the wedge the curving rocks of Grant's Hill made a rim of crust, scorched-looking, crimped with crevices and gullies. The whole surface of the crust was broken, as if somebody had jabbed it with a knife to cool it, so that here and there the filling showed through—raisin and green-apple filling—the green lumps of trees, the small darker lumps of cabins, and sleek narrow slices of the little ponds like citron.

The filling steamed. Smoke from the lumpy chimneys of the cabins mingled with the waver of mist rising from the marshes.

Forbes's road made a curving thin mark on the broken crust, as if a knife point had been drawn across it while the crust was still dough; and the little streams went angling off on both sides of the road like patternings on piecrust.

He was halfway down the cliff when he saw a figure on the far bank of the river, in the cove made by the creek that blustered down from Hogg's pond to the Mon.[1] He waved his arms and shouted, and an answering halloo came faintly. The figure disappeared behind the cleft bank. Presently a boat came drifting down. The creek shot it out into the river like a thrown knife—like a double-bladed clasp knife with its

---

[1]Referred to in *The Judas Tree* as Massacre Pond. Hogg's pond was the more commonly used name.

two blades open, one at each end. *Ramsey,* he thought. *By the Lord, it's Ramsey.*

The slim boat moved slantingly across the current. The man in it sat bent over. He looked idle, without either oars or paddle. But his legs were busy. Even at this distance it was possible to see his knees pump, first one knee and then the other. On both sides of him the turning wheels gleamed wetly. They beat at the surface of the river, lifting the brown water up into the sunlight in long dripping streams that were suddenly white, clean, and shining, and then, as they fell, were brown again and dirty.

The boat was coming fast. Ramsey would be waiting for him by the time he reached the river.

When he broke out through the matted alder thicket at the bottom of the cliff, the boat was fifty yards downstream and fifty yards out, and it was jerking back and forth upon the current like a waterbug—drifting, scuttling back upriver, drifting down again. Holden, hobbling through the crazy tumble of rocks and debris heaped up along the bank by old floods and ice jams, sent his voice ahead of him:

"Hello, Will!"

The wheels stopped. The boat slid away. The man in it shouted:

"Where's your rifle?"

"I haven't got one." He didn't blame the man for asking. Indians had a trick of laying a gun down across their moccasins and fetching it up quickly with a jerk of one foot. "It's all right. It's Holden. I'm Chris Holden."

The boat scuttled back three lengths and hung there, the wheels turning slowly. The man in it wasn't Ramsey. He called:

"Raise your arms up. Put them up high." The barrel of a gun lay on his thighs and jiggled as his legs worked. "Come out on the flat where I can see you."

He walked out into the dark slime of the mud flat.

"Can't you see I'm white?"

"If you're white, say Mary."

"Mary," Holden said. Most Indians couldn't make an "r" sound; they turned Mary into Mally. But the man wasn't satisfied yet.

"Say Merry Mary's marrowbone."

"God damn it!" Holden shouted at him. "What's the matter with you? Can't you see my whiskers?" But he said the words.

The man sitting on the square box in the middle of the boat began to run. His legs pumped furiously. The wheel paddles slapped the river and the boat shot forward, angling closer to the shore until it was within two perches of Chris Holden, and he saw that the stranger in it was a boy not more than seventeen or eighteen, and that he was frightened.

"You'll have to wade," the boy said. "There's snags hereabout. I don't want to tear a wheel off. I saw your whiskers, all right. But you could have been a half-breed. They're as bad as Indians, some of them."

"Yes," Holden said, knee deep in the river. "Some half-breeds can say Mary's marrowbone, too."

The boy looked at him sullenly.

"I know that." Then, sharp, as Chris lifted one foot in its soggy lump of wrappings: "Don't step on the gunwale! This thing tips right easy."

"I know. I've been in it. That's why I called you Will. I thought you were Ramsey."

"Ramsey's dead."

"Oh."

"He took smallpox. They gave me his cabin. I found the boat where he had left it. Nobody seemed to care about it, so I use it sometimes."

He leaned forward, shuffling his feet on the wooden treadles that protruded from the box he sat on. He began to pump the treadles.

His flying legs were like Pollexfen's—plump, soft-looking, powerful. But the rest of him was not at all like Ellerby Pollexfen. His hands, with the tiller lines clutched in them, were small, dirty, child's hands; and above the broad spread of his buttocks on the box his body narrowed to a thin chest and thin sloping shoulders that looked too small for his big head. He had a high-domed, bulging forehead and the kind of eyes that could be scraped off with a stick. Below them, the rest of his face diminished, as if his mouth and chin had not grown up. They did not look younger than his eyes; they only looked as if the things his eyes had seen to make them bulge had also terrified his mouth and chin and they were trying to withdraw themselves, to hide. His pale blue eyes peered up now under the dome of his forehead, and his voice was at the same time truculent and timid:

"Kenny says Will Ramsey had more brains than anybody this side of the mountains."

"He did, likely," Chris said. "Kenny . . ." Kenny was the young Quaker clerk who had been sent out by the Pennsylvania provincial government to run its trading house in Pitt's Town. "Is he still here? He told me that he wasn't staying."

"He keeps saying he won't stay. He stays, though. It's his doing that I'm out here. Some of the people—Colonel Burd and Trent and the Butlers and some others—thought there ought to be school in Pitt's Town. Burd said they could keep school in his cabin. They asked Kenny if he knew somebody they could get for teacher, and he wrote to me. I didn't know what it was going to be like."

"What is it like?"

"It's awful." The pale eyes slid away and came back, furtive and suspicious. "I've heard about you." Then, as if suddenly he had remembered manners: "My name's Ten Eyck." For a moment his inadequate face had a friendly, boyish, young look. Then the sullenness came back and it was old again and frightened. "I don't see why Kenny stays here. I don't see why anybody that's half decent stays in Pitt's Town! It's a pesthole! Smallpox. Dirt. Stinks. Brawls and fights. *Fleas* . . . You can't sleep nights for the fleas and brawling and the drunken Indians."

"I thought the army'd put a stop to that."

"Pfuhh!"

"When I was here last year there was an order out that any trader who sold whisky to an Indian would have his cabin torn down. They had torn some down already."

"They stopped doing it. Captain Ecuyer wanted Pitt's Town to be like a city. He said everybody had to have a number on his front door. They've got up to seventy-eight now, and the officer that's seeing to it says there are almost a hundred fifty houses. But if the army tears down any cabin that's already got a number, it makes all the rest wrong. So they quit it. Nobody seems to care now if the traders let the Indians have whisky."

"Are they letting them have powder too?"

"I don't know. Kenny thinks so. It's hard on him. He hasn't any trade left scarcely. All the Indians go to Bone's place—to the Gilded Beaver and George Croghan's and the Golden Eagle or Garth's Castle up the river."

"Is Garth in town?"

"I don't know. Some of his men are. They came in two weeks ago with wagons."

"Who? Bone . . . Hesselgart . . . Williamson?"

"Bone's one of them. I don't know if he's selling powder, but I know he's selling whisky. The Indians get drunk there, and then they come down to Kenny's wanting to lie on the store floor with their women. They raise hell because he doesn't let them. Night before last a whole pack of them hung around the store and yelled and threw rocks at it. It's enough to make a man go crazy." Ten Eyck shuddered. "One did."

"Who?"

"The surgeon, Miller. He cut his throat in his quarters one night. With two razors."

Holden felt a quick revulsion. Ten Eyck was a whiner—the worst kind of whiner, who remembered everything unpleasant to gloat over it. He was the kind that would worry at a hangnail, keeping it sore, getting perverse pleasure out of the small soreness. It was almost two years since poor crazy Miller killed himself. Holden's voice was brusque with irritation:

"It's a little late to worry about Miller. He was hypped to start with. Why not think about the new man? You won't catch him cutting his throat."

"No"—sullenly. "Boyd drinks, though. He's drunk all the time—almost all. When he isn't——"

Holden thought: *For God's sake. I'd cure him of that bitching if I had him in the rangers. But I wouldn't have him.* Then he was astonished. Ten Eyck had begun to giggle.

"When Boyd isn't drunk, he helps Kenny with his bones. That's funny. Bone . . . bones. When Kenny can't stand one Bone any more, he goes out and gets himself a sackful. He goes up to the battlefield and gathers them, and Boyd helps him sort them out. He's trying to get enough to make a skeleton—a whole one. It's not easy. They're all scattered, but Boyd says he can put the bones from different men together. Wouldn't you think the army would have buried those men? Just leaving them there that way . . . It's not decent."

"No, it isn't," Chris said. "I know how you feel. I went east by Braddock's road last summer." It had been the first time he had traveled that way since the massacre, and the sight of the white bones and skulls strewn through the underbrush had shocked him. He had seen one skull with a sassafras shoot growing through its clenched teeth. For four years, with an idle garrison only a few miles away in Fort Pitt, England had not bothered about burying the men who died with Braddock. He had stood there in the overgrown trail, cursing in wild anger, damning the ingratitude and callousness and cold brutality of a government that cared so little. Judas! He had been expecting too much. He had not known, then, anything about brutality and callousness. He had not seen England then. He had, now. He said: "They do worse in England. In London they dig up old graveyards when they want room. They throw the bones into carts and haul them to the edge of town and dump them."

"That's no worse," the boy said. "It's no worse than Boyd. When he's sober, he collects skulls. He must have two dozen in his quarters."

"He's a surgeon."

"But he doesn't study them. He keeps them under his bunk. Chamber pots, he calls them. He says they are his religion. He told Post, the missionary, that the only difference between Christianity and heathenism is that Christians had invented chamber pots. He says it was a bad mistake because it made them comfortable, and you can't be comfortable and a Christian at the same time. He says look at Job. He told Post that the only way to Christianize the people in Pitt's Town would be to make all of them use skulls for jordans—to keep them reminded that they're going to die. I'm not scared of dying. Not just dying. It's how."

"Indians, you mean?"

"Yes. They're not human. They're like animals. They even smell like animals." The boy's eyes, bulging under the dome of his forehead, were small, furtive animals too. "I wasn't scared of smallpox when they gave me Ramsey's cabin. But I wouldn't want the Indians to get me."

"Why the devil do you stay then?" He regretted instantly that he had said it. He had seen the same look—desperate and hopeless—on Will Ramsey's face. Ramsey, too, had lived in terror of the wilderness and yet had not dared to leave it: he had been sentenced to imprisonment for debt, in Maryland, and had escaped. But in his case it had not been an escape: it had been only the exchange of one dread for another. Ramsey never had been meant for the frontier. And this boy was not meant for it either. There were men like Ramsey and Jim Kenny and the surgeon, Miller, whose nerves lay too near the surface. Holden changed the subject:

"I'm looking for a man named McCoy. I was going to meet him at John Fraser's."

"He's not there. I don't know him, but I'd know it if he'd been there. Ramsey's cabin is the next one to the forge. You want to go there?"

"No. No, this is all right."

The high, gullied bank was slipping by. The spring flood, Holden saw, had torn great chunks out of the bank and dragged them down, and the Monongahela was devouring them now slowly. Where he remembered five log houses in a row, there was only one house. All the solid ground between it and the river had collapsed. It stood tilted on the edge of the deep cave-in, with its front wall leaning over nothing.

"That was Burkett's place," the boy said. "All the houses in the Lower Town were covered six feet. It was worse on the Allegheny side, though: all the houses there were washed away. Most of them are piled up in the island two miles down. Burkett had to crawl out his loft window. He was standing on his roof and hollering when I picked him up."

"You picked him up?"

"Sure. It's a good boat. Only the wheels weren't fixed like they ought to be, for ice. There was a lot of ice. Cakes of it kept getting caught between the gunwales and the wheels. That's why the wheels don't stick out so far now. I made the axle shorter." He said, pleased: "You didn't notice that."

"No." The boy, Holden thought, was full of contradictions. It was hard to think of him paddling about in a raging river full of floating ice, picking people off roofs. It had taken a good deal of courage.

The boat drifted past the mouth of a creek. Suddenly the bank was gone. It turned into piles of brown dirt like a row of dung heaps in a barnyard with another row of larger heaps behind them, and Chris Holden saw that Fraser had not been exaggerating when he said a man could walk into Fort Pitt without bothering about the bridge across the moat. The flood had broken through the riverbank and dug deep gouges in the dirt wall of the fort.

He could see the rear walls of the barracks through the gouges. Where the earth of the Monongahela curtain had washed down into the ditch, the bottom of the ditch was level with the lower places in the broken wall. And where the covered way had run along the glacis, with a row of upright sharpened logs protecting it, only a few logs leaned crookedly together like the old pilings of a wrecked wharf. A fatigue detail was puttering in the wreckage. Two men in overhauls pushed at a log half-heartedly; three others leaned on spades and watched them.

"How much do I owe you?"

"I don't want anything. The committee pays me sixty pounds the year for keeping school." He sounded proud. "I didn't mind fetching you across."

"I'm obliged, then." Holden stepped out. Behind him, as he floundered toward the shore, he heard Ten Eyck suck his breath in. *My back,* he thought. *The blood* . . .

He was red muck to the knees when he reached solid ground in front of the Flag bastion. His feet were two enormous lumps. He had to stop and dig the balled clay off them with a stick.

And then, when he went on again, around the bastion toward the King's Road, he felt the wrappings on his left foot coming undone. His impatient prodding with the stick had burst the strip of shirt that they were tied with, and a yard of the wet, mud-slimed leather trailed behind his heel. He stooped and ripped the filthy bundles off his feet. His feet looked about the way he had expected them to look—like pieces of boiled fat back, with red patternings of mud for streaks of lean.

The Flag bastion hid the ruins of the fort's south wall. The glacis had withstood the flood here. It was not smooth; it was veined with an infinity of crooked gullies; but it had not collapsed into the moat. The fraise, too, was intact; the slope of the glacis, rising gently, climbed just high enough to leave the ax-whittled tops of upright logs exposed in an irregular and jagged but unbroken palisade. Beyond them, across the fifty-foot ditch, the brick walls of the bastion sheered away in geometric angles under their gray-green stone copings.

Sodded parapets rose from the copings. Muzzles of brass cannon gleamed in the embrasures. A matross, squatting, slowly rubbed the stubby barrel of a cohorn with a rag. He stared down at Holden's grotesque figure, blew his nose into the dirty rag with two prolonged snorts that were like a comment, and took another slow swipe at the gun.

Ahead, the wall of the town curtain stretched away, straight, smooth, like the side of a brick warehouse tilted slightly backward, until it came to the projecting bulk of the next bastion—the great Grenadier, largest of the man-made hills that formed the five points of the star fort. The Grenadier was a substantial fortress in itself—a five-sided, flat-topped hill encased in brick and buttressed at each steeply slanting corner with rough blocks of hand-cut limestone. Twenty feet above the bottom of the moat, behind earth ramparts shoulder-high and twenty feet thick, iron guns from a royal frigate filled the gun ports with the ponderous square shoulders of their timber carriages. On the wall beyond the bastion loomed the gallows shapes of the squared-timber frames from which the main gate and the drawbridge were suspended. They were made of whole trees. You could hang a giant on them.

The town itself completed the illusion of solidity and permanence and safety. It had not changed. The only difference he could see was that the cabins were a little shabbier and dirtier than he remembered. They looked blurred, somehow, as if they had settled down into the landscape and become a part of it. Even the ax-gnawed stumps that dotted the flat ground between him and the road seemed shrunken, as if they were being absorbed slowly, being pulled inexorably back into the earth.

And now, coming to the wide curve of the King's Road where it swept around the bastion toward the bridges and the main gate, he realized that the brick walls of the Grenadier and the long brick curtain had the same blurred, bleared look. The flood had covered everything for days, and when the rivers finally receded they had left a film of muck upon the logs of all the cabins, on their shutter planks and slab roofs, on the stumps, and even on the red bricks of the fort. Where the grass had grown rank, last year, on the broad slopes of the sodded glacis, there was the same coating of silt, dry and cracking. It had been deposited so thickly that the carefully laid sod was buried; only a few stubborn tufts of grass were struggling through the crust.

The road narrowed to slip through the breach that had been left for it, a little wider than a wagon, in the outer earthworks. A log gate stood open. The road, passing through, ran out upon the twenty-foot shelf of the covered way behind the glacis and came to the first of the two wooden bridges.

The moat was more than a deep ditch here. It was a dry lake, two hundred feet wide, with an artificial island in it—a flatiron-shaped redan of red brick standing on a limestone trivet. The road curved across it, past a small squared-timber guardhouse. Every trick that European soldiers had learned in a thousand years of fighting had been used in building Fort Pitt. The very curving of the road was a shrewd minor part of its defenses. If the outer bridge were stormed and taken, those who took it could not fire upon the second bridge nor even see it till they reached the sharp bend of the road halfway across the bare top of the artificial island. And if they got there, the redan was built to trap them. Two of its three sides were lined with breastworks, but the third side toward the fort was open; cannon on two bastions and the curtain wall between were laid to pour shot into it from three directions.

Holden, running across the first bridge, had a feeling that the fort was pushing him back. It was hard to run. It was hard to feel that there was any need to hurry. Only an enemy who came with batteries of heavy field guns could beat down the fire of those brass howitzers and frigate cannon. Only troops with scaling ladders could get up those sheer walls. *Indians.* . . . No wonder Colonel Bouquet had smiled at the notion. Bouquet, sitting in the quiet elegance of the Apollo room three hundred miles away, had not seen what the flood did. Even Chris Holden, forcing his tired legs to run, found it hard to realize that the imposing cannon and the solid masonry and the whole complicated geometric pattern of redans and bastions had become a lie now—that behind them the dirt ramparts fronting the two rivers had turned into a spilled pudding of mud slowly drying in the ditches they had half filled.

The red-coated sentry in the guardroom doorway yawned at him and then grinned, with the yawn half finished, at his bare feet.

He was running doubled over, with his head and shoulders and his body leaning forward, making his legs hurry to keep up with him. He couldn't spare his hands to make his shirttail decent, he needed both his hands to hold him up. If he put his hands behind him to pull down his shirt, he was quite certain that his body would go sprawling headlong and would never get up.

He was past the second drawbridge. He was in the long, deep, slit-like passage that led through the curtain. It was narrow. It had stone walls. Soldiers lounged against the wall beside a windlass that was like a rimless cart wheel on a tree-trunk axle.

Gravel hurt his bare feet. The parade ground stretched ahead, enormous. The gray slab barracks and the governor's house against the far wall seemed to be a long way off. He ran toward the red brick house, and the house came to meet him. His hands found it unexpectedly. He put his hands against the brick wall and leaned there with his head between his arms.

Somewhere, a great distance off and a great height above him, somebody said "Garn!" The voice came again: "Garn! Get away now. Comin' here drunk . . ."

He lifted his head and looked up at the sentry on the steps.

"Ecuyer," he said. "I want to see Ecuyer."

"By God, ye *are* drunk! If it's the hair of the dog ye're wantin', ye'll not get it here. Ye'll get the cat's tail. Be off with ye now before an off'cer sees ye."

"I said take me to Ecuyer." The words felt stiff. Even to himself he sounded drunk.

"Have it y'r own way." The soldier's amiable face turned ugly. "Fifty lashes. That'll sober ye." He fumbled for the latch behind him. The door swung open of its own weight. "Corp'ral! Corp'ral of the guard . . ."

"What's all the chat about?" There were two soldiers on the steps now. "Who's he?"

"Another dish o' cat meat. Wants t' see the gov'nor. He thinks he does."

"He does, does he? What's your name, you?"

"Holden." There was more to it than that. You didn't just say *Holden* when you went calling on a governor. He took one hand away from the brick wall and rubbed his forehead with it. "Holden," he repeated. "Christopher Holden. Captain, First Regiment, Virginia Militia."

The corporal said angrily:

"You fool you, Farrell! Fetch him in here."

He was in the orderly room with its familiar split-log benches and its gunrack and the muskets leaning in a row against the rack and the headquarters orderlies leaning in a row upon the bench against the left-hand wall. He was looking at the door there in the wall. It had opened and then closed again behind the corporal, and it was familiar also. It had warped the winter it was hung and it was still warped; they had never changed it. But the room had changed. It was much darker than it used to be, with its white plaster walls.

He put both hands up to his head and dragged them down across his eyes, hard. The room was still dim and dingy-looking except for a streak like a plaster molding just below the ceiling. But his head was clearing. He looked at the white streak carefully, following it from wall to wall. It ran all the way around the room, as regular and even as a molding, and he realized that it was the original white plaster. From its lower edge down to the floor, the walls were covered with a dark stain. The rivers had been in the room; they had filled it almost to the ceiling.

The warped door, opening again, squawked like a hen disturbed upon her nest. The corporal said:

"Here. In here."

He was walking through the adjutant's bare office, past a paper-littered table, past a red-coated clerk who scratched an ear with the frayed end of a quill pen and stared at him morosely. There was yet another doorway with another warped door. He was looking at a big desk bastioned with precisely geometric piles of rep-taped and folded papers—at a small-paned window with a bleak view of another muddy brick wall— at a painting of snow-covered mountains in a gilt frame. Captain Simeon Ecuyer, the Swiss mercenary who commanded His Britannic Majesty's forces at the Forks of the Ohio, had brought his native mountains with him to the wilderness. But the officer behind the desk was not Ecuyer.

Chapter 26

The captain who sat between the dreary window and the painted mountains was years younger than Ecuyer. His face was a handsome, sulky boy's face, soft and pallid, and his back had none of Simeon Ecuyer's ramrod stiffness. He lounged indolently, sidewise, with one scarlet arm flung carelessly along the curving splint back of the chair and his hand dangling limply from the wrist lace. His other hand lay in a pool of lace upon the desk. One slender finger stroked the silver-chased butt of a pistol and his eyes watched it under curling lashes, dark in the unnatural pallor of his face. Only his face was stiff. It had the chalky white look of a freshly pipe-clayed crossbelt.

"Well?" The word came from somewhere high up in his nose. "You may report." His voice was like his face, stiff, colorless. It made the hollow, soft sound that a piece of chalk made, moving slowly on a thin slate.

"Captain Holden, First Virginia——"

"Yes. Yes. Yes. I know all that."

"Captain Ecuyer was expecting me."

"Captain Ecuyer is not here. You can see that, can't you? I am in command at present. Captain Steele, His Majesty's Royal American Regiment. Go on."

"Indians," he said. "The Indians . . . They're coming."

"I know that too."

"You know?" Holden sagged against the desk. His hands, hunting for a place where they could help him to stand up, blundered into one of the neat piles of papers. The pile toppled over. "You *know?*"

"Certainly we know—though not from you. We are not dependent upon hired provincials for our information. Fortunately we have other sources. *Very* fortunately." For the first time he looked up at Holden. "You left Williamsburg eight weeks ago. Perhaps you will be good enough to tell me where the devil you've been."

"The Maumee. I've come from the Maumee in eleven days." His legs shuddered and his tongue was clumsy. "Four hundred miles in eight days."

"Well, which is it? Eight days, or eleven? Oh, no matter. Let be. A small difference of three days—a mere trifle, doubtless, by militia standards." Steele's hand flicked the dangling wrist lace. He frowned at it delicately. "Your idea of orders seems to be about the same as your idea of information. A slight deviation doesn't matter. You are sent on an important confidential duty and you disappear for eight weeks."

"I——"

"Kindly do not interrupt me, Holden. We know all about you. Colonel Bouquet was at some pains to inform us—a most sensible precaution, in the circumstances. They were most peculiar circumstances. They were damned outrageous. The Ohio Company has the gall to summon the

188

king's Indian commissioner and dictate to him. It has the gall to summon the commanding officer of the Department of the West and harass him with trumped-up rumors and dragoon him and fob off its agents on him."

"Bouquet didn't say that."

"Indeed." Steele's frown deepened into two sharp creases with a welt of flesh between them. "So you give me the lie, do you?"

"Bouquet wouldn't say that. He would know it's not true."

"I see." Steele's hand moved, languid, toward the scattered papers. "It may interest you . . ." The effort was too great. His fingers drew back and collapsed into their pool of lace. "No matter. I remember what he said quite clearly. 'At a meeting called in Williamsburg on the third instant by the gentlemen of the Ohio Company . . .' Do you deny that?"

"They called it, but——"

"But! But! I suppose you'll tell me they did not insist on interfering with affairs that don't concern them. I suppose they didn't badger and bedevil Colonel Bouquet till he felt obliged to act against his own best judgment and Sir William Johnson's. It is not the colonel's practice to indulge in chitchat, Holden. When he writes dispatches in his own hand, you may be assured he has a purpose. In this case the purpose was to warn us so that we would understand the whole irregular proceeding. He named names. Washington, for one. That by itself was quite sufficient— Washington, the most notorious of the Ohio Company's whole pack of troublemakers. Colonel Bouquet wrote that he engaged you 'on the urgent representations of Colonel Washington and the other gentlemen there present.' *Gentlemen.* . . . Provincial bumpkins! Farmers and tobacco peddlers and slave drivers, village lawyers, placemen, speculators, your Ohio Company land-grabbers. And a blacksmith! Fraser, a back-country blacksmith, forced upon His Majesty's commissioner for Indian affairs and the commanding officer of a department. As an equal!"

"Fraser is an officer." He said it dully. He had no strength left for anger.

"Oh yes. Yes. Small wonder we must have an army out from England to protect your stinking worthless little colonies, when you make officers of blacksmiths." Steele's full underlip pushed out contemptuously as he added: "And land-company surveyors. Very clever, Holden. Using troops at government expense to cut roads through the mountains and build forts to hold your land claims. I've heard all about your Colonel Washington and how Forbes and Bouquet had to fight him, harder than they fought the French, to take the Forks of the Ohio. Gad's life, it's a marvel that Forbes didn't have him shot for insubordination."

Oh, for God's sake, Holden's mind protested. *Insubordination.* After five years, British officers were still mouthing that distorted story, using it to justify their stubborn distrust of provincial officers and their dislike of everything American. The soft, hectoring voice went on and on:

"If war wouldn't profit the Ohio Company, your precious Washington would have none of it. All that you Virginians wanted was a road built to your land grants. When Forbes and Bouquet decided not to truckle to you but to build the road through Pennsylvania instead, you snarled and snapped like dogs robbed of a bone. Your surveyor-speculator-colonel yapped and whimpered that it was impossible to build a road across the mountains, that he couldn't take supplies across the mountains."

Oh, for God's sake . . . stop it! Forbes had built his Pennsylvania road. For seven months, six thousand men had toiled and starved and struggled through the Allegheny wilderness, while all the time there was a road already built to within seven miles of the Ohio and the French fort at the Forks—a clear, level road that had already carried Braddock's endless wagon train and his artillery and even his fine borrowed London coach. Washington had never seen the sense of using a whole army and an entire summer for the building of a new and worse road. He had said so, logically, bluntly, and the British generals and colonels hadn't liked his bluntness or his logic either. They chose to ignore the fact that after six months of enormous labor, Forbes himself despaired of reaching Fort Dusquesne—that his officers in council had decided to go into winter quarters on the Loyal Hanna—that Forbes gave his cherished name of Pittsburgh to his camp there, a hog wallow of mud, slush, and misery, fifty miles east of the Forks of the Ohio. British officers chose to forget that after cautiously avoiding Braddock's road, as if the road itself was to be blamed for Braddock's massacre, they had contrived to blunder into the same kind of trap on Grant's Hill. And when the French, outnumbered thirty to one, burned Fort Duquesne and fled, Englishmen had taken the despaired-of victory as proof that Forbes had been right all along and Washington a pigheaded, selfish, calculating provincial who served himself first, the Ohio Company second, and his king third—if and when his duty to his king and country coincided with his other interests.

"That little game's played out now, Holden. Does the Ohio Company believe it can still use the army? Well, it can't! Trying to usurp the powers of government—sending its own agent to the Indians to speak for Johnson—trying to impress the tribes and cozen more land out of them and more trade." The smooth, pallid voice was wearing Holden's nerves thin. It was rasping on them like soft chalk with grit imbedded in it. "You were hired to carry messages to certain nations. The Shawnees, the Senecas, the Hurons"—Steele's slim fingers ticked the names off on the fat butt of the pistol—"Caughnawagas, Delawares . . . Yes, I remember the whole list distinctly. There was nothing in your orders about going to the Maumees. Can you tell me why you saw fit to exceed your orders?"

"Oh, for God's sake!" He had only half believed John Fraser's furious description of Steele's overbearing, vicious arrogance. He believed it now. But this last piece of ignorance was past believing. "The Maumee is a river. There's no nation called the Maumees."

"Don't swear at me! And don't quibble!" Steele's mouth tightened. But it did not harden. His lips, pushed out, became fuller, softer. "I don't care for quibbling, Holden. The Senecas who live along the Genesee River are still Senecas, but we call them Genesees. There is a Maumee River. Indians have towns there. Very well—they're Maumees."

Holden leaned on his braced arms and stared at him. It was not possible that this was happening. It was not possible that this was the climax of those days and nights when he had driven himself beyond exhaustion and beyond his last shred of endurance and yet kept on going. There was a thin, uneven, brittle-looking line above Steele's nose now, in the pallor of his forehead, like a crack in plaster. *God's teeth!* Steele was powdered like a macaroni. All he needed to complete him was a quizzing glass and a tall cane fashionably clouded. He did not belong here: he belonged in Ranelagh Gardens or St. James's among all the other white-faced, insolent, crimped, powdered, high-and-mighty elegants and lordlings and the dandiprats who aped the lordlings.

"Now, Holden . . ." The crack in the caked powder widened as the white flesh ridged into a welt again between the frowning creases. "Let's see whether you have *any* information that's worth hearing. You blurt out that the Indians are coming. It's been obvious for weeks that they are coming. That sort of intelligence is useless. Would it be expecting too much if I ask *how many* Indians are coming?"

"All of them. Every nation north of the Ohio and west to the Wabash. The Miamis. Sacs and Foxes. Even the Ojibway. That means the Hurons and the lake tribes. I don't know about the Eries and the Senecas. They're the only ones I——"

"*Pfaugh!* The Senecas! D'you imply that Johnson cannot manage the Six Nations? Don't provoke me, Holden. I didn't ask you which *tribes*. I don't want these generalities—I want to know how many of these mangy beasts are coming."

"I can't tell you. Nobody can tell you. Thousands."

"Thousands." Steele's voice mocked him. "Nonsense!"

"The Shawnees and Senecas alone can send a thousand. The Ottawas and Hurons can turn out as many. There aren't many Delawares left, and the Caughnawagas are a small tribe; but God knows what the Ojibway and the Potawotami are doing. I've only seen small parties. Indians don't travel in big bodies. They——"

"Guesswork. Generalities and guesswork. The plain fact is that you don't know. Thousands! Have you any idea what a thousand of those musk cats would mean, swarming in here? Dirty, squawling, thieving beggars! And we treat them better than if they were Englishmen. Gad's life, Holden, d'you know what a soldier gets for stealing? A thousand lashes. We've been too damnation tender with these thieving redskins. I'd make their skins red, I'll warrant! Tie 'em up and flog 'em. Hang a hundred or two of 'em. It would cost less, and they'd smell no worse dead. How they stink! This place is bad enough without 'em, but they'll stink it up like Bedlam. And we'll treat 'em as if they were lords and princes. Feed 'em! Feed 'em six months' rations in a week and go hungry ourselves to make up for it. That's what you have let us in for with your rumor-peddling to Sir William. Fetched 'em here to Fort Pitt when Sir William had arranged to meet 'em at Niagara."

"God Almighty!" Holden's voice was thin with incredulity. "They're not coming to a *meeting!* They're not coming to a council! It's war—*war!* I thought you knew. You said you didn't need my information. You said you had other sources." He felt his tongue stiff on his dry lips. He could hear it babbling: "I was too late. They'd already made their minds up. They burned the belts at Wakatomica. They threw them in the council fire and burned them. They tried to kill me on the Maumee—I had peace belts but they tried to kill me. I got away. I tried to get through to Sandusky, but they headed me; I couldn't. That was eleven days ago. I thought I'd be too late. I wasn't sure until this morning that they hadn't been here."

The white, vapid face did not change. It only stared at him without expression, without interest even.

"There's a reason why they haven't been here. The small posts . . . Le Boeuf . . . Venango . . . Ligonier and Red Stone. They've gone to hit the small posts and the settlements first. They'll cut the forts off and surround them and then go for the plantations—Clapham's, Byerly's at Bushy Run, the Turkey Foot, the Loyal Hanna. That's the reason they're not here yet. You've got to warn the forts! Venango and Le Boeuf won't have a chance. It may be too late already, but you've got to try! You've got to get those people in here. If you send men with spare horses for the women, Byerly's and Clapham's people can be in here in a few hours. A man on a good horse can be at Venango before morning, but he's got to start now! *Steele!*" He leaned closer to the still, emotionless face. His arms trembled as his weight came on them. "Steele, for God's sake . . . Don't just sit there! Don't you understand me?" The white face changed at last. It smiled.

"Yes. Yes, I believe I understand you. I would prefer not to." Steele straightened slowly. When he sat erect he was a tall man. "This is worse than I expected." The brief smile had left his mouth less sullen. It was pleased now. It was almost eager. "So you think the garrisons should be recalled from Fort Venango and Le Boeuf and Red Stone. Ligonier too. It takes a bold man to propose that, Holden."

"I didn't. I was thinking of the people in the little settlements, but . . ." It took courage for an officer in Steele's position even to consider giving up a fort. It took more than courage. Holden was aware of a small and remote sensation of surprise. *He's not a fool.* Steele's mind was not as empty as his face; it had gone swiftly and directly to the thing that he himself had not considered. "Ligonier may have a chance. The others haven't. A dozen men can't hold Le Boeuf or Red Stone. A platoon can't hold Venango—not against what's coming. I told Bouquet that Fort Venango couldn't be defended if it was attacked in earnest."

"Yes. He mentioned that. Then it *is* your idea that these posts should be abandoned?"

"Not Ligonier. There are too many settlers on the Loyal Hanna; the one chance they've got is to get into Ligonier. But the others, yes. They're useless."

"I suppose you realize that if I issue such an order I shall be court-martialed."

Holden nodded.

"Disobedience of orders. Cowardice. What would my defense be? That I acted upon your suggestion? That I gave up three forts in the face of danger—at the first suggestion that they were in danger? That I acted on a rumor——"

"Rumor!"

"Story, then. A story brought to me by one man. Any officer appointed as judge advocate to prosecute me would call that a rumor. What else could he call it? He would tell the court that one man's unsupported story threw me into a blind panic. The court would agree with him. It would be compelled to do so. You can see the difficulty, Holden."

"I see fifty men dead! Scalped! Burned! Tortured! And for nothing . . . *nothing!*"

"That still leaves me nothing, Holden. Nothing but an unsupported story brought to me by one man, without any proof whatever."

"If you want proof . . ." Holden pushed himself away from the desk. "My back . . ." He turned so that Steele could see it. "That's blood on my shirt. My head . . . A hatchet did that. Maybe you can't see—it's clotted."

"I don't doubt that you've had trouble. Even Croghan has had trouble. One of those red devils gave him a black eye, right here in Pitt's Town.[1] But it didn't mean war. I've seen bloody heads before this, Holden. If every brawl and broken head and black eye meant war . . . I can't let a bloody shirt outweigh our other information. As you say, I told you we have other sources. We have. Good ones. There is Calhoon on the Tuscarawas. Calhoon is a trader—an experienced one, Holden. He went into the Muskingum country last fall with a train of goods and twenty clerks and drivers. Isn't it strange that a man who wintered in the Shawnee towns should see no need to warn us? That he sees no sign of trouble?"

"But that was a month ago!"

"And it was *two* months ago that you told Johnson and Bouquet the Indians were plotting trouble. You were some hundreds of miles distant and you had only just returned from England, but you knew more then than Calhoon knew at Tuscarawas a month later. You knew more than Crawford on the Twightwee, or the interpreter—McKee, or Poulson at the Five Towns."

"Poulson knew. Poulson warned *me*. He was getting ready to pull out then. He had fourteen hundredweight of fur, but he was going to leave it and head for the Forks as fast as he could travel. When Nimwha took my belts, he waited. Nimwha is the chief of the five Lower Towns. He took the belts and said he wanted peace; he said he'd try to hold his young men. Poulson thought he might be strong enough to do it. That's why Poulson waited—to make certain."

"You amaze me, Holden. Three weeks ago a man as sound as Poulson wasn't certain. Just what was this *warning* that he gave you?"

"He said deputations from the Ottawas and Hurons had been in the Lower Towns, haranguing Nimwha's people, urging them to kill the traders. They said Pontiac intended to kill every white man and take back the country—the whole country. Drive the English into the Atlantic Ocean and destroy them."

"And you listen to such nonsense!"

"It's not nonsense to them. They believe it. They despise us, Steele! They know how weak we are. They know that they whipped us four times—that they helped to whip us. Trent at the old fort here, Washington at the Great Meadows, Braddock, and then Grant again here. Whipped

[1]The Indian who blacked George Croghan's eye was a Delaware chief, Tedyuscung.

us almost without trying! My God, Steele, it's not eight years since scalping parties were within thirty miles of Baltimore and the town was in a panic. It's not eight years since Annapolis was building breastworks to defend itself against the Indian attack that everyone believed was coming."

"Did it come?"

"No."

"No, of course not. D'you expect me to abandon three forts on the strength of things that happened eight years ago—that *didn't* happen? You dared to propose that I abandon three forts. You dared! Gad's life, you must have been desperate to try that! Well, the game's up. That's one trick you'll not take, Holden."

"Trick. . . ." He repeated the word stupidly. It had no meaning.

"Oh, drop it. Stop pretending, Holden. You're caught and you know it. D'you think I'm a ninny? D'you think I can't see what it would mean to your Ohio Company if we gave up those posts? What an uproar you could make about that! Danger . . . panic on the frontier . . . forts abandoned . . . that's *proof* of the danger . . . send us more troops . . . drive the Indians across the Allegheny . . . drive them off our precious land grants! It's the same old story."

Yes, Holden's mind repeated wearily, *the same old story.* The same threadbare lie. The old lie that had been worn thin before Steele ever heard it.

"More troops! Always more troops! You Virginians have squealed and yammered for ten years now." Even anger did not fill the hollow thinness of Steele's voice. "You've been squealing louder since the government shut out your settlers. That hurt, didn't it? That drove you frantic. You can't peddle your damned land grants!"

The words were a flood, slowly rising. It seemed to Holden that the spate of words was filling his brain, mingling with the flood of weariness and weakness and futility, closing over his head, and there was no longer any need to struggle. He could rest now, if that voice would stop. It didn't.

"This is not the first time tricks like this have been tried, Holden. When a tradesman sees a profit and thinks up a trick to get it, he can always find some bully to pull off the trick."

Steele was leaning forward, but it seemed to Holden that the pallid face was dimmer. It was blurred with its own shadow. It was not a face at all now. It was like a patch of fungus on a tree, dead-white and dry and lifeless. He knew that his mind was acting queerly.

"When the London merchants wanted the West Indies trade, they didn't stick at bringing on a war to get it. They——"

Oh, stop. Stop. Dammit. . . . He was interested in the odd behavior of his mind now. He was interested in the white face there below him. If he put his hand out, he could touch it. It would not be dry and stiff. It would feel the way the underside of a great round flat toadstool felt—flabby and a little moist and cold and lifeless and a little like flesh but not flesh that had life in it. It would feel like something that grew in a damp, dark place, as clammy and unpleasant as the dead-alive voice:

"—didn't stick at a cheap trick to get the war they needed . . . found a fellow that had lost an ear .. no difference to them that Captain Jenkins's ear had been cropped in the pillory for stealing or false swearing or some such small matter. . . ."

Holden only half heard. He had lost all interest in what the voice was saying. He was only interested in the pulpy red mouth. It reminded him of something.

". . . sent Jenkins into Parliament to swear the Spaniards cut his ear off . . . sent him into Commons with a piece of hog rind done up in a box to show off for his ear. This isn't '39 now, Holden. We fought one war over a man's ear, but we'll not fight another. The Ohio Company will have to think up something better than Captain Jenkins's ear or Captain Holden's sore head. What the devil do you find to laugh at?"

Holden was not laughing. He was only smiling. He knew now what the face was made of. It was not a fungus; he'd been wrong about that. The soft, petulant, pale-red lips gave Steele's face the look of the plant that grew in damp woods in springtime, bulging up through rotten leaf mold in unpleasant swellings that were like pale lumps of dead flesh. It was called the corpse plant. The lumps it made were formed of tightly clustered, delicately curled white stalks, dry-looking and stiff-looking. When you touched them, they were damp and flabby. And they turned black when you touched them; they were rotten. The corpse plant fed on rottenness—on dead leaves and decaying humus—and on the living roots of other plants.

Steele's tirade went on, on and on, in the same colorless, unchanging voice. It did not disturb him. Its monotony was almost soothing. He could think quite comfortably. Steele was like the corpse plant. Steele was one of those delicately elegant and perfect rotten things that grew out of the rottenness of England—out of the top layer of insolence and arrogance and place and wealth that covered England like decaying humus—out of the dull brutality and callousness that still burned women at the stake, and hanged young boys for stealing pinchbeck buckles, and permitted children to be sold or farmed out and made hideous with festering sores and set to begging on the steps of churches—out of a society that rode to church and gambling clubs and bagnios in enormous gilded coaches through streets heaped with ordure, and chained poor crazy people naked in their filth in Bedlam and went Sunday-picnicking to watch their antic sufferings and snuff their smells as if the stench of human filth was perfume and the sight of human misery a spectacle devised for their civilized enjoyment. Steele was one of those unpleasant parasites that flourished on corruption and decay, infesting palaces and ministries and armies, spreading their own rottenness while they sucked life out of what was good and strong in England.

". . . worse than Jenkins. No pretenses . . . common, ordinary fellow . . . bully." Holden heard the words in snatches. "You . . . gentleman . . . rich." *Rich.* Holden thought. *That's rich.* His mind went on about its interesting business. Even while a corpse plant grew, it was already dying, rotting. The decay appeared in pale-red splotches. As the splotches spread, the corpse plant twitched; the indolently drooping stalks uncurled and straightened; you could see them moving. He could see the pale-red lips move:

"Captain-liar Jenkins. Captain-bully Jenkins. Do you hear me, Holden?"

"Yes," Holden said.

"And you take it! My God, but you're shameless! You come in here with a clumsy lie, and when you're caught you try to bluff your way through. You try to bluff and bully a king's officer into abandoning the forts entrusted to him. Captain-liar-a-bully Holden. And you grin—you can stand there grinning! I dare say you'll not resent that either. You provincial *gentlemen* are all alike. You're all bluffs and bullies. Two of you in two days are enough to turn the stomach. You and Leslie—officers and gentlemen. And cowards. He——"

"Leslie?" Unexpectedly, Chris Holden found that Steele had said something interesting. "Major Leslie?"

"That's what he calls himself. These titles—pah! I wonder that His Majesty allows them. Not twenty-four hours ago this Major Leslie swaggered into this post, draggled-tailed and slovenly as you are, and provoked a brawl—a low brawl—publicly, on the parade ground. He had the effrontery to force a quarrel upon two of my officers—upon two captains of the Royals, by God!"

"Two?" This was very interesting. It was most amusing. *"Two?* That sounds like Leslie. That sounds like the proper odds for Leslie. I trust that your officers were able to protect themselves. May I inquire what happened?"

"He got his face slapped. That's what happened."

"By both of them?"

"By a girl! By a common tavern slut he followed all the way to Pittsburgh."

"I see." This was very funny. "Do I understand this slut is under the protection of *both* of these officers—both of them at the same time?"

"Why, damn you!"

"Interesting," Holden murmured. "Interesting." In Steele's face the splotch that was his mouth was spreading. The pale red was creeping up his cheeks now, it was showing through the pallor in two larger splotches. Holden watched them carefully, with an expectant scientific curiosity. In a moment or two Steele would unfold; he would get up out of the chair; he would stand erect and he would be all red—pale-red face and pale-red coat—like a corpse plant. It occurred to Holden that perhaps there was a way to hasten the unfolding. "Major Leslie—is he under orders?"

"He is not! One of you is a plenty."

"Well, then, I suggest a small experiment. You say all provincial gentlemen are cowards. I am not free to resent it. I suggest, though, you repeat your observation as it touches Leslie. I suggest that you repeat it to his face, sir."

Steele unfolded. He was on his feet, erect, and he was all red. Holden chuckled at him. *It worked. God's teeth and toenails—it worked!* He could not control himself. He didn't want to. It had been a long time since he'd felt so pleased and satisfied and tickled. The chuckle tickled in his throat and bubbled up into his mouth and he was laughing.

He leaned on the desk and shook with laughter till the desk began to swim away from him. He tried to hold it, but it was a big desk, sleek and smooth and slippery. There was nothing he could hold to, he could only try to keep up with it as it floated toward the window. But he was not worried. His mind was still clear and clever. The desk was much too big to float out through the window; when it got there, it would fetch up with a loud bump.

It did.

He pulled himself up close to it again and patted it and chuckled. Good desk. He approved of it. He approved of Steele too. Both of them had done exactly what they were supposed to do.

There was another loud bump. It annoyed him. There was no occasion for it. *Bump . . . bump . . .* Steele was pounding the desk with the fat butt of the pistol. The warped door screeched open. Steele said:

"Corporal, get this man out of here. Take him to the gate and throw him out. He's not to come in—tell Captain-Lieutenant Carre I said so. He is not to be allowed in under any circumstances. He is not to talk to any member of this garrison. D'you understand that, Holden? If I hear so much as one word of your rumor-peddling . . ."

Holden sniggered. A hand took him by the arm. The desk spun away. The warped door swirled toward him. Faces swam in a dark whirlpool. They revolved around him, faster, faster, but they were suspended somehow. They did not sink. He was sinking. He was being sucked down into the flood that had filled the orderly room higher than a man's head. It was whirling so fast that it glistened. It was blinding, like sun, and there were red splotches spreading and uncurling, turning black around the edges. He plunged through the spinning vortex into stunning brightness.

Chapter 27

The smell of burning roused him. It was thin and bitter. It was warm and gassy.

He awakened easily, completely. There was no reluctance and no struggle. There was no confusion. He knew instantly that he was in John Fraser's bed and that he had been sleeping a long time and that the awful clogging weariness was gone. His senses were alert. Even in his sleep they had run quickly to their places, and he lay motionless now, waiting for them to identify the thing that had alarmed them. Already they were telling him there was no danger in it, there was nothing that he had to do about it. But they couldn't tell him how he'd got to Fraser's cabin.

He snuffed curiously at the gassy odor. It was not unpleasant. It was only unfamiliar. But it must belong here. Everything else was as it should be—the peeled rafters slanting, the greased-paper window coppery with sunshine, the lighthearted rapid chatter of the water wheel that ran the bellows for John's forge. And there were small bustling hushed sounds in the next room.

Jackie Fraser always bustled. She liked noises and she liked to make them—busy, brisk broom noises, spoon-and-stewpan noises, lid-and-kettle noises. He knew that she was trying to be quiet now and let him sleep, but he imagined he could hear her sputtering.

The idea of Jackie Fraser being quiet was amusing. He smiled, and the smile felt loose. It felt as if his face had come unwrapped. He put his hand up and discovered that his face was naked. The stiff bristly mat of beard was gone. Someone had shaved him while he slept. His cheeks were as bare and raw as a parlor floor looked when its Brussels carpet had been taken up and it had been scrubbed thoroughly and sand-scoured. His face felt as if it had been scoured with sand.

He discovered that his arms and shoulders, too, were bare. And when he lifted the edge of the covers and looked under them, he saw that he was naked in the bed. The filthy leggins and the crusted shirt were gone and he was clean. His body was so white that it was luminous in the dim yellow cavern of the lifted linen.

He was not merely naked: he was a skeleton. He could see his ribs springing like hoops of a staved-in barrel, the skin sunken deep. His belly was a shallow dry pond, white and hollow-flat like the Ohio salt-lick ponds in summer.

He had not been hungry when he woke up. But now, at the sight of his ribs and his belly, he was famine-stricken, he was starved and ravenous. He knew what the warm mysterious smell was. It was something cooking, scorching. His belly mourned: *Jackie . . . Jackie . . . burned it . . . letting it burn . . . no!*

In one frantic motion he swung his legs over the edge of the bed and snatched the patchwork quilt and huddled it around him and went hurrying to prevent disaster.

The disaster was worse than he had feared. Mrs. Fraser was not cooking. She was ironing. She had his blue militia tunic spread out on the table and she was assailing it with an immense charcoal flatiron. The thin smell of burning was the charcoal gas emerging from the metal spout that stuck up from the front end of the flatiron like a long thick neck and curved into a round black empty hole. He felt as empty as the hollow spout, and his disappointment rose up thin and bitter. He said desolately: "Jackie!"

"Well," she said. "Well. I suppose you want your dinner. I never saw a man yet didn't want things of a woman at the wrong time." She wet a finger at her mouth and lifted up the iron and touched the wet tip of the finger to it. The iron sputtered. "It's heated just right. Just right—an' you wake up an' come slinkin' in here to be fed."

"You didn't need to iron that coat," he said.

"Carre thought you'd maybe want to wear it when Ecuyer got back. He said Ecuyer'd surely come today, because there's a ball down at the fort tonight—the king's birthday ball. It ain't in nature for the commandant to miss that."

"Stair Carre . . . is he here?" Chris saw, in his mind, the small, thin, beak-nosed face poised hawklike on the long thin neck. Of all the English officers he had known in nine years of war, Lieutenant Stair Campbell Carre was the only one who had become a close friend. "I haven't seen Stair since he relieved me at Venango."

198

"It's a lucky thing for you that he was off'cer of the day. If he hadn't seen you when you fell down the steps at headquarters——"

"I didn't." It was coming back now. "I didn't fall. They threw me."

"Yes. Stair saw 'em. It was him brought you here. Now go get some clo'es on. There's some things o' John's laid out. I burned ever'thing you had on, quick's I got it off you."

"*You* did?"

"Who'd you think did?"

"I thought John——"

"Stair sent John to find Ecuyer. 'Tain't the first time I undressed a man. Nor washed one, neither."

"Thanks, Jackie. How long did I sleep?"

"Round the clock an' four-five hours onto the next go-round."

"I thought you were getting breakfast. I thought you were cooking something—vinegar pie or something. It woke me up."

"Vinegar pie! For breakfast! You gone Pennsylvania Dutch? Anyway, it's hours past breakfast."

"Then we can have pie, can't we?" Ever since he first knew Jackie Fraser he had teased her in small foolish ways.

"You'll get no pie. You'll have more broth an' like it."

"More?"

"You had nearabout a gallon before you dropped off. In a couple hours I'll serve you up some stew. John got him a deer down to Shertee's, day 'fore yesterday."

He asked, carefully casual:

"Any sign of trouble?"

"There ain't been no shootin', if that's what you mean. There ain't been no heads peeled. But there will be."

"Yes? Go on. What's happened?"

"You might say there's signs. For one, the Munsees[1] up the Allegheny have pulled out. A couple men that had been huntin' came back to the Forks last night; they said the Munsee towns are empty—not man, woman, or child in 'em. For another sign, there was some Delawares come in yest'-day about noontime, tradin'. They had skins—a lot of them an' good ones, but they acted like they were in an almighty hurry. Took the first price offered an' went back down-river; but b'fore they went, their headman told McKee if he was goin' anywheres he oughtn't to be gone for more'n four days."

"Does Steele know that?"

"He knows, all right. Trent[2] told him. Trent's sure they're up to mischief. Him an' his men an' some others that he's told are keepin' their guns handy. They're carryin' their rifles ever'wheres they go, even when it's only out back. Steele don't like it. He was dead set on arrestin' you, soon's as he heard about it. Said you had been spreadin' wild talk, breakin' orders. Carre told him you'd been drinkin' an' had passed out so you couldn't talk. He figured 'twasn't in Steele's nature to believe any-

[1]Munsees—a branch of the Delaware nation.

[2]William Trent, brother-in-law and partner of George Croghan. This passage is based on the entry in his journal for May 27, 1763.

thing that was the plain truth, like you sleepin'. Land sakes, *will* you go an' get some clo'es on? That's my good quilt you're wipin' up the floor with."

He went back into the bedroom. In his anguished haste to keep imaginary food from scorching, he had noticed nothing, but he saw now that he must have had the instinct of a sleepwalker to escape breaking his neck, or his shins at least, on trunks and boxes. All his baggage was here —his old shabby field trunk, the new trunk that he had bought in London, and the other one with silver handles to its elegantly curved top.

His own London trunk was open and his traveling coat was spread out on it, the three capes hung carefully across the lid to smooth themselves of wrinkles. He wondered whether either of the Frasers had looked into the red-varnished trunk—and then remembered he had given the key to Diana Travers. To Diana Holden, he corrected himself, and waited for the hurt to come. He was surprised, a little, when it didn't.

On the rived plank bench beside the bed lay one of Fraser's hunting shirts, thrummed leggings, Mingo-beaded garters, a fresh doeskin clout folded into a square with its edges just so. A pair of moccasins squatted on the puncheon floor. He looked at them while he stood on one foot and then on the other, shoving his thin shanks into the enormous flapping sacks of Fraser's leggings. Trade moccasins, he thought. Fancy ones—not what a man would wear for serious business in the woods. The dyed quillwork was Shawnee.

But the moccasins fitted: his feet hadn't shrunk; for all their soakings, they were still as big as ever. His shoulders were still wide enough to fill the hunting shirt; but he was glad that it was cut more like a coat than like the linsey wrap-arounds that reached down to the knees and tied behind with strings. A shirt of that kind, if it fitted John, would go three times around Chris Holden's lankness now. When he had tied the garters at his knees, the leggings did not feel so much like grain sacks, but they felt as if he had a skirt on each leg; the folds he had to take in them made wide pleats underneath the garters.

He sat on the bench, frowning at them and listening to Jackie's spoon-and-kettle, fire-and-poker noises and the frantic clamor of his stomach. If he had a pipe . . . It was weeks since he had smoked. Weeks? Months. The stone pipes he had shared in Shawnee and Caughnawaga and Miami council lodges didn't count. The last time he had had a long clay in his mouth was that night at Selden Blount's, almost two months ago. Plague! All these trunks, and not a pipe in any of them, or a smidgen of tobacco.

But he might have left one in a pocket of his traveling coat. He got up from the bench and rummaged in it hopefully. There was tobacco in two pockets, crumbs and shreds to mock him. And there was a paper, folded, that got into his way. He jerked it out and wondered when and why he'd wadded a newspaper into the skirt pocket of his London coat to bulge it.

He looked at the heading in the streaked light of the window. There was a full-rigged ship sailing backward in one corner; in the other, a post-man on a horse with an impossibly crimped tail was galloping into an inky sunrise. Between them was a drawing of St. James's Street, complete with coach and strolling elegants and ladies. Below, five different kinds of letters said OWEN's Weekly Chronicle, or, UNIVERSAL JOURNAL. From Saturday, February 4, to Saturday, February 11, 1763.

It seemed impossible that he had been in London when this paper had been printed—that he had been walking in St. James's Street and looking at that palace.

"Chris! Chris Holden, ain't you dressed yet?"

"Coming," he called. He said, in the doorway: "I was waiting so to hear you. It sounds right good."

But he saw that the attempt at pleasantry had failed. Jackie's face seemed to be growing smaller. It was so small that it looked gone.

"John does that," she said. "He does that sometimes, just to plague me."

"He's a wise man. He knows you're the only woman he could stand hollering at him."

"I guess that's so."

"He knows too much for any Indian to get the better of him, Jackie."

"Yes." There was no agreement in her eyes. "A man's allowed so much luck in his life. Just so much. When he's used it up——"

"I didn't know you worried like that, Jackie."

"It's a thing men don't know."

"Carre should have sent a man that wasn't married. There's a plenty of them." He felt the need to defend himself against her fear and her unspoken accusation. "Why did he pick John?"

"Because he couldn't send a soldier and he knew Steele wouldn't send one. Oh, set *down!* What's that you got there?"

"What? Oh, this. A newspaper."

"Land, I ain't seen a newspaper in I don't know when."

"It's a London paper. It's an old one. I'd forgotten that I had it."

"London. Think of that, now. John said you didn't take to London. But you must have, to be readin' about it while your broth gets cold."

He handed her the paper.

"That's a picture of St. James's Street, there. You can see King George's palace at the far end."

"An' you've been there!"

"Not inside the palace. Anyway, I'd rather be here." He was positive about that as he sat down to the table with the blue bowl on it. He picked the bowl up greedily in both hands.

"Put that down, Chris Holden! Been to London, an' you fetch back manners like that! You eat that broth slow. *Slow.* You hear me?"

"Yes. I heard you." He grinned. "So did all of Pitt's Town."

"More of your fine manners—tellin' me I holler. Skulkin' in the bedroom so I'll have to holler. I allow the cat that went to London learned more manners than what you did." But she had forgotten, for a moment, to be worried. She was making a face at him. "What I should have done, I should have smacked you while I had you bare. I should have smacked you good."

"I wouldn't have known anything about it."

"You'd have known, all right. You'd have felt it till a month past Christmas, happen I'd laid into you the way I ought. My land alive, I ain't never seen a newspaper like this here one, Chris. 'The History of

Europe for This Week,' " she read. "That's what it says. Land alive, I thought history was something happened a long time ago, not just this week. It says 'Russia' at the top here, an' then it's got a T set in a garden of flowers, like, an' the other letters of a word alongside. It's right pretty. Only I can't say the next word." She spelled it.

"Czarina," Chris said.

"What's that?"

"The wife of the King of Russia. They call him the czar."

"C-z-a-r-i-n-a. What do they need the C for?"

"I don't know."

"I expect it's a mistake. I expect you couldn't look for them to spell things right, in English. They're foreign, ain't they? It says, 'The Czarina has long entertained a personal resentment against the King of Prussia . . .' Well, I never! Just like a woman! An' her married to a king, too! It says, 'The Russian Army, after taking possession of His Prussian Majesty's dominions in Poland, is now making an invasion upon his dominions in Germany. *Take and hold'*—they've got that in a different kind of letters; I expect that's so it will look more important—*'Take and hold* is the standing maxim in the Russian cabinet.' What does all that mean, Chris?"

"It means they've got wars over there too."

"I expect so. Then there's a place where it says 'Prussia' and then 'Sweden and Denmark.' There ain't nothing about London."

"Precious little. You'll find what there is if you turn over to the other side. All the London newspapers are the same. You look on the second page to see what's happening in London."

She turned the page. He was spooning the last drop of broth out of the bowl and slyly eyeing the pot on the hearth crane when she cried out so suddenly and loudly that she startled him:

"My great land alive!"

"What's the matter?"

"It's terrible!"

"What is?"

"London. It's a terrible place! Why, it's all robberies and murders, Chris. Listen to this: 'Yesterday evening two gentlemen returning out of Kent in a post chaise were stopped and robbed near New Cross Turnpike.' An' right after it there's this: 'Last night as Mr. Willis, an attorney of Chiswell Street, and Mr. Spackman, grocer, of the same place, were returning from Islington, they were attacked in the Spa fields by four footpads, who used them cruelly, and took from them their watches and about £2.' And then there's a piece about a man named Crawford that shot a minister's servant—'shot him dead upon the spot,' it says, and for no reason. Chris, is all that *true?*"

"I don't know."

"But in *London!* It's a city. It's got palaces and schools and churches, and it's where the king himself lives. I marvel he allows it."

"London's a big place. Almost anything can happen. People that have to be out on the streets at night take servants for a guard, or they arrange to go in parties, and they carry loaded canes or sword canes and some carry pistols. The post drivers take guns with them. London's a city, right enough, and it's been there a long time; but there are woods inside it that are right much like the woods around here, and swamps full of snipe, and . . . Jackie, is that venison stew ready?"

She was still absorbed. He helped himself from the pot on the crane.

"Here's a man stood in the pillory for beating a girl, an' here's a postmaster that had robbed the mails; he got fifty pounds, it says. I declare to goodness, I'm that glad you fetched this newspaper. It makes me feel a great way safer. London . . . I'd be scairt to death in London. Chris . . ."

"Uh?" He had his mouth full.

"Is this why you saved the paper—this here, where it says about the apples?"

"Apples?"

"It says 'Royal Mercy,' an' then underneath it says, 'We are informed that on Monday last a dozen apples were plucked from Tyburn Tree.' What kind of tree is that?"

"It's the gallows, on a hill called Tyburn. Tyburn Tree's a kind of joke, in London."

"A nice pleasant joke, I must say! It says, '. . . plucked from Tyburn Tree, when my Lord Justice Grenfell, sitting in Old Bailey, granted reprieves to twelve persons who had been condemned to be hanged for various offenses at the last assizes. These Beneficiaries of the Royal Mercy are to be transported to the province of Virginia, there to serve in the plantations of that Colony subject to the pains and penalties by the law provided for the breaches of terms of indenture.' Then it tells the names and what they did."

She began reading the names.

" 'Benjamin Dyckett, for the stealing of ten pair thread stockings; Margaret Dyckett, his wife, for abetting said crime; Fanny Swivens, widow, for abduction of a male child; Jeremy Love, for being a notorious budge rascal and pickpocket . . .' What ever's a budge rascal? Is that a joke too?"

"No. Not in London. There are too many of them. It means he was a thief."

"A thief. We've got *those*. Did you know somebody stole a thousand dollars, Pennsylvania currency, out of Captain Ecuyer's quarters? Almost a year ago now, an' they never found who done it. I allow they'd hang *him* if they caught him. They wouldn't let him off the way they done this Jack Rundle, here. 'For attempted robbery of the Romsey mail,' it says, an' then it says, 'Abigail Martha Hale, for the murder of a seaman, the said seaman being then about his duty under an impressment officer.' Chris, that's the one that you bought, ain't it?"

"So John told you what an idiot I was."

"I don't know's you were an idiot. John says you set her free. It ain't the only decent thing was ever done that went wrong—if that's why you bought her. You couldn't know she wasn't decent."

"A girl that had done murder?"

"It don't say she done murder. It says the judge changed her sentence on account she didn't. It says she was an ac—ac—*ac*complice, but that she didn't do the killin'."

"She confessed. That's what Pollexfen said. That's what Ellis said. Leach too. Everybody said so. She confessed to killing her own brother."

"John told me about that Pollexfen. I don't know them others, but it's plain they hadn't read what's in this newspaper. Ain't you read it neither?"

"No. I forgot I had it."

"Happen you weren't's interested in that girl's I thought you were. Or else . . ." She looked at him sharply. "Chris Holden, I'd give a pretty to know what happened. I allow *you'll* never tell. You came close, though. You talk in your sleep. D'you know that?"

"No." It alarmed him.

"You didn't use to. But you surely talked a plenty last night. Times I was a mind to wash your mouth out good with soft soap. Sluts an' bitches an' nightwalkers."

"I'm sorry," he said.

"What I'd like to know is what you're sorry about. *Something* happened." The paper hid the most part of her face. Her eyes peered at him shrewdly over the king's inky palace. "John told me you'd got quit of that tidewater frill that you were sweet on. He said seemed you didn't mind much. I don't know. Maybe it was her you laid them names to. I'd been thinkin' . . ."

Her eyes slid out of sight.

"Leave me read you what it says here. 'The reprieved girl'—that's her —'was condemned at the January assizes. On her trial, when asked if she had aught to say in her defense, she cried out, "I killed my brother! It's all my fault. If I hadn't made him come to London, it would not have happened. I did not kill the sailor and he didn't either. But I'm guilty of my brother's death. I am as guilty as if I had killed him with my own hand." ' "

It was wrong. It had to be wrong. She had confessed to murder; they'd all said so. She had picked his pocket. She was a girl off the London streets. She had been willing . . . too willing. And then she had gone to Garth. But now he saw her again, on the deck of the ship, with her young body caught and held and revealed in the wind's hard embrace.

"Anyway," he heard himself say, "I didn't follow her out here. I'm not that much a fool."

"I didn't say nothin' like that. What you talkin' about?"

"Steele—something he said. You remember Leslie?"

She nodded.

"Them that was on the frontier back in '56 ain't forgettin' the Maryland Rangers an' Arnie Leslie. It was him saved the Cumberland men when the Delawares had 'em surrounded on Sidelong Hill, after McCord's was burnt. What's he got to do with this?"

"He's here. Steele said he had followed a girl out to Pitt's Town—a girl that had been indented."

"That's likely, ain't it? Maryland gentry traipsin' acrost the mountains after a common bound girl! I know all about that. What happened was,

Arnie Leslie went down to the fort, an' the first thing he saw was a captain of Royals—Barent, his name is—tryin' to kiss this girl. Bein' a gentleman, nothin' will do but he's got to say Barent can't. An' then out of the officers' quarters comes Arnold—you know *him*—an' wants to protect her too. He's been hot after her for weeks."

"Arnold's got a girl."

"An' wishes he didn't, now that he's seen this new one. Anyway, there they were, rowin' like tomcats, until the redheaded chit gave Leslie a slap for his pains."

"Red? Did you say redheaded?"

"Redder'n that copper kettle." The newspaper crumpled. "My land, Chris! She ain't *that girl!*"

"No," he said slowly. "Her hair isn't red." He saw her hair blown by the wind. He saw her smiling at him, and then Ellerby Pollexfen pulling him away, and the smile dying. "It was more like a new-minted gold piece."

"I vow!" Mrs. Fraser got up abruptly. "I vow, Chris! D'you think tavern wenches an' bound girls an' fancy women are so scarce out here that the first one you hear about is *her*? There's a good twenty of 'em. A bad twenty, I mean." She seized the long poker leaning by the hearth and prodded at the half-burned logs. The sparks flew. "Every wagon train that comes acrost the mountains fetches in a woman or two—an' I don't mean wives. There's traders that make as much off girls they fetch in as they make off rum. My stars! In a garrison town? What with the new ones they fetched in this year, we've likely got more fancy women here now than there is in Norfolk or Annap'lis. That's not countin' squaws."

She turned toward him, and the poker spilled ash on the puncheons.

"Happen it was her, what difference would it make?"

"It might make a good deal," he said. "I thought she might be here. If she was, it would be Garth that brought her. And Garth's got a wife. I don't think Guyasuta's daughter would like sharing her bed with a white girl."

"Hannah? She's a Mingo, ain't she? There's a plenty Mingo women doublin' up with any white man that'll buy 'em a two-shillin' brooch an' feed 'em."

"She's no ordinary Mingo. Hannah holds herself high. Hannah's father is about as close to being chief of the whole Mingo nation as it's possible to get. He's one Seneca that's never bothered to pretend he doesn't hate the whites."

"It would help some if he hated Garth a little."

"That's what I've been thinking. Maybe he does."

"Givin' Garth his daughter? Givin' him twelve million acres?"

"He might have a reason. He could do that and still hate him. I thought Garth was using Guyasuta, but I've changed my mind. It's the other way round. Guyasuta's using Garth."

"Anyway, it ain't the same girl," she insisted.

"No. If it had been, I might have got my money's worth out of her. It would be worth a hundred and three pounds if she turned Hannah against

Garth. I was afraid he wouldn't risk it. All the same, I'd like to know where Garth is."

"Where d'you suppose he is? All his men are here, but he ain't. Where would you be about now, if you were up to what you think he's up to?"

"I'd be in Guyasuta's town. Thanks, Jackie."

"And you wouldn't have no white girl with you."

"No."

"That's likely why he sent her here."

"Here! You said——"

"I ain't said nothin' wasn't true, Chris. All I said was that the girl Val Arnold's after ain't the girl you bought. She ain't. But the other one's here. Now, Chris, you wait! Don't you go actin' hasty. There ain't nothin' you can do about it."

He was on his feet.

"Where is she?"

"John said I wasn't to say nothin', but you got to find out sometime. If she went to Garth, like John said, I allow he's had enough of her. He wouldn't leave no woman that he wanted at Dave Bone's place, amongst all them soldiers an' trail drivers. Garth's done with her. She's Bone's girl now. An' she's dirty—dirty as a squaw, Chris."

"So you've seen her. And John's seen her, and she *is* the girl?"

"Yes. Now you look here, Chris Holden! You ain't goin' to the Gilded Beaver!"

She whisked to the door and stood there with the long iron poker clutched in both hands.

"I believe you'd hit me," he said.

"I will!"

"There are two doors, Jackie." He grinned at her. "What you going to do about that?"

The poker clattered on the floor.

"Here, now! You can't shoot me."

She was lifting a long rifle from its wall pegs.

"You've been a fool about as often as you can afford, Chris. Oh, I know you're goin'. I can't stop you. If you got it in your mind you want her——"

"I don't want her, Jackie."

"What you goin' for, then?"

"I don't know. I've got a notion. A kind of a half a notion."

"You ain't goin' there without you take this rifle."

"That thing's no good," he said. "A rifle's no good in a place like that."

She nodded briskly.

"That's so. Like as not you wouldn't have room. Take your pistols."

"They're no good anyplace. They got wet and I didn't stop to clean them. It wasn't any use; my powder had got wet too."

"They're clean," she said. "I cleaned them soon as I got done with you. I put new flints in. They'll shoot."

He stood grinning at her.

"I'll bet there's one thing you forgot."

"Well, what?"

"You didn't scour my teeth."

"Oh, didn't I?"

"You didn't!"

"The next time I'll leave the sassafras twig sticking in your mouth, so you'll know."

"Don't," he said. "No, don't. I'd just as soon you didn't."

Chapter 28

The shortest way to the Gilded Beaver was along the bank of Hogg's Pond run to the King's Road. But the Gilded Beaver was on the far side of the run. To reach it by the road, he'd have to wade the ford. He didn't want to.

The reason, he told himself, was that he didn't want Dave Bone or any others of Garth's people to know that he had come from Fraser's. It wasn't a good reason. Anybody who was not a newcomer at the Forks would know that if Chris Holden was in town the likeliest place to find him was the Fraser cabin. But it was better than admitting to himself that he couldn't bear the thought of muddying and wetting these dry moccasins. This was the first time in weeks when he'd been clean and dry. He didn't want it spoiled.

He saw that John had built himself a kind of wharf—the half of a split log that rested on posts driven into the creek bottom. It made a walkway by which John could reach the water wheel and tinker with it.

He picked out a solid-looking piece of ground where grass grew on the opposite bank and ran out along the log and took a flying leap. It landed him on the grass. The sod sank in a little and the grass wiped greenish stains along the sole seams of the moccasins, but he had kept them dry. He looked back at the creek. It was a right good jump for a man who'd been through what he had been through, these last few days. He went down through the wooded pasture toward the lower run. When he came to it he saw the Perdue cabin on the farther bank.

Pitt's Town had another name for the Perdue house. It was called Perdition.

Nan Perdue, who lived there, was not married. Neither were the two girls who lived with her. There were a plenty of unmarried women in the town—some who claimed that they were wives to the men they lived with, and some who didn't bother about claims. But no men lived in Nan Perdue's house. They only visited.

The next step for that trollop he had bought, when Bone was finished with her, would be Nan's—if Nan would take her in.

As he turned up along the bank toward the King's Road, he noticed an odd thing about the Perdue cabin. One of the sticks near the top of its cat-clay chimney had put out a green shoot.

The chimney looked new. The flood probably had softened the clay in the old one and washed it away, and whoever built the new one had used green willow for the sticks. The sprout near the chimney top already had three leaves and it was going to have more. It would thrust roots into the wattled clay and they would twist and twine around the other sticks, wrenching and pulling them apart; and in a year or two the chimney would be cracked and ready to fall down.

It was a nice piece of irony. Those three fluttering green leaves summed everything up neatly—civilization and nature and the struggle that went on here endlessly between them.

Civilization! Its first achievement at the Forks of the Ohio had been to arrange for nine years of war, with more efficient instruments for killing. Now its own weapons, the steel knife and the hatchet and the gun, were being turned against it by civilized men who had become more savage than the savages. Its second achievement had been to turn nature itself into a successful business at Perdition—to establish the world's oldest trade in its own house before there was a schoolhouse or a church. And now, there too, nature was taking back its own. The wilderness was taking possession of Nan Perdue's house in the same way it repossessed the squatters' clearings and the soldiers' roads—and the squatters' and the soldiers' skeletons when they were dead—overrunning them and obliterating them with underbrush and suckers from the stumps and hiding every trace of them with vines and brambles.

There were piles of garbage in the King's Road. Gray-scummed pools in cabin dooryards overflowed the wheel tracks. A fish head stared at him with sunken eyes. Long wisps of raveled fiber hung down from the lynn-bark roofs like unkempt hair on the cheeks of Hogarth's slatterns in Gin Alley. Smells came from open doorways like the reek of fox dens—or of Billingsgate. Pitt's Town was doing its best to become as civilized as London.

An Indian was sitting on the ground in front of the Gilded Beaver and he was dead drunk—or looked it. His back was to the wall, his chin sagged on his chest and mostly hid the tattooed Turtle clan sign. His legs were spraddled out, the sure proof that an Indian was drunk.

Another Mingo was still on his feet, but he too leaned against the wall and was beginning to slide down; his blanket was hunched up behind as if he carried a papoose; his head drooped and jerked up again and drooped. He was an old man. His face was seamed with wrinkles. His paint, faded and dull with dirt since he had put it on, ran crosswise of his cheeks and skull; it lay in the wrinkles like the yellowish-red clay that chinked the cracks between the wall logs of the Gilded Beaver.

The plank sign hanging from a pole above him bore the figure of a beaver cut from brass. The brass was black with tarnish and the beaver was as crudely outlined as the turtle on the drunken Mingo's chest.

From either east or west, on the King's Road, the Gilded Beaver looked to be a stone house with two log-built wings. Actually the rough limestone wall that rose above the slab roofs of both wings was only a partition. And one of the wings was little better than a stable, finished hogpen fashion; the ends of the logs, sticking out at odd lengths from the corners, were just as the ax had left them. It was a storage room for trade goods, with a cockloft above it.

But the Gilded Beaver made some claim to elegance. Its front door had two handles. One was an iron bar curved into a semicircle, its ends bolted through the four-inch slabs. The other handle, just above it, was a loop of rope that served the purpose of a latchstring.

The low room was filled with soldiers of the Royals, some in tricornes, some in high-peaked grenadier caps, and they were not altogether sober. The tables around which they sat were round-topped and half a foot thick. No two were the same size. Table tops and stools alike had been sawed out of tree trunks, with the bark still on them.

A stairway of split logs climbed to a gallery where doors opened on the cockloft. The Gilded Beaver's second claim to elegance hung from the ceiling—a chandelier made of two pieces of peeled sapling, fixed crosswise of each other and suspended by chains of the sort used for snubbing wagon wheels on the steep mountain roads. At the four ends of the cross-pieces, tallow candles burned on the spikes of iron candleholders; the iron pans caught the drip till they were full; after that, they didn't. The yellow flames, dull in the pipe smoke, showed rust on the chains.

A barrel on a high shelf dribbled liquor into a canteen; the man who held the spigot was Jake Hesselgart. The half-naked man in the far corner was the fellow with the plucked skull and the pigtail who had all but broken Fraser's head at Williamsburg. The other plucked head and naked shoulders were an Indian's. He had let his blanket drop down; it hung from his clout string like a skirt. By the single feather in the crown of his red skullcap, the Indian was a Mingo. He was talking to a burly white man who stood almost inside the great stone fireplace, shadowed by it. Something passed between them. The white man was Dave Bone.

Holden moved closer to the bar, past the huddle of guns in the corner back of the slab door. He leaned against the wall. The bar was to his left. He could see only part of it. He could see only Jake Hesselgart's hand, jiggling at the spigot of the barrel on the overhead shelf, and the backs and fuzzed crests of two Delawares dickering over skins. He couldn't see the fellow they were dickering with. The stone wall had been laid up in angles, with a recess for the bar and a solid slab front coming up rib-high in front of it. The slabs made the bar into a kind of barricaded fort.

A grill of peeled poles swung from strap-iron hinges on a beam over-head. It was pulled up flat against the ceiling now, held there by a rope that passed through a ringbolt in the wall and was tied in a slipknot to a spike behind the counter. If there was trouble at the bar, a jerk on the loose end of the rope would fetch the grill swinging down into the faces of the troublemakers.

At the far end of the bar, where the stone wall jutted out again, there was a low door leading to a well house. Beyond that the trading counter ran along the wall. It had rows of shelves behind it, piled with folded blankets, strouding, calimanco, ribbons, silver and brass bracelets, bags of trade beads, powder flasks, knives and knife blades without handles, hatchets, bullet molds, and pigs of lead for bullets. There were buffalo horns and cow horns, some in the rough and some that had already been glassed down and stoppered. There were bales of furs and some few loose pelts that had not been packed yet.

Odds and ends of harness dangled from nails in the rafters. Felling axes and wide smoothing axes stood in a sheaf on a pile of meal sacks. Light fowling muskets and two decent-looking rifles leaned against the shelves. There weren't any of the usual trade muskets.

He saw Jake walk around the far end of the bar with a bottle in his hand. He saw Bone take the bottle and pass it to the Indian. The Indian began to worry at the cork. Bone made an angry motion with both hands. The Mingo pulled the red blanket up around his shoulders and tucked the bottle underneath the blanket. Dave had something in his hand. He couldn't make out, in the fireplace shadow, what it was.

Out of the tail of his eye he saw a girl come up the room from the far end. She was weaving through the helter-skelter of the tables and stools and the soldiers' sprawled legs, carrying mugs on a wooden tray. He recognized her, but he likely wouldn't have if Jackie Fraser hadn't told him she was here. Her dress was rags and she was dirty—dirtier than either of the frowsy women at the tables. Even her hair had lost its color with the dirt she'd gathered. What Jackie said was true: Garth was finished with her. His small hope of making use of her died out.

He knew that Jake was filling the mugs on the tray and that the girl was starting back across the room, but he kept watching Bone. A soldier lurched up from his stool and tried to kiss her. She dodged. The soldier pawed at her. She hooked a foot around one leg of the stool where he had been sitting and dragged the stool in front of him. He tripped on it. His hand, reaching for her bodice, hit the tray instead. The mugs went crashing down. The drunken Royal fell on top of them and lay there. His white-gaitered legs kicked foolishly.

Holden saw Jake threatening the Hale girl with his fist. He heard him bellow at her . . . *better ye spilled blood . . . bitch . . . wipe it . . . beat the Jesus out o' ye . . . Bone. . . .* Bone hadn't noticed. If he had, he wasn't doing anything about it. Hesselgart was dragging the soldier to his feet, shaking him, hustling him toward the door . . . *get out o' here . . . Bone'll charge ye f'r a bath . . . get goin'.*

The girl was fumbling at the well-house door. She undid the wooden button and went in. Water gurgled and splashed in a bucket. She was coming out again, her body weighed down by the bucket. Her other arm stretched out to balance her.

Bone was coming up the room now with the Indian. The girl's arm was in the Mingo's way. Bone flicked it with the back of his hand, with the knuckles. The girl cringed away and crouched down to wipe up the liquor. Holden moved along the wall.

He could see the mink skins spread out on the bar now, and the white man who was dickering with the Delawares. The man was the same fat, ragged rascal who had started all the trouble on the *Star of London* with his cardsharp trickery and his talk about a queen between two knaves. Jeremy Love. *Love.* . . . The name, too, was appropriate. Everything was appropriate today; love was a trickster and a cheat, and Jeremy Love was still the trickster and the cheat. His gab was as glib as ever. He was passing his hands over the five mink skins on the bar and talking to the Delawares in his smooth gentlemanly patter. He was calling the two Indians *gentlemen.* One of the pelts began to shrink. It crawled up under the palm of his moving hand and vanished in his sleeve.

"And so, gentlemen, you see that the mink skin is no longer a mink skin. It has become"—he turned the hand palm up—"a silver button!"

Holden wondered whose coat Love had pilfered of a button. He wondered what possessed Dave Bone to let that pudgy rogue play tricks on Indians. The Delawares were not amused.

"Where skin?"

Love spread his hands. The button was gone now. He smiled up into the dark threatening faces like a guileless child. One of the Indians made a grab for him. He wasn't there.

Bone swerved toward the bar.

"What the hell goes on here? What's the ruckus?"

"I'm sure I don't know, Mr. Bone. This . . . uh . . aborigine claims there were five minks. As you see for yourself, sir, there are only four."

"Bring five." One of the Indians held up his hand with the thumb and fingers spraddled. "He steal!"

"God damn ye, Love!" Bone reached across the bar and snatched the pelt out of the ragged sleeve. "Ye damned lard-bellied, worthless, thievin'—— Try that again, I'll gut ye!"

Holden heard the cursing, but he did not see Bone slash the pelt across the guileless face. The Mingo, making for the door, was only a few feet away. Holden's eyes were on the powder horn that stuck out from beneath his blanket.

He stepped out from the wall and got between the Mingo and the door. He took hold of the blanket and jerked it aside. On the bend of the powder horn he saw himself crouched in carved underbrush with two puffs of carved smoke spurting at him from behind trees. One of them was a sycamore, the other was a linn tree. Dan McCoy was dead.

The Indian reached for his knife, but Holden's hand was quicker. He set the point of the Mingo's knife against the copper belly. He said in Seneca:

"Walk backward."

He didn't want someone to open the wide door behind him and give the Indian a chance to make a jump for it. The Mingo hesitated. He put a little pressure on the knife.

"Move!"

The Indian began walking backward. His little hard brown eyes watched Holden's for his chance. Chris didn't give it to him. He guided the Mingo in among the tables with small turnings of the knife.

The girl was on her knees beside the bucket, sopping at the spilled rum. She might be some use to him yet. He might steer the Mingo into her so that a quick shove would trip him. An Indian flat on his back on a tavern floor was a drunken Indian. There'd be less notice taken. With the Mingo down and the knife at his throat, he might get something out of him.

It didn't work. Bone had already noticed. He was between the Indian and the bucket. He was stooping over and saying something to the girl. Now he was coming. He stopped just behind the Indian.

"Lookin' f'r somebody, Holden?"

"Yes. Garth. Where is he?"

"How the hell do I know?"

"This Mingo knows."

"Garth ain't been here. This Injun don't know nothin'. He's a Genesee. He just come in from up north."

"He knows something, Bone. So do you. You know he's carrying a dead man's powder horn."

"He ain't."

"Are you telling me McCoy's alive?"

"I ain't tellin' you nothin'. I don't know nothin' about McCoy. Ye can't tell nothin' by a powder horn. I got a couple hundred of 'em here."

"Not like this one, Bone." He flicked the knife across the rawhide string and took the horn. "There's only one like this."

Bone started for the bar. The knife flicked again. It quivered in the beam above Bone's head. Holden drew one of the pistols.

"That's right, Dave. Stop right there. Put your hands down on the bar, flat. Spread them out. Yours too, Jake." He backed the Mingo up against the bar. "I think Bone wants a drink, Jake. Get him one." Hesselgart's hand started down. "No, not private stock. Not a gun, either, if that's what you're after. That keg on the shelf will do."

Hesselgart filled a mug and put it on the bar.

"Drink it, Bone. Make out that you enjoy it. Take your time. It could be your last drink. Now. . . . This Indian killed Dan McCoy. McCoy was carrying a pouch. I want it."

"Go ahead an' want it."

"I want you to give it to me."

"Go to hell."

"This Mingo gave it to you."

"No."

"What did he give you?"

"Nothin'."

"Now I know you're lying." He saw Bone's eyes shift past him. Water splashed. He could hear it dripping.

"Is this what you're looking for?" The girl's voice was behind him, to one side. He couldn't turn his head. The water kept on dripping. He pulled out the other pistol.

"Drink your drink, Bone." He backed away till he could see the girl. She was holding up a fur pouch, black with water, dripping. So that was why Bone had stooped and spoken to her: he had put McCoy's pouch in the bucket. He heard Bone say:

"Damn ye! I'll cut the hide clean off o' ye f'r that. Stay where ye are."

"Get up——" He tried to think of the girl's name. Abigail Martha Hale. You didn't call a convict Mistress Hale. "Get up," he said, "Abigail." It sounded foolish. "Hold onto that pouch. Get behind me."

"Ye little bitch," Bone said. "Ye give him that, I'll break y'r arms."

"I don't think you will, Bone. I'm taking her along."

"Slave-stealin' . . ." Bone licked his lips. "That's hangin'."

"Yes. For you, it is. You should have thought of that a little sooner. Go to the door——" He couldn't say that foolish name again. But he heard her going. "Open it."

He felt air stirring on his neck. He backed up into the draft from the open doorway.

Some of the soldiers were looking at him. One of them had both hands on the table edge. He looked drunk enough to take on trouble that did not belong to him. Bone opened his mouth to yell.

"Don't," Holden said.

Bone yelled:

"Zeke! Zeke!"

That must be the name of the Swede-Turk. It was as foolish-sounding as the other name. It was curious how many odd things came into a man's mind when he wasn't thinking of them, when he had his mind on only one thing and his life depended on it. He looked at the Royal who was gathering himself to spring.

"Don't. I'll put a hole through anything that moves."

The Royal took his hands down from the table. Dave Bone moved. Chris fired. He put a hole in the slab front of the bar an inch from Dave Bone's ribs.

The smoke of the shot screened him for a moment. He put the empty pistol in his shirt and jumped back and felt the door come to his shoulder. He reached along the inside of the door and found the leaning guns. He snatched up a rifle and with the butt of it sent the other rifles and the muskets crashing to the floor.

He slipped around the door and pulled it shut and pushed the barrel of the rifle through the loop of the rope handle and down through the iron handle and dragged up on the barrel till the rifle was wedged hard, the butt against the door and the muzzle on the doorpost.

Inside, he could hear them shouting. Feet were pounding on the puncheons. The door rattled.

He gave the girl a push.

"Run! That way. . . . Bend down!"

He had told her just in time. Dry dirt trickled down the wall where she had been standing. The muzzle of a rifle came poking between the logs.

Chris slipped the other pistol into his belt and took the rifle muzzle with both hands and pulled. The barrel slid out past his chest. He threw his full weight on it and bore down and heard the barrel give way at the lock.

Then he doubled himself low and ran.

Chapter 29

The girl still clutched the bundled apron, and the apron dripped. It was making a pool on the floor of Jackie Fraser's kitchen. The heavy oak bar dropped into its slots across the door. Holden went to the first window and began to close the shutters.

"What's that for?" Jackie asked.

He took the powder horn out of his shirt and showed it to her.

"Dan's," she said. "God damn them." She said it as quietly as if she had been saying that it was a right nice horn. "Where'd you get it? Up there?"

"Yes. Off a Mingo." He moved to the other window. "There's something else, too. Abby's got it." Saying the girl's name that way surprised him. He had not been thinking of her name.

The sound of dripping changed. The drops were louder on the puddled floor.

"That's Joe's pouch," Jackie said.

"Dan was carrying it. He took it after Joe was killed. It had half of the seawan strings and peace belts in it."

"It's still nearabout full."

"Dan didn't get far." The shutter bar fell into place. He walked over to Jackie and the girl. He stood between them, looking at the wet mass of seawan in the pouch. "The Genesee towns. . . . Bone said the Mingo had come from the Genesee." He told Jackie how Bone tried to hide the pouch and how the girl had showed it to him. "I had to bring her with me, after that."

"Land alive! I'd skin you if you hadn't."

"I don't think they'll come here looking. But it's safer to close things up."

"I don't know," Jackie said. "I don't know if it is or not."

"Why?"

"If they come, and the cabin's shut tight, they'll know you're here and she's here. I think I'd undo those windows, Chris. They can't see in through the paper. I think I'd unbar the door and leave it open a crack."

"And let them walk in?"

"They won't walk very far. I been fetchin' water. I got everything about filled."

He saw now the biggest iron pot—half again as big as a bushel measure —hung on the heaviest crane, and the smaller pots smoking along the hearth, the buckets of water set every few feet all round the room close to the walls, and the waist-high tub pulled out from its corner behind the stone chimney. She had been getting ready for fire. She had been getting ready to hold the cabin alone, if the Indians came.

"The tub ain't quite full," she said, "but it's full enough. It's about all a man can handle. Roll it over there to the door and set it so's the door can't be opened more than just a crack. If they come, I'll be takin' a bath. That's one thing'll stop them. They can't see through them paper windows to know if I am or not."

He wrestled the tub over to the door. He unbarred the door and opened the window shutters. Jackie Fraser looked at the girl in the tawny light.

"There's one of us needs a bath," she said. "How long since you had one, honey?"

The girl looked as if she was going to cry. Then her chin went up. It quivered, but it was up.

"I was in prison," she said.

"You came 'crost the mountains. There's streams."

"The men. Bone and those. They were always around. I had chains on— my arms, not my legs. They chained me at night to a wheel."

"Don't you lie to me, child."

"Stop pestering her," Holden said. "She's had a bad enough time."

"You keep out o' this, Chris. It depends on her how bad the time was. There's some wouldn't mind. I ain't pesterin' her no more than I've got the right to. She's in my house an' I don't like dirt in my house. I can get the dirt off'n her outside, happen it's worth my while. But it ain't, till I know how dirty she is inside. All right—speak up, Abby."

"I'm not lying. I slept on the ground."

"It's right cold in the mountains, nights. How many blankets d'you have?"

"I had one, part of the time. Sometimes Bone wouldn't let me have it. I . . ." Her hands twisted the dirty wet apron around themselves. "You don't believe me. You couldn't. Nobody could." Her hands let the apron go. She drew from somewhere a pathetic dignity. "I'll go. I——"

"Where will you go?"

"There's Perdition," Holden said.

He saw that she knew what Perdition was. Her eyes were dark with something that looked like contempt and anger. Jackie, too, was angry.

"You keep out! I told you, Chris. Child, where would you go?"

There was sudden hope in the dirt-streaked face.

"If you'd let me stay till it's dark—so they couldn't see me—I'd get away."

"There's no place to get to. They'd find you. It's two hundred miles 'crost the mountains. You couldn't follow the road. A London girl in those woods—you'd be lost in an hour."

"I'm not. I'm not from London. I lived in the country. A little town. There were hills. I wouldn't get lost. What else can I do? I can't go back—there." She looked at Holden again. She said bitterly: "You did that. I had a chance. He was coming tonight. Now I can't go back."

"Who was coming?"

"Oh, what do you care? What difference does it make?"

"Who, Abby?"

"Mr. Garth. He was kind to me. That's more than you——"

"Kind! God's teeth, kind! He turned you over to Bone."

"No. Bone bought me."

"Bone. That's a joke."

"You ought to know," she said.

"I do. Dave Bone's a hired hand. He couldn't buy a Mingo squaw."

"He bought me. He bought all the convicts."

"I see," Chris said, and his mind began to tighten a little. His fingers began to tighten.

"Do you?" Her eyes were so dark they were almost black. *Like steel,* he thought. *Like steel in John's forge, when the heat turns it blue a little.* "I thought you did," she said.

"Go on."

"What's the good?"

"It might be some good." Jackie's tone was sharp. So was her face; it was like a terrier's face, alert and eager but not yet sure. She had picked up the sign, but she wasn't sure what it meant. "Go on. There's no harm in tellin', now you've started. Bone didn't fetch more'n three or four to the Forks. What happened to the rest?"

"He sold most of us. In that town, at the fair."

"Why not you?"

"He said I wasn't for sale. He said I was—bait. He made me stand on the platform while he sold the others. He was selling the Dycketts apart——"

"Which ones were the Dycketts?" Chris asked.

"They were married. They'd just been married a little while. Bone tried to sell them apart, and I stopped him." She saw the doubt. "I did! I told the man who was going to buy them, and then he wouldn't. Bone whipped me for it. He was whipping me when Mr. Garth came and made him stop. He tried to buy me and couldn't. Bone wanted too much, but Mr. Garth made him promise to keep me until he could get the money."

"I see," Holden said again. But he didn't see. The girl was a clever liar. "You've been well kept."

"That wasn't Mr. Garth's fault. He did try to buy me. That's why he was coming tonight. I think he must have got money enough to do it."

"Good God, you don't believe that? What would he want with you now?" He was purposely and coldly brutal. This might be the truth. "After Bone has had you."

"He hasn't—had me." Her face was scarlet. "You don't believe that either! I don't care what you believe!"

"You were with Dave Bone for six weeks."

"I wasn't the only one. I wasn't the only one that he didn't sell. There was Jeremy Love . . ."

That, at least, was the truth. He said cruelly:

"I suppose he protected you."

"He would have!" she cried. "He did all he could. When Bone was going to whip me, he tried. . . . Bone knocked him down. He knocked out some of his teeth. He hurt him. I thought he was going to kill him. It was somebody else."

"Who was somebody else?"

"I mean Bone didn't bother me. I think he was afraid. Mr. Garth told him . . . I heard Mr. Garth say, 'Don't forget she's mine. Keep your whip off her. Your hands, too.' Bone did. He had somebody else. He didn't sell Fanny Swivens."

"Which one was she?"

"The girl in blue taffetas. The one . . . You saw her, on the ship. Bone kept her. They"—her face burned—"they slept in one of the wagons." Suddenly she was crying. "When Bone wouldn't give me a blanket, Jeremy Love tried to make me take his. He's an old man. He's sick. You wouldn't know—he's so clever and gay. He hides it. He'd talk to me, nights. He'd recite. He'd make up speeches, trying t> keep me from being afraid."

"Speeches." Holden looked at the pouch on the table. "What kind of speeches?"

"The kind he made at the fair. In the Boukabekabus. They put him into that—that thing that they called the monster. They made him talk. Latin and French and Greek." Her head came up again in a sudden defiance.

"You think I'm dirty. I slept with Jeremy Love almost every night. They let me. It was a joke; they laughed. Bone said it was the best joke since you made out to buy me and I believed you did."

"I bought you," he said. "It wasn't a joke."

"You . . . bought . . . me?"

"Yes. I did."

"If he says so, child, it's true. Chris Holden's a middlin' great fool, but he ain't a liar. Get out o' here, Chris. This girl's had all she can stand. I'm goin' to clean her up an' then she's goin' to bed. If you got more questions to ask, likely they'll keep."

"There's one that won't. Abby, who told you that Garth is coming tonight?"

"His wife."

"Hannah! Where'd you see her?"

"At the Gilded Beaver. She came there last night."

For a moment he had a wild notion of going back to the tavern and finding Hannah and taking her out, of taking her to the fort. He thought of bringing her here, holding her here. She was Guyasuta's daughter. A hostage. . . . The girl said:

"She went away this morning."

"To meet Garth?"

"I don't know."

"Did she go alone?"

"I don't know. I heard horses going——"

"That'll do, Chris. You fetch the kettle off'n the crane an' pour it in the tub. Go on! I can't see what good you're doin', pesterin' at her."

He thought he saw. But he emptied the kettle into the tub and picked up the pouch and carried it through the bedroom into the forge. The forge door was barred and the shutters were barred. It was dark. But there were coals still alive in the bed of ashes on the raised hearth. When he stirred the ashes, they glowed. He took out the belts and seawan strings and hung them on the anvil. He hung the pouch up to dry. He reloaded the empty pistol. Then he sat down on a keg of nails to think.

There was no doubt in his mind about what he was going to do. Garth had killed Lovatt and Dan McCoy, and Garth would kill others unless he was stopped. There was only one sure way to stop him. Martin Garth must be killed.

There was no anger in the decision; his feeling had gone far past anger. It was not a decision at all. It was simply a fact. All he was thinking of now was how it could best be done. If the girl was telling the truth . . .

He got up from the keg and walked back into the bedroom. The door was closed. He rapped, but he didn't wait. He saw Jackie Fraser whisk herself quickly between the door and the tub.

"Land o' mighty, Chris! You turn right around an' march out! This girl ain't got a stitch to her body."

"She can scrooch down, then. She can do whatever she likes, but I'm coming in."

Jackie said: "Scrooch!"

There was nothing to see of the girl but her head behind the rim of the barrel. Her head was mostly soap. There was soap in her eyes and soap where her ears should be, and the rest was strands of wet hair plastered tightly to her head and cheeks. A bare arm came up. A dripping hand tugged at the strangly hair.

"You huddle yourself! You can act decent even if he doesn't."

"*Hhfff*. Soap. In my mouth." She was sputtering like Jackie.

"It ain't your mouth." Both of them were sputtering now. "I saw you fussin' at your hair. There's no need. He ain't goin' to look. If he does . . ." Jackie scooped up a handful of suds. The bare arm disappeared. "You know, Chris, she's a jemmy thing. She's put together right nice when you get down *to* her. Her skin's real pink."

"I might have a chance to save it, if you'll just hush. Abby, who told you I didn't buy you?"

"Mr. Garth."

"When?"

"Right after you left the ship."

"Did he come and tell you?"

"No. I told Jeremy I was free, and he wanted to know if I had a paper to prove it. I said *you* said Mr. Leach would give it to me, and Jeremy told me to go and get it. He said: 'Go right now.' He didn't believe you had freed me. I was frightened. I ran. They were in the cabin——"

"Who?"

"Mr. Garth. And Leach. And Bone. I told Mr. Leach you said he would give me my papers, and Mr. Garth said something about a joke. He said: 'First he pretends to buy the girl, and then he pretends to free her.' And Leach said: 'I'm sure the gentleman meant no harm.' And Mr. Garth said: 'That's carrying it too far. Even for Holden, that's going a little too low.' And then they said I had been sold to Bone, along with the rest." Her voice was small and hollow-sounding in the tub. "I remember it all. Every word. I've said them over and over. I couldn't believe anybody could be so cruel."

"If you remember every word they said, perhaps you'll remember this. When you went into the cabin, where were they? What were they doing?"

She said slowly:

"Bone opened the door. Leach was standing against a table, looking at something. It was a fur of some kind—I don't know. Mr. Garth was athirt the table."

"Garth was where?"

"On the other side of the table, sitting down. There were papers on the table. There was a candle lighted. Mr. Garth . . ." Her voice was slower and slower and more like a frightened child's with each word. She was seeing it all again, and feeling it all. "He had something in his mouth. Not a pipe. I don't know that either. It smelled like a pipe when it burned."

"A cigarro."

"I'd never seen one before. When . . . I remember now. When he said: 'That's carrying it too far,' he was twisting a piece of paper. And when they said I'd been sold to Bone . . . it was Mr. Garth said it. And then he put the paper into the candle flame, and when it was burning he used it to light the—— I don't remember what you said it was."

"God's breakfast! You remember everything else. You remember every word that was said two months ago, but you can't remember one a minute ago."

"Land alive, Chris! No wonder she can't. You glarin' at her like she had killed——" Jackie stopped, with a stricken face. "I'm sorry, child. You ain't goin' to be plagued no more this day, I vow."

"I bought her. She's mine. I don't intend to be robbed."

"Seems to me you're a little late with your don't intends."

"I'll plague her until I get at the truth. I've not got it yet. Bone didn't buy those convicts."

"She only said what they told her."

"I wish to God she'd remember something that I could use." All she had said so far was of no use at all. It was worse than useless. He had already guessed what happened, before he asked; and he was as far as ever from having proof. "There's got to be something! Think, Abby. What else did they say? What did Garth say when Bone whipped you? *Mmhh* . . . Jackie, *has* she been whipped?"

"She has. You can see if you want."

"No!" The girl crouched lower. "No, please!"

"Don't worry. I'm not going to look. What did he say?"

"I told you. Oh, let me be!"

"Think," he said.

"I can't. Except——"

"Except what?"

"Something Bone said. He said: 'You told me to gentle her.' But Mr. Garth didn't. . . ." The small chin came out of the water. It was stubborn, even with suds smeared on it. "He *was* kind. He was! He asked Bone not to put me in chains like the rest, when we came off the ship. He asked him not to sell me to anyone else. He told Bone not to touch me. That's the truth."

Holden went back to the forge to stare at the dulling coals and at a pouch two men had carried—two men who were dead because they had followed him. His mind went back to the accepted fact that Garth must be exterminated. He would kill Martin Garth exactly as he would a rattle-snake coiled in a cabin doorway. But he had no desire to die of the rattler's bite. He had no desire to be hanged for the killing of a snake.

He thought he saw now how it might be managed. The girl was telling the truth. He was certain of that. And if Garth still wanted her, there was a way to use her.

He fumbled among John's tools till he found a small iron bar. Then he walked into the bedroom and dragged the high-domed London trunk out from the wall. He thrust the bar through the padlock and twisted it and broke the lock. The lid was thrown back and his arms were full of the Forgel gown when he heard Mrs. Fraser say:

"John!"

He flung the gown at the bed. The stiff silk, collapsing there, made a sound that was like Jackie Fraser's breath running out in a long shudder of relief. Then she was calling to him:

"Chris! Chris, come here! John's back! You come here an' rassle this tub away so John can get in the door."

He came on the run. The girl didn't matter. He didn't see, till he'd wrestled the tub away, that the soapy water was gone and that Jackie had freshed the tub. The girl was trying to hide herself in clean water that showed the white gleam of her huddled arms and her knees. He looked quickly away from her as John Fraser walked in. It was John who stared.

"By the holy pink-toed prophets!"

"They're pink," Jackie said. "But you needn't gawk." Her tongue was sharp as a knife, whetted on the hard stone of fear that had been her heart. "Her toes ain't no matter f'r you—nor the rest of her, neither. Have you et?"

"Not no dish like that one." Then he sobered. "I told you not to tell him. That's Dave Bone's girl, ain't it?"

"No. She's the one Chris bought, but she ain't none o' Bone's. I had a good reason——"

"It can wait," Chris interrupted. "Did you find Ecuyer?"

"No. I had the trip f'r nothin'. Time I got to Ligonier he'd a'ready started back by way o' Clapham's. I just been down to the fort, though, an' he's there. Carre gave him your report. No—I don't know if he thinks it's true. But he's actin' like he thinks so. He's settin' up a night patrol around the town, an' he's ordered the whole garrison under arms at sundown. That's somethin'."

"Yes. Did you have any trouble, John?"

"Never saw an Indian track from here to Ligonier. That don't mean they ain't around. But I been consid'ble safer than what you've been, messin' round at Garth's place. Jumpin' Jupiter, Chris, ain't you been in enough messes over women?"

"I'm trying to clean one up."

"Yes, I see you are. I got eyes. But there's some dirt that don't clean so easy. It'll take more'n water to scrub off the dirt this girl's got on her. I mind what Garth said——"

"He lied, John. You tell him, Jackie. There's something I've got to do."

He was stooping over the trunk, taking out the silver slippers, when Fraser came and stood over him with the powder horn in his hands.

"So they got McCoy."

"Yes."

"I'd think you'd have gone after Garth instead o' stealin' his wench."

"I couldn't leave her, after she did what she did. And I'm not going after Garth. I'm going to bring him to me."

"With her? Is that what you mean?"

"Yes. I'm taking her to the ball at the fort tonight. I've not been invited but—well, I suppose they'll let me in. I hope Garth will follow us there. I think he will. I think he'll feel safe. I think he'd prefer to take her away from me there, in public. I think that's the way his mind works."

"What good will that be? What you aimin' to do?"

"Kill him."

"There? God A'mighty, they'll hang you!"

"Not if I force him to fight me."

"He won't. That ain't his way."

"I think he will. There are some things even Garth can't take. I don't think he can take the disgrace of refusing to fight, with a hundred people there to see him back down. That's his weakness. He thinks he's a gentleman. Go ahead. Snort. But that's what he wants to be. Foul as he is, he wants to be respectable—respected."

"He'll have you laywayed."

"He can't very well waylay me in the governor's ballroom."

"You've got to get there, first."

"This is one time you can go along, John. I think I'm right. I *am* right. But I've got to admit that it's sound tactics to have a good rear guard."

"What you'd ought to have in your rear is a damn good kick. I ain't go'n' to let you do it. I ain't go'n' to go."

"Then I'll go alone." He swept up the heap of silks and laces on the bed. "But I wish you'd have a look at Carroll's pistols. Jackie cleaned them. But"—he smiled at John's worried face—"I don't trust a woman. I missed Dave Bone by an inch."

"Jackie didn't say that."

"I didn't tell her. I didn't intend to hurt Bone very much, but I did want his trigger finger. The pistol hung fire just enough. I missed him."

He walked into the other room and heard Mrs. Fraser say *scrooch!* He threw the gown over the back of the nearest chair and still had a double armful of petticoats and ribbons, and his hands were full of slippers, pattens, stays, and green silk stockings.

He dumped the whole lot on the table and turned around. The girl had forgotten to scrooch. She scrooched now. He stood and looked at her, crouched in the tub.

"She's a little thing," he said. "You can sew up the dress, can't you, Jackie, so to make it fit? I don't know about the stays."

"Chris, have you gone stark crazy?"

"No. We're going somewhere else, and she can't go stark. Abby, d'you know how to dance?"

"I—I——" Her eyes were big over the rim of the tub.

"Well, do you?"

"Not really. Not really *dance,* at a ball. But I can! Oh, those beautiful clothes! That gown—and stockings and pattens to match." He looked at the table, surprised. He hadn't noticed that the wooden pattens were painted ice-green like the gown. "And slippers! And *side hoops!* Oh, you can't mean they're for *me!*"

"You can't dance at the king's birthday ball in your birthday clothes."

"But whose—whose are they?"

"Mrs. Holden's," he said, and his mouth went flat.

He walked to the wall and looked at the rifles that lay there across their pegs. He took one of them down. John Fraser went quickly to stand beside him.

"That there's the best rifle ever you laid hands on, Chris. It's the best rifle ever was made. Two barrels, over an' under. An' both of 'em true."

The men's faces, intent and absorbed, turned a little away from the gun at a cry from Jackie.

"What's the matter?"

"It's no never mind o' yours. It's nothin' a bachelor'd ought to see."

Their faces turned back to the rifle.

"I vow! Abby, there's drawers made o' silk. All my days I never thought I'd see a pair o' she-drawers. That's a something, ain't it?"

"You said——"

"What'd I say?"

"You said a bachelor oughtn't to see them. But they're—— He said *Mrs. Holden.*"

"That's his brother's wife."

"Oh!"

"The less said about her, the better. An' nothin', the best. Nothin' to him. D'you hear?"

"Yes."

"An' don't you go takin' notions. Chris Holden ain't got no more use for women than he's got for Martin Garth. He's just bein' kind on account of he's sorry about what he done to you."

Chapter 30

They were walking down the King's Road from the ford in the dark. The Frasers were just ahead. When they passed by the Gilded Beaver a thin blade of light reached out from the chink where the mud was gone. It gilded, a moment, the rifle on Fraser's arm.

The moment was like a nightmare to Abby. And then it was gone, and nothing had happened at all. She was safe.

She was walking in silver slippers, with pattens to keep them clean. She carried a fan in her hand—lace like a silver cobweb spun between ivory sticks. Her hand lay light on a gentleman's arm, and the arm was strong, and the gentleman very tall. The slippers had teetery heels and the wooden pattens went down into puddles she couldn't see. There were times when she had to clutch. Then, sometimes, the fan tapped the butt of the pistol in Captain Holden's belt. She never had dreamed of going to dance at the king's birthday ball with a man who wore pistols and carried a gun almost as tall as himself.

Her other hand clung to the silken gown so it wouldn't be spoiled by the road. It was hard to hold. There were so many billowing folds, and the silk was heavy and stiff.

She tried to cling to one thought so it wouldn't be spoiled. That was hard to hold too. But she clung to it desperately. She was safe . . . safe . . . *safe.* This was her wish, fulfilled by the laurel leaf. This was her dream, come true in the strangest way.

It was. And it wasn't.

She had dreamed of a silken gown—of a gown as blue as the sea. And wide. Not as wide as the sea but much—oh, *much*—too wide for a door.

The gown would be laced in front, all the way from the billowing rustle of silk at her feet to the swell of her breast, with blue satin ribbons that shimmered like ripples under a sunny wind. And then, at the top, there would be a whole froth of white ribbons like foam from a wind-blown wave. She had dreamed of her shoulders bare in the satiny foam, and of being as lovely as Venus rising out of the sea.

She had risen out of a tub that was made from a hollowed log.

She had dreamed of a painted coach and a palace ball, and linkboys with flaring torches, and liveried footmen more haughty than any ship captain or Dorsetshire baronet who ever had stopped at the Angel. She would step out of the coach and her pattens would go *t-tap* . . . *t-tap-tap* on the wide stone blocks of the London footway and up the stone stairs to the door, and the haughty footmen would all be flummocksed because the king's door was not as wide as her dress. She would stand at the drashel a minute and let them worry—but only a minute, because she would always be kind, no matter how fess and fine. She would touch the side hoops of the gown and the hoops would rise on their secret miraculous hinges and she would be as slim as a young beech tree. She would walk in between the dirns as lightly as any beech leaf sailing the wind, and even the king would be daddered to see her so slender and litty. Then the dress would be wide again. And the music would start.

Dreams changed. This was still a dream. *If only you never woke up.* . . .

But she was awake, and the other thoughts came crowding. This gown that she wore wasn't hers. It wasn't blue. It was green. But the sea was green. The sea was a beautiful thing. It had been such a lovely color that morning—the morning the *Star of London* came slowly into the wharf and she waited for Captain Holden. The sun like gold on the water, and sinking, and shining like sunken gold. . . .

She wished Mrs. Fraser hadn't put flour on her hair. When her hair was clean it was bright. Not as goldeny bright as the sun on the cool green water, but it would have looked nice, she thought, with the green silk gown. The thought was frightening somehow.

Such thoughts were wrong. It was wicked to wish for things that you couldn't have. She had wanted so many things. She had walked a dark road alone to the wishing well, with dread in her heart, but her thoughts had been wicked and greedy, and she had been terribly punished. And then she had walked another dark road with this man beside her, going with him through another dark town and turning in at a gate and thinking. . . . Being afraid and yet not afraid. Knowing. . . . And then not knowing. Wondering why he didn't. And knowing that, finally, too. Thinking that he had come home to his wife and loved her so much that he'd had no thought for a girl he bought and left on the garden steps.

She had not been afraid, after that, for a while. She had been happy that morning, walking back to the wharf and waiting there for Captain Holden to come and find her. Not much, but a little happy. After so long, a little had seemed a great deal.

And then he had come. She had been happier, truly, in the few minutes before he said she was free than she was in the short minutes afterward, while she believed she was free. She had been frightened then, without knowing why. *Afraid to be free. . . .*

Now she was frightened again, and once more she did not know why. It wasn't the same reason now. Captain Holden hadn't said she was free. He had only said he had bought her and paid for her and didn't intend to be robbed. And then he had stood and looked at her, crouched in the tub, as if he was seeing her all the way to her feet. Or as if he did not see her at all. She didn't know which. His face had been angry and stern, and his wide mouth was flattened against his teeth, and his eyes weren't the eyes of a man who looked at a girl he wanted.

She didn't want to be wanted. She knew that look now.

It was ugly and evil and dreadful. She'd seen it so many times—in Wynn Lulorth's eyes, and the eyes of the tannery men looking up at her on the scorched wet thatch of the Angel, and in the eyes of the bailiffs and Bow Street runners looking at her in her shift in that horrible place that was called a compter and smelled of slops, and in Dave Bone's eyes.

Her hand shuddered on Captain Holden's arm, but he didn't notice. He couldn't know what she was thinking. He wouldn't care. He hadn't spoken to her since they came out of the Frasers' cabin. He hadn't wanted to touch her. He'd carried Mrs. Fraser across the ford, and left her to Mr. Fraser.

If he'd only say one word. If he'd even swear. . . . It would help to crowd out the ugly thoughts and the dread. But he didn't. And suddenly, now, she knew that Captain Holden was an unhappy man. She had never seen him smiling and gay. He had smiled, that day on the ship, but it wasn't a randy smile. It had been mocking and grim and a little sad. No, more than a little sad. It had hidden some secret hurt. A hurt and a guilt. And she thought she knew now what the hurt and the guilt had been. If that girl was his brother's wife . . . He couldn't have taken her, knowing . . . *What do I know about him? If that girl hadn't been there, he would have taken me. I knew that he wanted to. I* . . . And what right had she to think that another woman was evil?

She felt naked now. She was wearing more clothes than she ever had worn. But the silken drawers close to her flesh gave her a feeling of being completely undressed and abandoned and wicked.

The road crossed a bridge of logs over a stream that rustled like silk. It was hard to walk, in pattens, on logs that she couldn't see. She stumbled and clutched Captain Holden's arm, and he didn't like it. She felt the muscles rise into knotty ridges under her hand, as if he had clenched his fist. Off to the left a cabin's greased-paper windows made orange smears in the dark. She couldn't know he was thinking: *Downhill to Perdition. It will be hell for her if this doesn't work.*

The road curved to the right. They had come to the lower town and the trees were gone. The road ran across level ground between rows of cabins. A fire was blazing beyond them. The leaping flames turned the cabins blacker than night with their solid shadows and reddened the logs of the walls that fronted the road. Soldiers stood by the fire. They were grenadiers of the Royals. Their scarlet tunics seemed to be part of the fire; the red light, sweeping up over their coats and their ruddy faces, gleamed on

the brass of their caps and turned the sharp-pointed peaks into tips of
flame. They leaned on their muskets, watching a circle of men in homespun and shag-hair and leather shirts who squatted around a blanket
spread in the road itself. Dice rattled. A face like a rusty hatchet thrust
itself into the circle to follow the cast.

She shrank. But Captain Holden was unconcerned; his arm was hard
under her hand, but it didn't bulge up into ridges now. Mr. Fraser looked
back.

"Did you see the buzzard, Chris?"

"I saw him. It looks as if it'll work."

"The ensign that's got the patrol is Hutchins. I know him. I better
make sure." Fraser drew his wife to the side of the road. "You wait inside,
Chris. You wait for me, understand?"

"I'll wait," Captain Holden said lightly. "I want to dance with Jackie."
They walked on past the Frasers.

There was a long plank bridge over a pit of darkness. Her pattens went
tap . . . t-tap-tap, almost as they ought to go. And the dream, coming
true, was only a little changed. There was a timbered gate that was like an
enormous door. There were torches that flared and dripped red smoky
light on the gate and the dirns. The linkboys who held the torches were
soldiers, and so were the liveried footmen; but no frigate captain or
baronet who ever had stopped at the Angel had been as haughty and stiff
as these sentries presenting arms. And the gate was wide, but the rigid
soldiers filled part of the space, *and there wasn't room for her dress!*

She let the silk drop from her one hand and took the other hand off
Captain Holden's arm. She touched the side hoops lightly—the gentlest
touch—and they rose on their secret hinges against her body and made
her slim, and she walked in as lightly as any beech leaf blown by the High
Stoy wind.

She heard the music beginning. Her throat was tight and she wanted to
cry and instead she was laughing in pure delight. There were stars in her
eyes because there were tears on her lashes. They shimmered in front of
her eyes because, as she walked half blind with this happiness, the road
curved across the redan and the high wooded hills beyond the Ohio drew
back and the waning moon poured its silver upon the river.

The road finished its turning and came to the farther side of the brick
redan that stood like an island in the dry moat and guarded the gate.
There was another bridge over a hollow darkness.

The bright laughter stilled in her mouth. Her heart made a sickening
lunge toward her throat and the laughter was thin there and thinner and
draining away. Her throat wasn't choked, it was empty. Her heart was
squeezed small. She could feel the brief happiness being drained out of
her, down and down into a bottomless pit of darkness and dread, all the
hope and the happiness going. Against the low moon the gaunt timber
frame of the gateway stood like a gallows, waiting. *Like Tyburn Tree
. . . like Tyburn Tree . . .* She was fruit from Tyburn Tree, and she had
no right to be happy.

There was the hollow sound of her feet on this other bridge, and her
heart was under her feet, somewhere in that awful pit.

There was a flame-lighted wall, red and black—red bricks and black dark, and the red flame dripping down from the pine knots in iron brackets and the black smoke dripping upward.

There was a long, deep passage between high walls—a drong like the narrow alley that led to the hollow, dead house in Turnmill Street. And she seemed to be standing again on the mended steps in her shift and the cold wind was blowing upward over her body, under the shift, from the open door and the foggy street, and a man hung by the nail driven into his neck and gurgled his life away. She could hear his life drip . . . and the gallows rose over her head, black and foreboding and waiting.

The deep passage came to an end. She walked out into flat acres of moonlight.

She was walking across the parade ground toward gleaming glass windows where candlelight poured through the moonlight and music splashed, and water splashed in the tub where ladies with powdered hair and bare shoulders sat on stools and washed their feet in the tub. The fine ladies of Pitt's Town didn't have pattens to wear, they had come to the ball barefooted. A soldier in a green tunic waited to hand them huck towels, and they dried their feet and put on their stockings and slippers. She heard the gurgle and drip in the tub.

Captain Holden stopped. They stood in the moonlight and waited. She watched the bare shoulders of women and bright-colored officers' tunics revolve past the lighted windows. The music was strong and quick, they seemed to float on the music. The ladies had powdered hair. The officers' coats were scarlet; goldeny things like ropes dangled over their shoulders; gorgets shaped like the waning moon hung under the lace at their throats. She thought: *Captain Holden wears a blue coat, his breeches are buff, I like blue and buff much better than scarlet.*

The Frasers came up behind them. Captain Holden and Mr. Fraser were talking together, low-toned. She heard Mr. Fraser say:

"Not yet." And something about a buzzard that flew the roost.

Captain Holden was touching her now. He had his hand under her arm, around her bare arm. The Frasers were walking toward the bright door, but Captain Holden was turning her toward the dark. He was talking to her at last:

"Don't you want to go up on the wall a minute? There's a plenty of time. You can see the moon. They'll be dancing all night, but the moon will be gone in a little while."

She wanted to go to the ball. But she was a piece of property, bought and paid for. She was walking up the ramp that led to the Grenadier bastion. She didn't know what a bastion was, and she didn't know that the smooth-packed slope was a ramp. There was a wooden platform under her feet. There was a level space, oddly shaped, with low walls all around. Soldiers sat on benches, they crouched on the planks at her feet. Cannon crouched at square holes in the wall. Now the soldiers were standing up. Captain Holden said a word. They flopped down again.

He led her toward one of the cannon that glistened like soft black velvet under the moon. He put both hands to her waist and lifted her off her feet and set her down on the gun.

226

"Lord!" He sounded surprised. "You're a little thing!"

"You said that before." Such an empty voice.

"I know. But you must have shrunk in the water."

Was he trying to say he had seen through the water and seen her and through her?

"What became of the stays?" he asked. "Did you wear them?"

She answered him with an absurd dignity, and knew that it was absurd.

"Captain Holden!" she said.

"After all, they're my stays."

"They were much too big."

"I thought so."

Why did he think so? His hands at her waist? His eyes—had they measured her so exactly while he stood and stared at her in the tub? She must hold to that dignity, foolish or not. She had to have something to hold to.

"Did you bring me here to inquire about stays, Captain Holden?"

He didn't trouble to answer. He said instead:

"You look like Venus rising out of the sea."

"Oh!"

"What's the matter? Don't you like being Venus?"

"I . . ." But she couldn't tell him. He'd laugh. He would think of the tub and the soap on her face, and her hair like sogged strings. "You didn't come all the way to Pitt's Town to tell me that." Her hand found a cord tied to the gun in a loop. She held to it. "Why did you come?"

"I'm a soldier," he said. "I came because I was ordered."

"Oh." Her hand tugged at the cord.

Suddenly, somewhere close by, a sentinel shouted.

"Main guard! Eleven o'clock, and all's well."

So late, she thought. It had taken Mrs. Fraser hours to sew her into the dress that was much too big. The shout echoed. It came back in other men's voices:

"Post number two! All's well."

". . . number three. All's well . . . well . . . well."

The echoes were echoes at last against the black river bluffs. They trembled there. The last echo of all was her voice repeating the words:

"All's well. It is—isn't it?"

He had wit enough to hear the desperate pleading that tried to be calm. But he didn't have wit enough now to comfort her with a lie. For some quite unreasonable reason he did not want to lie to this girl.

"It's quiet," he said.

"I like that."

"Sometimes things can be too quiet."

"I know." Quiet in an empty and ruined house. Quiet in a narrow alley that led out of Turnmill Street. Quiet as fog. The cord came loose in her hand. "It's Indians, isn't it? Guns. . . ." She looked at the rifle he leaned on. "I'm not frightened of Indians somehow."

How could she be frightened of them? She had never seen what they could do. *Even if she had,* he thought, *she's already seen worse. She's seen*

227

what white men can do. He didn't know all that she'd seen, and likely he never would. He saw the cord twisted around her fingers.

"Here. Here, now. You'll ruin the ordnance." He laid the rifle against the wooden gun carriage and took the cord out of her fingers. "You see, even cannon wear aprons. This lead plate's an apron. It's tied on the gun to cover the touchhole from rain."

"It's not raining," she said absurdly.

"The fog's bad as rain. It comes off the rivers at night. You can see it beginning, there in that patch of moonlight."

"Yes, Captain Holden."

He was leaning over her, tying the cord. Her hair smelled clean and the moonlight was turning it into pale gold.

"You might call me Chris."

"But . . . Wouldn't that be wrong? You said . . . I'm your property."

"Well, then, let's say I prefer my property to obey me."

He finished tying the thong of the cannon apron. He straightened up. "There."

"I'm sorry," she said, "Chris."

"Sorry? About what? It's fixed. There's nought to be sorry for." But there was. He was bitterly sorry now for the thing he had done to her, and for the thing that he was about to do.

"Chris?"

"Yes."

"You do—own me?"

"No one has a right to own anyone else." The words came with a sudden surprising conviction. He wondered whether George had succeeded in buying Jason. "By God," he said, "men and women weren't made to be bought like"—he couldn't compare this girl to a horse or a cow—"like yards of cloth. So help me, as long as I live I'll not own another slave."

"You mean . . ."

"Set you free? I don't know that I can. No, that's not true. I know that I can't. You——"

"I understand. A convict can't just be turned loose."

"That's the mistake I made. I did something that wasn't lawful. I did it because . . ." Why in the devil should he be showing himself to her for the fool that he was—the selfish, conceited, clumsy, blundering fool? "I did it because I was afraid of a woman," he said. "I thought she loved me. I thought she wouldn't like my buying a pretty girl. I thought she was going to marry my brother. That's why I went to London. When I came home, I thought she hadn't. Then I found out she had." There. He had said it now. She knew the whole ugly truth. "Believe me, I'd set you free if I could."

"I'm not sure I'd want that."

"Not sure you'd want what?"

"To be free from you."

"Why? My God, why?"

"You've been kind. You took me out of that awful place. You——"

"I got you into it. That was the least I could do."

"But you didn't intend . . . You're the only one in a long time who cared what became of me." She whispered, half to herself: "In such a long time."

"Abby—stop it. Listen to me. It wasn't kindness that made me bring you here."

"Then why——"

"I made a mistake." His voice was flat, and his mouth was flattened against his teeth. "I intend to correct it tonight. I brought you here because I think Garth will follow. When he sees you . . ." His hand touched the lace at her shoulder. It touched her hair as if it regretted something. "When he sees you like this, he'll try to take you back. That will be *his* mistake."

"You're going to kill him." Such small words. Such a small voice. But it said the short words so calmly.

"Yes."

"You can't." At last, now, the calmness broke. "Chris, you can't!" She thought of the gallows shape standing against the moon. "It's murder!"

"A duel? Hardly. I brought you here to make sure that he'll fight me."

"It's murder." She licked at her lips but the awful word stuck. "Oh no!"

"It's not on account of you," he said, "if that's what you're sniffling about." He was purposely brutal. "If it weren't for you, I'd find some other way. This way is surer, that's all. I've got other reasons for killing Garth. I've got two of them with me. This powder horn belonged to a man Garth killed. This pouch belonged to another." He showed it to her under the skirt of his coat.

"I don't believe you!"

"It isn't important," he said, "whether you do or not."

"Captain Holden . . ."

He turned. A gangly subaltern stood at his shoulder.

"Hello, Baillie. I'm glad to see you." Holden put out his hand. "Lieutenant at last! That's fine."

The lieutenant's hand slipped away quickly.

"By your leave, Abby—Lieutenant Baillie. Mistress Hale. She's from Dorsetshire." He knew Baillie wasn't. "She'll be a Virginian now. She's a distant relation of mine." A man had some sort of relation to what he owned. And Dorset was distant enough.

Baillie wriggled. His bow was hasty and awkward.

"Your servant, ma'am. Deuced sorry to interrupt. You're wanted at headquarters—Captain Ecuyer." He wriggled again and whispered, "Devilish nuisance. The dulcinea's given me itch."

"That's too bad. It's worse than a nuisance. So's this. I've been wanting to see Ecuyer, but I must say I wish he'd chosen a better time."

But he thought this was likely the first free time Ecuyer had had since he came back from Ligonier and Carre handed him the report. There had been a plenty for the commander of the Ohio frontier to do in the past few hours. And there was the old wound, still painful, that had ended his dancing days. Wound or not, Ecuyer wouldn't care much about dancing tonight, with that report on his mind.

"Will you come along now?" Baillie said.

They walked down the ramp and across the parade to the governor's house, into the light and the music. Her dress was too wide for the door. It was much too wide. But no one looked at her at all. There were officers inside the door, but their backs were turned; they stood in another doorway and watched the dancing, and all she could see past their heads was a picture that must be the king's and part of a little balcony where soldiers played violins and a cello moaned and a brass horn ba-aahed like a new born lamb.

"The rifle," she heard Baillie saying. "You'd best leave it here. Awkward, takin' that into the gov'nor's office."

She saw Captain Holden leaning the rifle against a long rack that was full of guns.

"I dare say Ecuyer won't mind if I bring Miss Hale."

"Oh no! No!" Baillie was sure about that. "No indeed!" His voice squirmed away into silence.

They were walking through other doorways, past soldiers stiffly on guard, not at all concerned because the governor's door was not as wide as her gown. She saw a picture of snow-covered mountains, and underneath it an officer sitting behind a desk. He had a high sloping forehead with wrinkles that ran across it; he had a wide mouth with an underlip too wide for the one above it. He was looking at her. He looked surprised.

There was another officer standing beside the desk. He had a small sullen mouth. It curled, and it seemed to mock her. He made a mocking bow.

Something was loud in the silence, rapping on hollow wood. *Tap . . . t-t-tap . . . tap. . . .* She'd forgotten to take off the pattens. This was the horrible end of her dream when she dreamed it asleep, not awake—when she walked into the ball with the pattens still on her feet, and tried to dance in the wooden clogs—the dreadful moment when everyone knew that the hoops of her gown were made from the hoops of a keg.

Over the sulky-faced officer's powdered wig, as he bowed, she saw a mud-spattered traveling cape laid across the back of a chair. She saw Martin Garth standing by it.

Chapter 31

"Is this the woman?"

"Yes," Garth said. "That's the woman, Captain Ecuyer." He picked up his traveling cape.

"One moment," Ecuyer said. "If you please, Mr. Garth. I have heard your side. We have here a matter of law. The law . . ." He smiled. The smile touched only his wide lip and left the rest of his face regretful. "In this place the law—it is me. I do not enjoy being a judge. *Alors,* it seems that one has no choice. To be a judge, Mr. Garth, one must hear both sides."

"There's no other side to this." Garth said it easily, smoothly, with the same deferent confidence he had used so well at the Raleigh.

"That is not possible. Everything has two sides. You mean, I think, that the other side is not good. If that is true, Mr. Garth, you will rest content while I hear it. So."

Ecuyer glanced at a much-creased paper. His cane lay on the desk. He picked it up and rolled it over the paper to smooth the creases. A second paper slid out from under the edge of the one on top. Ecuyer looked up at the girl.

"Your name—it is Abigail Martha Hale?"

"Yes," she said faintly. She felt the hard ridges under the cloth of Captain Holden's sleeve. They were a little comfort. His face was not. And his silence was frightening.

"You are under indenture?"

"Yes."

Holden was numb with surprise at this unexpected disaster. He hadn't been careless this time. He had been sure, when he saw Williamson throwing dice on the blanket spread in the road, that the fellow was there for a reason. He'd been sure that as soon as he passed, Williamson would be off on a run to tell Garth. But he had let Fraser go back to make doubly sure; and Ensign Hutchins had said Garth hadn't come to the fort; and Williamson had been gone. Even then he had let Fraser go ahead to make sure Garth wasn't already at the ball, and to let him know when Garth came. Now he heard the questions tightening slowly around the girl.

"You left the place called the Gilded Beaver today?"

"Yes."

"You were willing to go?"

"Yes! It was horrible! I——"

"If you please. You do not understand what I ask. You were not forced to go? Captain Holden did not compel you?"

"No."

"Captain Ecuyer . . ."

"One moment, Captain Holden. I come to you in a moment. One thing at a time. Mr. Garth has accused you of stealing his property. It is of a seriousness—such an accusation against an officer assigned to His Majesty's forces."

"I took her! Don't try to shield me! I took her because she's mine."

"Of a certainty, Captain Holden, I do not try to shield you. *Alors,* I do not wish to have it said that an officer under my orders is guilty of theft, unless it is true. The girl says she went willingly."

"She couldn't stay there! Bone threatened to flog her. He threatened to break her arms."

"So. Bone. He is a brute, this Bone. Mr. Garth, it is my opinion that Captain Holden did not force the girl to go with him. *Par consequent,* I do not put him under arrest. Now, Captain Holden, you say she belongs to you. Mr. Garth claims she is his."

"I don't *claim,*" Garth said. "You've got the indenture to prove it. You've got the bill of sale—Norfolk notary—sold to Bone—Bone to me."

"Yes. That is true." Ecuyer handed both papers to Steele. "You will look at them, if you please. They appear to be quite in order."

"Quite," Steele said.

"Perhaps Captain Holden would care to see them."

"I don't need to see them. They're false. I bought this girl on the *Star of London* two days out of Norfolk. Garth lies if he says I didn't. Garth forced the sale. I outbid him."

"May I ask you why?"

"Because I don't like bullies and cowards, and a man who bullies a helpless girl is the lowest form of coward God ever made. I came here tonight to tell Garth to his teeth he's a liar, a thief, and a coward." But this was not where he had meant to do it. He had intended to say these things in the crowded ballroom where Garth would have to resent them or take the shame of refusing the fight. "I bought this girl—which makes him a liar. He stole her—which makes him a thief. I'll answer for what I say with any weapon he chooses."

"You will answer," Ecuyer said, "but to me. Not to Mr. Garth. There will be no dueling here. So. Captain Holden, you say you bought this girl?"

"Yes, sir."

"You have then a bill of sale?"

"No, sir."

"No?"

"I set her free."

"So. You set her free. Mr. Steele, may I have the indenture? *Merci.*" He began to read. " 'Abigail Martha Hale, spinster, aged seventeen, tried and found guilty of murder, sentence of death by hanging commuted to transportation. . . .' You knew this?"

"I knew it, yes."

"You know a convicted felon may not be freed during her term of service?"

He felt the sweat drenching his stock and the lace at his wrists. Would he never be done with that selfish and careless and ugly day? He said, desperately, the one thing that might help her now:

"I intended to marry her."

"Pfaghh! That's the cap to the joke." He heard Garth's breathy laugh. "Marry her! God's life, Captain Ecuyer, he left her aboard the ship and went off with another woman."

"I think," Steele said, "the girl is the answer to that. There's no need to ask her. You've only to look at her face. Whatever he may have intended, he didn't tell *her*. Or else he'd fulfilled his intention—as far as it went."

Ecuyer's cane struck the desk.

"Captain Steele! You forget yourself. Withdraw the remark. That is an order, sir."

"Withdrawn," Steele said sullenly.

"Now, Captain Holden, we try again to come to the point. You have no proof that you bought this girl. Mr. Garth has proof."

"Those papers are false. They've got to be false! I bought her. The agent made out the indenture."

"That's true," Garth said. "I've been waiting for that. Here." He took another creased paper out of his pocket. "Read that."

"But this . . ." The long wrinkles deepened in Captain Ecuyer's forehead and curved down over his temples, around his eyes. *"Je ne le comprends pas.* It is made out to Captain Holden. The date is the thirtieth March, two days before Bone's. That is what Captain Holden said."

"Yes. The agent filled out the indenture, just as he said. But souldrivers don't sign indentures until the money's been paid."

"Ah!"

"You'll notice it hasn't been signed."

"I notice. *C'est fini.* The woman is yours, Mr. Garth. You may take her now."

Holden lunged toward the desk.

"You can't do that, sir! You don't know what they'll do to this girl. Indenture or not, Bone had no right to sell her to Garth. I know the Virginia law, and Pittsburgh is in Virginia. If you give him this girl, you're using the army to violate civil law. Bone forfeited all his rights weeks ago by unlawful abuse. She was made to walk barefoot across the mountains—four hundred miles from Williamsburg to the Forks. She was chained to a wagon wheel nights and made to sleep on the ground without even a blanket. She's been whipped without warrant of law."

"Not by me," Garth said. "That has nothing to do with me. There's no law that would penalize me for what somebody else may have done. I bought her to save her from Bone's abuse. She knew I was going to buy her. She wanted me to."

"I have said she is yours, Mr. Garth."

"Wait! You've not heard all of it yet. I went to the Gilded Beaver to look for this girl. I found something else. I found this!" Holden thrust the carved powder horn out the length of its cord. "This belonged to Sergeant McCoy of the Virginia Rangers. He's one of the men who started out with me by order of Colonel Bouquet. I took it away from a Mingo at Garth's place today. It means that McCoy's been killed. The same Mingo gave this to Bone." He pulled the pouch out from under his coat. "McCoy was carrying this. He took it when Lovatt, my other man, was killed by Seneca arrows on Laurel Ridge. Bone tried to hide it. He shoved it into a bucket of dirty water—a scrubbing bucket. I'd not have found it at all if this girl hadn't had the courage to show it to me. That's why Bone said he'd break her arms. You can't turn her over to them, sir. By God, you *can't!"*

"Very pretty," Garth said. "Very pretty indeed. First I'm to blame because somebody else mishandles a convict girl. Now I'm to blame for an Indian bringing a pouch and a powder horn into my trading store. I'm to blame for Bone hiding the pouch. Captain Ecuyer, this thing's gone so far that it's got to go farther. I'm tired of insinuations. I wish you would ask *Captain* Holden what day he left Williamsburg."

"That is not necessary," Ecuyer said. "I have his report. The third April."

"By your leave, then, I'd like to ask the girl a question or two. I'd like to ask her where she last saw me, and when."

"You may ask."

"Where was it, Abby?"

"In that town. They said it was Williamsburg."

"That is where Bone whipped you?"

"Yes."

"And what day was that?"

"I . . ." She looked at Captain Holden uncertainly. Something depended upon the answer. "I don't know," she said. That was the truth.

"I don't . . ." Captain Holden's face was still turned away, watching Garth with that deadly look. But the look was defeated, too. "It was three days, I think."

"You'll see that agrees with the bill of sale to Bone—the first day of April at Norfolk. Now, Abby, did you see me the day you were whipped?"

"Yes."

"And the next day?"

"Yes."

"And the next?"

"Yes."

"There, Captain Ecuyer. Holden has been insinuating that I'm to blame for his men being killed. I think that's answer enough."

"It's no answer at all." Holden fought on, without hope. "He had half a dozen men with him. Bone——"

"God's life! There's the rest of the answer. A while ago it was Bone who fetched the girl over the mountains."

"Garth had other men. His wife was with him in Williamsburg—she's Guyasuta's daughter. She didn't come there alone. There were Indians somewhere about. He sent word to them. We were ambushed the sixth day out—on the Nemacolin path. The path was mentioned when Garth was present."

"That's right," Garth said. "And none of this proves anything."

"It is sufficient. I do not care to hear more." Ecuyer picked up his cane. "Captain Holden, you have my permission to sit." He jabbed the cane at the chair where Garth's cape had been. "That is also an order. I know you by reputation. It has been good. I hope you do not compel me to place you under arrest. I give you the choice. I have none, if you disobey. There is not much that a man can do when he is locked in a dungeon."

Not much that a man can do. Holden thought Ecuyer was hinting that there was something he might yet do. He walked to the chair and sat down.

"Captain Steele, you will be so good as to see Mr. Garth to the door." He glanced at the girl's stricken face, and his lip hung loose. His face, for a moment, was sad. "I suggest you go quietly. It will be easier for you, I think."

Garth took her by the arm. Her piteous look went to Holden.

"Thank you," she said. Her mouth quivered; she made it be still. "I'll send the dress back. I can, can't I, Captain Ecuyer? It's his—property."

"No," Holden said. "It's not." He hated the sight of the dress. "I don't want it. Keep it."

234

The side hoops came to the door. She forgot to lift them. Garth thrust her out in a sound of silk crushing and tearing.

Chapter 32

The door, closing, shut out the sight and the sound of the silk. The sound of the music was not altogether shut out. It flowed thinly and brightly under the crack of the door and seeped through the flood-stained walls. Captain Ecuyer's cane tapped the desk in time to the violins gaily playing "Oh, London Is a Fine Town."

Holden remembered the tune. Snatches of that sardonic *Beggar's Opera* song came back to him now:

> *For she must have both hoods and gowns*
> *And hoops to swell her pride;*
> *And scarfs and stays . . .*

He still had the stays. She had been too small to wear them. Oh damn. Damn! *Damn!* She had been so proud of those hoops. She had loved that gown. And she had wanted to send it back. She had even thanked him. Alone and helpless and frightened—and she had *thanked* him!

"God damn it!"

The tapping stopped. Ecuyer said slowly:

"I know how you feel."

"The hell you do."

"You look at me as if you would like to shoot me. I do not mind, if it helps. To look, I mean. To shoot me—that is against regulations."

The music was ebbing away. The tip of Ecuyer's cane traced an aimless pattern across the desk.

"I make a joke," he said. "It is not a good joke. I have not the mood. I am sorry for what I have had to do. Tell me, Holden, did you plan to marry with her?"

"No."

"I did not think that you did."

"Not then."

"I understand. I thought, when you said it, that you were yourself surprised. You intended to lie, and you found that the lie had become the truth. *N'est-ce pas?*"

"Yes." Even now it surprised him. He hadn't known it until Ecuyer put this heartsickness into words. "If you understand . . ." His hands gripped the arms of the chair. "May I go?"

"No."

"For God's sake!"

"The law is the law. I am sorry, Holden. She is like—I do not know." Ecuyer's eyes went to the painted mountains and came back lonely. "Young. Fresh. Of a gracefulness. Like the flowing of wind across tree-tops. How a girl so young could do murder and yet seem to be so untouched——"

"She didn't do murder."

"No?"

Ecuyer listened gravely. But when Holden finished, he said:

"The court knew all that. It knew before you did, Captain. The law—we cannot change that. It is too late. I think we are both too late."

"Both?"

"This report that you made. I think now it is true. Mr. Garth came to me this evening. He had been to the Seneca town upriver—Guyasuta's town. He saw things that he did not like and he came to tell me he fears now that you are right."

"Judas! You believed him when you didn't me!" This was the last ugly irony. Once more Garth had covered his trail. He had used Johnson and Croghan and Carroll and other men, shielding himself with their own respectability. *Now he's using me. He's shielding himself with the very things that I've done to expose him.* "My God, don't you see what he's doing? Garth's using the truth as a lie to protect himself! Didn't Bouquet tell you *anything?* Didn't Carre tell you?"

"Carre told me, yes. It is difficult sometimes to know what is true. You yourself—you lied when you said you intended to marry with her. And then . . . *hélas!* If you do not know what is true in yourself, how am I to know? I tell you this. Before Garth came here tonight, I had taken your word. I have done what I can—the patrols, the garrison under arms, the messengers. About Garth I do not know. You do not have proof of that, either."

"No. But my sergeant is dead. *She* gave me the proof of that, and God knows what she risked. And you let him take her!"

"You are so sure about him?"

"Yes."

"I think you will not be so sure when I tell you something, but I think perhaps you will feel better about the girl. He has his wife with him."

"No. He hasn't. She was here last night, but she went away."

"I think you are wrong, my friend. He asked permission to bring her into the fort if we are attacked."

"He would! That's the way he works. Whether she comes to the fort or not, you'll still give him credit for asking. You'll still believe him."

"Sacré nom d'un chien!" Ecuyer got to his feet. "You are the stubborn one, Holden." He straightened the gorget over the frill at his throat. "Come. It is not good if I do not show myself at the ball. Under the circumstances, I must require that you stay beside me. I think, if I let you dance, you would be out the door the first time you came to it."

They walked through the adjutant's office together and crossed the hall. There were sentries in pairs at each door. There were soldiers standing with bayonets fixed beside every window. Ecuyer touched his arm.

"I am right. You look at the door. These preparations are not all for you, but they serve; they will keep you in. The king's birthday ball—it gives me a good excuse to be ready without making a great alarm. Every soldier who is not on guard or on town patrol is here at my headquarters. I have all the garrison in my hand. That is your doing, my friend." Ecuyer was trying to make amends. "There are many lives in our hands. You know that, Captain Holden. I cannot think of one only, no matter how precious. You also—you cannot think of yourself. Take heart. She will be safe, I think. You have seen Major Leslie, no? He was here for the hurly-burly. That is the—how do you say?—the mob scene, when they play tricks on each other. He is a good man, Leslie. But he is always in trouble. Every time he is in a fight, no matter how small, he gets himself wounded. Now, so they tell me, he has had a quarrel with two of my officers. You Americans—never quiet. Never content. Always the hurly-burly."

The music went gamboling into a gay new tune, and the room was a swirl of bright gowns and bright uniforms—scarlet coats and blue breeches of Royals and gilded gorgets and jiggling gold shoulder knots. There was one faded Virginia tunic with scarlet slashings; he recognized Captain Will Trent. The gowns that twirled to the music had not come from Paris. Nor even from London. Some of the women who wore them —officers' wives—had spent years in the barracks of wilderness forts, and some of the gowns looked made over and some looked homemade. But they were bright, swiftly whirling eddies of color under the candle sheen, and the powdered heads and bare shoulders swam in the pools of brightness.

The tune was an Irish trot, and a sad-faced young soldier stood by the balcony rail and sang in an Irish brogue:

> *I'm bubbled. Oh, how I am troubled!*
> *I'm bubbled, bamboozled, and bit . . .*

Holden's eyes were searching the ballroom for Fraser and Jackie and could not find them, and hope lunged up in his chest. John must have seen Garth take her out and he must have followed, and—if he had— he would know at least where she was. The soldier sang:

> *When you come to the tree,*
> *Should the hangman refuse,*
> *These fingers with pleasure*
> *Could fasten the noose. . . .*

They could dance to a song like that! They could laugh. They thought it was funny and gay. They didn't know he had come here to kill a man. If they knew, they would doubtless think that was funny too, because he had been so completely bamboozled and bit.

He had not dared to do what he should have done. Carroll's French pistols were in his belt. He could have shot Garth as he stood in Ecuyer's office. But the old habit of taking orders was strong, and so was the habit of living. He'd been so careful to keep his neck out of the noose. He hadn't known, until it was much too late, that Abby was worth all the risk. The music changed and the soldier sang:

> *If soon she be not made a wife,*
> *Her honor's singed and then for life*
> *She's what I dare not name.*

Chapter 33

Garth's body, behind her, pressed her against the door of the Gilded Beaver. His arms held her there, and his hands were quick and sure in the dark.

She shrank away from his hands and only pressed herself closer against him.

Body and arms, he was hard as iron. He was as hard as the thick iron hasp driven into the hewn-log doorpost. He was a hasp that held her pinned to the door. She could feel his hands seeking the slender hole that ran through the long shank of the padlock and fastened the chain between the hasp and the heavy iron handle sunk in the door.

She heard the repeated faint click of the key that turned many times like a screw in the lock. The door swung inward. Light tumbled out. Only a few candles burned in the tap of the Gilded Beaver. The tops of the tree-trunk tables floated on shadows as dirty and thick as the muddy Monongahela. But there was light enough for her to see the mud on the silver slippers and mud on the gown where Garth's boots had spattered it.

She heard the door close and the bolt slide into its socket. She started to walk toward the stairs.

"Abby."

She kept on walking. She wanted to run.

"Abby. *Come here.*"

She stopped at the foot of the split-log steps. Garth took her by both shoulders where the gown left them bare. He still had the chain of the door in his hand. It was cold on her flesh. He turned her around and held her.

"It's time you learned," he said. "I've given you time enough."

She heard herself pleading. Small voice lost in the empty room. Lost in enormous loneliness. Voice itself empty and hopeless.

"Please, Mr. Garth. I'll work. I'll serve my time. Fourteen years. . . . I'll be faithful."

"Yes. Yes, I think you will."

His hands slid down over her shoulders, stripping the silk away, and down over her arms. He forced her arms behind her, the wrists together. He wrapped the chain around her wrists and twisted it tight.

"You're mine. Do you understand? Just as my boots are mine. I can do with you as I want—anything I want."

He bent her backward over the rail with his weight upon her.

"No! *Please* . . ."

His mouth came down to her.

"I'm not going to punish you, Abby." Hot murmur pressed to her flesh. Coming through her flesh. In her. She felt it inside her own throat. "You'll know who you belong to, after tonight. You'll never forget."

"Ye picked the wrong night," Bone said, somewhere in the shadows.

She felt the stillness in all Garth's body against her. She felt him taking control of himself. He straightened. The chain slid away from her wrists. It clashed on the rail.

"Go upstairs," he said. "Dave, what are you doing here?"

"Waitin' f'r you." Bone came from behind the trade counter.

"I told you to go. I said to close up and get out."

"Sure. Sure ye did. I closed up, but not on account o' her."

"Didn't the stuff get out?"

"Sure. Sure."

"Were the wagons stopped?"

"Yeah. The guard stopped 'em, down by the gate. They didn't find nothin'. Took one look at that God-damned monster o' yours an' told Jake t' go on. They didn't bother t' look inside it."

"Then what's the trouble?"

"Ye been lookin' f'r trouble, Garth? Well, ye got it. There's five Mingoes waitin' f'r ye."

"Where are they?"

"I got 'em hid in the storeroom. They don't like it much."

"Go back there and keep them quiet. Tell them I'll talk to them pretty soon."

"Ye better make it pretty damn soon. One of 'em's Guyasuta."

"God damn it! Abby, go on upstairs. Watch her, Dave."

"I'll watch her." Bone grinned. "But there ain't no need." The candles laid dirty shadows over the grin. "Hannah's back. She's up there on the gallery, watchin'."

Garth kept his control of himself.

"How much did she see?"

"I dunno. I'd just come out o' the storeroom. I saw the loft door movin' when I come out."

"Hmmhhh."

"She's y'r end of it, too. I didn't marry her, Garth. I can't help if yo lost y'r taste f'r red meat. Maybe Hannah can She don't fancy y'r new piece o' white. Maybe that's why she fetched her father. Watch y'rself! Here they come."

The door back of the trade counter opened. Abby, huddled against the butt of the stairway pole, looked straight into Jeremy Love's frightened face. He seemed to be bowing to her.

Then she saw that he wasn't bowing. He was walking bent over because his arms were twisted high on his back and his wrists were held by a naked Indian towering behind him.

The Indian looked like a shadow streaked by the candlelight. But the streaks were paint. They glistened. They rippled like flames as he moved. Red and yellow bands ran up over his belly and over his chest, and the upper half of his face was a yellow mask that ran up over his naked skull, with red daubs on his cheekbones and over his eyes. A tufted crest of red deer's hair rose from the crown of his head. She didn't know it was deer's hair—it looked like the smoking tip of a candle flame. She didn't know that the feather dangling out of the crest was an eagle's feather.

There were four more Indians now, coming in single file up the narrow space back of the trading counter. They carried guns. They were painted. One whole face was the orange-red of a greased-paper window, but it was not dull as a window; it had the hard sleek shine of a ladybug's back and it was dotted with small round spots of black paint. Another face was painted in crooked red and black streaks that wriggled and crawled toward its nose, and one had two horrible mouths—a broad slash of red where its mouth should be and another from ear to ear just below the eyes—and one had a black mask of paint from its forehead down to its nose and the nose was a wide round splotch, crimson and flat.

All but the one with the painted snakes on his face wore the high fuzzed crests and the single long feather dangling; but he wore a red cloth cap that fitted close to his skull. Rows of short feathers went around and around it, and at the top of the cap a thing stood up that looked like a piece of bone. And it was a bone, but she didn't know what it was in her new growing terror. Whatever it was, there was another long feather stuck into the thing, and as the Indian walked the feather revolved.

He was thick and ugly and shorter than all of the others, but he was the one that Garth spoke to:

"Guyasuta is welcome. But why does he come? This was not our talk. It is dangerous here."

"Not dangerous. White men dance."

"The soldiers keep watch in the town," Garth said.

"Soldiers!" Guyasuta's voice was filled with a bitter contempt. "They walk always in the same place, like a horse that is tied. Tomorrow not walk."

"Tomorrow," Garth said.

Abby stared at his face. It was calm.

"You." She heard herself say the one word. *"You!"*

"Tonight," the Indian said, "the white man whose name is Clapham not walk. Dead. All people there dead. What Garth do with white woman?"

"She is my slave. This fat white man is also my slave. Guyasuta will keep him for me."

"Fat one no good."

"Yes. Good. He speaks many tongues." *Talk,* Garth was telling himself. *Talk. Keep on. Talk about this fat, cringing worm. They won't think the girl's so important.* "The white men pay many skins to hear this one speak in strange tongues."

"Hear talk."

"Jeremy. If you want to live, give them some Latin. Quick! Speak up."

"Pax vobiscum." Jeremy licked his lips. *"O tempora. O mores. Necessitas non habet legem. Ogni medaglia ha il suo rovescio.* For God's sake, Mr. Garth . . ."

"Guyasuta has heard. The fat one is worth more than many muskets."

"We take."

"The white woman also is worth more than many muskets. Already one white man has tried to steal her. She is a present for Hannah. She will be Hannah's slave."

"Good. We take."

"No. Hannah stays here. Hannah goes to the fort with me. The white one goes with her."

"Hannah stay. White one not stay."

"Yes. She stays."

"White man Garth's enemies, not?"

"Yes."

"Garth can protect wife from enemies?"

"Yes."

"Garth can cause white men to give up fort? Garth can cause soldiers to open gates by white flag that is red? Not?"

"Yes. If you cut off the roads, I can. When they begin to get hungry, I can make them open the gates."

"Good. Garth is strong. Garth can keep wife from white men. Guyasuta also is strong. Keep white one from Seneca men. *Oho!* Seneca man not lie with woman she belong other man." The red and black painted snakes crawled and squirmed around his contemptuous mouth. *"Ne Seneca haksa'dase'a then'en ne henes! Ne Seneca haksadase'a then'en dion'dak ne iagon'gwe Ononwan'da'a Ni'haia'do'den!* [A man of the Seneca is not a vile animal with a long tail! A man of the Seneca does not lie with a woman whose body is white!]"[1]

It was true. And if it had not been true, Garth knew he was caught. Guyasuta had built a neat trap for him with the wordy and roundabout logic that Indians loved. He knew that he had to yield now, or else risk all he had schemed and worked for and waited for in the fourteen years while he slowly and patiently won the Indians' trust—sucking on foul pipestems that had already been sucked by a thousand mouths, eating stewed dog, dipping his hands into food pots where feathers and entrails floated together.

"Take her," he said.

A naked arm reached for her. She screamed. She tried to run up the stairs and the pattens tripped her. She fell on her hands and knees and crouched there, trying to crawl and knowing that it was useless to crawl and looking at two quilled moccasins on the step just above her chin. The quills were red and yellow and blue. They made patterns of delicate flowers. She looked up into Hannah's face.

"Hannah, please! Make them let me go!"

Hannah put one foot on her face and pushed. She fell backward down the stairs. Two Indians caught her.

"Jeremy!"

A hand crushed the scream back into her mouth.

Jeremy broke away. He scuttled past Dave Bone's elbow and ran, dodging and twisting among the tables, trying to reach the door. The Indians cut him off easily. He ran back among the tables. He managed to knock down one table. Mamaultee leaped over the upset table and

[1]In the Seneca legend of creation, certain animals, birds, and insects were "impure" and symbols of evil. Among them was *ne henes*—the long-tailed cat-creature or panther, as well as the snake and the lizard, spiders whose very name stood for something repulsive, and screech owls, horned owls, and red-tailed hawks.

headed him off again. He tried for the storeroom door, but he saw a face with two mouths grinning at him and waiting.

There was only the well-room door left, but it was a door and Jeremy Love was half blind and half crazed with fear. He ran for the door like a hedgehog scuttering into its hole. He squealed as he ran. He got into the small stone room and pulled the door shut behind him and tried to hold it.

Mamaultee wrenched it open. Jeremy struck at him with the scrubbing bucket. The Indian snatched his hatchet out of his belt. It knocked the bottom out of the bucket and knocked the bucket from Jeremy's hands. It struck again and beat down the frantic hands. It made a sound on Jeremy's head like the thud of the broken bucket collapsing on the floor. Jeremy toppled over the low stone wall. The windlass spun.

Abby tried to cover her face with her hands. She couldn't. Her hands were held. She couldn't cover her ears. The spinning windlass made a sound that was like a long cry. Then she heard the splash. Mamaultee stuck his glistening yellow head out of the well room. He put his hatchet back into its loop and took out his knife.

"Bring light."

"No," Garth said loudly. "No. You can't scalp him here. He'll be found." Guyasuta beckoned Mamaultee.

"O'nen na'e [Now that is true]. Not scalp. White men know then Garth is much friend to the Seneca." He turned to Hannah, standing now at the foot of the steps. "We go."

Hannah reached for the candle that burned on the bar. She did not pick it up. She put her hand into the flame and held it there.

"Na'e," Guyasuta said. She took her hand out of the fire.

The Indians walked to the door. Hannah followed them. When the five Indians had slipped out, she bolted the door and stood there, silently waiting for Garth.

"Jesus!" Bone said. "Did ye see what she did?"

"What who did?"

"Hannah."

"Yes. Douse the candles, Dave."

"We'd ought t' haul that lump o' lard out'n the well."

"Let him be."

"He'll mess it up, rottin' there."

"If the damned fool fell in . . ."

"Accidental like, huh? What now?"

"Down to the fort."

"There's places I'd sooner be."

"That's the one place you're perfectly safe."

"There's your station upriver. They'll leave that alone."

"No, they won't. I told Guyasuta to burn it."

"Jesus!"

"I told him to burn those wagons too. They're worth more as ashes right now. If my station's the first one burned, nobody can say the Mingoes are favoring me. It'll stop any talk. Nobody will listen to Holden or Fraser either, after I've been burned out."

Bone began to blow out the candles. Garth followed him down the room. The last candle, burning in Dave Bone's hand, leaned the shadows of rifles and muskets against the wall behind the counter. The stacked shadows moved back and forth as the small flame moved.

"Why the hell didn't ye give Guyasuta them guns?"

"I've a better use for them."

"Yeah?"

"I'm going down and offer them to Ecuyer. I'm going to tell him to help himself to everything in the place—everything that's left."

"*Offer* 'em! Christ, he'll *take* 'em without no offers."

"Of course he will."

"By God!" Bone said it with admiration. "By God, but ye're slick. Ye'll get credit. Ye'll get the cash an' the credit too."

Chapter 34

Christopher Holden had been in the ballroom, a prisoner there, for almost an hour. Captain Ecuyer was sitting down now in a chair on the small railed dais under the gilt-framed portrait of George III, between the staffs where the garrison colors drooped—the King's Color with the gold cipher glinting on its pale red cross, and the dark blue regimental flag of the Sixtieth Foot. Holden, standing beside him, glared at the merry dancers. What in hell were they finding so funny now?

There was a swarm around the bucket of bombo, and Dr. Boyd was in the thick of the swarm. He was also nearest the bucket and helping himself to a drink for every two that he poured. He laid his head back on the cushion of fat at his neck and trolled out the catch:

> Man may escape from rope and gun;
> Nay, some have outlived the doctor's pill . . .

The crowd shook to a gale of laughter.

"Never mine!" Boyd shouted. He dipped the ladle full and emptied it at a gulp. "Never killed a man yet with a pill. Never gave 'im one! There'sh only one med'cine ain't poison. It don't come in pills."

He hiccuped. The crowd shook again.

Boyd peered at the ceiling, searching for something. He had mislaid the musicians.

"Where'sh music?" he bawled. "Wan' music!" He flourished his arms to still the delighted applause. "Wanna show ye somethin'. Med'cine—all nonshensh. 'S like song. Shilly. Sergeant, *play it again!* Now lishen!"

Boyd beat time with the ladle. He sang the two opening lines in a sweet clear tenor that didn't sound drunk at all. But he bellowed the third:

> Who takesh a woman must be undone . . .

"All nonshensh!" he announced. "All shilly! How c'n a man do that if he *ain't* undone?"

The room was an uproar. A girl shrieked with hysterical laughter.

"This doctor," Ecuyer murmured to Arnold, sitting beside him, "he goes too far sometimes. A strange man, Boyd, no? Skulls under his bed. A philosopher. And when he is drunk—*paillard*. What is the word? But yes—bawdy. One wonders what he will say next."

"Whatever it is," Arnold said, "they'll like it."

"Ah, *oui*. The flesh—it is close to earth. We are animals, no? Men and women too. But the animals—they do not make this sex business into a joke."

"Shilly!" Boyd roared again. "Tha'sh what it'd be. Shilly-shally." He stared solemnly at the crowd. "Shally. No." He shook his head sorrowfully, and swayed, and almost lost his balance. "No. Don' r'member Shally's lasht name."

The hysterical girl shrieked again.

Holden saw her. She stood near the door, clinging with both of her hands to the arm of a blushing subaltern. Her cheek lay on his shoulder. Her mouth was open. Her own shoulders shook with her uncontrollable laughter.

And then he saw her face beginning to freeze. Her body stopped shaking. Not all at once. Slowly. Her shoulders first. Then the pink flounces around and around her dress. She stood there stiff and suddenly fragile and brittle—a pink bisque doll with a mouth that no doll should have.

Her mouth was wide open and round, and too red because her face was growing as white as if it were really frozen. The sound that came out of her mouth was frozen. It was brittle. It snapped. When it began again it was still hysterical. But it was not laughter.

It was pure crystalline terror. Her scream was an icicle made of sound.

It hung suspended above the room for a moment, and then it fell and was shattered into the numberless small dull pieces of sound that a startled crowd made—exclamations and questions and slipper heels loud on the floor in the sudden silence.

The music had stopped. The musicians had been the first ones to see the woman who stood in the doorway.

Two men were holding the woman. One was John Fraser, the other a sergeant of Royals. The woman was holding a child in her arms. There was blood on the child. Her hair hung in two thin braids over the woman's arm, and one was the color of corn silk and one was dark. The dark braid dripped on the floor.

"She's dead." The woman's voice, too, was dying. "Ellen's dead." She began to sag. "They killed Joe."

"My God," a man cried, "it's Joe Pruitt's wife! Pruitt, that teamed for Clapham."

The woman said:

"Clapham's dead. They drove his scythe into his back. It come out'n his chest. They're all dead."

Lieutenant Baillie appeared in the doorway. He saw Ecuyer standing behind the rail, his hands gripping the rail, and began to walk hurriedly up the room. He looked as if he wanted badly to run, not to walk.

"We was haulin' the last o' th' fodder in, Joe an' me. Ellen an' little Joey was playin' b'hind th' barn. We seen 'em bust out'n th' woods. Joe didn't have no gun, but he went f'r th' kids. He whipped up the team an' he hollered f'r Ellen an' Joey t' run."

Mrs. Pruitt gasped between words. Baillie's heels were loud in the gasps.

"They shot Joey. They broke his leg. I guess. He fell down. Joe jumped off an' run f'r him. They shot Joe. There was two of 'em after Ellen. I had the fodder fork. I killed one. The fork stuck."

Baillie halted before Ecuyer, saluted, swallowed. His face was green-yellow and sick.

"Officer of the guard, sir." He swallowed and swallowed as if his throat were a pump and he had to prime it. "Delawares, sir. They hit Colonel Clapham's at two o'clock. Three men besides her got away. They think everyone else was killed. They say the other women——" Baillie vomited on the floor. Behind him, the voice continued to die.

". . . Joey wasn't dead. He was sculped, but he wasn't dead. The barn was afire. They threw him in."

The bisque-doll girl went to her with a steady face and quietly took the dead child out of her arms. The pink flounces began to turn red.

"The women were badly treated, sir," Baillie said.

"Yes. They do that."

"Mrs. Pruitt drove twenty miles with her little girl in the wagon. The child died just before they got here. She wouldn't believe it was dead, sir. She wanted a doctor. That's why she walked straight in."

"I understand, Mr. Baillie. Return to your post. Have the signal torch run up on the flagstaff. I will have also one gun, to wake up the town."

"——'s sir!" Baillie wheeled. He lurched as the doctor had done when he shook his head. He walked like a drunken man, very carefully. Boyd, bending over the child, looked sober.

"Sergeant," Ecuyer called. "I'll have a flam, if you please."

The drummer's sticks were already poised. The drum rattled. The crowd sound hushed. Ecuyer's wide lower lip turned out. It shaped itself like the French horn's curving mouth. His voice rang through the room.

"Ladies and gentlemen. Colonel Clapham's plantation was attacked by Indians early this afternoon. So far as we know, only four people got away." He was utterly calm. "Perhaps we shall be attacked. Perhaps not. I intend to act as if an attack was certain. All men, of this instant, are in the militia. Mr. Trent?"

"Here, sir."

"I make you the commandant for the militia."

A woman wailed.

"My children. I've got to get my children!" The sentinels at the door were keeping everyone in the room.

"One moment!" Ecuyer said. "Every man having property in the town will be permitted to go to his house and collect such belongings as he can carry. It is of an importance that you should bring all the food you have. All! Captain Arnold, see to it."

"Yes, sir."

"Lieutenant Donnellan . . . Lieutenant Grey. You will take each a demi-platoon and set a guard on both roads. You will let no one pass —out. Captain Lieutenant Carre, you will take your company and begin to tear down all the houses between the fort and the lower run. You understand? All! Leave nothing to give the savages cover."

"Yes, sir!"

"Mr. Trent, as you form the militia, you will also send details to haul in the logs of the houses. Floors, doors, everything. Captain Holden . . . Lieutenant Fraser . . . you will assist Mr. Trent. Captain Arnold, see to it that Captain Holden has three or four soldiers to back him up in seizing horses for hauling." *Or watch me,* Holden thought. He did not hear the rest. He was running. He caught Fraser's arm and drew him into the hall.

"D'you know where she is?"

"No. I seen ye come in. I seen Garth takin' her out. Steele was with 'em. We laid back a minute t' get clear o' him—Jackie an' me—but when we got t' the bridge we was stopped by the sentries. Steele's orders, they said. God damn him! You go'n' t' talk t' Trent?"

"Not now." He was snatching the heavy rifle out of the rack. The rack was already half empty. "You see Trent. I'm going to Garth's."

"You ain't goin' alone."

"Don't disobey orders, John. No use both of us being in trouble."

"Wait f'r them soldiers, Chris. We may need 'em at Garth's. We may need 'em bad."

The drummer boys of the guard stood in a row under the gleaming windows. The light, behind, pinched their young faces with shadows. The roll of "the general" throbbed through the tumult on the parade. Men in citizens' clothes hurried by. Their women trailed after them. Soldiers and officers ran with their wives to save what they could from their cabins in Lower Town.

The signal torch flared at the peak of the flagstaff. The pine knots in their woven iron basket dripped fire. Bits of blazing resin dribbled down on the bastion. The torch dribbled bits of red light over the crowd jammed at the mouth of the narrow passage under the timberwork of the gate.

The passage was filled with Royals—Grey's and Donnellan's details going out at the double to block the roads. A few civilians got through behind them. Burent, who built batteaux for the army. Hudson, his helper. McKee, the interpreter. Then Stair Carre's whole company surged through the crowd like a blunt-nosed barge, pushing it right and left and leaving a wash of people behind and a flotsam of men and women against the brick walls of the passage. Holden saw Captain Barnsley's wife with her back to the bricks, and Lieutenant Rosetidge's wife, Captain Mather's nigra servant, and young Will Clapham whose uncle was dead on his scythe.

There was a look on their faces—empty and gone. Nothing had happened to these people yet. But already they looked like people caught in some dreadful disaster—a flood or a fire. Already they had the look that was stamped on the faces of refugees.

Holden and Fraser crossed the bridges behind the double files of heavily running soldiers. There were lights yet behind the windows of Nan Perdue's. Other windows were springing out of the darkness in sudden bright squares of glass or the blurred-paper smears of orange.

Where the King's Road turned up the slope, they began to meet other hurrying people. And these were really refugees, from the town. They carried things in their arms and on their backs and trundled them in barrows that bumped and squealed—sleeping children and crying children and bundles and benches and spinning wheels, pots and kettles and blankets huddled up any which way, and sacks of meal, sides of bacon, and braids of corn. One man had a tall clock across his shoulder. Another man carried nothing except one shoe. Holden looked at his feet. He was wearing the other shoe.

Holden heard, as he ran, the hollow thumps of mauls against cabin doors, the straining creak of fence rails prying logs out of cabin walls, the thundering crash of a log coming down, the pursuing chatter of dry mud chinking that spattered on the dry ground and among the weeds. The soldiers were already tearing the nearest houses apart.

He saw a man crawl out of his cockloft window and drop to the ground: his house door was carefully barred inside, and probably blocked by a table and chest of drawers and a cupboard. He saw another man threading a chain through the hasp on his doorpost and through the hasp on the door. He heard the click of a padlock.

The utter absurdity of it—people carefully closing the doors and barring the shutters of houses that wouldn't be there in the morning. A man went a little insane, for a while, when he had to abandon his home, when he had to walk away and just leave it.

Through an open door now he saw William Guttery closing and barring his shutters. A pile of things lay on the sapling-trunk bed against the wall. A horn lantern hung on a bedpost. Mrs. Guttery stood in the dooryard, trying to make her hands meet and clasp around the shapeless bundle she held.

"Will!" she screeched. "They's sojers onto the roof!"

The soldiers had found Will Guttery's lean-to, out back. Two Royals came scrambling up to the ridgepole now. They began throwing down the rocks that held Guttery's cedar-bark shingles in place.

Will Guttery came to the door. His hands held to the jambs of the door as he looked up at the men on the roof. Then he let his hands fall. He went back into the cabin and gathered up the four corners of the blanket left on the bed. The pile of stuff on the bed came up with the blanket. A slab of the roof fell in. Guttery stood and looked at the piece of his roof on his floor. Then he took the lantern down from the bedpost and started to blow it out. A soldier shouted down through the hole in the roof:

"Leave it be!"

"It'll set things afire," Will said reasonably.

"What the hell d' you care? One way or other, ye ain't goin' t' have no house."

Sapling rafters began to roll down the roof. They clattered down into the dooryard and lay there like jackstraws piled up for a game. The soldiers were making a game of destroying the town. Fraser yelled at the men on the roof:

"Heave up that ridgepole! Get one o' them rafters under it. Give it a heave."

The ridge log came thundering down.

"Pick it up," Fraser said to the Royals with him. "Sling y'r muskets an' take a-holt." The four soldiers picked up the log. "Come on, Chris." They ran up the road.

The Gilded Beaver was dark. Holden tried the door.

"All right," he said. "Smash it in."

The Royals butted the end of Will Guttery's ridgepole against the door. It bounced and a hollow boom came out of the house. They swung the log back and drove it against the door and it bounced again.

"Here, Chris. Take this lantern. Gi' me a hold o' that log."

The log crashed into the door. Again. And again. At the third crash, the bolt gave. The rush of the log carried John and the Royals into the empty tap. Holden ran down the room and swung the lantern over the trading counter. He opened the storeroom door. He opened the well-room door.

"Here," Fraser called. "Gi' me a light t' this."

He had found the candlestick on the bar. Holden opened the lantern. The wick caught from the flame.

"There's a loft," Fraser said. He ran up the stairs and disappeared and came back. "No. Nothin'." He saw Holden stooping over. "What ye got, Chris?"

"This." He held it up. "It's a knot of ribbon. It's off her dress. She was here. He brought her here."

The soldiers were looking on curiously. One of them said:

"That rope moved. In the well house there."

They crowded into the tiny room. Holden opened the lantern again. He saw now the bucket smashed on the floor. He held the lantern over the coping. There was only the rope, dropping down to the round black glisten of water, and the well bucket floating there upside down. But the round black pool was stirring. Ripples spread out from the bucket.

"Haul it up!"

A soldier laid hold of the windlass handle. It took his whole weight to turn it. A hollow cry came from the well.

"Help! Kind sirs, help!"

There was still only the bucket. It tipped as the windlass groaned.

The dripping edge tilted up. Under it, gray hair hung in dripping strings. Fraser leaned over the coping and seized the rope. The windlass turned faster. Jeremy Love's arms were locked so tightly around the rope handle that when they dragged him over the top of the wall they had to pry his arms loose.

They carried him out and set him down on a stool and held him. The water that streamed down his face began to turn dark. Holden touched his head. He whimpered.

"Take it easy, Chris," Fraser said. "He's right bad."

"Not at all, gentlemen." Jeremy's eyes were closed and his voice was weak, but its habit of cheerful patter was strong. "Very happy to see you, gentlemen. Happy indeed. A most fortunate meeting for me."

"What happened, Jeremy?"

"Oh yes. Yes indeed. Indians. Unpleasant creatures. Truly horrible creatures. I almost gave them the slip. Still agile, you know. But one of them caught me a knock on the head with his hand ax. I fell backwards into the well. A wondrous invention, wells. A splendid example of man's ingenuity. As you saw, I held onto the bucket handle. That was my own ingenuity, gentlemen." His eyes slid open. He smiled his cherubic and guileless smile.

"No, to be frank, it was not. It was a phenomenon, gentlemen . . . a delicate matter of weight and balance. My weight on the handle caused the bucket to turn upside down. I was not observed.

"*What happened?* What did they do with her?"

"Her. Her. Obviously you are inquiring about a female." He slobbered. His babyish mouth blew bubbles. Holden wiped the drooling mouth with his handkerchief. "Humble thanks. Ah, Captain Holden. My thanks and apologies. Regret . . . too much water. Couldn't help swallowin' some."

"Jeremy, *think*. What happened?"

"They took her away. The Indians. Garth tried to stop them. He wanted to keep her here. His wife . . . I . . . ah . . . I assume she's his wife—she did not seem pleased."

"Hannah. Was Hannah here?"

"Yes. With her father."

"Not Guyasuta? Not here!"

"Garth called him Guyasuta. It sounded like that. Yes—I'm quite sure. I have a quick ear. No education whatever, but I have picked up Latin and——"

"Did they say what they'd do with her? Did Garth say?"

"The short one—the ugliest one—the one he called Guyasuta——"

"That's Guyasuta, a' right."

"—said Seneca men didn't lie with a woman that belonged to some other man."

"You see, Chris, she's a' right."

"I'm quite sure she will be all right. She's not Garth's any more. Garth gave her to Hannah. He said she was Hannah's slave."

Holden felt the blow in the pit of his stomach as if he'd been kicked. Jeremy Love pattered on:

"Mr. Garth said she would work for Hannah. He wanted to take them both to the fort. The Indian disagreed. He was quite positive. Quite. When the Indians started to take her, Abby ran up the stairs. Hannah stopped her. Oh!" Jeremy struggled up in their arms. "Oh, stripe me, sir! I remember now . . . Hannah kicked her. She put her foot in her face and pushed her back down the stairs."

Holden ran toward the back of the room where the trade counter was. He set the lantern clattering on the counter and vaulted over. He started rummaging on the shelves. Fraser was close behind him.

"What ye doin', Chris?"

"Food. I've got to have something. I——"

"Chris, ye ain't goin' t' Guyasuta's town!"

"Yes."

"Ye ain't sure she's there."

"She'll be there. If she isn't dead before they get her that far."

"They won't hurt her, Chris. She's Garth's, an' he's on their side."

"He gave her to Hannah. You know what that means. Hannah can do whatever she wants with her. She can have her burned."

"They don't burn women, Chris."

"They burned Katy Unger after Kittanning. I saw that."

"Ye can't help her, Chris. If that's what they're up to, ye'll only get fried along with her. Chris, ye're a God-damn fool."

"I have been, till now."

"Ye can't get through. Ecuyer's got the roads guarded."

"I won't use the roads."

"Ye can't get a horse up them rocks."

"I won't use a horse."

"It's forty miles, Chris."

"Forty." Forty miles weren't many, after four hundred miles in eight days. But the miles ahead stretched like four thousand now. "I'll cut up over Grant's Hill and come back to the river road."

"Ye can't! They'll be swarmin' in here by sunup."

"I've got to, John. I've got to be sure. I've got to find their tracks. I've got to have a look at Garth's station upriver. They might have taken her there. It's close on to daylight. I'll know, by the time I hit Croghan's and Garth's, which way they're heading. If they're not at Garth's Castle, I'll cut across country again. I'll strike the path about where the big falls are. There's a crossing there. Food. I've got to have food!"

Fraser gave up.

"It looks like they've cleaned the place out," he said. He was scrambling over the counter. "Here's a side o' bacon they missed. On the floor. It's been tramped some, but—— Here's somethin' else. A horn, an' it's full."

"I don't want——" Holden stopped. There was somebody in the shadows beyond the counter.

"Captain Holden . . ." Voice like a wavering shadow. Voice afraid of itself. "I've got to see you."

"Who are you?"

"I'm Ten Eyck. I asked the soldiers. They said you were back here."

Fraser lifted the lantern. The light pasted a yellowish fungus on Ten Eyck's face.

"Captain Holden, you didn't say there was danger. You didn't tell me. You told Kenny. Kenny's gone. He went off this afternoon. You might have told me."

"I haven't seen Kenny," Chris said.

"Jesus God!" Fraser cried. "Get out o' here!" Then he saw that the soldiers had followed the schoolteacher into the trading room. "Get rid o' this fool. Kick him out."

One of the soldiers took hold of Ten Eyck.

"You got a musket?" he asked. "Then go down to the fort an' draw one."

Ten Eyck's mouth sucked in. The fungus growth on his face seemed to shrivel. His small face seemed to be shrinking. There wasn't room for his eyes. They crawled farther and farther out of his head until they seemed ready to roll down his meager face.

"That's it," he whispered. "You said that, Holden. You said that's how I'd know if the trouble was bad."

"Get goin'," the soldier said. "You want I should boot you? Measly, cringin'—— By God, you're as yellow as gourd guts." He ran Ten Eyck up the room.

"Here—take the horn, Chris."

"I don't want the horn. I've got Dan's. I filled it today. I don't want but a hand of bacon."

"Ye're takin' that horn." Fraser was hacking the flitch of bacon. "Gi' me that pouch." He dragged out handfuls of strings and belts and dumped them on the counter. He thrust a slab of the bacon into the pouch and stuffed the seawan on top. "Ye don't know how long ye'll be or how far ye'll go. Chris, if ye find her, ye can't noways bring her back here."

He hadn't thought about that. He had thought only of finding her. Finding her like the girl in the song they sang at the ball—*her honor's singed and then for life she's what I dare not name.* Finding her like Kate Unger. He wouldn't care if another man had had her. He'd care, but it wouldn't matter, he'd love her as much. But they'd had to kill Kate. It was all they could do for her when they found her, too late.

Fraser was dragging his neckcloth from under his coat. He was wrapping slabs of meat in it, stuffing them into Holden's pockets.

"Listen, Chris. If ye find her, make f'r the Susquehanna. Stick t' the little streams. Even Indians can't follow tracks under water. There's runs all through that country up there. They mostly bear east of north. Ye got that compass, Chris?"

"Yes. I've got it."

"Them streams is like men sleepin' watch—head t' foot. Them that drains t' the Allegheny is head t' toe with them that runs east. One night ye'll slip over a hill an' the next creek ye hit will be runnin' east, 'stead o' west. Ye hearin' me, Chris?"

"Yes."

"Make f'r the settlements, Chris. Ye c'n do more good warnin' the settlements than ye could by comin' back here."

"Yes." He was miles ahead now. He was thinking of Philadelphia. Pollexfen waiting for him at the Indian Queen. Pollexfen had seen him pay the money to Leach, and Pollexfen could prove . . .

"Take care o' y'rself, ye damn fool."

"I will. I've got to. I've got to find her. I will." He hung onto that thought. He had to hang onto it. "I'll get through, John. You're going to need help. I'll get through to Bouquet."

"We're go'n' t' need a powerful amount o' help. The best thing ye c'n do f'r us is t' put a burr under Bouquet. Put a hot brick in his pants. Chris, way it looks t' me, ye'd best make it a ramrod. Ye'd best make it plenty hot."

Chapter 35

She was in a house. She hadn't known that Indians lived in houses.

She hadn't thought much about it, but when she had wondered at all she had thought that they lived as the beasts of the field. But this house was built of logs, like a white man's house. It was bigger than any cabin in Pitt's Town, and many times bigger than most. The difference was that the logs of this Indian house were not laid up one on another, with ends sticking out any which way. These logs stood on end, neatly and side by side. And the bark roof was arched, not pointed or flat. It fitted down closely over the tops of the logs, like a mobcap without much frill.

There was the smell, but the smell wasn't any worse. It was only different. It wasn't sour like the smell of white cabins along the King's Road at the Forks, or the loft where she'd slept, or of Dave Bone's taproom when it was crowded with sweating soldiers and batteau men.

It was not even new. It was something she'd smelled before, and she tried now to think what it was. If she tried hard enough it kept her, some parts of the time, from thinking of other things. Of Captain Holden's defeated and hopeless face—of the silver slippers, gone—and she didn't know where—of the beautiful gown, torn by brambles and bushes now and stained to her knees and even above her knees and still damp from the last creek they'd dragged her through.

Part of the time her hands had been tied behind her and part of the time there had been a rope made of plaited leathery cords looped around her neck and tied to the belt of a savage who rode a horse. Now her arms were spread out at the height of her shoulders and tied to the ends of a curving bow that cut into her shoulder blades, and her arms and her back were aching because she'd been tied so long. Hours. She didn't know how many hours.

The sun had been bright and hot over the trees when she came to the town, and now it was dark and it had been dark a long time and the drums still throbbed.

The drums had begun at dusk and they'd never stopped. She could feel them throb in her head and in the ache of her back and her arms and her wrists where the cords dug in. But the cords were no worse than the chains had been, and the bow in her back was no worse than the rusty iron, and this house was much cleaner than Newgate prison. But it was a prison. They were keeping her here for Garth. *Don't think about that. Garth's wife won't let him* . . . Hannah was not here. Garth might come alone. *Don't. Don't think.* Maybe Captain Holden would come. But he couldn't. She knew he couldn't. *Think about the queer town.* She tried hard to remember how the town looked when they brought her here.

There weren't any chimneys! That was one reason the houses looked queer. She had seen, coming into the town, the little curved separate roofs set athirt the roofs of the houses. She had seen, in the afternoon twilight inside this house, the holes high up in the arch of the roof, and the smutted stones that lay on the floor like hearths without chimney places. The holes in the roof were for smoke. And the little roofs, set crosswise, kept the rain out. But the smoke didn't always go out through the holes. It hung under the ceiling and sooted the bark and made the house smell like a charred cask with the dregs of rum still in it. The sweet smell must be from the people who lived here. She'd noticed the smell, a little, when Indians came to the Gilded Beaver to trade.

She had been amazed by the Indian town. It was bigger than Pitt's Town. There weren't more houses, there weren't as many. But they were so big. They looked as if fifty people or more could live in each house. They were long, and their length made them narrow, but they were wider even than the Frasers' cabin.

There wasn't a street, but the houses were ranged in more orderly fashion than those in Pitt's Town. They stood wide apart, in two rows, with a broad grassless trampled space between them almost like a village square. There was a red-painted post in the square. She remembered that, and how slivered it looked—as if horses had gnawed it or someone had been hacking on it, trying to cut it down—and the splinters lying around and trampled into the dirt. She had not come anigh to the post. They had taken her straight to this house. And again she had been amazed in spite of her fear.

The Indians slept in four-poster beds that had canopies over them. Anyway, that was how it looked, the one glimpse she had of the shadowy length of the house when they brought her in.[1] The Indians' beds had posts made of saplings, the same as the Frasers', and the canopies seemed to be made out of sheets of bark. But the Frasers' bed didn't have any canopy at all. The Indians' beds seemed to be all one against one, end to end, on both sides of the house; but they had blankets on them the same as white people's beds, and fur robes spread over or under the blankets.

She was in one of the bed places now, only it wasn't used for a bed. The space here at the end of the house was a kind of storeroom, and there were things of the same kind you'd find in a white man's attic—big wooden buckets and small ones, and noggins made out of bark, and the same braids of corn hung from the roof poles, the same kind of bundles of furs on the floor.

The Indians had a mortar and pestle, too. The mortar part was made from a hollowed tree trunk. It looked like the Frasers' tub. Tears came to her eyes when she thought of the moment when Captain Holden came into the room and tumbled the lovely dress over the chair and the other things on the table.

Her dream had come true—almost exactly true—the terrible one that she dreamed in her sleep. She had forgotten to take off the pattens, she'd gone to the ball with the wooden clogs on her feet, and they had known right away that she wasn't a lady, and she hadn't been let to dance.

Her eyes were still blinded by tears when the women came in. She

[1]To Abby, in her ignorance of Seneca ways, the continuous dwelling platforms for families in the lodge looked like beds set end to end. Her mistake is hardly surprising.

hardly saw them untying the long braided leather rope that fastened the bow to one of the upright posts. She didn't know she could move until one of the Indian women jerked the rope, pulling upward on it, and three or four others lifted her to her feet.

They walked her the length of the empty dark house to the door at the farther end. The woman who held the rope jerked it again. It twisted her arms about, still tied to the bow, so that she went out sidewise through the door, and neither the ends of the bow nor her side hoops caught.

Something important seemed to be going on, with bonfires burning and all. It looked like the streets in that town when the bonfires were lighted at night. Williamsburg, it had been.

There were a many fires. One, it seemed, was for women. One, the biggest, was for the men. And there was another where a great iron kettle steamed and bubbled on a thick pole laid across forked stakes.

There was even an orchestra. It was only drums—three of them, low and flat, in a row on the ground by the fire where the men were gathered. On a many such evenings as this she'd stood by herself on the Angel's little back gallery, dreaming, imagining that the shadowy coach yard was a stage and that it would soon be lighted and filled with people, and that the play would begin. This was like a stage-set for a play—the lights flaring, the whole street, or square, or whatever it was, filled with characters strangely dressed.

She saw one who had horns on his head. They stuck out from each side of a shaggy band that she thought must be surely the fur of a bear. The horned Indian wasn't tall, but he seemed important. He carried a kind of scepter thing in his hand. It was heavy. He rested the head of it in the crook of his other arm.

There was another odd player who looked like a royal jester. He had a fool's cap on his head—-that was what it looked like. He pranced and capered and waved the long wands in his hands. One of them looked like a long-handled warming pan.

It was like seeing *Othello* begin, or the *Merchant of Venice,* and wondering what the people in far-off places were like and how they dressed. She had seen a play once. She had seen it begin . . . No No! *No!* Of course she hadn't. She had stood at the gallery rail of the Angel and seen an old, dreadful game beginning again, and it had seemed like a play.

She mustn't get mixed up now, in her head. She mustn't. She needed her wits. She didn't know what she could do with her wits, but she mustn't lose them. She mustn't go mad with this fear that was growing and growing and thrusting its little roots down into her mind and into her heart and all through her.

And now, as the women led her closer and closer to the biggest fire and the rows upon rows of eyes glittering at her out of the painted faces, she saw that the short, squatty, important man was the one who had been at the Gilded Beaver. The thing he held wasn't a scepter. It was a club with a heavy, round, brutal head.

And the jester wasn't a jester at all and his cap was not a fool's cap. He and the crest on his head both were horrible things. The crest was made of the head of an animal and the wings of a bird. The bird's wings were spread wide from the back of his neck and his face peered out from under a dried wolf's head. The dead shriveled lips were drawn back and grinning above the fangs, and the Indian's face looked as shriveled and dead as the wolf's.

She saw the sticks in his hands and they, too, were dreadful. The one that had looked at first like a warming pan had a turtle's carcass tied to its upper end, with the shrunken head and the dead claws dangling. The other was wrapped round and round with a dried rattlesnake. The head stuck out at the top.

The weazened old Indian capered and chanted. He flourished the rattle-snake wand back and forth in front of her face. The women shrank back, but their hands still held her. There were dozens of clutching hands. They clung to her arms, to her hair, to her dress. They seemed to be waiting for something.

It came. The short, ugly Indian made a sign with his hand.

The women swarmed on her with hideous screeches. Their hands clawed and tore. She felt their nails on her flesh. She heard the gown being ripped apart. She heard the silk itself crying out in thin screeches—thin and pitiful cries torn out of the dress.

The heaving and surging weight of the squaws bore her down. The mass of fighting and screaming women was crushing her into the ground and she couldn't breathe, and her stomach heaved to be rid of the awful weight of their stench.

And then they were gone. She lay there quite peacefully on the ground, all alone, and heard the Indans laughing. She saw part of her dress on a squaw, running wildly, with other squaws chasing her. Some of the men had joined in the game. They were cavorting and prancing and flourishing pieces of silk and lace.

She saw one young Indian, painted vermilion and black, dancing a crazy dance. He was wearing her side hoops. And as he danced he was working the hoops up and down on their hinges over his naked thighs and over his painted ribs.

She looked at herself then, lying there on the ground. The dress was gone. The petticoats had been ripped away. The stockings were gone, and even the drawers were gone. She was on her back, and her arms were still stretched to the tips of the bow, and she was completely naked.

The rows of eyes glittered at her. Two old, wrinkled women came and bent over her and lifted her to her feet.

They held her. She couldn't have stood by herself. But she saw that in their mad fight for her clothes the squaws had dragged her a little away from the fires. The short, ugly Indian was walking toward her, and he was Hannah's father and that was why this terrible thing had happened. He still had the red feathered cap on his head, under the band of bearskin and under the horns. He still had the one long feather stuck in the hollow bone that stood up from the crown of the cap. The feather revolved as he walked.

She stood there and stared and stared at the one slowly twirling feather.

The Indian looked at her. She saw the hate in his eyes. He said a word.

The women led her away. *He understands English,* she thought. He had said a few English words to Garth. *I can talk to him.*

But the thought came too late. She turned her head. There were only the faces of women behind her. She cried wildly, desperately:

"I'm not Garth's! *Not Garth's!* I belong to another man!"

A squaw struck at her with a stick. It broke on her cheek. The women led her away toward the end of the street. She saw now, beyond the men's fire, the two trees that had been cut off a few feet from the ground. They had been trees with branches and leaves a few hours ago. She knew it. She hadn't seen any ugly, hacked stumps like that.

The realization did not come all at once. It came like water out of an icy bucket, being poured into and through her slowly. It numbed her, body and brain. She said very calmly:

"What are they going to do?"

And then, still calmly, she thought: *That's silly. They can't understand what I say.* But one of the women answered, a single word:

"Burn."

The word was not new. She had known it as soon as she saw the stakes. And she was still cold and numbed by the icy shock pouring through her.

She looked for the woman who spoke, and found her—an old, bent hag with a face as dark and withered and wrinkled as a potato dug up but not found and left all year on the ground. She said:

"Make it quick. Please tell them to make it quick."

The numbness was draining away and the awful fear was being poured into her slowly, not all at once. But it filled every part of her as the numbness made room for it.

"Tago aween," the old woman said. Then her leathery lips felt for another word. They rubbed. You could hear them rub. "Not quick," she said. "Never quick."

Abby knew with a sudden horror that the old woman was white.

The squaws led her toward the stakes. There were heaps of wood in a circle around them. There was a kind of passageway left in the circling heaps of branches and brush. The squaws turned her around. They clung to her while they untied the bow from her wrists. Their nails sank deep into her arms.

They tied her by one of her wrists to the stub of a branch on the hacked-off stump of one tree. The braided green hide of the cord raised her arm over her head. They tied her other wrist to the other tree. Then they left her.[2]

She hung by her wrists from the cords. The drums . . . the drums . . . if the awful drums would stop . . . if they would stop for only a minute, she'd know that this wasn't so.

This was somebody else who stood here naked under the eyes of a

[2]The conventional picture of Indian torture, familiar to most Americans, almost invariably shows a single stake, as neatly rounded as if it had just been bought from a turning mill, and the captive also still neat and unharmed and always respectable in a clean white loincloth, with hands tied precisely behind. But anyone who has read even a few eye-witness accounts knows that the Indians were highly ingenious impresarios at this sort of entertainment. The methods of torture varied from tribe to tribe and also from time to time, as different masters of ceremonies took charge.

hundred men. And it wasn't like being looked at naked by men. They weren't men. They were animals, crouching and waiting. They were the werewolves she'd read about. They were the *loups-garous* in the old French tales her father had told.

This was a play. It was still a play. And she was a part of the play. It was a puppet show. She was one of the puppets. She hung by strings. She could feel the strings on her wrists.

That was all she could feel. Her body was stuffed with sawdust—her arms and her legs and her head. There was no feeling in her at all except the feeling that this was unreal, that she wasn't real, that this couldn't be happening. Then she thought: *Sawdust burns.*

Chapter 36

They couldn't be going to burn her. The men seemed to be so good-natured. They were having a wonderful time. They were chuckling and laughing together, and making jokes. The things they said as they looked at her must be jokes.

If only the drums would stop. They went on and on, a monotonous, changeless, remorseless throb.

The older women had settled themselves by their fire. They had knives. They were whittling sticks. She could see the sticks whiten. They had sharp points. The squaws laid them into neat piles with the sharpened ends all the same way.

One of the old women had something that wasn't a stick. She held it up now. She shook it toward the white girl. It was a gourd or something.

The old woman held it against the front of her filthy shirt. The thing that she held was shaped like a young girl's breast. It was round and full. There was even a nipple where the small stem still clung.

The woman picked up a stick from the pile of whittled sticks on the ground. She drove the sharp point of it into the thing that was shaped like a breast.

She picked up another stick and pushed it in with a vicious jab. She continued to pick up the white sharp sticks and to jab till the breast-shaped gourd was bristling with long pine splinters. Then she dragged herself up.

She was very old. She walked, bent, toward the fire, and spoke to the men. Some of them looked up and laughed. They set the bristling thing on a long slim stick and thrust it into the fire. The splinters burst into flame.

The old woman came hobbling toward the heaped wood and the naked girl. She stood in the gap in the circling heat and held the stick out toward Abby until the splinters burned down and the gourd was blackened and scorched.

The younger women were bringing more wood. They were throwing it on the piles. The encircling heap was as high as her knees. It rose to her thighs, to her hips.

As each squaw dropped her armload of wood, she stooped and picked out one stick. She threw the stick at the girl. Sometimes the sticks missed. But they came from every direction—in front, and behind, from all sides. She couldn't dodge. The sticks didn't hurt much. But her body was welted and scratched. The squaws gibbered and screeched.

And the children were joining in. The small naked boys ran off into the woods and came back with pine cones and pieces of birch bark and sticks. They set the cones on the sticks. They wrapped the ends of the sticks in the curls of bark. They thrust them into the fire, and the cones and the bark burst into fierce little tongues of flame. The boys came running. They flipped the sticks at her, over the heaps of brush.

Some of them struck her. They scorched her before they fell. They fell on the ground around her. The few wisps of grass caught fire. They burned to the roots. The ground all around her bare feet was strewn with the burning cones and the glowing wisps of burned bark and the coals from the lighted sticks. They thickened into a carpet of fire at her feet.

There were sparks in her hair. There was a small fierce ember stuck to her flesh in the hollow between her breasts. Her body writhed. The ember, darkening slowly, slowly let go of her flesh. It dropped to the ground and winked out. But there was a fiery pain at the base of her throat. It stayed. A spark was caught in her flesh there too. It ate into her flesh.

A new agony came. It wrapped itself tightly around her body. One of the younger women, carrying wood for the fire, brought a long, limber branch. She thrust it into the fire, and when it burst into flame along its whole length she ran into the circle and struck at the tethered white body. The burning branch curled around Abby's waist.

She screamed, then, the first time. The Indians yelled.

The circle of men had changed. It was only the three-quarters part of a circle now. It was open, toward the girl, so all of the men could see her. She could see them. She could see what they were doing.

They were still laughing and joking. They kept poking the fire, like a lot of small boys. They kept stirring the pot. They were heating things in the fire.

The horrible witchlike creature with feathers behind his head was tottering toward the fire where the kettle boiled. He picked up a ladle made of a bone—long bone that must be the thigh of a man. He dipped it into the kettle and stirred and brought it out dripping and bubbling. A young, clouted Indian came with a pine cone impaled on a ramrod. The thing in feathers poured some of the bubbling stuff onto the cone. It burst into flame.

As if that were another signal, one of the savages plucked a hatchet out of the coals. It smoked. Even the handle was hot. He shifted his hold on the haft, and the other savages hooted and laughed. He was coming toward her, the smoking hatchet coming closer and closer. The handle was scorched from the fire. Little curling trails of scorch ran up toward the Indian's hand where the coals had set the long handle ablaze and the flames had licked it.

She could move a little. She backed away till her arms, drawn up by the plaited green strips of hide, were raised in a pleading gesture.

The Indian walked through the gap in the circle of faggots. He stood in front of her now, and the hot iron head of the hatchet glowed cherry red through the gray of the ashes with which it was smeared.

The Indian lifted the hatchet. *God, please . . . please mak'en to go away . . . please mak'en not to zweal me!* He laid the glowing hatchet against her flesh where the thong raised her arm.

The searing pain flashed through her body and up through her throat and it was a scream in her throat.

All the Indians screeched when she screamed.

But God was helping her bear the pain. After the first long cry, she could bear it. The pain was still there, pressed against her side. But the hatchet was gone. The Indian was walking away; she could see his shoulder blades sticking out through his back.

He walked as if he had failed at something. He had. There was nothing so very clever in clapping a hatchet against the ribs. Half the crazy screeches were mocking him because he was stupid and timid. It wasn't often the Seneca burned a woman. But when they did, there were certain exquisite refinements of degradation and torment. The mean-looking, thin little man had achieved nothing but the routine.

The yelling and laughter ceased. Even the women were quiet. Only the children still hooted and scrambled about. There was a curious, waiting tenseness among the men. They seemed to be waiting for something. They were. But she couldn't know these small beginnings of torture were a contest, a game in which they were taking turns. She could not know that the real game came later—much later—the really ingenious torture.

They were waiting to see what the next, in his turn, meant to do.

He got up from his place. He was a dull-looking fellow, thick-shouldered and heavy-bellied. He walked slowly across the open space to the women. He stooped and picked up a handful of the white, whittled splinters. He took a long time selecting the one that he wanted. The Indians started to yell, but their yells were not loud. They had plenty of time. They were only chafing him.

The Indian finally picked out a splinter. He walked to the iron pot, seething over the fire, and plunged the stick in. It came out dripping and dark. He turned and began to walk toward her. His belly wagged as he walked.

She didn't know what he intended to do. The thin splinter looked harmless, after the glowing hatchet. She did not know that sometimes, when Indians tortured a woman, they filled her whole body with long thin pine splinters that had been dipped in pitch, and that when she was quilled like a porcupine, head to foot, they set the splinters afire and turned her into a living torch.

She didn't know how long it took to drive in enough slivers, or what happened in between. She didn't know that sometimes, after the splinters burned down to the flesh and into the flesh, the woman was still alive and they could devise new clever tortures that her seared flesh would still be able to feel.

The Indian walked up to her until his belly was almost touching her body. Her arms, raised by the thongs, almost embraced him. His arm went back over his shoulder.

And then she remembered the gourd. In the waiting quiet, her voice was the only sound—a sound so sharp that it hurt like knives in her throat and her ears and her head. She hardly felt the splinter driving into her flesh.

She saw it there.

He had missed the breast. All the other Indians hooted.

The pain and the terror seemed to explode in her mind, in a blinding flash.

But the Indian wasn't going. He was standing there, half turned away. His hands hung down at his sides. And the yelling had stopped. She knew that, when her own cry stopped. The thick-bellied Indian seemed to crouch there in front of her like an animal, doubled up, ready to run.

He stared and stared at the thick white cloud that hung in the trees where the path came up from the river.

And then she knew that she had gone mad at last. She was glad. She was grateful to God. People always said that the mad ones in Bedlam did not feel pain.

Where the flash had been, she saw Captain Holden standing, wrapped in the cloud.

He stood there so still and so calm that she knew he was not there at all. But his head was thrown back and his thumbs were hooked into the sash at his waist. And she heard him speak:

"*Tohne waktan'ha!*"

She didn't know what he said, but the voice was his.

"*O'nen ni'a hau'!* Here I stand. Now I am coming."

He threw off the cloud like a blanket and walked up the street toward the painted post. He had something white in his hand. As he walked, it wavered and moved. She thought wildly that it was a piece he had torn from the wavering, drifting cloud.

Chapter 37

Christopher Holden walked into the Indian town quickly and casually. He hoped he was striking the proper balance between briskness and nonchalance. It was a delicate balance.

He looked at the painted and splintered post as if it had only the slightest interest for him. He looked once at the naked girl and the live coals strewn at her feet and the piles of faggots and brush that encircled her. Then he looked away.

He came to the pack of savages crowded around the fire and the pack gave way. He stepped through toward the fire and the pack closed in. He stood quite calmly among them, carelessly swinging the long white thing that he held in his hand.

"*He'onwe Hadi'nonge ne Seneca* [Where are the Seneca]?" He made his voice light and scornful. "*He'onwe hadi'nonge ne ha'sennowa'nen Guyasuta* [Where the chief Guyasuta]?"

The short ugly Indian spoke:

"*Ieiensdon'gwa! Sgaga'di! Dedji'aon'gwa!* [On your right! On the other side! All around you!] *I'iet Guyasuta* [Guyasuta stands next to you]."

Holden laughed.

"*De'osthon!*" He said it loudly. He hoped he had found the right word. He hoped that it meant what he wanted to say. If it did, it meant "not even a little." It was the Seneca version of "not by a long shot."

He had chosen it as a deliberate insult. His one chance was to catch their attention and hold it. He'd caught it, at least. He heard them sucking their breath, and that was the sign of amazement. *Make them mad. Make them so mad they can't think.*

"I was sent by the king my father to bring a belt to the Seneca. I was sent to tell them of presents being prepared."

He looked down at the belt in his hands and wagged it provocatively.

"But now! What do I find when I come with belts from my father the king? I find women! Women painted to look like men! Ha-*ha!*" It was not the false laughter now. It was the Seneca cry of contempt. "Paint cannot hide the truth. You have become as women! Foolishly painted women fit only to torture a woman!"

Again the in-sucking breath of amazement. They would take a good deal from a man who held a belt in his hands and talked their own language, in symbols they understood.

"I cannot believe that all of the Seneca fighting men have become as women. *Then'en!* No! It must be this *ha'sennowa'nen*—this chief." He was sarcastic now. "This great chief! This mighty one called Guyasuta!"

The time had come for the speech he had been rehearsing for forty miles. The next ten minutes would do it. And if they didn't, the white body forgotten now in the circle of faggots would writhe and scream and turn slowly into a shriveled and awful thing, and he would die of the fire in his turn.

"Listen to me! *Ne gwa, gi'on, hadi'nonge ne hen'non'gwe.*" He launched into the ancient oration, the ancient Seneca legend. "In the beginning, so it is said, man-beings dwelt on the other side of the sky. So, in the midst of the village, the lodge of the chief stood." He interrupted the story: "His name was not Guyasuta!"

They laughed. By the Lord, they *laughed!* He had them. They might burn him yet, but for the time being this was an entertainment. The next act could wait.

"Therein dwelt the chief and his wife and one child, a girl they two had. But the chief was surprised that he began to be lonesome. Now, furthermore, he the Ancient One became very lean. His bones dried. And this was because he was much displeased that they two had a child. One would think that the chief was jealous."

He came at last to the place in the legend where the jealous man-dweller-beyond-the-sky pushed his wife through a hole in the sky and she fell on the back of a turtle and made the earth and became its grandmother, she the Ancient One, she the first woman-being. All savage religion was based on that story. It was not always the same religion; it varied from tribe to tribe. But it accounted for many things—for the fact that family, clan, and inheritance came from the woman and not from the man—for the fact that women sat in the Indians' councils as they were not permitted to sit in the white men's councils—for Hannah's power. It even accounted for the turtle-shell rattle set on the end of the shaman's wand as the symbol of the Great Spirit, contending always against the Evil Spirit. This wrinkled shaman, he noticed, was taking no chances; he had the symbol of evil, the rattlesnake wand, in his other hand.

Holden went on reciting the ancient Seneca gospel. He was into it now. His voice rose and fell in the Seneca chant and the words came freely. Thank God he'd had nothing to read those long winter nights at Venango. Thank God he'd sat by the fire in his hut and poured rum into another old, wrinkled shaman and listened and learned. He had done it then for a joke. He'd thought it would be excruciatingly funny to stand for the House of Burgesses sometime and make a harangue on the hustings in Seneca. He'd thought it would make as much sense as most of the politicians' speeches he'd heard.

He was telling now how the grandmother of the earth gave birth to a girl man-being, and how the girl child in her turn was delivered of twins. The legend accounted for that. The Seneca had their own version of the immaculate conception. His voice rose and fell in the sonorous cadences:

"There on the grass she would kneel. The wind entered into her body. It was delightful. The wind was enclosed in her body."

On and on, through the birth of twin male man-beings to the maiden made pregnant by the delightful wind, and how one man-being was rightly born but the other sprang from his mother's navel and was short and ugly and known as the Warty One. He told how the maiden died, and the grandmother of the earth cared for the two man-beings, and how the elder one fashioned the animals, each in its different shape—how he made the deer from his bow and the wolf from an arrow—how he took the upper teeth out of the mouths of the buffalo and the elk—and how he made the mink long and slender by stripping it through his hands.

The legend went on to tell how the *otgon*—the dread powers of magic —had slain the younger brother, him the Warty One, and how it came to be thought that the elder brother had killed him. And then he came to the curse that the elder brother had put on the grandmother of the earth, her the Ancient One:

"*Waa'gen he'onwe Odinon'sot ne Nangannia'go.* He saw a place where beavers had built a lodge. He saw one standing there. He shot it and killed it. So then he placed its body on his back by means of the forehead strap and he departed for home. There where his grandmother sat he cast it. So now out of doors they two skinned it. When they were nearly through there was a pool of blood on the green hide." The Ancient One, for a joke, took up a handful of blood and cast it upon her grandson. "But now he took up a handful of blood and cast it between the thighs of his grandmother. Now he said: 'Ye, ye females, shall be affected thus every month.' So now she, the Ancient-bodied, began to weep, and she said: 'For how long will it be thus as a habitual thing?' Then the youth said: 'As many days as there are spots on the fawn.'[1]

"Now again she began to weep, she the Ancient One. So now she said: 'It is not possible for me to consent that it shall be thus. I would accept the number of stripes on the back of a chipmunk.' The youth said: 'So be it.' So then he said: 'Customarily, four days shall a woman-being remain out of doors. Then, customarily, she shall re-enter the place where they her family live.'"

They had listened to him this long, they would be expecting that he would finish. But Holden did not go on with the legend. He stood silent as long as he dared, dragging the waiting out until he thought it was ready to break. Then he raised his voice angrily, scornfully:

"I speak now to this mighty chief, Guyasuta. I speak now to *Honon'-hi'dael*"

The Indians chuckled. He had called Guyasuta the Warty, the Ugly One. The Seneca thought it was funny. He heard the deep belly chuckles go on and on. Ho'*ho*. Ho'*ho*. By the way they were taking it, they weren't overfond of the thick, squatty, long-faced chief.

"I was sent by the king my father to bring a present to Guyasuta. The king my father knows all. He speaks every day with *ne sga't Hawennio*, the Great Spirit."

Holden found himself wondering now, with some remote part of his mind, whether George III ever said his prayers. The squalor and vice of London did not look as if anyone ever had bothered to pray about them, least of all the king. They burned women in London, too, alive, at the stake. *Go on, Holden. This is the test. This is what you've been working up to.*

"Continue to listen! The king my father asked the Great Spirit to say what would be the most suitable present to send Guyasuta. The Great Spirit told him. He has sent a suitable present. He has sent Guyasuta a needle!"

The in-sucked breath made a sound like the wind.

"Continue to listen! Is not a needle a woman's tool? Why does Hawennio say to the king my father that Guyasuta should have a needle? *Da! Onen!* So now I will tell you. The king my father is very angry. Hawennio is very angry. They know that the Seneca are not women. They also know that Guyasuta, their chief, has become as a woman. This is no white man's needle! It comes from *ne Eia'dagen'tci*, the Ancient One, the grandmother of the earth. *Na'e!* It is the truth! You shall see that this needle is magic. You shall see with your eyes whether I speak with the tongue that is forked like the snake—with the tongue of *ne ge'gach'ys*, the lizard."

Thank God! He had thought of the lizard part of the Indian superstition.

[1]The entire portion of this chapter dealing with the Seneca version of the cosmology has been based on, and largely adopted verbatim from, the translation of the Seneca issued, with an introduction by J. N. B. Hewitt, as a part of the 21st annual report of the Bureau of American Ethnology to the secretary of the Smithsonian Institution for 1899-1900, and published by the United States Government Printing Office in 1903.

"Now I will show you the needle."

He took the compass out of his pocket and held it up so they all could see. He could only hope that none of these Mingoes had seen a surveyor's compass before.

"Continue to listen! The needle is in this box. Be not afraid." *Keep on saying that, Holden. Say it often enough and they may not know how afraid you are.* "The needle I hold in this box is like unto the lizard that creeps into the mouth of a man and eats of his heart."

Again, now, the indrawn breath of amazement.

"Be not afraid. The king my father has given me power to control the needle that eats a man's heart. Now I will show you that it is a magic needle. I will prove it is I who control it."

He opened the lid and glanced at the compass quickly. He picked out a ragged lightning-scorched pine that stood to the north, by itself, at the end of the street. He picked out three warriors crouched on the inside edge of the circle.

"You and you and you. Lay down your guns and come here."

They hesitated. He laughed.

"Are you afraid? I will not let the box harm you."

The Indians laid down their guns and came warily toward him.

"Come closer. Look into the box. Do you see the needle?" He turned the compass to keep the needle moving.

"*Na'e.* It is true. We see."

"Now behold. Do you see that tree?" He held the compass still on the palm of his hand. He spoke to it. "Listen to me. Turn thyself now to the tree."

The needle steadied. It pointed straight to the blasted pine. The three Indians murmured incredulously.

"*Na'e! Na'e!*" They turned to the tense, waiting circle. "*Na'e!* It is even so!"

"The Seneca men are strong," Holden said tauntingly. "But they are not strong enough to make the small woman-needle point at anything else but the tree. Come—try it."

He thrust the compass into the nearest coppery hand. The hand trembled. The needle swung.

"The strong Seneca shakes like a leaf! Put the box on the ground. Now turn it. Make the needle point somewhere else. Ha-*ha!*" Holden was not laughing nor even pretending to laugh. He was using the Senecas' own expressive, derisive word. "Weaklings! Are all of the Senecas women? Where is *ne Shadodiowe'go'wa,* the medicine man, the magician? Let him show the Seneca magic. Let him call upon the Great Spirit and on *ne Hanisheonon'ge,* the evil He-Who-Dwells-in-Caves. Is he, too, afraid?"

"Sioto," Guyasuta said loudly, "make needle turn."

The medicine man rose reluctantly. He tottered across the circle, and as he walked the pebbles inside his turtle-shell wand rattled as if his own bones were rattling. He peered down at the compass.

"Turn," he commanded. "Turn! Point to fire!"

The needle hung steady.

"Turn it yourself," Holden jeered. "Move it. Kick it. Be not afraid. I will not let it harm you."

Sioto passed the shell of the turtle over the compass and muttered. He shook the rattle. Holden jeered again.

"Seneca magic no good. Call on *ne Hanisheonon'ge*. Call on the Evil One." He looked at Guyasuta and pointed. "Make the needle go to *him*." He saw Guyasuta shrink ever so little. It gave him an idea.

The medicine man was muttering incantations. He was passing the rattlesnake wand over the compass now.

"Ha-*ha!*" Holden cried. "Sioto calls upon both Him-Who-Is-Master and Him-Who-Dwell-in-Caves. They do not answer Sioto."

"Not magic," Sioto said. He drew himself up in a rustle of feathers. His venomous face looked at Holden under the dried wolf head. "Needle always point the same way. Always point at tree."

"White man lie!" Guyasuta said. *"Ne Shadiowe'go'wa* says needle points always to pine tree."

Holden pretended that he was enormously weary. It did not require much pretending. He bent and picked up the compass.

"Sioto lies," he said. "And Guyasuta believes him. It is as the king my father thought. Guyasuta is not a chief but a woman! Now I will prove it. A needle is not a thing for a man. I ask you, O Seneca, will a woman-needle go to a man? I will make it go to *him*."

The Indians' breath, sucking in, was louder than ever now.

"But the king my father is just. He is merciful. He told me to give Guyasuta one chance to prove he is not a woman. Now, therefore, let Guyasuta have weapons. Arm yourself, Guyasuta!"

Holden's voice rang through the town.

"Give him your hatchet, Mamaultee! Give him your musket which you have had from the king my father. I know it is his. See—his mark is upon it. My father's totem is on it." His finger touched the Tower insignia sunk in the barrel. "I knew that Mamaultee possessed a gun which was stolen from my father the king. But my father gives it now as a gift to Mamaultee. More weapons! Quickly! Make haste!" He was snatching muskets and hatchets out of the Indians' hands and out of their belts, and he was piling them into Guyasuta's arms, and this couldn't go on, it was too fantastic. "Guyasuta must prove that he is more strong than a woman's magic. Guyasuta, stand where you are! If you move . . ."

He had never dreamed, when he sat in the room with the comb-backed chair and the pitcher that had a cracked nose, when he ate cold mutton as Washington carved, that he would be using Washington's compass like this. Even George might be a little surprised. He might even *look* surprised.

Guyasuta had muskets in both his hands. His hands were clutched to his painted belly. They had to clutch to hold the other guns and the hatchets that Holden had thrust upon him. He held enough weapons now to arm a demi-platoon.

"See! I give the needle to Guyasuta." That was the gamble. That was the turn of the final card. If the ugly Indian moved or dropped the metal he held . . .

Guyasuta shrank back. But he didn't move. He stood there as if his feet had grown into the ground. He couldn't take the compass. His hands were too full. But every glittering pair of eyes in the circling rows could see him shrink. They could see that he did not dare to accept the box.

"Ha-*ha!*" Holden repeated the Seneca cry of contempt. "Ha-*ha!* Already this mighty chief is fixed to the earth. He is held where he is by the needle. The needle has not yet touched him."

He took one step and stood where the Indian's breath was a foulness upon his face. He took one of the muskets out of Guyasuta's hands and thrust it against his body where his forearm could clutch it.

"Now we shall see!" He thrust the compass into the Indian's hand. "Behold! It directs its sharp point to the heart of Guyasuta. Continue to stand there! If you move, Guyasuta, the needle will leap from the box like the lizard that eats the heart!"

The Indian stared at the flat brown box in his hand.

"Otgon!" he muttered.

"Yes," Holden cried. *"Otgon!* Evil and magic."

The Indian's hand was shaking. He would bear torture without a quiver, but *otgon . . . Otgon,* the disembodied. *Otgon,* the evil spirits who slew him the Warty One, him the Ugly One.

Holden spoke to the shaking box.

"O needle of *ne Eia'dagen'tci!* Quiver! Dart thy blue tongue at this Ugly One!" The trembling blue point of the compass needle looked a good deal like a flickering tongue. "I know thou art hungry. Thou shalt be fed on the heart of this female man-being. The name of this female man-being is He Who Fights Women. His heart should be as tender as the boiled tail of a beaver."

The quivering needle was still. It was fixed toward the cluster of toma-hawk heads in the ugly Indian's belt.

"Now I speak to you, He Who Fights Women! I ask you a question— you who were once Guyasuta. Shall I permit the needle to leap from the box? See, it crouches! It waits! Shall I permit it to spring into your mouth, you who were once Guyasuta?"

He saw the quick hope in the Indian's little eyes.

"Then'en. No. You take."

"Ho! Ho'*ho!*" He imitated the Senecas' belly chuckles. "He Who Fights Women does not like his gift. He is afraid, *non.*" There was another odd thing. The French word for *no* was the same as the Seneca word for *perhaps.* But there was no perhaps about Guyasuta's fear. He stood shamed before his own people. *Don't go too far, Holden. You've gone far enough. You've torn him down. Now put him together again.* "All these things were known to the king my father. He knew that Mamaultee possessed a gun that was stolen. My father knew also that Guyasuta possessed a young woman who had been stolen."

Stealing women was not a crime. It wasn't a sign of weakness. *You've got to do better than that.*

"Continue to listen! Know now that the king my father never takes back his presents. He Who Fights Women must keep the needle! Know also that this Ugly One is himself evil and *otgon.*"

266

That was a mistake. He knew it the instant the word came out of his mouth. He had said Guyasuta possessed magic powers, for *otgon* meant evil and magic in one. *Let's see you get out of that, Holden. Quick!* That one slip of the tongue was enough to kill him and her, slowly and horribly.

"I say that He Who Fights Women is *otgon!* This was well known to the king my father and to her, the Ancient One. *Na'e!* Verily, that is true! Now let him who was called Guyasuta prove that it is not true! He who was once Guyasuta has stolen a maiden from *Eia'dagen'tci,* the grandmother of the earth. She is even as *ne Gaha'ciendie'tha Ononwan'da'dan Ni'haia, do'den.* She is even as the fire dragon whose body is made of pure white."

That, too, was a part of the Seneca superstition-religion. But he was stretching it thin. He shouted:

"Let him who was once Guyasuta prove that *this* is not true! Let him fight with this woman-needle. Let him contend against it. If he be not a woman—if she whom he has stolen be not as the dragon of fire—let him make the needle point to her whose body is white!

"Continue to listen! If he who was called Guyasuta can make the needle go to the woman, she dies by the fire. And I also die, because I speak with the tongue of the lizard. But if he fails, the woman goes. She goes from the town with me. Is that not just?"

He heard the deep grunts of approval. The Seneca liked a gamble as much as they liked an oration or burning a woman.

"*Onen,* thou puny one, Guyasuta! *Onen!* Now prove thyself! Make the woman-needle leave thee and go to her."

Guyasuta tried. He had no choice but to try.

"Little needle, go to the woman! Leave me, O needle! Go to her the White Bodied!"

The needle pointed steadily at the hatchets stuck in his belt.

"Try again," Holden urged. "Call upon Him-Who-Is-Master. Call on the Evil One!"

Guyasuta called. The needle point did not move.

"*Na'e!*" Holden made a gesture of utter contempt. "It is even so. They do not reply. Now I will take the woman and go."

He turned his back upon Guyasuta. The circle gave way before him. He walked slowly, confidently, across the bare, fire-stained ground where the shadows reached for him. He walked into the circle of piled-up wood. He took a knife from inside his coat.

He had been miles down the river, below the big falls, when he saw the fire stain spreading against the sky. He had known then that something was going on in Guyasuta's town. Something special. It was too late at night for a fire like that, unless there was something special. It could be a council, debating. It also could be . . .

Even then he had kept control of himself. Even then he had taken the time to find the down tree and hide the rifle under the trunk and cover the lock as well as he could. He had left one of the pistols also, and the flask that went with them, and the horn of powder that Fraser had forced him to take. Where he was going, he would have little need for weapons. He kept the pouch with the belts, because the one chance was to talk—to make them listen when he began to talk. He kept McCoy's powder horn too. He had thought that perhaps it might come in handy as proof that the Mingoes were killing the king's young men.

It had come in handy, but not in the way he had thought it might. It had made them listen, seeing him step from the flash and smoke of a whole horn of powder.

He cut the thongs at her wrists. He took his time doing it. While he cut, he talked:

"When you're loose, don't move. Stand right here. Don't move! For God's sake, don't act like you're scared. For God's sake, don't run!" One arm fell down at her side. She used it to cover herself. "You'll be loose in a minute now. When you're loose, start to walk. No matter how badly they've hurt you, walk. Walk toward that tree at the other end of the town. *Now. . . .*"

She obeyed him. She walked.

She would have obeyed him now if he told her to turn and go back to the stakes and be burned. She had seen him perform a miracle. To her he was like a young god.

They had the full length of the town to walk.

The girl kept her eyes on the blasted pine. She did not look once at the glittering eyes or the painted bodies. Holden also ignored them. He walked with his hands in his pockets. He had the knife in one hand. If this went wrong now, he would drive the knife into the small white body that walked before him.

That was his only thought of this girl's imagined body, revealed to him now completely. That—and the far-off thought that she was so small. He hadn't realized that she was so small, not even in Frasers' tub.

They passed the last house of the town. They came to the bend of the path that led down to the river. They made the turn of the path.

"Walk a little faster now," Holden said quietly. "Not much faster. A little. No running. They'll hear if you run."

He moved up a little closer behind her. If she ran, he would knock her down. He'd have to. But she didn't run. He slid the knife into his waistcoat. He took off his coat and hung it over her shoulders. Her hands took it and lapped it around in front and held it. He untied the sash from his waist and hung it across his left shoulder.

Sooner or later the Mingoes would find out the trick. At least they'd find out that it *was* a trick. Sooner or later some buck would come to look at the compass in Guyasuta's hand, and the buck would have a hatchet stuck into his bellyband, and the needle would turn.

But it hadn't happened yet. They still hadn't found out. He would know by the yells when they did.

The river was just ahead. He could see it, steel gray through the trees. And he thought: *Thank God. . . .* He thanked God for the dawn. He hadn't known it was morning. He hadn't been thinking of that. Now he would have light for the thing that he meant to do. He corrected himself. *For the thing I'm going to try.* It couldn't be done. But he'd try.

He tied the sash in a hard knot at his right hip. He tied it again and drew the knot hard. He pulled it with all his strength.

The tails of the blue coat dragged on the ground just ahead. She looked even smaller, in the blue coat, than naked.

The knots ought to hold her. The silk-mesh sash was made to carry the man who had worn it, when he was wounded. It ought to hold a girl who was more a child than a woman.

Chapter 38

He was tearing up the canoes on the riverbank when he heard them yell. The trick had worked about as long as he had any right to expect.

The screeching kept on. But he knew that they weren't all wasting their wind on yelling. He knew that some of the young men had taken out for the river path at the first sign that it was a trick. They'd be coming fast.

But he wasn't finished with tearing up their canoes. He was running along the shore, ripping the bark with his knife. All he had time for was one quick, turning slash of the blade. It would be simpler and quicker to give each canoe a heave and a kick and set it adrift. But there was a bend and an eddy below. Some of them might drift in toward the bank and lazy there till the Indians swam out and fetched them.

He figured he still had the quarter part of a minute, but there were more canoes left than he could tear up. He cried at the girl, stumbling after him over the shale:

"Wreck them! You see what I'm doing. Pick up a stone! Smash them in!"

She picked up a stone. The coat fell from her shoulders. It lay in a huddle around her feet. She dropped the stone and reached for the coat.

"For God's *sake!*" He was enraged. "Is that all women think about? I don't give a damn for your body!"

She picked up the stone again. She smashed one canoe.

Then he heard them coming, pounding along the path. He began to run down the shore, kicking canoes into the stream as he went.

The last one went skittering out across the band of slack water. The current fumbled at it and caught it and took it away. He felt a surge of triumph. He had never believed he would have the time to wreck all their canoes or set them adrift. He had never believed the nonsensical trick with the compass would hold them so long. Instead of one chance in a hundred thousand, there was suddenly now one chance in a thousand— perhaps even one in a hundred. If he could reach the opposite bank of the river before they fetched back a drifting canoe and the pursuit began . . .

Then his brief triumph died. They would have other canoes drawn up high on the bank, out of sight, concealed in the brush. The pursuit would be on before he had gained a hundred yards. If he got to the opposite bank with a hundred-yard lead, he might run away from them. He might —not the girl. They would wear her down in half an hour. They would track her and find her in spite of every trick that he knew.

He was running back up the shore. He was gathering paddles now as he ran. The girl was following him. She had the coat huddled around her again, and it made him mad. He had seen her once. What the hell did it matter?

"Come on! Run!"

He was still picking up paddles. He had a whole armload of them by the time he came to the small, slim birchbark he'd picked out at the beginning and left on the bank. He flung it into the water and held it.

"Get in. No!" God Almighty, she didn't know the one end from the other. "Not there—in front!"

She spoke to him once:

"We can't. We can't get away."

He knew that. She needn't tell him. He snarled at her savagely:

"We can't if you think we can't. We probably can't. But water's better than fire. We can die more comfortably."

He laid the armload of paddles carefully in the canoe. The thin bark was precious. He laid the paddles so he could reach them easily where he would crouch in the stern.

He thrust the light canoe out with a push of his leg and settled himself. The shove carried it through the slack water. The current took it and turned it.

The canoe made no sound. It was part of the hurrying river, seized and absorbed by the river as lightly as any leaf. He did not drive for the opposite bank. He drove downstream with lunging and powerful strokes.

The Mingoes would be bursting out of the woods any moment now. They'd begin to shoot. One lucky shot, ripping the frail bark open, and it would be finished. They wouldn't have even the chance to drown. They would be dragged out alive and revived and saved for the fire.

The first of the Indians reached the shore. Their howls were savage. They didn't like what they'd found. Some of them started to shoot. He heard the big muskets, but he was out of range now. Even close, in an Indian's hands, a trade musket was just about as dangerous as the yells.

But they had rifles too. He heard the tiny report, like a fiddlestring plucked. He never knew where the ball went.

He kicked the canoe with the paddle and turned it out, quartering into the current. When he looked over his shoulder again, he saw them carrying birchbarks out of the woods and laying them in the slack water along the shore.

He counted them. Three . . . four . . . five . . . six canoes. And two of them were big. They weren't the forty-foot giants used on the lakes—canots du maître, the French called them—with fourteen or sixteen paddlers. But they were a plenty big. They were "half-canoes"—the bâtards or bastards, called so because they were of an off size. But they would have at least eight men at their paddles.

Well, that was that. Calmly, without any feeling at all, he saw one of his two chances go. There was no chance, now, of getting away by land. There never had been. He'd only been culling himself.

It was going to be the falls. It would have to be. Nothing else was left. It would be a race for the falls.

He was in the swift current now. He laid his paddle across his thighs and picked up one from the pile in the bottom of the canoe. He waved it and yelled. Then he threw it into the river as far as he could. The Indians howled.

He picked up the rest of the paddles and brandished them and hurled them away from him, end over end. As each paddle flew, he yelled tauntingly. *Make them mad. Make them so mad they can't see straight. Make them so mad they can't see what happens under their dirty noses.*

He turned the canoe more sharply across the current and set himself to a race that he dared not win by more than two hundred yards. They must be so close, when he won, that their own eyes would see him lose.

He had figured it all in his mind as he ran the path to the Indian town, the seven miles up from the falls. It all had to be done by guesswork. He didn't know how fast the current ran yonder, close to the opposite bank. He didn't know the speed of the plunge of the river over the falls. He didn't know what would happen after the plunge. He thought—he *hoped* that he knew.

The notion had come to him as he crossed the river where he'd told Fraser he'd cross it, below the falls. He had seen the falls plunging into the roaring gorge. He had seen the cloud of mist like a pillar of fire rising above the gorge, high above the rocks and the forest, towering above the tremulous earth and fierily burning with the sunset upon it.

And then he had seen the tree. And the notion had come. It was the wildest notion he'd ever had. But dying by water was better than dying by fire. He had gone back across the rocks of the gorge and hidden the rifle and one of the pistols and the extra horn that John Fraser had made him take. He'd almost certainly never use them again. But the act of hiding them made his idea respectable somehow. It showed that he meant to try.

The river was curving now to the right. It ran hard and sleek and swift and steel gray as a smoothing ax slashing into the forest. It left the dark line of the trees on both sides.

The sky was the same steely gray. It wasn't touched yet by the sun. But downstream—to the west, not the east—there was the beginning of sunrise. The mist that always hung above the great falls was golden and rose. *A false dawn. The last one I'll ever see, and it's got to be fake.*

He was drenched with sweat. Already, without the sun on the river, the day was hot. *Where you're going, Holden, it'll be hotter than this.*

The canoe began making a different sound—a quick, slapping sound. And it shook. The shaking was different from the vibration of his strong paddle strokes.

The new, slapping sounds were little hard waves beating against the bark. But the waves weren't made by wind. They were made by the river, already beginning to gather itself for the plunge over the falls.

The banks on both sides were becoming higher and rockier. A man alone might make a good fight in those rocks—a man with weapons. He had nothing now but the knife and the pistol. But if he was alone, he might make a run for it yet, and a fight. But he wasn't alone.

The current was beginning to boil. Gouts of water came over the bows. He saw the girl's body wince. Cold water lashing her naked burned flesh . . . But he couldn't think about that.

Every stroke gained him a little toward the far bank. He held the paddle with his left hand low to the blade, his right hand on the rounded top of the haft. Perhaps, if he paddled on the left side, they wouldn't guess so soon that he was intending to try for the farther bank.

They guessed soon enough. He heard the shout go keening across the water.

"*Sgaga'di! Sgaga'di!* [The other side!]"

The pursuit split up. Two of the small canoes swung ever so little toward the right bank, to cut him off if he made a quick dash to land there. The two war canoes—the bastards—began to work over toward the left bank. That was good. That was fine. The space of gray rushing water between him and them had widened by ever so little.

Then it narrowed again as the *bâtards* turned straight downstream. They were sure they could cut him off now if he tried to land. He threw his weight into the paddle at every stroke. That two hundred yards—he had to keep that slim lead.

Two of the small canoes were still holding on behind him, still in midstream. They were using the same hard current that he was using, to catch him. He still didn't think they could do it. But the Mingoes were sure of him now. If he tried either bank, they would catch him. And if he didn't . . . They screeched triumphantly as they herded him toward the falls.

Two or three, in each of the big canoes, were laying their paddles down. They were picking up guns, and suddenly there was a cloud of white smoke drifting over the river, behind the *bâtards*. He had not heard the shots. He saw the Indians' mouths wide open, yelling. He did not hear the yells.

He realized, then, that his ears were already filled with the roar of the falls.

The race was almost finished. The two war canoes were swinging in toward the bank. On the other side the two smaller canoes already had landed. The Indians in them were running along the shore, hopping fallen trees and scrambling over the rocks. He had waited almost too long to make his drive for the bank. One of the two canoes behind him was pulling away. The other held on.

He looked for the swale he had seen on the opposite bank—the one with the great white boulder that looked like a cow lying down. It was there. It was closer than he'd dared to hope. He was more than two thirds of the way across. But the falls were close; the roar was already enormous and overwhelming.

He swung the paddle across to the other gunwale so quickly and smoothly that he did not lose a stroke. He pointed the bows at the rock that looked like a cow and held them there steadily.

He had picked that white rock last night as his aiming point. It was just about three hundred yards from the brink of the falls. He would need that three hundred yards, for the girl.

He must come within twenty feet of the bank where that fat rock lay. He must make his turn there. He couldn't think of the girl till he'd made the turn. She'd have to stay in the bows till the last thin minute. She was his ballast. He couldn't quarter this current if she weren't there in the bows.

He could see the lip of the falls. It was shaped like Captain Ecuyer's odd lower lip, pushed out in the middle, pulled in at the corners a little.

The convulsed cloud of mist was beyond the brink. It towered up out of the roaring chasm, and up and up.

He could see no top to it now. It was still half a mile away, but it overhung the canoe. It was a storm cloud high in the sky, convulsed with wind —but it was not dark like a storm cloud. It was bright. It gleamed with a myriad crystals holding the sun.

Most of the river was hard and steely and dull, and yet somehow it, too, was bright. It was even dazzling. Such swiftness could not be dull. It was like the stroke of an ax—after the stroke is finished and there is only the knowledge that there was a flash.

The river was moving so fast that it did not seem to be moving. It came to the brink of the falls and bent and hung there as if it was one solid piece.

The river and the canoe, the pursuing canoes, even the rocks and the forest seemed rushing madly along, careening toward one inescapable fate —the plunge of the roaring water.

It was not the river only that plunged. He could see that now. The forest itself seemed to plunge. It disappeared. It was lost in the mist. The rocky shores also curved and turned downward and disappeared with the same final abruptness of the river itself. There was nothing beyond the falls but the writhing mist.

The mist moved with a convulsive, digestive motion, as if there the whole of creation was being swallowed and consumed and absorbed.

He felt no special emotion. He had faced death before. The only difference was that now there was time to think. What he was thinking was that he felt exactly as he had felt a hundred times in a canoe, using his utmost strength and his utmost skill—exactly as he had felt a dozen or two dozen times before, racing with Indians, and death at the end of the race.

The only difference now seemed to be that the outcome was certain, and that did not seem to be making any great difference in how he felt. It was very strange. It was almost worth dying, he thought, to find out that you didn't mind it.

The girl . . . He refused to think of the girl at all. He shut her out of his mind. There could be no emotion in this. Rushing down the implacable river, with Indians in pursuit and Indians cutting him off on both banks, he was trying to solve a more intricate problem than any he'd ever been given at William and Mary. He was trying to calculate the sum of a dozen forces. And all of the forces themselves were incalculable. And the sum was death. But his mind knotted itself to the problem.

He was trying to calculate the speed of the current—and the difference of the speed of this light canoe with only two people in it and the speed of the crowded *bâtards*—and the speed he was losing by cutting diagonally across the drive of the river, thwarting its will—and the greater speed of the war canoes which, although deeper and heavier, had four paddles driving hard on each side—and the relative loss of the war canoes' speed as they too tried to cut through the current and reach the opposite bank without reducing too far the chance of reaching the bank before they were irredeemably caught in the powerful current.

Another quick backward glance told him why the *bâtards* were aiming for the bank higher up the river than he.

One of the smaller Mingo canoes had turned away too late. It was caught in that hard, inexorable current. Out of the tail of his eye Holden saw it sweeping downstream.

The water was smooth around it. The canoe rode as if on a quiet pond. But the Indians knew they were lost. They had laid down their paddles. They sat on their heels and chanted their song of death. Holden saw their lips move. He heard nothing except the bellowing crash of the falls.

Both canoes were moving so fast that the Mingo canoe seemed almost to be standing still. It passed with incredible slowness.

It came to the brilliant hard lip of the falls and there the bows caught on a rock where the water ran thin. The stern swung. The three Indians toppled sidewise over the brink. Even then they seemed to fall slowly. He saw, for a moment, their red deer-hair crests and their slanting feathers blackly and sharply outlined against the rose, white, gold, and pale green of the mist. All three of the feathers were twirling as they went down.

He thought: *That's good. They'll probably find the bodies. It'll give them something to do*. Where he intended to hit the falls, he thought, no bodies would ever be found. There were too many rocks below.

He still had to calculate—to guess—the loss of speed and stability and the sudden increase in the difficulty of steering, when he called Abby back to the stern. She must stay where she was till the last. But she must not stay there a tenth of a second too long; she must not begin to crawl to the stern a tenth of a second too late.

And she was another incalculable. He didn't know how much courage was still left in her. He couldn't be sure that she'd hear, or that if she heard she would heed him. If he misjudged the moment, or if she failed to hear him and understand and obey, everything he had done would be useless. He had to take the chance that she wouldn't hear, that she was frozen with fear, that she wouldn't move fast enough, that she'd cling to that foolish coat as if her nakedness mattered when in a minute or two . . .

He began to shout against the roar of the river.

"Abby! Abby, listen to me. Drop the coat. Never mind the coat. You've got to do something for me." He repeated that. "For me! For me, do you understand?

He saw her nod. *Thank God!*

"Drop the coat. Let it go."

She dropped it obediently.

"Turn around. Carefully. Take your time."

The canoe was pitching now in the unpredictable waves spouting up from the hidden rocks. But she was turning around. She knelt, facing him, with her hands holding the gunwales.

"Begin to crawl toward me! Be careful. Take your time. Crawl to me. Crawl!"

She understood. She started to crawl on her knees. Her hands walked along the gunwales.

And Holden realized that he had made a miscalculation. There was an unexpected force that was suddenly helping him. Driving at an angle across the furious current, he had gained a small unexpected advantage from the shift of her weight from the bows. By a small but perceptible trifle, it was easier now to steer. It shouldn't be, but it was. *It's because she's so small,* he thought. The slight shifting of balance made only the slightest difference, but it was actually easier now to hold the canoe's head from swinging downstream.

He took a last hurried look over his shoulder. It was going to be close. The two war canoes were touching the bank together. The Mingoes were scrambling out. They were beginning to run down the bank.

They still thought he was trying to land. They were racing to head him off. They had their guns in their hands. There could still be one shot to rip the birchbark wide open and leave them helpless here in the shallow water. It was going to be very close.

The girl was crawling over the last thwart now. She knelt at his feet and looked up.

He knew that she knew she was going to die. But he saw the look in her face and it startled him. *She's looking at me as if she thinks that I'm God.* He had never seen a look like that on anyone's face before.

"Come closer," he shouted. The roar of the falls was deafening, blinding, and overpowering. "Closer!"

She crouched on her naked haunches between his knees. And still that look. That look. *I'm not God. I've got to be, now. She thinks I am going to save her. My God . . .* He finished it: *Help me.*

He shouted at her again.

"Put your hands underneath my sash, on each side. Now twist them around it. Twist both your arms around it. It's strong. It'll hold."

He felt her arms twisting themselves around and around, in and under the sash. It brought her close to him. She leaned against him, and yet he knew she was trying to lean away, to give him the freedom to move his arms. Her head was against his stomach. He saw the scorch in her hair.

"Abby!" he shouted down at her head. "Abby!"

She turned her face up. He felt her chin digging in. She said, so steadily that he was aware of an enormous amazement:

"Yes?"

"There's only a moment left. There's a chance. It's not a good chance. It's all we've got."

"Yes." Her face waited.

"When I say *Now!* lock your hands behind me. Lock them hard. No matter what happens, hold on! Do you understand?"

"Yes."

He looked over her head. He would never speak to her again. But there was a second left. It would have to do.

"I love you," he said.

If she answered, he didn't hear her. It didn't matter.

He fought the canoe and the spouting waves. He drove the canoe straight toward the wildest water of all, close in to the shore, where the lip of the falls drew back over teeth of rocks. The river poured through the rocks in a furious seething uproar—it would be an uproar, except for the awful immensity of the sound that came out of the gorge beyond.

But there was one place where the water ran smooth in the midst of the turbulence. It was almost too small to see. Sometimes the spray from the wild broken water on either side concealed it completely.

That was the place that he had to hit. He had to hit it exactly. That was his only chance. *Chance!* He mocked at himself. It wasn't a chance. It was just that he'd always thought, when his time came at last, he'd like to fight on till the last grain of powder was gone and the knife broken short in his hand. There wasn't a chance in a hundred thousand to live.

But that chance would go if he missed the smooth place between the rocks and the crazily spouting water took possession of the canoe. It would be swamped, or whirled end over end, or be flattened into sheets of torn bark and cedar roots before it was ever swept over the falls.

At least it was going to be quick. And it wouldn't hurt. He wondered whether he ought to tell her.

The plunge would almost certainly kill them. And if it didn't, there was the crazy boil and seethe of the water to drown them, there was fury of rapids to batter them on the rocks. The rocks and the river would beat a human body to shapeless pulp within minutes. This perfect small body, kneeling before him . . .

"*Now!*" he said.

She obeyed him. She rose on her knees. Her body pressed closely against him. He felt the sash taking her weight. He felt her hands locking behind his back.

The high bark prow sliced like a knife between the two perpetual bursts of exploding water. It shot over the smooth glassy lip of the falls. The canoe began to tilt.

He rose to his feet. He dragged the girl's body with him. She was no weight at all. He was hardly conscious that she was there, crouching against him, her knees bent a little, her face pressed against his stomach, her arms twisted into the sash.

He stood with his own knees bent in the tilting canoe. At the last second, as if in a crazed despair, he flung up his arms.

As the canoe went completely over the brink, he used his bent legs and his arms, the speed of the plunging river, the thrust of the falling canoe, to throw himself forward and outward.

It was the last thing that he remembered—the thought held for hours —the knowledge, hoarded against this instant, that the falls did not plunge straight down—that they curved outward, away from the lip—that he had to hurl himself clear of the plunging water or it would carry them down and beat them to pieces upon the rocks. If he fell with the bulging water, the high curving stern of the Mingo canoe would probably break his back. If he fell with the plunging falls, he would miss the birch tree that grew on the bank—the old raddled hag of a tree that had shown him their one chance to live.

He saw the tree growing out of the rocky bank halfway down the face of the falls. He was going to miss it.

He felt the canoe smash by. The stern raked his back. It flung him outward. He blessed it.

There was the tree, falling upward to meet him. The tree looked frail. It looked like a rotten tree—soaked forever with water.

It looked like a metal tree. Its branches would snap like an old rusted iron ramrod. It was black where the bark was scoured off. It was rusty in patches where the bark clung. And the rusty branches would break—if he got his hands on a branch.

They were dripping. He saw that now. There was no time to see it. The tree was coming too fast. He had seen its dripping branches before. They would be too slippery to hold.

A branch slashed him across the eyes. He was blind. His hands groped in the roaring dark. They came to another branch. It was wet and slippery. The bark peeled away. He could feel it go. He felt the branch go. He felt an enormous blow on the back of his neck.

The roaring was instantly hushed.

The wet, limber branch of the birch swung through the plunging falls. For half of its length it was hidden in water that turned into yellow hard foam as it beat on the branch.

The birch limb withdrew itself slowly out of the falls. It quivered a little and then it was still. It dripped.

Chapter 39

Christopher Holden was never to know how long he lay stunned by the blow of the falls on the back of his head and his neck and spine.

His first conscious thought—the first thought he remembered later—was that he had gone to bed in his boots. He wasn't sure. The only thing he was sure about was that there was a terrible roaring inside his head.

It was likely the finest head he had ever brought home—if he had come home. He didn't know where he was.

He wiggled his toes. They moved, but it wasn't wiggling. It was too slow to be that. Their motion, ponderous, slow, and remote, confirmed his suspicions about the boots. *Filthy habit,* he thought. *Getting be gentleman. Made up mind wouldn't.* There was some weighty reason why he had made up his mind, but he couldn't think now what it was.

What he was lying on didn't feel like a bed. It was smooth and hard and flat. He felt of it carefully. His hand, too, was very slow. It didn't feel, it patted. It went up and down in preposterous ponderous motions he couldn't control.

He opened his eyes—and saw nothing at all. There was only a grayness that flowed past his eyes, down, always down, always down, down . . . He was dizzy and sick. He thought he was also blind. *Blind drunk.* He'd never been quite that bad. Never as bad as this.

The endlessly downward dizzying motion was like a gray curtain in front of his eyes, and he couldn't see and it made the dizziness worse and the roaring worse. From somewhere a long way away he heard his mind telling him: *Don' look't it. Let self go.* It seemed like a good idea. He let himself go. His eyes followed the gray pouring downward until they came to his boots.

The boots were on his feet, and his feet were lying in a puddle of some kind. *Gen'leman, sure enough. Didn' even get home. Fell down inna street. Shamed y'rself.*

It required an enormous effort to sit up and look at the boots. It required an impossible effort to drag them off. They were full of water. He emptied them carefully and set them up side by side, neatly, at the edge of the puddle. They fell over. It took him quite a long time to get them set up again.

But he couldn't blame them. When he tried to stand up himself, he fell down.

He fell on his knees and elbows. He still couldn't see very well. Everything was dullish and gray. But the curtain was no longer being pulled down in front of his eyes. His head roared, but he wasn't so dizzy.

It was then that he noticed the girl. He'd not only tumbled into bed in his boots, he had tumbled in with a wench. She didn't have a stitch on.

It came back to him slowly. No, not *slowly*. It was all there, waiting for him to know it. But the blow on the back of his head and neck had done something to him. All his thinking was slow. All his seeing was slow. Even the water plunging downward and always downward a few yards away seemed to be falling slowly, it seemed to hang. But he understood how it was. He remembered now that the river had seemed to hang, curved and motionless, over the falls.

Even when he began to know that he was perfectly sober, it was hard to remember exactly what happened. He remembered that he owned the girl. He'd bought her. They'd tried to steal her. He'd got her back. *'S funny. Some kind of row.* He was quite definitely put out with her. Hadn't he given her a whole trunkful of clothes? What'd she done with them? Look at her there, the trollop.

The roaring inside his head became what it was—the thunderous roar of the falls. The dizzying downward gray motion that poured past his eyes became what it was—the plunge of the river.

He knew a moment of panic. The Mingoes. They would be hunting for bodies among the rocks, in the rapids that gushed through the rocks. They might find the three Indian bodies; where the Mingo canoe had gone over, the river plunged into a pool—into a kind of well it had dug for itself in the rock. But they would find no white bodies. They'd follow the river all the way down through the gorge, and when they found nothing they might come back. Indians were insatiably curious. If they weren't, they would never have let him begin that trick with the compass, let alone finish it.

They would likely think that his body and the girl's were caught in an eddy behind the falls. They would want to be sure. They would want the scalps too.

He hunted frantically for the knife and found it where it should be, in the water-soaked sheath inside the armhole of his waistcoat. He stood with the knife in his hand, trying to think. His thoughts still moved very slowly, and there were so many of them. They kept running into each other, and when that happened they simply flattened and disappeared like the ripples along the sand at his feet.

There were so many things that he had to attend to. He couldn't think of them all. He tried to follow one ripple across his mind. *Keep Mingoes out*. That was it. *Kill them*.

But even his stupefied mind knew that was absurd. You couldn't kill many Mingoes with only one man and one knife. There was something else. Something very important. *Kill girl*. That seemed a more reasonable idea. That wouldn't be so hard to do. But she ought to be reasonable too. She ought not to be lying there in plain sight on the sand, where a Mingo could see her the instant his head came up out of the pool.

He knelt down beside her and shook her. He shook her slowly. He couldn't seem to do anything quickly. Her head only rolled on the sand. Her hand flopped on the sand. *Can't leave her here*. But his body was answering the demands of his mind reluctantly, grudgingly. Slowly and quite impersonally, he picked her up in his arms. He held her there, on his knees. It took him quite a long time to make his legs lift him up with the girl in his arms.

The cavern under the falls ran back a long way.[1] He carried her as far into it as he could, stooping under the rock as it slanted. When he laid her down, he was surprised by the feel of the sand underneath his hands. It was dry. It was loose and soft. Even the roar of the falls was not so loud here.

His first really lucid thought came into his mind. They were buried under the river, but they were dry. Anyway, they could be. It was quite a remarkable thing.

He sat on his haunches awhile and considered it soberly. His conclusion remained the same. It really was quite a thing.

His mind now was beginning to function. Taking off his boots had been nothing but repetition, unconscious. Hiding the girl had been instinct, only half conscious. But now he began to think about her.

His first thought was that she was dirty. Even the pounding falls had not washed all of the sooty smears from her skin. Then he saw the burn on her side. It was the perfect profile of an English trade hatchet, raised in angry red flesh. God! No wonder she'd screamed.

Deliberately, he rolled her over. He had to know how much worse she was hurt. There were small welts and bruises and burns down her back and legs. There was one long burn that crossed her body from hip to hip, as if she'd been whipped with a flaming stick, but the burn wasn't deep. None of them was deep.

They would heal of themselves. Only the hatchet burn was bad. If it

---

[1] The waterfall and the cavern under it are not in existence. The thin shelf of rock over which the river plunged collapsed long ago. I remember, when a boy, descending into the misty, thundering gorge of Minnehaha Falls; but within twenty years those famous falls had shrunk and vanished as the lakes and streams that fed them dwindled.—N.H.S.

mortified . . . He looked at the soles of her feet. They were cut and bruised, but not burned. Already he had begun to think about getting away. The burn on her side wouldn't keep her from traveling—not with her kind of courage.

It did not occur to him that the same crashing blow of the water that numbed his brain might have numbed hers forever.

She was breathing. Her breast rose and fell. He felt her heart under his hand.

He turned her again on her back and got to his feet and walked to the edge of the pool. He had the knife in his hand, but he thought, now, that no Mingo head would rise from the pool. He thought he had lain on the sand unconscious for hours. If it was possible to come under the falls, and if the Mingoes had wanted to come, they certainly would have come while he lay there senseless and helpless. That danger, he thought, was past.

He saw, now, what had happened. They had not fallen together. The blow of the water had broken her hold on the sash. He saw the prints of their fall in the sand that felt hard to the hand but was yielding and wet.

They had fallen, both, on their feet. And then on their knees. And then headlong. Her hands had been clenched as she fell. He saw the small prints of her fists.

He unbuttoned his waistcoat and took it off and sopped it into the pool. It was already wet. More water didn't matter. He washed it carefully, inside and out, until he was sure that no sand still clung.

For the first time, walking back to her, he was acutely conscious that she was naked. It was not her nakedness that he thought of—as nakedness. It was her helplessness, and his helplessness.

He stood over her, shocked for a moment, while he took stock of their meager possessions. He had the knife. He had the pistol, soaked and quite useless now. He had the pouch. There was bacon in it. How much, he didn't know; but God bless John Fraser for being a stubborn man. He had his waistcoat and shirt and sash, his breeches, his stockings, his boots—that was all. That was the sum.

The shirt—he could give her that. He could cover her with the shirt and the silken sash. He was already planning to use the waistcoat to make her a bed. She was small enough. It would do. It would keep her burned, beaten flesh from the sand. Thank God for the regulations that made an officer's waistcoat two thirds the length of a bedgown. It came halfway to his knees, when he had it on. It would be almost big enough for the whole of her body. He smoothed and hollowed a bed for her in the sand and spread the waistcoat over the hollow he made. He picked her up and laid her carefully on the waistcoat. She pleased him. She fitted it very well.

He stripped off his shirt and washed that also in the pool to rid it of sand. He spread the shirt over her. Then he began to untie the knots in the sash. He was tired. He had to sit down to do it. The silk was wet and the knots were as hard as iron. But he got them undone at last, and he washed the sash. It made, he thought, a very nice coverlet. She looked like a child asleep in a darkening room—a child who had gone to bed with her face unwashed and her hair uncombed. There were marks of tears on her face.

He hoped she would stay unconscious until he had done the little he could for her burns. He opened the pouch and took out the handfuls of beads and belts, and dumped them upon the sand. The pouch smelled of wolverine, and the bacon smelled of it too. But he had to do something for her. That hatchet burn was deep. He cut off a fatty piece of the bacon.

He drew back the sash and the shirt and crouched over her. She cried out, once, as he smeared the fat on the burn. But she did not rouse. He greased the long burn that curled round her hips, and the other small burns he could find, and then covered her and went and sat down on the sand.

He was shaking, he had to sit down. He thought, at first, that the shaking was from exhaustion. Then he realized that he was shuddering with the cold.

The clammy breeches clung to his legs like slush. He stood up and leaned with his shoulder against the rock while he stripped them off. *Dry,* he thought. *Dry. The sand's dry. Some current of air* . . . It was dark in the cavern now. He fumbled along the rock and found a knob where he thought the breeches might dry. He stripped off the soaked stockings and hung them somewhere and sat down again on the sand. He was a little warmer without his clothes. *Tomorrow,* he thought. *Tomorrow.* It was too dark now to look for a place where a human body could pass through that pounding water and live. If there wasn't a place . . .

He heard her whimpering in the dark. And when he went to her and knelt beside her, he found her shivering under the clammy silk and cambric shirt.

He loved her and she was his. He had told Ecuyer he wanted to marry her. And what difference did it make, if tomorrow morning he found there was no way out?

He lay down beside her, slowly and carefully, lifted the wet silk and cambric, and drew her into his arms and held her and covered her with his body as well as he could without hurting her burns.

She lay like a child in his arms, and he held her as if she were a small child, sick and hurt and cold. He felt her body slowly grow warmer against him, and even the stuff of the shirt, lying over them, turning a little dry. She stopped shuddering, sometime before he slept.

Chapter 40

She was still asleep when he woke. She had come even closer to him. Her head lay on his shoulder. Her hand was curled under his chin. He thought: *She's all right. She's going to be all right.* This was sleep, not unconsciousness.

He himself felt strong and new. The miracle of sleep never failed to restore him. But he lay now a long time, not stirring, looking at the girl's face on his shoulder and thinking: *So this is the one. Out of all the women in all the world, she is the one.* It seemed to be both a very simple and a very remarkable thing.

He drew himself away from her at last, very carefully, so not to wake her, and covered her again. Whether from the heat of their bodies during the night or from some odd current of air, the shirt and the sash were quite dry. He tucked them gently around her.

His breeches, hung on the rock, were still damp. He decided to leave them hanging. What he intended to do would only soak them again.

He walked down to the edge of the pool and saw his boots standing there. He had hidden the girl and himself as well as he could in the depths of the cave and then left the boots in plain sight.

But no harm had been done. The Mingoes had not come under the falls. There was a logic in that. It had an obvious, merciless meaning. If the Mingoes could not come under the falls, it meant that nobody could. And if nobody could come in, alive, then nobody could get out.

But he had to make sure. He stood by the pool and looked at the falls. The plunging water was no longer gray. It was golden and green. It seemed to be filled with light. He must have slept all of the night and more than half of the day. There must be a time in the afternoon when the sun, for a little while—for an hour or perhaps only minutes—shone full down the gorge of the falls. This must be the time.

The roar no longer disturbed him. Already, in a few hours, his ears had become adjusted to the enormous sound. It occurred to him now that the roaring was actually louder outside, in the gorge, than it was here beneath the river. And most of the mist, like most of the sound, was outside. There was only a little mist in the cave. It drifted up, faint wisps of vapor, and disappeared in the immensity overhead. It turned into water somewhere, far up, out of sight. Water ran down the rocks of the cave—little silent trickles.

A few yards in front of him the plunging river collapsed in thunder and seething, leathery, yellow foam and furious waves. But the waves also collapsed. By the time they had crossed the pool they were the gentlest of ripples. They hardly left marks on the sand. It was impossible, unbelievable, that a few yards away from the downcrashing river and the thunder it made and the waves it flung up and the foam it beat out of itself, such calmness and peace could exist.

The cavern itself was shaped like the mouth of a monstrous reptile. A long tongue of rock thrust out from its depths, almost to the edge of the pool. It was moist, and it was split at the end.

Perhaps it was the reptilian tongue that gave the cavern its look of a patiently waiting mouth. But it also had great crunching jaws. At either side of the cataract, rocks like long fangs stuck up. And other fanged rocks thrust down.

The river came writhing helplessly down upon these rocks and was instantly crunched to pieces. It clung to the monstrous jaws like slaver—yellow and thick. He would never get out by way of the rocks at the sides of the cavern. They had been his first and his biggest hope. He had thought he might clamber up there. But the rocks and the river were mortar and pestle. Nothing could live. If there was a place to get out, it was somewhere under the thick, creamy masses of foam at the farther edge of the pool.

He waded out, shoulder deep, and began to dive under the foam, into the battering-ram of the river. He dived again and again. And again and again he was thrown back, pounded and beaten and dazed.

The girl was alone when she woke. She had seen, once, a breath-catching negligee fashioned of crimson tabby so crusted with delicate silver threads that it looked as if silver spiders had spun their webs over the cloth. She lay for drowsy long moments in her warm nest of sand, contentedly puzzled.

The cloth that covered her now wasn't tabby, but it was light and it was almost like a cobweb. It was made out of silken mesh. And it wasn't woven with silver. But over her head the moisture that trickled across the rocks was spangly and silvery now. And she was covered somehow with the daintiest, smoothest cloth she had ever felt—excepting the silken drawers.

Recollection came back with a rush, and terror came with it.

She could see only half of the cave. The long tongue of rock hid the rest. She thought she was all alone. She saw the downpouring water. It was the last thing she remembered. They had been in it together. She sprang up and ran toward the water.

The shirt dropped. She clung to the sash. She used it to cover herself. But she couldn't see him. He'd died in the falls. Somehow she had lived, but he'd died.

Holden was shoulder deep in the pool when he heard her cry out. She came from behind the rock and saw him rise from the water. The soft goldeny light fell through the falls upon him. It clung to his whole wet body.

To her, in that moment, he was luminous, godlike. Without will, her arms reached out toward him. Her hands forgot the sash. It dropped and she did not know it. She moved toward him as if he were a great light and a warmth that drew her.

This was the moment toward which all her life had been flowing. She didn't think. She knew it. This was her reason for being. She murmured against him:

"Oh, Chris. I thought you had died. I thought I was all alone." And then, fiercely, clinging to him: "I want to be close to you, Chris, I want to be closer . . . closer . . ." Her face searched his. "Oh, Chris, never leave me. Never."

She looked confused, bewildered, and almost blind. He thought, at first, that she wasn't yet quite awake. He had never seen that look on a woman's face until now—the look of a woman consumed by her love.

Perhaps the confusion was in himself. But he did not think so. He could see the rest of her clearly. Not a line was blurred. He could see her much too distinctly for his self-control.

But her features seemed to be blurring before his eyes. It was as if they were melting in some inner heat and fusing. That was it. Not confused. Fused.

She was not bewildered. She wasn't still half asleep. She wasn't blind. Her eyes were worshiping him. She was flowing toward him within the clasp of his arms—a strong flowing of her whole body that was like a wave sweeping over him, into him.

Her body settled against him. Her arms flowed around him. With a long sigh, a collapsing of breath that was like the long, slow collapse of a wave on the shore, she let her weight lie upon him.

Her indistinct, blinded face came close to his. But not blindly. Surely. Her mouth was warm. He was being swept away by an inexorable wave. He was being carried under, absorbed, made a part of it. He was being fused with her, mingled with her, and overwhelmed.

They were in the grip of something that plunged like the falls and was as remorseless and as resistless, something so strong that it made even death unimportant, so strong that it shut out the past and the future, all memory, all apprehension.

He was being drawn down and down as the plunging river had drawn him down into the unbelievable depths of the pool . . . down and down . . . lost and gone . . . and he was spending the whole of his strength in a blind desperate striving . . . they were striving together for life. And then they were cast up together as the river had cast him up, exhausted and spent. He could still hear the tumult within him, the roaring that filled the world. But the desperate striving was over.

They lay motionless, clasped together, as if asleep. They were not asleep. They were shaken and awed by the nameless immensity that had seized them and drawn them under and let them go.

He turned on his side and drew her strongly against him and smoothed her hair back from her face and looked at her as if he were seeing her now for the first unbelievable time. Her face lay on his arm. Her parted lips touched his shoulder. Her breath ran over his flesh like little warm waves advancing—like shy quiet waves on a shore when the storm that swept it is gone—like the sea itself panting after its passion is spent.

Her head was thrown back on his arm and her throat was arched, and her eyes now were dark with love as they had been wont to darken with anger. They were the deep dark blue that she had inherited out of the long-gone past, the blue black of the deep Norse fjords. And she lay and looked at him as if her eyes had drawn him into her deeply, absorbed him and held him and kept him—as if her eyes were themselves a part of the nameless immensity that had possessed them.

They lay looking deeply and steadily into each other's eyes until at last he smiled at her for the sheer joy that welled up through him, slowly and powerfully. She began to smile, answering, understanding. But there were tears on her cheeks.

She had known she must die. She had known she must suffer torment. Her body had known the foretaste of torment but her mind had denied it. Seeing, feeling, and knowing, she had yet been unable to comprehend wholly the horror that waited for her. Now she could not comprehend or believe this either.

Remembering, she could not yet quite remember. She had felt the hot coals on her flesh; when the agony passed, she knew it had been there, she knew it was coming again, and yet she could not quite believe it would happen again. Now she could not believe that this happiness would ever, could ever happen again. Her whole body arched like a swiftly drawn bow that pressed tensely against him. Her mouth sought his blindly again.

For her, what had happened had been a simple and natural thing—as natural and as instinctive and savage and primitive, in its way, as the Cerne Abbas giant, that symbol of life carved into the Dorset hillside so long ago that the people who carved it there had left no other record of their existence.

And it was given to Holden to know that her conduct had been that of innocence—not of ignorance, but of instinct, a primitive naturalness. And he wondered: *Will it ever be like that again? Can it happen more than once? Is it possible that what has happened to us can last all of our lives?*

He was not thinking about her body. He was thinking of the force that had suddenly lifted and moved them and brought them together.

Nothing, he thought, had been more remote from his mind at that moment. And nothing, he thought, had been more remote from hers.

Abruptly, inevitably, he was remembering Diana Travers. And the strangest part of the recollection was that he was suddenly sorry for her, for his brother James, and for all men and women who sought something in life and, never finding it, never knew what it was that they sought. He himself had not known until now. There had been something desperate about his love for Diana. Had it been love? There had been a greediness in it—a hard, seeking selfishness. He had thought of himself, not Diana. He had been as selfish, he thought now, as she had been.

This was different. The difference astounded him, because it was so enormous. This had been hunger, not appetite. The one was deep, fundamental, and necessary; the other was artificial. The one was the need of food, the other was only a craving to please the taste. The difference, until now, had been beyond his comprehension.

He did not like the man who had thought deliberately of possessing this girl's helpless body. Walking with her in the dark Norfolk street, seeing only the glimmer of her white blouse beside him, he had undressed her in his mind. In the last twenty-four hours, seeing her naked body, holding it in his arms, he had not thought of her in that way. If he had thought of her so, it had not been a dominant thought; it had been a small thought, quickly pushed away. Even when she came toward him across the sand and he saw her, as he had imagined seeing her, with her arms lifted to him, he had not thought of her as a body. He had loved *her,* and the flesh that clothed her had not been merely a woman's body.

What had happened to them had been an overpowering sense of belonging, of being drawn inexorably and irresistibly together. It had been a fusing that had almost nothing to do with the mingling of their bodies that had given it its expression.

He lay listening in the dark to the everlasting plunge of the river. He thought of love like a river, tumultuous, overpowering, and unexhausted. No matter how much it gave to the falls, it always remained. And he thought of the peace and the safety that dwelt here so strangely in the midst of the tumult and that were caused by the tumult. Now, so long as they lived, he would have inexhaustible love. No matter how much he took of her love, it would always be there.

He knew that their lives might be ending. But now, in the deep peace that followed the tumult and came from the tumult, he lay looking into the darkness without despair.

Chapter 41

She was demure in the cambric shirt. It covered her quite to her knees.

She sat on a cushion and sewed a fine seam, as a well-bred lady should do. With Christopher Holden at work beside her at the edge of the pool, they were as sedate as any soberly wedded pair intent on important domestic tasks.

True, the cushion was made of sand, and the sand was damp. The lady had pulled up the tail of the shirt, behind, so to keep it dry. True, also, the seam that she sewed was not the finest seam in the world, because she was stitching in wolverine fur and using a sliver instead of a needle. She sat cross-legged, digging her bare toes into the sand. Her toes gripped the sand intently and purposefully when the thread disappeared—as it often did—in the shapeless pieces of fur.

Holden, too, sat cross-legged. He had a wet log between his knees, salvaged out of the pool. His knife was driven deep into the blackened wood. He was trimming pieces of leather by drawing them toward him against the edge of the knife.

The pieces of leather had come from his belt. He had four pieces, each with a pattern drawn on it with the point of the knife—a pattern the shape of her small bare foot. If he made no mistakes, he would have the soles for two pairs of moccasins. But there would be only one pair of uppers. The shapeless pieces of fur that lay in her lap had been cut from Joe Lovatt's pouch. He had gouged a row of almost invisible holes around the edge of the hide. When the scarlet thread was drawn double through every hole and the matching hole in the sole, Joe's pouch would make two furry sacks for her feet.

He had no expectation that she ever would wear these pieces of leather. Making the moccasin was a deliberate pretense. He had not found, yet, the courage to tell her that she was going to die.

"Stand up," he said.

It also seemed strange to be able to talk in this endless, deafening uproar. But they had discovered that by pitching their voices low, only a little above a whisper, they could talk to each other easily, almost naturally.

She stood up. He took one foot in his hand and laid the knife-cobbled sole against it. And then, as he saw that the leather would fit and let it drop on the sand, he still held her ankle. She balanced herself with a hand on his shoulder, smiling down at him. He kissed her toes, one by one. Then, because he was so completely unhappy and in despair, his masculine notion of humor made him brush his unshaven cheek against the sole of her foot.

She squealed. He kissed the sole of her foot. A shiver ran through her body. He felt it against his lips, and felt it run through his body also. And he thought: *So strange. So strange.* Life and death, so close together. He had never been so alive, and never so certain of death. On his knees in the wet yielding sand, he put his arms around her and held her strongly. Love and life and death, intermingled. He had found his life and his love and his death all at the one time.

And he wondered why a river should go on for ages, a pestle beating and beating into the mortar of rocks, when a man lived so short a time. Nothing could come from that tumult and violence. But out of the tumult and violence they had known, something could come. Out of this pestle and mortar of human bodies, a new life could come. The idea shocked him profoundly. He had not thought about that until now.

It was a shock wholly different from the shock of seeing the girl he loved tied to a torture stake, or the shock of knowing he loved her—and hearing it first from another man's lips. It was wholly different from the blow of the falls on his senses. It shocked him awake—wide awake.

He realized, with a sharp amazement, that he had been resigned. He had given up. He had admitted that there was no way to escape.

"By God!" He sprang up. There must be a way. If there wasn't a way, he would make one. He would not permit this woman, this perfect flesh and the valiant spirit it held and the other life it might hold, to be destroyed. "By God, I'll not!"

He didn't know he had shouted defiance at death. Neither did she, except that she saw him suddenly leap to his feet and his lips move strongly and angrily. She could not hear a shout in the cave. It was possible only to hear a tone just a trifle above a whisper. But he was honest with her at last. He stood with his arms around her and told her, quietly, what he intended to do.

"There must be a way to get out. I've looked. I haven't found one. I'm going to try again. There must be a way."

She smiled up at him with a worshiping faith in her face.

"If you say there is," she said, "then there is."

"I'll have to dive. Don't be afraid if you don't see me for quite a while. I know how to swim and dive. I've been doing it ever since"—he measured her with his eyes—"ever since I was knee high to the woman I love."

She looked very soberly down at her bare, scratched leg.

"You weren't very big," she said.

She sat down again at the edge of the pool and took up one of the pieces of fur and one of the scraps of leather cobbled to match her foot. She found the sliver that was her needle. She was carefully pushing a scarlet thread through the wolverine hide and the piece of belt, beginning to draw them together, as he waded out into the water.

Holden marveled at her—at her calmness, and at her small sober face bent over her task. *She won't let me see she's afraid. She's showing me that she believes.* He did not believe, himself, that he would find a way out. But he was grateful to God for her faith and the calmness and courage that matched her faith.

He dived again and again under and into the terrible ram of water driving endlessly into the pool. It flung him back again and again, beaten and battered and almost senseless and drowned, almost too stupefied to swim to the shallow water and wade to the edge of the pool.

She put the silk aside then and held his head on her lap and stroked his face, and stroked the slavery foam from his hair and his arms. And when he was strong again, she let him go without a word of protest.

He came back at last triumphant.

"I've found it!" He lay on the sand while the breath came back into his beaten body. "I didn't think . . . I'd about given up."

"No," she murmured, "you hadn't. You never give up." She spoke with a prescience now. "Someday I'll wish that you would. It will kill you, someday, this not giving up."

"The rocks break the force of the water, just where it looks the worst. There's a place no wider than this." He spread his arms on the sand. "I came up on the other side of the falls—outside. I was in a panic. I wasn't sure I'd get back." But he had got back. He would always get back to her. "There wasn't a sign of life. They've given up looking for us." He sat up. "Tonight we'll go."

He began to tell her what he intended to do. He drew a map on the sand at her knee—the river itself and the falls and the gorge, the log where his weapons were hidden, the streams that would lead them at last to the Susquehanna. He told her about Pollexfen, waiting in Philadelphia. He told her that once they had found Pollexfen, she would belong to him.

"But I do," she said. She held up the moccasin in her hand. "It's finished," she said.

She put the moccasins on her feet. She stood up in them as proudly as if they were silver slippers. He thought, when she walked away from him, that she was showing how well they fitted. Instead she was bending over the tangled pile of seawan, the strings and belts that he had dragged out of the pouch and left on the sand.

She picked out a belt and tied it around her waist. It made his shirt fit her almost as if it had been a dress. Anyway, it seemed so to him. He thought she looked beautiful in it. But young—so young, with her slender legs showing under the hem of the shirt, and her bare toes digging into the sand like a child's.

It was impossible to think of her, so, as a woman grown—as the woman whose body he had held in his arms, whose body had answered his. But when the belt was drawn tightly to her small waist, the shirt showed her breasts rising softly rounded and full, and the white frill of the shirt, lying between them, somehow insisted upon them instead of concealing them.

She whirled about to show him how fine a dress she had made of the shirt, and he saw through the thin cambric the body that he remembered.

But she was full of her own concerns. She knelt again over the heap of beads, and he couldn't think what she was looking for until she stood up with one long string in her hands.

"See! A necklace!" she cried.

He nodded and smiled at the necklace. It was a risk, he thought, but a very small risk. The beads were dull, they wouldn't shine in the dark. If the necklace pleased her so much, there was no great reason for her not to have it. It was so small a thing to give her such great delight—and he didn't know yet that this was a woman who would somehow find delight in the small things if great ones could not be had. She did not know it either. She did not realize yet how much she had changed from the girl who dreamed greedy dreams.

She said, almost as if she were thinking of something else:

"Must we go tonight?"

He looked up at her. Her face was serene.

"The sooner the better," he said.

"No. I want one more night." And he had thought there was nothing in her mind but her child's delight in a beaded belt and a necklace, and her childish pride in the queer furry moccasins that she had helped to make. "Am I wicked? I don't feel wicked. I want to stay one more night. It's important. Truly it is. It may be the whole of our lives. It may, mayn't it?"

"Yes," he said honestly.

He kissed her knees, kneeling there. Her hands reached down for his hands. They walked hand in hand back into the depths of the cave.

Chapter 42

He had made all his preparations for going. There were not many to make.

He stood on the darkening sand and looked down at what he had done. The girl stood quietly by him. Her hand lay lightly in his, and it did not tremble. He marveled again at her courage. The preparations seemed puny and futile against the malevolent might of the river.

There was the pack he had made of their meager possessions—his boots, the foul-smelling and precious bacon, the useless pistol, the extra moccasin soles he had cut from his belt. They were all jumbled together and wrapped in his waistcoat and lashed with the sinews of seawan belts from which he had stripped the beads. There was the smaller pack that was only her moccasins bundled up in his breeches, with a harness to carry it high on her shoulders. The sinews would cut her flesh, but the pack might break the stunning blow of the falls on the back of her neck.

The sash was completely gone now. Instead there was the loop of rope he had plaited, hour after hour, from the raveled threads.

There was the water-soaked log he had used as a cobbler's bench. He had dragged it along the edge of the pool almost to the thundering rocks. It lay solidly on the sand, pointed exactly at the one place where the falls were thin. A single silk thread, knotted from ravelings of the sash, stretched taut from a crack in the log and disappeared into the water. It was tied at the other end, at the bottom of the pool, to a rock he had carried out and placed at the spot where his dive must begin. When the touch of the thread on his ankle guided him to it, he could stand on the rock with his toes curled over the edge and know that he would dive in the right direction.

The falls were no longer filled with light, dazzling and luminous. They were gray. They were turning black. The water did not look like water.

It looked too solid for water. It fell like a great dark mountain crumbling and sliding in one endless avalanche and exploding against his eyes and his ears.

The place where they must break through—the one possible place—was in some ways the worst place of all. It was close to the slavering jaws of rock under the falls. And outside it was close to the right-hand wall of the gorge. The wall was sheer. The river ran swift and deep—so swift that its surface was ridged like ropes and quivered like tautened ropes.

He knew that he could make only the feeblest fight against that furious current. But he must struggle across it somehow and reach the rock wall. He must use his hands and his feet, his elbows and knees, to check their mad progress a little. Unless he checked it enough, they would be dashed on the rocks of the rapids below, knocked senseless, and crushed.

It would be a short fight. The great rocks that lay in the river like steppingstones were a quarter mile down from the falls. In half a minute after they dove under the falls, they might both be dead. Or one might be dead and the other terribly hurt. And he might be the one to die, and she the one to be left hurt and alone and helpless.

There was an awful temptation to stay here and wait for death, slowly and comfortably. After today, the thing he intended to do was like being driven from Eden. *It takes a long time to die of starvation.* They would have many days together. They would have every minute together—a lifetime of days.

Outside, there was only certain danger and possible death and probable hurt—and if he did not find Pollexfen, this girl belonged to another man. And Pollexfen was four hundred miles away, and the tribes were up, and there was no food but a handful of stinking hog meat. *Stay. . . . Stay! If you live fifty years, there will never be days like this. Never this again. Never quite like this.*

It had been, he thought, the pleasantest day of his life. They had spent it in getting acquainted—a process which frequently follows love and not infrequently ends it.

The day had been filled with surprises for both of them. The girl discovered a man who was not always grim and whose love was not merely passion. She found, instead, a man who was gentle and patient and gay. This was the first day he had tended her burns when she was awake, and she was amazed that his hard, bony hands were as gentle as Susannah Ingle's had been, and his face gentler yet. She saw his lips wince as he touched the bacon fat to the angry red mark of the hatchet.

"It doesn't hurt," she comforted him. "I think it's much better. I was burned worse than this, once, a long time ago." It was only eight months ago. It seemed like as many years. "Much worse. Do you know what I did? I put on a new dress." She remembered how it had hurt her fingers to fasten the dress. "I walked out alone in the dark to a wishing well, and I made a wish."

"What kind of a wish?"

"It was a secret. They have to be secrets. Didn't you know?" He was greasing the long thin burn that curved over her hips. She lay with her head on her arms. When she lifted her head to look up at him, over her shoulder, her mouth was a child's mouth teasing him, playing a game. "You have to be careful. One little hint, and it's spoiled."

He helped her to play the game.

"Do they always come true if you keep them secrets?"

"Not always the way you expect. I was a greedy one. You know, when you wish, you pluck a leaf off the laurel tree and make it into a cup to drink from the well. I made such a many wishes that the poor laurel tree had almost no leaves at all. I wanted beautiful clothes. I wanted to be a fine lady. I wanted so many things! They couldn't all have come true. But they did."

"All of them?"

"Yes. I know, now. They were all one wish. Every wish was for you."

"If you want so to be a fine lady . . ." he said. "Fine ladies have breakfast in bed. D'you think you'd like that?"

She thought he was joking. He disappeared. He was gone a long time. And she was amazed again, when he reappeared. For he had a thin flat rock for a tray, and he had found a few pale, almost colorless fronds of fern growing in crevices in the walls, and her tiny portion of bacon lay neatly cubed on the fern. He served her, so solemnly comical that she laughed in delight. It was a joke, but it was a much gayer, happier, tenderer joke than she possibly could have expected.

He sat down before her and made a table out of his knees. She looked at it haughtily.

"It will do, I suppose." She mimicked the highty-tighty voices of ladies sipping their wine by the Angel's chimney place. "Of course it is not at all what one would expect in London. Slitterkins, no!"

He grinned. He had heard such voices. He'd wanted to strangle the throats that made them.

"It smells a deal better," he said.

"Really! How provincial! I think London charming. Oh, a bit gamy, of course." She broke down completely in laughter. But when she sobered she said: "I thought it was beautiful, when I first saw it—all soft and hazy, like gauze on a lovely gown."

"That coal smoke? Ugh! Your London looked more to me like a swarm of gnats over a swamp. It's dirty. It's foul. I know now why Englishmen swarm all over the world. They can't endure London."

"I know. I knew it and still I loved it. I could have loved it." Her face was wistful. "John Gay saw it and smelled it and made fun of it, but he always sounded as if he enjoyed it so much. Here's part of the London you didn't like. . . .

> "Who that rugged street would traverse o'er,
> That stretches, O Fleet-ditch, from thy black shore
> To the Tower's moated walls? Here steams ascend
> That, in mix'd fumes, the wrinkled nose offend.
> . . . when rains the passage hide,
> Oft the loose stone spirts up a muddy tide
> Beneath thy careless foot. . . ."

"That's poetry," Holden said. He hadn't expected poetry from a girl who had been transported, no matter how unjust the sentence. "Where'd you learn that?"

"From my father. He loved books so much. He used to read to me. He taught me Latin and Greek. That's why . . ."

Chris did not hear her say that she'd hoped to have her own school in London. He was too much astounded by what he had already heard to hear any more, for a minute or two. He had seen her in chains. He had seen her in rags, mopping a tavern floor. And even when he knew that he loved her, he had not really thought *about* her, but only of her. If he had stopped to think, he would not have supposed that she knew how to read or write. Now, as if it was nothing at all, she was telling him that she had more education than he, although he had spent his four years at William and Mary and drunk his full share of learning from Wetherburn's punch bowl in the Apollo room.

He began to listen again. She was smiling a little sadly, not looking at him as she murmured:

"We used to read plays. I think I liked *Othello* the best. But you made me think of *Hamlet.*"

"I made you . . ." he mumbled. "I . . . Why?"

"It was the knife, I think."

"The knife?" He repeated it stupidly. Then he remembered the day he bought her.

"It was a sort of dagger," she said. "My father thought Hamlet would wear a dagger, not a great sword like Henry the Eighth. But you looked like a prince; that was another reason. And you looked so unhappy. You were."

"I thought I was."

"That's the same thing," she said wisely. And then she came to the inevitable question of a woman in love. "Chris, was there ever anyone else?"

"No one that mattered," he said.

And so she knew that there had been someone who mattered—and knew, now, that what she had thought was true. She wished that she didn't know, because she saw in his face that he did not want her to know. She saw a kind of relief in his face when he thought she knew nothing about the girl in the house in Norfolk. *He'll never know that I know. I don't mind.* But she did. *It must have been awful for him. He isn't that kind of man,* she thought, with her absolute sureness about him. *It doesn't matter.* It did. But it seemed to her that keeping her knowledge from him was one small proof she could give of her love— a proof he would never know.

Now, as the last light was squeezed from the falls and the darkness rushed out of the cavern and crowded around them, she gave him another proof of her love. He stooped and picked up the thin loop of silken rope, and she admitted at last that she was afraid—for him.

"I don't want to be tied," she said. "Please. Let me go alone."

"You can't," he said. "You can't swim."

"I'll just drag you down."

He took her face gently between his hands.

"Sweetheart, have you forgotten? We're together—in everything."

"Yes," she whispered. "Yes."

"You're not going to be tied. If you didn't love me, I'd have to. You see, if you're not still with me when I get through, I'll have to come back. If you want me to live . . ."

"I'll hold on. I promise, Chris."

He tied the small pack to her shoulders. He harnessed the larger pack to his own. He put the silk rope over his head, so that it lay against the back of his neck and passed under his arms and hung at the small of his back. He held her closely a moment. Then they were wading out into the darkness that rose, cold, higher and higher around them.

His foot found the rock. His head went under as he stooped and pulled the string loose. He jerked it free from the log and stood winding it carefully on his wrist, around and around. Even these few knotted threads were precious; they had to be saved for mending her moccasins. He felt her body beginning to shudder with cold. Where she stood, behind him, the water was up to her chin. The wet end of the thread flopped against his chest. He made it fast on his wrist

"Now," he said.

Her arms twisted into the silken rope. Her hands, gripping the rope, were fists on his ribs. He stepped up on the rock and fitted his toes to its edge. He dove with all of his strength for the bottom. His hands felt the water thickening with the sand that bubbled and seethed there. It pattered against his face—everything upside down—earth raining upward through water and striking his face.

His fingers found solider sand. They dug into it, clawed it. He was crawling along the bottom on his hands and his face, and his legs were driving him down and keeping him down. But he couldn't tell how fast he was crawling, or whether he moved at all. The sand was liquid. It dribbled away through his hands.

And then the blow came. It drove his face into the sand. It pinioned his arms. He threshed out with his legs and felt himself being tumbled, head downward, the rest of his body rising. He knew he had failed.

He was being spun heels over head in a somersault, and the smothering weight was not on the back of his head, it was on his face, and he could not feel the pull of the rope at all, he could not feel her hands or her arms. *She let go. She lied . . . she meant to let go. She thought it would save me.*

He was hopelessly lost. All sense of direction was gone. He had been turned completely over. Perhaps more than once. Perhaps several times. The massive weight of the water was on his back again now.

It was crushing him down and down. His strength was as nothing against it. His arms and his legs were bound with the ridged, taut ropes of the water. His body was bound and it was being helplessly dragged. *Back under the falls,* he thought. *I can stand it.* His lungs were only beginning to hurt. *But she can't. Where is she . . . where . . . where?*

He felt a solid blow on his back. His hands dug for the sand of the bottom. He tried to crawl. There was no bottom to crawl on.

He felt the small prickling patter against his face. There ought to be sand. But there wasn't. His hands felt nothing at all. *Stunned*. His mind considered the matter coldly. *No feeling. No arms. No legs.* Being stunned was quite comfortable. But he had to breathe. *Go ahead. Breathe. It can't make any difference now.*

He opened his mouth and breathed. The small pattering prickled against his tongue. He drew moist air deep into his body and held it and waited for it to drown him. It didn't. He breathed again.

And then he discovered that he was lying flat on his back on a smooth, gently sloping rock, and that he was being held on the rock by ropes that ran under his arms. He heard a voice crying his name.

"Chris! Chris!" Pale, wailing ghost of a voice. He could see the ghost. It floated above him, immense and formless. Not white. A pale darkness. *"Chris!"*

The ropes cut into his arms. They dragged him over the rock. He felt the water sliding away from his body. His hands dabbled in it. They came to the ropes that bound him, and recognized them at last. They were only the silken cord he had made.

He put his hands down on smooth rock, under a silken smoothness of water steadily flowing across his ribs. He raised himself up with his hands. The motion drew a cold body against him. He sat on the rock, only chest deep in the river, and felt Abby's knees pressing into his back.

The river moved strongly. It wrestled with him. It tried to lift him off of the rock. He braced himself hard with one hand and turned slowly, still sitting down, and got his arm around the cold backs of her knees and held her. He felt the weak shudders begin in her knees. Her hands let go of the silken rope. They found his face. They drew his head back against her and held it. He felt their desperate clinging and the quiver of fear that comes when the reason for fear is gone.

Slowly, carefully, he got to his feet on the rock. He stood braced against the current, holding the small shaken body against him.

Sensations came pouring now, like water washing across him. And they were all wrong. They were as wrong as the river.

The river should be an irresistible torrent, ropy and hard and deep. It was shallow. It came only to his thighs. It was smooth, it was almost slow. And his first sensation was not of relief or of thankfulness or of being safe. It was, strangely, of warmth and light.

There was no light, but the darkness was visible. It towered high above him. It was solid and wet and it pattered against his face and he knew that he stood in the cloud of mist that rose from the falls. He thought, without thinking: *It looks like spilled milk.* There was even a smell that belonged to milk, and the smell was a part of the warmth. Coming out of the cavern into the gorge was like coming out of a cool springhouse into the warmth of a rainy night. Only the milk was not in the springhouse. It was here, outside. Under the wavering paleness of mist, the river moved in a wavering paleness of creamy foam. He could feel it cling to his thighs. And he began, now, to understand what had happened. He was remembering, now, how the river had looked four days ago from the path at the top of the gorge.

Half the river had seemed to be flowing against itself. The part near the wall of the gorge was like wet, straining hawsers. But farther out, in midstream, it had been creamy and pale; it had been covered thinly with yellowish foam; it had looked like a round iron griddle covered with melted butter. He remembered now that the melted-buttery foam went around and around in an enormous circle—a circle so big that he had thought nothing of it. He had been thinking, then, of the furious chute that rushed past the sheer rock wall. He had not realized that two thirds of the river, below the falls, was one great whirlpool in which the water hurtling down through the chute was thrown back by the reef of rocks a quarter mile down and turned upstream again in a powerful eddy that moved smoothly and slowly because it was immense.

Some freak of the current had thrown them into the eddy, and she had dragged him out on the rock and held him until his senses came back. He was not surprised. It was she who had had the courage and strength and the sureness of body and mind to demand him.

Swimming the eddy was nothing at all to him now. He was filled with an exultation that was like an explosion of strength. His sureness was like her love. He went straight to the log where his weapons were hidden. He found the stream that came tumbling out through the north wall of the gorge.

They climbed it, through pouring water, on stair steps of limestone ledges, and the banks of a wooded ravine closed around them. The roar of the river grew fainter behind them. They heard it, inside their ears, long after their ears could not hear it.

Chapter 43

They had followed the streams for days. Nights, rather. Never by daylight. Both the great east-west Indian paths were behind them now. They had crossed the Kiskeminetas path the first night after they left the falls, and they crossed the Kittanning path on the tenth or eleventh night. He wasn't sure which. The nights of wading the endless streams, the days of watching, the days and nights of fear for this woman he loved, had blurred into one another.

It gave him a queerish feeling to stand ankle deep in the ford of the path to Kittanning. It gave him a sense of his life repeating itself. A little less than eight years ago he had wet his feet in that stream on the Pennsylvania farmers' desperate march to wipe out the Delaware town. Things had happened on that expedition that must not be repeated now. Finding the path reminded him of Kate Unger, the girl he'd found dying but not quite dead in the Delaware torture fire.

He was taking no chances now. He was taking no risk that could possibly be avoided. When they had to move from one stream to the next, they'd done all their travel by dusk, in late evening or early dawn, and they'd traveled the shaly hills where tracks would show least. When they crawled into thickets or underneath fallen trees, before day, he had used every trick that he knew to cover their tracks. And when they crept out, at dark, he had treated their hiding places with all the care that a formal box garden was ever likely to get. He had rearranged leaves so that they would not look disturbed; he had brushed the grass with his hands so it wouldn't look crushed by their knees; he had brushed sandy beaches with bunches of twigs and washed out their footprints on muddy banks with water scooped up in his hands.

But the country was changing now. The little streams came from the north. Every stream that they followed now was taking them farther away from the one real safety for her—Philadelphia, and Pollexfen, and proof that he'd bought her and paid for her and she couldn't belong to Garth. He knew, by the course of the creeks, that the Allegheny had turned to the west—that they were well to the north of the great bend of the river.

The time had come now when he had to find a stream that came from the east. It would have to be almost a river, one that would lead him deep into the tangled watershed where, as John Fraser said, the streams that ran to the Susquehanna lay head to toe with those that ran to the Allegheny. It meant leaving the creeks that had covered their tracks. It meant a long piece of travel across the hills, and they would have to travel by daylight; he'd have to have light to pick out the ground that would show their tracks least.

The decision, tonight, made itself. He stopped traveling while there were still hours of darkness left, because the small run they were following was already petering out and because he found a shelter that tempted him. A still smaller run came flowing into the stream, and he smelled the wild azalea in bloom on the hill beyond. He followed the little run and came to a thicket so dense that the tangle was almost impenetrable. The azalea climbed a steep slope, and it was still dense when they came to the rounded top of the hill. From here, in the morning, he might be able to see the country that lay to the north.

"We'll stop here," he whispered.

He took the first watch. It was one thing on which he'd insisted. The dawn, he said, was the most dangerous time. But it was more an excuse than a reason. The real reason was that he knew she was close to exhaustion after a night of struggling through water she couldn't see. She lay down obediently. But it was still dark when he felt her stirring beside him, and then she was whispering close to his ear:

"I'm awake. I can't sleep any more. I'll watch now."

He knew that she had not been asleep more than two or three hours. He knew that she had willed herself to wake up.

There was a strength in her beyond any strength he had known or suspected in women. This was not an easy journey, even for him—wading night after night up invisible creeks, sometimes only ankle deep and sometimes more than head deep in the sudden pools. She had fallen more often than he on the sliding and treacherous shale. She had crawled through as many jagged and tangled snags. She had been whipped by as many branches slashing out from the banks in the dark, and torn by as many brambles. She was as hungry as he, and she had even a greater reason for terror: she had felt the Indian fire.

And she was helpless. Strong and young and filled with life, she was yet dependent entirely on somebody else for her very existence—on somebody else's judgment and knowledge and skill. That, he thought, was the thing that would drive him crazy. But her steadiness never faltered. There was never a whimper from her. Never a plea to rest. She was doing her utmost to carry her share of the load. And because she had no means of knowing how big the load was, and because she loved him, she was trying to carry more than her share. She was trying to shield and spare him, he knew, as he was trying to shield and spare her.

Their mouths met briefly. There was no time for even a proper kiss. While their mouths were mingled, the fatal moment might come.

"Lie down," she whispered. "Sleep."

He lay down. He did not protest. He knew that her giving was part of her strength. He also knew that a moment might come when her life would depend on the last small reserve of his strength.

He lay with his head in her lap, the rifle on the ground by his leg, where his hand could come instantly to the slim stock, and a pistol thrust through the beaded belt. She had the other pistol. It was already cocked, so that if they were followed into their hiding place, the click of the lock pulling back would not disclose where they lay.

With her other hand she was stroking his forehead slowly, his temples, his eyelids. But she was not looking at him. He saw the outline of her face against the dim sheen of the starlight, with a tangle of branches around it. Her face was lifted and listening. It was quiet and calm.

He thought: *She is like the earth, still and deep and strong.* It didn't seem odd at all to compare this girl with the earth itself, though the earth was so large and she was so small. Her fingers touched his eyelids again. They were soft and gentle. They were firm and sure. They were as sure as she had been when she came to him. They were warm and soothing. He thought: *There is peace in her.* It seemed a strange thing to think, in the same moment when he was thinking how she had come to him. And yet it was true. . . .

He awakened in a pink world. For a moment he thought it was early morning, the whole world was flushed with sunrise. He was lying on his back, and the sky above him was strewn with little fluted pale-pink clouds and intricately patterned with soft rosy yellow and gold-greenish streakings. And then he realized that the high sun was pouring down on him and that the arch of sky was not sky at all. It was a densely woven fabric of azalea branches filled with goldeny green leaves and clustered blooms on delicate green stems.

Abby's hand was lying lightly on his mouth. Her face was turned away. It was as if she had not moved since he first fell asleep; she sat there in the same listening attitude. He lay motionless and heard nothing but the infinitely faint stirring of wind in the leaves. The touch of the girl's fingers on his mouth became a firmer pressure. She was trying to arouse him in the way he had taught her. He moved his lips against her hand to tell her that he was awake.

"I didn't want to wake you," she whispered, "but you said I should if I heard anything I didn't understand. There's a wolf howling. There. . . ."

He heard the drawn-out, quavering sound.

"That's not a wolf." The cry came again, with a thin whimper in it. "That's a dog." The dog sounded hurt.

"A dog," Abby breathed. "Then there must be people, Chris."

The wailing came at intervals. Sometimes it was almost human.

"The poor thing," Abby murmured. "Can't we——"

"No!" Whatever had happened to make that dog howl might have happened in the last hour. The wind shifted quickly in these jumbled hills; a trick of wind could have dulled even the sound of shots and screams and savage hootings. If Indians had anything to do with the dog's wailing, they might be coming south now.

But there was no need to tell the girl what he was thinking. There was nothing to do but keep hidden. There was nothing useful he could do but urge her to lie down and sleep. She lay down obediently, but for a long time she did not sleep. She pretended, though, to please him, and he knew by the irregular quick motion of her breast that she was pretending. She was holding her breath for a half minute at a time to listen. But at last she was lulled by her own pretending. Her mouth softened and the fingers that had been tight childish fists uncurled. She slept.

Motionless, he listened to the dismal wailing and the silence into which the wailing dribbled. Something was wrong. Not even the worst zany of a dog would yell like that in daytime—endlessly, monotonously —for nothing.

The dog was a complication. Abby was expecting him to do something about the poor brute, but the only sensible thing to do was to keep clear away from it. The last thing he wanted was to have a dog get their scent and come tearing at them with a crazy burst of yelping. Any Indian who heard a racket like that would be curious.

There were other noises. Once there was a rustling that came closer steadily, and his eyes hunted vainly for a stick. The only sticks within reach were small, dead, dry-rotten. He slipped his hatchet from his belt as a snake slithered toward him, twining through the humped azalea roots. Its eyes glittered at him. The rustling stopped. He slid the hatchet back into its loop. The king snake's body made a loop around a root hump as it turned. It slid away from him.

A mother skunk with her pups trailing after her came ambling upwind through the thicket. They passed in procession a few yards away, a black, white-striped, noiseless shadow with four duplicate small shadows tumbling after it.

A gray squirrel came tree-hopping, springing from one oak branch to another, playing a game—swinging on each branch until it had stopped swaying. The squirrel finally discovered something wrong in the azalea thicket and sat on a limb directly overhead and screamed about it. If Indians heard it, this shrill indignation could be as dangerous as a dog's barking. Chris waited for the squirrel to get tired. When it didn't, he risked throwing a stick at it, and it went away with one last gibbering outburst of profanity.

The sun was far down when the girl awakened. He saw the listening expression on her face before she opened her eyes: she had wondered about the dog as soon as she woke up. The hurt touched her mouth now.

"Chris . . . Can't we?"

He nodded.

"We'll go. But we'll eat first."

He gave her a thin strip of the strong meat in his pocket. When he took a strip out for himself, there were two left.

"Chew it," he said. "Make it last."

She smiled at him. He thought she knew that he was dragging out the time, putting off the moment of departure. But she ate so slowly that he finished his fragment of the bacon before hers was gone. He gave her both the pistols.

"Stay here," he whispered. "I'll be back in a few minutes, or you'll hear a tree frog."

He crawled downhill through the covert on hands and knees, studying the next few inches of the ground ahead as if it were a map he must remember, lifting his rifle, pushing it ahead six inches, laying it down, drawing one knee after it and then the other. He picked every twig out of the space ahead before he moved his left hand forward and let his weight come on it.

His progress was less noisy than the king snake's had been, but it was much slower. It took him half an hour to find the edge of the azalea tangle, because he crept around the shoulder of the hill to see south, down the draw, as well as north.

The shoulder of the hill fell away, clean under sassafras and pin oaks. The draw below him widened into a small meadow and then narrowed again, northward, between two more round hills. He lay looking at them, his eyes moving from one tree trunk to another, trying to miss nothing. There was nothing. He croaked like a tree frog, once.

The girl was only a few yards behind him when he heard her coming. She was learning. She had learned more, these two weeks, than some men learned in ten years in the forest, even when they knew that their lives depended on learning.

When they came to the top of the next hill they saw its north slope dropping down to aspen thickets and bright glints of water through the quiver of the bronze leaves. The sliding glints moved steadily to meet a long, low, slanting shaft of sun. They slid underneath it and he lost them in the dazzle. He had a notion that there was a bend to northward, in the woods downstream. He wasn't certain, and it didn't matter. There below him the creek flowed from east to west, straight, and as far as he could make out from the foldings of the wooded hills to eastward, it ran straight for a long way. This might be the stream he wanted—the one that would take them to the watershed where the creeks that fed the Allegheny overlapped the ones that ran east to the Susquehanna.

He crawled through a patch of buckthorn, with the girl behind him, and lay in the edge of it and studied the stream and the aspens and the woods beyond. He found, presently, two things that interested him. There was a little open space among the aspens, near the creek bank, and there was a whitish splotch there that might be a boulder almost buried in the earth. If it was a boulder, they could jump from it into the water. And on the other side, a perch or two upstream, a tiny run came trickling from the bank. There would be a chance to break their trail and tangle and confuse it.

He crawled out of the buckthorn and led the way down to the aspen thicket. It was good, close cover. The white splotch was the boulder he thought it was. And, as he had thought, there was a band of soft gray sand below the lip of the near bank. He stood just inside the thicket, listening, and then he walked up on the rock and jumped. He hit the water smoothly, beyond the strip of bare sand, and the splash he made was not much louder than a fish would make, jumping for a bug. He waded to the far bank and crouched down there, listening. The dog howled again. It was very close now.

He beckoned to the girl. She came up on the rock barefooted, carrying her moccasins in her hands. She jumped, and her sure slender legs made less noise in the water than he had made. His hand reached out to her. They waded soundlessly upstream and turned into the run. It was bottomed thick with old leaves under a thin shine of water. Their tracks would not last more than a few minutes.

There was a band of alders here, and then thick woods and underbrush on both sides of the gully. They worked up the run. It made a sharp turn past the mossy trunk of an old oak and then, abruptly, ended in a slanting bank. The bank was dark with loam and stringy with a mass of exposed roots through which water seeped and dribbled from an underground spring.

Holden peered over the bank. A few yards ahead the woods ended as abruptly as the gully. He was looking out across a small, pathetic clearing filled with charred, hacked stumps. Off to the left a bark-roofed cabin squatted. He could only see one end of it, blank, windowless. The logs still had the bark on.

The ground amongst the stumps was clean. It showed crooked rows and hillings where young corn was growing. Except for the dog, mourning off there in the woods behind the house, there was no sign of life.

The split-log door was standing halfway open. He could see the inside of the cabin, a dark shadow, almost solid; and he thought now that the people who had lived here had been warned or frightened and had pulled out in a hurry. Only people in a tearing hurry would have gone away and left the door unfastened. It was a thing that people didn't do.

There might be food in the cabin. He thought of the two thin bits of foul meat in his pocket. He was hungry and he knew the girl was hungry. In another day or two he'd have to risk a shot to get food. He didn't like the feeling of this place. He didn't want to stay here. But a quick look into the abandoned cabin would be much less risky than the racket of the rifle.

He went back down the gully to a place where he could lift himself out by the limb of a swamp ash, without leaving marks on the bank.

He leaned down, clinging to the limb, and gripped Abby's hand and swung her up. He left her in a burrow of thimbleberry vines, with both the pistols, and began to circle the clearing, working downstream through the woods.

The howling stopped. He thought the dog had heard him, and he was astonished and relieved because it didn't raise some different kind of row.

He came out into the trail abruptly. It was not a proper path cleared through the brush. It was as narrow and as crooked as a game trail, only not as plain. Then he saw the scuffed leaves and the trodden ground, and places on each side where the bushes looked a little shabby, and then places lower down where the thin bark of the alders had been scratched and scruffed. The scratches were about where a bucket would have dragged against the bushes. The man who settled here had surely been a fool. He had not only built his cabin in the midst of the dense woods, he had built it at least two hundred yards away from the stream and then hadn't bothered to clear out a decent path for fetching water.

He heard a scuttering in dry leaves, somewhere toward the creek, and then a whimper. The dog again. It was a queer way for a dog to act—howling all day, and then hushing, and now scuttling off and making that one quick, thin whimper.

A few paces down the slope the faint path twisted out of sight. He eased into the brush, inching through it, and came back cautiously and slowly to the trail a rod beyond the turn.

A dead Indian lay there, face down. The hind flap of his clout had flipped up as he fell; it covered half his back. The other half was covered with dried blood. The blood had run down the gullies of his ribs. There was a hole in his back—a kind of scooped-out place the size of a small gourd, a round, shallow puddle that had been filled with his blood and then had dried and shrunk. A musket ball made that kind of a hole in a man's body when it went clean through him. The Indian was a Huron, by his feathers. The gun beside him was an old French musket.

Around the next turning of the path Holden found the woman. She, too, lay face down. She had black hair. The only way of telling she was white was by her hands and legs. The back of her head had been crushed in, and her whole head and neck and the cheek he could see were a black crust of blood.

He came to the doll next. He couldn't tell whether it was face up or face down. It was a homemade doll—a piece of calico that had been stuffed with something, with dry moss or ravelings of cedar bark. It had two peeled sticks for arms and two more for its legs. It had no face at all.

The girl lay just beyond. She had two thin bleached-looking sticks for arms. Like the doll, she had no face. He couldn't see her legs. The second Indian lay dead on top of her, and his stone maul with the dried blood on it was there on the leaves where he had dropped it after he crushed her face.

Holden felt sick. He understood now what had happened. The man who lived in the cabin had seen Indians or heard them, and he and his wife and child had made a run for the creek. Perhaps they had a canoe there. They had made their break in daytime. Otherwise these two Wyandots would not be lying here, dead. The man who killed them had had light to aim by.

He found the man, then, and read the whole story. The man had gone ahead. The Indians had jumped them from behind, or chased them, and the man had gone back and shot two of them—too late. And then a third Wyandot had jumped him. They had fought it out, and the white man had lost. The Indian's knife had gone into his eye.

But the Indian had been hurt too. He had crawled away, leaving spatters of blood on the leaves and great gouts of it where he had stopped crawling for a while and then gone on. He had been crawling downhill, following the path. Holden found him ten yards from the creek bank, in a scabbed pool of blood that he had coughed up.

It wasn't hard to tell that the white man's knife had found his lungs. And it wasn't hard to tell that the three Wyandots had been all there were. A clumsy poplar dugout and a birch canoe were drawn up on the bank. The Indians lay as they died, and nothing had been taken. Their guns and powder horns and pouches and knives were all there beside them—all except the knife stuck in the white man's face and the musket that the Indian who used the knife had dropped before they grappled. He knew, without looking, that the musket had been fired. The Indian had missed. He went back up the path and looked, and it was so.

There was no need, now, to circle the whole clearing. But he did it. If he came back to Abby from the same direction, she might wonder. There was no need for her to know.

Chapter 44

The sun was gone. The sky still held its light as they went toward the cabin. In a broad band above the forest, the sky now was the color of wild azaleas. The tops of the walnut trees arched black against it and the glow came through the young leaves. It clung to them in a million tiny halos. But already the thick shadows of the woods were shouldering across the clearing, hiding the hacked stumps and the pathetic corn rows. The earth itself seemed to be rising, swelling upward until it was level with the stump tops, filling all the space between them. The woods crowded closer. The small clearing shrank.

It was as if the wilderness could not wait to take back its own, to hurl itself upon the cabin and the corn and blot them out with shadows of itself.

Already the cabin was only a darker shadow. Just above it the thin crescent of the new moon began to whiten like a bleached rib among the bones on Braddock's field. There was a bleached spot on the cabin door. It was dry and brittle under Holden's fingers.

He pulled out the splinter that was stuck into a crack between the half logs. He pulled it out carefully so not to tear the piece of birch bark it held. There was barely enough light to read the crude lettering on the bark.

Injuns riz. Me and Missus gone to Venango. You beter git thar to if you can read this.

BEN SALTER

So that was his name. Ben Salter had been a brave man. He had also been a foolish one. If he hadn't stopped to write that note, he might have got away safe with his wife and child. It was hard, sometimes, to tell the difference between a brave man and a fool.

Holden put the piece of birch bark back where it had been. He slid into the cabin without opening the door any farther: he didn't want those leather hinges squealing.

It was pitch dark inside, but there wouldn't be much, in Salter's one-room cabin, to stumble over.

It took him no more than a minute to find what there was. The floor was dirt. It was pretty well packed, but it wasn't even. There was a slab table set with wooden bowls and noggins. He could feel the marks of Ben's knife on them. There was a four-poster bed, and Ben had made that too; the posts were only the peeled trunks of saplings. All the covers were still on the bed—a crazy quilt on top and two blankets over a coarse ticking mattress. The mattress had a hollow in the middle. They had slept there together long enough to shape it with their bodies.

A stool rapped his shin. It didn't hurt. He'd been expecting that and he was moving slowly. There was a higher stool—the child's. There was a cupboard with its door ajar, and he wondered how Ben Salter had fetched a cupboard to this lonely place. Then, touching it, he found it was made of split saplings with the flat sides outward. The flat sides were smooth, the edges fitted snugly. Salter must have loved the woman. He had spent months scraping down those saplings with his knife and sanding them to make the cupboard for her.

There was a row of pegs inside it. Most of them were empty; but they, too, were smooth. Clothes hung on the others. A woman's dress. A man's greatcoat: Salter had come from some town, then. Even in the dark he knew the coat was threadbare. His fingers felt the worn weave.

"Abby." She was beside him. He guided her hand to the cupboard. "There's a dress here. Maybe you can wear it." He was sure she could. The woman in the path was a small woman.

"Do you think I ought?"

"Of course." His hand had found soft leather on another peg. "I'm taking one of Salter's hunting shirts. If I could find some moccasins . . ." He found them, three pairs, on the cupboard floor. He left the smallest pair and took the others. "Here. Can you wear the dress?"

"Yes. She wasn't very tall."

He almost said "No." He said instead:

"Move over to the table. When you take off the shirt, put it on the table so there'll be no trouble finding it again. I don't want to leave anything behind to show we've been here."

"Can't we stay here? Can't we stay the night? It would be so wonderful, Chris."

"No. We're not staying fifteen minutes."

He heard the quick beginning of a protest. It was no more than an indrawn breath. She did not give it words. This girl knew that he knew more about some things than she did; she was willing to admit it. She didn't think, because they had shared love equally, that she had a right to share equally in everything else and that she must enforce the right.

She was moving toward the table. Her body made a white blur in the dark. Then the blur was gone. She had put on the dress.

"Are you ready?"

"Yes."

"Stand by the door and listen. Not in the doorway—to one side. There ought to be food here somewhere."

He stooped to the hearth. It was powdery with ashes. An iron kettle stood on a flat stone: the Salters hadn't owned a crane or a trivet. He wiped his hands on his breeches and felt of the kettle. There was corn mush in it, a cold, stiff mass. Mrs. Salter had been getting breakfast. They had left the kettle on the hearth and the fire burning, and before it had burned out the mush boiled over. The outside of the kettle was smeared with cold mush, crusted over. His tongue swam in sudden juices.

He straightened up. His hand touched the sapling rafters and followed them. It brushed stiff, rustling, swinging things—a cluster of dried onions, ears of corn hung by their braided husks. There wasn't much corn, and the ears were puny. The Salters would have been hungry long before the new corn tasseled, unless Ben had had luck in his hunting.

He didn't want to take the corn or onions. Other Indians might come by.

A little farther on along the rafter poles he found what he had hoped for—long strips of smoked deermeat dangling. The meat was badly cured. The strips were hard as leather. They were stiff as warped laths. But they were food and he could take them. The onions and the corn would be enough to keep the cabin looking the way it had been left—all its pitiful possessions hurriedly abandoned, touched by no one.

He moved to the table now, with Ben Salter's shirt across his arm. The shirt was a leather wrap-around. It was a good thing that it was: his shoulders were considerably wider than Salter's. When he had the shirt on, the thrums at the top of the sleeves hit him halfway along his collarbones. But there was enough of it to tie around his middle.

He took one blanket off the bed. He tucked the other blanket smoothly at the foot and spread the quilt over it again. Then he laid the blanket he had taken on the floor and laid the lathlike strips of dried meat on it. He lifted the iron kettle from the hearth and blew the ashes off it so they would not leave a trail across the floor, and used the back of his hand to brush the ashes in the chimney place so there would be no mark to show that there had been a kettle.

He put the kettle on the blanket. Piece by piece, so to be sure that he dropped nothing, he fetched the discarded shirt, the shoepacks, and his boots and piled all of them around the kettle. Then he went to the door for a quick look at the clearing.

His hand touched the girl. Her body answered him. The meeting, the brief touch of his hand and the warm instant answer, was like an embrace. That much of her was better than everything of all other women in the world.

"Darling, I——" His whisper stopped. He heard a rustle outside. There was a quick scrambling rush. A white blur drifted across the starshine. It disappeared beyond the door and then came back again, moving slowly. It seemed to double upon itself. Claws rattled on the still log. The dog came sidling in. He saw the flutter of its high-held white tail.

"Oh-hh . . ." Abby was on her knees. Her arms were around the dog. "He's hurt," she breathed. "Oh, Chris, he's badly hurt. He's been cut all across his shoulders." He heard the dog's tongue busy on her face. "Chris, he fetched something. He had it in his mouth." Her breath caught. "It's . . . it's a doll. A cloth doll. The Salters . . . They didn't get away. They didn't, did they?"

"No."

He saw the dim blur of her face, lifted toward him. The starshine glimmered on it in two streaks. He knew she was crying. She had not cried for herself.

The dog came to him now with a noisy rush and stood up to him. It wasn't a big dog; its front paws came no higher than mid-thigh. He put his hand on the smooth head and felt the quick upthrusting of its nose, the eager licking of its tongue. Its nose and tongue were hot and dry as pine chips in the sun. He slid his hand down to its shoulders, feeling the wound there. The gaping lips of the cut were dry and hot too.

The dog whimpered faintly. Then it was gone. He heard it lapping water from the bucket by the chimney. He heard Abby whisper:

"The poor thing. He's thirsty."

It was the first piece of woman-foolishness he'd heard her say. With a whole creek full of water, there was no reason for the dog being thirsty. Drinking from the bucket was a habit, likely. The Salters must have set right much store by that dog. And it had set right much store by them too. It had tried to help them. It deserved something better than being left behind. But he would have to leave it. He couldn't have the best dog in the world trailing along after them, crashing in the bushes or letting out a yelp at the worst time.

He knelt by the blanket, gathering the ends together, knotting them. Behind him he heard Abby murmuring to the dog. When he had finished tying the ends of the blanket he went to her with the bundle in his hand. She stood up.

"Now?"

"Yes."

"But the Salters . . . They're here, aren't they? They're not far away? You saw them?"

"Yes."

"Can't we . . . We can't just go away and leave them. We can't take their things and leave them."

He knew what she meant.

"There's no time. It doesn't matter to them. If it happened to me, I'd rather have the sun and wind. I wouldn't care about the burying. There's a canoe. We can be at Fort Venango in the morning."

"You mean we ought to warn the fort."

"Yes. But it's dangerous, Abby. You've got to know that."

"It's all dangerous, isn't it?"

"I don't mean Indians. I mean, if the fort's still there, a runner may have got through from Fort Pitt. They may know about us."

"About me."

"Yes. I don't know the commandant. I'll have to handle him the best I can. We'll say you're Mrs. Holden. You are."

She moved close to him. He had the rifle in one hand and the blanket bundle in the other, but he bent and laid his cheek against hers.

"You're crying! Abby, are you frightened? We'll not go. It's either too late or the fort's been warned. We'll follow the creek east. That's what I meant to do."

"No. No, I'm not frightened. I'm just happy, Chris. I'm so full of happiness that it runs over."

Her arms came up around his neck. They tightened. She clung to him, and her mouth was wet. The kiss was salty with her tears. Her arms slipped down. Her fingers came to touch his mouth.

"Oh, Chris." Her whisper trembled. "I didn't mean . . ." She brushed the wetness from his lips.

"I like it," he said. "Things keep when they're put down in salt. They last for a long time."

The dog followed them out of the cabin. But when Chris struck across the clearing toward the run, it hesitated. It sat down and whined, came on a little way, and stopped and whined again. It howled, once, as they pushed into the woods.

They followed the run to the creek and waded with the current till it brought them to Ben Salter's landing. They left the clumsy dugout where it lay and took the high-prowed Wyandot canoe. The creek was dark and crooked. Trees shut out the stars. The current quickened. Holden let it have its way with the canoe. In two twisting miles it fetched them to the Allegheny. He turned the prow upstream into the hollow darkness close against the east bank.

Chapter 45

All night he had paddled with the circling short stroke that the Wyandots themselves used, never lifting the blade from the water. Even the faint sound of water dripping from a paddle could be heard a long way on that silent river.

Now, in the last deep dark before dawn, he left the protecting shadows of the eastern bank and drove hard for the Venango shore. He knew exactly where he was—he hoped he knew. He would come to the west bank about a mile below the mouth of French Creek, a mile and a quarter through the woods from Fort Venango. There was a brambled gully he remembered.

"Abby." He murmured her name. She answered instantly. As he thought, she hadn't been asleep. "We're crossing over. There's a place to hide the canoe, if I can find it."

His eyes were fitted to the dark now. He could see her take the pistols from the folds of Mrs. Salter's skirt where she had kept them dry against the river damp. He let the paddle run.

There were no shadows here. The bank was steep and bare. Its color was beginning to show in the pale light. It was about the color of the bark canoe. He crouched low so to make no moving blur against the bank. In minutes now it would be daylight. And there was no cover at the foot of the high bank, except those few half-drowned willows by the bend there.

The prow drifted past the willows. He heard water chuckling. Here were the two vine-hung trees, the small stream tumbling over their sprawled roots, the deep cleft in the bank behind them. After two years, he had come back to it in the dark. He had missed it by no more than fifty yards.

He thrust the paddle down into the sand and put his weight on it and made a quick roll out of the canoe. He lighted on his feet and caught the gunwale as it slid by. He held it with his knee while he laid the paddle on the bottom. With one hand he slid the canoe up against the current, past him, till the girl was at his knees.

It was the first look he'd had at Mrs. Salter's dress. The dress was a dark-grounded calimanco of the sleazy sort that the poorest planters bought for house slaves. It had a bodice with a round neck and wood buttons, and the bodice fitted her too tightly. His shirt had been more becoming to her. But the calimanco wouldn't show up in the woods. He was thankful that Ben Salter hadn't had the money for gay patterns.

"Pull up your skirt," he whispered. "Keep it dry so it won't drip."

He took one of the pistols and put it in his belt. The girl stepped out beside him, the skirt pulled to her thighs and bundled tightly in one hand.

"In there." He motioned toward the trees. "The vines make a cave, like."

She walked quickly through the fan of running water, and he saw the water busying itself with filling up her footprints in the sand. He should have told her not to step on the sprawled roots. Their soaked bark was soft; a touch would peel it. But she knew. He saw her setting her feet carefully between the roots.

Then she turned. She was unbuttoning the bodice. She slipped the barrel of the pistol into it, between her breasts. She was kilting the skirt, tucking it under the waist of the bodice. Her hand was offering to help him.

He hadn't asked for help. Without a word, she'd known she could be useful.

He lifted the canoe out of the river, just clear of the water, holding it there until the most part of the drip was done with. The canoe was light, but guiding it between the trees was easier with her hand under the prow, taking part of the weight.

Behind the trees the sides of the ravine were low, but they narrowed quickly until they were like the sharp notch of a gun sight. Ferns grew thickly, pale green in the twilight. The rough, ropy vine trunks hung like a ship's cordage from the frost-grape tangle high above. New slender shoots of swamp blackberry curved down from a woody mass of older growth so interlaced and matted that it covered the ravine from bank to bank. The little stream flowed underneath a wattled roof of thorned stems, dead and living. The roof was two feet thick in places and four feet in others. It was tough and springy. It was strong enough to bear a man's weight: he had walked upon it. Each summer the new growth was lacing deeper into the ravine and creeping closer to the river. In a few more seasons it would close the entrance with a barbed door.

The girl had to stoop now. There was not quite room enough for the high prow of the canoe; they had to tilt it. But the roof was higher, inside. A few yards from the entrance Abby could stand upright.

The canoe settled snugly to the drowned-leaf bottom. The ravine was wider here. Being in it was like being in a dim, cool cellar where a spring bubbled in one corner and preserves in stone jars stood in rows along the earthen shelves. It smelled of moist earth and of fruit, as if the wild blackberries that grew here had steeped it in their juices.

He crouched in the running water, carefully arranging the vines to hide the faint signs of their passage. He plucked off two blackberry leaves that looked a little twisted on their stems and might be bruised, and wilt, and be seen from the river. He brought the leaves with him in his hand and put them carefully in the canoe. Even a plucked leaf, floating down the river, could be dangerous.

He laid the rifle down across the gunwales and went to the girl and took her in his arms. It was the first time since they left the falls that he had really kissed her. *Oh God,* he prayed, *let me come back.* It was the first time he had done that. *Darling . . . darling . . .*

"I'll come for you in an hour," he told her.

"No. I'm going with you."

He protested quickly. Her arms held him.

"No," she whispered. "No. Together. Always . . . *all ways.* . . ."

He yielded to her. It was wrong and foolish. It was the first unnecessary risk he'd taken. He could not deny her.

They came to the end of their hiding place and waited, listening; parted the brambly curtain of young vines; went on along the narrowing ravine. Like so many other streams that they had followed, this one ended in a hillside and a tumble of loose rock below the steeply slanted face of a ledge buried in the hill but exposed, here, by the relentless flowing of the springs within it. There was no sound whatever but the trickling water.

Chris stooped to one shining trickle. With handfuls of water he washed the loam and mold and bits of dead leaves from Ben Salter's moccasins before he stepped out on the clean wet rocks. He stood waiting while the girl washed hers. When she straightened up she drew the pistol from the bodice of Ben Salter's wife's dress, and he saw, deep-printed in her flesh, the outline of the pistol lock and knew that he had hurt her with his hard embrace. He knew she had not minded being hurt.

She began buttoning the bodice.

"No," he said. "Don't."

The dress was cheap and ugly. It was too tight. The round neck was not becoming. For some reasonless deep reason, he could not abide it. He said again, smiling down at her:

"Don't."

For a moment her hand stayed, surprised, the fingers curled around one wooden button. Her eyes questioned him. There was a trouble in them. Her smile was uncertain. Then she took her hand down. The graceless bodice, loosed from the three topmost buttons, yielded to the fullness of her young breasts.

Holden stood looking at her and he was no longer smiling. He was looking into her and through her.

Suddenly her face was scarlet. Under the intimacy of his eyes, the blush suffused her neck and the curves of her shoulders and the soft curving of her breasts. She felt it sweeping her whole body. *Why? Why now? I didn't feel this way before, when . . . He's pleased about it. Why is he so very pleased now? Three wooden buttons . . .*

He smiled at her.

"Mrs. Holden," he said, and turned to climb the rock.

He knew this ground. Off to the left a hundred perches was the army road that ran south from Fort Venango eighty miles to Fort Pitt. Beyond it was the Indian path from Custaloga's town to Pematuning and Kuskuski at the forks of the Big Beaver. A mile ahead the military road came out on French Creek—or Beef River, if you called it by the name the French had given it—and turned up the bank, past the batteau landing and the bullock pens, past the ruins of the Frenchmen's dam and their sawmill that he'd turned into a sheepshed, and the garden where he'd wasted months of labor and got nothing because all the seed sent up from Port Pitt had been worthless.

He would have to cross the road to reach the stockade, or else follow it across the open ground after it had made its turning. Either way was bad, if there were Indians around.

There was a break here in the treetops. There was a patch of clean blue sky that suddenly was clean no longer. Something black and ragged swirled across it. Something like a piece of charred bark, whirled above the high heat of a fire and dropping in slow blundering circles. And there was another—and another—scorched leaves circling in strong updrafts, flakes of black soot falling.

There was no fire. There was only the faint smell of old fire.

He knew, now, why there had been no buzzards at the Salters'. They were at Venango.

Other smells were curdled with the smoke taint—a sick-sweet smell that was like the stench of corpse plants when they rotted, and a smell like scorched meat on a spit. He knew what he was going to see.

The first thing that he saw across the open ground was the old sawmill. It had been burned, but it was still standing. The roof was gone. He could see right through the log walls. There was daylight in broad streaks between the logs. They looked like ribs. The fire had eaten out the dry moss chinking; it had wrapped itself around the logs and eaten them awhile and then gone out.

The next thing he saw was the potato patch. It marched across the bottomland in sturdy files that were the dark green color of a Pennsylvania militia coat, only the Pennsylvanians never got their ranks as straight as that. There was a regiment of corn, knee tall. The thin breeze, drawing down the valley, overflowed the low bank of the Beef and washed across the garden. The green thrums of carrot tops and turnips fluttered in it.

To the right of them the batteau landing showed three broad, flat smears of black that narrowed into points. There had been three batteaux, and they had all been burned. To leftward, up beyond the garden, the rail fence of the bullock pen was gone. Not torn down—gone.

He stepped out from the shelter of the trees and saw the fort. He could see right through the fort, too.

There was no gate. He thought: *They never sent the hinges for the gate.*

He looked through the gateway, across the parade ground, into the woods beyond. Where the blockhouse should have been, there was a flattish heap of charred wood. Behind the blockhouse the fire had eaten a great hole in the stockade.

On both sides of the gateway the twelve-foot logs stood as they had always stood; they'd never been quite even at the top. But they were black now. There was a soft sheen upon them. They were velvety with char.

The dust was deep here in the rutted road. It was patterned every which way with Indians' tracks. There'd been a lot of them. He heard the padding of the girl's feet in the dust. In the woods he hadn't heard it. She was likely too scared now to think of being quiet.

He saw he had been wrong about the gate. It had been hung. The Indians had smashed it in. It was lying on the ground inside the stockade with its top against the upright logs. It made a kind of low roof, like a lean-to. The fire had been here too. The gate logs had been eaten to the core. They lay there like pole rafters of a burned-out cabin.

There was a charred body underneath them. A small body. It lay face up, its head in the edge of the roadway. All you could tell about it was that the scalp had been ripped off.

He didn't want to look at it. He looked up at the hewn beam that had been planted for the gate to swing on, and he saw that he had been right, after all—the army hadn't bothered to send hinges for the gate. Stair Carre or Gordon or somebody had devised a way to hang it. They had used one flimsy door hinge at the top, and a musket barrel thrust down through an auger hole into a block of wood spiked to the bottoms of the stockade logs. It hadn't done much good. The musket barrel lay there on the ground, bent, twisted, futile.

There were other bodies inside the stockade. There was life also. Black shadows slid down the charred walls and skimmed swiftly out across the small parade ground. When they stopped, they shuddered and became immediately smaller, blacker. As if Fort Venango still burned, whirling the fragments of its cedar-shake roofs high above it to fall down again in aimlessly blind swoops and circlings, the buzzards swooped and circled and dropped, fluttered their wings, and settled on the bodies. Like bats out of a foul-smelling cave, he thought. Like bats out of hell. The smell was overpowering.

There was an army ration wagon. The wagon box had burned through in the middle and collapsed. The wheels still had mud on them from the last swamp they had rolled through. The mud was baked onto the spokes. The rims were streaked with dull red that showed through the flame smut. They looked as if they were still hot. They weren't. But they were loose on the fire-licked wheels.

The tilt cover had been burned off and some of the hoops had burned through at the curve. They looked like the ribs of a skeleton that had been jumped on, its chest crushed down against the backbone.

The bodies on the ground didn't look like soldiers' bodies. They looked like sacks of meal spilled from the wagon and scorched by the fire. He couldn't see their scarlet tunics and he thought: *Of course. The Indians stripped them. They've been lying in the sun. That's why they're black.* But that was not the reason. When he walked over to the nearest body, it was covered with a blackish crust that glistened because it was moving. It was crusted thick with flies.

He started toward the wagon. There was something white on the ground beyond it—something that did not belong there. When he moved, the glistening crust moved on the body at his feet. It peeled away in chunks. It became a low dark buzzing cloud about his knees. It thinned and settled, and a part of it was crawling on him. His insides turned over.

The wagon bucket still hung on its hook. It was smutched with tongue-like smears, but it had not burned. There was still a little water in it. The driver hadn't got around to emptying the bucket before he was killed.

Holden stepped across the wagon tongue. The thing lying on the ground there was a piece of white cloth—it had been white once; it was dirty now with footprints, with the dirt trampled in. It was tied by two corners to a willow pole. The pole was broken. It sagged and bent double when he picked it up.

The cloth was linen. One edge was uneven. It was the torn-off half of a hand-woven bed sheet. It was like the sheets he had waked up in, in John Fraser's cabin, in the Frasers' bed. It could have been a piece torn from one of the sheets that Jackie Fraser wove and put into her marriage chest. He showed it to Abby. He said:

"They'd surrendered."

She took the trampled linen and stood looking at it. When he moved, she followed him.

His arm thrust her back. But it was too late. She had already seen the stake set in the ground beyond the wagon, and the shapeless thing that hung there, and the circle of dead embers and the charred ends of rails. *That's where the bullock pen went,* Holden thought. *They used the rails to roast him.* He drew Abby back around the wagon where she could not see the thing, but she still saw it. She would always see it.

"Who . . ." Her lips moved stiffly. Her tongue would not move at all. "Who is it?"

"I don't know. Gordon, likely." He thought of a stake in Guyasuta's town, and the circle of brush, piling higher. He heard Abby saying:

"You were here once. You were in command here. It could have been you."

"Stop it," he said. "Stop."

It seemed to her that everything had stopped—everything inside her, like the workings of a clock that had stopped—not broken, not needing to be wound, needing only to be jarred to start again. There was an enormous stillness. Inside of her. Outside. A dead stillness everywhere. She did not want to be jarred. She wanted the stillness to continue, to go on forever. She did not want this horror to become real.

Then she heard it. *Tup-tup. Tup-tup.* It was like the ticking of a clock behind a closed door. A big clock in a big room with a thick door. *Tup-tup.* It was muffled, hollow-sounding. The sound jarred her and the stillness in her was completely shattered and the realization lunged upon her sickeningly and her whole body was a scream that she must shut in somehow. She began to sob without sound, with hard wrenching shudders. *Tup-tup. Tup-tup.* She felt Holden's arm around her shaking shoulders.

"It's a drum," he said. "It's underneath the gate. Someone's alive."

She wanted to scream at him that it was a trick, that there were Indians under the wrecked gate, that they were waiting to kill him. He had already left her.

He was walking swiftly toward the leaning gate with his rifle ready. He was going around behind it. She did not scream. She cocked the pistol. When she caught up with him, he was on his knees and another man was lying on the ground there—a man in a fringed hunting shirt and leggings striped with shadows and with the bright streaks of sunlight that came through between the burned logs. She went down on her knees beside him.

He was a big man. He was almost fat. And he was old. His hair was yellow-gray. His fleshy face was covered with inch-long bristles of the same yellowish-stained gray, and his flesh underneath was the same color except where blood running from his mouth had run down among the hairs and hid the skin. His lips were pale gray and shiny, like bullet lead when it was scraped.

His shirt looked burned. It was black and crusty-looking. But when she touched him, the black was not burned leather; it was char and dirt and blood together, plastered on him. It was dry and stiff in places. In other places it was soft and slippery. One of the big legs moved. *Tup.* She saw the drum lying on its side. It was wedged in against the bottom of the gate. Where one streak of sunlight touched it, the paint was swelled up into yellow blisters. The old man's moccasined foot touched it. *Tup.* His shiny lips moved.

"Ye taken y'r time gettin' here. I seen ye when ye come out o' the woods. I tried to signal ye then."

"I didn't hear it," Holden said. Then he realized that he had heard the muffled padding of the drum. He had thought the sound was Abby's footsteps.

"The damn drum slipped. I had it shoved up close't against the boy there. I kept the flies off him pretty well, but he ain't stiff like he was. The drum got away from me. It rolled."

"Boy," Abby said.

"Yes, ma'am. He tried to save his drum. He must of. They caught him easy, but the drum was in a patch o' weeds outside the wall. He must of throwed it just afore they got him. No, ma'am. Don't lift my head. I'm better like I am. Time was I'd give a winter's catch to have one pretty as you lay my head into her lap. They kind of broke me up. They kind of broke this whole place up. Le Boeuf, too. The same night. Ye c'd see it burnin'."

"Water?" Holden muttered. "Do you want some water?"

"I ain't that dead. If ye had some whisky . . ."

"We haven't."

"No matter. What's one drink o' whisky in a man's life? I've had a plenty. Just as glad I didn't know the last one was the last one." His eyelids slid down, wrinkled. The skin of his cheeks pinched up to meet them. His eyes peered up at Holden out of two puckered sacks. "I know ye. I seen ye afore, some'res. Ye was one o' them Virginny Rangers with old Iron Head. Hold on, now. Don't tell me." A look of shrewd triumph slid into his eyes. "Hold on . . . Holden. That's it! Ye're Cap'n Holden."

"That's right."

"I'm Mike Cassaday. Don't it beat all? I mean how a man's brain keeps on workin' when the rest of him's stopped. I e'er wondered would I be man enough to make a joke when I was dyin'. I done it."

"We'll fix you up. You're not going to die."

"The hell I ain't. I know more about it than what you do. I got a hole clean through me. I put sassafras leaves on the hole in front, with a pad o' moss around t' sop the blood, but ye could chink a cabin with the moss ye'd need to fill the hole that ball made in my back. Hold on. . . ." He was still pleased with his joke. "Seems to me I heard tell ye was in command here, two-three years back."

"Yes."

"The place has changed some." A tough grin twitched the gray-yellow bristles on the gray lips. "They made quite a farm here. Old Colonel Clapham didn't have no better." Cassaday snorted. Two trickles of blood ran brightly from his nostrils. "Gordon sure was hell on them potatoes."

The blood dribbled down his chin. Abby wiped it with a corner of the sheet.

"I thank ye, ma'am. Gordon was a savin' man. An' he liked his vittals. He was always scared the rations wouldn't come up from Fort Pitt an' he'd starve to death. Mostly the rations didn't come. Way it turned out, though, he needn't to of worried."

"Could you eat something? We've got some corn mush."

"Me? Hell, no. Puttin' corn mush into me would be all the same as pourin' meal into a busted sack. Them big musket balls sure tear a man apart. I'd been dead five days ago except I set my mind."

"Five days!"

"That's when it happened. I ain't been under here that long. They'd of found me if I'd been here that long, or else I'd of cooked. This gate burned nearabout all night. I wasn't here," he insisted. "Not f'r the start of it. I could of maybe stopped it. I dunno. I dunno if Gordon would of listened. I was acrost the Beef four-five miles when it started. I been shootin' deer-meat f'r the sojers. They was payin' me a penny the pound, dressed out. A penny the pound, Pennsylvany money." An angry strength came into Cassaday's thin voice. "What d'ye think o' that? Gordon was a nigglin' Scotchman. He was paying twicet that to them mangy Delawares o' Custaloga's!" His voice rang out, loud and wrathy.

Holden looked back across his shoulder.

"Ye're a' right," Cassaday said. "There ain't no Injins now. They been gone two days."

"There could be others."

" 'Tain't likely. Not here. Them that ain't gone south a'ready will be travelin' by river or else by the Kuskuski path." But he apologized: "There ain't no call f'r me to holler. Only Gordon riled me. Time was when he wouldn't pay me nothin' f'r the meat I fetched in. He had orders to buy from the Injins—he said."

"That's right. I had the same orders. Only," he remembered, "the officer that sent the order didn't send the money."

"Ain't that like 'em? Figger they c'n keep a couple thousand Injins peaceable by buyin' meat from maybe ten or twenty—an' then not payin' 'em. Ne'er a pound o' meat did Gordon get out o' the red bastards the whole winter." He looked at Abby. "Excuse me, ma'am. I can't help they're bastards. What riles me is men like Ecuyer an' Bouquet an' Croghan has knowed all along they're bastards, but they've treated 'em like they was dumbhead Palatines an' Swedes that could be cheated eight days in a week an' kicked in the behind come Sunday. Like I said, I was shootin' meat. I'd got me a nice deer up north o' the savannah, t' other side the Beef, an' I was comin' down along the edge o' the river woods when I seen the creek bank lined with elms an' birchbarks. There must of been forty of 'em. The Injins was all crowded up around the gate—Delawares an' Mingoes mostly, but there was some few Hurons an' Ojibways. They had a white flag tied onto a pole."

"This?"

"I'll be—— A sheet, ain't it?"

"Half of one."

Cassaday felt the edge of the cloth with bloody fingers.

"Don't that beat hell? I thought it was a piece of wagon cover. Now where in hell'd them mangy bastards get a linen bed sheet?"

"If the Ojibway have come down this far, they've likely cleaned out everything up north."

"They said they had. They told Gordon that. They said they'd took Detroit an' Mackinac an' Sandusky an' Niag'ra an' Presque Isle—the whole lot."

"Good God!"

"They're the damnedest liars. They're a'most as bad as white men. They told Gordon that the forts had give up an' they was takin' all the people in 'em to Sir William Johnson. They said they wasn't hurtin' nobody. Ye know that's a lie. The rest of it could be. 'Twouldn't be no wonder if they'd got them forts, though, if they worked the same trick that they worked here.

"I saw the whole thing. Gordon was up on the firin' platform, an' Killbuck was makin' a harangue t' be let in an' have a council. He was sayin' about how the other forts had give up an' all the whites was movin' back east. 'Go in peace,' he hollers. 'Take y'r people an' y'r cattle. All we want's our huntin' ground.' The mangy weasel—I could of shot him easy. I would of, if I'd knowed what was go'n' to happen. But I couldn't figger that a man that wouldn't give up tuppence would give up a whole fort. I thought any minute Gordon would cut loose on 'em. One good blizzard would of physicked 'em. It would of cleaned 'em out good, they was jam-packed that tight. Of a sudden, Gordon jumps down, an' I think, 'Now he'll let 'em have it.' An' then the gate starts to open, an' the Injins pile into it, swingin' it wide, an' the whole lot of 'em is pourin' in, an' the screechin' starts. They closed the gate so nobody'd get out. It didn't take 'em more'n about two minutes."

"Didn't anybody get into the blockhouse?"

"I dunno. If they did, it didn't do 'em no good. It was a sheep-killin'. Gordon didn't have no sojers that could stand up to a growed man. His sergeant wasn't no more good than an old woman, an' the men was runts. There wasn't one of 'em that had the strength of a tame cat.[1] They went crazy. The best I know, only one man fired his musket. He fired through a loophole, crazy like, when all the Injins was a'ready inside. I ran right into it."

"You mean a soldier shot you?"

"Nobody but. I could see his red coat through the palin's, an' his musket poke out, an' then he let go." He saw the doubt in Holden's face. "I was runnin' f'r the wall. I thought I might get me a few of 'em from the outside, through the loopholes, afore they caught on."

"Brave," Abby whispered. "So brave."

"No, ma'am. I was just mad at Gordon bein' cullied that way. I'd told him an' I'd told him. I done my best to learn him about Injins. All I could do was crawl away. I smeared the blood out in the dirt, much as I could, as I went along. They didn't trail me. They was havin' too much fun. I laid under a down tree f'r three nights till they had got done with Gordon. They pulled out then—some of 'em down the crick an' the rest down the road. I laid under the tree awhile more, till it got dark, an' then I crawled back here. I should of done it soon as they pulled out. Come mornin', there was hard-shoe tracks around the gate. Sojers, they must of been. There ain't nobody wears hard shoes but sojers. They come in the night.

[1]These words are not an author's slighting comment on men who died in fear and agony. The language used here is Lieutenant Gordon's, taken from a dispatch he wrote to Colonel Bouquet from Venango on August 18, 1762. "Everything," he wrote then, "has a Glumee Aspect."

From Le Boeuf or Presque Isle, likely. I must of dozed off. They sure wasn't makin' no noise, an' they didn't hang around. They took one look in at the gate an' then high-tailed. I been layin' here e'er since, waitin' f'r some more to come along an' tryin' not to die. Well, I done it. I al'ays was a one to hit my mark. Ye got to git to Fort Pitt, Cap'n. Ye got to git there quick."

"We came from there."

"My God, they ain't took Pitt!"

"No. But the Indians hit Clapham's three weeks ago. They killed Clap-ham and most of his people. The fort's been warned."

"I got a canoe hid, t' other side the crick. The river's runnin' high. Ye c'n make it down to Pitt in two days."

"We've got a canoe. But we're going east. We're making for the Susque-hanna."

"Hold on." It was not a joke now. "Ye can't do that. Ye got to let 'em know, down to the Forks."

"There's no need," Chris said. "A man wouldn't have a chance of get-ting through. They're swarming all around the Forks by now. There's no need," he insisted. "I'm not risking this girl's life for nothing. Fort Pitt's been warned for weeks."

"Warned! *Warned!* Gordon had been warned too. I warned him—an' ye see what happened. It's the white-flag business. It's this talk about the other forts bein' give up. 'Twouldn't fool old Iron Head or Bouquet, but there's too damn many o' these new off'cers that will b'lieve an Injin's lies about pertectin' 'em if they give up. Ye know that, Holden. Ye got to go. Ye got to! That's what I stayed alive f'r. Ye got to show 'em that there sheet an' tell 'em what ye seen."

"Yes," Abby whispered. "The white flag that is red. I heard them say that. At the Gilded Beaver."

Cassaday seemed not to hear her.

"Tell 'em not to heed no white flag nor no talk of lettin' 'em go safe. Tell 'em no matter how bad things look, there ain't nothin' c'n be worse'n what'll happen if they let 'em in!"

"We'll go," Abby said. "We'll tell them."

"Good girl! Let that be shame to ye, Holden."

"No," she said. "You don't know what he's done. He's done more than his share. He's done a hundred times more. It was him warned them first—before Clapham's. They wouldn't listen to him. He went to the Indian towns to try to stop it and they almost killed him."

"Is that a fact? I draw back what I said. It riled me, thinkin' a Virginny Ranger would——"

"Don't try to talk."

"Why not, ma'am? It's the last chance I got. I couldn't hung on much longer. Not till sundown, even. I got kind o' lonesome layin' here. I ain't been a one t' think about what happens after—hell-fire an' such. But listenin' t' Gordon got me thinkin'." He raised up on one elbow and looked full at Abby. "D'ye think there's a hell, ma'am?"

"I don't know," she said. "No! No, there isn't! It would make God like an Indian."

"I thought o' that. I fed 'em!" he said loudly. "Fort Pitt didn't send no rations the whole winter. I fed Gordon's men all winter." His eyes saddened. The lids slid down over them. "I can't claim no credit f'r that. I got paid. Pa-a-aid . . ."

His mouth fell away from the word. His fleshy cheeks slid down across the angles of his jaws. They made a roll of puffy gray meat that pushed against the lobes of his ears. Without a sound, the blood welled up into his mouth and filled it and ran over.

Chapter 46

The shots broke like a bundle of sticks being broken. They made a sound as if a man had gathered up a handful of dead sticks to start a fire and was breaking all of them at once across his knee. In the fog, the sticks sounded wet.

Relief welled up in him and took him by the throat and shook him. They were still fighting at the Forks. Fort Pitt had not been taken.

After the first small bundle of shots, the others broke one at a time. Some of them were close together. Sometimes there were long aching minutes in between. He couldn't tell how far away they were. The smothering fog on the river twisted everything. He didn't know yet where the fort was, or how he was going to know when he came to it. He thought that if he hadn't heard the shots he might have drifted past it without knowing. He might yet.

The fog was so thick that it turned the black dark into twilight. It was gray-white, and he had a feeling that he should be able to see in it. But being in it was like pulling a wet shirt over your head. It was like the shirt sticking to your arms and shoulders so you couldn't get your head out. Only you would get the shirt off, somehow, in a minute or two. They'd been in the fog for hours.

He snuffed the wet fog up into his nose and down into his throat, smelling it and tasting it for smoke, for the odor and the taste of damp bricks in the fort's walls, for the smell of white men. The only smell was the sour mud along the bank, and all it told him was that he was close in to the shore. There was no way of knowing whether it was the real bank of the river or an island. The last bend above the Forks was full of islands.

Anywhere he tried to land, he might run into Indians. All the tribes in the Ohio country must be camped around the Forks now. In four days he had seen more Indians than he had seen in any four months since the massacre of Braddock's army. He had counted thirty-two canoeloads. It was incredible. It was an Indian migration—whole towns coming down the Allegheny—men, women, children, even dogs. And those thirty-two canoes were only the ones he had seen in four of the ten days since he and Abby left Venango—the four days when they had been in hiding places from which he could watch the river.

Suddenly his heart was hammering. His nose pinched to the smell of coal gas. *Coal.* . . . Stone coal burning in the Fort Pitt barracks in the small hours of the morning, in midsummer heat. . . . It wasn't possible. And then he thought of charcoal burning in a brazier, and the Ashantee woman dropping herbs upon the charcoal. It *was* possible. Mosquitoes were a plague in Pitt's Town. They hung over the fort in whining clouds.

He took one slow twisting stroke and held the paddle still and felt it slice through mud. The soft mud took the bows of the canoe with a faint hiss.

This was the moment he had dreaded, when he would have to leave Abby while he searched the bank. But she knew what he had to do. She knew that she must wait here, holding the canoe lightly to the shore, till he came back. He didn't dare to take her with him, and he didn't dare to pull the canoe higher on the mud. He might bump into them and come back fast. He might not have the moment it would take to shove off.

His hand touched her cheek. Then he was walking across the mud flat, and each step was taking minutes, and each minute was a lifetime as he set one foot down and let his weight come upon it slowly and then pulled the other foot out of the sucking ooze. The mud flat was wide. He could almost tell, by the stiffening of the mud from step to step, how much the river had gone down each day.

He came to the cut bank. Nettles stung his fingers. If it was the patch of nettles that grew by the corner of the garden where the French had planted peach trees . . . It was. When he moved a dozen steps downstream, the bank was gone. The long arm of the fort's ditch came out to the river here. Four hundred feet away the Music bastion jutted into it. Four hundred feet. . . . They were that close to safety.

He went back to the canoe. More endless minutes in the sucking mud. More lifetimes of minutes as they worked back to the ditch together. And then they were in it and across it, crouching, listening, and hearing nothing. They were feeling the ground through their moccasins before each step, setting each foot down slowly, crushing the dry crumbles of clay slowly, smothering the sound with the wet leather.

Halfway from the river to the bastion there was a bridge where the river road crossed. Holden waited for it to come to them. It did not come. His hand, feeling for the side of the ditch, touched a sloping brick wall. For an instant he felt foolish. He'd been waiting for the bridge. There wasn't any. The soldiers would have taken up the bridge the night the refugees came in from Clapham's. He had come to the foot of the Music bastion while he thought that it was still two hundred feet away. *Thank God.* . . .

He took another step along the sloping wall. His hand touched naked flesh. It slid away.

He struck downward with the rifle barrel and hit nothing. A shoulder drove into his belly while he was off balance. It drove the rifle lock into his groin. Arms locked around him. They bound his own arms helplessly against his sides.

He tried to break the hold and couldn't. The Indian was stronger than he. He knew it in the first hard straining of their bodies.

The realization hit him like the shoulder in his belly. Somehow, after

318

the Monongahela, he had had a notion that no Indian could beat him in a hand-to-hand fight. He had thought he might be killed, but not this way.

This was the old nightmare, true now—the same sour-sweet smell of rancid grease and sweat and the musk like an animal's, the same smothering of his breath, the same sleek writhing flesh, the same pain gouging up his chest. The Indian's jaw was grinding into the old scar. The naked skull was underneath his chin. It slid up along his cheek.

He felt the stiff brush of the scalplock on his mouth. He tried for it with his teeth and got it, but he didn't get enough of it to hold. It slipped away between his clamped teeth and he had a mouthful of the greasy hair.

The Indian wasn't trying for his knife; he wasn't trying to get a leg behind Holden's legs and throw him; he was just hanging on. That meant there were more Indians in the ditch. All this one had to do was hang on till one of the others found the leather shirt and drove a knife into it from behind.

He gouged for the Indian's crotch with the rifle lock and knew he was too low. He tried to twist the barrel of the rifle down between the Indian's legs and trip him, but he couldn't. The brick wall was his only chance to break that hold in time.

He let go of the gun and flung his body backward in an arch and dragged up on his arms. They reeled across hard, crumbly dirt. His heels hit the hewn-stone footing of the bastion. He teetered. His back hit the ridged bricks. The Indian was on top of him, but the locked arms were underneath. He ground them on the bricks.

The crushing grip eased. Then it crushed again. But he had got one arm loose. He felt for the Indian's face with his hand and found it. He felt the dry bars of paint across the oily face. They guided him. His fingers drove in for the eyes. The Indian's head went back. Chris got his other arm free. He got both hands around the slippery throat. His thumbs dug in.

They lay there straining. The Indian was big and solid. His weight kept Holden pinned against the wall.

He heard another Indian coming—the faint, crumbly sound of dry dirt under moccasins. A hand fumbled at his sleeve. There was only one thing he could do now. He yelled:

"Help! Help! On the bastion there . . . help!"

The hand fumbled up his arm. It came to his neck. The second Indian knew where his throat was now. The knife . . . He yelled again and could not hear his yell. The shot wiped out the sound. It pushed the noise back hard into his mouth. It filled his mouth and nose and throat with the hot griping stink of powder. The body pressed upon him jerked. Then it began to sag. The arms still clung to him, but they were loose. The Indian slid down between his legs and hung there. The arms, caught between his body and the wall, still held the Indian up. He heard Abby's voice.

"Chris . . . Chris . . ."

She was close to him. He put out his hand and found her. His fingers felt the pistol in her hand. He wondered at it. *I was going to save her. She saved me.*

He heard a thud on the dry bottom of the ditch. He saw the red wink of a spark and then a fuzzy sputter of red winks. He seized Abby's arm and twisted it. He forced her down. He heaved himself away from the brick wall and felt the Indian's arms slide down across his buttocks. The body collapsed at his feet. It tripped him. He fell forward and felt Abby's body with his elbow as he hit the dirt. He flung himself on top of her and wrapped his arms around her head. He tried to make his body bigger than it was.

His eyes watched the sputtering. *Don't do that.* . . . He pushed his face into the dirt. The dirt turned red.

He could see every detail of it. There was a dry crooked crack. It looked deep. The dirt under his eyes were dry grains like the dirt that earthworms left behind them. Every grain had its own shadow.

A clap of metal thunder smashed against his head on both sides. It squeezed his ears into his skull. They were inside it, pushed together. He could hear the ringing in them, far inside his head. It was not a solid ringing. It was broken into pieces. He could hear the pieces clanging.

A hard blow took him on the back. The red light went out. He couldn't see the small black grainy shadows. Everything was black again and solid. *A grenade,* he thought. *They threw down a grenade.* He yelled again: "The bastion! You, there! We're white! *White!*"

A clear voice agreed with him. It said:

"That's a white man."

Other voices rustled, grumbled, muttered. Bodies rustled. Feet made hollow grumblings, gritty mutterings. Feet in hard shoes, running on the planks of the gun platform, grinding dry dirt into them. Clear voice again . . . *rope . . . make fast . . . cohorn men . . . pull . . .*

Sound came crawling. Indians. In the ditch, close. Creeping along the wall. He crouched back on his knees, with the girl between them. He pulled out his knife. The crawling sound was closer. Not an Indian. The rope, slithering down the wall.

He got up on his feet, first one foot, then the other. He found Abby's arm and pulled her up beside him. He tried to step across the Indian and stepped on his belly. The dead Indian sighed.

The sound crawled in the dirt. He stooped down and found it. He picked up the rope. He held his knife between his teeth while he looped the rope around Abby's waist and tied it. She was still clinging to the pistol. He took it out of her hand and guided her hand to the rope. He put the empty pistol in his shirt.

"Carre," he whispered, louder. "Carre."

Whisper came back . . . *yes . . . yes?*

"Carre, you'll have to pull. Be careful. She can't climb, be careful."

Hoarse whisper, not Carre's:

"Jesus! It's a woman!"

The rope went taut. He stooped again and got his arms around her legs and lifted her. He held her as high as he could. If the rope dragged her over the rough edges of those bricks . . . She was gone. He took the knife out of his mouth and turned to face the ditch. He set his backside to the wall and pressed against it, ready to spring. He drew one foot up and set the heel onto the top edge of one brick. He listened.

The rope came back. They didn't pay out slowly, now that they were sure that it was not an Indian trick. It flopped down onto his back, between him and the wall. He fumbled on the ground and found the rifle. He put the knife between his teeth again and took hold of the rope and jerked. They hauled him up. He tried to walk the wall, but he lost his footing. He came up to the gun port on his knees and fell into the bastion on his hands.

Chapter 47

They were all around him in the dark. He could not see them, but their low guarded voices and their hands were facts. His fingers tingled from their eager and astonished welcome—Stair Carre's hand thin and dry and bony, Fraser's big fist crunching, and Tom Yeardley's even bigger.

He felt no surprise that these friends of his should be here, almost as if they had been waiting for him. It was not even a surprise that Tom should be here; Yeardley and Arnett Leslie were like Lovatt and McCoy—they were the way McCoy and Lovatt had been; where one was, you would likely find the other pretty soon.

He could not see Abby, but he thought John was hugging her. He had a notion that Carre, too, had hugged her and then been embarrassed because his surprise had tricked him into a show of emotion. Fraser was muttering to her now.

"God A'mighty, girl, I'm glad you're safe. Chris . . . my God, where'd you find her?"

"Guyasuta's town."

"An' got her out!"

"We walked out."

"Just like that," Carre said.

"It's weeks," Fraser husked. "Where you been, Chris?"

"Venango." In the immense relief of being here, he had almost forgotten why he came. "It's gone. They wiped out everybody in it. They burned Gordon. Le Boeuf's gone too. I don't know whether anybody got away or not."

"Price got away," Carre said. "He got all his people out. They got out through a window at the back while the blockhouse was on fire and the Indians were waiting at the door. Price came in a week ago with most of his men and a woman. They'd passed by Venango."

Holden thought: *They made the tracks that Cassaday saw. He was alive when they came by.* Carre's thin, transparent whisper went on.

"Presque Isle's taken too. Christie surrendered—God knows why."

"The Indians told Gordon all the forts were gone," Chris said. "Sandusky, Detroit and Niagara—everything."

"They tell us the same thing. Every day or so there's a deputation waving British flags or white flags and wanting to make talk. They've all got a different story. One day Detroit's been burned and everybody in it has been killed. The next, Gladwyn has surrendered and his whole garrison is being taken east."

"That's what they told Gordon. He believed them. They came with a white flag and . . ." Holden undid his shirt. He pulled out the cloth wrapped around his body. "Here—here's the flag they used to cully Gordon. It's half of somebody's bed sheet. I came back to bring it. I thought Ecuyer ought to know."

As he held it out toward Carre, his hand went through a long tear in the cloth. The tear had not been there. It was there now. He remembered the blow on his back. When he put his hand behind him, his hand went through a long tear in Ben Salter's shirt. The shirt was slashed across. Under the slash the meat of his back was swelled up in a hard, raw ridge. He took his hand away, but there were fingers on his back.

"Chris!" Abby cried, and smothered the cry quickly. "Chris, you're hurt!"

"No. It's a scratch. It's nothing. A piece of that grenade." He had broken the Indian's hold just in time. He had flung Abby down and thrown himself upon her just in time.

Then he remembered that it was she who broke the Indian's hold. It was she who had saved both of them. *Brave,* she had said to Cassaday. *So brave.* He felt the violent trembling of her body.

He felt his own body trembling with an awful sickness. It had all been unnecessary. He had risked her life for nothing. He had brought her back for nothing. The people in Fort Pitt knew everything that he knew—more than he knew. Carre was whispering to him again:

"You must be outworn. You'd best take her to the women's quarters. They're just down the ramp—the northwest barracks."

"No," Abby said. "I'm all right."

He felt the dread in her. She was thinking about Garth.

"Stay, if you like. We can't leave the wall till daylight. We're spread a little thin."

A man came hurrying along the firing step. His heels came down hard on the planking of the bastion platform.

"What's going on here? Are they in the ditch again?"

"They were," Carre said. "We had a bit of fishing. Here's a friend of yours we fished out, Trent."

"Good morning, Will." Holden put out his hand.

Will Trent came close to peer into his face.

"Holden! By the pearly gates!" His hand was cold and hard.

"He didn't miss them pearly gates much," Fraser said. "He walked up the ditch."

"I must say you picked the hardest way of getting in."

"Anything Chris Holden does, he'll do the hard way. It's God's wonder you got through, Chris. We've got beaver traps set. Crow's-feet too. Part o' y'r new wagon's down there in that ditch, Chris. I used the iron off'n it to make crowfoot traps—three toes down an' a sharp prong stickin' up to gouge the foot of any redstick that steps on it. All y'r hoes an' hinges an' such have been cut up to make langrage. About all you've got left is y'r anvil an' y'r clo'es, Chris. But I guess you can be thankful that you've got a carcass to put clo'es on."

"He can do better than that," Trent said. "He can put in his claim. He ought to be in style."

"What kind of claim?"

"For your wagon and your hardware," Trent said. "And your anvil."

"John says I've still got the anvil."

"It's been damaged, hasn't it? Of course it has. Don't ask me how an anvil can get damaged. It's got to be damaged. You'd be surprised how much damage Indians can do to anvils that they haven't even seen yet."

"Ay," Yeardley chimed in plantively, "and don't forget your grandma's stewpan, or the diaper you were born in, or your great-aunt's second cousin's second-best queue ribbon. He'd ought to put them in, oughtn't he, Will?"

"Certainly."

"You think we're jokin', don't you?" Fraser rumbled. "Well, we ain't. By God, there's claims stacked up in Ecuyer's office higher'n I am. Ever' scut of a wagoner an' pack-train driver an' sawmill hand an' batteau carpenter has put in a claim f'r his cabin that Ecuyer tore down—f'r the logs that's bein' used to save their hides. They've put in claims f'r more mahogany tables an' four-poster beds an' silver candleholders than there ever was in Williamsburg an' Norfolk put t'gether."

"Speaking of hides," Trent said, "Nan Perdue has put in *her* claim. On top of losing her house, she and her girls can't peddle their hides any more. They're——"

"Shut up," Fraser told him. "There's a lady here."

"A lady?" Trent's tricorne came off. "Your pardon, ma'am. I didn't realize . . . If you're where I think you are, you're so small you must forgive me for not seeing you. Chris, I've some excuse for my bad manners. What's yours? You might introduce me."

"Captain Trent——"

"He ain't," Fraser broke in. "He's been promoted. He's the major-commandant of the militia."

"—Mistress Hale."

"Oh, I——" Trent checked himself. "Your servant, ma'am." It was obvious that he knew she was the convict girl out of the Gilded Beaver.

"Speakin' of hides," Fraser said abruptly, "you'd ought to have heard them traders holler when Ecuyer grabbed their fur bales to make breastworks. They like to bu'sted themselves, yellin' to be paid. There was only four that didn't holler. Trent, here, an' McKee—you know him, Chris. He's a kind of Indian agent f'r Ecuyer now. An' him they called Hellward Bound, that ran that Golden Eagle—he's dead, so he couldn't holler. An' Garth was the other. It ain't Garth's way; he let Dave an' Williamson an' Hesselgart put up the holler. But he's got his claim in. God A'mighty, ye'd think them hides was solid gold. Ye'd think they was eatable, by God. Are you folks hungry?"

"No. We found food in a cabin, a few days ago."

"You still got some?"

"There was a little jerky. I left it in the canoe."

"Left it," Fraser said. "He left it."

"Is it that bad?"

"It's worse. The men are on half rations now. The women get thirds, an' the children get a quarter. Chris, how much you got in that canoe?"

"Three strips of jerky and part of another."

"Jesus! That'd keep thirty men alive f'r one more day. When that time comes it'd be enough f'r sixty, they'll be so shrunk up in the belly. Carre, I'm go'n' to try it."

"No," Chris said. "I'm the one that left it."

"You ain't messin' round amongst them traps again. You didn't have no right to get through 'em in the first place. I set 'em, an' it makes me look bad. Where's the rope?"

Fraser lapped the rope around his chest once, with the short end of it in his left hand. He leaned against it and stepped out of the embrasure, walking down the steep slant of the bastion wall. The glow of the gun matcn in its bucket of sand touched fingers of fog closing in behind him. They drew him down. Two matrosses, kneeling under the blunt barrel of the cohorn, payed out rope. It slacked and hung loose in their hands. They sat back on their haunches, waiting.

It seemed to Holden that the darkness had become a little less dark on the bastion. But east, up the hill beyond the unseen ruins of the town, and south across the Mon, it was getting darker. It was close to day. The loom of Grant's Hill and the Monongahela bluff had taken on a substance solider and blacker than the night.

The matrosses hunched forward on their knees. They began hauling on the rope. Fraser came walking up the wall.

"The canoe's gone," he said. "Them red bastards got it."

"Well," Trent said. "Well. Do you know what day this is, Chris?"

"No." He wondered why it mattered.

"It's July fourth. Nine years ago this morning we were starting our retreat from the Great Meadows. We were a licked lot that morning. Carrying our wounded. And rain coming down in buckets. And the Indians running crazy, trying to set fire to the stockade. Things aren't as bad now as they were then."

"We could use some of that rain, Will," Fraser said.

"We've got two wells. We'll have water, if they don't go dry."

"My God," Fraser said.

"Now what's wrong?"

"I was just thinkin'. Less'n four months ago, right where we are now, we were standin' to our necks in water. Ice water," Fraser added. "This is go'n' to be another scorcher." He bent his head into the hollow of his arm and wiped his face.

It was as if he'd wiped the night off of his face. When his arm dropped and his head came up, Holden saw him plainly. All the faces of the men standing on the platform were becoming plain now—Trent's, clean-shaven, hard, sharp, grimly humorous; Tom Yeardley's, plump and child-like under tousled blond curls, and yet somehow like a worried buffalo's face because his forehead bulged just underneath the curls as if two horns were trying to push through; Carre's, smaller than ever beside Tom's; and John Fraser's gaunt and stubborn.

He couldn't see their shoulders yet. The night was sinking slowly. It was being drained away like water. These four tall men still stood neck deep in darkness.

The squared tree-trunk timbers of the gate emerged. They looked more than ever like a gallows. The log roofs of the barracks floated on the ebbing dark. Low, slanting, with the long binding poles laid crosswise of the logs, they looked like badly made rafts being sucked down into the black eddy of the fort's parade ground.

There was no light in the sky yet, but away beyond the gate frame you could see a piece of the Monongahela like a chunk of pig lead. In the opposite direction, out across the flat ground, the Allegheny made a long streak, dull, lead-colored. You could see, picked out against it, the tops of logs in a long palisade.

"Well," Trent said, "what d'you think of our new fort, Chris? Where the dirt bastions had been washed into the ditch, we made walls out of whisky barrels with dirt in them. Of course we had to take the whisky out. It was a sinful waste. You can still see a man, now and again, with his nose shoved tight against one of those barrels. We built a stockade on the Ohio and Monongahela curtains—on what there was left of them. About half the town is in it—the wall logs of cabins, the doors, rafters, tables, benches, bedposts, wagon boxes . . ."

Trent's voice drifted off. He went on talking, but Chris Holden was no longer listening. He was hearing the slow current that moved in the shoaling dark of the parade ground. He could see it moving. It was people coming from the barracks. They were making a crowd. Women. Children. They were drifting along past the barracks toward the Music bastion as if, somehow, they knew something had been happening here. Their faces, upturned, made a shapeless mass of pale blobs at the foot of the ramp that climbed up to the bastion.

They stood there, silent at first, and then they began to whisper. The whispering grew louder and became a murmur. And then, as if the daylight washing down across the walls released them somehow from the need of silence, they were talking out loud. Children chased each other. Horses stamped. A cow mooed. And a girl laughed—a clear, ringing peal of laughter. Chris Holden felt an almost overpowering need to rush down the ramp and clap his hand across that foolish mouth. But for a moment, he thought, he could not have moved. He stood numbed by the impossible fact of sound—loud, careless, normal sound.

It was unbelievable. Here were people walking about in the open, with no vines to hide them, with no willow thickets, no dead tree trunks to crouch under, no azalea tangles. He let his breath run out in a long shaking sigh of relief that was almost like laughter, and felt Abby's body going limp against him. And then she was laughing as the other girl laughed—and she could not stop.

He saw a woman come out of the crowd and walk quickly up the ramp. She was a small, brisk woman.

"Hello, Jackie," he said.

"Hello, Chris."

She put her arms around Abby and held her as the uncontrollable bright laughter turned to hard sobs.

He heard Carre say suddenly:

"Mrs. Fraser, take her to the women's barracks. Now!"

They were moving away from him. As they went down the ramp he saw what Carre had seen. A straggle of militiamen was coming from the Ohio bastion. They were leather-shirted, linsey-shirted, homespun-coated, or half naked and breechclouted. Martin Garth was with them.

He saw Garth step out of the ragged column and start walking rapidly across the parade. He was not walking toward the girl and Mrs. Fraser. He was hurrying to get between them and the women's barracks.

All for nothing . . . nothing. All for worse than nothing. Holden suddenly felt all the bony structure of his face and jaws so plainly that it was as if he saw them—saw the flesh gone and his skull bare. His teeth were clenched so tightly that the pressure ran through all the bones inside his face and made him conscious of them. *Dead,* he thought. *Dead. They'll hang me for this. I've thought about it for a long time. Now it's come.*

His thumb hooked around the rifle lock and pulled it back.

Chapter 48

Stair Carre's hand went to the lock of Holden's rifle. His middle finger got between the hammer and the cock.

"For God's sake, Chris, don't make it any worse."

"Can it be worse?" Holden's hoarse cry was no louder than Carre's low, urgent warning.

He wrenched at the rifle. The flint drew a gash across Carre's knuckle. Beads of blood welled up as Carre's grip tightened.

"You can't help her this way."

"I can set her free of him!"

"She'd still be a convict and a slave, Chris. She'd be sold again. The Lord knows who'd get her. Not you, if you were in irons waiting to be tried. Look . . ."

Garth was closer to the barrack door than Jackie Fraser and the girl. He had headed them off. But he was being headed off himself now. A woman stepped down from the doorway, and it was as if the door itself had come away. She was as tall as Garth and broader—not with panniered skirts but with flat, bony hips and shoulders. She planted herself squarely in Garth's way.

"You see," Carre said, "how foolish it would be. There's nothing Garth can do—no men allowed in the women's quarters. And that's Captain Jones's widow. Mistress Rawbones Jones—that's Boyd's name for her." Garth stood looking at the woman. He had to look up a little. Around them now there was a growing crowd of women and a growing sound of laughter. Holden saw Garth's furious and futile gesture as he turned away. Carre's voice was going on, unhurried, casual. "It will take an order from Ecuyer to get Garth inside five paces of that doorway. That's the deadline she's set. And I mean set. I've seen her set a man flat on his backside for coming too close to the door to talk to his own wife."

"Thanks," Holden said. "Thanks. I—I—— My God, Stair, I didn't have to come back here. I didn't have to bring her back. We could have got away, east. But she wouldn't go. We came to bring *that*." He touched the dirty bundle under Carre's arm. "I'm going to marry her."

"I see," Carre said. But it was plain he didn't.

"She's free. She was convicted of murder and transported because a sailor in a press gang got killed trying to take up her brother. All she was guilty of was being where it happened."

"That's right," Fraser said. "All that's in a newspaper that Chris fetched from London. Jackie's got it safe, Chris."

"She's free!" he repeated. "I bought her and I set her free. If it wasn't lawful, she's still mine. Garth burned her papers. The indenture agent double-sold her."

"Can you prove that?"

"I can if I'm given time. Six people know what happened. Garth. Bone. Leach, the indenture agent. Abby."

"And that far it's your word and hers against Dave Bone's and Garth's. And Garth has indenture papers, and he'll lie."

"He has lied. Bone will lie; he knew what he was doing; he could hang for it. The agent would lie. They could both hang. But there's the captain of the ship we came in, and a man named Pollexfen—Ellerby Pollexfen. They've no interest in it. They both saw me buy her. They both saw me pay the money. A court would believe them."

"Do you know where they are?"

"God knows where Captain Brookes is. At sea, likely, or else back in England. But Pollexfen's somewhere in the colonies. He was going to meet me at the Indian Queen in Philadelphia——" Holden stopped. The words came back to him: *Three months from this.* The day had been All Fool's Day. *If that dog hadn't howled . . . if I hadn't gone to Salter's . . . if I'd turned east up that stream . . . eleven days . . .* In eleven days he might have been in Philadelphia. Carre saw the sudden anguish in his face.

"Easy does it, Chris. I'll see Ecuyer. I'll give him my oath that you can furnish proof if you are given time. No. Don't thank me. You can thank Major Leslie that you had the chance to tell me. But for him, you'd be in irons this minute. You'd be twenty feet below ground, waiting for a drumhead court to shoot you for desertion. Gape all you like, Chris. They arrested Leslie."

"For what?"

"For desertion. Disobedience of orders. Cowardice."

"Leslie . . . *cowardice!*"

"I know. But they tried him. And he pleaded guilty. Oh, they turned him loose. On a technicality. Boyd defended him, and Boyd's as sharp as one of his own scalpels. The defense was that the court had no power over Leslie, innocent or guilty. Leslie wasn't on militia duty. Even if he had been, as a field officer of militia he had no rank in a regular garrison. And he was not an officer. He didn't know it at the time, but the governor of Maryland had canceled his commission. If it hadn't been for that . . ."

"What had he done?"

"The same damn-fool thing that you did," Fraser answered. "Only he didn't walk into no Mingo town, an' he didn't walk into Venango. He an' the girl he fetched back came in with a part of Ensign Price's men from Fort Le Boeuf. It was Arnold pushed the charges. An' the court knew why he pushed 'em. Arnold wanted the girl. Carre, you don't think . . ."

"Charges against Chris? No. It would have been possible to draw new charges against Leslie that a court *could* deal with, but nobody had the stomach for it. I don't think Ecuyer'd stomach any more such nonsense. I'll go see him now."

"We might as well walk down to quarters," Trent said. "Yeardley's sleeping on his feet, and I imagine it's been some time since Chris has slept in a bed—even in a plank one."

They went down the ramp together. Fraser thrust a big fist under Holden's elbow.

"Quit y'r frettin', Chris. Ecuyer'll listen to what Carre says. Ever'thing else that you told turned out true. Coulson got in from the Lower Towns the first day you were gone. He'd been a prisoner f'r weeks. Two of Calhoon's men came in next day; an' the day after, Calhoon himself turned up. Shingess an' some more chiefs—Wingenum an' Windahola—had disarmed him an' his people an' then started 'em east with some Delawares to protect 'em. They protected 'em! They led 'em into a trap at the Beaver Creek ford. Four out o' fourteen got away."

They turned in at the door of a brick-faced barrack. Air thick with the smell of sweat-soaked leather, dirty clothes, and unwashed bodies pushed against their faces. Men snored in two layers in the double tier of plank bunks. Fraser led the way to the far corner.

"We ain't much f'r rank in the militia. Off'cers bunk in with the men. These three bunks are mine an' Tom's an' Leslie's. You can take that there one." They sat down, two and two, their shoulders hunched beneath the edges of the top bunks and their heads together in the space between. "Ye've seen Indian wars, Chris, but ye ain't never seen no war like this one. It gets on a man's nerves. It's like they were teasin' us. They've been at it f'r two months now, an' we ain't had one good fight yet. They crawl up in the garden an' take pot shots at us, an' a half hour later they're walkin' in the King's Road wavin' strings o' wampum an' hollerin' to McKee. They shoot us up, an' then they come whinin' that they're hungry. Will, you got that ledger of yours on you? Let Chris read it. A man just nat'rally can't believe what's happened, hearin' of it. It all sounds like lies. It looks truer when it's wrote out."

Trent pulled a small account book from his pocket and began to thumb the pages.

"I don't know if you can read it, Chris. I've been in right much of a hurry most times. There's some things that don't make sense. Like this. Here's the first of June. 'This morning an order was issued by the to pull down and burn all the outhouses.' I left out 'officer commanding.' "

'You see," Fraser said. "I told you it was crazy. He leaves out Ecuyer an' puts in about outhouses."

"I meant the upper town," Trent said. "I meant the outlying houses."

"Outhouses is a good enough word. It fits the most of 'em." Fraser's hands, lying on his thighs, swelled into fists. He said heavily: "It don't fit my forge, though."

"Did they burn that?"

"No. I tore it down m'self. I built it, by God, an' I tore it down. The most part of it's in the stockade. There ain't no better logs in it nowheres than what they are. Oak. Folks said I was hypped, usin' oak logs f'r a house. They'll be standin' when them soft-wood timbers out of Butler's house an' Bassett's an' the rest has burned. Them red devils ain't tried fire yet. Give 'em time. We ain't had no rain in seven weeks. Them pine palisades'll go like kindlin'. An' them roofs—they'd ought to built troughs on them roofs to drench 'em when the bastards start in with fire arrows."

"Christie had troughs on the roof at Presque Isle," Yeardley said. "They burnt Presque Isle."

"Here," Trent said. He held out the open ledger. "You might start in here, Chris. I think maybe the fifth June will interest you." His thumb marked the place. Holden read:

5th, 2 o'clock at night one Benjamin Sutton came in, who says he left Redstone two days ago and found that place evacuated, and saw a number of shoe tracks going towards Fort Cumberland which he supposes was the garrison, that there was with him there a white man named Hicks and an Indian named Kecois, who would have burnt the fort had he not persuaded them from it. That Hicks told him that an Indian war had broken out and that he would kill the white people wherever he found them.

"You see," Trent said, "Garth's not the only one—if he *is* one. John told me what you think."

"What do you think, Will?"

"I don't know what to think. He didn't have to stay here. If he knew what was coming, he could have stayed away; he could have left after we got word of Clapham's. But here he is, and his wife with him."

"He brought Hannah here?"

"He's got a room in the officers' barracks. He's living here with Hannah while her father's killing every white man he can get his hands on." Trent stood up. "I've got to go along. There's always a fight or two around this time in the morning. It's my job to stop 'em. If it isn't some man that's been cheated on his rations, it's his wife claiming he's been cheated. A man's got to take his wife's word, hasn't he?" Trent laughed grimly. "Her word—or her words. You ought to hear 'em. I hope, when the time comes, those married men will fight Indians half as hard as some of their wives fight amongst themselves." He stood scowling thoughtfully at nothing. "You know, John's right. This is a crazy mix-up. I was never one for Nan Perdue's kind. But . . . You know, whores can be right useful people. Nan and those girls of hers and that Peggy Sargent that Val Arnold pushed out of his bed—they do more work than almost any twenty of those married women. Cooking. Washing. Tending other people's children. And no fuss about it. I don't know what in time gets into a woman when she gets to be called missis."

Trent went away. Tom Yeardley stretched out on the bunk and closed his eyes. Fraser fell to picking the flint of his rifle. Holden turned back to Trent's journal:

9th, By a great smoke which rose up the river, we suppose the enemy has burnt Mr. Croghan's house, the smoke rising where we imagined his house stood. Nine o'clock, two more expresses were sent to Venango.

June 11th, At break of day some Indians were discovered among the ruins of the upper town. About 10 o'clock they set fire to a house, on which a shell was thrown among them, some time after Indians were seen in the lower town and some hallooing heard at a small distance from the fort.

12th, An Indian was discovered from the garden; about 11 o'clock a party, out cutting spelts, saw two Indians and fired on them, on which a number more appeared and fired on our people, who returned it; on some round shot being fired from the cannon in the fort the Indians ran off.

13th and 14th, Nothing worth notice.

15th, A party was sent to cut spelts and were fired on. Sergeant Miller of the militia, contrary to orders, with three others advanced to Grant's Hill, and just as they had gained the summit, Miller was shot dead, a party advancing drove the enemy off and prevented their scalping him.

18th, The enemy set fire to another house up the Ohio.

21st, About 11 o'clock at night the Indians on the opposite side of the Monongahela repeated all's well after our sentinels.

24th, The Turtle's Heart, a principal warrior of the Delawares, and Mamaultee came within a small distance of the fort, Mr. McKee went out and they made a speech, letting us know that all our posts and Ligonier was destroyed, that great numbers of Indians was advancing, but that out of regard to us they had prevailed on six nations of Indians not to attack us but give us time to go down the country, and they desired we should set off immediately . . .

Holden swore savagely. Fraser left off picking at his rifle flint.

"What's the matter with you? You found somethin' you don't like?"

"Mamaultee. That speech he made to Alec McKee. It's the same thing Killbuck said to Gordon. 'Go down the country'! That's all they need—to get two hundred women and children strung out along the Forbes road. Maybe it's a good thing I came back. Maybe that bed sheet Killbuck used to cully Gordon will do some good."

"Maybe," Fraser said. "So long's nothin' happens to Ecuyer. He's onto 'em. Ecuyer gave Mamaultee what was comin' to him. Read the rest of it."

The commanding officer thanked them, let them know that we had everything we wanted, that we could defend it against all the Indians in the woods, that we had three large armies marching to chastise those Indians that had struck us. Out of our regard to them we gave them two blankets and a handkerchief out of the Small Pox Hospital. I hope it will have the desired effect.

"Three large armies," Chris said. "Where'd they come from?"

"Out of Ecuyer's head, most likely. That's about the only place they could have come from. Bouquet said all he had was sick men shipped up from Havana. You remember that, don't you? We're go'n' to be right hungry by the time he gets here. *If* he gets here. That smallpox better work almighty fast. D'you see what happened yest'day an' the day b'fore?"

"You mean this?" Holden read aloud. " 'They came into the cornfield, drove off a number of cows and shot several.' God's breath, John, can't the cattle be kept close enough so they can't get at them?"

"We ain't had no rain in seven weeks. I told you that. There ain't no grass left in the flat ground. The only feed is up past Perdition, where the woods begins. That ain't the whole of it. Look at yest'day."

" 'At ten o'clock this morning as a party of men went to the garden for greens, et cetera, they were fired on by some Indians who had hidden within thirty yards of the fort.' They know we're hungry. They know we can't hang on without them cattle an' the garden stuff. Go on—read the rest of it."

At 10 o'clock two guns were heard on the opposite side of the Allegheny, and immediately four Indians appeared naked and their bodies painted different colors, singing as they came along according to their custom when appearing as friends; they had two small sets of British colors. Mr. McKee went down and asked who they were and what their business was; they answered him they were Ottawas and came from D'Troit ten days ago, where they said everything was settled between them and us at that place and therefore desired to be brought over.

Notwithstanding the fair appearance they came under, McKee directed them to go up the river and cross at a place where the Indians were frequently seen crossing. When they came over Mr. McKee went and met them a small distance from the fort. They informed him that their chiefs had come to the opposite side of the river and desired them to deliver the following speech:

"Brother the Commanding Officer: By this string of wampum we open your ears, wipe the tears from your eyes, and remove everything that is bad from your heart, that you may hear and receive them in friendship tomorrow." Gave a string painted with blue clay. Mr. McKee gave them some bread and tobacco and they returned across the river.

"So the fort's near to starving, and we feed them," Chris said.

"I told you it was the God-damnedest thing. Folks didn't like it much. You should've heard 'em when they saw them loaves of bread go out. It sounded like the whole fort was groanin'. An' then they cussed Ecuyer. The militia did. Anything they don't like, they lay it to Ecuyer. An' there's a plenty they don't like. If they knew Ecuyer was God in a red coat, they'd still damn him. They don't like red coats. Way they talk, they'd sooner trust a Mingo's red hide than a reg'lar's uniform. It ain't good. It's damn bad. I wish I knew how much Garth's buzzards have to do with stirrin' up the talk against Ecuyer an' the Royals." Fraser opened the pan of his rifle and looked at the priming. "I wish I knew how we're fixed f'r powder. We got orders not to waste a grain."

"That's sense."

"Sure it's sense. But it kind o' pinches in y'r belly, not knowin' if the powder ye've got in y'r horn is all ye're go'n' to get. I know we ain't fixed good f'r cannon shot. Ever' time a man goes outside the fort, he's supposed to pick up ever' stone he sees an' fetch back his pockets full. We're that short, Chris." Fraser got up from the bunk. "Well, come on. We might's well draw our rations."

At the barracks door they met Carre coming in.

"I saw Ecuyer," Carre said. "I gave him the bed sheet. He'll not be cozened by that kind of trick. I told him what you said about the other. When this is over, he'll see that you have time to furnish proof. A reasonable time, he said."

Chapter 49

The siege of Fort Pitt was not like a war. It was more like a disease. It was like the slow inexorable progress of a disease that was painful only at times—that wasted men's and women's bodies and their nerves and courage—that burned them as if with a fever.

Hunger pinched their faces. The sun turned them black. You could see the skulls emerging.

A few men died: not many. But now, in the last week of July, the fort was like a sickroom in which four hundred and thirty men and women had begun to know that they, too, probably were dying. After two months of siege it was as if already they had died a little.

They were no longer in the world they knew. Yet living, they had passed beyond it. The fever that possessed them was an intermittent fever. It rose from despair to hope and sank into despair again. From the slow hours in which nothing happened it burned into moments when men died obscenely.

But the worst part was the waiting . . . waiting . . . waiting. Waiting for the help that did not come. Waiting for the next burst of crazy screeching from the rank weeds in the garden. Waiting for the next shot. Each single shot now was a small stroke of paralysis that twitched the muscles —a small numbing of the will—a sudden gathering and pulling of the nerves as if nerves were fiddlestrings and an angry hand had seized them, silenced them, and let them go. For an instant life itself stopped. Then it lurched on again.

An order posted on the hoardings at the barrack doorways said there must be no loud talking. Women were forbidden to quarrel, lest their noisy squabblings keep men on the walls from hearing officers' commands. Even the dogs were forbidden to bark.

The one order was as useful as the other. Captain Ecuyer ordered the dogs killed. He could only threaten women. He could only shut them up in their own quarters.

Nothing could shut out the smell. As the rivers dwindled, the Monongahela mud flats reeked and festered. Mud boils swelled, enormous, till their pent-up gases burst them, and the nauseating odor mingled with the stench of the latrines, and with the smells of unwashed bodies in the barracks where men slept in puddles of their sweat, and with the smells that came out of the casemate where the children had been put for safety. There were no latrines there for the hundred and six children.

To Abby the fort was a kind of Newgate—only better. Much, much better. The smell wasn't any worse. The half ration that kept other folk complaining was more food than she had ever had in prison. She even felt safe: Chris was here. She didn't know that Hannah was her real protection.

She was lying awake now in the top bunk over Mrs. Fraser's. It was dark yet, but she always woke up in time to watch the daylight draw its thin line down the joining of the shutters. There had been a time when she thought evenings were the best part of the day. But the mornings were the best now. That was when the shutters of the women's barracks were unbarred, and the men who had been at the loopholes all night came down from the walls. She sat up and began to dress. It was a kind of ceremony. First she took off the beaded necklace and the belt. She wore them even when she went to bed. Now she took Mrs. Salter's skirt and blouse down from the pegs in the beam overhead and wriggled into them. Then, slowly, carefully, loving them, she put on the necklace and the belt. They were her courage. They were like a wedding ring—*two* wedding rings. They were like Chris's arms around her.

But this morning, when the shutters opened, Chris was not there. Abby knew a moment of blind panic. Then someone said that the day and night watches had changed off, and she realized that all the faces of the men outside the windows were new. Her hands caressed the smooth beads as she waited for Peggy Sargent to read out the names of the women to fetch water for the barrels on the walls. Her name was not called. It meant that today she wouldn't see him.

To Chris Holden the fort was a kind of Bedlam. It was not a normal place. People were shut up in it, and some of them were no longer normal people. Their blank stillnesses were abnormal. And the stillnesses were ripped to pieces, every now and then, by the sudden insane ravings of the naked creatures crouching in the weed-smothered garden, in the cellars of the torn-down houses and the burrows they had dug into the riverbanks. Gunshots, slamming on the brick walls, made a clangor like that he had heard in Bedlam when the naked madmen and madwomen chained there beat the stone floor with their leg irons.

The sky was clean and hard this morning. It was blue-glazed like the bowl in which Jackie Fraser fed him broth the morning he fell down the governor's steps. It was as hot, too. Even now, at sunrise, sweat stood out on John Fraser's forehead and on Ten Eyck's like the globules of grease in a hot broth. The heat haze was already rising. The burned town seemed still to be burning. A brassy vapor seemed to flow up from the chimney of the Perdue house. The house was gone, but the men who wrecked it had not bothered with the chimney. The willow shoot that grew out of it was considerably longer. It had seven leaves now. They quivered in the upward flowing of the haze.

"We'd ought to have torn down that chimney," Ten Eyck said.

"It don't make no diff'rence," Fraser told him. "It ain't in musket shot."

"They've got rifles. Some of them have. It was a rifle that killed Huggins on the Monongahela bastion—all the way across the river. It could make a difference when they attack. They——"

"What the hell would they do that for? It's been two months, an' they ain't attacked yet. All they got t' do is wait f'r us t' come out or t' get so weak that they c'n walk in."

"It's not that they use it——" Ten Eyck stopped. His mouth and chin seemed to have shrunk smaller in his meager face. His eyes bulged more than ever. The sun put a brassy glitter on them. "It's that sprout. I keep thinking of those skulls on the hill, there, with weeds growing through them."

"Oh, for God's sake," Fraser said.

"We'd ought to have torn it down. It's like a sign from God. God sent an olive leaf to Noah."

"Seems to me it set Noah up considerable."

"It's not the same. It's a blasphemy, like. Or it could be God's warning. Growing on Perdition that way."

The man on the other side of Ten Eyck snarled:

"Ahhh—shut up! You ain't no missionary."

There was an argument a little farther down the wall. Tell you Bouquet's comin'. He's at Bedford. He ain't. He's at Ligonier. Feller that come in last night—he come from Bouquet at Fort Ligonier. Dave Bone's nasal voice:

"He come from Ligonier, a'right, but he didn't come from Bouquet. There ain't no army there. There ain't none at Bedford, neither. I bet ye a pound he ain't even started."

"Make it a pound o' beef," a man said, and laughed harshly.

"Yah." Nasal sneer. "If ye lost, ye couldn't pay up. There ain't no more beef left than there is an army comin'."

"Ye can take y'r pay in horse meat, if ye go an' fetch it. Look at." A bay horse had walked out of the woods behind the ruins of the Gilded Beaver. It began to graze on the swamp grass at the edge of Hogg's Pond. "That's Thompson's horse. D'ye see that white foreleg?"

"Yah. I wonder c'd ye make soup f'r five hundred people out'n one horse. By God! There's Thompson! He's a-goin' after it. Ecuyer'll skin him."

"Not if he brings in the horse."

They watched Thompson walking up the slope between the charred smears of the cabins. He was a middle-aged, farmerish-looking man and he had a stubborn way of walking. His bent shoulders seemed to push a heavy barrow. He had a looped rope in his hand. Somebody said: *hang himself, by God*.

The grazing horse flung up its head. You could hear Thompson talking to it. The horse moved away a few steps. You could almost hear its feet drag out of the swamp muck. You could see Thompson moving slowly and more slowly, pulling his feet out. He got the rope around the horse's neck. The horse jerked back. The rope jerked Thompson off his feet. He clung to it. The horse dragged him a few yards.

Then the shot came. The horse screamed. On the wall a woman screamed. *God A'mighty, that's her. That's his wife.* Thompson still clung to the rope. You could see him lifting his head, you could see him lifting himself on one elbow. You could see the dark stream gushing from the horse's belly. Musket smoke coiled upward from the trees. The Indians came out of the woods as silently as smoke. There were seven of them. They did not screech until they were one jump from Thompson. Then you couldn't tell their screeches from his. But you could see the knives work. They worked on Thompson and the horse at the same time. The knives cut steaks off the living horse. They cut Thompson into ribbons of flesh, like meat being cut in strips for jerky.

They left him lying there. He lay there all day in the sun. Ecuyer would not risk men's lives to bring in human bodies. There was not enough left of the horse to matter.

By the middle of the afternoon the flies were a solid black cloud. On the firing step of the Town curtain men's talk made an angry buzzing. Nobody wanted to go up the hill and fetch Thompson's body in. But it made a noble argument. It was something new to jaw about. *Oughtn't to be left there . . . ain't decent, with his wife knowin' . . . Anyways, we'd ought t' have a service.*

Ye can't have no burial service without ye've got somethin' t' bury. *Why the hell not?* It made another argument. The more they talked about it, the more it seemed to be a good idea. It was easier to bury a man who didn't need a hole dug for him. Nobody'd have to break his back. All it took was words. Fetch the missionary. *Ahh, his kid's sick, leave him be.* There's a plenty o' kids sick. Mine's one o' them. Muller can't do nothin' f'r 'em. He ain't no doctor. *He's a better doctor than what Boyd is.* They can't neither of 'em feed the kids. *Muller tells 'em stories. Bible stories.* He can quit it f'r five minutes, can't he? *I don't knows he'd want to.*

They had another argument about whether Muller would be willing to say a burial service for a man they couldn't bury. *What's wrong with the teacher? He's got all th' gab.* Hey, Ten Eyck, you know how the words go? *Hell, anybody knows that.* I allow it'd be a comfort t' th' widow. *Ask her.* So they asked her.

Two women brought her to the firing step. Ten Eyck said the words. The most of them were right. Mrs. Thompson held her face with both hands and her sobbing came between them. The men turned to watch the women leading her away. They didn't know whether it had been a good idea or not.

Nobody missed Ten Eyck till a gunner on the Flag bastion saw him climbing up the far wall of the ditch away down at the Mon end where the earth had caved in. He had an ax in his hands. Lieutenant Greber shouted at him, but he kept on going. *Crazy fool . . .*

Ten Eyck walked steadily across the open ground until he came to the chimney of Perdition. He began to batter at it. He was clumsy with the ax. The chimney clay was baked hard. He had only made some gouges in it when the first Indian rose up from the bank of the stream behind Perdition. A dozen rifles cut loose at him, but he used the chimney as a shield. He hid behind it. Another Indian and another and another sprang up from the bank. They had crept up the dry gully from the river. Now, one behind another, they ran for the chimney.

Ten Eyck kept on chopping. He looked back across his shoulder, once, toward the hullabaloo on the wall; but he did not seem to understand it. The uproar of shouting kept him from hearing the small noises that the Indians made, running. On the Grenadier bastion, matrosses set hand-spikes to the carriage of a frigate cannon. An officer bawled at them:

"No! No! The cohorn! *Use the cohorn, blast you!* Break the fuse short——"

The four Indians slid out from behind the chimney while the matross was still blowing on his match. John Fraser and Chris Holden fired together. Other rifles went *whap*. Muskets hammered.

The first Indian died standing up. The shots nailed him to the chimney. But the other three swarmed over Ten Eyck. He tried to run and strike out with the ax at the same time. It made a bright streak as it flew out of his hands. He was down, with the three Indians on top of him, when the cohorn went off. You could see the shell climbing, turning, smoking. It began to drop, a small black ball rolling down the shimmer of the heat haze.

One of the Indians rose to his knees. He lifted the torn scrap of flesh with the blood running from it. The shell burst almost in his belly. It lifted him. He hung in the air a moment while his body came to pieces. The top half of it toppled backward. The other half still stood there with blood spouting from it. The pouring blood pulled red drawers down its legs in the instant before it toppled forward. A third Indian was sprawled over Ten Eyck. The fourth was crawling. Muskets pinned him to the earth. He kept on moving minutes after he was dead.

Men kept on shooting at him in a frenzy, and their savage howling beat down the shouts of officers who cursed them for their waste of powder. They had not killed four Indians at one time since the siege began. They thought a lot of Ten Eyck, now that he was dead. They wouldn't let *him* lie there. No, by God! If Ecuyer wouldn't lower the drawbridge, they'd go down the wall.

Ecuyer ordered the bridge lowered. Four militiamen went out. They carried Ten Eyck in by arms and legs and laid him on the ground inside the gate. He wasn't cut up much. Just scalped. They weren't sure he was dead. They thought so, but they stood waiting for Boyd to come and see for sure. The flies came first. They danced around the raw place on the schoolteacher's big head.

A woman knelt and brushed at the hovering flies. One of the militiamen said: "God! Somebody'd ought to have kept Thompson's widow in the barracks." But the insane yelling had fetched all the women out of quarters.

Boyd elbowed through the crowd.

"What devil's business is this, now?"

"I allow he thought it was God's business. He was tryin' to finish off Perdition."

"Ay, was he, now? He might have known." Boyd thrust a foot out toward the swarming flies. "That's all the halo he'll be gettin' for it."

Mrs. Thompson looked up at him. Her mouth moved in slow convulsions but no sound came. Two women took her by the arms and lifted her and walked her through the crowd. When they came to the edge of it the sound that she had tried to make tore loose. She screamed and broke away. Before anyone knew what she was about she snatched the knife that hung in a sweat-black sheath at a militiaman's neck. His name was John Maycamp. The string that held the sheath was a rolled rawhide cord. It broke. While John Maycamp stared after her and felt his neck, Thompson's widow turned and ran across the parade ground. She ran in swaying jumps that lifted her body sidewise, first one side and then the other. Each jump lifted a wild cry out of her body. She pulled the knife clear of the sheath.

Hannah had just come out of the officers' quarters at the west end of the governor's house. She had closed the door and was standing by it. When she saw Mrs. Thompson coming she turned to the door again and tried to open it. It stuck. The knife went into her back. It came out and went in again. She slumped against the door. It opened for her then. She lay across the sill.

Mrs. Thompson stood there. She did not look at Hannah. She looked at the knife and threw it from her. She put her hands up to her head and swayed it.

John Maycamp walked across to where his knife lay. He picked it up and wiped it on his leg. Coming back, he picked up the sheath. He slid the knife into it and began to knot the broken cord.

"By God," he said to no one in particular, "she done right." He hung the knife around his neck. "Mingo bitch. . . ." He looked around the crowd. "You—Williamson. You can tell Garth I said so. Feedin' Mingo bitches."

" 'Tweren't none of Garth's doin', Maycamp. He'd of turned her out. It was Ecuyer made him keep her. Ecuyer figgered she'd pertect us. He figgered Guyasuta wouldn't get rough long as she was in here."

Something said *wunch!* Glass fell, brittle spattering on the pebbled dirt. The whole sash of a window in the upper story of the south barracks had burst outwards. A body hung there with sharp splinters of glass digging slowly into it.

The splinters broke. The body bowed across the sill. Its arms reached down for the parade. Then it slid a little. It fell with a soggy sound that brittled as the fallen glass was broken into smaller pieces on the pebbles. An arrow stood up in the middle of the broad back.

The crowd leaned backward. Leaned forward. Began to run. Face at the bursted window, its mouth twisting. *Came in through the window on the other side!* Officer's feet pounding. His voice bawling: *Who opened those shutters?* Lieutenant Donnellan went thudding up the ramp to the Monongahela bastion. *Who opened . . . shutters . . . God damn shut 'em. . . .* He ran doubled over, as if he too had an arrow in his guts. His voice wailed along the firing step on the far side of the barracks. *Shut 'em . . . shuttum . . . whowoo . . . ooo. . . .* Shutters banging. Jumble of cries in the circle thickening around the soldier's body. The cries spread in widening circles. *Fire arrow! Fire arrow!* Woman's wail now. *Oh God, help us . . .*

It was the first time the Indians had used fire. You could see the little bundle of scorched grass pushed halfway up the arrow. You could see the flake of birch bark, crisp, black, sticking to the blood on the dead man's shirt.

A soldier who wore no shirt came to the broken window. He threw out a wadded blanket. They spread it over the body. The blanket stuck up like a tent. It was somehow more dreadful to see that tent-peak of blanket than to see the arrow. They stared at it with a morbid fascination, seeing themselves under it.

Wild shout now. *They're comin'!* Sudden scramble of drums . . . the sticks scudding. . . . Other shout. *Water detail! Water detail! Women not on water . . . inside!* Feet scudding, scattering. Curves of pale fire arching over the roofs, flickering down, skittering across the baked earth, going out. One sticking in the ground, smoking, the shaft burning. Donnellan's wail keening up beyond the barracks. *Water . . . water. . . . The roof's caught.*

You could see smoke rising in three places. Three blue-black wisps, standing straight up. You could see the first tongues of the fire lick at the ridgepole. All the roofs were lightwood. They were tinder. You could hear the first faint crackling.

Then the muskets on the Allegheny wall began to crackle. The sound spread around to the Ohio bastion. Spread the other way to the Town curtain and licked swiftly down the stockade on the Mon side. The fort was a circle of fierce cracklings and a circle of smoke swelling. Outside— larger, looser, coiling, undulating—another circle of smoke formed.

It was the first time the people in Fort Pitt had realized how many Indians there were around them. There had been a plenty to cut all the roads, to drive off the horse herd and destroy the cattle, and to set a man's life as the price of a carrot from the garden or a handful of grain from the spelt field. There had been a plenty to encircle the Forks with the dotted line of camp smoke—and a plenty more to burn Venango and Le Boeuf and Presque Isle and God only knew how many other forts or which ones. But the camps were hidden, they were in the hills a mile or more away. The warriors who came down from the camps were hidden before daylight; at thirty yards, in the weed-grown garden and behind the Mon bank, they had been invisible. In nine weeks the people in the fort had seen no more than twenty at one time. But now . . . *my God, there's an army of them.* Only guns by hundreds could weave that continuously broken but unbroken pattern of pale flashes in the soiled smoke. There was a mob of savages in the lower town, all the way from the Rosgruge yard to the place where Captain Basset's house had stood. Another mob behind the banks of both the rivers. And another in the garden. *Jesus, there must be four hundred of 'em. Five . . . six hundred.* They would never know exactly. But there were almost as many savages around Fort Pitt now as had followed Beaujeau to the massacre of Braddock's army.

The fire arrows began falling short. The Indians were blinded by the smoke of their own muskets. But one arrow found Ecuyer about five o'clock.

It came in through a gun embrasure on the Music bastion and drove deep into the muscles of his left thigh. It made a sound as if he had been kicked. He did not lose his feet, but his shoulders jerked back and his loins jerked forward, his buttocks shrank beneath the shocked arch of his body.

He was commandant and governor of the Ohio frontier, but they took his breeches down in public. Boyd had to break the arrow shaft to do it.

Strange to see the bare flesh of his legs. So white. There was not much blood. The stump of the arrow fitted the wound tightly. Boyd said:

"Pick him up. Fetch him to his quarters."

"*Non!*"

"I'll be givin' of the orders. It's a small head on that arrow—the kind they'll be after usin' with a bit of poison. No chance for the blood to run and purge it. There's some carvin' I'll be doin' on ye—an' no corkscrew." Boyd was mournful. And then vainly hopeful: "Ye'll not have a bit of rum left for the snake bite?"

"*Non.* And none for the doctor, either." As they picked him up, Ecuyer gave an order: "Mr. Hutchins, have the drums beat cease fire. The men— they are wasting powder. They are making the noise only." He was thinking of the empty powder barrels. The thought was a harder shaft of pain inside him. "Tell them: not a shot until they have a fair mark. Mr. Hutchins . . ."

"Yes, sir."

"If you please, tell Captain Steele that he is in command for the time being."

The drums tried to make themselves heard in the uproar. *Cease fire . . . cease fire. . . .* Officers ran along the stockade, pounding the backs of militiamen and soldiers. *Cease fire! Stop it . . . stop it!*

The inner circle of smoke seeped slowly upward. But the outer circle thickened. As it swelled, it bulged in toward the fort. Its coils seemed to tighten. It was still there when the sun went down. The musket flashes gave it red and orange scales. The fire arrows flickered out of it like red tongues darting.

Chapter 50

The flames died on the drenched roofs. But the fever that possessed the fort burned higher.

A corporal and a private of the Royals died of it that night. Loose excrement of smoke on the parade ground, steaming. Char-like puddles of black vomit on the roofs. Dribbles of it clinging stiffly to the scorched eaves. Bloody flux of Sergeant Hermon's coughing . . . lungs torn by a bullet. A bone-breaking fever now . . . Marcus Hulings' right leg broken by a musket ball . . . a grenadier's leg broken in three places.

In the morning all the men and women in the fort knew that this was the crisis of their sickness. The attack did not abate with daylight. Its ferocity increased. The air you breathed was torn before it reached your lungs.

The fort itself was taken with convulsions. The guns on the Music bastion had begun to plow the garden. *Little early for fall plowing.* . . . The guns on the river bastions pushed their furrows toward the banks. Crooked furrows. Shallow. The baked earth was iron-hard. The sixpounder iron balls bounced and skittered. But the watchers at the loopholes cheered the plowmen.

Indians were being killed and wounded. You could see the iron balls make new cave-ins on the caved banks of the rivers . . . burrows suddenly collapsing . . . the dark bodies spinning. You could see the bodies being torn to pieces, their flesh shredded, and sometimes the next ball trampled the same body. *Like squaws tramping pemmican, by Jesus.* Grinding shredded flesh into a paste of putrid mud and water.

There were hundreds of dark living bodies, and you couldn't see them. The fabric of their musket firing was so tightly woven that there was no thinnest space of silence. And how could you possibly hear anything except the muskets and the cannon and the roaring in your own head? But other sounds soaked through the fabric. The moist gobbling yells drooled through the crevices between the logs of the stockade . . . throaty wet sounds . . . liquid oozing between snags of teeth . . . thin slaver of sound dripping like foam from a mad dog's mouth. There were hundreds of mad dogs, all yelping, howling.

For the first half hour of daylight you could see—a little—through the gun smoke. Then the red sun seemed to dry it and it was opaque again. The blinded gunners swabbed their pieces and went scuttling out of the embrasures. They ran on all fours to the shelter of the breastworks.

In the afternoon a faint breeze began drawing up the valleys. It was hot: you couldn't feel it. You could only see it tugging at the fabric of the smoke. The smoke raveled slowly. You could see Indians running, hunting for more solid cover. While they ran, the fabric of the sound was looser; it was frayed a little as their firing slackened.

Through the ravelings of smoke Chris Holden saw that there was only half a chimney at Perdition. The cohorn shell that tore the Indian in two had torn the top half off the chimney also. It had hung the other half with trailing vines, a tangle of the Indian's intestines. The willow sprout was gone. *Gone yesterday.* . . . He hadn't noticed it until now.

It made no difference now. The wilderness no longer was content with the slow processes of life in taking back its own. It would be satisfied with nothing less than death.

New slender sprout grew suddenly where the chimney top had been. It had leaves like a willow . . . long thin slender pale leaves . . . they were flattened to the stem by a hard wind. *Can't do that.* Absurd thought. *Wind not hard enough to do that.* The arrow made its own wind as it climbed. When it curved and fell, it fluttered its pale leaves. The little flames slapped forward as it struck the roof. They lay flat to the shingles for an instant. And then they were growing. *Water . . . water!*

Chris saw women running. Saw one woman only. She was quicker than the others. She began to climb the ladder. She was standing on the roof top, waiting, and her feet were bare.

The little leaves had grown into a burning bush when the first bucket came. Abby cut it down with a curved sickle of bright water.

But the arrows came much faster than the buckets. There were other bushes of flame growing. There was only a six-foot space between the barracks and the shoulders of men along the stockade. If the roofs burned, the fierce heat would drive them from the loopholes. The stockade would go.

Tear the roofs off! No use . . . there's the floors . . . go up like touchwood . . . can't get at fires if they start inside the barracks . . . if the floors catch . . . Goddam bunks are kindlin'. *Tear the bunks out! Throw them out the windows. Throw the mattresses out. Make a pile of them on the parade ground. Burn them where they can't hurt.* No! Don't burn them! Pull the stuffing out . . . the hay out. Burn that. Small piles . . . *small ones!* Save the ticking. Soak it to beat out the roof fires.

The women began harvesting the mattress hay. They piled it in small cocks on the parade ground, but a large stack would have done no damage. The hay was moldy-damp with sweat. It burned slowly, with a greasy black smoke.

The Indians set up a fiercer screeching when the thick smoke rolled across the roof tops. They began to pop out of their burrows. They stood upright in the garden. An Ojibway with a turkey-feather tailpiece started a convulsive dance. The men on the walls applauded him with rifles. He died of his own convulsions. Three or four more died before they understood that it was not the whole fort that was burning.

The women sopped the mattress ticks and piled them at the bottoms of the ladders.

The sun went down. The night was starless, but the stars fell. The burning arrows came at intervals all night. Single red streaks curving, falling. Whole flights of shooting stars—and anyone knew that a falling star was the sure sign that a life was ending.

No reliefs, now. Every man was on the walls. No sleep. No respite.

Indians worming their way closer in the darkness. Musket flash . . . and flash . . . flash . . . and the last flash always nearer. Sudden unseen rushes. Scurry, scuffle, trample on the dirt walls that lay spilled into the ditches. Allegheny curtain . . . Mon wall . . . the Ohio bastion.

The most of the rushes never reached the stockade. Some did. Hack and thrust between the palings. Silent unseen hatchets chopping downward over the points of the palings. And then, suddenly, the dry dirt crushing, sliding . . . the feet going . . . the yells going crazy as the young bucks flopped into their coverts. But you never knew how many had stayed, lying motionless and soundless at the bottom of the stockade, waiting for a soldier to stir at his loophole, listening for a white man's guarded breathing.

John Maycamp had been careful with his breathing. It wasn't till he moved to ease his belly cramps that the knife came through the crack between two logs. It got him in the ribs. If the Indian had held the knife flat, it likely would have killed him. But his ribs stopped the blade an inch beyond the point. Maycamp dropped his rifle. He took the Indian's arm in both hands and dragged it through the crack and bent it till it broke. He held it with one hand while he slid his own knife through the crack. His first try found the throat.

But the rest was not so easy. He had to work the arm down till he could get his knee to it, against a log, and work both of his hands out through the crack to peel the scalp. Then he moved along the wall to do a little bragging.

It took him five steps to come to the nearest man. Even now, with the Mon redoubt and the redan in front of the main gate abandoned, there was upwards of half a mile of bastion wall and stockade to be guarded. On the Allegheny curtain the men stood fifteen and eighteen feet apart.

Five days. Five nights. Endless hours of madness. The whole fort afflicted with an ague now. The glass in the windows chattering like teeth at each concussion of the cannon. The endless muskets wracking the parade ground . . . wrenching at it . . . tilting it at crazy angles . . . lifting it and letting it go. The baked earth too brittle to endure the strain . . . the earth and men's nerves too brittle to endure it . . . cracking. The parade ground sounded hollow under running feet. *Felt* hollow. You could hear it in the vibrance of your tired legs.

The cracks in the parade were spreading. They were longer, wider. Weary shuffling feet tripped in them. It was an illusion that smoke came out of the deep cracks, as if fire was waiting under the thin crust of earth. It had to be illusion. But on the last day of July illusion had become more real than the reality. It was also better. It was better than the moments of terrifying sanity in which men knew that they had gone insane.

In such moments they knew that this was not happening. It was impossible. It was against all nature and all reason. Indians did not have patience for long sieges. Indians would not face musketry from breastworks. They would not face cannon. Indians did not dig trenches. The fact that Indians were doing all of these things beat against men's reason.

Will Guttery had two such moments. Some officer or other—he did not know which one, in the dark—had moved him to a new place on the wall. When day came he saw that he had found his table. He knew it couldn't be here, but it was.

The soldiers that had torn his house down, the night the news came from Clapham's, hadn't done the table much hurt. They hadn't even broke the legs off. They had set it up on end with the legs wedged through the cracks between the pickets, and it made about the safest place that there was anywheres along the stockade on the Allegheny side. It was wide enough to cover four cracks, and the puncheons were a plenty thick to stop trade-musket balls or even rifle bullets. There wasn't any way an Indian could slide a knife into you, like had happened to John Maycamp.

Finding that table all in one piece made Will Guttery think better of the Royals. They'd set it into the wall, solid, with two sawed boards spiked across it; but the spikes were in the logs on either side. The only hurt that had been done to it was cutting out that loophole between two of the puncheons. But he figured the hole wouldn't show much. It wasn't so big that a candleholder wouldn't cover it. He began to wonder if his wife had fetched the candleholder from the house before the soldiers

342

wrecked it. And then, for the first time, he thought about his ridgepole—about seeing soldiers running with it, going up the King's Road in the opposite direction from the fort. Might be it hadn't been cut into ten-foot pieces to make pickets for the stockade. Might be he could find it, after this was over. With a table and a ridgepole, he would have a right good start towards a new home.

Somebody yelled. You couldn't make out, in the racket, what the yelling was about. He took a quick look through the loophole in his table and saw the ridgepole coming toward him. It wasn't twenty yards away, and it was rolling. There were Indians behind it, squirming on their bellies, shoving the log in front of them. All he could see was their heels, jerking as they shoved.

Will Guttery screamed at them. He poured a delirium of filthy babble through the loophole as he fired and fired. Other men were shooting at the log now. You could hear the pat-pat of the bullets, soft and useless in the uproar. The Indians worked the log up to the top of a mound of flood-heaped dirt and started burrowing behind it. In a few minutes they had dug themselves in, and their muskets poked out underneath the log. It was a thing that Indians did not do. But they did it.

In the afternoon the Indians started bringing canoes down both the rivers. On the Flag bastion the six-pounder field gun jumped and ran back. The lieutenant in command there jumped.

"Damn and blast you!" He raved at the gun crew. "Firing without orders! Have you to the halberds. . . ."

The ball made a white streak in the brown Monongahela, far beyond the nearest elm-bark.

"Flog you bloody . . . know you can't hit a canoe at that range . . . solid shot. . . ."

The second splash came. It was rounder, slower. The lieutenant stared with his mouth open.

The Indians were throwing themselves out of their canoes. Only one knelt motionless. He had no head.

It was one more thing that could not happen. You could not believe that you had seen it.

The headless Indian swayed at last. His red-painted copper body slid so smoothly to the copper water that you hardly saw it going. Then, for a few yards, the river also had its paint.

On the Allegheny side the canoes kept close in to the bank. The high bank and the orchard hid them. A few canoes worked up the near bank, hidden until they were out of gunshot, and then crossed the river. The Indians were taking off their wounded. You could see the sagging bodies being lifted out and carried through the shallows. But nobody felt like cheering. There weren't enough of them to cheer about.

Nobody seemed to realize that the Indians' firing had slacked off. There were only enough shots now to keep men's heads down and nerves jerking. The people in the fort hardly realized, now, that their nerves jerked. They were used to it. They stood numbed in the numb silences between the random shots.

Sunset bloodied the Ohio. While the water blackened slowly there, the Allegheny and the Mon turned gray. Fog crept in from both the rivers and down from the marshes. It hung in thick bands across the flat ground. You could see the legs of Indians underneath it—their legs only, walking, trotting or just standing. You couldn't see their bodies.

But a little later, when the dusk grew darker than the fog, the Indians came closer. You could hear sounds like tree branches breaking, leafy branches making *whssh* sounds. You could hear the noise of chopping. Now and again, dimly against the fog that whitened in the growing darkness, you could see Indians hacking at trees in the orchard and the Rosgruge garden and at saplings on the riverbanks. You could make out that they'd lopped the branches and were trimming the trunks, peeling the bark off them. *My Christ . . . gettin' ready . . . gettin' fixed f'r somethin'.* Ain't that what the 'Jibways do t' women? Ain't that what they was a-fixin' t' do with that Gail girl? *Name ain't Gail. It's Gaillard.* It ain't only 'Jibways, neither. *Cut a sapling trunk an' peel it . . . sharpen the top end . . . make a stake, like, with the roots still in the ground. Set a woman on it . . . run the sharp end into her an' leave her stand there while they burn her. . . .* Ahhh, shut up! God A'mighty, *shut up!*

The Indians began lighting fires. It was the first time they had built fires so close to the fort. The cannon on the walls could reach them easily, but the gunners only crouched and waited. There were too many fires. It might be a trick to make the fort waste powder.

The men on the walls watched dully. They couldn't know for sure what any of these things meant—the Indians carrying away their wounded, the canoes being gathered, the muskets slacking off, the young trees being hacked, the fires.

But they knew the meaning of the other thing that had just happened. The flour had run out. They had eaten their last bread—not bread enough to matter—and some woman on the ration detail been telling that the only food left in the fort was four legs of beef. Four legs wouldn't go far amongst five hundred and forty people, all of them half starved already.

Hour after hour there was nothing but the glow of the embers in the fires. They were like red eyes that watched the fort. They even blinked— an Indian, passing a fire, closed that one eye for a moment. It was after midnight when the fires began to move.

You could see Indians running—quick gleams of their bodies in the red flare of the torches that they carried. The flames made a bobbing, weaving pattern in the darkness. *Look at them . . . look . . . going to rush us . . . try to burn the stockade. . . .*

The rush did not come. But the fire did. All along the riverbanks and in the orchard and the Rosgruge garden, sudden fiercer fires exploded. They made hard round bundles of flame. You could see the Indians around the saplings they had trimmed, now. You could see the saplings bending, redly lighted bodies pulling them down, the tight bundles burning in the crotches where the branches had been hacked short. You could see the Indians let go.

The balls of flames shot upward. They seemed to hang. And then they rushed upon the fort.

Not merely the stars falling now. Fiery meteors . . . and always meteors had been the portent of the world's end. Even this lost world into which the people in the fort had passed was ending.

The meteors began to fall inside the walls. They burned with a smell of pitch and resin. Some struck the roofs and rolled off. But others stuck. And some burst as they fell. They strewed the roofs with blazing fragments—cattails, wads of corn leaves, dry grass soaked in resin, pine knots.

Women climbed the ladders. They formed bucket lines from the two wells to all the buildings. But there were not enough women. The lines were so long that they must be thin. The buckets came so slowly, slowly. The first shower of fireballs set four roofs to blazing in a dozen places. The governor's house was on fire. The east barracks was on fire. The roof of the officers' quarters by the Town wall caught. *Water . . . water!* The cries wailing up and breaking. Thin with fear and growing thinner. Sharpening themselves into hysteria.

The Indians were screeching now. They were getting bolder. They were not troubling to fetch fire to their sapling slingshots from the piles of embers. They were building new fires close by. The crackle of the rifles on the wall now blended with the crackling of flame as it wrapped itself around the roof poles. But there was not a minute when there was not at least one bundle of fire arching through the sky. Sometimes there were five or six together, trailing showers of sparks behind them, trailing smoke that you could see now by the flames that stood up on the roof tops.

And then the attack came. Not where anyone expected. Not the way that anyone expected. The savages who had used white men's tactics—siege and rifle pits and rolling breastworks—used another now.

Muskets flickered from the burrows in the riverbanks and from the weedy coverts in the garden. Bullets rapped against the stockade. But the first warning of the real attack was the curved prow of a canoe thrust into an embrasure, grating, sliding, hooking itself over the planks of the platform. Wild shout . . . *the ditch . . . they're in the ditch again!* And then another, wilder . . . *look out . . . they're coming up . . . great Jesus . . . they've got ladders . . . ladders!* They did not have ladders. The momentary flambeau of the first grenade showed the moat in front of the Town curtain swarming, and canoes laid against the wall like scaling ladders. Every canoe had a row of Indians upon it, climbing.

From behind the parapet, you could not stop them. Could not even see till they reached the top. Then the glare of the flames above the roof tops showed them plainly. As the first heads rose above the ramparts that had been so safe, the people in the fort said *gahhh!*

It was not a single sound. It was the sum of all conscious and unconscious human noises—fear, astonishment and anger, desperation, hopelessness and frenzy, resignation, terror. It was not an outcry. Not an exclamation, even. It was a hard sigh—a sucking in of life in one long gasp, a letting go of life.

No one ever knew a great deal of what happened. Scenes leaped out at you in flashes, redly. The night leaped upon them blackly. Blotted them out.

All the scenes were nightmares filled with monsters that crawled upward toward you. You could hear their claws scrape. You could hear them hissing. You could see the upturned bottoms of elm-bark canoes like scaly monsters that reared on invisible hind legs and thrust beaked snouts into the embrasures. Other monsters crawled upon them, fingers digging into the bark, moccasined feet scratching. The panting of the Indians as they climbed was like the hissing in a snake den. The moat was a writhing snake pit. The things that came slithering up out of it were colored like snakes—shining brown snakes, wriggling upward—patterned scalily with red and black, blue, yellow, green and orange.

The men all along the wall rose up to meet them. Climbed the parapet and rushed to meet them—musket butts and bayonets, clubbed rifles, knives and hatchets. No man who lived through the next few minutes could remember more than one or two things that had happened. Glimpses. . . .

A militiaman in clout and leggings, shirtless, hacking and hacking with a hatchet at the prow of a canoe, his rifle jerking in his left hand . . . dropping the hatchet . . . swinging the rifle up in both hands and setting the curved butt against the gunwale, shoving . . . the Indian who clung to the canoe just lying there and looking at him . . . and then reaching out and slipping a brown finger through the trigger guard and jerking on the trigger. The rifle going off . . . the butt dropping away, the rifle sliding down the brick wall . . . the man standing there and staring at the hole blown in his belly. And then the blood coming. The man trying to hold it with his fingers. He was holding it with both hands, one clutched on the other, when he fell. He was still staring at his belly and still not believing that there was a hole there.

A Shawnee with a red and green face . . . mouth wide open, yelling, as he leaped from the prow of another canoe to the parapet. A soldier jabbing at him with a bayoneted musket . . . and the bayonet going neatly and precisely into the open mouth, a small thin spurt of steely red light. The bayonet withdrawing . . . and, like a counterthrust, a thin spurt of bright blood following it from the mouth, still open.

Fireball falling squarely on a drumhead . . . the boy with the drum hung to his neck just standing there while the fire licked at his white crossbelts . . . never knew how long he stood there.

Holden saw John Fraser split a Mingo's head wide open with an ax. Saw another Mingo seize the string of Fraser's bullet holder . . . Fraser's head jerk forward . . . Indian pulling himself up the parapet . . . or else Fraser dragging him up by the cord around his own neck. No room for the ax. The Indian's maul lifted. Holden slashed his knife across the cord. The Indian toppled backward off the wall.

John Fraser saw Chris Holden leaning over the wall. Reaching. Seizing a Shawnee by his braided scalplock, hauling him off the bottom of an elm-bark, lifting him up . . . Didn't see what happened. Too damned many of the squawling, crawling devils. Fingers clutching at the stone edge of the ramparts. The ax slicing through one set of fingers. Gun butt smashing other fingers. Red mash . . . look out . . . slippery. . . .

The flames on the barrack roofs were not licking tongues now. They were rags blowing on a shrieking harridan's skirt. They were torn and tattered. You could hear them tearing. They burned with long ripping sounds in the dry shingles. The roof of the officers' barracks behind Holden wore a garment of flame. When he threw himself back from the parapet edge, once, he saw a woman's bare feet in the garment. *Abby . . . Abby . . .* He did not know. For him, that was the worst of the madness, the last awfulness of the delirium.

It was over in ten minutes. As quickly as they came, the painted faces were gone from the parapets. The bodies slithered down the sloping walls. They dropped into the dark pit and you saw them briefly, running, in the burst of a grenade. When the next grenade exploded there was only the smoke writhing and the dark carcasses of the canoes piled crazily, their snouts smashed and twisted, their backs broken, scaly hides torn and the ribs protruding.

The roofs burned for a long time after the last shot was fired. When morning came the Indians were gone.

Chris Holden looked at Fraser, leaning with his chest against the parapet and his head hanging as if he had just been sick. His face looked yellow. There was a long cut down one cheek, a straight gully through the underbrush of whiskers. Where it crossed his jaw, the flesh had pulled apart. The bone showed above the lump of dried blood plastered to his chin. The bone was not white, it was yellow. Every minute or two another drop of blood ran slowly down the gully and dripped over his jawbone. Holden wanted to ask how the cut had happened, but he thought that John was sleeping on his feet.

When he looked along the wall, he saw that all the faces had the same yellow-sick look. They were pinched, drawn, wasted, shrunken, puffy, swollen, red-eyed. They belonged to people who had been sick for a long time.

Holden was looking at the gash in Fraser's cheek again, wondering vaguely why the blood kept dripping, when the two Royals came along the wall and halted just behind him. He didn't know that they were there till one of them reached out and took his rifle. When he turned, Baillie was standing with his heels together and his round chin lifted so high that the skin on his neck was pulled tight. His neck was very dirty.

Baillie looked steadily at something over Holden's head.

"Sorry, sir," he said. "You are under arrest."

"Uh?"

"Will you come along, sir?"

Fraser did not wake up as they marched him off.

The descent into the dungeon shocked him. Not because he was arrested and they were going to lock him up there, nor because the Royals' heels made no sound on the last six steps—steps too thickly plastered with old flood silt. He was shocked because it was so cool and damp. *Cool.* He had forgotten there was such a thing as coolness.

Chapter 51

Stair Carre had only half a face. The flambeau he carried laid its red light on the one side of his forehead and his nose and left the other side in darkness.

Like that Mingo, Chris thought. *The one that John killed.* His head felt like the silted floor, thick, soft, crusted over. He could not break through the crust of sleep upon it. Stupidly, and knowing he was being stupid, he put up his hand and tried to push away the dark and see the whole of Carre's face. But the dark was solid. It was made of metal. *An ax,* he thought. He took his hand down from the bars.

"Punishment cell," Carre said. "Hurrying things, rather. Might have waited till you've been found guilty. Still—daresay it's sensible. It saves a sentry. No need for a guard here."

"Have you seen her? Does she know, Stair?"

"Yes, I've seen her. She knows. She sends you her love." Carre added: "I suppose you know the charges."

"Baillie read them to me."

"He gets all the dirtiest assignments. Who d'you want for counsel?"

"I hadn't thought." He thought now. He had seen enough of British army cliques and jealousies and favoritism to know how little a man's merit counted. Stair Carre was a regular officer, his whole life was the army. But Stair lacked the two essentials for promotion—influential friends and money to buy higher rank; after seventeen years he was still only a captain lieutenant by Ecuyer's temporary order. Defending a provincial on these ugly charges might well mean, for Carre, the end of his career. "Leslie," he said. "Leslie has been through it."

"Leslie's gone. He slipped out last night to try to get a message to Bouquet. The last message, likely. The food magazine is empty. We're done, Chris, unless help comes this week." Then, irrelevantly: "Leslie's married. On the Ohio bastion, three hours before he went. His wife doesn't know yet that he's gone. Thank God I'll not be the one to tell her. He hasn't got a chance."

"No." *I'd not have done that. Go, yes. But not that way.* Abby would not want somebody else to tell her. *Together.* It was her word. She had said it when he tried to leave her in the ravine below Venango. *Together . . . always . . . all ways.*

"Well." Carre was brusque. He was damning himself for the careless cruelty of talking about marriage. "Leslie *is* gone."

"Boyd, then. Boyd defended Leslie."

"He'll not leave Ecuyer."

"As bad as that?"

"He's afraid it was a poisoned arrow. See here, Chris, maybe I went off at half-cock. Took it for granted, rather. Shouldn't have, but—— D'you see, I've already told Burns that I'll be your counsel."

"Thanks, Stair. You shouldn't have. But I'd be lying if I said I didn't want you. Burns—wasn't he judge advocate at Leslie's trial?"

"He was. What's more, he's the one who said, when it was over, that charges could have been drawn up to convict Leslie."

"They acquitted Leslie."

"Of desertion, yes."

"Cowardice, too."

"You're not charged with that. Arnold was a fool. The man who drew these charges isn't. Don't forget that Leslie was acquitted on a technicality—a whole string of technicalities. Not one of them applies to you. You were on active duty, assigned to regular troops—to Bouquet himself. Even on the one charge of desertion, it could be a near thing."

"I came back."

"Yes." Carre's whistle made a thin wail in the tunnel. "That may help. It's the other charges."

"Aren't they all the same thing?"

"I don't know. And I can't find out. I asked Captain Ehrlich—he's assigned as the judge advocate. He said if I wanted explanations, I should ask you—you'd know what you'd done. I don't like it. These charges took a bit of doing. They weren't drawn up in five minutes. They've been ready, waiting for the proper moment. That's what shogs me. That, and the way they're worded. 'Willful disobedience of orders' could be part of the first charge. But 'gross neglect of duty to the peril of His Majesty's garrisons on the Ohio frontier' can't be. I know what your orders were. I heard 'em. You and Fraser were assigned to help Major Trent seize horses and haul in the timber from the houses. Damn it, Chris, you could have disobeyed those orders twenty times without imperiling the garrison. And it's not *one* garrison—it's plural. 'To the peril of His Majesty's *garrisons*.' That doesn't mean desertion, Chris. There's something else. There's got to be. But what? What?"

"You said Leslie's married."

"What's that got to do with it?"

"Nothing—with the charges. A good deal, with Abby. She's mine, Stair. I bought her and I paid for her. Ecuyer said he'd give me time to prove it. Hold him to his promise. No matter what happens, hold him to it until Bouquet gets here. I've just thought that Bouquet knows about her. He heard Garth admit in public that I'd bought her. In Williamsburg—on the steps of the Raleigh Tavern. Colonel Washington heard him too. So did Richard Henry Lee and Daniel of St. Thomas Jenifer and Nehemiah Andrews. They'll remember. They'll remember the price—a hundred and three pounds and sixpence. Jenifer said, 'That's ten hogsheads, prime.' Tobacco, he meant."

"Bouquet would be a plenty. But——"

"You're thinking that Bouquet won't get here."

"No. That's one thing I'll *not* think. I'm thinking about what you said: 'No matter what happens.' If it goes wrong, Chris——"

"I know. She'll still be a convict, to be sold again."

"Yes."

"There's a way, Stair." Then, suddenly, he was not sure. "Who married Leslie?"

"Why, the girl he——"

"No. No. Who performed the service?"

"The little missionary, Muller."

"Then there *is* a way. I thought Steele might have done it, as the acting governor. . . . You said there's no sentry. If somebody could bring Muller . . . No, not you, Stair. You've too much to lose. John Fraser———"

"Fraser couldn't get her out of barracks, Chris. I can—and I will. But why? What's the good? It might make things worse for her."

"If they shoot me? No. It would be her one chance. If it's proved I own her . . . Don't you see, Stair? If it's proved she's married to the man who owned her, she'd be free."

He heard them coming. *Careful . . . being careful.* No torch, this time. Only footsteps, soft, slow. They made little crunchings on the silt crust. They made little suckings. Only two sets of footsteps. Neither one hers. *Carre couldn't get her out.*

"Chris. . . ." John Fraser's whisper, thick as darkness. Fingers touching his face. Abby's fingers. "I'm carryin' her. Carre's waitin' up above in case somebody comes. We got t' make it quick. They're puttin' on a sentry at taptoo. It's near dark a'ready." He had supposed it was the middle of the night.

Other whisper. Thick, too. Hurrying . . . trying to hurry. Johann Muller's tongue made little suckings in its hurry.

"Do you, Christopher Holden, take this woman———"

"Yes." He held the slim hand tight against his mouth. *"Yes."* Her fingers heard him.

"Do you, Abigail Martha Hale———"

"Yes."

Her hand gone. Her mouth there instead.

". . . no man put asunder."

And her mouth gone now. The careful footsteps going. He thought: *Every time I've kissed her I knew it might be the last time.*

Chapter 52

The court-martial of Major Arnett Leslie on June twenty-sixth had been a military spectacle—a ritual for drums and halberds. With such pomp and circumstance as the resources of the fort allowed, it followed the impressive ceremonial form prescribed to lend the King's own majesty to the King's regulations.

It had been a form in more than one sense. Some of the questions asked at Leslie's trial suggest that even the judge advocate knew what was coming and helped Boyd prepare his climax.[1]

[1] The story of Major Leslie's trial, his sudden plea of guilty that terrified Diantha Gaillard, and the maneuver by which Dr. Boyd turned the prosecution's evidence into a defense, is told in *The Judas Tree*. It may seem remarkable that in a besieged fort the time and strength of officers was spent on two courts-martial. The fact is that between June twenty-sixth and August fifth there were not merely two, but five.

But there was no pomp at the trial of Captain Christopher Holden on the fifth of August. Forty days of siege had changed things.

There was no flour now to white the hair of the five officers who sat as judges at the table facing the railed platform and the portrait of the King. They were men who had gone sleepless almost to the end of their endurance. They were men who had fought to the end of hope, and past it. Their bellies gnawed them, and their minds were gnawed now by the dread of what was coming if Bouquet did not come quickly.

Two of them were wounded. Three had wives in Fort Pitt, and two of the three had children. The judge advocate had seven children. He, too, had been wounded. His right arm, broken between wrist and elbow by a hatchet, was a bundle of soiled rags and slivery splints chopped from the staves of a brine barrel. He had taken the arm out of its sling and laid it carefully on the small table that flanked the row of judges, and his left hand nursed it as he stared out through a shattered window.

In the silence, unbelievable after the five days and nights of constant guns, the crying of the children crawled out of the casemates. It came through the broken windows and lay in the room. It changed as little as the smutted shapes of smoke upon the wall. But it had been changed: it was not as loud as it was a week ago.

The court sat at two o'clock. Nobody in Fort Pitt knew that at one o'clock Bouquet's relieving column had been ambushed.

Captain Ehrlich stooped and slid the black sling at his neck around his splinted arm. His empty sleeve flapped as he rose to summon his first witness.

"I call Major Trent."

Stair Carre leaned to Holden at their own small table facing Ehrlich's.

"Shrewd," he whispered. "You see what he's up to. He could use any one of twenty officers to prove the same things he can get from Trent. But Trent's your friend and the court knows it."

Trent came in escorted by a sergeant of the grenadiers. He looked straight at Holden as he took the oath. And then, when it was finished, his hand moved to the salute.

"By the Lord," Carre murmured, "the court knows where *he* stands."

Chris Holden was aware of a sudden tightness in his throat. He was aware also of an enormous irony as Trent turned to the platform. It was to be a witness box now. And he was being tried for doing what Ecuyer had compelled him to do by keeping him on that platform, a prisoner, while Garth took Abby to the Gilded Beaver.

Ehrlich's opening questions were routine. Name . . . rank . . . inform the court of any unusual occurrences that came to your attention on the night of May twenty-eighth . . . inform the court concerning any orders given to you. . . .

"Were certain officers placed under your direction, Major?"

"Yes, sir."

"Name them to the court."

"Captain Holden and Lieutenant Fraser."

"What were their duties?"

"To assist me."

"And did they assist you?"

"They did."

"Indeed. State the nature of the assistance you received from Captain Holden."

"He got through to Fort Venango when nobody else could."

"I see. You regard that as assistance, Major?"

"I do. He was too late to warn the garrison, but he returned to Fort Pitt with important information."

"Is it not true that the same information had already been received?"

"It is not, sir. Captain Holden brought the first intelligence of the means by which the fort was taken."

"Captain Holden is accused of deserting his post."

"He did not desert it. What he did has my complete approval."

"Do you wish the court to understand that you ordered him to go?"

"No, sir. I approved his going."

"I see." Ehrlich's thumb and finger picked at a frayed edge of bandage. "Major Trent, *when* did you give your approval?"

"Immediately, sir. As soon as I was told of his intention."

"Captain Holden told you?"

"No. Lieutenant Fraser."

"At that time, Major, where was Captain Holden?"

"In Pitt's Town."

"Did you see him?"

"It did not occur to me to see him. Fraser told me Captain Holden hoped to get through to Bouquet. I believed if anyone could do it, he could. I repeat, sir, I approved his conduct. I did and I do, sir."

"That will be all, Major. You may stand down. I ask the court to instruct Major Trent to hold no communication with other witnesses. Sergeant, call Lieutenant Fraser."

"It's too good," Carre whispered. "Too good. Talk of angels standing on a needle! That's the thinnest truth that a man ever stood on. If he'd only told me! Or if he told John . . . But I'd swear he didn't see how he could use the truth to help you until Ehrlich asked that question about ordering you to go."

A torn scrap of gray cartridge paper hid the gash in Fraser's cheek. The dried blood held it, but the edges wriggled as he took the oath. He leaned with both hands on the railing, his big head thrust forward. At the first question he was fighting.

"When and where did you last see the accused on——"

"On the east wall, day b'fore yest'day." It was true. The dungeon, last night, had been much too dark for seeing. "He was fightin' like ten wildcats. He'd just histed up a Shawnee by the back hair an'——"

Ehrlich cut him short.

"The witness will be silent till the question is completed. The question is: when and where did you see Captain Holden on the night of May twenty-eighth?"

"Right here. He was standin' right here where I'm standin'."

"Did you or did you not see Captain Holden in the Gilded Beaver?"

"Yes. It was the twenty-ninth, though. It was gettin' on towards mornin'." Maybe that would make the court think Chris had carried out the most part of his orders.

"What was he doing?"

"He was tryin' t' find a white girl that a British officer had turned over to a polecat an'——"

"The witness will use proper language."

"That's the properest language I c'n think of f'r a white man that'd hand a woman over t' th' Mingoes."

Ehrlich broke in with another sharp admonishment, but Fraser plunged ahead.

"By God, I swore t' tell th' truth. I'm tellin' it! You ain't go'n' t' like it, but it's back o' this whole business. There's a witness. Love, his name is. He was there when Martin Garth turned her over. He saw Guyasuta in the Gilded Beaver."

"Guyasuta." Ehrlich smiled. There were other brief smiles on the weary faces in the row along the table. The idea of Guyasuta being in town on the night of the massacre at Clapham's was preposterous. "Now, Lieutenant, you say it was getting on toward morning when you were with Captain Holden at the Gilded Beaver."

"That's right."

"You went there together?"

"That's right."

"Directly from the fort?"

"Yes." What in hell was Ehrlich trying to get at?

"I see. You were with the accused continuously from the time you saw him in this room until you, or one of you, left the Gilded Beaver. Inform the court whether during that time either of you spoke to Major Trent."

"No."

"That will be all. You may stand down."

"All! I ain't even started! I ain't told you——"

"The witness possibly has told the court more than he intended. Stand down, Mr. Fraser." Ehrlich turned to the long table. "I ask the court to notice that this testimony makes it clear that Major Trent used the word 'approval' in a very broad sense. Quite obviously he did not give his approval to the conduct of the accused in advance. He had no knowledge of it. The man Love mentioned by Lieutenant Fraser is already on the list of witnesses. Sergeant, bring in Jeremy Love."

Question . . . question . . . *convict* . . . *thief* . . . *pickpocket* . . . *bond slave* . . . came to Pitt's Town in May . . . *yes* . . . perhaps you were previously acquainted with Guyasuta . . . *heard his name*. Question. Answer. Question. And then:

"I see. You were thrown down the well. And from the bottom of the well you saw Mr. Garth turn this woman over to these Indians. A soldier who swears falsely may be punished with a thousand lashes. A transported felon——" Ehrlich shrugged. "Did you see Captain Holden leave the Gilded Beaver?"

"Yes."

"Where was he going?"

"I don't know."

"Oh. You don't know. Did you hear any conversation between the accused and Mr. Fraser?"

"No, sir."

"I will ask the court to warn the witness. Now, Love—you have one more chance to answer."

"They were talking, but I didn't hear them." Jeremy Love's face was the color of the cartridge paper on John Fraser's cheek. His face was grayish strips between its wrinkles. His sweat glued the strips together. "A gentleman does not eavesdrop." His attempt at dignity was neither funny nor pathetic. It was merely absurd. In the end Captain Ehrlich got what he was after. Jeremy Love, in his anxious dodging, tripped himself on his own shrewdness. He said Fraser had told Captain Holden that the roads were guarded.

"That will do. Remove him, Sergeant. I ask the court to notice that by the testimony of this friendly witness the accused was planning to desert. He discussed the means with Fraser. His desertion was deliberate and willful disobedience of orders. I call Ensign Price."

Price was haggard. He spoke firmly, but his hand shook as he took the oath. He, too, one day would be facing a court-martial.

"You were the officer commanding Fort Le Boeuf?"

"Yes, sir."

"Your post was attacked by Indians on the night of June the eighteenth?"

"On the eighteenth, yes, sir. But it was in the morning. We held them off till——"

"You are not upon your trial, sir. *Before* you were attacked were you invited to surrender?"

"No, sir. They——"

"Confine yourself to answering the questions. The savages did not come to you with a white flag?"

"No, sir."

"When you withdrew from Fort Le Boeuf, did you pass Fort Venango?"

"Yes, sir."

"What was its condition?"

"It had been burned, sir. The gate had been broken down. The garrison had been wiped out. We counted fourteen bodies."

"Did you see a white flag?"

"No, sir."

Ehrlich picked up from the table a small packet neatly tied with red tape. He undid the tape and dropped it and unfolded slowly the torn half of a bed sheet.

"Did you see this?"

"No, sir."

"Captain Holden claims he found it lying in plain sight on the parade ground at Venango. You are quite sure that you did not see it?"

"Yes, sir."

"You . . . did . . . not . . . see it?"

"No, sir."

354

Stair Carre leaned to Chris. His face was cheerful but his murmur anxious.

"I was right. They're not counting on desertion. The white flag business . . . Ehrlich's trying to discredit you. He's leading up to something. Whatever it is, it'll come now."

It came.

"Sergeant, bring in the woman known as Abigail Martha Hale."

"Steady, Chris." Carre's knee touched Holden's. "They were bound to call her. Maybe I'm wrong. Maybe they've got nothing but desertion. There's nothing else that she can testify to. If that's all, she'll help you."

She came in with her head high, but her legs were trembling. She looked at Chris once and then looked away. *Don't . . . don't let them see how much I love him. They'll know that I'd lie for him.* If only she knew which lies were the right ones. But she didn't.

Her legs were heavy as she climbed the two steps to the platform. They were almost as slow and heavy as when the iron bars were on them. She was in the dock again. It was wooden like the dock in the Old Bailey. *But it's lower.* There were no tall iron spikes in the railing. There was nothing to hold on by. She held tightly to the beaded necklace. *There are spikes, though.* They were on the muzzles of the soldiers' muskets. Muskets like bars, upright, black against the windows. No glass in the windows. *It's like Newgate.* Judges in a row. She counted them. Five. *I had three.* Five red coats. *I had only one judge that wore red.*

The officer with his arm in a black sling was walking toward her. *The judge had a black cap.* He was laying the arm on the rail beside her. The ends of the splints curved up out of the dirty bandage. They had little grooves. Pieces of a barrel. *I came to dance in this room, but they wouldn't let me. I had side hoops. Steel ones. But they wouldn't let me.*

"You are Abigail Martha Hale?"

"Yes." *I'm not. I'm Abigail Martha Holden.* But both Mr. Fraser and Captain Lieutenant Carre had told her that she must not say so.

"You are a convicted felon?"

"Yes."

"State the crime for which you were convicted."

"Murder." That shamed whisper! Mrs. Christopher Holden, felon. All her life there would be whispers. *My life.* Her life didn't count now. *I killed my brother. Now they want me to help kill my husband.*

"Murder." He was saying the word over. "You are not a thief?"

"No!"

His hand leaped out at her.

"Then where did you get this?" His fingers closed around the necklace.

"I didn't steal it!"

"Pah! I suppose you'll tell me Captain Holden gave it to you."

"Yes. He did."

"And this?" He touched the white belt.

"Yes."

"Oh well. If he gave them to you . . . I daresay he had more."

She knew now that she had said the wrong thing. It was true. She didn't know why it was wrong. She looked at Chris and he was smiling at her, warmly, loving her with his smile. Maybe what she'd said was right. It must be.

"Did he have more?"

"Yes."

"How many?"

"I don't know."

"Do you mean you didn't see them?"

"No. I didn't count them."

"Oh! There were so many that it would be needful to take count." His hand reached again. "Give me the belt."

"No!"

"Sergeant. . . . Remove that necklace and that belt. Put them on the table."

They had been her courage. They were gone now. *Chris. . . . Chris. . . . What have I done to you?* He was still smiling at her as they took her out. But Carre was not smiling.

Ehrlich walked slowly to the table. He picked up the belt and necklace. He dangled them as he talked:

"Witnesses have attempted to show that the accused did not desert his post. I ask the court to notice that desertion is not necessarily absence from a place of duty. It may also be abandonment of duty. Under the circumstances, the court might see fit to regard the charge of desertion as technical and to dismiss it—if it concerned only Captain Holden's absence from this post. It is much more serious."

The beads clashed on the table. Ehrlich picked up a folded paper.

"Here is an official letter addressed to Captain Ecuyer and signed by Colonel Bouquet. It sets forth the nature of a special duty to which Captain Holden was assigned. He was entrusted with a mission of the gravest importance. He was entrusted with peace belts and with strings of seawan to be delivered to the sachems of the Senecas, the Delawares, the Shawnees. . . ." Ehrlich threw the paper down. *"He did not deliver them!* He did not try to deliver them! He gave two of them to a female convict. There they are! She testified that he had many more.

"By leaving *this* post, Captain Holden put his own life in peril. He followed the woman to the Gilded Beaver. He attempted to escape with her. He was guilty of desertion. The just penalty is death. But before he left Fort Pitt he was already guilty of desertion by abandoning his duty. He was guilty of disobedience of orders. He was guilty of a gross neglect of duty to the peril of His Majesty's garrisons. Some of those garrisons are dead." Ehrlich's fist closed on the beads. "They are dead because the man on whom their lives depended used *these* to adorn a woman!"

Chapter 53

It took them until after dark to finish with him. He knew, long before they finished, what the end would be. Not one scrap of evidence for his defense. Joe Lovatt's pouch, cut up for Abby's feet. Dan McCoy's carved powder horn, left in the woods by Guyasuta's town. Dave Bone testifying . . . no pouch . . . no powder horn. The pouch, dripping from the bucket, wrapped in Abby's apron, hidden, and no one but she and he to swear it. Garth on the stand, adding details to that letter from Bouquet. Suave, regretful, keeping a hard hold on his indignation, letting it show just enough for show. The court believing him: his wife was dead, and somehow that was all the warranty he needed. No—nothing said in Williamsburg about McCoy or Lovatt. Their names never mentioned by Bouquet or Holden either. And Lovatt and McCoy were skeletons, the vines were tugging at them.

Likely it was fair that he should die. He had killed Joe and Dan in the same way Abby killed her brother. If she had not gone to London . . . If he had not gone to Williamsburg . . . *No,* he thought, *it started before that. If I hadn't gone to London, they would be alive.*

He had a moment with Carre while the guard was being called in, after it was finished. Carre saying:

"Not done yet. The verdict isn't final. It will be reviewed."

"Who will review it?"

"Under ord'n'ry circumstances, Amherst."

"They're not ordinary."

"No. It could be the officer commanding the department. It could be Bouquet. My God! Cut off, with Ecuyer wounded, it could be Steele."

He had looked at death a many times before and been afraid. He was afraid now.

He had waited for it through a many nights as dark as this one. Walked toward it, when that was the thing to do. Slept quite comfortably, sometimes, while he waited for it in uncomfortable places. Neither the one thing nor the other had a great deal to do with courage. It was a matter of balance: a second fear to counterweight the other. He had always been a little more afraid of being afraid.

The counterweight was gone now. There were still two fears, but both were on the same side of the balance. His own death. Abby's life. Of all the deaths a man could die, shooting was the easiest and quickest. And when you were dead it likely didn't make much difference who had done the shooting. If Stair Carre lived and Ecuyer lived and kept his promise, Abby would be safe. She would have the house in Norfolk and the land at World's End.

The grating of the key in the rust-fouled lock fetched him awake. *Key.* He did not know how long he had been sleeping. *Cut off . . . Ecuyer wounded . . . it could be Steele.* He had thought that even Steele would take a decent time about it. *Dark.* They wouldn't come for him without a flambeau. The door opening. Too dark to see it. Panting whisper:

"Captain Holden."

He felt along the wall to find the door. His hand touched a bundle of damp rags with an arm inside it.

357

"Jeremy Love, sir. At your service, sir. A most fortunate accident. I found some keys. Keys always fascinate me. Couldn't resist——"

"Found them?" This was some of Stair Carre's doing.

"Yes, sir. The officer of the guard jostled me, sir—quite unavoidable. A black night. A very black night. I found keys in my hand. Quite a number of them."

"Who is officer of the guard?"

"Lieutenant Baillie, sir."

Baillie!

"Did he know you took them?"

"I explained, sir. It was an accident. Never fear—he shall have the keys back and no one the wiser. No end of people bumping into each other on a night like this."

"He'll get the blame."

"Oh no. No indeed. I have a bit of iron in my cuff, sir. In fact, two bits. Pieces of Mr. Fraser's crowfoots—crows'-feet. Confusing, these new names, to an old man, sir. I shall leave one in the lock of this door and another on the floor of the tunnel to the postern. Most fortunate about the keys, sir. Mr. Fraser fetched the trap and bent the iron, but it might have taken a deal of experiment. We could not be certain how much time we had, sir. Come along. To the foot of the steps first."

"The sentry. . . ."

"He will . . . ah . . . be removed. Oh, not violently. No indeed, sir. Merely distracted for the moment. He already has been, long enough for me to slip in. You have friends, sir. Many of them. When the guard passes on its next rounds a pebble will be tossed down the steps. We shall have a good half minute. Twenty steps, ten seconds—more than ample to cut by the sentry. Timing is the essence of deception. Then three minutes to the postern, walking slowly. I shall count, sir. The guard requires two and a half minutes from the dungeon entrance to the west end of the governor's house. When it has gone by, there will be another small distraction."

"Jeremy, does she know about this?"

"Oh no, sir. It would be the greatest happiness of my life to tell her. You recall that I brought this trouble on her—on you both, sir—aboard ship. But it seemed best to avoid the least chance of suspicion. Chive me, sir, I was near forgetting. A pistol—in my waistcoat. There you are, sir. And a knife. We considered a rifle, but——" A small sound spatted on the trampled silt. "Now, sir."

The door of the sally port closed behind him. He stood with his back to the narrow door and waited. Made himself wait until he heard the gritty-solid rhythm of the guard passing on its next rounds. With its sound to cover him, he took the footbridge in a hard burst of running.

He lay still for a long time, listening. So quiet. The least noise enormous in the quiet. Sound like a tired sigh; a mud boil collapsing as the gas inside it oozed out. *Even hear the mud flats breathing.* Sudden bottle of sound being opened. Hollow sound. Being opened in a cellar. Only the cry of a shitepoke in a swamp downriver, but it sounded as if a deep-chested man was being strangled, as if he had squeezed one wild sound past the hands that choked him.

Chris began to crawl. The dry dirt slid. It talked excitedly about him. *Can't crawl. Quieter to walk.* He stood up and began to walk. Slow step. Foot feeling for the talkative earth, the earth saying *hssh.* Step and wait and slow step. The ground smooth and hard now. The Monongahela mud flat baked to a brick hardness in the sun's kiln.

The earth softening. Sloping gently downward, turning moist. Wet, suddenly. Water a thin coolness under his feet. He walked up the gully of the stream that came down past Perdition. Wherever the Indians were, they wouldn't be lying in this gully. If they hadn't quit or gone to meet Bouquet, they likely had pulled back into their camps. He heard Ehrlich's voice, sarcastic: *walked right into Guyasuta's town and out again.*

When he came to the place where the log bridge had been, he climbed up into the King's Road. He walked up the road. Ehrlich probably would not believe that either.

He was on the hills above the Turtle Creek gorge when he heard the firing.

It was not like firing. It was more like a man muttering in his sleep, slobbering a little, his tongue going *tl'hh . . . tl'hh* in his sticky mouth. Chewing his teeth, dull clicks and grindings. Waking himself with his own sleep noises, turning over, muttering again. And then snoring in hard, rasping snorts. There were sinking, bubbly gasps between them.

Only one kind of firing made a sound like that. Disciplined guns. Musket fire by demi-platoons. Echoes shuddering between the volleys.

Ambushed. That was why the Indians were gone from Fort Pitt.

Turtle Creek gorge was a trap—a box trap fifteen miles long. He had taken to the hills at daylight because a man had small chance in that narrow, rock-walled, twisting valley. Little chance for one man in that rabbit burrow. Less chance for many men, in column on a road. He began to run toward the sound of firing.

As he ran, it ceased.

He burst out of the woods and looked down across the naked shoulder of a hill into the deep gash of the gorge. You could see how the gash had been made: the bright blade that had cut through the hills was still there in the wound: Turtle Creek was a thin steely gleam. The road lay beside it, narrow shadow cast by the thin blade. But the road was empty and the gorge was empty. He began to run again across the open ground. He climbed the ridge above the gullet of the gorge. A dark juice trickled through it.

He went down on his face on the rim rock and watched the brown slobber of Indians dribbling down the road. They came in a thin stream with a kind of froth upon it—deer-hair crests of Mingoes, fuzzy Shawnee scalplocks, the Ojibway wolf tails, the horned Ottawas, feathers twirling in bone sockets, feathers sticking upright in hair roached with mud, dangling Huron feathers. There were hundreds of them, trotting. There was something purposeful about them. *Going back to Fort Pitt.*

There were other matters in the froth that floated on the brown stream. Scalps on sticks, not dry yet, dangling wetly. Other hairy things tied to the muzzles of their muskets: Highland sporrans. Other feathers drooping from dark Highland bonnets. *Going back to finish.* . . .

All the coils of his insides were crawling. They were squirming upward, trying to escape from the hot sickness that possessed them. They squeezed a scalding juice into his throat. He pressed his face into the rock and let it come. When the earth stopped squirming under him, he raised his head. The brown stream in the gorge was gone. There was another on the rock where his face had been lying. He wiped his mouth. His hand was like a claw. It was rigid from its clutching at the rock. The finger ends were white.

The bodies lay on the slope of a low hill. They had no legs. He thought, at first, they were white boulders.

The Highlanders on the slope had fallen as they charged. They lay face down. Their kilts had been flung forward as they fell. Their sunburned legs were the same color as the sun-scorched grass. Only their buttocks gleamed white in the sun.

Beyond them, men lived. He did not believe it. But they moved. They walked through the thickets, searching. Now and then they stopped. They stooped. They turned and went back up the hill, bent over, carrying other men who must be living.

He came to the first swathe of dead and saw that they had not been scalped. *Beat them,* he thought. *Beat them!* There were naked bodies that did not gleam whitely. Burned-grass-colored bodies.

Trees at the top of the hill. More dead men. Decently dead. Laid out in a row with their kilts to cover them. But the white shine of bone above their foreheads, trickles of blood down their faces, squirming there like knots of black worms. So many dead Highlanders. So few Indians among them. *So few living white men.* This had not been a massacre. It had not been Braddock's ford or Grant's Hill. But he knew, before he came to the meal-sack breastworks and the dead horses and the rows of wounded, that this was a crippled army. The men who moved dazedly about this hilltop would not make a column half as long as that savage stream he had seen rushing westward toward the Forks.

The meal sacks made a kind of low wall that ran crookedly around the hilltop. Not a whole wall—pieces. Gaps were patched with hacked-off tree limbs and packsaddles, a half-rotten log, a horse's body with an Indian dead in the embrace of its forelegs.

The wounded lay in rows behind the barricade. The dead horses were everywhere. You could see how the attack had started: the wreckage of the pack train was strewn down the east side of the hill on both sides of the road and in it. The horses that had been saved were roped together here, inside the barricade; the reek of the soaked ground and human filth washed over the long rows of wounded men.

Bouquet was sitting on a log with a drum between his legs and his dispatch case on the drumhead. A big man in a brown hunting shirt with darker brown thrums on the sleeves and shoulders sat beside him.

They looked up, and Chris Holden thought again of Ehrlich. *Have me shot twice if I told him this.* The big man was Pollexfen.

Bouquet was first to his feet. His hand was eager.

"Captain Holden! From Fort Pitt?"

"Yes, sir. I escaped."

"Escaped! It is not taken?"

"No." He hadn't meant to use that word. "Not yet. But it can't last long. There's been no food for three days. We had them at us night and day from the twenty-eighth——"

"Yes. Yes, I know. Major Leslie came to us by Stony Creek. I am writing now a message to Ecuyer."

"Writing!"

"You think, then, I should go on. It is impossible."

"It's not impossible for Indians. They're making for Fort Pitt. They'll be there tonight. One more night like the last one——"

"For Indians it is possible. For us, no. I have lost a quarter of my army. I have fifty dead men. Perhaps more; I do not yet know."

"My God, sir! You're not turning back?"

"No. The army will remain here. I have also sixty wounded. I do not intend to leave them. I have left my wagons at Fort Ligonier. So soon as they can be brought, we will move. Perhaps in three days. Until then, no. But the Royals—they will hold on. This letter that I write will help."

"They can't eat a letter."

"But yes! My Royals? Of a certainty they can!"

"May I take it, sir?"

"Ah! You do not change, Captain. You speak the mind and then ask for trouble."

"I was wrong. The letter's more important than food."

"Yes. I have already one man who has volunteered. The man called Miller, who came yesterday from Fort Pitt."

"It's been easy to get out these last three nights. It may not be tomorrow. I got in once when it wasn't. I can get in again."

"Good. Good. In an hour. This quartermaster that you sent me—I think if you ask him he will feed you."

"Certainly I'm quartermaster." Ellerby Pollexfen's face was cherry red from sunscald, but it had lost nothing of its plumpness or its bland assurance. "Good one. Best one in whole army, likely."

"It's impossible. You're not here, Polly."

"What's impossible about it? You're here."

"But for God's sake, why? How?"

"Your fault. Waited for you in Philadelphia. Didn't come. Heard Indians were up. Thought you might be in it. Heard Bouquet was in town. Went to see him, found out where you'd gone. Found out something else, too. Colonies may be diff'rent from England every other way—government the same. Slow. Blind. Stupid. Lazy. Damn it, Chris, the Pennsylvania assembly and the gov'nor's council wouldn't lift a hand to help him. Wouldn't lift their backsides off their chairs to go see whether he was tellin' truth. Said he was exaggeratin'. Said Indians were nice people.

361

Mustn't hurt 'em. Mustn't be too hasty about sendin' troops—might hurt their feelin's."

"I've heard that before."

"Bouquet needed wagons. Needed horses—wanted four hundred. All he'd got was twelve. Needed powder, flour, shoes. Needed everything. Couldn't get it. Merchants wouldn't help. Said they doubted Bouquet had authority to pay 'em. Said they wouldn't get their money. Thing he needed most was man of business to be quartermaster. Took me."

"Polly, you fool! You told *me* it was dangerous to go wandering around by myself in London."

"Was. Got head broken. Diff'rent with me. Wasn't by myself. Wasn't wanderin'. Knew where I was goin'. Went." Holden knew what Pollexfen was going to say. He said it: "Simple."

Chapter 54

An hour after daylight a white flag poked up from the cellar hole of Captain Basset's house. It stayed there for a while, not moving. Nothing moved.

There was no sound anywhere except the breathy mutter of men's cursing as they watched it. But that one sound, all the mutters put together, made a kind of moaning. That white thing hanging there was hard to bear. In the last five days of quiet, the hope that the Indians weren't coming back had grown almost into a conviction.

Now a Mingo's head poked up beside the flag. You could see his single feather twirling. When he was dead sure that he wasn't going to be shot at, he climbed out of the cellar and began to twirl the white cloth. The way it fluttered, it looked like the half of a man's ruffled shirt. The sleeves were gone, but you could see there had been places for them.

The Mingo started calling for McKee. When the interpreter stood up on the rampart of the Grenadier, five other Indians climbed out. McKee spoke to them in Seneca. Then he turned and looked down at Steele in the group of officers behind him.

"They want to talk again. All six of 'em."

"Who are they?"

Contempt showed in McKee's face. Steele was one of those blind-stupid officers that had never learned to tell one redstick from another.

"They've all of 'em been here two-three times a'ready. Guyasuta. White Eyes. Custaloga. Wingenum and Windahola. Shingess." There was something else Steele ought to know. He'd ought to know it without being told. "They're all Delawares and Mingoes."

"Very well." Steele's voice was more than ever like a thin slate. His tongue scrawled on it dryly. "I'll talk to them as long as they will talk." The thin slate was laid over an enormous emptiness. "Any time that we can gain . . . A few hours . . ." He seemed to be talking to himself. He seemed to be listening to answers only he could hear. "Better than fighting . . . Let them in. . . ."

362

"Let them in!" Trent and Ehrlich and Carre echoed him together. All the echoes hollow-sounding. It was Ehrlich who protested: "You don't mean surrender?"

"I don't know. I'll hear what they have to say."

"What can they say except the same old lies?"

"Lies!" The chalk broke on the slate. Steele's tongue was thicker. "We don't know they're lying. Mr. McKee gives great credit[1] to what they told Ecuyer." He stared hard at Trent. "I believe you have been concerned in two surrenders. The Indians kept their word both times."

"Not the Indians," Trent said. "The French. I didn't surrender Fort Prince George. I wasn't there when it happened. It——"

"It was surrendered," Steele said.

"There was no choice. There was none at Fort Necessity. But it was the French who kept the Indians off us afterwards. If they hadn't——"

"No choice," Steele repeated. "You admit that there are times when there is no choice. Mr. McKee, tell the chiefs they may come in."

"You can't do that!" All the blood was gone from Stair Carre's face. The sun had burned his face too deeply for it to turn white. But the tight parchment of his skin aged suddenly. It yellowed. Even his hooked nose went yellow at the tip, the rest of it stayed brown. He tried to lick his dry lips, but his tongue felt stiff. It would not quite reach. "If you let them in, they'll see how near we are to being done."

"Captain Ehrlich, I will have the Royals formed on the parade. A square. Three sides—open toward the gate. The grenadier company excepted, Captain. Mr. Carre, you will have the grenadiers distributed along the Town wall. No militia on the Town curtain—I'll have no damned civilians firing on a flag of truce. Matrosses to remain on the bastions. Mr. Phillips, all militiamen to the other walls. No shooting—I make you responsible. Tell them that any man who fires a shot without command will never fire another. Mr. Hutchins, double sentries at the door of every barracks. That will make a better showing. Show them we have men to spare. . . . Better showing, better terms."

"For God's sake, sir!"

"Mr. Carre, I will remind you that you are a soldier. You will carry out your orders. Mr. Baillie, all the shutters to be closed. All the women to be kept in barracks. And a messenger to Mr. Garth. He may be useful. Guyasuta does not know his daughter has been killed."

"If you're going to let the chiefs in," Trent said, "we might make a show of breakfast." Someone laughed. Harsh, short sound. Bitter. "I mean it," Trent insisted. "If they see some of the women at the ovens and the cook fires——"

"You can't fool them that way. They've got noses."

"Beaver," Trent said. "Drop some beaver pelts into the kettles. *They'll* smell."

The drawbridge screeched. As it began to fall, the Indians outside set up a screeching. It was hard to tell the one sound from the other.

The Royals made a hollow square inside the gate. The square was not

[1]These words appear in a dispatch written by Ecuyer on June 18.

large. Its three sides were thin. Counting the eight drummer boys drawn out in a long rank in front of the right-hand side of the square, there were fewer than a hundred Royals.

A small table had been fetched out from the governor's house. It stood unevenly on the pebbly ground. Steele, sitting at the table, faced the gate. McKee sat on the other stool. Burns, Garth, Trent, and Ehrlich stood behind them. Five lieutenants and two ensigns made a longer row—Baillie, Greber, Fleming, Davenport and Christie, Price and Hutchins. They made the bottom of the square look thicker.

The windlass groaned. The ropes strained. The gate swung slowly upward, the bridge slowly downward. When the first streak of daylight showed between, the Indians screeched again, then were still.

The men at the windlass were not as strong as they had been. The bridge got away from them. It dropped the last few feet . . . *uhhhh.* Tired sound. Spent. Exhausted. There was a finality about it. The chains rattled hoarsely.

The six chiefs began to walk across the bridge.

"Guns," Burns said under his breath. "They've got guns. *God——*"

All the guns had bayonets fixed to them.

The chiefs held the muskets in their right hands, with the butts up. They stopped in front of the table. One by one, they drove the bayonets into the earth. The Tower muskets quivered on the slender steel. Guyasuta laid the white flag on the table; it had not been a shirt: it was a piece torn from a woman's underclothes. He began talking slowly. Loudly, so that every man in ranks could hear him.

"White man's army." Every word slow. Gritty. Each word like the dry crunch that the bayonets made, driving into the hard earth. "Not come. *He'onwe!*" His hand pointed at one of the muskets. "White man's army *there.*" He pointed at another and another. "There! There! All dead."

Guyasuta pulled a Highland bonnet from beneath his blanket. He hung it on one of the musket butts. Windahola hung another bonnet on another musket.

"White man's army—women." White Eyes drew a kilt from underneath his blanket. Guyasuta took it. He flung it at the gun that still swayed, with the Highland feather swaying. The kilt wrapped itself around the barrel, clung, slipped, and fell limply. "Dead. All dead."

Shingess threw a sporran down beside it. Wingenum stepped forward, and now a third musket had a bonnet. But the bonnet would not stay there. It was too small. It was dry and shriveling already. The stiff scalp fell off the musket butt. It lay red-and-black side up on the red and black plaid of the kilt.

A boy in the row of drummers said *uhhhh.* Then he fell, doubled over on his drum. The sticks made a dry rattling as they rolled.

Stair Carre stood in the embrasure on the Grenadier bastion that overlooked the gate and the redan, the bridges and the road cut through the glacis. There were Indians on the redan. Not many. More of them standing on both banks above the sunken roadway. The sun was behind them and their shadowed bodies looked black. *Buzzards,* he thought. A whole flock of buzzards at the turning of the King's Road. Other flock perched on the edges of the gully that ran past Perdition. *Carrion there for them.* He could smell the dark vines rotting on the chimney.

He looked down at the gunners kneeling by their pieces. Four guns. Cohorn loaded with shell. Grapeshot in the others—double loaded. Matches ready. *Why not?* You killed buzzards without even thinking. *Bastards.* . . . The two words ran together in his mind. *To hell with their white flag.* After all these weeks of lies and treachery and murder, the Indians still counted upon white men to return them good for evil. *To be damned fools.* . . . Their own promises were lies, but they still trusted white men's. *White men's honor.* . . . It had been the Indians' best weapon. Damned-fool white men thinking that all other men had the same odd notions about honor. The smell of the gunners' matches prickled in Carre's nostrils. The temptation prickled.

Blow them to hell. More vines for that chimney. He began to laugh. *Whole God-damned arbor. A grape arbor, by God!* He saw the gunners looking at him.

Stair Carre had, then, his own terrrifying moment of clear sanity. *Mutiny,* he thought. *That would be mutiny.* After seventeen disciplined years, he was standing here quite calmly and insanely planning how to disobey an order thoroughly and finally, completely.

But he knew he would not give the word to fire. Not now. He did not know what he'd do if Steele decided to surrender. *Think about that.* . . . There was something he could do about it. Not much. Gain time. *Time for what?* He didn't know that, either. But he walked to the Flag bastion quickly. He walked to the flagstaff and untied the halyards. He began to jerk them. Little ripples ran along the ropes. The flag jerked, slid a little. *Jam the halyards . . . can't be shot for that.* There . . . that did it. *Off the pulley.* . . . *Have to send somebody up to clear it . . . take time . . . give Steele time to change his mind.* Familiar voice behind him. Name it said also familiar. *Of course,* he thought wisely. *My own name.* The sergeant repeated it: "Captain Carre, sir. . . ."

He turned from the flagstaff, and the sergeant pointed. White men walking in the King's Road. Three white men, and they had no right to be there. Penalty for walking in that road. Death.

The three white men were not soldiers. They were the same color as the dusty road. Drab. Their shadows were more clearly outlined than their bodies . . . black shapes, face down in the dust.

Their shadows crawled in front of them. *No . . . moving too fast. Running on their bellies.* Smooth and quick and easy. *Hypped,* he thought. *I'm as hypped as Dr. Miller when he cut his throat. Seeing ghosts in day-light.* But the three men were still there. Still there . . . not ghosts. It didn't matter. They would be ghosts in a minute. They were almost to the gully by Perdition. Indians were all around them.

They would never run that gantlet. *Run it?* They were *walking* the gantlet of a hundred savages in war paint—walking calmly, side by side, between the two long rows that did not dare to lay a hand on them because the chiefs were in the fort.

But there was no telling about Indians. One crazy Indian could start it. Carre's body and mind ached with the desire to shout at them. *Run! Run!* He knew that if they ran they would be killed. It was their own calmness that was keeping them alive. If they ran, not even the lives of the six chiefs inside the fort would save them.

The three men came to the turning of the road. Their bodies made the turn. Their shadows didn't. The three quickly crawling shadows made one shadow now that moved along beside them. He saw that the nearest man was Miller. *Insane.* . . . It was a man named Miller that had cut his own throat, and all men named Miller must be insane.

The man in the middle wore a brown linen hunting shirt with darker brown fringe. The fringe swung confidently. He was a big man—more than a head taller than the man named Miller. He had a bright red face. Even at this distance it looked placid. He was so big that he hid the third man till they came to the last curving of the road. Stair Carre had only one quick glimpse of Holden. Then the sunken roadway hid all but the top half of the big man's head.

The three white men were on the inner bridge before the chiefs knew they were coming. Holden and Pollexfen halted under the gate timbers. Miller shouldered roughly between Wingenum and Shingess. His voice thrust against the aching stillness.

"A dispatch from Colonel Bouquet!" He handed it to Steele. "Bouquet fought them for two days and beat them!" He stared into unbelieving faces. "Great God in the mountain, can't you hear me? Can't you understand? Bouquet beat the breechclouts off 'em! He's only a day's march away. He's got food! *Food!* Four hundred horseloads!"

There was a sound at last, a long sigh running through the ranks of Royals. At Miller's shout the women left their make-believe of cooking. They were edging forward. And then they were running. Holden, searching for Abby's face among them, did not find it. But he saw Garth watching him across Trent's shoulder. Garth's face showed exactly nothing. The deep lines still tied it firmly.

Steele was saying something: *reasons for not trusting Captain Holden.* Miller stormed at him.

"Reasons! Reasons! You've got reasons, have you? If you'd listened to him in the first place—— Bouquet trusts him! Bouquet sent him back here. No, by God! He didn't send him. Holden *offered* to come back here. It's him that had the gall to walk right in here through that pack o' redsticks. Maybe if he hadn't, we'd of been too late." Miller snatched the torn white shift from the table. "What you doin' with this, Steele? I got a wife here! I went out an' risked my neck to save her an' you—— Good Christ, were you goin' to knuckle down to a few measly Delawares an' Mingoes? That's all there is out there! This here was their last trick. They're bluffin'! They're done an' they know it. And you'd ought to known it! There ain't an Ottawa or an Ojibway or a Shawnee or a Huron out there. They've pulled out. They crossed the river three miles up. Holden followed 'em across last night. They're gone, an' they ain't comin' back. They're splittin' up. They're makin' for their towns. *Good Christ!* Can't you read? Don't you know Bouquet's own writin'?"

Steele was staring at the paper as if he could not believe that it was in his hands. Miller flung himself around.

"Holden, tell this damned fool who we fetched in with us!"

"Colonel Bouquet's quartermaster." Still the numb, dazed, doubtful faces. *God . . . God . . .* would men never listen to the truth? Lies. It was lies they wanted. "Bouquet's got a thousand men! He'll be here in two hours!"

They believed that. He could see the blankness peeling off the faces of the Royals. They were disciplined men. After that first long sigh they made no sound at all. But there was other sound. He saw it beginning —the scream starting in a woman's scrawny throat, shaking the loose skin there. And he had seen that face before . . . before . . . It made no difference, but he remembered. Mrs. Pruitt hadn't screamed the night she brought her dead child to the King's birthday ball.

There were other faces. Young woman's face beginning to smile. Tears sliding crookedly into the creases. Whole face sliding downward. She was on her knees behind the Royals. *Thank God. Oh, thank God. Thank you, God. . . .* Men's faces too, now. Wolfish faces. Hairy, but the hair like animals' fur on them—their cheeks so sunken that the hair was matted tightly and the bones showed long and gaunt beneath it. Head back. Narrow jaws wide open. Black hair rippling on a long neck. Wild yell tearing at the roots of all the hairs.

The yell set off others. Barracks doors burst open. Shutters slammed back. Women running. Women at the windows. A crowd gathering behind the Royals. Bedlam now behind the upright bars of muskets. Screeches as insane as all the whoopings that would haunt this place forever. Howlings. Gun butts pounding the earth. Hollow earth a drum now, thudding.

The chiefs turned and walked slowly through the gallows frame of the gate timbers. Wilder howlings pealed up. *No . . . no! Bloody bastards! Don't lettem out . . . don't lettem!* The militiamen surged against the Royals' backs. The three sides of the square sagged inward. Then they steadied. The savage howling followed the six Indians across the bridges.

Holden, one hand gripped by both of Will Trent's and the other by Captain Lieutenant Burns and Price's at the same time, looked for the one face he wanted. Could not find it. Could not find Garth's either. *Where . . . where . . . here a minute ago. . . .* Who? Saw him. Walked off. Going toward the women's barracks. *Women's barracks. . . .* He was dragging his hands free. He was running. Salter's hunting shirt and leggings clung to him, soaked, soggy with his sweat. They flopped, and he was soaking them with more sweat as he ran. But he was cold. *Nothing Garth could do now.* But he ran as he had run the morning when the Ottawas had tried to kill him. His fear drenched him with the icy coldness of that pond where he had hidden.

He stood in the doorway of the women's barracks and called to her. Heard her voice, faint, somewhere. Not here in the barracks. Outside somewhere. And then heard the shot.

Chris Holden, who had suffered by the inability of others to believe the truth, would have been utterly unable to believe the truth about Garth —if he could have known it—at the moment Miller shouted: "Bouquet fought them for two days and beat them!"

To Martin Garth that was the moment toward which he had bent his life. It was success, complete. It was all that he had hoped for. In his careful scheming, the relief of Fort Pitt had been the one imponderable. It had been the one thing left to chance entirely.

He knew Indians too well to believe that if Fort Pitt surrendered, he or any other white man could prevent a massacre. He would have tried—and failed. He had not feared for his own life. Other lives did not concern him greatly. But attempting to prevent a massacre and failing would have showed how little real power he possessed. And not making the attempt would have been even worse. To achieve his whole ambition, the respect and confidence of his own people was as vital to him as the confidence and favor of the Indians. He would have both, now.

His land deeds were at least as valid as they ever had been. In credit alone, in London, they were worth a fortune. And this bloody summer would keep settlers out for a long time. The land would multiply in value. He was in no hurry. The Indians believed that they had used him. Let them. He had used them for purposes that they could not suspect—to compel the army to send in enough troops to keep settlers off his land claims—to wear out the patience of the Ohio Company with endless waiting—to make the Indians so hated that he would be the only strong friend that they had among the white men.

He had not kept his promise to make Fort Pitt open its gates. He had never meant to keep it. But the tribes had not kept their part of the bargain—they had not prevented the relief from coming. He would still stand higher in the Indians' regard than any other trader. While he waited for the Indians' own lands to make one fortune for him, he would make another from their trade. In the end there would be another province in America, and Martin Garth would be proprietor and governor—as powerful as the Penns and Calverts. There was no good reason why he shouldn't succeed Sir William Johnson.

Chris Holden's escape had not disturbed him greatly, nor his sudden reappearance in the gateway. Holden was still under sentence for desertion. Even if Bouquet or Amherst spared his life, Chris Holden was discredited. Let Holden talk: he never would find proof. The only white man who could swear that Martin Garth had broken any law was Dave Bone.

Hannah was dead. There would be no nonsense now about the women being kept in barracks. There would soon be Abby. . . .

And then he had recognized Pollexfen.

One moment, everything. The next moment, nothing. But Garth held himself as tightly in complete disaster as he had in absolute success. He knew instantly what he must do, and did it. He made his excuses calmly to McKee and Trent and Ehrlich, turned, walked briskly—but not hurrying—toward the women's barracks. He walked past it almost without thinking about Abby. There were other women. She was not important. Bone was.

He found Dave on the Ohio bastion, took him by the arm, and walked him up the firing step along the Allegheny curtain. There were only four or five militiamen along the whole stockade, here; the rest had rushed to the parade ground. When he came to Will Guttery's table, Garth stopped.

"We're getting out of here, Dave."

"Gettin' out? Amongst them red hellions, now they've had their tails pinched? No, by God! I ain't goin'!"

"There's the little matter of Ecuyer's money."

"You're in that as much as I am."

"My neck won't save yours, Dave. There's the other little matter of the girl, too."

"I ain't goin' out amongst them Mingoes, girl or no girl. All I got t' do is say what happened."

"We went over that once, Bone. *You* bought her. And *you* sold her. You knew Holden had already bought her."

"There ain't nobody believed him when he said so. Nor her, neither. An' there ain't nobody else can say so. Not here."

"Yes. There is. He came in with Holden. It just happens he's the owner of the ship. I'm leaving, and you're leaving with me. Move! Get over that wall, Dave. The table's a good place."

Bone looked down at the pistol in Garth's hand.

"A'right." He climbed the two sawed boards that made steps, spiked across the table. He put one foot in the angle between the sharpened points of two logs in the stockade. With his rifle in one hand, he reached out with the other for one of the table legs and swung himself over. He hung dangling for a moment and then dropped.

Garth was climbing up the table. His thick body made a solid smooth bulge, fitted to the loophole. Dave Bone nudged it with the muzzle of his rifle.

"That's your belly, ain't it?"

He nudged it again. Pulled the trigger. Stood and looked up at the hands clenched on the top end of the table. Watched them loosen. Watched the daylight come between the loophole and Garth's body. Watched the crooked circle of the daylight make a broader bright patch on the tawny leather—bright patch covered suddenly with pouring darkness.

Then his pent-up hate came pouring. He drove the rifle barrel through the loophole with a panting fury. The lock broke. Splinters gouged his hand. The end of the snapped lock loosened a long splinter down the crack between the puncheons. He could see Garth huddled in the dirt, his face bowed against the table. He pulled the rifle barrel halfway out and threw his weight against it. The crack widened and he got the barrel into it. The planks wrenched apart. He was gouging Garth's face with the muzzle when Chris Holden dragged the rifle out of his hands.

Bone made no attempt to get away. He stood with his face pressed to the split between the planks and babbled.

"He knew I was goin' t' do it. He was scairt just b'fore I done it. He was scairt o' me, I tell ye. He knew I was goin' t' do it."

The four or five militiamen who had come running at the sound of Bone's shot leaned on their rifles, listening.

Holden looked down at the man he had intended to kill. *Like a snake.* That was the way Bone had killed him.

John Maycamp looked at the wrecked table. He said:

"Guttery ain't go'n' t' like this. Cap'n, I allow Bone done ye quite a favor."

"No," Holden said. "He was too late."

"Too late?" All the faces soberly concerned. "Ain't she all right?"

"I don't know." *Meant Garth was finished.* "I haven't found her."

"She's all right. Ain't nothin' happened since ye got away."

Chris Holden had a faint awareness of surprise. No reason for it. The whole fort knew about Abby, likely. About him and Abby. But he wondered whether these haggard farmerishlike men had had a part in his escape. He wondered whether Jeremy Love—his childish brain as unexpectedly shrewd, sometimes, as his childish hands—had gone to some of these men, knowing they were hostile and suspicious toward all Indian traders, knowing that such men as these would hardly be suspected of opening dungeon doors and sally ports and tricking sentries, knowing also that such officers as Steele would be incapable of understanding or suspecting the existence of so much kindliness and shrewdness and casual courage in these ordinary men.

"They still figgerin' t' shoot ye, Cap'n?"

"I don't know. I'm still under sentence."

"Then we'd best fetch Bone in," Maycamp said. "Might be he'll talk straighter now. Might be ye c'n use him."

"Thanks." He hadn't thought of that.

Other men were waiting for him on the Ohio bastion—John Fraser and Stair Carre, Yeardley and Pollexfen. They had Abby with them. She was almost lost among these tall men. They were shielding her. They knew what had happened by Will Guttery's table: they were keeping her from seeing.

He had her, now. He knew her so well. He had loved her so long— almost ten weeks—all existence. All life, all desire, all past, and all future in this one small body in his arms. And her arms so fierce in their love and gladness—and their fear for him. Her mouth trembling as she kissed him. Her eyes steady though her lips were shaken.

"It's all right . . . all right. . . . Love you. *Love you.* . . ."

Gone again, now. Always something came between them.

He was walking with Stair Carre. They were crossing the parade ground. Holden turned toward the dark doorway of the prison.

"No!" Stair was sharp about it. "There'll be none of that. I told Steele we'd not have you in that blasted snake pit of a dungeon. Yes—killed seven rattlers down there. Only food there's been, these last five days. No, I wasn't taking chances when I told Steele. There were a good many of us. Burns, Trent, Phillips. Ehrlich, too. Anyway, it won't be Steele much longer. Ecuyer's better—well enough to sit up if Boyd had left him anything to sit with. He's a butcher, Boyd is. But a good one."

Stair Carre took him to the officers' barracks by the Town wall and upstairs to his own quarters. Half the ceiling of Carre's room was gone, the roof burned away. There was a litter of burned shingles on the floor. Pieces of charred rafters were piled in one corner.

"I've seen stouter jails," Chris said.

Chapter 55

He was in the room for three days. It was not a bad place to be. This was the first time in months he had slept in a bed.

He saw, on the first afternoon, a column of Royals marching out to meet Colonel Bouquet—the gaunt men, the hungry men. Their scarlet tunics were faded and ragged now, and some were brown with scorch and the scorched cloth had crumbled away. They marched with bare arms or bare legs that belonged to skeletons, not to men.

The next day, from the small eastern window under the gable, he saw the carpenters floundering into the muck of the Mon, trying to raise the sunken bateaux. And young Baillie, when he came in as officer of the guard to make sure that the prisoner hadn't escaped, was enormously daring. He said there was talk of an expedition to punish the Indians, to wipe out their towns and crush them for once and all.

"As soon as Bouquet comes in," Baillie said. "Yes, sir! Bouquet's got a thousand men. We can let him have two hundred more. That's twelve hundred troops to move up the Allegheny and clean out the towns as they go. Cannon, too—cohorns and field guns mounted on the bateaux. We'll give them a proper lesson."

He went away. Twelve hundred men, Holden thought—and Bouquet had four hundred and sixty when he marched out of Carlisle. He had three hundred and fifty now, and sixty of those were wounded, and some of the wounded would die. Bouquet did not have two hundred men who were fit for a new campaign. And cohorns on the bateaux—the first shot would knock those cranky and flimsy things into huddles of floating planks, if they'd float at all after three months of being sunk.

But the spirit was there, no matter how weak the flesh and the means possessed by the flesh. And Holden found himself thinking now of the Royals' motto—*Celer et Audax*. Swift and audacious. And it was true.

It was true in young Baillie, who'd never got over his blushing and always caught itch in the summer. It was true of the men who were going out to meet Bouquet's crippled column. And Holden thought now of another thing that had not come into his mind in years. The Sixtieth Foot might wear scarlet coats. It might be a regiment number neatly set down on the British Army list. But it wasn't a British regiment.

Everyone always called them Royals, but that was only the half of their name. They were the Royal Americans.

They were different, too, from any other troops in the British Army. They were the only regiment that had never worn lace—and that, he thought, was about as large an exception as any politician in London could be expected to make to tradition and things-as-they-always-were.

The small concession was not important. The important thing now, to Holden, was that the Sixtieth Foot had been raised in the colonies. The men who had held the frontier for five desperate years and three of the bloodiest months in all Indian war were not British soldiers at all. They were Americans!

Some of their officers were English and some were bad, like Steele; and some good, like young Baillie; and some were the finest and bravest gentlemen God ever made, like Stair Carre. But a many were foreigners. *Foreigners.* What did that mean?

They were Germans and Swiss and Dutch and Swedes and the Lord knew what. And the most of the settlers west of the Susquehanna were Germans, or Scotch from the north of Ireland. And they were Americans. They were men of the breed who had marched to Kittanning—three hundred militia—to strike at the source of the Indian raids when Braddock had failed with three thousand. These were the men—Royals or traders or settlers or bateaux makers—who had held the frontier through the worst that the savage tribes could do.

They were hard men to beat. You could beat them but they wouldn't know it. They wouldn't stay beaten.

Their homes were gone. They would rebuild their homes.

Pitt's Town would rise again. It would be a little better than the town that had been torn down and burned—not much, but a little better. There would be fewer cabins with hogpen ends and cedar-bark roofs held in place with stones, and fewer floors of packed dirt. It was always so, after each disaster. You had to kill these people, to stop them.

The three days were peaceful days. There was nothing for him to do —nothing that he could do. Whatever needed doing was being done by Carre and Pollexfen and Fraser and—he smiled to himself, deeply happy —by the woman he loved.

On the third morning it rained—a hard, driving, hammering rain. It poured through the hole in the roof in a waterfall. He stripped and stood in the pouring water and let the rain whip him and pound him. He dried himself on one of Stair's blankets and looked at Stair's mirror and basin and box of razors. He filled the basin with water still spouting into the room from the hole in the roof. Then he stood in front of the mirror and shaved, and a face emerged. He scarce knew it. He had stood like this before—years ago, more than four months ago—and looked at his face in another mirror and he had disliked it intensely. The face had mocked him. It had been sardonic and grim, leering at him with one lifted eyebrow.

The eyebrow was lifted still, but the face did not mock him now. It was thin, but it grinned at him.

He threw himself down on Carre's bunk, and he was asleep when Stair Carre unlocked the door and came in.

"Get your clothes on, man! You're wanted. Ecuyer's waiting."

Holden had a feeling that Carre was excited. It didn't seem sensible; Stair Carre was never excited. The feeling persisted.

He had got himself into clout and leggings when Carre asked abruptly:
"What would you give to know who has the room next to you?"

"Not——" He stopped with his shirt half over his head.

"No. *Not* Mrs. Holden. Steele."

"Steele's under arrest?"

"Quite. Oh, I daresay they'll not hang him. He did too well. He fought like a tiger when it was touch and go. No, I'd say they will probably shoot him."

"How can they? He didn't surrender. After all, Price abandoned his post." Holden laughed, and laughter was harsh. The bitterness still was there. "Such a post as it was—a log hut in a bog. And burning down over his head. Surely they'll not punish Price!"

"They'll try him, of course. He may be acquitted and given a pat on the back. They'll try Christie too, for surrendering. Steele . . . it's not just that Steele had notions about surrender. As a matter of fact, there's some doubt that he favored it," Carre said with a careful carelessness. "I don't remember. Everything was such a hell of a mess. How could I remember, to swear it?"

"I have no cause to love Steele," Holden said. "But I'd likely forget, myself. This shooting a man in cold blood——" He had almost forgotten already that he had intended to shoot Martin Garth, and that his blood had felt cold.

"That's the only way," Carre protested. "It's the only sensible way. For five years now I've pounded that into my men. Keep cold. Like ice. Imagine you're one solid cake of ice, you can't move your trigger finger until you see what color an Indian's painted. Now we've got to start over again. We've got to teach 'em to shoot at a mark after they have been shooting for weeks at live Indians." Carre made a weary gesture. "They're not going to like it. It's funny. It's the same after every war. Every war is always the last one. Now they're saying we've given the Indians such a whipping they'll never come back."

"They'll come," Chris said. "There are more tribes out yonder than in the Ohio country. I've heard the Miamis talk. They're not cowards—but they're a plenty scared of the tribes that live to the west."

"I wish to God Steele was out there. I think he wishes so too, even if they flayed him alive, or burned him the way they did Gordon. D'you see, Chris, he stole."

"Stole what?"

"Money out of Ecuyer's office. A thousand dollars in Pennsylvania money. It was money Bouquet had sent to pay Burent's carpenters."

"But why? I thought he was right well off."

"Was ever a man well off that plays another man's game? Steele did. He played with Garth, nights, up at Nan Perdue's. And he lost and he lost. He was stony and worse than stony. He had his pride, Steele had. Good family . . . sisters . . . all that. It's one thing to be hustled away from England and into the army. It's something else to be cashiered for a gambling debt and then thrown into jail. I think that's what Steele was afraid of, really. He took the money. He gave most of it to Bone."

"Bone!"

"Why does that surprise you? You know that Garth never worked in the light. He was like a beaver that comes out only at night."

"They don't," Chris said wearily. "They work in the day."

"Do they, now! No matter. . . . You'd know Garth would never have taken stolen money from Steele. He took it through Bone. And Bone has confessed. It's odd how many men break at the very last minute, when there's no longer the need. Ecuyer found he'd been gouging the townfolk on meal. He ordered Bone flogged. Only thirty lashes. But Bone broke down after the fourth. He began to yawp about Steele. They found the money—Steele's share. In the cohorn on the Mon bastion—the howitz that was so old we'd never have dared to fire it. We put it there for show. I suppose Steele thought that was one place nobody would ever look."

"Bone could have put it there."

"Oh, quite. Quite. The rub is, Steele admitted it. He needn't have, but he did. His nerves were in rags, I suppose."

Carre dragged at his fob, and his watch popped out of his breeches.

"Come along, Chris. The prisoner will be escorted to the headquarters of the officer commanding. That's what the order says. I've got it in writing here, if you want to look. It says three o'clock. It's three less a quarter now. Oh, the devil with it! I'm not going to wait fifteen minutes. *My* nerves are ragged too. I'm going to tell you. Ecuyer has disapproved the court's findings."

"I'm free, then. I will be. Where is she, Stair?"

"Headquarters." Carre reached for his fob. "No, dammit! I'll not look at that watch again. Bad habit. I've looked at it nine thousand times, in these last three months, to see how much longer I'd lived than I had expected to. In a few minutes—ten or twelve, I'd guess—Abby'll be free, officially. I can't say as much for you. It's Ecuyer's idea. He has the authority. It's his notion of making amends. Don't spoil it for him. It's not illegal to marry the same woman twice."

"D'you mean *now?*"

"I do not. I mean three o'clock. Can't you wait nine minutes to marry her again?"

"No!"

They walked down the stairs together and out onto the parade and along the front of the officers' barracks to the governor's house. The eaves had been burned away. The house had a kind of blank look, like a face with its eyebrows gone.

Holden felt a tumult rising inside him as they went up the steps. He had walked up these steps one night with a golden-haired girl in a Forgel gown on his arm, not caring too much what happened to either the girl or the gown so long as they served their purpose. And he had come down the steps again, not so many hours later, and she was the only thing in the world that mattered.

They walked into a different tumult. The hall of the governor's house was filled with men and the smell of men. All of them were civilians—traders and wagoners, bateaux makers, sawmill hands, men from the town that had been.

The small space was hot. The men were drenched with their sweat. The stench of their bodies, unwashed for months, was as thick as the turgid Mon.

The men stewed in their sweat. Their talk made a low seething bubbling sound. It was angry talk. The seething exploded, loud and profane and obscene, when Captain Lieutenant Carre coolly elbowed his way to the door of the adjutant's office and the sentinels let him in and let Holden in. The door, closing, put a lid on the sound.

Carre left him and went to the sentry beside the opposite door. He came back again.

"One moment," he said. "With Ecuyer it's always *un moment*. She's in there. Pollexfen's there, and the Frasers. But Ecuyer's still signing orders."

The noise in the hall boiled louder. Carre grinned.

"Those people haven't changed, have they? D'you know what they're yelling about? They want to be paid for saving their own damned hides. Claims! Claims! *Claims!* Every man of them wants to rebuild his house. They want their claim money to do it. By the Lord, we can't keep them quiet. An officer can't walk across the parade without having a mob around him. That's why we let them into the hall. They're a little quieter there—I think. What are you grinning at?"

"At the notion of keeping them quiet," Chris said.

Those clamoring, unwashed, unshaven, foul-smelling, and foul-talking men had surged over five mountain ranges in profane and matter-of-fact disregard of savage nations and savage nature. They had clung to this poor mud heap of a fort and its frail wooden walls that were made of their own wrecked homes. They had held it in spite of flood and heat and hunger and all the tribes with the fierce fighting names—Seneca, Caughnawaga and Shawnee, Ottawa, Huron, Miami, Winnebago, Ojibway.

And it seemed to Chris Holden now that he was seeing these people more clearly than ever before, though there was a wall between them and him, and the door was closed. This tumult, this surging violence, was a part of them. They were direct, not devious. And he thought, now, that that was why Garth had failed—why Garth was condemned to failure when first he descended into that alien deviousness and found in it a satisfaction he did not find in outrightness and violence. Garth had been sly and intricate—and therefore alien. He had been European, not an American.

Holden smiled faintly again. The Ohio Company was American enough. It had pretended deviousness and even had practiced it. But its deviousness had been transparent; everyone saw through it instantly; it had been the naïve deviousness of a child—and therefore essentially crude, bold, and shameless, direct, even violent. It had been a part of this people.

This people was new—clamoring, threatening, jostling, impatient and restless, resistless. Whence they had come meant little. They had been changed. They were somehow a different breed.

They were not always pleasant people. They were not always admirable. But they weren't easy to conquer—they believed too deeply that whatever they wanted was right and was theirs by right. The outright noisy demanding, the bold ruthless taking, the quick forgetting of hardship and danger and death, the land lust and the greed—it was all a part of their confident fierce belief in the right to do what they pleased. It had put its mark on them. It was stamped on their pinched, hungry faces.

Hungry . . . There were other hungers. The girl he loved was beyond that door, waiting. There was one hunger that was not like any other. It would never be gone. He would satisfy it, but he would yet be unsatisfied. No. Not unsatisfied . . . *wanting.* There was a difference. He knew, now, that it was very great.

No matter how often or long, how far into the days and the years of days that were left to him, the hunger would always remain. And there would always be food. He would be fed forever by the love in her steadfast eyes, and nourish himself with her body and spirit. *Body and spirit. Body and soul.* They were so close together that there was no way to tell them apart, no way to keep them apart. One was somehow a part of the other, and he and she were somehow a part of each other.

The door opened. The sentry beckoned at last.